CALEB WILLIAMS

CALEB WILLIAMS

William Godwin

edited by *Gary Handwerk*
& A. A. Markley

broadview literary texts

Canadian Cataloguing in Publication Data
Godwin, William, 1756–1836
    Caleb Williams

(Broadview literary texts)
Originally published under title: Things as they are, or, The adventures of Caleb Williams.
Includes bibliographical references.
ISBN 1-55111-249-3

I. Markley, A.A. (Arnold Albert), 1964– . II. Handwerk, Gary J., 1954– .
III. Title. IV. Series.

PR4722.C3 2000   823'.6   C00-931805-4

Broadview Press Ltd., is an independent, international publishing house, incorporated in 1985.

North America:
P.O. Box 1243, Peterborough, Ontario, Canada K9J 7H5
3576 California Road, Orchard Park, NY 14127
TEL: (705) 743-8990; FAX: (705) 743-8353;
E-MAIL: customerservice@broadviewpress.com

United Kingdom:
Turpin Distribution Services Ltd.,
Blackhorse Rd., Letchworth, Hertfordshire SG6 1HN
TEL: (1462) 672555; FAX (1462) 480947; E-MAIL: turpin@rsc.org

Australia:
St. Clair Press, P.O. Box 287, Rozelle, NSW 2039
TEL: (02) 818-1942; FAX: (02) 418-1923

www.broadviewpress.com

Broadview Press gratefully acknowledges the financial support of the Book Publishing Industry Development Program, Ministry of Canadian Heritage, Government of Canada.

Broadview Press is grateful to Professor Eugene Benson for advice on editorial matters for the Broadview Literary Texts series.

Text design and composition by George Kirkpatrick

PRINTED IN CANADA

Contents

Acknowledgements

This volume would not have reached publication without the considerable support of many people. We are particularly grateful to Pamela Clemit for invaluable advice at several phases of the project, and we owe a considerable debt to recent editors of *Caleb Williams*, David McCracken, Maurice Hindle, and Pamela Clemit. Our thanks to colleagues for help and advice, among them Phyllis Cole, Carol Kessler, Elizabeth Buckmaster, Adam Sorkin, George Franz, Edward Tomezsko, and David McCracken. And to Don LePan for encouraging the project, to Mical Moser and Barbara Conolly of Broadview Press for editorial assistance, and to Dr. Eugene Benson.

We gratefully acknowledge assistance from the Rare Books Collection at Duke University for allowing us access to microfilm copies of Godwin's journals from the Abinger Collection in the Bodleian Library, Oxford University; the National Art Library, Victorian and Albert Museum, for access to the original manuscript of the novel; the Interlibrary Loan Office at Suzzallo Library, University of Washington, for locating a copy of the 1831 edition of the novel; and Sandy Stelts of the Pattee Library, Penn State University, for providing a copy of the title page from the 1794 edition of *Caleb Williams*. We are also grateful to Pickering & Chatto for allowing us to reprint Godwin's original ending to the novel and his "Of History and Romance" from their editions of his *Collected Novels and Memoirs* and *Political and Philosophical Writings*, respectively.

Our task was made far easier by the help of Loretta Catanzaro, Pearl Shannon, Frauke Plummer, Petia Parpoulova, and George Rueckert in preparing the manuscript and by Susan Ware, Jean Sphar, Steven Severance, Lucy Morrison, and Sara Whildin in assisting our library research.

And finally, personal thanks to Jeanne Moskal, Nora Crook, Richard Kopley, Julia D. Markley, Holley Markley, Brian Meyer, and Nancy Strom.

Introduction

Despite being William Godwin's first substantial venture into
fiction, *Caleb Williams* proved to be the most important and
influential novel published in Britain during the 1790s. It was
both a popular and a critical success, a novel of equal significance for political and for literary history, even though reactions to it were sharply marked by the polemical divisions
among its readership. It achieved such distinction because it
was the first wholly successful political novel within the European narrative tradition. Taking as its task the presentation of a
"review of the modes of domestic and unrecorded despotism,"[1]
Caleb Williams became the first text to blend fully the aesthetic
potential of the fictional form with the highly charged political
debates of its particular era.

    Caleb Williams was not without predecessors, to be sure, and
can be usefully characterized as part of what came to be called
Jacobin fiction – "Jacobin" being the term used by British conservatives to discredit expressions of political critique by associating them with the most radical strand of French revolutionary politics. *Caleb Williams* is indeed radical in its critical perspective on British society, yet it stands apart even from similar
novels for its innovative use of the techniques of fiction to
explore the intricate interplay of psychology and politics that
sustains political repression. Its analysis focused, in Godwin's
own terms, upon the way that "[government] insinuates itself
into our personal dispositions, and insensibly communicates its
own spirit to our private transactions."[2] In his fiction, as also in
his political philosophy, Godwin anticipated more recent
accounts of how political ideology permeates the recesses of
personal identity, how our inner selves are shaped "in ways not
fully accessible to our own understanding" by socially constituted values and prejudices. Although his particular program
for change, a highly rationalist, liberal anarchism anticipating

---

1   Godwin's preface to the 1832 edition of *Fleetwood*, p. 443 of this volume.
2   William Godwin, *Enquiry Concerning Political Justice and Its Influence on Morals and
    Happiness*, ed. F.E.L. Priestley (Toronto: 1946) [1797 edition], Book I, Chapter 1, 4.

"the euthanasia of government," did not become a widely shared political platform, it did have considerable impact upon a number of prominent writers and political figures of his own era. Still, Godwin's diagnosis of the difficulties involved in establishing social justice even in ostensibly "liberal" political orders remains as relevant today as it was in his own time.

When *Caleb Williams* appeared in 1794, William Godwin had already reached what would prove to be the high point of his personal fame. The publication of his *Enquiry Concerning Political Justice* in February 1793 had made him one of the most prominent political philosophers in Britain, and an essay published in October 1794, "Cursory Strictures," dealing with the treason trials of a dozen prominent British radicals, had demonstrated that he could have significant influence upon current political events as well. His reputation peaked at a time of tremendous political ferment, as British society at all levels struggled to come to terms with the legacy of the French Revolution and to determine what its relevance could or should be for Britain. As a force intervening in these debates, the timing of *Caleb Williams* could not have been better. Godwin gave the novel's original preface (suppressed by his publisher due to its polemical tone) the date of May 12, 1794, the same day on which the British Prime Minister, William Pitt, had suspended habeas corpus and launched the first of a series of preemptive arrests of prominent British radicals.

Godwin had written three short novels prior to *Caleb Williams*, but none since 1784. The impulse behind Godwin's return to fiction was his desire to convey the message of *Political Justice* to a wider audience than his lengthy philosophical treatise was likely to reach. As the novel's original preface stated, "It is now known to philosophers, that the spirit and character of the government intrudes itself into every rank of society. But this is a truth, highly worthy to be communicated, to persons, whom books of philosophy and science are never likely to reach."[1] It was quite explicitly, then, a work aiming to fuel public debates about the legitimacy of the existing political

---

1   See Appendix B.

order. Yet *Caleb Williams* was not simply a piece of didactic fiction, a description that might more justifiably be used for a number of other Jacobin novels. Instead, its highly original synthesis of available literary models made it an essential step on the way to nineteenth-century social realism and the heyday of the novel in the Victorian era.

Political Justice had already laid a foundation for the novel's form as well as for its objectives. Its critique of the power of government to shape the character of its citizens was virtually a blueprint for political fiction, where the psychological basis for and consequences of political oppression could be closely depicted, and where the effects of such oppression upon character over time could be carefully followed. Godwin's goal in this novel was to show how the "mind-forg'd manacles" described in a poem like Blake's "London" came to be created and, even more importantly, how it was that they had managed to persist for so long. The interest of *Caleb Williams* lies in how it succeeds on two levels – as political criticism and as psychological analysis – blending its dual themes together with great power and showing their essential interdependence.

Great Britain in the 1790s

The early 1790s were a period of intense political upheaval in Great Britain. The outbreak of the French Revolution on July 14, 1789, had inspired politicians who opposed the contemporary government under King George III and Prime Minister William Pitt to intensify their efforts towards political reform in Britain. Many political activists felt the time had come to push for similarly radical steps toward democratizing the political institutions and equalizing the grossly unbalanced distribution of power and wealth in their own country. By November 1789, the prominent Dissenting minister, Richard Price, had published a widely circulated treatise, *Discourse on the Love of our Country*, that gave new immediacy to long-running political arguments by welcoming the changes brought by the French Revolution. Price's text argued for the people's right to liberty in matters pertaining to religious choices and for their right to resist oppressive governments and to form new ones. The response of political conservatives to texts such as these, which they saw as politically incendiary, was equally rapid. Edmund Burke's *Reflections on the Revolution in France and on the Proceedings in Certain Societies in London Relative to that Event* (1790) became a touchstone for this debate, with many of the most prominent radical texts, from Mary Wollstonecraft's *A Vindication of the Rights of Men* (1790) and *A Vindication of the Rights of Woman* (1792) to Thomas Paine's *Rights of Man* (1791) and Godwin's *Political Justice,* responding directly to Burke's attacks upon political change.

Questioning whether the French were to be congratulated on the early stages of a political turmoil born of violence and irreverence, Burke argued that it was too early to determine whether or not the changes in France were really to be regarded as a positive or necessary step toward greater freedom. He contended that the beginnings of revolution in France might well lead to increasingly widespread violence, which would do no more to foster civic freedoms than the regime that was being overthrown had done. Burke sharply contrasted the situation in France to that in Britain, where he argued that previous constitutional reforms had created a government that was already more equitable and progressive than any comparable regime in Europe. His rebuke of political agitation set off a flurry of pamphlets in which hundreds of reformers and conservatives debated the issue of reform as it pertained both to France and to England. As events began to confirm some of Burke's predictions, the tone of the attacks upon those who, in Burke's eyes, would slavishly follow a French model became increasingly shrill.

Yet an independent foundation for political change had already been established in England prior to the French Revolution. A number of political societies throughout England had come together to celebrate the centennial of the deposition of King James II, the "Glorious Revolution" of 1688 that figures across the political spectrum took as Britain's own exemplary model for political change. Many of these groups saw the revolution in France as a parallel step toward political liberty, and that revolution in turn helped speed the growth of new political societies in Britain. Thus, the Society for Constitutional Information, a long-standing group whose numbers had dwindled severely during the 1780s, experienced a dramatic increase in membership in 1791 and 1792. The more moderate Society of Friends of the People was launched in order to encourage debate pertaining to the English Constitution, specifically concerning the electoral system and political representation.

Most worrisome for the government was the extension of these debates into the working class, a group that had previously been largely excluded from political participation. Their most prominent and effective organization was the London Corresponding Society, founded in January 1792 and organized into many small divisions throughout London. Its low dues allowed working men to join, and it took as one specific goal the widening of political debate – a goal it pursued through regular correspondence with other political groups throughout Britain and through the publication of inexpensive political pamphlets on such topics as Parliamentary reform. Many reform societies were closely linked to others, working together to disseminate political literature, organize meetings, and petition the government. Their activities stretched into continental European politics as well, with various groups sending letters of congratulation to the revolutionaries in France on their success in overthrowing an oppressive government. From the government's perspective, the threat to the established order lay less in the existence of political debate than in the scale and spread of these debates. The larger danger lay in the way these groups succeeded in harnessing new print and communications technologies to foster political discontent across social classes and to organize what seemed likely to become truly national agitation.

Increasingly worried that what they saw happening in France might repeat itself in Britain, Pitt and the members of his government came to feel more and more anxious about what they viewed as the growing radicalism of the voices for revolution in England. Government officials and magistrates were encouraged to take aggressive steps to quell any activity that could be considered riotous or seditious. An early target of this harassment was Thomas Paine, whose arguments in favor of the American and the French revolutions became widely known through inexpensive editions of his *Rights of Man*. Paine was forced to flee England under threat of arrest after publishing a second part of this work in 1792. The government's anxieties were further increased by the execution in Paris of Louis XVI on January 21, 1793, and by the French government's declaration of war against England on February 1, 1793. Charges of seditious libel began to be lodged against numerous individuals and groups suspected of inciting political dissension or simply of criticizing either the government or the king.

William Godwin's first public intervention in these political matters was sparked by the trial in early 1793 of a candle-maker by the name of Daniel Crichton. Crichton had left Scotland to pursue his trade in London and, on a day's outing, had been drinking prior to touring the Tower of London. Upon seeing the royal armory and munitions, the intoxicated Crichton proclaimed, "Damn the King; we have no King in Scotland, and we will soon have no King in England." Crichton soon found himself arrested, enchained, and ultimately sentenced to three months imprisonment and a heavy fine. In response to this and related events, Godwin published four letters in February and March of 1793 in the *Morning Chronicle* (extracts from the letters can be found in Appendix B). In these letters, Godwin angrily argued that recent government proceedings violated the most basic principles of the British Constitution, its guarantee of civil and personal liberty and its protection of free speech. He pointed out that the Crichton case provided an ominous precedent for similar prosecutions, and he deftly turned the conservatives' arguments about conspiracies against the government against them by contending that the main threat to the British Constitution came not from radicals, but from an orchestrated campaign of political repression aiming to silence all political dissent.

In the second of these letters, Godwin attacked John Reeves, who in the fall of 1792 had founded the "Association for the Preservation of Liberty and Property against Republicans and

Levellers." This association dedicated itself to suppressing any publications deemed seditious and to discrediting the reformers and their efforts, and it encouraged the founding of similar societies in other parts of the country. Reeves had hardly invented the tactics of political repression; the Birmingham riots of 1791, for instance, which led to the destruction of the houses and property of numerous prominent Dissenters, had been sparked by similar loyalist agitation. But Godwin worried about the systematic nature of the repression Reeves' association and others sought to foster and their barely concealed complicity with governmental intentions. Calling Reeves "the assassin of the Liberties of Englishmen," Godwin criticized him for the hypocritical way in which he had worked to discredit Thomas Paine. At the time of Paine's trial in absentia for sedition, Reeves sought to discredit Paine by using the very methods of popular agitation that he claimed were tactics of political instability when used by political reformers. In *Caleb Williams,* Falkland adopts these same tactics of "hand-bills, ballads, and misrepresentation" to destroy Caleb's credibility.

Godwin's final letter makes the most explicit case for the principles of political truth and rational discussion that Godwin promotes in both *Political Justice* and *Caleb Williams*. It sought to directly influence the Crichton case by appealing specifically to those "persons as may be appointed to serve upon juries for the trial of seditious and treasonable words." Godwin puts his faith in the power of a single individual, placed in the circumstances that an event like this trial had created, to reverse the entire tide of political repression. He argued that, "One upright and intelligent juryman might put a close to that scene of persecution which is the disgrace of Britain." That person, if "endowed with moderation, intrepidity, and benevolence" and willing to rely upon a "clear, simple, unornamented understanding" in telling "a plain and artless tale," would inevitably succeed in bringing his fellow jurymen to accept the case for liberty of speech.

Despite appeals like Godwin's, the arrest and conviction of reformers continued throughout Great Britain. The government pursued political figures such as John Frost, the secretary of the London Corresponding Society, who was imprisoned for six months for engaging in what was considered a seditious conversation. It also sought to muzzle political debate by putting publishers and booksellers on trial for printing and distributing reformist literature. Lord Braxfield, a prominent Scottish judge, proclaimed publicly that, because the English Constitution was "perfect," any proposal for changing it should be regarded as treasonous. Even relatively moderate, middle-class figures, such as Thomas Muir, a founder of the Scottish "Friends of the People," and Thomas Palmer, a Scottish Unitarian, were targeted. Both were tried and harshly sentenced by Braxfield (to fourteen and seven years of transportation respectively) for relatively mild expressions of political dissent. Godwin wrote a letter attacking their treatment as ordinary felons and visited them while they awaited transportation to Australia. In light of the miserable condition of British prisons and the even harsher living conditions prisoners faced when transported to a distant location in the British Empire, these sentences were often little different from the death penalty.

Still, the reformers moved forward with an attempt to disseminate their message by organizing large conventions in London for the election of delegates and by debating specific plans for resisting government repression. In the fall of 1793, a third "British Convention of the Delegates of the Friends of the People associated to obtain Universal Suffrage and Annual Parliaments" was held in Edinburgh. The convention was quickly disbanded, and several of its leaders were arrested and charged with sedition, including a new friend of Godwin's, Joseph Gerrald. Godwin visited Gerrald in prison and discussed with him at length how Gerrald might best handle his defense. On January 23, 1794, Godwin wrote to Gerrald, praising him for his devotion to the cause of reform and pointing out to him the great opportunity he had for altering public opinion by calmly defending his right to work toward non-violent change. This letter, reprinted in Appendix B, reflects Godwin's faith in the irresistible power of truth to effect political change. In a blow to such philosophical optimism, however, Gerrald's self-defense failed. He was convicted and sentenced by Judge

Braxfield to transportation for fourteen years, dying of an already-present tuberculosis before he could return to England.

In May of 1794, just as *Caleb Williams* was coming off the press, the Pitt government launched a major strike against the reformers. Having carefully watched the publications of such groups as the London Corresponding Society and the Society for Constitutional Information and having infiltrated society meetings with spies, government officials finally believed they had uncovered evidence that another English Convention was being planned, and that the reformers were taking steps towards arming themselves for military action. Twelve of the leading members of the Corresponding and Constitutional Societies were arrested for high treason, among them Godwin's acquaintances, John Horne Tooke and John Thelwall, and, later that year, his close friend, Thomas Holcroft. Even though the full pressure of the government was brought to bear in the effort to secure convictions, only three of these figures were actually brought to trial and all were acquitted, thus escaping the almost certain execution that would have followed a guilty verdict. Godwin's contribution to this outcome was considerable. On October 21, in the midst of the trial, he published in the *Morning Chronicle* an extremely influential, anonymous analysis of the case, entitled "Cursory Strictures on the Charge delivered by Lord Chief Justice Eyre." In this essay, Godwin demonstrated that the government's attempt to arraign and convict these men for high treason had no viable foundation under English law. A charge of high treason required evidence of intent to use armed force against the government, something that the government remained unable to prove.

Despite its failure to secure convictions in specific cases such as this one, Pitt's government continued to take advantage of the climate that they helped create in order to push for even more rigorous restraints upon political liberty. In May 1794 the Habeas Corpus Act was suspended, allowing the government to hold suspected criminals indefinitely without having to bring formal charges against them. In December 1795, the Seditious Meetings Act outlawed meetings or lectures involving more than fifty people without approval from local

governmental officials, and the Treasonable Practices Act outlawed speaking against the king or the Constitution, as well as
any attempt to appeal to Parliament on the subject of political
reform. Thus, the period during which *Caleb Williams* was
composed and disseminated was a time of extreme personal
danger for anyone who supported political reform in Great
Britain. As Godwin wrote in a note about his original preface
to the novel, "Terror was the order of the day." Indeed, the
political issues that Godwin addresses in *Caleb Williams* – issues
pertaining to truth, freedom, authority, and power – were quite
literally matters of life and death in 1794.

Godwin's *Political Justice*

Amid this atmosphere of political crisis, William Godwin first
came to widespread public attention with the appearance of his
Enquiry Concerning Political Justice in February 1793. By 1793,
Godwin had been living in London for ten years and at work
for much of the preceding two years almost exclusively upon
this text. Prior to 1791, he had supported himself primarily as a
political journalist, with his most consistent income deriving
from his contributions to the *New Annual Register*, a comprehensive survey of current events that provided one of the most
visible voices of the Dissenting community. Godwin's affilia-
tion with this journal was apt, since his own intellectual roots
linked him closely to the long tradition of British Dissent, those
independent Protestant denominations that stood in active
intellectual and social opposition to the dominant, state-spon-
sored Anglican Church. For many reasons, including the political disenfranchisement of its members, the Dissenting move-
ment had long been a source of political and social critique in
Britain.

During his involvement with the *New Annual Register*,
Godwin had particular responsibility for the sections on
contemporary British and European politics, which had forced
him for several years to pay careful attention to daily political
events. While work on this journal thus contributed to Godwin's political expertise, it was both time-consuming and

tedious, since he was expected primarily to report rather than comment upon events. Hence Godwin entered eagerly into the contract that the publisher George Robinson offered him in July 1791 to produce a major work of political philosophy. In return for publication rights upon completion of the text, Robinson agreed to the quite unusual step of paying Godwin's living expenses for the time that it took Godwin to finish his manuscript (which turned out to be one and one-half years). When it appeared, less than a month after the execution of King Louis XVI in France, the reception had to have been enormously gratifying to the thirty-six-year-old Godwin. The book was widely and generally favorably reviewed as a significant contribution to ongoing political debates. It went through three editions within five years and circulated even more widely in other forms – large extracts were published in reviews and inexpensive editions, several pirated editions appeared, and many copies were broadly circulated by subscription libraries. Indeed, within a short time nearly everyone conversant with contemporary political discussion was aware of Godwin's importance as a political philosopher.

Yet *Political Justice* is a curious text, its principles hard to define neatly and its coherence hard to assess among the extensive revisions that Godwin made for both the second and third editions.[1] The work is a combination of Enlightenment rationalism and visionary idealism, a mix of scrupulous analysis and utopian dreams. On the one hand, *Political Justice* presents a strongly determinist account of human behavior; its first principle is "that the actions and dispositions of mankind are the offspring of circumstances and events, and not of any original determination they bring into the world" (I.4.26 [1796]; the 1793 edition speaks of "incidents" and "impressions" rather than "circumstances"). On the other hand, *Political Justice* dis-

---

1   Quotations from *Political Justice* in our introduction are generally taken from the 1793 edition as edited by Mark Philp for the Pickering edition of Godwin's works, and are given by book, chapter, and page number in that edition. Occasional quotations from the 1796 edition come from F.E.L. Priestley's 1946 facsimile edition of the text and are likewise given by book, chapter, and page number. The most thorough analysis of Godwin's revisions among the three editions of *Political Justice* can be found in Philp's *Godwin's Political Justice*, especially chapters 6, 7, and 9.

plays Godwin's conviction that circumstances, since they are in many ways human contrivances, are susceptible to change and improvement. The text is by turns utilitarian, seeing human happiness as calculable in an impersonal and collective way, and what Mark Philp has aptly termed "perfectionist," concerned for the moral development of every individual.

What most struck contemporary readers of its first edition, however, was the blunt manner in which Godwin derived consequences from the pure rationalism of his principles. *Political Justice* became most notorious, perhaps, for the relative worth it ascribed to human lives in its example of the famous seventeenth-century cleric and author, François Fénelon, and the fire. "The illustrious archbishop of Cambray," Godwin asserted, "was of more worth than his chambermaid, and there are few of us that would hesitate to pronounce, if his palace were in flames, and the life of only one of them could be preserved, which of the two ought to be preferred." This holds equally true even, "Supposing the chambermaid had been my wife, my mother or my benefactor. This would not alter the truth of the proposition. The life of Fenelon would still be more valuable than that of the chambermaid; and justice, pure, unadulterated justice ... would have taught me to save the life of Fenelon at the expence of the other" (II.2.50). But *Political Justice* included a series of equally scandalous criticisms of conventional morality and accepted calculations of social justice. It argued that "marriage is an affair of property, and the worst of all properties," the "most odious of monopolies" in its despotic control over women's destinies. Hence marriage as an institution should simply be abolished (VIII.6.453–54). And it asserted that the act of promising, taken by many philosophers as the basis for social ethics, is absurd. Promises are fundamentally irrational because they bind our future behavior even though we can never know how altered circumstances may change our judgment about the most desirable course of action (III.3.87–89).

The preface to the 1793 edition of *Political Justice* described its aims as updating the science of politics to take account of "a great change that has been produced in men's minds" by the recent revolutions in America and France, an updating made necessary in this, as in all fields of inquiry, because "the human mind in every enlightened age is progressive" (Preface, iii). As its full title – *Enquiry Concerning Political Justice and its Influence on General Virtue and Happiness* – indicates, Godwin's work takes political and ethical philosophy to be intimately related. "Political society ... is founded in the principles of morality and justice. It is impossible for intellectual beings to be brought into coalition and intercourse, without a certain mode of conduct ... immediately becoming a duty incumbent on the parties concerned" (II.5.66). This emphasis in the *Enquiry* means that it is finally less a theory of political institutions and processes (although it does include much about both) than a theory of political psychology and social education.

In contemporary terms, we might most aptly characterize *Political Justice* as a work of ideology critique. Governments inculcate certain values in their citizens and do so all the better for being so pervasive in their operation. "Politics and modes of government ... educate and infect us all. They poison our minds, before we can resist, or so much as suspect their malignity" (I.4.49 [1796]). The novelty of Godwin's critique of politics lies in part in his insistence upon the fact that the unobtrusive effects of government may be even more powerful than its explicit aims and policies. "It may fairly be questioned, whether government be not still more considerable in its incidental effects, than in those intended to be produced" (I.1.3). Those incidental effects – how governments shape our beliefs and values and judgments – can coerce citizens far more efficiently than the more obviously intrusive measures (such as regulating commerce or taxation) that are typically the subject of public debate. From its theoretical starting point, *Political Justice* develops an empirical critique of current political systems, analyzing the psychological consequences of the imbalances of power and inequities of wealth that characterized every contemporary political order.

From Godwin's perspective, government invariably exerts a bad influence because it operates as a fundamentally conservative force, obstructing the natural processes of change that would otherwise lead to the improvement of human nature.

Government is the perpetual enemy of change because "It gives substance and permanence to our errors" (I.4.21). It institutionalizes values and judgments that prove, over time, to be nothing more than local prejudices. Even when the dictates of government are not in error, they routinize moral behavior and inhibit the cultivation of self-reflection that is, for Godwin, an essential part of our worth as human beings. "Men are so successfully reduced to a common standard by the operation of positive law, that, in most countries, they are capable of little more than, like parrots, repeating each other" (II.6.76). The general aim of political philosophy and of practical political activity must therefore be the "euthanasia of government," an outcome, Godwin assured his 1796 readers, that "ought not to be contemplated with alarm" (III.6.238 [1796]). In the meantime, living under political orders that exhibit all the despotism that Godwin associated with even relatively benevolent systems, a citizen should only "Obey; this may be right; but beware of reverence" (III.6.230 [1796]).

In the prevailing political climate, when the fundamental arrangements of British society were being called into question, Godwin's system represented an explosive philosophy. Its liberal anarchism was radical even within the spectrum of political opinions in the era and the bluntness of its assertions – contending, for instance, that "All government corresponds, in a certain degree, to what the Greeks denominated a tyranny" (V.23.308) – made its revolutionary potential perfectly clear. According to his daughter's, Mary Shelley's, later account, Godwin was saved from prosecution by the government only by the high price of his weighty treatise, since its cost would presumably limit its dissemination and influence. Yet the very extremism (or one might say, the logical consistency) of Godwin's arguments that magnified their immediate impact also served to limit the long-term impact of his ideas both as political theory and as practical political advice. Over the subsequent decade, the rising tide of reactionary political opinion in Britain carried both author and text into relative obscurity. Nor does the world seem more ready now than in 1793 to contemplate seriously the abolition of government.

Yet as one of the earliest studies of how political ideology functions, *Political Justice* deserves to rank with the works of Machiavelli, Hobbes, and other classics of modern political philosophy. It articulated as well as any work of its era the fundamental political questions then confronting European societies. It served as one of the most important statements on the question raised by Burke's *Reflections on the Revolution in France* – whether government should appeal to and rely upon human prejudices (Burke's term for what he saw as a valuable accretion of social experience) to guarantee its stability, or whether it should instead base its justification and appeal upon strictly rational principles.

Viewed as a program for political change, however, *Political Justice* appears as a much less radical intervention in those debates. From the start, Godwin insisted that "The true instruments for changing the opinions of men are argument and persuasion" (IV.2.115). The "revolution of opinions" (VIII.2.441 [1796]) that he envisioned fell far short of the aspirations of many of his fellow radicals, a gradualism that became even more strongly marked in his revisions of the text for its second and third editions. *Political Justice* rests its faith upon the inevitable power of truth, clearly articulated, to carry conviction to the minds of its hearers. It asserts that, "If there be such a thing as truth, it must infallibly be struck out by the collision of mind with mind" (I.4.15). For Godwin, political theory ought to be based upon moral truths, truths that he felt were objective, accessible by reason, and fully communicable and shareable. As Mark Philp points out, this "teleological" or "perfectionist" account of moral and social obligation diverges fundamentally from utilitarian accounts that assess actions according to their outcomes. "The perfectionist argues that we are duty-bound to realise our natures as self-perfecting autonomous agents" (86), indeed, that this is our highest purpose in life.[1] Both the science and practice of politics should therefore be aligned with these overriding moral aims.

---

1 See *Godwin's Political Justice*, especially pp. 53–57 and 83–89.

Philp's account particularly lays stress on Godwin's intellectual debt to the indigenous British tradition of Rational Dissent, contrasting this with what he sees as the lesser influence of the French *philosophes* to whom *Political Justice* often refers directly. This perspective also brings to light, however, Godwin's affinity with contemporary German thought, specifically with the idea of *Bildung* (education or cultivation) that was central to the reformist agenda of both German Classicism and German Romanticism. Unlike most competing versions of political life, perfectionism sets a higher standard for social life than self-interest (however sublimated or collectivized a version of self-interest one might present). It opposes itself most explicitly to the social contract theories of Hobbes, Locke, Rousseau, and other prominent liberal or romantic philosophers.

Godwin's perfectionism can be clearly traced to his own intellectual roots in the milieu of British Dissent. In particular, Godwin's stress upon the primacy of private judgment in moral deliberation has obvious affinities with the radical Protestant assertion of the primacy of personal conscience in one's relation to God. Godwin's own upbringing brought him for a considerable portion of his education under the direct influence of Sandemanianism, a particularly rationalist strand of Calvinism that retained the Calvinist doctrine of predestination, while emphasizing the importance of rational understanding over faith and works alike in determining one's suitability for salvation. As Philp notes, *Political Justice* can be read in many respects as a translation into secular political terms of an intellectual framework adopted from Dissenting theology. "He seems to have substituted truth for God, while retaining the framework of assumptions and arguments which accompanied theistic accounts of our moral duty" (33).

This shift is particularly noticeable in the centrality that Godwin gives to private judgment as the source of our understanding of both the principles of political justice and the obligation that its principles lay upon us. He says, "Every man is bound by the exertion of his faculties in the discovery of right, and to the carrying into effect all the right with which he is acquainted.... So that from this reasoning it ultimately appears,

that no man is obliged to conform to any rule of conduct, farther than the rule is consistent with justice" (II.6.76). Having
ascertained what our own inner understanding tells us to be
the truth, we are for Godwin under an equal obligation to convey those judgments to other people with utter frankness. We
have a duty to tell others all that we think on all matters
including, perhaps most problematically, all that we think about
them and their behavior. "How extensive an effect would be
produced," Godwin muses, "if every man were sure of meeting
in his neighbour the ingenuous censor, who would tell to himself, and publish to the world, his virtues, his good deeds, his
meannesses and his follies?" (IV.4.136). Godwin may be a shade
too optimistic here, but a key principle of his philosophy is that
sincerity of this kind is the surest mechanism for creating conviction about the sort of truths that he sought to convey.
"There is an energy in the sincerity of a virtuous mind that
nothing human can resist" (IV.4.137), a moral claim that lies at
the core of *Caleb Williams*.

Conviction of this kind, for Godwin, produces an immediate and inevitable impact upon behavior. "It remains true that,
when the understanding clearly perceives rectitude, propriety
and eligibility to belong to a certain conduct ... that conduct
will infallibly be adopted" (I.5.69 [1796]). As for Plato (and
unlike conventional Christian belief), we cannot in Godwin's
eyes choose anything we understand to be false or evil. What
we think to be good and true, however, remains subject to the
partial nature of our understanding as individuals. Hence communication of our judgments is important for another reason as
well. "If there be such a thing as truth, it must infallibly be
struck out by the collision of mind with mind" (I.4.15).[1]

One might indeed ask whether proposals such as these, the
only mechanism that Godwin really provides for carrying his
principles into practice, are finally political at all. Even though
his aversion to political violence becomes more pronounced in
later editions, it is clear that from the start Godwin envisaged
political change as a peaceful process, a matter of thoughtful

---

1   The affinity with John Stuart Mill's later liberal statements is striking. See, for
    instance, Chapter II of *On Liberty*, "Of Thought and Discussion."

deliberation and gradually widening consensus taking place outside the arena of parliamentary politics. "When the most considerable part of a nation, either for numbers or influence, becomes convinced of the flagrant absurdity of its institutions, the whole will soon be prepared tranquilly and by a sort of common consent to supersede them" (I.4.16). Given Caleb Williams' own experiences with prison, the metaphor offered by Godwin to illustrate this idea is particularly interesting. He imagines "ten thousand men of sound intellect, shut up in a madhouse, and superintended by a set of three or four keepers." Initially convinced of their own insanity, "They had therefore submitted to whips and straw and bread and water, and perhaps imagined this tyranny to be a blessing." As they instead become convinced that they are the ones whose understanding is correct, "the chains fall off of themselves, when the magic of opinion is dissolved" and the prisoners "quietly leave the mansion where they were hitherto immured" (I.7.38-39). Godwin explicitly rejects force even in the face of governmental oppression or resistance to change. "Force has already appeared to be an odious weapon; and, if the use of it be to be regretted in the hands of government, it does not change its nature though wielded by a band of patriots" (IV.1.111). Indeed, the preeminence accorded to *private* judgment in Godwin's thought is such that any sort of organized political activity is as bad as government itself. The 1796 edition of *Political Justice* states more emphatically a point already present in the 1793 edition. "All confederate action is of the nature of government, and ... consequently every argument of this work, which is calculated to display the evils of government ... is equally hostile to political association" (IV.3.293 [1796]).

As one can readily see, *Caleb Williams* involves both an exposition and a critical examination of the political principles Godwin articulated in the *Enquiry Concerning Political Justice*. The rationalism of his philosophical work undergoes significant modifications as it gets worked through on the plane of human psychology, where the power of human desires and emotions significantly complicates the capacity of characters to follow the dictates of reason. Mark Philp has noted how *Caleb*

Williams shows the mechanics of rational truth to depend upon the language of sensibility and thus indicates its debt to the literature as well as the philosophy of the eighteenth century. "Although the moral truth revealed to Falkland and Caleb is still objective truth, and although sincerity is allowed to triumph, the mechanics of the revelation and communication of truth and sincerity rely on the language of sentiment and sensibility" (116). Godwin's experience as novelist can thus be seen as one major influence, along with the intellectual and personal relationship that he would develop over the next few years with Mary Wollstonecraft, in modifying the rationalism of *Political Justice*. It prepares the way for the major revisions that Godwin made in both the second and third editions of *Political Justice*. Yet one could also contend that this shift was already implicit in Godwin's philosophy itself, which had been from the start an analysis of the social and personal psychology of political life. The utopian dimensions of his thought demand a shift like the one that led Godwin, as novelist, to meditate much more deeply upon the obstacles that lay in the way of the euthanasia of government, or even the more modest goal of an absolute sincerity in human communication.

Literary Influences on the Composition of *Caleb Williams*

In the early 1830s, toward the end of Godwin's life, publisher Richard Bentley chose to include both *Caleb Williams* and Godwin's 1805 novel *Fleetwood* in the first series of "Bentley's Standard Novels" (1831–55). After the success of the new edition of *Caleb Williams*, Bentley asked Godwin to provide an account of how he came to write his most famous novel, to be published as a preface for the 1832 edition of *Fleetwood*. This preface presents a selective version of the novel's origins, stressing the literary influences that shaped the text at the expense of the political motives behind Godwin's project. It was in that sense crafted to suit the more conservative public climate and readership of the 1830s, who were more likely to welcome a "book of fictitious adventure" than an explicit political allegory. Nonetheless, the preface makes a good starting point for examining the narrative structure of *Caleb Williams*, letting us trace specific literary influences upon the text's composition far better than we can with most novels. *Caleb Williams* becomes an even more impressive literary achievement once we have seen how rich an array of influences Godwin managed to weave into the texture of his novel.

In that account (included in Appendix A), Godwin explains how the reception of *Political Justice* encouraged him to strive to carry his political beliefs to a wider audience of readers – this time with "a book of fictitious adventure, that should in some way be distinguished by a very powerful interest." Godwin provides a detailed glimpse into his mode of composing the novel, explaining how he plotted the events of the book beginning with the third volume before then working backwards, why he adopted the first person confessional format rather than the more common third person narration, and what he did to maintain "a high state of excitement" in his mind during the long months of composition. As in writing *Political Justice*, his quite explicit goal was to change the beliefs of his audience, to create a tale "that shall constitute an epoch in the mind of the reader, that no one, after he has read it, shall ever be exactly the same man that he was before."

In pursuing this goal, Godwin turned to a number of literary predecessors for ideas about how to construct his tale. Along with the journals that Godwin kept for many years, the preface provides us with a detailed picture of his voracious reading habits and gives us a sense of how he drew upon earlier narratives in shaping his own. "It was ever my method," he explains, "to get about me any productions of former authors that seemed to bear on my subject." Godwin credits a variety of literary texts with inspiring him in the enterprise of "exploring the entrails of mind and motive, and in tracing the various rencontres and clashes that may occur between man and man in the diversified scene of human life." Throughout his life, for instance, Godwin read widely in Elizabethan and Jacobean tragedies, which doubtless influenced the suspenseful and dramatic aspects of his own tale of pursuit and revenge. But he was equally well read in contemporary fiction and non-fictional prose. Not only was he familiar with the novels of Richardson and Fielding, he also consulted quite different texts such as Jonathan Swift's *Gulliver's Travels* (1726), and Tobias Smollett's *Roderick Random* (1748), *Peregrine Pickle* (1751), and *Humphry Clinker* (1771) while composing *Caleb Williams*. Indeed, there seem to have been few available literary genres from which Godwin did not draw some significant features in composing *Caleb Williams*.

Godwin's preface first credits two particular texts with helping him to achieve the air of suspense surrounding Falkland's relentless pursuit of Caleb – both of them religious rather than political. The first of these was an ostensibly autobiographical Protestant polemic, *The History of Mademoiselle de St. Phale, Giving a Full account of the Miraculous Conversion of a Noble French Lady and her Daughter to the Reformed Religion, With the Defeat of the Intrigues of a Jesuit their Confessor* (1690). Using the first person confessional mode, Mlle. Justine de St. Phale describes her childhood in seventeenth-century France as the daughter of a Huguenot father and a strictly Catholic mother. Because her parents have agreed to raise their sons as Protestants and their daughters as Catholics, Justine has been brought up as a Catholic. Justine's mother, goaded by her corrupt and scheming confessor, persuades her to attempt to convert her brother Ferdinand to the Catholic faith. Instead, Justine's discussions with her brother convince her of the rightness of the Protestant faith. The excerpt in Appendix D details the first of a series of harrowing adventures as Justine is abducted and tormented by the henchmen of her vengeful mother. Godwin also mentions a second religious tract, *God's Revenge against Murder and Adultery* (1770). In this series of "tragical histories," an omniscient and wrathful God tracks down and punishes those who have sinned against him with all the vengefulness that an offended Falkland exhibits in *Caleb Williams*.

The vivid details of Caleb's own adventures owe a great deal to a quite different category of narratives, the factual and fictional accounts of the lives of criminals that were enormously popular during this period. Godwin specifically mentions two of the former, the "Lives of the Pirates," that is, Daniel

Defoe's *A General History of the Robberies and Murders of the Most Notorious Pyrates* (1724), and *The Newgate Calendar,* published as *The Malefactor's Register; or The Newgate and Tyburn Calendar ... from the Year 1700 to Lady-Day 1779*, an extensive collection of the exploits and punishments of actual British criminals. *The Newgate Calendar* played a particularly important role in the conception of Caleb's experiences as a fugitive. The elaborate prison escapes described in the history of Jack Sheppard provided many specific details for Caleb's own escapes and his attempts at disguising himself while evading arrest. More generally, these documents gave Godwin ideas for depicting the adventures of criminals such as Captain Raymond and his gang, with whom the fugitive Caleb lodges for a short time.

In addition to factual narratives of criminal lives, Godwin relied heavily on literary treatments of this topic. These fictional accounts trace their lineage back to seventeenth-century Spanish picaresque fiction, loosely linked tales of the adventures of a socially marginal *picaro* in his skirmishes with the prevailing social order. These texts were widely available, with Mateo Alemán's *Guzmán De Alfarache* (1599-1602), for instance, translated into English as *The Rogue* as early as 1622 (see Appendix D). In this work, Guzmán satirically observes society as he passes through multiple social roles. He plays the parts of beggar, thief, soldier, and gentleman in turn, employing disguises in a way that Caleb himself will imitate. When Caleb attempts to make a living for himself in London as a writer of criminal tales, he draws on his own past reading of *Guzmán De Alfarache* for inspiration. Henry Fielding's *True and Genuine Account of the Life and Actions of the late Jonathan Wild* (1743), another text mentioned in Godwin's novel, uses the real life story of a thief for more explicitly political purposes. By drawing a parallel between the lives of criminals and the actions of "the great," particularly politicians, it turns its tale of "fictitious adventures" toward the sort of political critique that Godwin sought to provide in *Caleb Williams.*

Yet the conservative Fielding was ultimately not sympathetic toward the criminal lifestyle nor inclined to examine the relation of crime to general social conditions, unlike another writer who was far closer to Godwin in these respects, Daniel Defoe. Defoe's heroes and heroines describe with journalistic precision their fall into crime and, most often, their ultimate reform. *Roxana* (1724) and *Moll Flanders* (1722), for instance, raise the very Godwinian question of whether those oppressed by their social circumstances are justified in revenging themselves by criminal acts upon the social order that has mistreated them. A selection from *The History and Remarkable Life of the Truly Honourable Colonel Jacque, Commonly Call'd Colonel Jack* (1722), included in Appendix D, shows how self-reflective about these issues Defoe's narrators can become. In this passage from early in the novel, the youthful Jack grows increasingly concerned about the evils of the life of pickpocketing and petty theft into which he had fallen as an abandoned child. His discomfort with the life he has been leading increases as he becomes aware of the distinction that society gives to those denominated "gentlemen." Godwin's gentleman-robber, Captain Raymond, echoes Colonel Jack's analysis in his debates with Caleb about the moral and political issues at stake in choosing the life of a criminal.

Godwin was less interested in the sensationalist features of the life of crime, however, than in the way that the lives and minds of criminals were shaped by their encounters with the criminal justice system. That system, he felt, made individuals into confirmed criminals and contributed to, rather than hindering, the spread of vice. Hence Godwin was extremely interested in the work of John Howard, an influential prison reformer who visited jails and prisons all over England and throughout the British Empire. Howard published an important critique of the English prison system, *The State of the Prisons in England and Wales*, in 1777. The excerpts from *The State of the Prisons* in Appendix C show the kind of issues that Howard raised by depicting inhumane prison conditions, where prisoners often lacked sufficient nourishment, clean water, and sanitary sleeping conditions. Unconvicted prisoners might be forced to live in these circumstances for months before they could expect a trial under the system of assizes, in which trials could be conducted only at times when a travelling judge was passing through town. Godwin also knew the play of his close friend Elizabeth Inchbald, *Such Things Are* (1787), which gives a laudatory portrait of John Howard in its main character, Haswell. Inchbald's title may well have suggested to Godwin the original title of *Caleb Williams, Things As They Are*. Godwin refers specifically to *The State of the Prisons* in his novel, underscoring the sense of common purpose between his fiction and Howard's project of social reform.

Although these accounts of criminals and the criminal justice system deeply shaped the moral and political framework of *Caleb Williams*, the psychological texture of the novel ultimately owes more to two other strands of contemporary narrative – the novel of sensibility and the Gothic novel. Falkland, in particular, is a victim of his own sensibility – a term that recurs repeatedly in describing him – but the entire relation between Falkland and Caleb is marked by an emotional intensity characteristic of sentimental fiction. Jean-Jacques Rousseau's *La Nouvelle Héloïse* (1761) and Henry Mackenzie's *The Man of Feeling* (1771) were important works in the rise of the novel of sensibility, but the preeminent creator of this genre in England was Samuel Richardson. Richardson's widely read epistolary novels clearly affected the dramatic features of Godwin's novel. As the excerpt from *Pamela* (1740-41) in Appendix D illustrates, Richardson's portrayal of conflicts between an aristocratic employer and a servant bold enough to challenge her employer's behavior is strikingly like the scenes of confrontation between Falkland and Caleb. Just as Mr. B— invokes his aristocratic rank to convince others of his truthfulness and to discredit Pamela's allegations that he has tried to seduce her, so does Falkland rely upon his status in society to ruin Caleb's reputation and credibility. Equally important for Godwin, though, was the way Richardson set the landscape of sensibility into the framework of the class distinctions that so sharply marked British society. Godwin also drew specific plot features from Richardson, basing many of the details of Falkland's adventures abroad, for instance, on Richardson's *Sir Charles Grandison* (1753-54), a novel in which the hero travels to Italy and courts a sought-after heiress. Richardson's *Clarissa* (1747-48) shows particularly close parallels with Godwin's original ending for the novel. Clarissa's final letters reveal her gradually mounting insanity and imminent death after her abduction and rape by her wicked suitor, Lovelace. The fragmentation and incoherence of her language strongly resemble the style of Caleb's prose as he struggles to comprehend how his pursuers have captured and drugged him.

Caleb Williams has particularly interesting affinities with one of the most popular genres of the era, the Gothic novel. Just as Gothic plots are driven by pervasive uncertainties about characters' motives, so the central relationship between Caleb and Falkland in Godwin's text is defined by awkward efforts of each to fathom the character of the other. As typified by such texts as Horace Walpole's *The Castle of Otranto* (1764), William Beckford's *Vathek* (1786) and Ann Radcliffe's novels, particularly *The Mysteries of Udolpho* (1794), the Gothic novel made use of a host of atmospheric features designed to maximize suspense and terror. The action in such novels frequently takes place in a dark, mysterious castle or monastery, falling into ruin, but offering an endless assortment of secret doors, subterranean passageways, and hidden chambers, a setting that parallels the twists and turns of a complicated story line. Their plots typically involve the pursuit and imprisonment of a helpless young heroine at the hands of a merciless tyrant or an evil monk, and her eventual rescue by a highly idealized young hero. Employing many aspects of the supernatural – ghosts, demons, portraits that walk out of their frames, or statues that bleed – Gothic novels reflected the attraction and the antipathy the British felt towards Roman Catholic religion and the cultures of Mediterranean Europe, particularly Italy and Spain.

While Godwin borrows some of these atmospheric elements, his real innovation in regard to Gothic is to make explicit the ideological implications lying beneath the surface of its literary forms. Like those novels, *Caleb Williams* functions as a pursuit narrative in which Caleb assumes the role of the typical Gothic heroine, constantly fleeing the machinations of a much more powerful villain. The suspense that Godwin achieves in narrating the graphic details of Caleb's imprisonments and his harrowing escapes is often intensified by using Gothic character types, such as the witch-like crone affiliated with Captain Raymond's gang, or Gothic narrative devices, such as the reliance upon accident in shaping the plot. In the deeply ambivalent mixture of love and hatred that Caleb feels for his tormenter Falkland, *Caleb Williams* also reflects an important trend of the Gothic novel as it became more concerned with psychological analysis. Caleb and Falkland can readily be interpreted as doubles or alter-egos, with their relationship exhibiting a strong degree of homoerotic or homosocial desire.

The most striking omission from Godwin's 1832 preface, however, is the absence of any reference to the explicitly programmatic novels and plays produced by the Jacobin writers who were his closest friends and collaborators during the 1790s. Their texts provided the most immediate models for his fictional enterprise and the closest analogue to his own political purposes. In response to the political fervor occasioned by the French Revolution, many writers of this period identified the novel and the stage as vehicles for promoting political discussion and reform. There they could hope to avoid the more direct censorship and repression that the government increasingly exerted against explicitly political tracts. Although these figures formed only a loose literary group, many of them, such as Godwin, the noted actress and playwright Elizabeth Inchbald, and the writer and novelist, Thomas Holcroft, were part of the same social circle. They actively read and critiqued one another's works, often at the manuscript stage. Godwin's diaries indicate his own careful study of such current works as Inchbald's *A Simple Story* (1791), Robert Bage's *Man As He Is* (1792), and Holcroft's *Anna St. Ives* (1792). Godwin and Holcroft enjoyed almost daily interaction throughout the period when Godwin was writing *Caleb Williams* and commented extensively on each other's narrative projects. Godwin's diaries indicate that he read, critiqued, and often revised sections of the manuscript of Holcroft's *The Adventures of Hugh Trevor* (1794) at precisely the time that he was finishing *Caleb Williams*.

While some Jacobin texts, such as Inchbald's play about John Howard, aimed explicitly at social reform, the greater number tended to focus more narrowly upon the domestic scene, depicted as a place where the consequences of the prevailing political order could readily be seen and assessed. As with Godwin's *Political Justice*, their agenda for reform was thus educational rather than overtly political in orientation, with change envisaged as a result of the moral reform of particular individuals. Inchbald's *A Simple Story* is typical in this regard, tracing the lapses of its female heroine and the tragedies that follow to the defects of her boarding school education. Holcroft's *Anna St. Ives* is an even more explicitly didactic text, heavily dependent upon the plot contrivances and stylistic modes of eighteenth-century predecessors. It contains long stretches of philosophical debate, and the twists and turns of its plot seem quite obviously intended to give illustrative force to its ideas.

Godwin doubtless learned a good deal from both Inchbald and Holcroft, recognizing, for instance, the skill that both had gained from their experience in the theater in building and sustaining dramatic tension. Yet his most significant debt is to the psychological realism that both sought to depict in their narratives. Despite the sometimes contrived or didactic nature of their plots, both of these writers tried to give depth to their characters' feelings, depicting complex shifts in mood and showing, with considerable originality, the difficulty even for intelligent individuals in clearly understanding their own motives and suppressed emotions. They traced with considerable specificity the effects of social circumstance upon individual thought and behavior, thereby making a significant contribution to the developing novel tradition in England. Maria Edgeworth's letter to Elizabeth Inchbald about *A Simple Story* makes it clear that contemporary literary figures perceived the importance of Jacobin fiction in this regard. "I never read any novel that affected me so strongly, or that so completely possessed me with the belief in the real existence of all the people it represents.... I believed all to be real, and was affected as I should be by the real scenes if they had passed before my eyes."[1] The Jacobin writers achieved this realistic effect in part by showing less; they leave more for characters (and thus also for readers) to discern, forcing them, as Fanny Burney and other recent predecessors had done, to read thoughts and motives from the external signs of visage and behavior.

Much as Godwin learned from his fellow Jacobin writers, *Caleb Williams* stands apart from them in several significant respects. It is less overtly didactic; Godwin subordinates debate to plot, and what debate it does contain grows naturally out of Caleb's situation (his reflections on prison, for instance, or his and Captain Raymond's discussion of the life of crime). In addition, Godwin typically leaves the broader philosophical implications of the events for us as readers to deduce; analysis, where it does occur, is Caleb's rather than the author's and thus remains rooted in the particularity of Caleb's situation. The greatest formal contrast with Godwin's fellow writers, however, comes from his decision to adopt a first-person, confessional mode of narration, a change that his 1832 preface describes him falling into almost by accident. The first-person form was of course not completely new; both epistolary fiction and confessional narratives of all kinds had made extensive use of it in European literature for centuries. Yet Godwin deployed it in particularly effective ways, recognizing the substantial impact it could have in creating psychological uncertainty and narrative suspense. He uses this device not only to give us insight into Caleb's state of mind, but also to limit his access to the minds of other characters. This is particularly evident and effective in Caleb's relation with Falkland, where so many of their respective actions are based upon misapprehension of the thoughts and intentions of the other person, but it also affects Caleb's relations with Forester, Laura Denison, and most other figures. Caleb is forced to speculate upon and even to invent Falkland's

---

1   Quoted from James Boaden, *Memoirs of Mrs. Inchbald; including her Familiar Correspondence with the Most Distinguished Persons of her Time* (London: 1833), II, 152.

mind and motives, putting him for the purposes of the narrative in a position much like our position as readers of the text.

Caleb Williams: Impact and Influence

Caleb Williams was one of the literary sensations of the 1790s, a widely popular text that proved to be Godwin's greatest commercial success as a writer. Sales in Britain were rapid; it went through three editions by 1797 and became one of the first texts selected for Bentley's Standard Novels series in 1831. Godwin himself oversaw the first five editions in England, including the 1831 edition that we have used as the basis for this edition, and made substantial revisions for the second and third editions. Irish and American editions appeared in 1795, and by 1797 it had appeared in multiple French and German translations. Twenty-six editions in three different languages appeared during his lifetime, and it was reprinted steadily throughout the nineteenth century.

The novel reached an even wider audience thanks to the success of a 1796 stage adaptation by George Colman the Younger, The Iron Chest. Although Colman changed the characters' names and substantially altered the plot, he drew the full dramatic effect from Caleb's gradual detection of his employer's secret and the emotionally charged confrontations between Falkland and Caleb. The climactic scene from The Iron Chest in Appendix E indicates how much Colman's dramatization owes to Godwin. To make the tale suitable for the stage, Colman had to transform the confessional format of Caleb's narration into dramatic dialogue. But he also made an intentional choice to minimize the political resonance of the novel, stripping away the more general social implications of the personal struggle between Caleb and Falkland.

Encouraged by the success of Caleb Williams, Godwin continued to write novels for the rest of his life. All of them, from St. Leon in 1799 to Deloraine in 1833 exhibit the same blending of psychological analysis and social commentary that had made Caleb Williams such a powerful and innovative text. St. Leon and Mandeville (1817) are historical novels set in the sixteenth and seventeenth centuries respectively, examining how social circumstances and upbringing shape an individual's identity and ideological orientation. Like Godwin's other novels, *Fleetwood* (1805), *Cloudesley* (1830), and *Deloraine* (1833), they focus upon the ways in which human ties of marriage, friendship, and kinship are marked, indeed, often warped, by the power relations that dominate society. They stress the importance of early education in marking character in unalterable ways.

Caleb Williams proved the most durable and influential of these texts. As Pamela Clemit has demonstrated, it provided the model for a school of Godwinian fiction in the early nineteenth century. The novel exerted a powerful influence on many other writers, especially those who became part of Godwin's immediate circle and who shared his aspiration of using fiction to contribute to political debate and reform. Mary Wollstonecraft's unfinished final work of fiction, *The Wrongs of Woman: or, Maria*, which Godwin published among her *Posthumous Works* in 1798, shows particularly close affinities with Godwin's narrative style and political concerns. Just as Godwin turned to fiction to disseminate ideas from *Political Justice*, Wollstonecraft set aside her plans for a second volume of her *Vindication of the Rights of Woman* (1792) in order to write a novel illustrating the difficulty for women of gaining rights within a culture of male privilege and power. Her novel's first-person narrator tells the history of her abuse within the institution of marriage, leading to her eventual imprisonment in a madhouse at the hands of her dissolute husband. Maria speaks of her marriage as having "bastilled" her for life, and echoes Caleb Williams' language as she describes the feeling of being hunted by her husband's accessories when she tries to escape her marriage.

Although Wollstonecraft's notes for the unwritten final chapters of *The Wrongs of Woman* are sketchy, they suggest how she might have resolved her version of this Godwinian plot. They imply that Maria, like Caleb, would fail to find impartial justice in appealing to the British court system for assistance. Maria's argument that her rights as a human being should outweigh her husband's rights over her as a wife fall on deaf ears, as do Caleb's attempts to use reason alone to convey the truth of his situation in a legal setting. Wollstonecraft's drafts parallel the original ending of *Caleb Williams*, with one plot climax showing the gradual fragmentation of Maria's narrative as she begins to lose consciousness after poisoning herself. Although *The Wrongs of Woman* was never completed, Wollstonecraft's project was shared and continued by other writers such as Mary Hays, another member of the Godwin-Wollstonecraft circle. Hays's first novel, *Memoirs of Emma Courtney* (1796), deals with the frustrations that arise from society's confinement of female aspirations and desires, and includes a figure modeled directly on Godwin. Her next novel, *The Victim of Prejudice* (1799), attacks the pervasive double standard that governs male and female sexual behavior. It shows how even a woman of great virtue faces insurmountable obstacles to overcoming an illegitimate birth and how vulnerable to corrupt men such status makes her.

Caleb Williams proved an equally strong influence on a figure who came to be known as the "Godwin of America," Charles Brockden Brown. Brown was an attentive reader and critic of Godwin's philosophy who followed Godwin's lead in using fiction to present his speculations on politics and morality. In his 1798 novel, *Wieland; or, The Transformation*, Clara Wieland unfolds the story of her idyllic family's destruction when a mysterious stranger intrudes upon their lives and begins to torment the various family members with his uncanny abilities as a ventriloquist. The Wieland family's vulnerability to this stranger's manipulation indicates just how superficial had been the veneer of reason that they saw as shaping their lives. Even the minds of educated, liberal individuals, Brown implies, remain susceptible to a resurgence of a deeply-seated political conservatism and to the use of religious fanaticism and brutal physical violence. Set in the rustic Philadelphia of the 1760s, *Wieland* serves as a fascinating exploration of the human psyche in the context of the emerging American democratic state. Brown continued to explore characters at the social margins and psychological extremes in his subsequent novels, from *Ormond, or The Secret Witness* (1799) through *Stephen Calvert* (1815).

Godwin's direct influence persisted into the mid-nineteenth

century through his contact with writers such as Edward Bulwer Lytton. Especially in his early novels, Bulwer Lytton adopts the form of fiction to foster the same sorts of social and political reforms that he was to pursue actively as a Member of Parliament. *Paul Clifford*'s (1830) "gentleman" thief and *Lucretia*'s (1846) female poisoner indicate his interest in the social circumstances that produce a criminal mind. His 1832 novel, *Eugene Aram* (1832) comes closest to the Godwinian prototype, being based upon an account in *The Newgate Calendar* that Godwin himself had considered using for a fictional work. A scholar who murdered a friend whom he suspected of having committed adultery with his wife, Aram continued to lead a normal life for fourteen years, only to be implicated, and then tried, convicted, and executed when his accomplice Houseman was brought to trial in 1759.

Godwin's most deeply felt influence as a novelist, however, may be found in the works of his daughter, Mary Wollstonecraft Shelley. Mary Shelley's masterpiece, *Frankenstein* (1818), is visibly indebted to Godwin for its confessional form and for its use of Gothic conventions to engage in social critique, and it shares Godwin's interests in close psychological scrutiny and in education. Although the novel appeared anonymously, reviewers such as Sir Walter Scott readily characterized it as having been written in the "Godwinian" vein. Victor Frankenstein's intemperate ambition, his instrumental use of others, his inability either to escape or to acknowledge his own tragic mistake are all features that bear the stamp of the Godwinian hero. Likewise, the structure of Mary Shelley's best-known work, with its depiction of the tortured love/hate relationship between creator and creature and of the different turns that each character takes as pursuer and pursued, owes much to the model of *Caleb Williams*. Shelley reconfigured Godwinian formulas for her subsequent novels as well, from the early *Valperga* (1823) and *The Last Man* (1826) to *Lodore* (1835) and *Falkner* (1837). Her flawed protagonists frequently fit the type of the Godwinian hero; their fates most often produce tragedy and solitude.

Both Godwin's political philosophy and his novels influenced many of the most prominent British Romantic writers, with the most visible instance being his son-in-law, Percy Bysshe Shelley. The visionary radicalism of Shelley's poetry and prose show clear affiliations with Godwin's *Political Justice*, a work of which Shelley was a devoted reader. Although Shelley's poetry relied more heavily upon the poetic logic of imagery and upon allegorical abstractions than Godwin's narratives, one can readily see in both the same concern with exploring and exploding the power relations pervasive in society. Godwin's trauma-shaped protagonists also played a seminal role in producing what came to be known as the Byronic hero – a character type that enjoyed immense popularity from the time of Byron's publication of the first two cantos of *Childe Harold's Pilgrimage* in 1812. Byron reshaped and revalued the Gothic villain to depict a series of brooding, world-weary, yet highly self-assertive figures, proudly defiant of social conventions, morality, and even fate. Byron greatly admired Godwin's characterization of Ferdinando Falkland, and he identified Falkland in his letters as an important influence on his own fictional protagonists. Byron's *Manfred* (1817) typifies this new type of Romantic hero. Tormented by a past crime that may well have been incest and by the death of his beloved, Manfred summons the spirits of the universe to help him find release from his pains. Refusing to accept the dichotomies of conventional morality and to go either to heaven or to hell, Manfred insists upon attaining a state of complete oblivion and wins out over death itself. Byron's rebels gave birth in turn to such Victorian heirs as Emily Brontë's Heathcliff (*Wuthering Heights*, 1847), and Charlotte Brontë's Rochester (*Jane Eyre*, 1847).

Critical Reactions to the Novel

Initial reactions to *Caleb Williams* were mixed, with the tenor of the judgment typically reflecting the politics of the reviewer. Yet most reviewers recognized it as a highly important novel, and even those who criticized its politics or its morals conceded that it possessed considerable narrative power. Thus, the *Analytical Review* (a moderate Whig journal) described *Caleb*

Williams as "a work in which the powers of genius and philosophy are strongly united," though the reviewer felt compelled to mark his own reservations elsewhere with the message he felt the book contained. The *Critical Review* (another Whig journal) applauded the moral of the work, while criticizing Godwin for neglecting to adopt a more religious tone in his critique of human behavior, and suggesting that most of the political content of the novel be deleted in future editions. Conservative critics were less generous. The reviewer for the *British Critic* (a journal funded in part by government secret service money) wrote that the novel provided "a striking example of the evil use which may be made of considerable talents," and saw Godwin's depiction of British society as an "odious" and "noxious" misrepresentation. The more radical *Analytical Review* acknowledged the "power of genius" in the work, yet even that reviewer criticized Godwin for abandoning the traditional "rules of composition" and bitterly attacked the moral tenor of the work as a whole. Typical of the era, these responses frequently focused upon the moral effect that *Caleb Williams* might be expected to have upon its readers. Although they attended very little to questions of form, they thus raised an issue that has been of great importance in recent discussion of the novel, the ways in which it attempts to reshape the values of its readers.

Despite the reservations expressed by some early critics, *Caleb Williams* came to be considered during the Romantic era as one of the finest novels in the English literary tradition. In an 1815 review of Godwin's *Lives of Edward and John Philips*, James Mackintosh praised *Caleb Williams* at length, calling its author the greatest male novelist of the age – the best, at least, since Oliver Goldsmith. Mackintosh wrote that although the novel was written with a "temporary purpose," it would hold its interest for readers long after its historical implications had ceased to be commonly understood. In *The Spirit of the Age* (1830), William Hazlitt, one of the pre-eminent critics of the era, termed the novel a masterpiece, ranking it second only to Cervantes' *Don Quixote* for the brilliant manner in which the relationship between its two main characters is delineated. "We conceive no one ever began *Caleb Williams* that did not read it through," Hazlitt wrote; "no one that ever read it could possibly forget it."

Yet there were few Romantic novelists whose reputation managed to sustain itself during the age of high realism that followed. Though they continued to praise Jane Austen and Sir Walter Scott, critics of the Victorian era tended to discount other Romantic fiction, leaving *Caleb Williams*, along with most Jacobin and Gothic novels, outside the generally acknowledged line of literary history. This judgment was in part political; Jacobin fiction, in particular, remained too radical in tone and content for a more conservative age. But it also reflected Victorian aesthetic reservations about works that seemed to them too declamatory in style, too implausible in plot, or too sensationalist in content. By 1932, we find even a sympathetic critic such as J. M. S. Tompkins summing up received opinion in this way. "Between the work of the four great novelists of the mid-eighteenth century and that of Jane Austen and Scott there are no names which posterity has consented to call great."[1] Between the 1830s and the 1970s, one finds relatively little critical literature on *Caleb Williams*, nor any new editions between 1926 and 1970.

By contrast, the last few decades have seen a renewed and immensely fruitful critical engagement with *Caleb Williams*. Four new English-language editions have appeared since 1970, including one edited by Pamela Clemit as part of Pickering's *Collected Novels and Memoirs of William Godwin*, and a host of interpretations have followed upon the more ready availability of the text. This revival of interest owes something to a more general renewal of attention to neglected writers of the Romantic age. But it owes something as well to an accident of literary history. In 1966, D. Gilbert Dumas announced the discovery of an earlier ending for the novel altogether different from the one in published versions of the text. In that original ending, Caleb is imprisoned, poisoned, and ultimately driven to madness by Falkland's agents. Caleb's fate in that ending is –

---

1 J.M.S. Tompkins, *The Popular Novel in England, 1770-1800* (London: 1932), vii.

though not necessarily more tragic than the rewritten version – far more pessimistic about his power as an individual to withstand the forces of political repression. Having the alternative version made it easier for critics to see and to debate the significance of Godwin's choice in ending the novel as he ultimately chose to do. Attending to this particular ambivalence in the text opened the door in turn to consideration of the further depths in Godwin's text, the structural and psychological complexity that has produced intense critical debate over the last few decades.

An important initial task in this critical revival was to restore to the novel a sense of its political immediacy and force. David McCracken, whose 1970 edition of *Caleb Williams* was the first to include the original ending, also wrote a pair of articles linking Godwin and Burke, as well as the first study of Godwin's important theoretical essay "Of History and Romance." Gary Kelly and Marilyn Butler did ground-breaking work in framing their interpretations of *Caleb Williams* within detailed consideration of its historical context. Kelly's work on Jacobin fiction helped generate a new appreciation for these novels, and his *English Fiction of the Romantic Period* provides an indispensable guide to the broader topic of Romantic fiction. Butler's studies focused upon locating Godwin within the political debates of the era; she also co-authored the general introduction to *The Collected Novels and Memoirs of William Godwin* (1992). Later critics have contextualized *Caleb Williams* in additional ways, Ian Ousby looking at its links to detective fiction, Randa Helfield at the legal dimensions of the novel, and Jon Klancher and Garrett A. Sullivan at its relation to the print culture and publishing climate of the period.

A central question for these historically oriented interpretations has been the degree to which *Caleb Williams* embodies or diverges from the principles of *Political Justice*. Can the novel, that is, be seen in the terms Godwin suggested, as an attempt to give wider audience to his political philosophy, or did the fictional mode lead him, intentionally or not, to revise or critique those principles? This perspective is particularly evident in studies that focus upon Godwin's political philosophy, such as the works by Mark Philp and Don Locke, and also dominates the analyses in the two recent biographies of Godwin by Peter H. Marshall and William St. Clair. But this angle has also proven fruitful for literary critics, including Kenneth Graham and Gary Handwerk, who have taken up the question of how the translation of Godwin's ideas from philosophy into fiction may have caused him to rethink those ideas.

Equally important in reestablishing the reputation of *Caleb Williams* was a fuller appreciation for its formal and technical innovations, and thus for its contributions to the development of the novel in England. Robert Kiely was an early advocate for Godwin's importance in this regard, as was B.J. Tysdahl, and Gary Kelly closely analyzed the coherence between character and plot in *Caleb Williams*. Recent critics have brought to light two particularly innovative features of Godwin's text, its highly original combination and recasting of available generic models (Kenneth Graham and Donald Wehrs) and its use of first-person narration to create both psychological depth and psychological ambiguity (Pamela Clemit and Gerard Barker).

Differing critical readings of the novel can often be measured by what they make of its ending, where what should have been a moment of triumph for Caleb turns somehow into his defeat and self-denigration. In a certain way, the original ending follows more consistently from all that has gone before, concluding as it does with the dominant political order largely unmoved by Caleb's rebellion. The revised ending, in contrast, offers a more wrenching and ambiguous close. Caleb gains his freedom, yet remains wracked by a guilt that seems to internalize within his own consciousness many of the features of the ideological apparatus that had previously been oppressing him from without. Mitzi Myers has argued for the superiority of the second ending because it foregrounds for the reader the ambiguity of Caleb's moral status, claiming that, "The numerous political reflections and the brilliant psychological analyses cannot be considered in isolation from the basic moral pattern that forms the core of the novel." Eric Rothstein has also analyzed how guilt and innocence, or the characters' perceptions of these states, are as much at the heart of the novel as epistemological issues of truth and falsehood or political issues of power and persuasion. Tilottama Rajan's "Wollstonecraft and Godwin: Reading the Secrets of the Political Novel" offers a particularly subtle reading of the conclusion in light of Godwin's own theory of fiction, suggesting that the reader's role is to read past the ending in which Caleb remains trapped. Deconstructive critics such as Karl Simms and Leland Warren have stressed more strongly the irreducible ambiguity of the ending as a measure of Godwin's uncertainty about or inability to achieve his own didactic purposes.

As for early critics, the emotional intensity of the central relationship between Caleb and Falkland has remained a dominant theme. Caleb's attitude as it vacillates between admiration for and detestation of Falkland is not a stance for which Godwin gives us any easy interpretive key. Some critics, such as Andrew Scheiber, have examined the pair as dialectical counterpoints for radically opposed values, while others, such as Masao Miyoshi and Robert Uphaus, have argued that Falkland and Caleb ultimately blur together, becoming doubles for each other's behavior and attitudes. More recently, the specifically homosocial and homoerotic dimensions of their relationship have been explored by Alex Gold and Robert Corber.

This array of recent criticism can remind us of how well Godwin's novel works, and of the many levels on which it works at the same time. The aesthetic coherence and analytical rigor of *Caleb Williams* go hand in hand in conveying the deeply unsettling picture that Godwin sought to portray of how ideology and character intersect. It is in that sense most especially a novel for our age, an age of pervasive and intrusive ideological manipulations. To have seen the world of modern politics in the making, at one of its moments of revolutionary origin, and to have depicted it with all the clarity of vision that he could command, was Godwin's gift as a novelist.

William Godwin: A Brief Chronology

1756   Born on March 3 in Wisbech, North Cam-
        bridgeshire, to Reverend John and Ann Hull
        Godwin, the seventh of thirteen children in a
        middle-class, Dissenting household.

1767   Becomes a pupil of Reverend Samuel Newton, an
        earnest and severe adherent of the strictly Calvinist
        Sandemanian Protestant sect.

1773   Enrolls at Hoxton Academy, one of the most
        prominent and best Dissenting academies in the
        country.

1778   Upon graduation from Hoxton, begins a five-year
        career as a Dissenting minister, marked by doctrinal
        and practical dissension with his congregations.

1783   Gives up the ministry, moves to London and begins
        a literary career; publishes a series of political, his-
        torical, and educational pamphlets while seeking
        regular journalist employment.

1784   Publishes two short sentimental novels, *Damon and
        Delia* and *Italian Letters*. Gains regular work as a
        contributor to the *English Review* and *The New
        Annual Register*, writing for the latter the section on
        "British and Foreign History."

1785   Writes for a new Whig journal, the *Political Herald
        and Review*, and eventually edits it until its demise
        in 1787.

1786   Meets Thomas Holcroft, who quickly became one
        of Godwin's closest friends.

1788   Begins keeping a daily journal, which he continues
        until his death.

1789   With the seizure of the Bastille on July 14, the
        French Revolution begins; on November 4,
        Richard Price delivers his pro-revolutionary ser-
        mon, *Discourse on the Idea of Our Country*.

1790   On November 1, Edmund Burke publishes *Reflec-
        tions on the Revolution in France*; on November 29,

Mary Wollstonecraft publishes *A Vindication of the Rights of Men.*

1791   Meets Mary Wollstonecraft. Thomas Paine publishes *Rights of Man;* in July, Godwin signs contract with George Robinson to write a lengthy work of political philosophy, which eventually becomes *Political Justice.*

1792   London Corresponding Society formed; Mary Wollstonecraft publishes *A Vindication of the Rights of Woman*; Paine flees England under threat of prosecution after publishing Part 2 of the *Rights of Man.*

1793   Louis XVI of France is executed on January 21; France declares war on Britain on February 1; Godwin publishes *Enquiry Concerning Political Justice* on Feburary 14 and begins writing *Caleb Williams*; publishes "Letters of Mucius" in the *Morning Chronicle.*

1794   Pitt suspends *habeas corpus* on May 12 and soon has a dozen of the most prominent British radicals arrested for treason; *Things As They Are; or, The Adventures of Caleb Williams* published on May 26; in October, Godwin's *Cursory Strictures* contributes to the acquittal of the radicals on trial; Godwin meets William Hazlitt and Samuel Coleridge; Mary Wollstonecraft gives birth to a daughter, Fanny, by her lover, Gilbert Imlay.

1796   Meets Mary Wollstonecraft again; they become friends, then lovers in August; George Colman's *The Iron Chest* is first performed.

1797   Publishes *The Enquirer, Reflections on Education, Manners and Literature*; Mary Wollstonecraft becomes pregnant, and they marry on March 29; a daughter, also named Mary, is born on August 30, but Wollstonecraft dies of post-delivery complications on September 10.

1798   Publishes his *Memoirs* of Mary Wollstonecraft and her *Posthumous Works*, the former harshly abused by the press and by friends for its frank recounting of her life.

1799   Publishes a second novel, *St. Leon: A Tale of the Sixteenth Century*.

1801   Meets and quickly marries Mary Jane Clairmont, who brings her daughter Jane (Claire) and son Charles into Godwin's home.

1803   William Godwin, Jr. born on March 28; publishes multi-volume *Life of Chaucer*.

1805   Publishes a third novel, *Fleetwood: or, The New Man of Feeling*; establishes with his wife the Juvenile Library, a publishing house for children's literature; over the next twenty years, writes a series of mostly historical works for children under the pseudonyms Edward Baldwin and Theophilus Marcliffe.

1812   Becomes acquainted with Percy Bysshe Shelley and his wife Harriet.

1813   Meets Lord Byron.

1814   Shelley elopes with Godwin's daughter Mary to the Continent, accompanied by Godwin's stepdaughter Claire.

1815   Publishes *The Lives of Edward and John Philips*.

1816   Travels to Edinburgh and meets Sir Walter Scott; Fanny Godwin commits suicide in October; Percy Bysshe Shelley marries Mary Godwin in December after the suicide of his first wife.

1817   Publishes *Mandeville, A Tale of the Seventeenth Century in England*.

1818   Mary Shelley publishes *Frankenstein*.

1820   Publishes *Of Population*, a rebuttal of Thomas Malthus's *Essay on the Principle of Population* (1798).

1822   On July 8, Percy Bysshe Shelley drowns in the Bay of Spezia, Italy.

1823   Mary Shelley and her son, Percy Florence Shelley, return to England.

1824   Begins publishing multi-volume *History of the Commonwealth of England* (through 1828).

1825   Declared bankrupt and forced to close publishing house.

1830   Publishes *Cloudesley: a novel*.

1831   Publishes *Thoughts on Man*, his first philosophical
        work since *The Enquirer*.
1832   First major parliamentary Reform Bill passed;
        William Godwin, Jr. dies of cholera in September.
1833   Godwin's final novel, *Deloraine*, appears; offered a
        sinecure post as "Office Keeper and Yeoman Usher
        of the Exchequer" by the government.
1834   Publishes *Lives of the Necromancers*, and William
        Godwin, Jr.'s novel, *Transfusion*, with a memoir of
        his son.
1836   Dies in London on April 7 at the age of 80.

A Note on the Text

The text used for this edition of *Caleb Williams* is the fifth edition of the novel, published in 1831 as part of Colburn and Bentley's "Standard Novels" series. This was the last edition published during Godwin's lifetime and incorporates the many changes he made in the text over the first five editions. The Pickering edition of *Caleb Williams*, edited by Pamela Clemit and incorporating variants collated by Maurice Hindle, lists over 1200 such changes. The large majority of these changes were stylistic or grammatical in nature, typically involving single words or short phrases. The names of several characters were changed after the 1794 edition, with "Doctor Arnold" becoming "Doctor Wilson," "Jones" becoming "Gines," "Gines" becoming "Warnes," and "Barton" becoming "Jeckols." A number of other changes were made in an effort to have characters such as Tyrrel and Grimes speak in language that more accurately reflects their social standing and education.

Godwin also made a number of more substantial revisions for the second and third editions. Readers who wish to study these variants in detail should consult the Pickering edition, Volume 3 of the *Collected Novels and Memoirs of William Godwin* (London, 1992). The most characteristic tendency of the major revisions is to sharpen or clarify the motives of various characters at key moments in the text, often by expanding upon their thought processes. In the first volume, for instance, Godwin added material describing in more detail Emily's feelings toward Falkland and his reactions to her, especially at the moment of her death. As revised, his rescue of her from the fire takes on a more explicitly erotic dimension than had been the case in the first edition. The motives of both Falkland and Tyrrel in their quarrel with each other also get expanded, with the effect of these changes being to emphasize Falkland's greater self-restraint and ethical superiority to Tyrrel. Godwin also made a structural change in the first volume for the third edition, reversing the order of the stories of Emily Melville and Hawkins so that the former precedes the latter. Probably in response to criticism of the novel, Godwin revised a number of passages dealing with legal issues, making clear, for example, that after Tyrrel's death Falkland is called before the magistrates simply for an informal hearing. A formal trial at that point would have made a subsequent trial, as occurs at the end of the novel, legally impossible.

In Volume 2, Godwin similarly added detail to his initial description of Forester's character and Caleb's response to him, and also expanded upon Forester's judgment of Caleb at their private interview. He inserted the details about the secret apartment where Caleb hides his possessions when he flees Falkland's house, further description of Caleb's state of mind when overtaken by a pursuer, more detail on Brightwel's character, and a brief conclusion for the tale of the peasant whose murder case had come before Falkland earlier in the novel.

The most significant changes occur in Volume 3, where Godwin adds several passages that indicate how Caleb's despair brings him to thoughts of suicide. Several paragraphs are added to Chapter 8 and another to Chapter 11, in which Caleb reflects upon how Falkland has been able to use the power of social institutions to rob him of his freedom. The largest single addition involves the passages on Laura Denison and her family, which underscore how successfully Falkland can undermine Caleb's efforts to convince anyone, even a figure of Laura's upright nature, of his innocence.

These alterations contribute to the psychological depth of the novel, and thus accord with the description of its purpose that Godwin emphasized in the preface he wrote for the fifth edition. They do not, however, diminish in any way the political resonance of the novel. There were no major omissions of material from the first edition in subsequent editions, so that the political implications of Caleb's fate remain as vividly present in revised editions as in the 1794 edition. As when Godwin first produced his text, politics and psychology continue to go hand in hand.

With only minor exceptions, we have retained both the spelling and punctuation of Godwin's 1831 text. These indicate Godwin's idiosyncratic but considered attitude toward the English language and, more importantly, reflect his sense of the rhythm and inflections of his prose.

THINGS AS THEY ARE;

OR, THE

ADVENTURES

OF

CALEB WILLIAMS.

BY WILLIAM GODWIN.

IN THREE VOLUMES.

VOL. I.

Amidst the woods the leopard knows his kind;
The tyger preys not on the tyger brood:
Man only is the common foe of man.

———

LONDON:
PRINTED FOR B. CROSBY, STATIONERS-COURT,
LUDGATE-STREET.
1794.

PREFACE

THE following narrative is intended to answer a purpose more general and important than immediately appears upon the face of it. The question now afloat in the world respecting *Things As They Are* is the most interesting that can be presented to the human mind. While one party pleads for reformation and change, the other extols in the warmest terms the existing constitution of society. It seemed as if something would be gained for the decision of this question, if that constitution were faithfully developed in its practical effects. What is now presented to the public is no refined and abstract speculation; it is a study and delineation of things passing in the moral world. It is but of late that the inestimable importance of political principles has been adequately apprehended. It is now known to philosophers, that the spirit and character of the government intrudes itself into every rank of society. But this is a truth highly worthy to be communicated to persons whom books of philosophy and science are never likely to reach. Accordingly it was proposed, in the invention of the following work, to comprehend, as far as the progressive nature of a single story would allow, a general review of the modes of domestic and unrecorded despotism by which man becomes the destroyer of man. If the author shall have taught a valuable lesson, without subtracting from the interest and passion by which a performance of this sort ought to be characterised, he will have reason to congratulate himself upon the vehicle he has chosen.

12 May 1794

THIS preface was withdrawn in the original edition, in compliance with the alarms of booksellers. "Caleb Williams" made his first appearance in the world, in the same month in which the sanguinary plot broke out against the liberties of Englishmen, which was happily terminated by the acquittal of its first intended victims, in the close of that year. Terror was the order of the day; and it was feared that even the humble novelist might be shown to be constructively a traitor.

29 October 1795

VOLUME THE FIRST

CHAPTER I

My life has for several years been a theatre of calamity. I have been a mark for the vigilance of tyranny, and I could not escape. My fairest prospects have been blasted. My enemy has shown himself inaccessible to entreaties, and untired in persecution. My fame, as well as my happiness, has become his victim. Every one, as far as my story has been known, has refused to assist me in my distress, and has execrated my name. I have not deserved this treatment. My own conscience witnesses in behalf of that innocence, my pretensions to which are regarded in the world as incredible. There is now, however, little hope that I shall escape from the toils that universally beset me. I am incited to the penning of these memoirs only by a desire to divert my mind from the deplorableness of my situation, and a faint idea that posterity may by their means be induced to render me a justice which my contemporaries refuse. My story will, at least, appear to have that consistency which is seldom attendant but upon truth.

I was born of humble parents, in a remote county of England. Their occupations were such as usually fall to the lot of peasants, and they had no portion to give me, but an education free from the usual sources of depravity, and the inheritance, long since lost by their unfortunate progeny! of an honest fame. I was taught the rudiments of no science, except reading, writing, and arithmetic. But I had an inquisitive mind, and neglected no means of information from conversation or books. My improvement was greater than my condition in life afforded room to expect.

There are other circumstances deserving to be mentioned as having influenced the history of my future life. I was somewhat above the middle stature. Without being particularly athletic in appearance, or large in my dimensions, I was uncommonly vigorous and active. My joints were supple, and I was formed to excel in youthful sports. The habits of my mind, however, were to a certain degree at war with the dictates of boyish vanity. I had considerable aversion to the boisterous gaiety of the village gallants, and contrived to satisfy my love of praise with an unfrequent apparition at their amusements. My excellence in these respects, however, gave a turn to my meditations. I delighted to read of feats of activity, and was particularly interested by tales in which corporeal ingenuity or strength are the means resorted to for supplying resources and conquering difficulties. I inured myself to mechanical pursuits, and devoted much of my time to an endeavour after mechanical invention.

The spring of action which, perhaps more than any other, characterised the whole train of my life, was curiosity. It was this that gave me my mechanical turn; I was desirous of tracing the variety of effects which might be produced from given causes. It was this that made me a sort of natural philosopher; I could not rest till I had acquainted myself with the solutions that had been invented for the phenomena of the universe. In fine, this produced in me an invincible attachment to books of narrative and romance. I panted for the unravelling of an adventure with an anxiety, perhaps almost equal to that of the man whose future happiness or misery depended on its issue. I read, I devoured compositions of this sort. They took possession of my soul; and the effects they produced were frequently discernible in my external appearance and my health. My curiosity, however, was not entirely ignoble: village anecdotes and scandal had no charms for me: my imagination must be excited; and when that was not done, my curiosity was dormant.

The residence of my parents was within the manor of Ferdinando Falkland, a country squire of considerable opulence. At an early age I attracted the favourable notice of Mr. Collins, this gentleman's steward, who used to call in occasionally at my father's. He observed the particulars of my progress with approbation, and made a favourable report to his master of my industry and genius.

In the summer of the year —, Mr. Falkland visited his estate in our county after an absence of several months. This was a period of misfortune to me. I was then eighteen years of age. My father lay dead in our cottage. I had lost my mother some years before. In this forlorn situation I was surprised with a message from the squire, ordering me to repair to the mansion-house the morning after my father's funeral.

Though I was not a stranger to books, I had no practical acquaintance with men. I had never had occasion to address a person of this elevated rank, and I felt no small uneasiness and awe on the present occasion. I found Mr. Falkland a man of small stature, with an extreme delicacy of form and appearance. In place of the hard-favoured and inflexible visages I had been accustomed to observe, every muscle and petty line of his countenance seemed to be in an inconceivable degree pregnant with meaning. His manner was kind, attentive, and humane. His eye was full of animation; but there was a grave and sad solemnity in his air, which, for want of experience, I imagined was the inheritance of the great, and the instrument by which the distance between them and their inferiors was maintained. His look bespoke the unquietness of his mind, and frequently wandered with an expression of disconsolateness and anxiety.

My reception was as gracious and encouraging as I could possibly desire. Mr. Falkland questioned me respecting my learning, and my conceptions of men and things, and listened to my answers with condescension and approbation. This kindness soon restored to me a considerable part of my self-possession, though I still felt restrained by the graceful, but unaltered dignity of his carriage. When Mr. Falkland had satisfied his curiosity, he proceeded to inform me that he was in want of a secretary, that I appeared to him sufficiently qualified for that office, and that, if, in my present change of situation, occasioned by the death of my father, I approved of the employment, he would take me into his family.

I felt highly flattered by the proposal, and was warm in the expression of my acknowledgments. I set eagerly about the disposal of the little property my father had left, in which I was assisted by Mr. Collins. I had not now a relation in the world, upon whose kindness and interposition I had any direct claim. But, far from regarding this deserted situation with terror, I formed golden visions of the station I was about to occupy. I little suspected that the gaiety and lightness of heart I had hitherto enjoyed were upon the point of leaving me for ever, and that the rest of my days were devoted to misery and alarm.

My employment was easy and agreeable. It consisted partly in the transcribing and arranging certain papers, and partly in writing from my master's dictation letters of business, as well as sketches of literary composition. Many of these latter consisted of an analytical survey of the plans of different authors and conjectural speculations upon hints they afforded, tending either to the detection of their errors, or the carrying forward their discoveries. All of them bore powerful marks of a profound and elegant mind, well stored with literature, and possessed of an uncommon share of activity and discrimination.

My station was in that part of the house which was appropriated for the reception of books, it being my duty to perform the functions of librarian as well as secretary. Here my hours would have glided in tranquillity and peace, had not my situation included in it circumstances totally different from those which attended me in my father's cottage. In early life my mind had been much engrossed by reading and reflection: my intercourse with my fellow mortals was occasional and short. But, in my new residence, I was excited by every motive of interest and novelty to study my master's character; and I found in it an ample field for speculation and conjecture.

His mode of living was in the utmost degree recluse and solitary. He had no inclination to scenes of revelry and mirth. He avoided the busy haunts of men; nor did he seem desirous to compensate for this privation by the confidence of friendship. He appeared a total stranger to every thing which usually bears the appellation of pleasure. His features were scarcely ever relaxed into a smile, nor did that air which spoke the unhappiness of his mind at any time forsake them: yet his manners were by no means such as denoted moroseness and misanthropy. He was compassionate and considerate for others, though the stateliness of his carriage and the reserve of his temper were at no time interrupted. His appearance and general behaviour might have strongly interested all persons in his favour; but the coldness of his address, and the impenetrableness of his sentiments, seemed to forbid those demonstrations of kindness to which one might otherwise have been prompted.

Such was the general appearance of Mr. Falkland: but his disposition was extremely unequal. The distemper which afflicted him with incessant gloom had its paroxysms. Sometimes he was hasty, peevish, and tyrannical; but this proceeded rather from the torment of his mind than an unfeeling disposition; and when reflection recurred, he appeared willing that the weight of his misfortune should fall wholly upon himself. Sometimes he entirely lost his self-possession, and his behaviour was changed into frenzy: he would strike his forehead, his brows became knit, his features distorted, and his teeth ground one against the other. When he felt the approach of these symptoms, he would suddenly rise, and, leaving the occupation, whatever it was, in which he was engaged, hasten into a solitude upon which no person dared to intrude.

It must not be supposed that the whole of what I am describing was visible to the persons about him; nor, indeed, was I acquainted with it in the extent here stated but after a considerable time, and in gradual succession. With respect to the domestics in general, they saw but little of their master. None of them, except myself, from the nature of my functions, and Mr. Collins, from the antiquity of his service and the respectableness of his character, approached Mr. Falkland, but at stated seasons and for a very short interval. They knew him only by the benevolence of his actions, and the principles of inflexible integrity by which he was ordinarily guided; and though they would sometimes indulge their conjectures respecting his singularities, they regarded him upon the whole with veneration, as a being of a superior order.

One day, when I had been about three months in the service of my patron, I went to a closet, or small apartment, which was separated from the library by a narrow gallery that was lighted by a small window near the roof. I had conceived that there was no person in the room, and intended only to put any thing in order that I might find out of its place. As I opened the door, I heard at the same instant a deep groan, expressive of intolerable anguish. The sound of the door in opening seemed to alarm the person within; I heard the lid of a trunk hastily shut, and the noise as of fastening a lock. I conceived that Mr. Falkland was there, and was going instantly to retire; but at that moment a voice, that seemed supernaturally tremendous, exclaimed, "Who is there?" The voice was Mr. Falkland's. The sound of it thrilled my very vitals. I endeavoured to answer, but my speech failed, and being incapable of any other reply, I instinctively advanced within the door into the room. Mr. Falkland was just risen from the floor upon which he had been sitting or kneeling. His face betrayed strong symptoms of confusion. With a violent effort, however, these symptoms vanished, and instantaneously gave place to a countenance sparkling with rage. "Villain!" cried he, "what has brought you here?" I hesitated a confused and irresolute answer. "Wretch!" interrupted Mr. Falkland, with uncontrollable impatience, "you want to ruin me. You set yourself as a spy upon my actions; but bitterly shall you repent your insolence. Do you think you shall watch my privacies with impunity?" I attempted to defend myself. "Begone, devil!" rejoined he. "Quit the room, or I will trample you into atoms." Saying this, he advanced towards me. But I was already sufficiently terrified, and vanished in a moment. I heard the door shut after me with violence; and thus ended this extraordinary scene.

I saw him again in the evening, and he was then tolerably composed. His behaviour, which was always kind, was now doubly attentive and soothing. He seemed to have something of which he wished to disburthen his mind, but to want words in which to convey it. I looked at him with anxiety and affection. He made two unsuccessful efforts, shook his head, and then putting five guineas into my hand, pressed it in a manner that I could feel proceeded from a mind pregnant with various emotions, though I could not interpret them. Having done this, he seemed immediately to recollect himself, and to take refuge in the usual distance and solemnity of his manner.

I easily understood that secrecy was one of the things expected from me; and, indeed, my mind was too much disposed to meditate upon what I had heard and seen, to make it a topic of indiscriminate communication. Mr. Collins, however, and myself happened to sup together that evening, which was but seldom the case, his avocations obliging him to be much abroad. He could not help observing an uncommon dejection and anxiety in my countenance, and affectionately enquired into the reason. I endeavoured to evade his questions, but my youth and ignorance of the world gave me little advantage for that purpose. Beside this, I had been accustomed to view Mr. Collins with considerable attachment, and I conceived from the nature of his situation that there could be small impropriety in making him my confident in the present instance. I repeated to him minutely every thing that had passed, and concluded with a solemn declaration that, though treated with caprice, I was not anxious for myself; no inconvenience or danger should ever lead me to a pusillanimous behaviour; and I felt only for my patron, who, with every advantage for happiness, and being in the highest degree worthy of it, seemed destined to undergo unmerited distress.

In answer to my communication, Mr. Collins informed me that some incidents, of a nature similar to that which I related, had fallen under his own knowledge, and that from the whole he could not help concluding that our unfortunate patron, was at times disordered in his intellects. "Alas!" continued he, "it was not always thus! Ferdinando Falkland was once the gayest of the gay. Not indeed of that frothy sort, who excite contempt instead of admiration, and whose levity argues thoughtlessness rather than felicity. His gaiety was always accompanied with dignity. It was the gaiety of the hero and the scholar. It was chastened with reflection and sensibility, and never lost sight either of good taste or humanity. Such as it was however, it denoted a genuine hilarity of heart, imparted an inconceivable brilliancy to his company and conversation, and rendered him the perpetual delight of the diversified circles he then willingly frequented. You see nothing of him, my dear Williams, but the ruin of that Falkland who was courted by sages, and adored by the fair. His youth, distinguished in its outset by the most unusual promise, is tarnished. His sensibility is shrunk up and withered by events the most disgustful to his feelings. His mind was fraught with all the rhapsodies of visionary honour; and, in his sense, nothing but the grosser part, the mere shell of Falkland, was capable of surviving the wound that his pride has sustained."

These reflections of my friend Collins strongly tended to inflame my curiosity, and I requested him to enter into a more copious explanation. With this request he readily complied; as conceiving that whatever delicacy it became him to exercise in ordinary cases, it would be out of place in my situation; and thinking it not improbable that Mr. Falkland, but for the disturbance and inflammation of his mind, would be disposed to a similar communication. I shall interweave with Mr. Collins's story various information which I afterwards received from other quarters, that I may give all possible perspicuity to the series of events. To avoid confusion in my narrative, I shall drop the person of Collins, and assume to be myself the historian of our patron. To the reader it may appear at first sight as if this detail of the preceding life of Mr. Falkland were foreign to my history. Alas! I know from bitter experience that it is otherwise. My heart bleeds at the recollection of his misfortunes, as if they were my own. How can it fail to do so? To his story the whole fortune of my life was linked; because he was miserable, my happiness, my name, and my existence have been irretrievably blasted.

CHAPTER II

AMONG the favourite authors of his early years were the heroic poets of Italy. From them he imbibed the love of chivalry and romance. He had too much good sense to regret the times of Charlemagne and Arthur. But, while his imagination was purged by a certain infusion of philosophy, he conceived that there was in the manners depicted by these celebrated poets something to imitate, as well as something to avoid. He believed that nothing was so well calculated to make men deli-cate, gallant, and humane, as a temper perpetually alive to the sentiments of birth and honour. The opinions he entertained upon these topics were illustrated in his conduct, which was assiduously conformed to the model of heroism that his fancy suggested.

With these sentiments he set out upon his travels, at the age at which the grand tour is usually made; and they were rather confirmed than shaken by the adventures that befel him. By inclination he was led to make his longest stay in Italy; and here he fell into company with several young noblemen whose studies and principles were congenial to his own. By them he was assiduously courted, and treated with the most distinguished applause. They were delighted to meet with a foreigner, who had imbibed all the peculiarities of the most lib-eral and honourable among themselves. Nor was he less favoured and admired by the softer sex. Though his stature was small, his person had an air of uncommon dignity. His dignity was then heightened by certain additions which were after-wards obliterated, – an expression of frankness, ingenuity, and unreserve, and a spirit of the most ardent enthusiasm. Perhaps no Englishman was ever in an equal degree idolised by the inhabitants of Italy.

It was not possible for him to have drunk so deeply of the fountain of chivalry without being engaged occasionally in affairs of honour, all of which were terminated in a manner that would not have disgraced the chevalier Bayard himself.[1] In

---

1   Pierre Terrail, seigneur de Bayard (1476–1524), one of the most renowned soldiers of his age, whose valor earned him the name *chevalier sans peur et sans reproche*, the chevalier without fear and above reproach.

Italy, the young men of rank divide themselves into two classes, – those who adhere to the pure principles of ancient gallantry, and those who, being actuated by the same acute sense of injury and insult, accustom themselves to the employment of hired bravoes as their instruments of vengeance. The whole difference, indeed, consists in the precarious application of a generally received distinction. The most generous Italian conceives that there are certain persons whom it would be contamination for him to call into the open field. He nevertheless believes that an indignity cannot be expiated but with blood, and is persuaded that the life of a man is a trifling consideration, in comparison of the indemnification to be made to his injured honour. There is, therefore, scarcely any Italian that would upon some occasions scruple assassination. Men of spirit among them, notwithstanding the prejudices of their education, cannot fail to have a secret conviction of its baseness, and will be desirous of extending as far as possible the cartel of honour. Real or affected arrogance teaches others to regard almost the whole species as their inferiors, and of consequence incites them to gratify their vengeance without danger to their persons. Mr. Falkland met with some of these. But his undaunted spirit and resolute temper gave him a decisive advantage even in such perilous rencounters. One instance, among many, of his manner of conducting himself among this proud and high-spirited people it may be proper to relate. Mr. Falkland is the principal agent in my history; and Mr. Falkland in the autumn and decay of his vigour, such as I found him, cannot be completely understood without a knowledge of his previous character, as it was in all the gloss of youth, yet unassailed by adversity, and unbroken in upon by anguish or remorse.

At Rome he was received with particular distinction at the house of Marquis Pisani, who had an only daughter, the heir of his immense fortune, and the admiration of all the young nobility of that metropolis. Lady Lucretia Pisani was tall, of a dignified form, and uncommonly beautiful. She was not deficient in amiable qualities, but her soul was haughty, and her carriage not unfrequently contemptuous. Her pride was nourished by the consciousness of her charms, by her elevated rank, and the universal adoration she was accustomed to receive.

Among her numerous lovers Count Malvesi was the individual most favoured by her father, nor did his addresses seem indifferent to her. The Count was a man of considerable accomplishments, and of great integrity and benevolence of disposition. But he was too ardent a lover, to be able always to preserve the affability of his temper. The admirers whose addresses were a source of gratification to his mistress, were a perpetual uneasiness to him. Placing his whole happiness in the possession of this imperious beauty, the most trifling circumstances were capable of alarming him for the security of his pretensions. But most of all he was jealous of the English cavalier. Marquis Pisani, who had spent many years in France, was by no means partial to the suspicious precautions of Italian fathers, and indulged his daughter in considerable freedoms. His house and his daughter, within certain judicious restraints, were open to the resort of male visitants. But, above all, Mr. Falkland, as a foreigner, and a person little likely to form pretensions to the hand of Lucretia, was received upon a footing of great familiarity. The lady herself, conscious of innocence, entertained no scruple about trifles, and acted with the confidence and frankness of one who is superior to suspicion.

Mr. Falkland, after a residence of several weeks at Rome, proceeded to Naples. Meanwhile certain incidents occurred that delayed the intended nuptials of the heiress of Pisani. When he returned to Rome Count Malvesi was absent. Lady Lucretia, who had been considerably amused before with the conversation of Mr. Falkland, and who had an active and enquiring mind, had conceived, in the interval between his first and second residence at Rome, a desire to be acquainted with the English language, inspired by the lively and ardent encomiums of our best authors that she had heard from their countryman. She had provided herself with the usual materials for that purpose, and had made some progress during his absence. But upon his return she was forward to make use of the opportunity, which, if missed, might never occur again with equal advantage, of reading select passages of our poets with an Englishman of uncommon taste and capacity.

This proposal necessarily led to a more frequent intercourse. When Count Malvesi returned, he found Mr. Falkland established almost as an inmate of the Pisani palace. His mind could not fail to be struck with the criticalness of the situation. He was perhaps secretly conscious that the qualifications of the Englishman were superior to his own; and he trembled for the progress that each party might have made in the affection of the other, even before they were aware of the danger. He believed that the match was in every respect such as to flatter the ambition of Mr. Falkland; and he was stung even to madness by the idea of being deprived of the object dearest to his heart by this tramontane upstart.

He had, however, sufficient discretion first to demand an explanation of Lady Lucretia. She, in the gaiety of her heart, trifled with his anxiety. His patience was already exhausted, and he proceeded in his expostulation, in language that she was by no means prepared to endure with apathy. Lady Lucretia had always been accustomed to deference and submission; and, having got over something like terror, that was at first inspired by the imperious manner in which she was now catechised, her next feeling was that of the warmest resentment. She disdained to satisfy so insolent a questioner, and even indulged herself in certain oblique hints calculated to strengthen his suspicions. For some time she described his folly and presumption in terms of the most ludicrous sarcasm, and then, suddenly changing her style, bid him never let her see him more except upon the footing of the most distant acquaintance, as she was determined never again to subject herself to so unworthy a treatment. She was happy that he had at length disclosed to her his true character, and would know how to profit of her present experience to avoid a repetition of the same danger. All this passed in the full career of passion on both sides, and Lady Lucretia had no time to reflect upon what might be the consequence of thus exasperating her lover.

Count Malvesi left her in all the torments of frenzy. He believed that this was a premeditated scene, to find a pretence for breaking off an engagement that was already all but concluded; or, rather, his mind was racked with a thousand conjectures: he alternately thought that the injustice might be hers or his own; and he quarrelled with Lady Lucretia, himself, and the whole world. In this temper he hastened to the hotel of the English cavalier. The season of expostulation was now over, and he found himself irresistibly impelled to justify his precipitation with the lady, by taking for granted that the subject of his suspicion was beyond the reach of doubt.

Mr. Falkland was at home. The first words of the Count were an abrupt accusation of duplicity in the affair of Lady Lucretia, and a challenge. The Englishman had an unaffected esteem for Malvesi, who was in reality a man of considerable merit, and who had been one of Mr. Falkland's earliest Italian acquaintance, they having originally met at Milan. But more than this, the possible consequence of a duel in the present instance burst upon his mind. He had the warmest admiration for Lady Lucretia, though his feelings were not those of a lover; and he knew that, however her haughtiness might endeavour to disguise it, she was impressed with a tender regard for Count Malvesi. He could not bear to think that any misconduct of his should interrupt the prospects of so deserving a pair. Guided by these sentiments, he endeavoured to expostulate with the Italian. But his attempts were ineffectual. His antagonist was drunk with choler, and would not listen to a word that tended to check the impetuosity of his thoughts. He traversed the room with perturbed steps, and even foamed with anguish and fury. Mr. Falkland, finding that all was to no purpose, told the Count that, if he would return tomorrow at the same hour, he would attend him to any scene of action he should think proper to select.

From Count Malvesi Mr. Falkland immediately proceeded to the palace of Pisani. Here he found considerable difficulty in appeasing the indignation of Lady Lucretia. His ideas of honour would by no means allow him to win her to his purpose by disclosing the cartel he had received; otherwise that disclosure would immediately have operated as the strongest motive that could have been offered to this disdainful beauty. But, though she dreaded such an event, the vague apprehension was not strong enough to induce her instantly to surrender all the stateliness of her resentment. Mr. Falkland, however, drew so interesting a picture of the disturbance of Count Malvesi's mind, and accounted in so flattering a manner for the abruptness of his conduct, that this, together with the arguments he adduced, completed the conquest of Lady Lucretia's resentment. Having thus far accomplished his purpose, he proceeded to disclose to her every thing that had passed.

The next day Count Malvesi appeared, punctual to his appointment, at Mr. Falkland's hotel. Mr. Falkland came to the door to receive him, but requested him to enter the house for a moment, as he had still an affair of three minutes to despatch. They proceeded to a parlour. Here Mr. Falkland left him, and presently returned leading in Lady Lucretia herself, adorned in all her charms, and those charms heightened upon the present occasion by a consciousness of the spirited and generous condescension she was exerting. Mr. Falkland led her up to the astonished Count; and she, gently laying her hand upon the arm of her lover, exclaimed with the most attractive grace, "Will you allow me to retract the precipitate haughtiness into which I was betrayed?" The enraptured Count, scarcely able to believe his senses, threw himself upon his knees before her, and stammered out his reply, signifying that the precipitation had been all his own, that he only had any forgiveness to demand, and, though they might pardon, he could never pardon himself for the sacrilege he had committed against her and this godlike Englishman. As soon as the first tumults of his joy had subsided, Mr. Falkland addressed him thus:

"Count Malvesi, I feel the utmost pleasure in having thus by peaceful means disarmed your resentment, and effected your happiness. But I must confess, you put me to a severe trial. My temper is not less impetuous and fiery than your own, and it is not at all times that I should have been thus able to subdue it. But I considered that in reality the original blame was mine.

Though your suspicion was groundless, it was not absurd. We have been trifling too much in the face of danger. I ought not, under the present weakness of our nature and forms of society, to have been so assiduous in my attendance upon this enchanting woman. It would have been little wonder, if, having so many opportunities, and playing the preceptor with her as I have done, I had been entangled before I was aware, and harboured a wish which I might not afterwards have had courage to subdue. I owed you an atonement for this imprudence.

"But the laws of honour are in the utmost degree rigid; and there was reason to fear that, however anxious I were to be your friend, I might be obliged to be your murderer. Fortunately, the reputation of my courage is sufficiently established, not to expose it to any impeachment by my declining your present defiance. It was lucky, however, that in our interview of yesterday you found me alone, and that accident by that means threw the management of the affair into my disposal. If the transaction should become known, the conclusion will now become known along with the provocation, and I am satisfied. But if the challenge had been public, the proofs I had formerly given of courage would not have excused my present moderation; and, though desirous to have avoided the combat, it would not have been in my power. Let us hence each of us learn to avoid haste and indiscretion, the consequences of which may be inexpiable but with blood; and may Heaven bless you in a consort of whom I deem you every way worthy!"

I have already said that this was by no means the only instance, in the course of his travels, in which Mr. Falkland acquitted himself in the most brilliant manner as a man of gallantry and virtue. He continued abroad during several years, every one of which brought some fresh accession to the estimation in which he was held, as well as to his own impatience of stain or dishonour. At length he thought proper to return to England, with the intention of spending the rest of his days at the residence of his ancestors.

CHAPTER III

FROM the moment he entered upon the execution of this purpose, dictated as it probably was by an unaffected principle of duty, his misfortunes took their commencement. All I have further to state of his history is the uninterrupted persecution of a malignant destiny, a series of adventures that seemed to take their rise in various accidents, but pointing to one termination. Him they overwhelmed with an anguish he was of all others least qualified to bear; and these waters of bitterness, extending beyond him, poured their deadly venom upon others, I being myself the most unfortunate of their victims.

The person in whom these calamities originated was Mr. Falkland's nearest neighbour, a man of estate equal to his own, by name Barnabas Tyrrel. This man one might at first have supposed of all others least qualified from instruction, or inclined by the habits of his life, to disturb the enjoyments of a mind so richly endowed as that of Mr. Falkland. Mr. Tyrrel might have passed for a true model of the English squire. He was early left under the tuition of his mother, a woman of narrow capacity, and who had no other child. The only remaining member of the family it may be necessary to notice was Miss Emily Melville, the orphan daughter of Mr. Tyrrel's paternal aunt; who now resided in the family mansion, and was wholly dependent on the benevolence of its proprietors.

Mrs. Tyrrel appeared to think that there was nothing in the world so precious as her hopeful Barnabas. Every thing must give way to his accommodation and advantage; every one must yield the most servile obedience to his commands. He must not be teased or restricted by any forms of instruction; and of consequence his proficiency, even in the arts of writing and reading, was extremely slender. From his birth he was muscular and sturdy; and, confined to the *ruelle*[1] of his mother, he made much such a figure as the whelp-lion that a barbarian might have given for a lap-dog to his mistress.

But he soon broke loose from these trammels, and formed

---

1 Sixteenth- and seventeenth-century term for the area in a bedroom containing the bed, a space where people of rank sometimes received guests.

an acquaintance with the groom and the game-keeper. Under their instruction he proved as ready a scholar, as he had been indocile and restive to the pedant who held the office of his tutor. It was now evident that his small proficiency in literature was by no means to be ascribed to want of capacity. He discovered no contemptible sagacity and quick-wittedness in the science of horse-flesh, and was eminently expert in the arts of shooting, fishing, and hunting. Nor did he confine himself to these, but added the theory and practice of boxing, cudgel play, and quarter-staff. These exercises added tenfold robustness and vigour to his former qualifications.

His stature, when grown, was somewhat more than five feet ten inches in height, and his form might have been selected by a painter as a model for that hero of antiquity, whose prowess consisted in felling an ox with his fist, and devouring him at a meal. Conscious of his advantage in this respect, he was insupportably arrogant, tyrannical to his inferiors, and insolent to his equals. The activity of his mind being diverted from the genuine field of utility and distinction, showed itself in the rude tricks of an overgrown lubber. Here, as in all his other qualifications, he rose above his competitors; and if it had been possible to overlook the callous and unrelenting disposition which they manifested, one could scarcely have denied his applause to the invention these freaks displayed, and the rough, sarcastic wit with which they were accompanied.

Mr. Tyrrel was by no means inclined to permit these extraordinary merits to rust in oblivion. There was a weekly assembly at the nearest market-town, the resort of all the rural gentry. Here he had hitherto figured to the greatest advantage as grand master of the *coterie*,[1] no one having an equal share of opulence, and the majority, though still pretending to the rank of gentry, greatly his inferior in this essential article. The young men in this circle looked up to this insolent bashaw with timid respect, conscious of the comparative eminence that unquestionably belonged to the powers of his mind; and he well knew how to maintain his rank with an inflexible hand. Frequently indeed

---

1 A select or exclusive social circle.

he relaxed his features, and assumed a temporary appearance of affableness and familiarity; but they found by experience, that if any one, encouraged by his condescension, forgot the deference which Mr. Tyrrel considered as his due, he was soon taught to repent his presumption. It was a tiger that thought proper to toy with a mouse, the little animal every moment in danger of being crushed by the fangs of his ferocious associate. As Mr. Tyrrel had considerable copiousness of speech, and a rich, but undisciplined imagination, he was always sure of an audience. His neighbours crowded round, and joined in the ready laugh, partly from obsequiousness, and partly from unfeigned admiration. It frequently happened, however, that, in the midst of his good humour, a characteristic refinement of tyranny would suggest itself to his mind. When his subjects, encouraged by his familiarity, had discarded their precaution, the wayward fit would seize him, a sudden cloud overspread his brow, his voice transform from the pleasant to the terrible, and a quarrel of a straw immediately ensue with the first man whose face he did not like. The pleasure that resulted to others from the exuberant sallies of his imagination was, therefore, not unalloyed with sudden qualms of apprehension and terror. It may be believed that this despotism did not gain its final ascendancy without being contested in the outset. But all opposition was quelled with a high hand by this rural Antæus.[1] By the ascendancy of his fortune, and his character among his neighbours, he always reduced his adversary to the necessity of encountering him at his own weapons, and did not dismiss him without making him feel his presumption through every joint in his frame. The tyranny of Mr. Tyrrel would not have been so patiently endured, had not his colloquial accomplishments perpetually come in aid of that authority which his rank and prowess originally obtained.

The situation of our squire with the fair was still more enviable than that which he maintained among persons of his own sex. Every mother taught her daughter to consider the hand of Mr. Tyrrel as the highest object of her ambition. Every

---

1 A powerful giant, son of Poseidon and Gaia (mother earth), who was invincible as long as his body remained in contact with the earth who had borne him.

daughter regarded his athletic form and his acknowledged prowess with a favourable eye. A form eminently athletic is, perhaps, always well proportioned; and one of the qualifications that women are early taught to look for in the male sex, is that of a protector. As no man was adventurous enough to contest his superiority, so scarcely any woman in this provincial circle would have scrupled to prefer his addresses to those of any other admirer. His boisterous wit had peculiar charms for them; and there was no spectacle more flattering to their vanity, than seeing this Hercules exchange his club for a distaff. It was pleasing to them to consider, that the fangs of this wild beast, the very idea of which inspired trepidation into the boldest hearts, might be played with by them with the utmost security.

Such was the rival that Fortune, in her caprice, had reserved for the accomplished Falkland. This untamed, though not undiscerning brute, was found capable of destroying the prospects of a man the most eminently qualified to enjoy and to communicate happiness. The feud that sprung up between them was nourished by concurring circumstances, till it attained a magnitude difficult to be paralleled; and, because they regarded each other with a deadly hatred, I have become an object of misery and abhorrence.

The arrival of Mr. Falkland gave an alarming shock to the authority of Mr. Tyrrel in the village assembly and in all scenes of indiscriminate resort. His disposition by no means inclined him to withhold himself from scenes of fashionable amusement; and he and his competitor were like two stars fated never to appear at once above the horizon. The advantages Mr. Falkland possessed in the comparison are palpable; and had it been otherwise, the subjects of his rural neighbour were sufficiently disposed to revolt against his merciless dominion. They had hitherto submitted from fear, and not from love; and, if they had not rebelled, it was only for want of a leader. Even the ladies regarded Mr. Falkland with particular complacence. His polished manners were peculiarly in harmony with feminine delicacy. The sallies of his wit were far beyond those of Mr. Tyrrel in variety and vigour; in addition to which they had the advantage of having their spontaneous exuberance guided and restrained by the sagacity of a cultivated mind. The graces of his person were enhanced by the elegance of his deportment; and the benevolence and liberality of his temper were upon all occasions conspicuous. It was common indeed to Mr. Tyrrel, together with Mr. Falkland, to be little accessible to sentiments of awkwardness and confusion. But for this Mr. Tyrrel was indebted to a self-satisfied effrontery, and a boisterous and over-bearing elocution, by which he was accustomed to discomfit his assailants; while Mr. Falkland, with great ingenuity and candour of mind, was enabled by his extensive knowledge of the world and acquaintance with his own resources, to perceive almost instantaneously the proceeding it most became him to adopt.

Mr. Tyrrel contemplated the progress of his rival with uneasiness and aversion. He often commented upon it to his particular confidents as a thing altogether inconceivable. Mr. Falkland he described as an animal that was beneath contempt. Diminutive and dwarfish in his form, he wanted to set up a new standard of human nature, adapted to his miserable condition. He wished to persuade people that the human species were made to be nailed to a chair, and to pore over books. He would have them exchange those robust exercises which make us joyous in the performance and vigorous in the consequences, for the wise labour of scratching our heads for a rhyme and counting our fingers for a verse. Monkeys were as good men as these. A nation of such animals would have no chance with a single regiment of the old English votaries of beef and pudding. He never saw any thing come of learning but to make people foppish and impertinent; and a sensible man would not wish a worse calamity to the enemies of his nation than to see them run mad after such pernicious absurd-ities. It was impossible that people could seriously feel any liking for such a ridiculous piece of goods as this outlandish foreign-made Englishman. But he knew very well how it was: it was a miserable piece of mummery that was played only in spite of him. But God for ever blast his soul, if he were not bitterly revenged upon them all!

If such were the sentiments of Mr. Tyrrel, his patience found ample exercise in the language which was held by the rest of his neighbours on the same subject. While he saw nothing in Mr. Falkland but matter of contempt, they appeared to be never weary of recounting his praises. Such dignity, such affability, so perpetual an attention to the happiness of others, such delicacy of sentiment and expression! Learned without ostentation, refined without foppery, elegant without effeminacy! Perpetually anxious to prevent his superiority from being painfully felt, it was so much the more certainly felt to be real, and excited congratulation instead of envy in the spectator. It is scarcely necessary to remark, that the revolution of sentiment in this rural vicinity belongs to one of the most obvious features of the human mind. The rudest exhibition of art is at first admired, till a nobler is presented, and we are taught to wonder at the facility with which before we had been satisfied. Mr. Tyrrel thought there would be no end to the commendation; and expected when their common acquaintance would fall down and adore the intruder. The most inadvertent expression of applause inflicted upon him the torment of demons. He writhed with agony, his features became distorted, and his looks inspired terror. Such suffering would probably have soured the kindest temper; what must have been its effect upon Mr. Tyrrel's, always fierce, unrelenting, and abrupt?

The advantages of Mr. Falkland seemed by no means to diminish with their novelty. Every new sufferer from Mr. Tyrrel's tyranny immediately went over to the standard of his adversary. The ladies, though treated by their rustic swain with more gentleness than the men, were occasionally exposed to his capriciousness and insolence. They could not help remarking the contrast between these two leaders in the fields of chivalry, the one of whom paid no attention to any one's pleasure but his own, while the other seemed all good-humour and benevolence. It was in vain that Mr. Tyrrel endeavoured to restrain the ruggedness of his character. His motive was impatience, his thoughts were gloomy, and his courtship was like the pawings of an elephant. It appeared as if his temper had been more human while he indulged in its free bent, than now that he sullenly endeavoured to put fetters upon its excesses.

Among the ladies of the village-assembly already mentioned, there was none that seemed to engage more of the kindness of Mr. Tyrrel than Miss Hardingham. She was also one of the few that had not yet gone over to the enemy, either because she really preferred the gentleman who was her oldest acquaintance, or that she conceived from calculation this conduct best adapted to insure her success in a husband. One day, however, she thought proper, probably only by way of experiment, to show Mr. Tyrrel that she could engage in hostilities, if he should at any time give her sufficient provocation. She so adjusted her manoeuvres as to be engaged by Mr. Falkland as his partner for the dance of the evening, though without the smallest intention on the part of that gentleman (who was unpardonably deficient in the sciences of anecdote and match-making) of giving offence to his country neighbour. Though the manners of Mr. Falkland were condescending and attentive, his hours of retirement were principally occupied in contemplations too dignified for scandal, and too large for the altercations of a vestry, or the politics of an election-borough.

A short time before the dances began, Mr. Tyrrel went up to his fair inamorata, and entered into some trifling conversation with her to fill up the time, as intending in a few minutes to lead her forward to the field. He had accustomed himself to neglect the ceremony of soliciting beforehand a promise in his favour, as not supposing it possible that any one would dare dispute his behests; and, had it been otherwise, he would have thought the formality unnecessary in this case, his general preference to Miss Hardingham being notorious.

While he was thus engaged, Mr. Falkland came up. Mr. Tyrrel always regarded him with aversion and loathing. Mr. Falkland, however, slided in a graceful and unaffected manner into the conversation already begun; and the animated ingenuousness of his manner was such, as might for the time have disarmed the devil of his malice. Mr. Tyrrel probably conceived that his accosting Miss Hardingham was an accidental piece of general ceremony, and expected every moment when he would withdraw to another part of the room.

The company now began to be in motion for the dance, and Mr. Falkland signified as much to Miss Hardingham. "Sir," interrupted Mr. Tyrrel abruptly, "that lady is my partner." – "I believe not, sir: that lady has been so obliging as to accept my invitation." – "I tell you, sir, no. Sir, I have an interest in that lady's affections; and I will suffer no man to intrude upon my claims." – "The lady's affections are not the subject of the present question." – "Sir, it is to no purpose to parley. Make room, sir!" – Mr. Falkland gently repelled his antagonist. "Mr. Tyrrel!" returned he, with some firmness, "let us have no altercation in this business: the master of the ceremonies is the proper person to decide in a difference of this sort, if we cannot adjust it: we can neither of us intend to exhibit our valour before the ladies, and shall therefore cheerfully submit to his verdict." – "Damn me, sir, if I understand." – "Softly, Mr. Tyrrel; I intended you no offence. But, sir, no man shall prevent my asserting that to which I have once acquired a claim!"

Mr. Falkland uttered these words with the most unruffled temper in the world. The tone in which he spoke had acquired elevation, but neither roughness nor impatience. There was a fascination in his manner that made the ferociousness of his antagonist subside into impotence. Miss Hardingham had begun to repent of her experiment, but her alarm was speedily quieted by the dignified composure of her new partner. Mr. Tyrrel walked away without answering a word. He muttered curses as he went, which the laws of honour did not oblige Mr. Falkland to overhear, and which indeed it would have been no easy task to have overheard with accuracy. Mr. Tyrrel would not, perhaps, have so easily given up his point, had not his own good sense presently taught him, that, however eager he might be for revenge, this was not the ground he should desire to occupy. But, though he could not openly resent this rebellion against his authority, he brooded over it in the recesses of a malignant mind; and it was evident enough that he was accumulating materials for a bitter account, to which he trusted his adversary should one day be brought.

CHAPTER IV

THIS was only one out of innumerable instances, that every day seemed to multiply, of petty mortifications which Mr. Tyrrel was destined to endure on the part of Mr. Falkland. In all of them Mr. Falkland conducted himself with such unaffected propriety, as perpetually to add to the stock of his reputation. The more Mr. Tyrrel struggled with his misfortune, the more conspicuous and inveterate it became. A thousand times he cursed his stars, which took, as he apprehended, a malicious pleasure in making Mr. Falkland, at every turn, the instrument of his humiliation. Smarting under a succession of untoward events, he appeared to feel, in the most exquisite manner, the distinctions paid to his adversary, even in those points in which he had not the slightest pretensions. An instance of this now occurred.

Mr. Clare, a poet whose works have done immortal honour to the country that produced him, had lately retired, after a life spent in the sublimest efforts of genius, to enjoy the produce of his economy, and the reputation he had acquired, in this very neighbourhood. Such an inmate was looked up to by the country gentlemen with a degree of adoration. They felt a conscious pride in recollecting that the boast of England was a native of their vicinity; and they were by no means deficient in gratitude when they saw him, who had left them an adventurer, return into the midst of them, in the close of his days, crowned with honours and opulence. The reader is acquainted with his works: he has, probably, dwelt upon them with transport; and I need not remind him of their excellence: but he is, perhaps, a stranger to his personal qualifications; he does not know that his productions were scarcely more admirable than his conversation. In company he seemed to be the only person ignorant of the greatness of his fame. To the world his writings will long remain a kind of specimen of what the human mind is capable of performing; but no man perceived their defects so acutely as he, or saw so distinctly how much yet remained to be effected: he alone appeared to look upon his works with superiority and indifference. One of the features that most eminently distinguished him was a perpetual suavity of manners, a comprehensiveness of mind, that regarded the errors of others without a particle of resentment, and made it impossible for any one to be his enemy. He pointed out to men their mistakes with frankness and unreserve: his remonstrances produced astonishment and conviction, but without uneasiness, in the party to whom they were addressed: they felt the instrument that was employed to correct their irregularities, but it never mangled what it was intended to heal. Such were the moral qualities that distinguished him among his acquaintance. The intellectual accomplishments he exhibited were, principally, a tranquil and mild enthusiasm, and a richness of conception which dictated spontaneously to his tongue, and flowed with so much ease, that it was only by retrospect you could be made aware of the amazing variety of ideas that had been presented.

Mr. Clare certainly found few men in this remote situation that were capable of participating in his ideas and amusements. It has been among the weaknesses of great men to fly to solitude, and converse with woods and groves, rather than with a circle of strong and comprehensive minds like their own. From the moment of Mr. Falkland's arrival in the neighbourhood, Mr. Clare distinguished him in the most flattering manner. To so penetrating a genius there was no need of long experience and patient observation to discover the merits and defects of any character that presented itself. The materials of his judgment had long since been accumulated; and at the close of so illustrious a life, he might almost be said to see through nature at a glance. What wonder that he took some interest in a mind in a certain degree congenial with his own? But to Mr. Tyrrel's diseased imagination, every distinction bestowed on his neighbour seemed to be expressly intended as an insult to him. On the other hand, Mr. Clare, though gentle and benevolent in his remonstrances to a degree that made the taking offence impossible, was by no means parsimonious of praise, or slow to make use of the deference that was paid him, for the purpose of procuring justice to merit.

It happened at one of those public meetings at which Mr. Falkland and Mr. Tyrrel were present, that the conversation, in one of the most numerous sets into which the company was broken, turned upon the poetical talents of the former. A lady, who was present, and was distinguished for the acuteness of her understanding, said, she had been favoured with a sight of a poem he had just written, entitled *An Ode to the Genius of Chivalry*, which appeared to her of exquisite merit. The curiosity of the company was immediately excited, and the lady added, she had a copy in her pocket, which was much at their service, provided its being thus produced would not be disagreeable to the author. The whole circle immediately entreated Mr. Falkland to comply with their wishes, and Mr. Clare, who was one of the company, enforced their petition. Nothing gave this gentleman so much pleasure as to have an opportunity of witnessing and doing justice to the exhibition of intellectual excellence. Mr. Falkland had no false modesty or affectation, and therefore readily yielded his consent.

Mr. Tyrrel accidentally sat at the extremity of this circle. It cannot be supposed that the turn the conversation had taken was by any means agreeable to him. He appeared to wish to withdraw himself, but there seemed to be some unknown power that, as it were by enchantment, retained him in his place, and made him consent to drink to the dregs the bitter potion which envy had prepared for him.

The poem was read to the rest of the company by Mr. Clare, whose elocution was scarcely inferior to his other accomplishments. Simplicity, discrimination, and energy constantly attended him in the act of reading, and it is not easy to conceive a more refined delight than fell to the lot of those who had the good fortune to be his auditors. The beauties of Mr. Falkland's poem were accordingly exhibited with every advantage. The successive passions of the author were communicated to the hearer. What was impetuous, and what was solemn, were delivered with a responsive feeling, and a flowing and unlaboured tone. The pictures conjured up by the creative fancy of the poet were placed full to view, at one time overwhelming the soul with superstitious awe, and at another transporting it with luxuriant beauty.

The character of the hearers upon this occasion has already been described. They were, for the most part, plain, unlettered, and of little refinement. Poetry in general they read, when read at all, from the mere force of imitation, and with few sensations of pleasure; but this poem had a peculiar vein of glowing inspiration. This very poem would probably have been seen by many of them with little effect; but the accents of Mr. Clare carried it home to the heart. He ended: and, as the countenances of his auditors had before sympathised with the passions of the composition, so now they emulated each other in declaring their approbation. Their sensations were of a sort to which they were little accustomed. One spoke, and another followed by a sort of uncontrollable impulse; and the rude and broken manner of their commendations rendered them the more singular and remarkable. But what was least to be endured was the behaviour of Mr. Clare. He returned the manuscript to the lady from whom he had received it, and then, addressing Mr. Falkland, said with emphasis and animation, "Ha! this is as it should be. It is of the right stamp. I have seen too many hard essays strained from the labour of a pedant, and pastoral ditties distressed in lack of a meaning. They are such as you, sir, that we want. Do not forget, however, that the Muse was not given to add refinements to idleness, but for the highest and most invaluable purposes. Act up to the magnitude of your destiny."

A moment after, Mr. Clare quitted his seat, and with Mr. Falkland and two or three more withdrew. As soon as they were gone, Mr. Tyrrel edged further into the circle. He had sat silent so long that he seemed ready to burst with gall and indignation. "Mighty pretty verses!" said he, half talking to himself, and not addressing any particular person: "why, ay, the verses are well enough. Damnation! I should like to know what a ship-load of such stuff is good for."

"Why, surely," said the lady who had introduced Mr. Falkland's Ode on the present occasion, "you must allow that poetry is an agreeable and elegant amusement."

"Elegant, quotha! − Why, look at this Falkland! A puny bit of a thing! In the devil's name, madam, do you think he would write poetry if he could do any thing better?"

The conversation did not stop here. The lady expostulated. Several other persons, fresh from the sensation they had felt, contributed their share. Mr. Tyrrel grew more violent in his invectives, and found ease in uttering them. The persons who were able in any degree to check his vehemence were with-drawn. One speaker after another shrunk back into silence, too timid to oppose, or too indolent to contend with, the fierceness of his passion. He found the appearance of his old ascendancy; but he felt its deceitfulness and uncertainty, and was gloomily dissatisfied.

In his return from this assembly he was accompanied by a young man, whom similitude of manners had rendered one of his principal confidents, and whose road home was in part the same as his own. One might have thought that Mr. Tyrrel had sufficiently vented his spleen in the dialogue he had just been holding. But he was unable to dismiss from his recollection the anguish he had endured. "Damn Falkland!" said he. "What a pitiful scoundrel is here to make all this bustle about! But women and fools always will be fools; there is no help for that! Those that set them on have most to answer for; and most of all, Mr. Clare. He is a man that ought to know something of the world, and past being duped by gewgaws and tinsel. He seemed, too, to have some notion of things: I should not have suspected him of hallooing to a cry of mongrels without hon-esty or reason. But the world is all alike. Those that seem better than their neighbours, are only more artful. They mean the same thing, though they take a different road. He deceived me for a while, but it is all out now. They are the makers of the mischief. Fools might blunder, but they would not persist, if people that ought to set them right did not encourage them to go wrong."

A few days after this adventure Mr. Tyrrel was surprised to receive a visit from Mr. Falkland. Mr. Falkland proceeded, without ceremony, to explain the motive of his coming.

"Mr. Tyrrel," said he, "I am come to have an amicable expla-nation with you."

"Explanation! What is my offence?"

"None in the world, sir; and for that reason I conceive this the fittest time to come to a right understanding."

"You are in a devil of a hurry, sir. Are you clear that this haste will not mar, instead of make an understanding?"

"I think I am, sir. I have great faith in the purity of my intentions, and I will not doubt, when you perceive the view with which I come, that you will willingly co-operate with it."

"Mayhap, Mr. Falkland, we may not agree about that. One man thinks one way, and another man thinks another. Mayhap I do not think I have any great reason to be pleased with you already."

"It may be so. I cannot, however, charge myself with having given you reason to be displeased."

"Well, sir, you have no right to put me out of humour with myself. If you come to play upon me, and try what sort of a fellow you shall have to deal with, damn me if you shall have any reason to hug yourself upon the experiment."

"Nothing, sir, is more easy for us than to quarrel. If you desire that, there is no fear that you will find opportunities."

"Damn me, sir, if I do not believe you are come to bully me."

"Mr. Tyrrel! sir – have a care!"

"Of what, sir! – Do you threaten me? Damn my soul! who are you? what do you come here for?"

The fieriness of Mr. Tyrrel brought Mr. Falkland to his recollection.

"I am wrong," said he. "I confess it. I came for purposes of peace. With that view I have taken the liberty to visit you. Whatever therefore might be my feelings upon another occasion, I am bound to suppress them now."

"Ho! – Well, sir: and what have you further to offer?"

"Mr. Tyrrel," proceeded Mr. Falkland, "you will readily imagine that the cause that brought me was not a slight one. I would not have troubled you with a visit, but for important reasons. My coming is a pledge how deeply I am myself impressed with what I have to communicate.

"We are in a critical situation. We are upon the brink of a whirlpool which, if once it get hold of us, will render all further deliberation impotent. An unfortunate jealousy seems to have insinuated itself between us, which I would willingly remove; and I come to ask your assistance. We are both of us nice of temper; we are both apt to kindle, and warm of resentment. Precaution in this stage can be dishonourable to neither; the time may come when we shall wish we had employed it, and find it too late. Why should we be enemies? Our tastes are different; our pursuits need not interfere. We both of us amply possess the means of happiness; we may be respected by all, and spend a long life of tranquillity and enjoyment. Will it be wise in us to exchange this prospect for the fruits of strife? A strife between persons with our peculiarities and our weaknesses, includes consequences that I shudder to think of. I fear, sir, that it is pregnant with death at least to one of us, and with misfortune and remorse to the survivor."

"Upon my soul, you are a strange man! Why trouble me with your prophecies and forebodings?"

"Because it is necessary to your happiness! Because it becomes me to tell you of our danger now, rather than wait till my character will allow this tranquillity no longer!

"By quarrelling we shall but imitate the great mass of mankind, who could easily quarrel in our place. Let us do better. Let us show that we have the magnanimity to contemn petty misunderstandings. By thus judging we shall do ourselves most substantial honour. By a contrary conduct we shall merely present a comedy for the amusement of our acquaintance."

"Do you think so? There may be something in that. Damn me, if I consent to be the jest of any man living."

"You are right, Mr. Tyrrel. Let us each act in the manner best calculated to excite respect. We neither of us wish to change roads; let us each suffer the other to pursue his own track unmolested. Be this our compact; and by mutual forbearance let us preserve mutual peace."

Saying this, Mr. Falkland offered his hand to Mr. Tyrrel in token of fellowship. But the gesture was too significant. The wayward rustic, who seemed to have been somewhat impressed by what had preceded, taken as he now was by surprise, shrunk back. Mr. Falkland was again ready to take fire upon this new slight, but he checked himself.

"All this is very unaccountable," cried Mr. Tyrrel. "What the devil can have made you so forward, if you had not some sly purpose to answer by which I am to be overreached?"

"My purpose," replied Mr. Falkland, "is a manly and an honest purpose. Why should you refuse a proposition dictated by reason, and an equal regard to the interest of each?"

Mr. Tyrrel had had an opportunity for pause, and fell back into his habitual character.

"Well, sir, in all this I must own there is some frankness. Now I will return you like for like. It is no matter how I came by it, my temper is rough, and will not be controlled. Mayhap you may think it is a weakness, but I do not desire to see it altered. Till you came, I found myself very well: I liked my neighbours, and my neighbours humoured me. But now the case is entirely altered; and, as long as I cannot stir abroad without meeting with some mortification in which you are directly or remotely concerned, I am determined to hate you. Now, sir, if you will only go out of the county or the kingdom, to the devil if you please, so as I may never hear of you any more, I will promise never to quarrel with you as long as I live. Your rhymes and your rebusses, your quirks and your conundrums, may then be every thing that is grand for what I care."

"Mr. Tyrrel, be reasonable! Might not I as well desire you to leave the county, as you desire me? I come to you, not as to a master, but an equal. In the society of men we must have something to endure, as well as to enjoy. No man must think that the world was made for him. Let us take things as we find them; and accommodate ourselves as we can to unavoidable circumstances."

"True, sir; all this is fine talking. But I return to my text: we are as God made us. I am neither a philosopher nor a poet, to set out upon a wild-goose chase of making myself a different man from what you find me. As for consequences, what must be must be. As we brew we must bake. And so, do you see? I shall not trouble myself about what is to be, but stand up to it with a stout heart when it comes. Only this I can tell you, that as long as I find you thrust into my dish every day I shall hate you as bad as senna and valerian.[1] And damn me, if I do not think I hate you the more for coming to-day in this pragmatical way, when nobody sent for you, on purpose to show how much wiser you are than all the world besides."

"Mr. Tyrrel, I have done, I foresaw consequences, and came as a friend. I had hoped that, by mutual explanation, we should

---

[1] Medicinal plants, senna being used as a purgative, valerian as both a stimulant and a sedative.

have come to a better understanding. I am disappointed; but perhaps, when you coolly reflect on what has passed, you will give me credit for my intentions, and think that my proposal was not an unreasonable one."

Having said this, Mr. Falkland departed. Through the interview he, no doubt, conducted himself in a way that did him peculiar credit. Yet the warmth of his temper could not be entirely suppressed: and even when he was most exemplary, there was an apparent loftiness in his manner that was calculated to irritate; and the very grandeur with which he suppressed his passions, operated indirectly as a taunt to his opponent. The interview was prompted by the noblest sentiments; but it unquestionably served to widen the breach it was intended to heal.

For Mr. Tyrrel, he had recourse to his old expedient, and unburthened the tumult of his thoughts to his confidential friend. "This," cried he, "is a new artifice of the fellow, to prove his imagined superiority. We knew well enough that he had the gift of the gab. To be sure, if the world were to be governed by words, he would be in the right box. Oh, yes, he had it all hollow! But what signifies prating? Business must be done in another guess way than that. I wonder what possessed me that I did not kick him! But that is all to come. This is only a new debt added to the score, which he shall one day richly pay. This Falkland haunts me like a demon. I cannot wake but I think of him. I cannot sleep but I see him. He poisons all my pleasures. I should be glad to see him torn with tenter-hooks, and to grind his heart-strings with my teeth. I shall know no joy till I see him ruined. There may be some things right about him; but he is my perpetual torment. The thought of him hangs like a dead weight upon my heart, and I have a right to shake it off. Does he think I will feel all that I endure for nothing?"

In spite of the acerbity of Mr. Tyrrel's feelings, it is probable, however, he did some justice to his rival. He regarded him, indeed, with added dislike; but he no longer regarded him as a despicable foe. He avoided his encounter; he forbore to treat him with random hostility; he seemed to lie in wait for his victim, and to collect his venom for a mortal assault.

CHAPTER V

IT was not long after that a malignant distemper broke out in the neighbourhood, which proved fatal to many of the inhabitants, and was of unexampled rapidity in its effects. One of the first persons that was seized with it was Mr. Clare. It may be conceived, what grief and alarm this incident spread through the vicinity. Mr. Clare was considered by them as something more than mortal. The equanimity of his behaviour, his unassuming carriage, his exuberant benevolence and goodness of heart, joined with his talents, his inoffensive wit, and the comprehensiveness of his intelligence, made him the idol of all that knew him. In the scene of his rural retreat, at least, he had no enemy. All mourned the danger that now threatened him. He appeared to have had the prospect of long life, and of going down to his grave full of years and of honour. Perhaps these appearances were deceitful. Perhaps the intellectual efforts he had made, which were occasionally more sudden, violent, and unintermitted, than a strict regard to health would have dictated, had laid the seed of future disease. But a sanguine observer would infallibly have predicted, that his temperate habits, activity of mind, and unabated cheerfulness, would be able even to keep death at bay for a time, and baffle the attacks of distemper, provided their approach were not uncommonly rapid and violent. The general affliction, therefore, was doubly pungent upon the present occasion.

But no one was so much affected as Mr. Falkland. Perhaps no man so well understood the value of the life that was now at stake. He immediately hastened to the spot; but he found some difficulty in gaining admission. Mr. Clare, aware of the infectious nature of his disease, had given directions that as few persons as possible should approach him. Mr. Falkland sent up his name. He was told that he was included in the general orders. He was not, however, of a temper to be easily repulsed; he persisted with obstinacy, and at length carried his point, being only reminded in the first instance to employ those precautions which experience has proved most effectual for counteracting infection.

He found Mr. Clare in his bed-chamber, but not in bed. He was sitting in his night-gown at a bureau near the window. His appearance was composed and cheerful, but death was in his countenance. "I had a great inclination, Falkland," said he, "not to have suffered you to come in; and yet there is not a person in the world it could give me more pleasure to see. But, upon second thoughts, I believe there are few people that could run into a danger of this kind with a better prospect of escaping. In your case, at least, the garrison will not, I trust, be taken through the treachery of the commander. I cannot tell how it is that I, who can preach wisdom to you, have myself been caught. But do not be discouraged by my example. I had no notice of my danger, or I would have acquitted myself better."

Mr. Falkland having once established himself in the apartment of his friend, would upon no terms consent to retire. Mr. Clare considered that there was perhaps less danger in this choice, than in the frequent change from the extremes of a pure to a tainted air, and desisted from expostulation. "Falkland," said he, "when you came in, I had just finished making my will. I was not pleased with what I had formerly drawn up upon that subject, and I did not choose in my present situation to call in an attorney. In fact, it would be strange if a man of sense, with pure and direct intentions, should not be able to perform such a function for himself."

Mr. Clare continued to act in the same easy and disengaged manner as in perfect health. To judge from the cheerfulness of his tone and the firmness of his manner, the thought would never once have occurred that he was dying. He walked, he reasoned, he jested, in a way that argued the most perfect self-possession. But his appearance changed perceptibly for the worse every quarter of an hour. Mr. Falkland kept his eye perpetually fixed upon him, with mingled sentiments of anxiety and admiration.

"Falkland," said he, after having appeared for a short period absorbed in thought, "I feel that I am dying. This is a strange distemper of mine. Yesterday I seemed in perfect health, and tomorrow I shall be an insensible corpse. How curious is the line that separates life and death to mortal men! To be at one moment active, gay, penetrating, with stores of knowledge at one's command, capable of delighting, instructing, and animating mankind, and the next, lifeless and loathsome, an incumbrance upon the face of the earth! Such is the history of many men, and such will be mine.

"I feel as if I had yet much to do in the world; but it will not be. I must be contented with what is past. It is in vain that I muster all my spirits to my heart. The enemy is too mighty and too merciless for me; he will not give me time so much as to breathe. These things are not yet at least in our power: they are parts of a great series that is perpetually flowing. The general welfare, the great business of the universe, will go on, though I bear no further share in promoting it. That task is reserved for younger strengths, for you, Falkland, and such as you. We should be contemptible indeed if the prospect of human improvement did not yield us a pure and perfect delight, independently of the question of our existing to partake of it. Mankind would have little to envy to future ages, if they had all enjoyed a serenity as perfect as mine has been for the latter half of my existence."

Mr. Clare sat up through the whole day, indulging himself in easy and cheerful exertions, which were perhaps better calculated to refresh and invigorate the frame, than if he had sought repose in its direct form. Now and then he was visited with a sudden pang; but it was no sooner felt, than he seemed to rise above it, and smiled at the impotence of these attacks. They might destroy him, but they could not disturb. Three or four times he was bedewed with profuse sweats; and these again were succeeded by an extreme dryness and burning heat of the skin. He was next covered with small livid spots: symptoms of shivering followed, but these he drove away with a determined resolution. He then became tranquil and composed, and, after some time, decided to go to bed, it being already night. "Falkland," said he, pressing his hand, "the task of dying is not so difficult as some imagine. When one looks back from the brink of it, one wonders that so total a subversion can take place at so easy a price."

He had now been some time in bed, and, as every thing was

still, Mr. Falkland hoped that he slept; but in that he was mistaken. Presently Mr. Clare threw back the curtain, and looked
in the countenance of his friend. "I cannot sleep," said he. "No,
if I could sleep, it would be the same thing as to recover; and I
am destined to have the worst in this battle.

"Falkland, I have been thinking about you. I do not know
any one whose future usefulness I contemplate with greater
hope. Take care of yourself. Do not let the world be defrauded
of your virtues. I am acquainted with your weakness as well as
your strength. You have an impetuosity, and an impatience of
imagined dishonour, that, if once set wrong, may make you as
eminently mischievous as you will otherwise be useful. Think
seriously of exterminating this error!

"But if I cannot, in the brief expostulation my present situation will allow, produce this desirable change in you, there is at
least one thing I can do. I can put you upon your guard against
a mischief I foresee to be imminent. Beware of Mr. Tyrrel. Do
not commit the mistake of despising him as an unequal opponent. Petty causes may produce great mischiefs. Mr. Tyrrel is
boisterous, rugged, and unfeeling; and you are too passionate,
too acutely sensible of injury. It would be truly to be lamented,
if a man so inferior, so utterly unworthy to be compared with
you, should be capable of changing your whole history into
misery and guilt. I have a painful presentiment upon my heart,
as if something dreadful would reach you from that quarter.
Think of this. I exact no promise from you. I would not shack-
le you with the fetters of superstition; I would have you governed by justice and reason."

Mr. Falkland was deeply affected with this expostulation.
His sense of the generous attention of Mr. Clare at such a
moment, was so great as almost to deprive him of utterance. He
spoke in short sentences, and with visible effort. "I will behave
better," replied he. "Never fear me! Your admonitions shall not
be thrown away upon me."

Mr. Clare adverted to another subject. "I have made you my
executor; you will not refuse me this last office of friendship. It
is but a short time that I have had the happiness of knowing
you; but in that short time I have examined you well, and see

you thoroughly. Do not disappoint the sanguine hope I have entertained!

"I have left some legacies. My former connections, while I lived amidst the busy haunts of men, as many of them as were intimate, are all of them dear to me. I have not had time to summon them about me upon the present occasion, nor did I desire it. The remembrances of me will, I hope, answer a better purpose than such as are usually thought of on similar occasions."

Mr. Clare, having thus unburthened his mind, spoke no more for several hours. Towards morning Mr. Falkland quietly withdrew the curtain, and looked at the dying man. His eyes were open, and were now gently turned towards his young friend. His countenance was sunk, and of a death-like appearance. "I hope you are better," said Falkland in a half whisper, as if afraid of disturbing him. Mr. Clare drew his hand from the bed-clothes, and stretched it forward; Mr. Falkland advanced, and took hold of it. "Much better," said Mr. Clare in a voice inward and hardly articulate; "the struggle is now over; I have finished my part; farewell! remember!" These were his last words. He lived still a few hours; his lips were sometimes seen to move; he expired without a groan.

Mr. Falkland had witnessed the scene with much anxiety. His hopes of a favourable crisis, and his fear of disturbing the last moments of his friend, had held him dumb. For the last half hour he had stood up, with his eyes intently fixed upon Mr. Clare. He witnessed the last gasp, the last little convulsive motion of the frame. He continued to look; he sometimes imagined that he saw life renewed. At length he could deceive himself no longer, and exclaimed with a distracted accent, "And is this all?" He would have thrown himself upon the body of his friend; the attendants withheld, and would have forced him into another apartment. But he struggled from them, and hung fondly over the bed. "Is this the end of genius, virtue, and excellence? Is the luminary of the world thus for ever gone? Oh, yesterday! yesterday! Clare, why could not I have died in your stead? Dreadful moment! Irreparable loss! Lost in the very maturity and vigour of his mind! Cut off from a usefulness ten thousand times greater than any he had already exhibited! Oh, his was a mind to have instructed sages, and guided the moral world! This is all we have left of him! The eloquence of those lips is gone! The incessant activity of that heart is still! The best and wisest of men is gone, and the world is insensible of its loss!"

Mr. Tyrrel heard the intelligence of Mr. Clare's death with emotion, but of a different kind. He avowed that he had not forgiven him his partial attachment to Mr. Falkland, and therefore could not recall his remembrance with kindness. But if he could have overlooked his past injustice, sufficient care, it seems, was taken to keep alive his resentment. "Falkland, forsooth, attended him on his death-bed, as if nobody else were worthy of his confidential communications." But what was worst of all was this executorship. "In every thing this pragmatical rascal throws me behind. Contemptible wretch, that has nothing of the man about him! Must he perpetually trample upon his betters? Is every body incapable of saying what kind of stuff a man is made of? caught with mere outside? choosing the flimsy before the substantial? And upon his death-bed too! [Mr. Tyrrel with his uncultivated brutality mixed, as usually happens, certain rude notions of religion.] Sure the sense of his situation might have shamed him. Poor wretch! his soul has a great deal to answer for. He has made my pillow uneasy; and, whatever may be the consequences, it is he we have to thank for them."

The death of Mr. Clare removed the person who could most effectually have moderated the animosities of the contending parties, and took away the great operative check upon the excesses of Mr. Tyrrel. This rustic tyrant had been held in involuntary restraint by the intellectual ascendancy of his celebrated neighbour; and, notwithstanding the general ferocity of his temper, he did not appear till lately to have entertained a hatred against him. In the short time that had elapsed from the period in which Mr. Clare had fixed his residence in the neighbourhood, to that of the arrival of Mr. Falkland from the Continent, the conduct of Mr. Tyrrel had even shown tokens of improvement. He would indeed have been better satisfied not to have had even this intruder into a circle where he had been accustomed to reign. But with Mr. Clare he could have no rivalship; the venerable character of Mr. Clare disposed him to submission: this great man seemed to have survived all the acrimony of contention, and all the jealous subtleties of a mistaken honour.

The effects of Mr. Clare's suavity however, so far as related to Mr. Tyrrel, had been in a certain degree suspended by considerations of rivalship between this gentleman and Mr. Falkland. And, now that the influence of Mr. Clare's presence and virtues was entirely removed, Mr. Tyrrel's temper broke out into more criminal excesses than ever. The added gloom which Mr. Falkland's neighbourhood inspired, overflowed upon all his connections; and the new examples of his sullenness and tyranny which every day afforded, reflected back upon this accumulated and portentous feud.

CHAPTER VI

THE consequences of all this speedily manifested themselves. The very next incident in the story was in some degree decisive of the catastrophe. Hitherto I have spoken only of preliminary matters, seemingly unconnected with each other, though leading to that state of mind in both parties which had such fatal effects. But all that remains is rapid and tremendous. The death-dealing mischief advances with an accelerated motion, appearing to defy human wisdom and strength to obstruct its operation.

The vices of Mr. Tyrrel, in their present state of augmentation, were peculiarly exercised upon his domestics and dependents. But the principal sufferer was the young lady mentioned on a former occasion, the orphan daughter of his father's sister. Miss Melville's mother had married imprudently, or rather unfortunately, against the consent of her relations, all of whom had agreed to withdraw their countenance from her in consequence of that precipitate step. Her husband had turned out to be no better than an adventurer; had spent her fortune, which in consequence of the irreconcilableness of her family was less than he expected, and had broken her heart. Her infant daughter was left without any resource. In this situation the representations of the people with whom she happened to be placed, prevailed upon Mrs. Tyrrel, the mother of the squire, to receive her into her family. In equity, perhaps, she was entitled to that portion of fortune which her mother had forfeited by her imprudence, and which had gone to swell the property of the male representative. But this idea had never entered into the conceptions of either mother or son. Mrs. Tyrrel conceived that she performed an act of the most exalted benevolence in admitting Miss Emily into a sort of equivocal situation, which was neither precisely that of a domestic, nor yet marked with the treatment that might seem due to one of the family.

She had not, however, at first been sensible of all the mortifications that might have been expected from her condition. Mrs. Tyrrel, though proud and imperious, was not ill-natured. The female, who lived in the family in the capacity of housekeeper, was a person who had seen better days, and whose disposition was extremely upright and amiable. She early contracted a friendship for the little Emily, who was indeed for the most part committed to her care. Emily, on her side, fully repaid the affection of her instructress, and learned with great docility the few accomplishments Mrs. Jakeman was able to communicate. But most of all she imbibed her cheerful and artless temper, that extracted the agreeable and encouraging from all events, and prompted her to communicate her sentiments, which were never of the cynical cast, without modification or disguise. Besides the advantages Emily derived from Mrs. Jakeman, she was permitted to take lessons from the masters who were employed at Tyrrel Place for the instruction of her cousin; and indeed, as the young gentleman was most frequently indisposed to attend to them, they would commonly have had nothing to do, had it not been for the fortunate presence of Miss Melville. Mrs. Tyrrel therefore encouraged the studies of Emily on that score; in addition to which she imagined that this living exhibition of instruction might operate as an indirect allurement to her darling Barnabas, the only species of motive she would suffer to be presented. Force she absolutely forbade; and of the intrinsic allurements of literature and knowledge she had no conception.

Emily, as she grew up, displayed an uncommon degree of sensibility, which under her circumstances would have been a source of perpetual dissatisfaction, had it not been qualified with an extreme sweetness and easiness of temper. She was far from being entitled to the appellation of a beauty. Her person was *petite* and trivial; her complexion savoured of the *brunette*; and her face was marked with the small-pox, sufficiently to destroy its evenness and polish, though not enough to destroy its expression. But, though her appearance was not beautiful, it did not fail to be in a high degree engaging. Her complexion was at once healthful and delicate; her long dark eyebrows adapted themselves with facility to the various conceptions of her mind; and her looks bore the united impression of an active discernment and a good-humoured frankness. The instruction she had received, as it was entirely of a casual nature, exempted her from the evils of untutored ignorance, but not from a sort of native wildness, arguing a mind incapable of guile itself, or of suspecting it in others. She amused, without seeming conscious of the refined sense which her observations contained; or rather, having never been debauched with applause, she set light by her own qualifications, and talked from the pure gaiety of a youthful heart acting upon the stores of a just understanding, and not with any expectation of being distinguished and admired.

The death of her aunt made very little change in her situation. This prudent lady, who would have thought it little less than sacrilege to have considered Miss Melville as a branch of the stock of the Tyrrels, took no more notice of her in her will than barely putting her down for one hundred pounds in a catalogue of legacies to her servants. She had never been admitted into the intimacy and confidence of Mrs. Tyrrel; and the young squire, now that she was left under his sole protection, seemed inclined to treat her with even more liberality than his mother had done. He had seen her grow up under his eye, and therefore, though there were but six years difference in their ages, he felt a kind of paternal interest in her welfare. Habit had rendered her in a manner necessary to him, and, in every recess from the occupations of the field and the pleasures of the table, he found himself solitary and forlorn without the society of Miss Melville. Nearness of kindred, and Emily's want of personal beauty, prevented him from ever looking on her with the eyes of desire. Her accomplishments were chiefly of the customary and superficial kind, dancing and music. Her skill in the first led him sometimes to indulge her with a vacant corner in his carriage, when he went to the neighbouring assembly; and, in whatever light he might himself think proper to regard her, he would have imagined his chambermaid, introduced by him, entitled to an undoubted place in the most splendid circle. Her musical talents were frequently employed for his amusement. She had the honour occasionally of playing him to sleep after the fatigues of the chase; and as he had some relish for harmonious sounds, she was frequently able to soothe him by their means from the perturbations of which his gloomy disposition was so eminently a slave. Upon the whole, she might be considered as in some sort his favourite. She was the mediator to whom his tenants and domestics, when they had incurred his displeasure, were accustomed to apply; the privileged companion, that could approach this lion with impunity in the midst of his roarings. She spoke to him without fear; her solicitations were always good-natured and disinterested; and when he repulsed her, he disarmed himself of half his terrors, and was contented to smile at her presumption.

Such had been for some years the situation of Miss Melville. Its precariousness had been beguiled by the uncommon forbearance with which she was treated by her savage protector. But his disposition, always brutal, had acquired a gradual accession of ferocity since the settlement of Mr. Falkland in his neighbourhood. He now frequently forgot the gentleness with which he had been accustomed to treat his good-natured cousin. Her little playful arts were not always successful in softening his rage; and he would sometimes turn upon her blandishments with an impatient sternness that made her tremble. The careless ease of her disposition, however, soon effaced these impressions, and she fell without variation into her old habits.

A circumstance occurred about this time which gave peculiar strength to the acrimony of Mr. Tyrrel, and ultimately brought to its close the felicity that Miss Melville, in spite of the frowns of fortune, had hitherto enjoyed. Emily was exactly seventeen when Mr. Falkland returned from the Continent. At this age she was peculiarly susceptible of the charms of beauty, grace, and moral excellence, when united in a person of the other sex. She was imprudent, precisely because her own heart was incapable of guile. She had never yet felt the sting of the poverty to which she was condemned, and had not reflected on the insuperable distance that custom has placed between the opulent and the poorer classes of the community. She beheld Mr. Falkland, whenever he was thrown in her way at any of the public meetings, with admiration; and, without having precisely explained to herself the sentiments she indulged, her eyes followed him through all the changes of the scene, with eagerness and impatience. She did not see him, as the rest of the assembly did, born to one of the amplest estates in the county, and qualified to assert his title to the richest heiress. She thought only of Falkland, with those advantages which were most intimately his own, and of which no persecution of adverse fortune had the ability to deprive him. In a word, she was transported when he was present; he was the perpetual subject of her reveries and her dreams; but his image excited no sentiment in her mind beyond that of the immediate pleasure she took in his idea.

The notice Mr. Falkland bestowed on her in return, appeared sufficiently encouraging to a mind so full of prepossession as that of Emily. There was a particular complacency in his looks when directed towards her. He had said in a company, of which one of the persons present repeated his remarks to Miss Melville, that she appeared to him amiable and interesting; that he felt for her unprovided and destitute situation; and that he should have been glad to be more particular in his attention to her, had he not been apprehensive of doing her a prejudice in the suspicious mind of Mr. Tyrrel. All this she considered as the ravishing condescension of a superior nature; for, if she did not recollect with sufficient assiduity his gifts of fortune, she was, on the other hand, filled with reverence for his unrivalled accomplishments. But, while she thus seemingly disclaimed all comparison between Mr. Falkland and herself, she probably cherished a confused feeling as if some event, that was yet in the womb of fate, might reconcile things apparently the most incompatible. Fraught with these prepossessions, the civilities that had once or twice occurred in the bustle of a public circle, the restoring her fan which she had dropped, or the disembarrassing her of an empty tea-cup, made her heart palpitate, and gave birth to the wildest chimeras in her deluded imagination.

About this time an event happened that helped to give a precise determination to the fluctuations of Miss Melville's mind. One evening, a short time after the death of Mr. Clare, Mr. Falkland had been at the house of his deceased friend in his quality of executor, and, by some accidents of little intrinsic importance, had been detained three or four hours later than he expected. He did not set out upon his return till two o'clock in the morning. At this time, in a situation so remote from the metropolis, every thing is as silent as it would be in a region wholly uninhabited. The moon shone bright; and the objects around being marked with strong variations of light and shade, gave a kind of sacred solemnity to the scene. Mr. Falkland had taken Collins with him, the business to be settled at Mr. Clare's being in some respects similar to that to which this faithful domestic had been accustomed in the routine of his ordinary service. They had entered into some conversation, for Mr. Falkland was not then in the habit of obliging the persons about him by formality and reserve to recollect who he was. The attractive solemnity of the scene made him break off the talk somewhat abruptly, that he might enjoy it without interruption. They had not ridden far, before a hollow wind seemed to rise at a distance, and they could hear the hoarse roarings of the sea. Presently the sky on one side assumed the appearance of a reddish brown, and a sudden angle in the road placed this phenomenon directly before them. As they proceeded, it became more distinct, and it was at length sufficiently visible that it was occasioned by a fire. Mr. Falkland put spurs to his horse; and, as they approached, the object presented every instant a more alarming appearance. The flames ascended with fierceness; they embraced a large portion of the horizon; and, as they carried up with them numerous little fragments of the materials that fed them, impregnated with fire, and of an extremely bright and luminous colour, they presented some feeble image of the tremendous eruption of a volcano.

The flames proceeded from a village directly in their road. There were eight or ten houses already on fire, and the whole seemed to be threatened with immediate destruction. The inhabitants were in the utmost consternation, having had no previous experience of a similar calamity. They conveyed with haste their moveables and furniture into the adjoining fields. When any of them had effected this as far as it could be attempted with safety, they were unable to conceive any further remedy, but stood wringing their hands, and contemplating the ravages of the fire in an agony of powerless despair. The water that could be procured, in any mode practised in that place, was but as a drop contending with an element in arms. The wind in the mean time was rising, and the flames spread with more and more rapidity.

Mr. Falkland contemplated this scene for a few moments, as if ruminating with himself as to what could be done. He then directed some of the country people about him to pull down a house, next to one that was wholly on fire, but which itself was yet untouched. They seemed astonished at a direction which implied a voluntary destruction of property, and considered the task as too much in the heart of the danger to be undertaken. Observing that they were motionless, he dismounted from his horse, and called upon them in an authoritative voice to follow him. He ascended the house in an instant, and presently appeared upon the top of it, as if in the midst of the flames. Having, with the assistance of two or three of the persons that followed him most closely, and who by this time had supplied themselves with whatever tools came next to hand, loosened the support of a stack of chimneys, he pushed them headlong into the midst of the fire. He passed and repassed along the roof; and, having set people to work in all parts, descended in order to see what could be done in any other quarter.

At this moment an elderly woman burst from the midst of a house in flames: the utmost consternation was painted in her looks; and, as soon as she could recollect herself enough to have a proper idea of her situation, the subject of her anxiety seemed, in an instant, to be totally changed. "Where is my child? cried she, and cast an anxious and piercing look among the surrounding crowd. Oh, she is lost! she is in the midst of flames! Save her! save her! my child!" She filled the air with heart-rending shrieks. She turned towards the house. The people that were near endeavoured to prevent her, but she shook them off in a moment. She entered the passage; viewed the hideous ruin; and was then going to plunge into the blazing staircase. Mr. Falkland saw, pursued, and seized her by the arm; it was Mrs. Jakeman. "Stop!" he cried, with a voice of grand, yet benevolent authority. "Remain you in the street! I will seek, and will save her!" Mrs. Jakeman obeyed. He charged the persons who were near to detain her; he enquired which was the apartment of Emily. Mrs. Jakeman was upon a visit to a sister who lived in the village, and had brought Emily along with her. Mr. Falkland ascended a neighbouring house, and entered that in which Emily was, by a window in the roof.

He found her already awaked from her sleep; and, becoming sensible of her danger, she had that instant wrapped a loose gown round her. Such is the almost irresistible result of feminine habits; but having done this, she examined the surrounding objects with the wildness of despair. Mr. Falkland entered the chamber. She flew into his arms with the rapidity of lightning. She embraced and clung to him, with an impulse that did not wait to consult the dictates of her understanding. Her emotions were indescribable. In a few short moments she had lived an age in love. In two minutes Mr. Falkland was again in the street with his lovely, half-naked burthen in his arms. Having restored her to her affectionate protector, snatched from the immediate grasp of death, from which, if he had not, none would have delivered her, he returned to his former task. By his presence of mind, by his indefatigable humanity and incessant exertions, he saved three fourths of the village from destruction.

The conflagration being at length abated, he sought again Mrs. Jakeman and Emily, who by this time had obtained a substitute for the garments she had lost in the fire. He displayed the tenderest solicitude for the young lady's safety, and directed Collins to go with as much speed as he could, and send his chariot to attend her. More than an hour elapsed in this interval. Miss Melville had never seen so much of Mr. Falkland upon any former occasion; and the spectacle of such humanity, delicacy, firmness, and justice in the form of man, as he crowded into this small space, was altogether new to her, and in the highest degree fascinating. She had a confused feeling as if there had been something indecorous in her behaviour or appearance, when Mr. Falkland had appeared to her relief; and this combined with her other emotions to render the whole critical and intoxicating.

Emily no sooner arrived at the family mansion, than Mr. Tyrrel ran out to receive her. He had just heard of the melancholy accident that had taken place at the village, and was terrified for the safety of his good-humoured cousin. He displayed those unpremeditated emotions which are common to almost every individual of the human race. He was greatly shocked at the suspicion that Emily might possibly have become the victim of a catastrophe which had thus broken out in the dead of night. His sensations were of the most pleasing sort when he folded her in his arms, and fearful apprehension was instantaneously converted into joyous certainty. Emily no sooner entered under the well known roof than her spirits were brisk, and her tongue incessant in describing her danger and her deliverance. Mr. Tyrrel had formerly been tortured with the innocent eulogiums she pronounced of Mr. Falkland. But these were tameness itself, compared with the rich and various eloquence that now flowed from her lips. Love had not the same effect upon her, especially at the present moment, which it would have had upon a person instructed to feign a blush, and inured to a consciousness of wrong. She described his activity and resources, the promptitude with which every thing was conceived, and the cautious but daring wisdom with which it was executed. All was fairy-land and enchantment in the tenour of her artless tale; you saw a beneficent genius surveying and controlling the whole, but could have no notion of any human means by which his purposes were effected.

Mr. Tyrrel listened for a while to these innocent effusions with patience; he could even bear to hear the man applauded, by whom he had just obtained so considerable a benefit. But the theme by amplification became nauseous, and he at length with some roughness put an end to the tale. Probably, upon recollection, it appeared still more insolent and intolerable than while it was passing; the sensation of gratitude wore off, but the hyperbolical praise that had been bestowed still haunted his memory, and sounded in his ear; – Emily had entered into the confederacy that disturbed his repose. For herself, she was wholly unconscious of offence, and upon every occasion quoted Mr. Falkland as the model of elegant manners and true wisdom. She was a total stranger to dissimulation; and she could not conceive that any one beheld the subject of her admiration with less partiality than herself. Her artless love became more fervent than ever. She flattered herself that nothing less than a reciprocal passion could have prompted Mr. Falkland to the desperate attempt of saving her from the flames; and she trusted that this passion would speedily declare itself, as well as induce the object of her adoration to overlook her comparative unworthiness.

Mr. Tyrrel endeavoured at first with some moderation to check Miss Melville in her applauses, and to convince her by various tokens that the subject was disagreeable to him. He was accustomed to treat her with kindness. Emily, on her part, was disposed to yield an unreluctant obedience, and therefore it was not difficult to restrain her. But upon the very next occasion her favourite topic would force its way to her lips. Her obedience was the acquiescence of a frank and benevolent heart; but it was the most difficult thing in the world to inspire her with fear. Conscious herself that she would not hurt a worm, she could not conceive that any one would harbour cruelty and rancour against her. Her temper had preserved her from obstinate contention with the persons under whose protection she was placed; and, as her compliance was unhesitating, she had no experience of a severe and rigorous treatment. As Mr. Tyrrel's objection to the very name of Falkland became more palpable and uniform, Miss Melville increased in her precaution. She would stop herself in the half-pronounced sentences that were meant to his praise. This circumstance had necessarily an ungracious effect; it was a cutting satire upon the imbecility of her kinsman. Upon these occasions she would sometimes venture upon a good-humoured expostulation: – "Dear sir! well, I wonder how you can be so ill-natured! I am sure Mr. Falkland would do you any good office in the world:" – till she was checked by some gesture of impatience and fierceness.

At length she wholly conquered her heedlessness and inattention. But it was too late. Mr. Tyrrel already suspected the existence of that passion which she had thoughtlessly imbibed. His imagination, ingenious in torment, suggested to him all the different openings in conversation, in which she would have introduced the praise of Mr. Falkland, had she not been placed under this unnatural restraint. Her present reserve upon the subject was even more insufferable than her former loquacity. All his kindness for this unhappy orphan gradually subsided. Her partiality for the man who was the object of his unbounded abhorrence, appeared to him as the last persecution of a malicious destiny. He figured himself as about to be deserted by every creature in human form; all men, under the influence of a fatal enchantment, approving only what was sophisticated and artificial, and holding the rude and genuine offspring of nature in mortal antipathy. Impressed with these gloomy presages, he saw Miss Melville with no sentiments but those of rancorous aversion; and, accustomed as he was to the uncontrolled indulgence of his propensities, he determined to wreak upon her a signal revenge.

CHAPTER VII

MR. TYRREL consulted his old confident respecting the plan he should pursue; who, sympathising as he did in the brutality and insolence of his friend, had no idea that an insignificant girl, without either wealth or beauty, ought to be allowed for a moment to stand in the way of the gratifications of a man of Mr. Tyrrel's importance. The first idea of her now unrelenting kinsman was to thrust her from his doors, and leave her to seek her bread as she could. But he was conscious that this proceeding would involve him in considerable obloquy; and he at length fixed upon a scheme which, at the same time that he believed it would sufficiently shelter his reputation, would much more certainly secure her mortification and punishment.

For this purpose he fixed upon a young man of twenty, the son of one Grimes, who occupied a small farm, the property of his confident. This fellow he resolved to impose as a husband on Miss Melville, who, he shrewdly suspected, guided by the tender sentiments she had unfortunately conceived for Mr. Falkland, would listen with reluctance to any matrimonial proposal. Grimes he selected as being in all respects the diametrical reverse of Mr. Falkland. He was not precisely a lad of vicious propensities, but in an inconceivable degree boorish and uncouth. His complexion was scarcely human; his features were coarse, and strangely discordant and disjointed from each other. His lips were thick, and the tone of his voice broad and unmodulated. His legs were of equal size from one end to the other, and his feet misshapen and clumsy. He had nothing spiteful or malicious in his disposition, but he was a total stranger to tenderness; he could not feel for those refinements in others, of which he had no experience in himself. He was an expert boxer: his inclination led him to such amusements as were most boisterous; and he delighted in a sort of manual sarcasm, which he could not conceive to be very injurious, as it left no traces behind it. His general manners were noisy and obstreperous; inattentive to others; and obstinate and unyielding, not from any cruelty and ruggedness of temper, but from an incapacity to conceive those finer feelings, that make so large a part of the history of persons who are cast in a gentler mould.

Such was the uncouth and half-civilised animal, which the industrious malice of Mr. Tyrrel fixed upon as most happily adapted to his purpose. Emily had hitherto been in an unusual degree exempted from the oppression of despotism. Her happy insignificance had served her as a protection. No one thought it worth his while to fetter her with those numerous petty restrictions with which the daughters of opulence are commonly tormented. She had the wildness, as well as the delicate frame, of the bird that warbles unmolested in its native groves.

When therefore she heard from her kinsman the proposal of Mr. Grimes for a husband, she was for a moment silent with astonishment at so unexpected a suggestion. But as soon as she recovered her speech, she replied, "No, sir, I do not want a husband."

"You do! Are not you always hankering after the men? It is high time you should be settled."

"Mr. Grimes! No, indeed! when I do have a husband, it shall not be such a man as Mr. Grimes neither."

"Be silent! How dare you give yourself such unaccountable liberties?"

"Lord, I wonder what I should do with him. You might as well give me your great rough water-dog, and bid me make him a silk cushion to lie in my dressing-room. Besides, sir, Grimes is a common labouring man, and I am sure I have always heard my aunt say that ours is a very great family."

"It is a lie! Our family! have you the impudence to think yourself one of our family?"

"Why, sir, was not your grandpapa my grandpapa? How then can we be of a different family?"

"From the strongest reason in the world. You are the daughter of a rascally Scotchman, who spent every shilling of my aunt Lucy's fortune, and left you a beggar. You have got an hundred pounds, and Grimes's father promises to give him as much. How dare you look down upon your equals?"

"Indeed, sir, I am not proud. But, indeed and indeed, I can never love Mr. Grimes. I am very happy as I am: why should I be married?"

"Silence your prating! Grimes will be here this afternoon. Look that you behave well to him. If you do not, he will remember and repay, when you least like it."

"Nay, I am sure, sir – you are not in earnest?"

"Not in earnest! Damn me, but we will see that. I can tell what you would be at. You had rather be Mr. Falkland's miss, than the wife of a plain downright yeoman. But I shall take care of you. – Ay, this comes of indulgence. You must be taken down, miss. You must be taught the difference between high-flown notions and realities. Mayhap you may take it a little in dudgeon or so; but never mind that. Pride always wants a little smarting. If you should be brought to shame, it is I that shall bear the blame of it."

The tone in which Mr. Tyrrel spoke was so different from any thing to which Miss Melville had been accustomed, that she felt herself wholly unable to determine what construction to put upon it. Sometimes she thought he had really formed a plan for imposing upon her a condition that she could not bear so much as to think of. But presently she rejected this idea as an unworthy imputation upon her kinsman, and concluded that it was only his way, and that all he meant was to try her. To be resolved however, she determined to consult her constant adviser, Mrs. Jakeman, and accordingly repeated to her what had passed. Mrs. Jakeman saw the whole in a very different light from that in which Emily had conceived it, and trembled for the future peace of her beloved ward.

"Lord bless me, my dear mamma!" cried Emily, (this was the appellation she delighted to bestow upon the good housekeeper) "you cannot think so? But I do not care. I will never marry Grimes, happen what will."

"But how will you help yourself? My master will oblige you."

"Nay, now you think you are talking to a child indeed. It is I am to have the man, not Mr. Tyrrel. Do you think I will let any body else choose a husband for me? I am not such a fool as that neither."

"Ah, Emily! you little know the disadvantages of your situation. Your cousin is a violent man, and perhaps will turn you out of doors, if you oppose him."

"Oh, mamma! it is very wicked of you to say so. I am sure Mr. Tyrrel is a very good man, though he be a little cross now and then. He knows very well that I am right to have a will of my own in such a thing as this, and nobody is punished for doing what is right."

"Nobody ought, my dear child. But there are very wicked and tyrannical men in the world."

"Well, well, I will never believe my cousin is one of these."

"I hope he is not."

"And if he were, what then? To be sure I should be very sorry to make him angry."

"What then! Why then my poor Emily would be a beggar. Do you think I could bear to see that?"

"No, no. Mr. Tyrrel has just told me that I have a hundred pounds. But if I had no fortune, is not that the case with a thousand other folks? Why should I grieve, for what they bear and are merry? Do not make yourself uneasy, mamma. I am determined that I will do any thing rather than marry Grimes; that is what I will."

Mrs. Jakeman could not bear the uneasy state of suspense in which this conversation left her mind, and went immediately to the squire to have her doubts resolved. The manner in which she proposed the question, sufficiently indicated the judgment she had formed of the match.

"That is true," said Mr. Tyrrel, "I wanted to speak to you about this affair. The girl has got unaccountable notions in her head, that will be the ruin of her. You perhaps can tell where she had them. But, be that as it will, it is high time something should be done. The shortest way is the best, and to keep things well while they are well. In short, I am determined she shall marry this lad: you do not know any harm of him, do you? You have a good deal of influence with her, and I desire, do you see, that you will employ it to lead her to her good: you had best, I can tell you. She is a pert vixen! By and by she would be a whore, and at last no better than a common trull, and rot upon a dunghill, if I were not at all these pains to save her from destruction. I would make her an honest farmer's wife, and my pretty miss cannot bear the thoughts of it!"

In the afternoon Grimes came according to appointment, and was left alone with the young lady.

"Well, miss," said he, "it seems the squire has a mind to make us man and wife. For my part, I cannot say I should have thought of it. But, being as how the squire has broke the ice, if so be as you like of the match, why I am your man. Speak the word; a nod is as good as a wink to a blind horse."

Emily was already sufficiently mortified at the unexpected proposal of Mr. Tyrrel. She was confounded at the novelty of the situation, and still more at the uncultivated rudeness of her lover, which even exceeded her expectation. This confusion was interpreted by Grimes into diffidence.

"Come, come, never be cast down. Put a good face upon it. What though? My first sweetheart was Bet Butterfield, but what of that? What must be must be; grief will never fill the belly. She was a fine strapping wench, that is the truth of it! five foot ten inches, and as stout as a trooper. Oh, she would do a power of work! Up early and down late; milked ten cows with her own hands; on with her cardinal, rode to market between her panniers, fair weather and foul, hail, blow, or snow. It would have done your heart good to have seen her frost-bitten cheeks, as red as a beefen from her own orchard! Ah! she was a maid of mettle; would romp with the harvestmen, slap one upon the back, wrestle with another, and had a rogue's trick and a joke for all round. Poor girl! she broke her neck down stairs at a christening. To be sure I shall never meet with her fellow! But never you mind that; I do not doubt that I shall find more in you upon further acquaintance. As coy and bashful as you seem, I dare say you are rogue enough at bottom. When I have touzled and rumpled you a little, we shall see. I am no chicken, miss, whatever you may think. I know what is what, and can see as far into a millstone as another. Ay, ay; you will come to. The fish will snap at the bait, never doubt it. Yes, yes, we shall rub on main well together."

Emily by this time had in some degree mustered up her spirits and began, though with hesitation, to thank Mr. Grimes for his good opinion, but to confess that she could never be brought to favour his addresses. She therefore entreated him to desist from all further application. This remonstrance on her part would have become more intelligible, had it not been for his boisterous manners and extravagant cheerfulness, which indisposed him to silence, and made him suppose that at half a word he had sufficient intimation of another's meaning. Mr. Tyrrel, in the mean time, was too impatient not to interrupt the scene before they could have time to proceed far in explanation; and he was studious in the sequel to prevent the young folks from being too intimately acquainted with each other's inclinations. Grimes, of consequence, attributed the reluctance of Miss Melville to maiden coyness, and the skittish shyness of an unbroken filly. Indeed, had it been otherwise, it is not probable that it would have made any effectual impression upon him; as he was always accustomed to consider women as made for the recreation of the men, and to exclaim against the weakness of people who taught them to imagine they were to judge for themselves.

As the suit proceeded, and Miss Melville saw more of her new admirer, her antipathy increased. But, though her character was unspoiled by those false wants, which frequently make people of family miserable while they have every thing that nature requires within their reach, yet she had been little used to opposition, and was terrified at the growing sternness of her kinsman. Sometimes she thought of flying from a house which was now become her dungeon; but the habits of her youth, and her ignorance of the world, made her shrink from this project when she contemplated it more nearly. Mrs. Jakeman, indeed, could not think with patience of young Grimes as a husband for her darling Emily; but her prudence determined her to resist with all her might the idea on the part of the young lady of proceeding to extremities. She could not believe that Mr. Tyrrel would persist in such an unaccountable persecution, and she exhorted Miss Melville to forget for a moment the unaffected independence of her character, and pathetically to deprecate her cousin's obstinacy. She had great confidence in the ingenuous eloquence of her ward. Mrs. Jakeman did not know what was passing in the breast of the tyrant.

Miss Melville complied with the suggestion of her mamma. One morning immediately after breakfast, she went to her harpsichord, and played one after another several of those airs that were most the favourites of Mr. Tyrrel. Mrs. Jakeman had retired; the servants were gone to their respective employments. Mr. Tyrrel would have gone also; his mind was untuned, and he did not take the pleasure he had been accustomed to take in the musical performances of Emily. But her finger was now more tasteful than common. Her mind was probably wrought up to a firmer and bolder tone, by the recollection of the cause she was going to plead; at the same time that it was exempt from those incapacitating tremors which would have been felt by one that dared not look poverty in the face. Mr. Tyrrel was unable to leave the apartment. Sometimes he traversed it with impatient steps; then he hung over the poor innocent whose powers were exerted to please him; at length he threw himself in a chair opposite, with his eyes turned towards Emily. It was easy to trace the progress of his emotions. The furrows into which his countenance was contracted were gradually relaxed; his features were brightened into a smile; the kindness with which he had upon former occasions contemplated Emily seemed to revive in his heart.

Emily watched her opportunity. As soon as she had finished one of the pieces, she rose and went to Mr. Tyrrel.

"Now, have not I done it nicely? and after this will not you give me a reward?"

"A reward! Ay, come here, and I will give you a kiss."

"No, that is not it. And yet you have not kissed me this many a day. Formerly you said you loved me, and called me your Emily. I am sure you did not love me better than I loved you. You have not forgot all the kindness you once had for me?" added she anxiously.

"Forgot? No, no. How can you ask such a question? You shall be my dear Emily still!"

"Ah, those were happy times!" she replied, a little mournful-ly. "Do you know, cousin, I wish I could wake, and find that the last month – only about a month – was a dream?"

"What do you mean by that?" said Mr. Tyrrel with an altered voice. "Have a care! Do not put me out of humour. Do not come with your romantic notions now."

"No, no: I have no romantic notions in my head. I speak of

something upon which the happiness of my life depends."

"I see what you would be at. Be silent. You know it is to no purpose to plague me with your stubbornness. You will not let me be in good humour with you for a moment. What my mind is determined upon about Grimes, all the world shall not move me to give up."

"Dear, dear cousin! why, but consider now. Grimes is a rough rustic lout, like Orson[1] in the story-book. He wants a wife like himself. He would be as uneasy and as much at a loss with me, as I with him. Why should we both of us be forced to do what neither of us is inclined to? I cannot think what could ever have put it into your head. But now, for goodness' sake, give it up! Marriage is a serious thing. You should not think of joining two people for a whim, who are neither of them fit for one another in any respect in the world. We should feel mortified and disappointed all our lives. Month would go after month, and year after year, and I could never hope to be my own, but by the death of a person I ought to love. I am sure, sir, you cannot mean me all this harm. What have I done, that I should deserve to have you for an enemy?"

"I am not your enemy. I tell you that it is necessary to put you out of harm's way. But, if I were your enemy, I could not be a worse torment to you than you are to me. Are not you continually singing the praises of Falkland? Are not you in love with Falkland? That man is a legion of devils to me! I might as well have been a beggar! I might as well have been a dwarf or a monster! Time was when I was thought entitled to respect. But now, debauched by this Frenchified rascal, they call me rude, surly, a tyrant! It is true that I cannot talk in finical phrases, flatter people with hypocritical praise, or suppress the real feelings of my mind. The scoundrel knows his pitiful advantages, and insults me upon them without ceasing. He is my rival and my persecutor; and, at last, as if all this were not enough, he has found means to spread the pestilence in my own family. You,

---

1   A character in a fifteenth-century French prose romance, *Valentin et Orson*, frequently translated and reprinted in England in the seventeenth and eighteenth centuries. After his mother is banished from Constantinople, Orson is raised by a family of bears.

whom we took up out of charity, the chance-born brat of a stolen marriage! you must turn upon your benefactor, and wound me in the point that of all others I could least bear. If I were your enemy, should not I have reason? Could I ever inflict upon you such injuries as you have made me suffer? And who are you? The lives of fifty such cannot atone for an hour of my uneasiness. If you were to linger for twenty years upon the rack, you would never feel what I have felt. But I am your friend. I see which way you are going; and I am determined to save you from this thief, this hypocritical destroyer of us all. Every moment that the mischief is left to itself, it does but make bad worse; and I am determined to save you out of hand."

The angry expostulations of Mr. Tyrrel suggested new ideas to the tender mind of Miss Melville. He had never confessed the emotions of his soul so explicitly before; but the tempest of his thoughts suffered him to be no longer master of himself. She saw with astonishment that he was the irreconcilable foe of Mr. Falkland, whom she had fondly imagined it was the same thing to know and admire; and that he harboured a deep and rooted resentment against herself. She recoiled, without well knowing why, before the ferocious passions of her kinsman, and was convinced that she had nothing to hope from his implacable temper. But her alarm was the prelude of firmness, and not of cowardice.

"No, sir," replied she, "indeed I will not be driven any way that you happen to like. I have been used to obey you, and, in all that is reasonable, I will obey you still. But you urge me too far. What do you tell me of Mr. Falkland? Have I ever done any thing to deserve your unkind suspicions? I am innocent, and will continue innocent. Mr. Grimes is well enough, and will no doubt find women that like him; but he is not fit for me, and torture shall not force me to be his wife."

Mr. Tyrrel was not a little astonished at the spirit which Emily displayed upon this occasion. He had calculated too securely upon the general mildness and suavity of her disposition. He now endeavoured to qualify the harshness of his former sentiments.

"God damn my soul! And so you can scold, can you? You expect every body to turn out of his way, and fetch and carry, just as you please? I could find in my heart – But you know my mind. I insist upon it that you let Grimes court you, and that you lay aside your sulks, and give him a fair hearing. Will you do that? If then you persist in your wilfulness, why there, I suppose, is an end of the matter. Do not think that any body is going to marry you, whether you will or no. You are no such mighty prize, I assure you. If you knew your own interest, you would be glad to take the young fellow while he is willing."

Miss Melville rejoiced in the prospect, which the last words of her kinsman afforded her, of a termination at no great distance to her present persecutions. Mrs. Jakeman, to whom she communicated them, congratulated Emily on the returning moderation and good sense of the squire, and herself on her prudence in having urged the young lady to this happy expostulation. But their mutual felicitations lasted not long. Mr. Tyrrel informed Mrs. Jakeman of the necessity in which he found himself of sending her to a distance, upon a business which would not fail to detain her several weeks; and, though the errand by no means wore an artificial or ambiguous face, the two friends drew a melancholy presage from this ill-timed separation. Mrs. Jakeman, in the mean time, exhorted her ward to persevere, reminded her of the compunction which had already been manifested by her kinsman, and encouraged her to hope every thing from her courage and good temper. Emily, on her part, though grieved at the absence of her protector and counsellor at so interesting a crisis, was unable to suspect Mr. Tyrrel of such a degree either of malice or duplicity as could afford ground for serious alarm. She congratulated herself upon her delivery from so alarming a persecution, and drew a prognostic of future success from this happy termination of the first serious affair of her life. She exchanged a state of fortitude and alarm for her former pleasing dreams respecting Mr. Falkland. These she bore without impatience. She was even taught by the uncertainty of the event to desire to prolong, rather than abridge, a situation which might be delusive, but which was not without its pleasures.

CHAPTER VIII

No thing could be further from Mr. Tyrrel's intention than to suffer his project to be thus terminated. No sooner was he freed from the fear of his housekeeper's interference, than he changed the whole system of his conduct. He ordered Miss Melville to be closely confined to her apartment, and deprived of all means of communicating her situation to any one out of his own house. He placed over her a female servant, in whose discretion he could confide, and who, having formerly been honoured with the amorous notices of the squire, considered the distinctions that were paid to Emily at Tyrrel Place as an usurpation upon her more reasonable claims. The squire himself did every thing in his power to blast the young lady's reputation, and represented to his attendants these precautions as necessary, to prevent her from eloping to his neighbour, and plunging herself in total ruin.

As soon as Miss Melville had been twenty-four hours in durance, and there was some reason to suppose that her spirit might be subdued to the emergency of her situation, Mr. Tyrrel thought proper to go to her, to explain the grounds of her present treatment, and acquaint her with the only means by which she could hope for a change. Emily no sooner saw him, than she turned towards him with an air of greater firmness than perhaps she had ever assumed in her life, and accosted him thus: –

"Well, sir, is it you? I wanted to see you. It seems I am shut up here by your orders. What does this mean? What right have you to make a prisoner of me? What do I owe you? Your mother left me a hundred pounds: have you ever offered to make any addition to my fortune? But, if you had, I do not want it. I do not pretend to be better than the children of other poor parents; I can maintain myself as they do. I prefer liberty to wealth. I see you are surprised at the resolution I exert. But ought I not to turn again, when I am trampled upon? I should have left you before now, if Mrs. Jakeman had not overpersuaded me, and if I had not thought better of you than by your present behaviour I find you deserve. But now, sir, I intend to leave your house this moment, and insist upon it, that you do not endeavour to prevent me."

Thus saying, she rose, and went towards the door, while Mr. Tyrrel stood thunderstruck at her magnanimity. Seeing, however, that she was upon the point of being out of the reach of his power, he recovered himself, and pulled her back.

"What is in the wind now? Do you think, strumpet, that you shall get the better of me by sheer impudence? Sit down! rest you satisfied! – So you want to know by what right you are here, do you? By the right of possession. This house is mine, and you are in my power. There is no Mrs. Jakeman now to spirit you away; no, nor no Falkland to bully for you. I have countermined you, damn me! and blown up your schemes. Do you think I will be contradicted and opposed for nothing? When did you ever know any body resist my will without being made to repent? And shall I now be brow-beaten by a chitty-faced girl? – I have not given you a fortune! Damn you! who brought you up? I will make you a bill for clothing and lodging. Do not you know that every creditor has a right to stop his runaway debtor? You may think as you please; but here you are till you marry Grimes. Heaven and earth shall not prevent but I will get the better of your obstinacy!"

"Ungenerous, unmerciful man! and so it is enough for you that I have nobody to defend me! But I am not so helpless as you may imagine. You may imprison my body, but you cannot conquer my mind. Marry Mr. Grimes! And is this the way to bring me to your purpose? Every hardship I suffer puts still further distant the end for which I am thus unjustly treated. You are not used to have your will contradicted! When did I ever contradict it? And, in a concern that is so completely my own, shall my will go for nothing? Would you lay down this rule for yourself, and suffer no other creature to take the benefit of it? I want nothing of you: how dare you refuse me the privilege of a reasonable being, to live unmolested in poverty and innocence? What sort of a man do you show yourself, you that lay claim to the respect and applause of every one that knows you?"

The spirited reproaches of Emily had at first the effect to fill Mr. Tyrrel with astonishment, and make him feel abashed and overawed in the presence of this unprotected innocent. But his confusion was the result of surprise. When the first emotion wore off, he cursed himself for being moved by her expostulations; and was ten times more exasperated against her, for daring to defy his resentment at a time when she had every thing to fear. His despotic and unforgiving propensities stimulated him to a degree little short of madness. At the same time his habits, which were pensive and gloomy, led him to meditate a variety of schemes to punish her obstinacy. He began to suspect that there was little hope of succeeding by open force, and therefore determined to have recourse to treachery.

He found in Grimes an instrument sufficiently adapted to his purpose. This fellow, without an atom of intentional malice, was fitted, by the mere coarseness of his perceptions, for the perpetration of the greatest injuries. He regarded both injury and advantage merely as they related to the gratifications of appetite; and considered it an essential in true wisdom, to treat with insult the effeminacy of those who suffer themselves to be tormented with ideal misfortunes. He believed that no happier destiny could befall a young woman than to be his wife; and he conceived that that termination would amply compensate for any calamities she might suppose herself to undergo in the interval. He was therefore easily prevailed upon, by certain temptations which Mr. Tyrrel knew how to employ, to take part in the plot into which Miss Melville was meant to be betrayed.

Matters being thus prepared, Mr. Tyrrel proceeded, through the means of the gaoler (for the experience he already had of personal discussion did not incline him to repeat his visits), to play upon the fears of his prisoner. This woman, sometimes under the pretence of friendship, and sometimes with open malice, informed Emily, from time to time, of the preparations that were making for her marriage. One day, "the squire had rode over to look at a neat little farm which was destined for the habitation of the new-married couple;" and at another, "a quantity of live stock and household furniture was procured, that every thing might be ready for their reception." She then told her "of a licence that was bought, a parson in readiness, and a day fixed for the nuptials." When Emily endeavoured, though with increased misgivings, to ridicule these proceedings as absolutely nugatory without her consent, her artful gouvernante related several stories of forced marriages, and assured her that neither protestations, nor silence, nor fainting, would be of any avail, either to suspend the ceremony, or to set it aside when performed.

The situation of Miss Melville was in an eminent degree pitiable. She had no intercourse but with her persecutors. She had not a human being with whom to consult, who might afford her the smallest degree of consolation and encouragement. She had fortitude; but it was neither confirmed nor directed by the dictates of experience. It could not therefore be expected to be so inflexible, as with better information it would, no doubt, have been found. She had a clear and noble spirit; but she had some of her sex's errors. Her mind sunk under the uniform terrors with which she was assailed, and her health became visibly impaired.

Her firmness being thus far undermined, Grimes, in pursuance of his instructions, took care in his next interview, to throw out an insinuation that, for his own part, he had never cared for the match, and since she was so averse to it, would be better pleased that it should never take place. Between one and the other however, he was got into a scrape, and now he supposed he must marry, will he, nill he. The two squires would infallibly ruin him upon the least appearance of backwardness on his part, as they were accustomed to do every inferior that resisted their will. Emily was rejoiced to find her admirer in so favourable a disposition; and earnestly pressed him to give effect to this humane declaration. Her representations were full of eloquence and energy. Grimes appeared to be moved at the fervency of her manner; but objected the resentment of Mr. Tyrrel and his landlord. At length, however, he suggested a project, in consequence of which he might assist her in her escape, without its ever coming to their knowledge, as, indeed, there was no likelihood that their suspicions would fix upon him. "To be sure," said he, "you have refused me in a disdainful sort of a way, as a man may say. Mayhap you thought I was no better 'an a brute: but I bear you no malice, and I will show you that I am more kind-hearted 'an you have been willing to think. It is a strange sort of a vagary you have taken, to stand in your own light, and disoblige all your friends. But if you are resolute, do you see? I scorn to be the husband of a lass that is not every bit as willing as I; and so I will even help to put you in a condition to follow your own inclinations."

Emily listened to these suggestions at first with eagerness and approbation. But her fervency somewhat abated, when they came to discuss the minute parts of the undertaking. It was necessary, as Grimes informed her, that her escape should be effected in the dead of the night. He would conceal himself for that purpose in the garden, and be provided with false keys, by which to deliver her from her prison. These circumstances were by no means adapted to calm her perturbed imagination. To throw herself into the arms of the man whose intercourse she was employing every method to avoid, and whom, under the idea of a partner for life, she could least of all men endure, was, no doubt, an extraordinary proceeding. The attendant circumstances of darkness and solitude aggravated the picture. The situation of Tyrrel Place was uncommonly lonely; it was three miles from the nearest village, and not less than seven from that in which Mrs. Jakeman's sister resided, under whose protection Miss Melville was desirous of placing herself. The ingenuous character of Emily did not allow her once to suspect Grimes of intending to make an ungenerous and brutal advantage of these circumstances; but her mind involuntarily revolted against the idea of committing herself, alone, to the disposal of a man, whom she had lately been accustomed to consider as the instrument of her treacherous relation.

After having for some time revolved these considerations, she thought of the expedient of desiring Grimes to engage Mrs. Jakeman's sister to wait for her at the outside of the garden. But this Grimes peremptorily refused. He even flew into a passion at the proposal. It showed very little gratitude, to desire him to disclose to other people his concern in this dangerous affair. For his part, he was determined, in consideration of his own safety, never to appear in it to any living soul. If

Miss did not believe him, when he made this proposal out of pure good-nature, and would not trust him a single inch, she might even see to the consequences herself. He was resolved to condescend no further to the whims of a person who, in her treatment of him, had shown herself as proud as Lucifer himself.

Emily exerted herself to appease his resentment; but all the eloquence of her new confederate could not prevail upon her instantly to give up her objection. She desired till the next day to consider of it. The day after was fixed by Mr. Tyrrel for the marriage ceremony. In the mean time she was pestered with intimations, in a thousand forms, of the fate that so nearly awaited her. The preparations were so continued, methodical, and regular, as to produce in her the most painful and aching anxiety. If her heart attained a moment's intermission upon the subject, her female attendant was sure, by some sly hint or sarcastical remark, to put a speedy termination to her tranquillity. She felt herself, as she afterwards remarked, alone, uninstructed, just broken loose, as it were, from the trammels of infancy, without one single creature to concern himself in her fate. She, who till then never knew an enemy, had now, for three weeks, not seen the glimpse of a human countenance, that she had not good reason to consider as wholly estranged to her at least, if not unrelentingly bent on her destruction. She now, for the first time, experienced the anguish of never having known her parents, and being cast upon the charity of people with whom she had too little equality, to hope to receive from them the offices of friendship.

The succeeding night was filled with the most anxious thoughts. When a momentary oblivion stole upon her senses, her distempered imagination conjured up a thousand images of violence and falsehood; she saw herself in the hands of her determined enemies, who did not hesitate by the most daring treachery to complete her ruin. Her waking thoughts were not more consoling. The struggle was too great for her constitution. As morning approached, she resolved, at all hazards, to put herself into the hands of Grimes. This determination was no sooner made, than she felt her heart sensibly lightened. She could not conceive any evil which could result from this proceeding, that deserved to be put in the balance against those which, under the roof of her kinsman, appeared unavoidable.

When she communicated her determination to Grimes, it was not possible to say whether he received pleasure or pain from the intimation. He smiled indeed; but his smile was accompanied by a certain abrupt ruggedness of countenance, so that it might equally well be the smile of sarcasm or of congratulation. He, however, renewed his assurances of fidelity to his engagements and punctuality of execution. Meanwhile the day was interspersed with nuptial presents and preparations, all indicating the firmness as well as security of the directors of the scene. Emily had hoped that, as the crisis approached, they might have remitted something of their usual diligence. She was resolved, in that case, if a fair opportunity had offered, to give the slip both to her jailors, and to her new and reluctantly chosen confederate. But, though extremely vigilant for that purpose, she found the execution of the idea impracticable.

At length the night, so critical to her happiness, approached. The mind of Emily could not fail, on this occasion, to be extremely agitated. She had first exerted all her perspicacity to elude the vigilance of her attendant. This insolent and unfeeling tyrant, instead of any relentings, had only sought to make sport of her anxiety. Accordingly, in one instance she hid herself, and, suffering Emily to suppose that the coast was clear, met her at the end of the gallery, near the top of the staircase. "How do you do, my dear?" said she, with an insulting tone. "And so the little dear thought itself cunning enough to outwit me, did it? Oh, it was a sly little gipsy! Go, go back, love; troop!" Emily felt deeply the trick that was played upon her. She sighed, but disdained to return any answer to this low vulgarity. Being once more in her chamber, she sat down in a chair, and remained buried in reverie for more than two hours. After this she went to her drawers, and turned over, in a hurrying confused way, her linen and clothes, having in her mind the provision it would be necessary to make for her elopement. Her jailor officiously followed her from place to place, and observed what she did for the present in silence. It was now the hour of rest. "Good night, child," said this saucy girl, in the act of retiring. "It is time to lock up. For the few next hours, the time is your own. Make the best use of it! Do'ee think ee can creep out at the key-hole, lovey? At eight o'clock you see me again. And then, and then," added she, clapping her hands, "it is all over. The sun is not surer to rise, than you and your honest man to be made one."

There was something in the tone with which this slut uttered her farewell, that suggested the question to Emily, "What does she mean? Is it possible that she should know what has been planned for the few next hours?" – This was the first moment that suspicion had offered itself, and its continuance was short. With an aching heart she folded up the few necessaries she intended to take with her. She instinctively listened, with an anxiety that would almost have enabled her to hear the stirring of a leaf. From time to time she thought her ear was struck with the sound of feet; but the treading, if treading it were, was so soft, that she could never ascertain whether it were a real sound, or the mere creature of the fancy. Then all was still, as if the universal motion had been at rest. By and by she conceived she overheard a noise as of buzzing and low-muttered speech. Her heart palpitated; for a second time she began to doubt the honesty of Grimes. The suggestion was now more anxious than before; but it was too late. Presently she heard the sound of a key in her chamber-door, and the rustic made his appearance. She started, and cried, "Are we discovered? did not I hear you speak?" Grimes advanced on tiptoe with his finger to his lip. "No, no," replied he, "all is safe!" He took her by the hand, led her in silence out of the house, and then across the garden. Emily examined with her eye the doors and passages as they proceeded, and looked on all sides with fearful suspicion; but every thing was as vacant and still as she herself could have wished. Grimes opened a back-door of the garden already unlocked, that led into an unfrequented lane. There stood two horses ready equipped for the journey, and fastened by their bridles to a post not six yards distant from the garden. Grimes pushed the door after them. "By Gemini," said he, "my heart was in my mouth. As I comed along to you, I saw Mun, coachey, pop along from the back-door to the stables. He was within a hop, step, and jump of me. But he had a lanthorn in his hand, and he did not see me, being as I was darkling." Saying this, he assisted Miss Melville to mount. He troubled her little during the route; on the contrary, he was remarkably silent and contemplative, a circumstance by no means disagreeable to Emily, to whom his conversation had never been acceptable.

After having proceeded about two miles, they turned into a wood, through which the road led to the place of their destination. The night was extremely dark, at the same time that the air was soft and mild, it being now the middle of summer. Under pretence of exploring the way, Grimes contrived, when they had already penetrated into the midst of this gloomy solitude, to get his horse abreast with that of Miss Melville, and then, suddenly reaching out his hand, seized hold of her bridle. "I think we may as well stop here a bit," said he.

"Stop!" exclaimed Emily with surprise; "why should we stop? Mr. Grimes, what do you mean?"

"Come, come," said he, "never trouble yourself to wonder. Did you think I were such a goose, to take all this trouble merely to gratify your whim? I' faith, nobody shall find me a pack-horse, to go of other folks' errands without knowing a reason why. I cannot say that I much minded to have you at first; but your ways are enough to stir the blood of my grand-dad. Far-fetched and dear-bought is always relishing. Your consent was so hard to gain that squire thought it was surest asking in the dark. A' said however, a' would have no such doings in his house, and so, do ye see, we are comed here."

"For God's sake, Mr. Grimes, think what you are about! You cannot be base enough to ruin a poor creature who has put herself under your protection!"

"Ruin! No, no, I will make an honest woman of you, when all is done. Nay, none of your airs; no tricks upon travellers! I have you here as safe as a horse in a pound; there is not a house nor a shed within a mile of us; and, if I miss the opportunity, call me spade. Faith, you are a delicate morsel, and there is no time to be lost!"

Miss Melville had but an instant in which to collect her thoughts. She felt that there was little hope of softening the obstinate and insensible brute in whose power she was placed.

But the presence of mind and intrepidity annexed to her character did not now desert her. Grimes had scarcely finished his harangue, when, with a strong and unexpected jerk, she disengaged the bridle from his grasp and at the same time put her horse upon full speed. She had scarcely advanced twice the length of her horse, when Grimes recovered from his surprise and pursued her, inexpressibly mortified at being so easily overreached. The sound of his horse behind served but to rouse more completely the mettle of that of Emily; whether by accident or sagacity, the animal pursued without a fault the narrow and winding way; and the chase continued the whole length of the wood.

At the extremity of this wood there was a gate. The recollection of this softened a little the cutting disappointment of Grimes, as he thought himself secure of putting an end, by its assistance, to the career of Emily; nor was it very probable that any body would appear to interrupt his designs, in such a place, and in the dead and silence of the night. By the most extraordinary accident, however, they found a man on horseback in wait at this gate. "Help, help!" exclaimed the affrighted Emily; "thieves! murder! help!" The man was Mr. Falkland. Grimes knew his voice; and therefore, though he attempted a sort of sullen resistance, it was feebly made. Two other men, whom, by reason of the darkness, he had not at first seen, and who were Mr. Falkland's servants, hearing the bustle of the rencounter, and alarmed for the safety of their master, rode up; and then Grimes, disappointed at the loss of his gratification, and admonished by conscious guilt, shrunk from farther parley, and rode off in silence.

It may seem strange that Mr. Falkland should thus a second time have been the saviour of Miss Melville, and that under circumstances the most unexpected and singular. But in this instance it is easily to be accounted for. He had heard of a man who lurked about this wood for robbery or some other bad design, and that it was conjectured this man was Hawkins, another of the victims of Mr. Tyrrel's rural tyranny, whom I shall immediately have occasion to introduce. Mr. Falkland's compassion had already been strongly excited in favour of

Hawkins; he had in vain endeavoured to find him, and do him good; and he easily conceived that, if the conjecture which had been made in this instance proved true, he might have it in his power not only to do what he had always intended, but further, to save from a perilous offence against the laws and society a man who appeared to have strongly imbibed the principles of justice and virtue. He took with him two servants, because, going with the express design of encountering robbers, if robbers should be found, he believed he should be inexcusable if he did not go provided against possible accidents. But he had directed them, at the same time that they kept within call, to be out of the reach of being seen; and it was only the eagerness of their zeal that had brought them up thus early in the present encounter.

This new adventure promised something extraordinary. Mr. Falkland did not immediately recognize Miss Melville; and the person of Grimes was that of a total stranger, whom he did not recollect to have ever seen. But it was easy to understand the merits of the case, and the propriety of interfering. The resolute manner of Mr. Falkland, combined with the dread which Grimes, oppressed with a sense of wrong, entertained of the opposition of so elevated a personage, speedily put the ravisher to flight. Emily was left alone with her deliverer. He found her much more collected and calm, than could reasonably have been expected from a person who had been, a moment before, in the most alarming situation. She told him of the place to which she desired to be conveyed, and he immediately undertook to escort her. As they went along, she recovered that state of mind which inclined her to make a person to whom she had such repeated obligations, and who was so eminently the object of her admiration, acquainted with the events that had recently befallen her. Mr. Falkland listened with eagerness and surprise. Though he had already known various instances of Mr. Tyrrel's mean jealousy and unfeeling tyranny, this surpassed them all; and he could scarcely credit his ears while he heard the tale. His brutal neighbour seemed to realise all that has been told of the passions of fiends. Miss Melville was obliged to repeat, in the course of her tale, her kinsman's rude accusation against her, of entertaining a passion for Mr. Falkland; and this she did with the most bewitching simplicity and charming confusion. Though this part of the tale was a source of real pain to her deliverer, yet it is not to be supposed but that the flattering partiality of this unhappy girl increased the interest he felt in her welfare, and the indignation he conceived against her infernal kinsman.

They arrived without accident at the house of the good lady under whose protection Emily desired to place herself. Here Mr. Falkland willingly left her as in a place of security. Such conspiracies as that of which she was intended to have been the victim, depend for their success upon the person against whom they are formed being out of the reach of help; and the moment they are detected, they are annihilated. Such reasoning will, no doubt, be generally found sufficiently solid; and it appeared to Mr. Falkland perfectly applicable to the present case. But he was mistaken.

CHAPTER IX

Mr. Falkland had experienced the nullity of all expostulation with Mr. Tyrrel, and was therefore content in the present case with confining his attention to the intended victim. The indignation with which he thought of his neighbour's character was now grown to such a height, as to fill him with reluctance to the idea of a voluntary interview. There was indeed another affair which had been contemporary with this, that had once more brought these mortal enemies into a state of contest, and had contributed to raise into a temper little short of madness, the already inflamed and corrosive bitterness of Mr. Tyrrel.

There was a tenant of Mr. Tyrrel, one Hawkins; – I cannot mention his name without recollecting the painful tragedies that are annexed to it! This Hawkins had originally been taken up by Mr. Tyrrel, with a view of protecting him from the arbitrary proceedings of a neighbouring squire, though he had now in his turn become an object of persecution to Mr. Tyrrel himself. The first ground of their connection was this: – Hawkins, beside a farm which he rented under the above-mentioned squire, had a small freehold estate that he inherited from his father. This of course entitled him to a vote in the county elections; and, a warmly contested election having occurred, he was required by his landlord to vote for the candidate in whose favour he had himself engaged. Hawkins refused to obey the mandate, and soon after received notice to quit the farm he at that time rented.

It happened that Mr. Tyrrel had interested himself strongly in behalf of the opposite candidate; and, as Mr. Tyrrel's estate bordered upon the seat of Hawkins's present residence, the ejected countryman could think of no better expedient than that of riding over to this gentleman's mansion and relating the case to him. Mr. Tyrrel heard him through with attention. "Well, friend," said he, "it is very true that I wished Mr. Jackman to carry his election; but you know it is usual in these cases for tenants to vote just as their landlords please. I do not think proper to encourage rebellion." – "All that is very right, and please you," replied Hawkins, "and I would have voted at my landlord's bidding for any other man in the kingdom but Squire Marlow. You must know one day his huntsman rode over my fence, and so through my best field of standing corn. It was not above a dozen yards about if he had kept the cart-road. The fellow had served me the same sauce, an it please your honour, three or four times before. So I only asked him what he did that for, and whether he had not more conscience than to spoil people's crops o' that fashion? Presently the squire came up. He is but a poor, weazen-face chicken of a gentle-man, saving your honour's reverence. And so he flew into a woundy passion, and threatened to horsewhip me. I will do as much in reason to pleasure my landlord as arr a tenant he has; but I will not give my vote to a man that threatens to horse-whip me. And so, your honour, I and my wife and three children are to be turned out of house and home, and what I am to do to maintain them God knows. I have been a hard-working man, and have always lived well, and I do think the case is main hard. Squire Underwood turns me out of my farm; and if your honour do not take me in, I know none of the neighbouring gentry will, for fear, as they say, of encouraging their own tenants to run rusty too."

This representation was not without its effect upon Mr. Tyrrel. "Well, well, man," replied he, "we will see what can be done. Order and subordination are very good things; but people should know how much to require. As you tell the story, I cannot see that you are greatly to blame. Marlow is a coxcombical prig, that is the truth on't; and if a man will expose himself, why, he must even take what follows. I do hate a Frenchified fop with all my soul; and I cannot say that I am much pleased with my neighbour Underwood for taking the part of such a rascal. Hawkins, I think, is your name? You may call on Barnes, my steward, tomorrow, and he shall speak to you."

While Mr. Tyrrel was speaking, he recollected that he had a farm vacant, of nearly the same value as that which Hawkins at present rented under Mr. Underwood. He immediately con-sulted his steward, and finding the thing suitable in every respect, Hawkins was installed out of hand in the catalogue of

Mr. Tyrrel's tenants. Mr. Underwood extremely resented this proceeding, which indeed, as being contrary to the understood conventions of the country gentlemen, few people but Mr. Tyrrel would have ventured upon. There was an end, said Mr. Underwood, to all regulation, if tenants were to be encouraged in such disobedience. It was not a question of this or that candidate, seeing that any gentleman, who was a true friend to his country, would rather lose his election than do a thing which, if once established into a practice, would deprive them for ever of the power of managing any election. The labouring people were sturdy and resolute enough of their own accord; it became every day more difficult to keep them under any subordination; and, if the gentlemen were so ill advised as to neglect the public good, and encourage them in their insolence, there was no foreseeing where it would end.

Mr. Tyrrel was not of a stamp to be influenced by these remonstrances. Their general spirit was sufficiently conformable to the sentiments he himself entertained; but he was of too vehement a temper to maintain the character of a consistent politician; and, however wrong his conduct might be, he would by no means admit of its being set right by the suggestions of others. The more his patronage of Hawkins was criticized, the more inflexibly he adhered to it; and he was at no loss in clubs and other assemblies to overbear and silence, if not to confute, his censurers. Beside which, Hawkins had certain accomplishments which qualified him to be a favourite with Mr. Tyrrel. The bluntness of his manner and the ruggedness of his temper gave him some resemblance to his landlord; and, as these qualities were likely to be more frequently exercised on such persons as had incurred Mr. Tyrrel's displeasure than upon Mr. Tyrrel himself, they were not observed without some degree of complacency. In a word, he every day received new marks of distinction from his patron, and after some time was appointed coadjutor to Mr. Barnes under the denomination of bailiff. It was about the same period that he obtained a lease of the farm of which he was tenant.

Mr. Tyrrel determined, as occasion offered, to promote every part of the family of this favoured dependent. Hawkins had a son, a lad of seventeen, of an agreeable person, a ruddy complexion, and of quick and lively parts. This lad was in an uncommon degree the favourite of his father, who seemed to have nothing so much at heart as the future welfare of his son. Mr. Tyrrel had noticed him two or three times with approbation; and the boy, being fond of the sports of the field, had occasionally followed the hounds, and displayed various instances, both of agility and sagacity, in presence of the squire. One day in particular he exhibited himself with uncommon advantage; and Mr. Tyrrel without further delay proposed to his father to take him into his family, and make him whipper-in[1] to his hounds, till he could provide him with some more lucrative appointment in his service.

This proposal was received by Hawkins with various marks of mortification. He excused himself with hesitation for not accepting the offered favour; said the lad was in many ways useful to him; and hoped his honour would not insist upon depriving him of his assistance. This apology might perhaps have been sufficient with any other man than Mr. Tyrrel; but it was frequently observed of this gentleman that, when he had once formed a determination, however slight, in favour of any measure, he was never afterwards known to give it up, and that the only effect of opposition was to make him eager and inflexible, in pursuit of that to which he had before been nearly indifferent. At first he seemed to receive the apology of Hawkins with good humour, and to see nothing in it but what was reasonable; but afterwards, every time he saw the boy, his desire of retaining him in his service was increased, and he more than once repeated to his father the good disposition in which he felt himself towards him. At length he observed that the lad was no more to be seen mingling in his favourite sports, and he began to suspect that this originated in a determination to thwart him in his projects.

Roused by this suspicion, which, to a man of Mr. Tyrrel's character was not of a nature to brook delay, he sent for Hawkins to confer with him. "Hawkins," said he, in a tone of displeasure, "I am not satisfied with you. I have spoken to you

---

1   A huntsman's assistant, responsible for keeping hounds from straying from the pack.

two or three times about this lad of yours, whom I am desirous of taking into favour. What is the reason, sir, that you seem unthankful and averse to my kindness? You ought to know that I am not to be trifled with. I shall not be contented, when I offer my favours to have them rejected by such fellows as you. I made you what you are; and, if I please, can make you more helpless and miserable than you were when I found you. Have a care!"

"An it please your honour," said Hawkins, "you have been a very good master to me, and I will tell you the whole truth. I hope you will na be angry. This lad is my favourite, my comfort, and the stay of my age."

"Well, and what then? Is that a reason you should hinder his preferment?"

"Nay, pray your honour, hear me. I may be very weak for aught I know in this case, but I cannot help it. My father was a clergyman. We have all of us lived in a creditable way; and I cannot bear to think that this poor lad of mine should go to service. For my part, I do not see any good that comes by servants. I do not know, your honour, but, I think, I should not like my Leonard to be such as they. God forgive me, if I wrong them! But this is a very dear case, and I cannot bear to risk my poor boy's welfare, when I can so easily, if you please, keep him out of harm's way. At present he is sober and industrious, and, without being pert or surly, knows what is due to him. I know, your honour, that it is main foolish of me to talk to you thus; but your honour has been a good master to me, and I cannot bear to tell you a lie."

Mr. Tyrrel had heard the whole of this harangue in silence, because he was too much astonished to open his mouth. If a thunderbolt had fallen at his feet, he could not have testified greater surprise. He had thought that Hawkins was so foolishly fond of his son, that he could not bear to trust him out of his presence; but had never in the slightest degree suspected what he now found to be the truth.

"Oh, ho, you are a gentleman, are you? A pretty gentleman truly! your father was a clergyman! Your family is too good to enter into my service! Why you impudent rascal! was it for this that I took you up, when Mr. Underwood dismissed you for your insolence to him? Have I been nursing a viper in my bosom? Pretty master's manners will be contaminated truly! He will not know what is due to him, but will be accustomed to obey orders! You insufferable villain! Get out of my sight! Depend upon it, I will have no gentlemen on my estate! I will off with them, root and branch, bag and baggage! So do you hear, sir? come to me to-morrow morning, bring your son, and ask my pardon; or, take my word for it, I will make you so miserable, you shall wish you had never been born."

This treatment was too much for Hawkins's patience. "There is no need, your honour, that I should come to you again about this affair. I have taken up my determination, and no time can make any change in it. I am main sorry to displease your worship, and I know that you can do me a great deal of mischief. But I hope you will not be so hardhearted as to ruin a father only for being fond of his child, even if so be that his fondness should make him do a foolish thing. But I cannot help it, your honour: you must do as you please. The poorest neger, as a man may say, has some point that he will not part with. I will lose all that I have, and go to day-labour, and my son too, if needs must; but I will not make a gentleman's servant of him."

"Very well, friend; very well!" replied Mr. Tyrrel, foaming with rage. "Depend upon it, I will remember you! Your pride shall have a downfall! God damn it! is it come to this? Shall a rascal that farms his forty acres, pretend to beard the lord of the manor? I will tread you into paste! Let me advise you, scoundrel, to shut up your house and fly, as if the devil was behind you! You may think yourself happy, if I be not too quick for you yet, if you escape in a whole skin! I would not suffer such a villain to remain upon my land a day longer, if I could gain the Indies by it!"

"Not so fast, your honour," answered Hawkins, sturdily. "I hope you will think better of it, and see that I have not been to blame. But if you should not, there is some harm that you can do me, and some harm that you cannot. Though I am a plain, working man, your honour, do you see? yet I am a man still.

No; I have got a lease of my farm, and I shall not quit it o' that-en. I hope there is some law for poor folk, as well as for rich."

Mr. Tyrrel, unused to contradiction, was provoked beyond bearing at the courage and independent spirit of his retainer. There was not a tenant upon his estate, or at least not one of Hawkins's mediocrity of fortune, whom the general policy of landowners, and still more the arbitrary and uncontrollable temper of Mr. Tyrrel, did not effectually restrain from acts of open defiance.

"Excellent, upon my soul! God damn my blood! but you are a rare fellow. You have a lease, have you? You will not quit, not you! a pretty pass things are come to, if a lease can protect such fellows as you against the lord of the manor! But you are for a trial of skill? Oh, very well, friend, very well! With all my soul! Since it is come to that, we will show you some pretty sport before we have done! But get out of my sight, you rascal! I have not another word to say to you! Never darken my doors again."

Hawkins (to borrow the language of the world) was guilty in this affair of a double imprudence. He talked to his landlord in a more peremptory manner than the constitution and practices of this country allow a dependent to assume. But above all, having been thus hurried away by his resentment, he ought to have foreseen the consequences. It was mere madness in him to think of contesting with a man of Mr. Tyrrel's eminence and fortune. It was a fawn contending with a lion. Nothing could have been more easy to predict, than that it was of no avail for him to have right on his side, when his adversary had influence and wealth, and therefore could so victoriously justify any extravagancies that he might think proper to commit. This maxim was completely illustrated in the sequel. Wealth and despotism easily know how to engage those laws as the coadju-tors of their oppression, which were perhaps at first intended [witless and miserable precaution!] for the safeguards of the poor.

From this moment Mr. Tyrrel was bent upon Hawkins's destruction; and he left no means unemployed that could either harass or injure the object of his persecution. He deprived him of his appointment of bailiff, and directed Barnes and his other dependents to do him ill offices upon all occasions. Mr. Tyrrel, by the tenure of his manor, was impropriator of the great tithes,[1] and this circumstance afforded him frequent opportunities of petty altercation. The land of one part of Hawkins's farm, though covered with corn, was lower than the rest; and consequently exposed to occasional inundations from a river by which it was bounded. Mr. Tyrrel had a dam belonging to this river privately cut, about a fortnight before the season of harvest, and laid the whole under water. He ordered his servants to pull away the fences of the higher ground during the night, and to turn in his cattle, to the utter destruction of the crop. These expedients, however, applied to only one part of the property of this unfortunate man. But Mr. Tyrrel did not stop here. A sudden mortality took place among Hawkins's live stock, attended with very suspicious circumstances. Hawkins's vigilance was strongly excited by this event, and he at length succeeded in tracing the matter so accurately, that he conceived he could bring it home to Mr. Tyrrel himself.

Hawkins had hitherto carefully avoided, notwithstanding the injuries he had suffered, the attempting to right himself by legal process; being of opinion that law was better adapted for a weapon of tyranny in the hands of the rich, than for a shield to protect the humbler part of the community against their usurpations. In this last instance however he conceived that the offence was so atrocious, as to make it impossible that any rank could protect the culprit against the severity of justice. In the sequel, he saw reason to applaud himself for his former inactivity in this respect, and to repent that any motive had been strong enough to persuade him into a contrary system.

This was the very point to which Mr. Tyrrel wanted to bring him, and he could scarcely credit his good fortune, when he was told that Hawkins had entered an action. His congratulation upon this occasion was immoderate, as he now conceived that the ruin of his late favourite was irretrievable. He consulted his attorney, and urged him by every motive he could devise, to employ the whole series of his subterfuges in

---

1   The person designated to receive as land-owner the tithes from his tenants that had originally been appropriated for the Catholic Church.

the present affair. The direct repelling of the charge exhibited against him was the least part of his care; the business was, by affidavits, motions, pleas, demurrers, flaws, and appeals, to protract the question from term to term, and from court to court. It would, as Mr. Tyrrel argued, be the disgrace of a civilized country, if a gentleman, when insolently attacked in law by the scum of the earth, could not convert the cause into a question of the longest purse, and stick in the skirts of his adversary till he had reduced him to beggary.

Mr. Tyrrel, however, was by no means so far engrossed by his law-suit as to neglect other methods of proceeding offensively against his tenant. Among the various expedients that suggested themselves, there was one, which, though it tended rather to torment than irreparably injure the sufferer, was not rejected. This was derived from the particular situation of Hawkins's house, barns, stacks, and outhouses. They were placed at the extremity of a slip of land connecting them with the rest of the farm, and were surrounded on three sides by fields, in the occupation of one of Mr. Tyrrel's tenants most devoted to the pleasures of his landlord. The road to the market-town ran at the bottom of the largest of these fields, and was directly in view of the front of the house. No inconvenience had yet arisen from that circumstance, as there had always been a broad path, that intersected this field, and led directly from Hawkins's house to the road. This path, or private road, was now, by concert of Mr. Tyrrel and his obliging tenant, shut up, so as to make Hawkins a sort of prisoner in his own domains, and oblige him to go near a mile about for the purposes of his traffic.

Young Hawkins, the lad who had been the original subject of dispute between his father and the squire, had much of his father's spirit, and felt an uncontrollable indignation against the successive acts of despotism of which he was a witness. His resentment was the greater, because the sufferings to which his parent was exposed, all of them flowed from affection to him, at the same time that he could not propose removing the ground of dispute, as by so doing he would seem to fly in the face of his father's paternal kindness. Upon the present occasion, without asking any counsel but of his own impatient resentment, he

went in the middle of the night, and removed all the obstruc-
tions that had been placed in the way of the old path, broke the
padlocks that had been fixed, and threw open the gates.

In these operations he did not proceed unobserved, and the
next day a warrant was issued for apprehending him. He was
accordingly carried before a meeting of justices, and by them
committed to the county gaol, to take his trial for the felony at
the next assizes. Mr. Tyrrel was determined to prosecute the
offence with the greatest severity; and his attorney, having made
the proper enquiries for that purpose, undertook to bring it
under that clause of the act 9 Geo. I. commonly called the
Black Act, which declares that "any person, armed with a
sword, or other offensive weapon, and having his face blackened, or being otherwise disguised, appearing in any warren or
place where hares or conies have been or shall be usually kept,
and being thereof duly convicted, shall be adjudged guilty of
felony, and shall suffer death, as in cases of felony, without
benefit of clergy."[1] Young Hawkins, it seemed, had buttoned
the cape of his great coat over his face, as soon as he perceived
himself to be observed, and he was furnished with a wrench-
ing-iron for the purpose of breaking the padlocks. The attorney further undertook to prove, by sufficient witnesses, that the
field in question was a warren in which hares were regularly
fed. Mr. Tyrrel seized upon these pretences with inexpressible
satisfaction. He prevailed upon the justices, by the picture he
drew of the obstinacy and insolence of the Hawkinses, fully to
commit the lad upon this miserable charge; and it was by no
means so certain as paternal affection would have desired, that
the same overpowering influence would not cause in the
sequel the penal clause to be executed in all its strictness.

---

1   Godwin refers here to the law of 9 George I c.22, passed in 1723 to punish those
    who carried weapons or concealed themselves while hunting or poaching on pri-
    vate land. Originally passed as short-term legislation and covering a narrow band
    of offenses against property, it was repeatedly renewed in later years and made per-
    petual in 1758. In the course of these renewals, it came to cover an increasing range
    of crimes (between 200 and 250 separate offenses) with the penalty of capital pun-
    ishment. As E.P. Thompson notes in *Whigs and Hunters* (London: 1975), it "sig-
    nalled the onset of the flood-tide of eighteenth-century retributive justice" (23).

This was the finishing stroke to Hawkins's miseries: as he was not deficient in courage, he had stood up against his other persecutions without flinching. He was not unaware of the advantages which our laws and customs give to the rich over the poor, in contentions of this kind. But, being once involved, there was a stubbornness in his nature that would not allow him to retract, and he suffered himself to hope, rather than expect, a favourable issue. But in this last event he was wounded in the point that was nearest his heart. He had feared to have his son contaminated and debased by a servile station, and he now saw him transferred to the seminary of a gaol. He was even uncertain as to the issue of his imprisonment, and trembled to think what the tyranny of wealth might effect to blast his hopes for ever.

From this moment his heart died within him. He had trusted to persevering industry and skill, to save the wreck of his little property from the vulgar spite of his landlord. But he had now no longer any spirit to exert those efforts which his situation more than ever required. Mr. Tyrrel proceeded without remission in his machinations; Hawkins's affairs every day grew more desperate, and the squire, watching the occasion, took the earliest opportunity of seizing upon his remaining property in the mode of a distress for rent.

It was precisely in this stage of the affair, that Mr. Falkland and Mr. Tyrrel accidentally met, in a private road near the habitation of the latter. They were on horseback, and Mr. Falkland was going to the house of the unfortunate tenant, who seemed upon the point of perishing under his landlord's malice. He had been just made acquainted with the tale of this persecution. It had indeed been an additional aggravation of Hawkins's calamity, that Mr. Falkland, whose interference might otherwise have saved him, had been absent from the neighbourhood for a considerable time. He had been three months in London, and from thence had gone to visit his estates in another part of the island. The proud and self-confident spirit of this poor fellow always disposed him to depend, as long as possible, upon his own exertions. He had avoided applying to Mr. Falkland, or indeed indulging himself in any manner in communicating and bewailing his hard hap, in the beginning of the contention; and, when the extremity grew more urgent, and he would have been willing to recede in some degree from the stubbornness of his measures, he found it no longer in his power. After an absence of considerable duration, Mr. Falkland at length returned somewhat unexpectedly; and having learned, among the first articles of country intelligence, the distresses of this unfortunate yeoman, he resolved to ride over to his house the next morning, and surprise him with all the relief it was in his power to bestow.

At sight of Mr. Tyrrel in this unexpected rencounter, his face reddened with indignation. His first feeling, as he afterwards said, was to avoid him; but finding that he must pass him, he conceived that it would be want of spirit not to acquaint him with his feelings on the present occasion.

"Mr. Tyrrel," said he, somewhat abruptly, "I am sorry for a piece of news which I have just heard."

"And pray, sir, what is your sorrow to me?"

"A great deal, sir: it is caused by the distresses of a poor tenant of yours, Hawkins. If your steward have proceeded without your authority, I think it right to inform you what he has done; and, if he have had your authority, I would gladly persuade you to think better of it."

"Mr. Falkland, it would be quite as well if you would mind your own business, and leave me to mind mine. I want no monitor, and I will have none."

"You mistake, Mr. Tyrrel; I am minding my own business. If I see you fall into a pit, it is my business to draw you out and save your life. If I see you pursuing a wrong mode of conduct, it is my business to set you right and save your honour."

"Zounds, sir, do not think to put your conundrums upon me! Is not the man my tenant? Is not my estate my own? What signifies calling it mine, if I am not to have the direction of it? Sir, I pay for what I have: I owe no man a penny; and I will not put my estate to nurse to you, nor the best he that wears a head."

"It is very true," said Mr. Falkland, avoiding any direct notice of the last words of Mr. Tyrrel, "that there is a distinction of ranks. I believe that distinction is a good thing, and necessary to the peace of mankind. But, however necessary it may be, we must acknowledge that it puts some hardship upon the lower orders of society. It makes one's heart ache to think, that one man is born to the inheritance of every superfluity, while the whole share of another, without any demerit of his, is drudgery and starving; and that all this is indispensable. We that are rich, Mr. Tyrrel, must do every thing in our power to lighten the yoke of these unfortunate people. We must not use the advantage that accident has given us with an unmerciful hand. Poor wretches! they are pressed almost beyond bearing as it is; and, if we unfeelingly give another turn to the machine, they will be crushed into atoms."

This picture was not without its effect, even upon the obdurate mind of Mr. Tyrrel. – "Well, sir, I am no tyrant. I know very well that tyranny is a bad thing. But you do not infer from thence that these people are to do as they please, and never meet with their deserts?"

"Mr. Tyrrel, I see that you are shaken in your animosity. Suffer me to hail the new-born benevolence of your nature. Go with me to Hawkins. Do not let us talk of his deserts! Poor fellow! he has suffered almost all that human nature can endure. Let your forgiveness upon this occasion be the earnest of good neighbourhood and friendship between you and me."

"No, sir, I will not go. I own there is something in what you say. I always knew you had the wit to make good your own story, and tell a plausible tale. But I will not be come over thus. It has been my character, when I had once conceived a scheme of vengeance, never to forego it; and I will not change that character. I took up Hawkins when every body forsook him, and made a man of him; and the ungrateful rascal has only insulted me for my pains. Curse me, if I ever forgive him! It would be a good jest indeed, if I were to forgive the insolence of my own creature at the desire of a man like you that has been my perpetual plague."

"For God's sake, Mr. Tyrrel, have some reason in your resentment! Let us suppose that Hawkins has behaved unjustifiably, and insulted you: is that an offence that never can be expiated? Must the father be ruined, and the son hanged, to glut your resentment?"

"Damn me, sir, but you may talk your heart out; you shall get nothing of me. I shall never forgive myself for having listened to you for a moment. I will suffer nobody to stop the stream of my resentment; if I ever were to forgive him, it should be at nobody's entreaty but my own. But, sir, I never will. If he and all his family were at my feet, I would order them all to be hanged the next minute, if my power were as good as my will."

"And this is your decision, is it? Mr. Tyrrel, I am ashamed of you! Almighty God! to hear you talk gives one a loathing for the institutions and regulations of society, and would induce one to fly the very face of man! But, no! society casts you out; man abominates you. No wealth, no rank, can buy out your stain. You will live deserted in the midst of your species; you will go into crowded societies, and no one will deign so much as to salute you. They will fly from your glance as they would from the gaze of a basilisk. Where do you expect to find the hearts of flint that shall sympathise with yours? You have the stamp of misery, incessant, undivided, unpitied misery!"

Thus saying, Mr. Falkland gave spurs to his horse, rudely pushed beside Mr. Tyrrel, and was presently out of sight. Flaming indignation annihilated even his favourite sense of honour, and he regarded his neighbour as a wretch, with whom it was impossible even to enter into contention. For the latter, he remained for the present motionless and petrified. The glowing enthusiasm of Mr. Falkland was such as might well have unnerved the stoutest foe. Mr. Tyrrel, in spite of himself, was blasted with the compunctions of guilt, and unable to string himself for the contest. The picture Mr. Falkland had drawn was prophetic. It described what Mr. Tyrrel chiefly feared; and what in its commencements he thought he already felt. It was responsive to the whispering of his own meditations; it simply gave body and voice to the spectre that haunted him, and to the terrors of which he was an hourly prey.

By and by, however, he recovered. The more he had been temporarily confounded, the fiercer was his resentment when he came to himself. Such hatred never existed in a human bosom without marking its progress with violence and death. Mr. Tyrrel, however, felt no inclination to have recourse to personal defiance. He was the furthest in the world from a coward; but his genius sunk before the genius of Falkland. He left his vengeance to the disposal of circumstances. He was secure that his animosity would never be forgotten nor diminished by the interposition of any time or events. Vengeance was his nightly dream, and the uppermost of his waking thoughts.

Mr. Falkland had departed from this conference with a confirmed disapprobation of the conduct of his neighbour, and an unalterable resolution to do every thing in his power to relieve the distresses of Hawkins. But he was too late. When he arrived, he found the house already evacuated by its master. The family was removed nobody knew whither; Hawkins had absconded, and, what was still more extraordinary, the boy Hawkins had escaped on the very same day from the county gaol. The enquiries Mr. Falkland set on foot after them were fruitless; no traces could be found of the catastrophe of these unhappy people. That catastrophe I shall shortly have occasion to relate, and it will be found pregnant with horror, beyond what the blackest misanthropy could readily have suggested.

I go on with my tale. I go on to relate those incidents in which my own fate was so mysteriously involved. I lift the curtain, and bring forward the last act of the tragedy.

CHAPTER X

It may easily be supposed, that the ill temper cherished by Mr. Tyrrel in his contention with Hawkins, and the increasing animosity between him and Mr. Falkland, added to the impatience with which he thought of the escape of Emily.

Mr. Tyrrel heard with astonishment of the miscarriage of an expedient, of the success of which he had not previously entertained the slightest suspicion. He became frantic with vexation. Grimes had not dared to signify the event of his expedition in person, and the footman whom he desired to announce to his master that Miss Melville was lost, the moment after fled from his presence with the most dreadful apprehensions. Presently he bellowed for Grimes, and the young man at last appeared before him, more dead than alive. Grimes he compelled to repeat the particulars of the tale; which he had no sooner done, than he once again slunk away, shocked at the execrations with which Mr. Tyrrel overwhelmed him. Grimes was no coward; but he reverenced the inborn divinity that attends upon rank, as Indians worship the devil. Nor was this all. The rage of Mr. Tyrrel was so ungovernable and fierce, that few hearts could have been found so stout, as not to have trembled before it with a sort of unconquerable inferiority.

He no sooner obtained a moment's pause than he began to recall to his tempestuous mind the various circumstances of the case. His complaints were bitter; and, in a tranquil observer, might have produced the united feeling of pity for his sufferings and horror at his depravity. He recollected all the precautions he had used; he could scarcely find a flaw in the process; and he cursed that blind and malicious power which delighted to cross his most deep-laid schemes. Of this malice he was beyond all other human beings the object. He was mocked with the shadow of power; and when he lifted his hand to smite, it was struck with sudden palsy. [In the bitterness of his anguish, he forgot his recent triumph over Hawkins, or perhaps he regarded it less as a triumph, than an overthrow, because it had failed of coming up to the extent of his malice.] To what purpose had Heaven given him a feeling of injury, and an instinct to resent, while he could in no case make his resentment felt! It was only necessary for him to be the enemy of any person, to insure that person's being safe against the reach of misfortune. What insults, the most shocking and repeated, had he received from this paltry girl! And by whom was she now torn from his indignation? By that devil that haunted him at every moment, that crossed him at every step, that fixed at pleasure his arrows in his heart, and made mows and mockery at his insufferable tortures.

There was one other reflection that increased his anguish, and made him careless and desperate as to his future conduct. It was in vain to conceal from himself that his reputation would be cruelly wounded by this event. He had imagined that, while Emily was forced into this odious marriage, she would be obliged by decorum, as soon as the event was decided, to draw a veil over the compulsion she had suffered. But this security was now lost, and Mr. Falkland would take a pride in publishing his dishonour. Though the provocations he had received from Miss Melville would, in his own opinion, have justified him in any treatment he should have thought proper to inflict, he was sensible the world would see the matter in a different light. This reflection augmented the violence of his resolutions, and determined him to refuse no means by which he could transfer the anguish that now preyed upon his own mind to that of another.

Meanwhile, the composure and magnanimity of Emily had considerably subsided, the moment she believed herself in a place of safety. While danger and injustice assailed her with their menaces, she found in herself a courage that disdained to yield. The succeeding appearance of calm was more fatal to her. There was nothing now, powerfully to foster her courage or excite her energy. She looked back at the trials she had passed, and her soul sickened at the recollection of that, which, while it was in act, she had had the fortitude to endure. Till the period at which Mr. Tyrrel had been inspired with this cruel antipathy, she had been in all instances a stranger to anxiety and fear. Uninured to misfortune, she had suddenly and without preparation been made the subject of the most infernal malignity. When a man of robust and vigorous constitution has a fit of sickness, it produces a more powerful effect, than the same indisposition upon a delicate valetudinarian. Such was the case with Miss Melville. She passed the succeeding night sleepless and uneasy, and was found in the morning with a high fever. Her distemper resisted for the present all attempts to assuage it, though there was reason to hope that the goodness of her constitution, assisted by tranquillity and the kindness of those about her, would ultimately surmount it. On the second day she was delirious. On the night of that day she was arrested at the suit of Mr. Tyrrel, for a debt contracted for board and necessaries for the last fourteen years.

The idea of this arrest, as the reader will perhaps recollect, first occurred, in the conversation between Mr. Tyrrel and Miss Melville, soon after he had thought proper to confine her to her chamber. But at that time he had probably no serious conception of ever being induced to carry it into execution. It had merely been mentioned by way of threat, and as the suggestion of a mind, whose habits had long been accustomed to contemplate every possible instrument of tyranny and revenge. But now, that the unlooked-for rescue and escape of his poor kinswoman had wrought up his thoughts to a degree of insanity, and that he revolved in the gloomy recesses of his mind, how he might best shake off the load of disappointment which oppressed him, the idea recurred with double force. He was not long in forming his resolution; and, calling for Barnes his steward, immediately gave him directions in what manner to proceed.

Barnes had been for several years the instrument of Mr. Tyrrel's injustice. His mind was hardened by use, and he could, without remorse, officiate as the spectator, or even as the author and director, of a scene of vulgar distress. But even he was somewhat startled upon the present occasion. The character and conduct of Emily in Mr. Tyrrel's family had been without a blot. She had not a single enemy; and it was impossible to contemplate her youth, her vivacity, and her guileless innocence, without emotions of sympathy and compassion.

"Your worship? – I do not understand you! – Arrest Miss – Miss Emily!"

"Yes, – I tell you! – What is the matter with you? – Go instantly to Swineard, the lawyer, and bid him finish the business out of hand!"

"Lord love your honour! Arrest her! Why she does not owe you a brass farthing: she always lived upon your charity!"

"Ass! Scoundrel! I tell you she does owe me, – owes me eleven hundred pounds. – The law justifies it. – What do you think laws were made for? I do nothing but right, and right I will have."

"Your honour, I never questioned your orders in my life; but I must now. I cannot see you ruin Miss Emily, poor girl! nay, and yourself too, for the matter of that, and not say which way you are going. I hope you will bear with me. Why, if she owed you ever so much, she cannot be arrested. She is not of age."

"Will you have done? – Do not tell me of – It cannot, and It can. It has been done before, – and it shall be done again. Let him dispute it that dares! I will do it now and stand to it afterwards. Tell Swineard, – if he make the least boggling, it is as much as his life is worth; – he shall starve by inches."

"Pray, your honour, think better of it. Upon my life, the whole country will cry shame of it."

"Barnes! – What do you mean? I am not used to be talked to, and I cannot bear it! You have been a good fellow to me upon many occasions. – But, if I find you out for making one with them that dispute my authority, damn my soul, if I do not make you sick of your life!"

"I have done, your honour. I will not say another word except this, – I have heard as how that Miss Emily is sick a-bed. You are determined, you say, to put her in jail. You do not mean to kill her, I take it."

"Let her die! I will not spare her for an hour. – I will not always be insulted. She had no consideration for me, and I have no mercy for her. – I am in for it! They have provoked me past bearing, – and they shall feel me! Tell Swineard, in bed or up, day or night, I will not hear of an instant's delay."

Such were the directions of Mr. Tyrrel, and in strict conformity to his directions were the proceedings of that respectable limb of the law he employed upon the present occasion. Miss Melville had been delirious, through a considerable part of the day on the evening of which the bailiff and his follower arrived. By the direction of the physician whom Mr. Falkland had ordered to attend her, a composing draught was administered; and, exhausted as she was by the wild and distracted images that for several hours had haunted her fancy, she was now sunk into a refreshing slumber. Mrs. Hammond, the sister of Mrs. Jakeman, was sitting by her bed-side, full of compassion for the lovely sufferer, and rejoicing in the calm tranquillity that had just taken possession of her, when a little girl, the only child of Mrs. Hammond, opened the street-door to the rap of the bailiff. He said he wanted to speak with Miss Melville, and the child answered that she would go tell her mother. So saying, she advanced to the door of the back-room upon the ground-floor, in which Emily lay; but the moment it was opened, instead of waiting for the appearance of the mother, the bailiff entered along with the girl.

Mrs. Hammond looked up. "Who are you?" said she. "Why do you come in here? Hush! be quiet!"

"I must speak with Miss Melville."

"Indeed, but you must not. Tell me your business. The poor child has been light-headed all day. She has just fallen asleep, and must not be disturbed."

"That is no business of mine. I must obey orders."

"Orders? Whose orders? What is it you mean?"

At this moment Emily opened her eyes. "What noise is that? Pray let me be quiet."

"Miss, I want to speak with you. I have got a writ against you for eleven hundred pounds at the suit of Squire Tyrrel."

At these words both Mrs. Hammond and Emily were dumb. The latter was scarcely able to annex any meaning to the intelligence; and, though Mrs. Hammond was somewhat better acquainted with the sort of language that was employed, yet in this strange and unexpected connection it was almost as mysterious to her as to poor Emily herself.

"A writ? How can she be in Mr. Tyrrel's debt? A writ against a child!"

"It is no signification putting your questions to us. We only do as we are directed. There is our authority. Look at it."

"Lord Almighty!" exclaimed Mrs. Hammond, "what does this mean? It is impossible Mr. Tyrrel should have sent you."

"Good woman, none of your jabber to us! Cannot you read?"

"This is all a trick! The paper is forged! It is a vile contrivance to get the poor orphan out of the hands of those with whom only she can be safe. Proceed upon it at your peril!"

"Rest you content; that is exactly what we mean to do. Take my word, we know very well what we are about."

"Why, you would not tear her from her bed? I tell you, she is in a high fever; she is light-headed; it would be death to remove her! You are bailiffs, are not you? You are not murderers?"

"The law says nothing about that. We have orders to take her sick or well. We will do her no harm; except so far as we must perform our office, be it how it will."

"Where would you take her? What is it you mean to do?"

"To the county jail. Bullock, go, order a post-chaise from the Griffin!"

"Stay, I say! Give no such orders! Wait only three hours; I will send off a messenger express to Squire Falkland, and I am sure he will satisfy you as to any harm that can come to you, without its being necessary to take the poor child to jail."

"We have particular directions against that. We are not at liberty to lose a minute. Why are not you gone? Order the horses to be put to immediately!"

Emily had listened to the course of this conversation, which had sufficiently explained to her whatever was enigmatical in the first appearance of the bailiffs. The painful and incredible reality that was thus presented effectually dissipated the illusions of frenzy to which she had just been a prey. "My dear Madam," said she to Mrs. Hammond, "do not harass yourself with useless efforts. I am very sorry for all the trouble I have given you. But my misfortune is inevitable. Sir, if you will step into the next room, I will dress myself, and attend you immediately."

Mrs. Hammond began to be equally aware that her struggles were to no purpose; but she could not be equally patient. At one moment she raved upon the brutality of Mr. Tyrrel, whom she affirmed to be a devil incarnate, and not a man. At another she expostulated, with bitter invective, against the hardheartedness of the bailiff, and exhorted him to mix some humanity and moderation with the discharge of his function; but he was impenetrable to all she could urge. In the mean while Emily yielded with the sweetest resignation to an inevitable evil. Mrs. Hammond insisted that, at least, they should permit her to attend her young lady in the chaise; and the bailiff, though the orders he had received were so peremptory that he dared not exercise his discretion as to the execution of the writ, began to have some apprehensions of danger, and was willing to admit of any precaution that was not in direct hostility to his functions. For the rest he understood, that it was in all cases dangerous to allow sickness, or apparent unfitness for removal, as a sufficient cause to interrupt a direct process; and that, accordingly, in all doubtful questions and presumptive murders, the practice of the law inclined, with a laudable partiality, to the vindication of its own officers. In addition to these general rules, he was influenced by the positive injunctions and assurances of Swineard, and the terror which, through a circle of many miles, was annexed to the name of Tyrrel. Before they departed, Mrs. Hammond despatched a messenger with a letter of three lines to Mr. Falkland, informing him of this extraordinary event. Mr. Falkland was from home when the messenger arrived, and not expected to return till the second day; accident seemed in this instance to favour the vengeance of Mr. Tyrrel, for he had himself been too much under the dominion of an uncontrollable fury, to take a circumstance of this sort into his estimate.

The forlorn state of these poor women, who were conducted, the one by compulsion, the other, a volunteer, to a scene so little adapted to their accommodation as that of a common jail, may easily be imagined. Mrs. Hammond, however, was endowed with a masculine courage and impetuosity of spirit, eminently necessary in the difficulties they had to encounter. She was in some degree fitted by a sanguine temper, and an impassioned sense of injustice, for the discharge of those very offices which sobriety and calm reflection might have prescribed. The health of Miss Melville was materially affected by the surprise and removal she had undergone at the very time that repose was most necessary for her preservation. Her fever became more violent; her delirium was stronger; and the tortures of her imagination were proportioned to the unfavourableness of the state in which the removal had been effected. It was highly improbable that she could recover.

In the moments of suspended reason she was perpetually calling on the name of Falkland. Mr. Falkland, she said, was her first and only love, and he should be her husband. A moment after she exclaimed upon him in a disconsolate, yet reproachful tone, for his unworthy deference to the prejudices of the world. It was very cruel of him to show himself so proud, and tell her that he would never consent to marry a beggar. But, if he were proud, she was determined to be proud too. He should see that she would not conduct herself like a slighted maiden, and that, though he could reject her, it was not in his power to break her heart. At another time she imagined she saw Mr. Tyrrel and his engine Grimes, their hands and garments dropping with blood; and the pathetic reproaches she vented against them might have affected a heart of stone. Then the figure of Falkland presented itself to her distracted fancy, deformed with wounds, and of a deadly paleness, and she shrieked with agony, while she exclaimed that such was the general hardheartedness, that no one would make the smallest exertion for his rescue. In such vicissitudes of pain, perpetually imagining to herself unkindness, insult, conspiracy, and murder, she passed a considerable part of two days.

On the evening of the second Mr. Falkland arrived, accompanied by Doctor Wilson, the physician by whom she had previously been attended. The scene he was called upon to witness was such as to be most exquisitely agonizing to a man of his acute sensibility. The news of the arrest had given him an inexpressible shock; he was transported out of himself at the unexampled malignity of its author. But, when he saw the figure of Miss Melville, haggard, and a warrant of death written in her countenance, a victim to the diabolical passions of her kinsman, it seemed too much to be endured. When he entered, she was in the midst of one of her fits of delirium, and immediately mistook her visitors for two assassins. She asked, where they had hid her Falkland, her lord, her life, her husband! and demanded that they should restore to her his mangled corpse, that she might embrace him with her dying arms, breathe her last upon his lips, and be buried in the same grave. She reproached them with the sordidness of their conduct in becoming the tools of her vile cousin, who had deprived her of her reason, and would never be contented till he had murdered her. Mr. Falkland tore himself away from this painful scene, and, leaving Doctor Wilson with his patient, desired him, when he had given the necessary directions, to follow him to his inn.

The perpetual hurry of spirits in which Miss Melville had been kept for several days, by the nature of her indisposition, was extremely exhausting to her; and, in about an hour from the visit of Mr. Falkland, her delirium subsided, and left her in so low a state as to render it difficult to perceive any signs of life. Doctor Wilson, who had withdrawn, to soothe, if possible, the disturbed and impatient thoughts of Mr. Falkland, was summoned afresh upon this change of symptoms, and sat by the bed-side during the remainder of the night. The situation of his patient was such, as to keep him in momentary apprehension of her decease. While Miss Melville lay in this feeble and exhausted condition, Mrs. Hammond betrayed every token of the tenderest anxiety. Her sensibility was habitually of the acutest sort, and the qualities of Emily were such as powerfully to fix her affection. She loved her like a mother. Upon the present occasion, every sound, every motion, made her tremble. Doctor Wilson had introduced another nurse, in consideration of the incessant fatigue Mrs. Hammond had undergone; and he endeavoured, by representations, and even by authority, to compel her to quit the apartment of the patient. But she was uncontrollable; and he at length found that he should probably do her more injury, by the violence that would be necessary to separate her from the suffering innocent, than by allowing her to follow her inclination. Her eye was a thousand times turned, with the most eager curiosity, upon the counte-nance of Doctor Wilson, without her daring to breathe a question respecting his opinion, lest he should answer her by a communication of the most fatal tidings. In the mean time she listened with the deepest attention to every thing that dropped either from the physician or the nurse, hoping to collect as it were from some oblique hint, the intelligence which she had not courage expressly to require.

Towards morning the state of the patient seemed to take a favourable turn. She dozed for near two hours, and, when she awoke, appeared perfectly calm and sensible. Understanding that Mr. Falkland had brought the physician to attend her, and was himself in her neighbourhood, she requested to see him. Mr. Falkland had gone in the mean time, with one of his ten-ants to bail the debt, and now entered the prison to enquire whether the young lady might be safely removed, from her pre-sent miserable residence, to a more airy and commodious apartment. When he appeared, the sight of him revived in the mind of Miss Melville an imperfect recollection of the wander-ings of her delirium. She covered her face with her fingers, and betrayed the most expressive confusion, while she thanked him, with her usual unaffected simplicity, for the trouble he had taken. She hoped she should not give him much more; she thought she should get better. It was a shame, she said, if a young and lively girl, as she was, could not contrive to outlive the trifling misfortunes to which she had been subjected. But, while she said this, she was still extremely weak. She tried to assume a cheerful countenance; but it was a faint effort, which the feeble state of her frame did not seem sufficient to support. Mr. Falkland and the doctor joined to request her to keep her-self quiet, and avoid for the present all occasions of exertion.

Encouraged by these appearances, Mrs. Hammond ventured to follow the two gentlemen out of the room, in order to learn from the physician what hopes he entertained. Doctor Wilson acknowledged, that he found his patient at first in a very unfavourable situation, that the symptoms were changed for the better, and that he was not without some expectation of her recovery. He added, however, that he could answer for nothing, that the next twelve hours would be exceedingly critical, but that if she did not grow worse before morning, he would then undertake for her life. Mrs. Hammond, who had hitherto seen nothing but despair, now became frantic with joy. She burst into tears of transport, blessed the physician in the most emphatic and impassioned terms, and uttered a thousand extravagancies. Doctor Wilson seized this opportunity to press her to give herself a little repose, to which she consented, a bed being first procured for her in the room next to Miss Melville's, she having charged the nurse to give her notice of any alteration in the state of the patient.

Mrs. Hammond enjoyed an uninterrupted sleep of several hours. It was already night, when she was awaked by an unusual bustle in the next room. She listened for a few moments, and then determined to go and discover the occasion of it. As she opened her door for that purpose, she met the nurse coming to her. The countenance of the messenger told her what it was she had to communicate, without the use of words. She hurried to the bed-side, and found Miss Melville expiring. The appearances that had at first been so encouraging were of short duration. The calm of the morning proved to be only a sort of lightening before death. In a few hours the patient grew worse. The bloom of her countenance faded; she drew her breath with difficulty; and her eyes became fixed. Doctor Wilson came in at this period, and immediately perceived that all was over. She was for some time in convulsions; but, these subsiding, she addressed the physician with a composed, though feeble voice. She thanked him for his attention; and expressed the most lively sense of her obligations to Mr. Falkland. She sincerely forgave her cousin, and hoped he might never be visited by too acute a recollection of his barbarity to her. She would have been contented to live. Few persons had a sincerer relish of the pleasures of life; but she was well pleased to die, rather than have become the wife of Grimes. As Mrs. Hammond entered, she turned her countenance towards her, and with an affectionate expression repeated her name. This was her last word; in less than two hours from that time she breathed her last in the arms of this faithful friend.

CHAPTER XI

SUCH was the fate of Miss Emily Melville. Perhaps tyranny never exhibited a more painful memorial of the detestation in which it deserves to be held. The idea irresistibly excited in every spectator of the scene, was that of regarding Mr. Tyrrel as the most diabolical wretch that had ever dishonoured the human form. The very attendants upon this house of oppression, for the scene was acted upon too public a stage not to be generally understood, expressed their astonishment and disgust at his unparalleled cruelty.

If such were the feelings of men bred to the commission of injustice, it is difficult to say what must have been those of Mr. Falkland. He raved, he swore, he beat his head, he rent up his hair. He was unable to continue in one posture, and to remain in one place. He burst away from the spot with vehemence, as if he sought to leave behind him his recollection and his existence. He seemed to tear up the ground with fierceness and rage. He returned soon again. He approached the sad remains of what had been Emily, and gazed on them with such intentness, that his eyes appeared ready to burst from their sockets. Acute and exquisite as were his notions of virtue and honour, he could not prevent himself from reproaching the system of nature, for having given birth to such a monster as Tyrrel. He was ashamed of himself for wearing the same form. He could not think of the human species with patience. He foamed with indignation against the laws of the universe, that did not permit him to crush such reptiles at a blow, as we would crush so many noxious insects. It was necessary to guard him like a madman.

The whole office of judging what was proper to be done under the present circumstances devolved upon Doctor Wilson. The doctor was a man of cool and methodical habits of acting. One of the first ideas that suggested itself to him was, that Miss Melville was a branch of the family of Tyrrel. He did not doubt of the willingness of Mr. Falkland to discharge every expense that might be further incident to the melancholy remains of this unfortunate victim; but he conceived that the laws of fashion and decorum required some notification of the event to be made to the head of the family. Perhaps, too, he had an eye to his interest in his profession, and was reluctant to expose himself to the resentment of a person of Mr. Tyrrel's consideration in the neighbourhood. But, with this weakness, he had nevertheless some feelings in common with the rest of the world, and must have suffered considerable violence, before he could have persuaded himself to be the messenger; beside which he did not think it right in the present situation to leave Mr. Falkland.

Doctor Wilson no sooner mentioned these ideas, than they seemed to make a sudden impression on Mrs. Hammond, and she earnestly requested that she might be permitted to carry the intelligence. The proposal was unexpected; but the doctor did not very obstinately refuse his assent. She was determined, she said, to see what sort of impression the catastrophe would make upon the author of it; and she promised to comport herself with moderation and civility. The journey was soon performed.

"I am come, sir," said she to Mr. Tyrrel, "to inform you that your cousin, Miss Melville, died this afternoon."

"Died?"

"Yes, sir. I saw her die. She died in these arms."

"Died? Who killed her? What do you mean?"

"Who? Is it for you to ask that question? Your cruelty and malice killed her!"

"Me? – my? – Poh! she is not dead – it cannot be – it is not a week since she left this house."

"Do not you believe me? I say she is dead!"

"Have a care, woman! this is no matter for jesting. No: though she used me ill, I would not believe her dead for all the world!"

Mrs. Hammond shook her head in a manner expressive at once of grief and indignation.

"No, no, no, no! I will never believe that! – No, never!"

"Will you come with me, and convince your eyes? It is a sight worthy of you; and will be a feast to such a heart as yours!" – Saying this, Mrs. Hammond offered her hand, as if to conduct him to the spot.

Mr. Tyrrel shrunk back.

"If she be dead, what is that to me? Am I to answer for every thing that goes wrong in the world? – What do you come here for? Why bring your messages to me?"

"To whom should I bring them but to her kinsman, – and her murderer."

"Murderer? – Did I employ knives or pistols? Did I give her poison? I did nothing but what the law allows. If she be dead, nobody can say that I am to blame!"

"To blame? – All the world will abhor and curse you. Were you such a fool as to think, because men pay respect to wealth and rank, this would extend to such a deed? They will laugh at so barefaced a cheat. The meanest beggar will spurn and spit at you. Ay, you may well stand confounded at what you have done. I will proclaim you to the whole world, and you will be obliged to fly the very face of a human creature!"

"Good woman," said Mr. Tyrrel, extremely humbled, "talk no more in this strain! – Emmy is not dead! I am sure – I hope – she is not dead! – Tell me that you have only been deceiving me, and I will forgive you every thing – I will forgive her – I will take her into favour – I will do any thing you please! – I never meant her any harm!"

"I tell you she is dead! You have murdered the sweetest innocent that lived! Can you bring her back to life, as you have driven her out of it? If you could, I would kneel to you twenty times a day! What is it you have done? – Miserable wretch! did you think you could do and undo, and change things this way and that, as you pleased?"

The reproaches of Mrs. Hammond were the first instance in which Mr. Tyrrel was made to drink the full cup of retribution. This was, however, only a specimen of a long series of contempt, abhorrence, and insult that was reserved for him. The words of Mrs. Hammond were prophetic. It evidently appeared, that though wealth and hereditary elevation operate as an apology for many delinquencies, there are some which so irresistibly address themselves to the indignation of mankind, that, like death, they level all distinctions, and reduce their perpetrator to an equality with the most indigent and squalid of his species. Against Mr. Tyrrel, as the tyrannical and unmanly murderer of Emily, those who dared not venture the unreserved avowal of their sentiments muttered curses, deep, not loud; while the rest joined in an universal cry of abhorrence and execration. He stood astonished at the novelty of his situation. Accustomed as he had been to the obedience and trembling homage of mankind, he had imagined they would be perpetual, and that no excess on his part would ever be potent enough to break the enchantment. Now he looked round, and saw sullen detestation in every face, which with difficulty restrained itself, and upon the slightest provocation broke forth with an impetuous tide, and swept away the mounds of subordination and fear. His large estate could not purchase civility from the gentry, the peasantry, scarcely from his own servants. In the indignation of all around him he found a ghost that haunted him with every change of place, and a remorse that stung his conscience, and exterminated his peace. The neighbourhood appeared more and more every day to be growing too hot for him to endure, and it became evident that he would ultimately be obliged to quit the country. Urged by the flagitiousness of this last example, people learned to recollect every other instance of his excesses, and it was, no doubt, a fearful catalogue that rose up in judgment against him. It seemed as if the sense of public resentment had long been gathering strength unperceived, and now burst forth into insuppressible violence.

There was scarcely a human being upon whom this sort of retribution could have sat more painfully than upon Mr. Tyrrel. Though he had not a consciousness of innocence prompting him continually to recoil from the detestation of mankind as a thing totally unallied to his character, yet the imperiousness of his temper and the constant experience he had had of the pliability of other men, prepared him to feel the general and undisguised condemnation into which he was sunk with uncommon emotions of anger and impatience. That he, at the beam of whose eye every countenance fell, and to whom in the fierceness of his wrath no one was daring enough to reply, should now be regarded with avowed dislike, and treated with unceremonious censure, was a thing he could not endure to recollect or believe. Symptoms of the universal disgust smote him at every instant, and at every blow he writhed with intolerable anguish. His rage was unbounded and raving. He repelled every attack with the fiercest indignation; while the more he struggled, the more desperate his situation appeared to become. At length he determined to collect his strength for a decisive effort, and to meet the whole tide of public opinion in a single scene.

In pursuance of these thoughts he resolved to repair, without delay, to the rural assembly which I have already mentioned in the course of my story. Miss Melville had now been dead one month. Mr. Falkland had been absent the last week in a distant part of the country, and was not expected to return for a week longer. Mr. Tyrrel willingly embraced the opportunity, trusting, if he could now effect his re-establishment, that he should easily preserve the ground he had gained, even in the face of his formidable rival. Mr. Tyrrel was not deficient in courage; but he conceived the present to be too important an epoch in his life to allow him to make any unnecessary risk in his chance for future ease and importance.

There was a sort of bustle that took place at his entrance into the assembly, it having been agreed by the gentlemen of the assembly, that Mr. Tyrrel was to be refused admittance, as a person with whom they did not choose to associate. This vote had already been notified to him by letter by the master of the ceremonies, but the intelligence was rather calculated, with a man of Mr. Tyrrel's disposition, to excite defiance than to overawe. At the door of the assembly he was personally met by the master of the ceremonies, who had perceived the arrival of an equipage, and who now endeavoured to repeat his prohibition: but he was thrust aside by Mr. Tyrrel with an air of native authority and ineffable contempt. As he entered, every eye was turned upon him. Presently all the gentlemen in the room assembled round him. Some endeavoured to hustle him, and others began to expostulate. But he found the secret effectually to silence the one set, and to shake off the other. His muscular form, the well-known eminence of his intellectual powers, the long habits to which every man was formed of acknowledging his ascendancy, were all in his favour. He considered himself as playing a desperate stake, and had roused all the energies he possessed, to enable him to do justice to so interesting a transaction. Disengaged from the insects that at first pestered him, he paced up and down the room with a magisterial stride, and flashed an angry glance on every side. He then broke silence. "If any one had any thing to say to him, he should know where and how to answer him. He would advise any such person, however, to consider well what he was about. If any man imagined he had any thing personally to complain of, it was very well. But he did expect that nobody there would be ignorant and raw enough to meddle with what was no business of theirs, and intrude into the concerns of any man's private family."

This being a sort of defiance, one and another gentleman advanced to answer it. He that was first began to speak; but Mr. Tyrrel, by the expression of his countenance and a peremptory tone, by well-timed interruptions and pertinent insinuations, caused him first to hesitate, and then to be silent. He seemed to be fast advancing to the triumph he had promised himself. The whole company were astonished. They felt the same abhorrence and condemnation of his character; but they could not help admiring the courage and resources he displayed upon the present occasion. They could without difficulty have concentred afresh their indignant feelings, but they seemed to want a leader.

At this critical moment Mr. Falkland entered the room. Mere accident had enabled him to return sooner than he expected.

Both he and Mr. Tyrrel reddened at sight of each other. He advanced towards Mr. Tyrrel without a moment's pause, and in a peremptory voice asked him what he did there?

"Here? What do you mean by that? This place is as free to me as you, and you are the last person to whom I shall deign to give an account of myself."

"Sir, the place is not free to you. Do not you know, you have been voted out? Whatever were your rights, your infamous conduct has forfeited them."

"Mr. what do you call yourself, if you have any thing to say to me, choose a proper time and place. Do not think to put on your bullying airs under shelter of this company! I will not endure it."

"You are mistaken, sir. This public scene is the only place where I can have any thing to say to you. If you would not hear the universal indignation of mankind, you must not come into the society of men. – Miss Melville! – Shame upon you, inhuman, unrelenting tyrant! Can you hear her name, and not sink into the earth? Can you retire into solitude, and not see her pale and patient ghost rising to reproach you? Can you recollect her virtues, her innocence, her spotless manners, her unresentful temper, and not run distracted with remorse? Have you not killed her in the first bloom of her youth? Can you bear to think that she now lies mouldering in the grave through your cursed contrivance, that deserved a crown, ten thousand times more than you deserve to live? And do you expect that mankind will ever forget, or forgive such a deed? Go, miserable wretch; think yourself too happy that you are permitted to fly the face of man! Why, what a pitiful figure do you make at this moment! Do you think that any thing could bring so hardened a wretch as you are to shrink from reproach, if your conscience were not in confederacy with them that reproached you? And were you fool enough to believe that any obstinacy, however determined, could enable you to despise the keen rebuke of justice? Go, shrink into your miserable self! Begone, and let me never be blasted with your sight again!"

And here, incredible as it may appear, Mr. Tyrrel began to obey his imperious censurer. His looks were full of wildness and horror; his limbs trembled; and his tongue refused its office. He felt no power of resisting the impetuous torrent of reproach that was poured upon him. He hesitated; he was ashamed of his own defeat; he seemed to wish to deny it. But his struggles were ineffectual; every attempt perished in the moment it was made. The general voice was eager to abash him. As his confusion became more visible, the outcry increased. It swelled gradually to hootings, tumult, and a deafening noise of indignation. At length he willingly retired from the public scene, unable any longer to endure the sensations it inflicted.

In about an hour and a half he returned. No precaution had been taken against this incident, for nothing could be more unexpected. In the interval he had intoxicated himself with large draughts of brandy. In a moment he was in a part of the room where Mr. Falkland was standing, and with one blow of his muscular arm levelled him with the earth. The blow however was not stunning, and Mr. Falkland rose again immediately. It is obvious to perceive how unequal he must have been in this species of contest. He was scarcely risen before Mr. Tyrrel repeated his blow. Mr. Falkland was now upon his guard, and did not fall. But the blows of his adversary were redoubled with a rapidity difficult to conceive, and Mr. Falkland was once again brought to the earth. In this situation Mr. Tyrrel kicked his prostrate enemy, and stooped apparently with the intention of dragging him along the floor. All this passed in a moment, and the gentlemen present had not time to recover their surprise. They now interfered, and Mr. Tyrrel once more quitted the apartment.

It is difficult to conceive any event more terrible to the individual upon whom it fell, than the treatment which Mr. Falkland in this instance experienced. Every passion of his life was calculated to make him feel it more acutely. He had repeatedly exerted an uncommon energy and prudence, to prevent the misunderstanding between Mr. Tyrrel and himself from proceeding to extremities; but in vain! It was closed with a catastrophe, exceeding all that he had feared, or that the most penetrating foresight could have suggested. To Mr. Falkland disgrace was worse than death. The slightest breath of dishonour would have stung him to the very soul. What must it have been with this complication of ignominy, base, humiliating, and public? Could Mr. Tyrrel have understood the evil he inflicted, even he, under all his circumstances of provocation, could scarcely have perpetrated it. Mr. Falkland's mind was full of uproar like the war of contending elements, and of such suffering as casts contempt on the refinements of inventive cruelty. He wished for annihilation, to lie down in eternal oblivion, in an insensibility, which, compared with what he experienced, was scarcely less enviable than beatitude itself. Horror, detestation, revenge, inexpressible longings to shake off the evil, and a persuasion that in this case all effort was powerless, filled his soul even to bursting.

One other event closed the transactions of this memorable evening. Mr. Falkland was baffled of the vengeance that yet remained to him. Mr. Tyrrel was found by some of the company dead in the street, having been murdered at the distance of a few yards from the assembly house.

CHAPTER XII

I SHALL endeavour to state the remainder of this narrative in the words of Mr. Collins. The reader has already had occasion to perceive that Mr. Collins was a man of no vulgar order; and his reflections on the subject were uncommonly judicious.

"This day was the crisis of Mr. Falkland's history. From hence took its beginning that gloomy and unsociable melancholy, of which he has since been the victim. No two characters can be in certain respects more strongly contrasted, than the Mr. Falkland of a date prior and subsequent to these events. Hitherto he had been attended by a fortune perpetually prosperous. His mind was sanguine; full of that undoubting confidence in its own powers which prosperity is qualified to produce. Though the habits of his life were those of a serious and sublime visionary, they were nevertheless full of cheerfulness and tranquillity. But from this moment, his pride, and the lofty adventurousness of his spirit, were effectually subdued. From an object of envy he was changed into an object of compassion. Life, which hitherto no one had more exquisitely enjoyed, became a burden to him. No more self-complacency, no more rapture, no more self-approving and heart-transporting benevolence! He who had lived beyond any man upon the grand and animating reveries of the imagination, seemed now to have no visions but of anguish and despair. His case was peculiarly worthy of sympathy, since, no doubt, if rectitude and purity of disposition could give a title to happiness, few men could exhibit a more consistent and powerful claim than Mr. Falkland.

"He was too deeply pervaded with the idle and groundless romances of chivalry, ever to forget the situation, humiliating and dishonourable according to his ideas, in which he had been placed upon this occasion. There is a mysterious sort of divinity annexed to the person of a true knight, that makes any species of brute violence committed upon it indelible and immortal. To be knocked down, cuffed, kicked, dragged along the floor! Sacred heaven, the memory of such a treatment was not to be endured! No future lustration could ever remove the stain: and, what was perhaps still worse in the present case, the offender having ceased to exist, the lustration which the laws of knight-errantry prescribe was rendered impossible.

"In some future period of human improvement, it is probable, that that calamity will be in a manner unintelligible, which in the present instance contributed to tarnish and wither the excellence of one of the most elevated and amiable of human minds. If Mr. Falkland had reflected with perfect accuracy upon the case, he would probably have been able to look down with indifference upon a wound, which, as it was, pierced to his very vitals. How much more dignity, than in the modern duellist, do we find in Themistocles, the most gallant of the Greeks; who, when Eurybiades, his commander in chief, in answer to some of his remonstrances, lifted his cane over him with a menacing air, accosted him in that noble apostrophe, 'Strike, but hear!'[1]

"How would a man of true discernment in such a case reply to his brutal assailant? 'I make it my boast that I can endure calamity and pain: shall I not be able to endure the trifling inconvenience that your folly can inflict upon me? Perhaps a human being would be more accomplished, if he understood the science of personal defence; but how few would be the occasions upon which he would be called to exert it? How few persons would he encounter so unjust and injurious as you, if his own conduct were directed by the principles of reason and benevolence? Beside, how narrow would be the use of this science when acquired? It will scarcely put the man of delicate make and petty stature upon a level with the athletic pugilist; and, if it did in some measure secure me against the malice of a single adversary, still my person and my life, so far as mere force is concerned, would always be at the mercy of two. Further than immediate defence against actual violence, it could never be of use to me. The man who can deliberately meet his adver-

---

1   Plutarch's life of Themistocles tells this tale. Eurybiades, the Spartan commanding the combined Greek fleet, sought to retreat from Salamis rather than fight the Persian fleet without the support of the Greek army. In his anger at Themistocles' refusal to abandon his arguments for fighting, Eurybiades threatened him with his staff. But Themistocles' moderation in responding with these words so impressed Eurybiades that he listened to and was ultimately persuaded by the arguments for battling the Persians there.

sary for the purpose of exposing the person of one or both of them to injury, tramples upon every principle of reason and equity. Duelling is the vilest of all egotism, treating the public, who has a claim to all my powers and exertions, as if it were nothing, and myself, or rather an unintelligible chimera I annex to myself, as if it were entitled to my exclusive attention. I am unable to cope with you: what then? Can that circumstance dishonour me? No; I can only be dishonoured by perpetrating an unjust action. My honour is in my own keeping, beyond the reach of all mankind. Strike! I am passive. No injury that you can inflict, shall provoke me to expose you or myself to unnecessary evil. I refuse that; but I am not therefore pusillanimous: when I refuse any danger or suffering by which the general good may be promoted, then brand me for a coward!'

"These reasonings, however simple and irresistible they must be found by a dispassionate enquirer, are little reflected on by the world at large, and were most of all uncongenial to the prejudices of Mr. Falkland.

"But the public disgrace and chastisement that had been imposed upon him, intolerable as they were to be recollected, were not the whole of the mischief that redounded to our unfortunate patron from the transactions of that day. It was presently whispered that he was no other than the murderer of his antagonist. This rumour was of too much importance to the very continuance of his life, to justify its being concealed from him. He heard it with inexpressible astonishment and horror; it formed a dreadful addition to the load of intellectual anguish that already oppressed him. No man had ever held his reputation more dear than Mr. Falkland; and now, in one day, he was fallen under the most exquisite calamities, a complicated personal insult, and the imputation of the foulest of crimes. He might have fled; for no one was forward to proceed against a man so adored as Mr. Falkland, or in revenge of one so universally execrated as Mr. Tyrrel. But flight he disdained. In the mean time the affair was of the most serious magnitude, and the rumour unchecked seemed daily to increase in strength. Mr. Falkland appeared sometimes inclined to adopt such steps as might have been best calculated to bring the imputation to a speedy trial. But he probably feared, by too direct an appeal to judicature, to render more precise an imputation, the memory of which he deprecated; at the same time that he was sufficiently willing to meet the severest scrutiny, and, if he could not hope to have it forgotten that he had ever been accused, to prove in the most satisfactory manner that the accusation was unjust.

"The neighbouring magistrates at length conceived it necessary to take some steps upon the subject. Without causing Mr. Falkland to be apprehended, they sent to desire he would appear before them at one of their meetings. The proceeding being thus opened, Mr. Falkland expressed his hope that, if the business were likely to stop there, their investigation might at least be rendered as solemn as possible. The meeting was numerous; every person of a respectable class in society was admitted to be an auditor; the whole town, one of the most considerable in the county, was apprised of the nature of the business. Few trials, invested with all the forms of judgment, have excited so general an interest. A trial, under the present circumstances, was scarcely attainable; and it seemed to be the wish both of principal and umpires, to give to this transaction all the momentary notoriety and decisiveness of a trial.

"The magistrates investigated the particulars of the story. Mr. Falkland, it appeared, had left the rooms immediately after his assailant; and though he had been attended by one or two of the gentlemen to his inn, it was proved that he had left them upon some slight occasion, as soon as he arrived at it, and that, when they enquired for him of the waiters, he had already mounted his horse and ridden home.

"By the nature of the case, no particular facts could be stated in balance against these. As soon as they had been sufficiently detailed, Mr. Falkland therefore proceeded to his defence. Several copies of his defence were made, and Mr. Falkland seemed, for a short time, to have had the idea of sending it to the press, though, for some reason or other, he afterwards suppressed it. I have one of the copies in my possession, and I will read it to you."

Saying this, Mr. Collins rose, and took it from a private drawer in his escritoire. During this action he appeared to recollect himself. He did not, in the strict sense of the word, hesitate; but he was prompted to make some apology for what he was doing.

"You seem never to have heard of this memorable transaction; and, indeed, that is little to be wondered at, since the good nature of the world is interested in suppressing it, and it is deemed a disgrace to a man to have defended himself from a criminal imputation, though with circumstances the most satisfactory and honourable. It may be supposed that this suppression is particularly acceptable to Mr. Falkland; and I should not have acted in contradiction to his modes of thinking in communicating the story to you, had there not been circumstances of peculiar urgency, that seemed to render the communication desirable." Saying this, he proceeded to read from the paper in his hand.

"Gentlemen,

"I stand here accused of a crime, the most black that any human creature is capable of perpetrating. I am innocent. I have no fear that I shall fail to make every person in this company acknowledge my innocence. In the mean time, what must be my feelings? Conscious as I am of deserving approbation and not censure, of having passed my life in acts of justice and philanthropy, can any thing be more deplorable than for me to answer to a charge of murder? So wretched is my situation, that I cannot accept your gratuitous acquittal, if you should be disposed to bestow it. I must answer to an imputation, the very thought of which is ten thousand times worse to me than death. I must exert the whole energy of my mind, to prevent my being ranked with the vilest of men.

"Gentlemen, this is a situation in which a man may be allowed to boast. Accursed situation! No man need envy me the vile and polluted triumph I am now to gain! I have called no witnesses to my character. Great God! what sort of character is that which must be supported by witnesses? But, if I must speak, look round the company, ask of every one present, enquire of your own hearts! Not one word of reproach was ever whispered against me. I do not hesitate to call upon those who have known me most, to afford me the most honourable testimony.

"My life has been spent in the keenest and most unintermitted sensibility to reputation. I am almost indifferent as to what shall be the event of this day. I would not open my mouth upon the occasion, if my life were the only thing that was at stake. It is not in the power of your decision to restore to me my unblemished reputation, to obliterate the disgrace I have suffered, or to prevent it from being remembered that I have been brought to examination upon a charge of murder. Your decision can never have the efficacy to prevent the miserable remains of my existence from being the most intolerable of all burthens.

"I am accused of having committed murder upon the body of Barnabas Tyrrel. I would most joyfully have given every farthing I possess, and devoted myself to perpetual beggary, to have preserved his life. His life was precious to me, beyond that of all mankind. In my opinion, the greatest injustice committed by his unknown assassin was that of defrauding me of my just revenge. I confess that I would have called him out to the field, and that our encounter should not have been terminated but by the death of one or both of us. This would have been a pitiful and inadequate compensation for his unparalleled insult, but it was all that remained.

"I ask for no pity, but I must openly declare that never was any misfortune so horrible as mine. I would willingly have taken refuge from the recollection of that night in a voluntary death. Life was now stripped of all those recommendations, for the sake of which it was dear to me. But even this consolation is denied me. I am compelled to drag for ever the intolerable load of existence, upon penalty, if at any period, however remote, I shake it off, of having that impatience regarded as confirming a charge of murder. Gentlemen, if by your decision you could take away my life, without that act being connected with my disgrace, I would bless the cord that stopped the breath of my existence for ever.

"You all know how easily I might have fled from this purgation. If I had been guilty, should I not have embraced the opportunity? But, as it was, I could not. Reputation has been the idol, the jewel of my life. I could never have borne to think that a human creature, in the remotest part of the globe, should believe that I was a criminal. Alas! what a deity it is that I have chosen for my worship! I have entailed upon myself everlasting agony and despair!

"I have but one word to add. Gentlemen, I charge you to do me the imperfect justice that is in your power! My life is a worthless thing. But my honour, the empty remains of honour I have now to boast, is in your judgment, and you will each of you, from this day, have imposed upon yourselves the task of its vindicators. It is little that you can do for me; but it is not less your duty to do that little. May that God who is the fountain of honour and good prosper and protect you! The man who now stands before you is devoted to perpetual barrenness and blast! He has nothing to hope for beyond the feeble consolation of this day!"

You will easily imagine that Mr. Falkland was discharged with every circumstance of credit. Nothing is more to be deplored in human institutions, than that the ideas of mankind should have annexed a sentiment of disgrace to a purgation thus satisfactory and decisive. No one entertained the shadow of a doubt upon the subject, and yet a mere concurrence of circumstances made it necessary that the best of men should be publicly put on his defence, as if really under suspicion of an atrocious crime. It may be granted indeed that Mr. Falkland had his faults, but those very faults placed him at a still further distance from the criminality in question. He was the fool of honour and fame: a man whom, in the pursuit of reputation, nothing could divert; who would have purchased the character of a true, gallant, and undaunted hero, at the expense of worlds, and who thought every calamity nominal but a stain upon his honour. How atrociously absurd to suppose any motive capable of inducing such a man to play the part of a lurking assassin? How unfeeling to oblige him to defend himself from such an imputation? Did any man, and, least of all, a man of the purest honour, ever pass in a moment, from a life unstained by a single act of injury, to the consummation of human depravity?

When the decision of the magistrates was declared, a general murmur of applause and involuntary transport burst forth from every one present. It was at first low, and gradually became louder. As it was the expression of rapturous delight, and an emotion disinterested and divine, so there was an indescribable something in the very sound, that carried it home to the heart, and convinced every spectator that there was no merely personal pleasure which ever existed, that would not be foolish and feeble in the comparison. Every one strove who should most express his esteem of the amiable accused. Mr. Falkland was no sooner withdrawn than the gentlemen present determined to give a still further sanction to the business by their congratulations. They immediately named a deputation to wait upon him for that purpose. Every one concurred to assist the general sentiment. It was a sort of sympathetic feeling that took hold upon all ranks and degrees. The multitude received him with huzzas, they took his horses from his carriage, dragged him along in triumph, and attended him many miles on his return to his own habitation. It seemed as if a public examination upon a criminal charge, which had hitherto been considered in every event as a brand of disgrace, was converted, in the present instance, into an occasion of enthusiastic adoration and unexampled honour.

Nothing could reach the heart of Mr. Falkland. He was not insensible to the general kindness and exertions; but it was too evident that the melancholy that had taken hold of his mind was invincible.

It was only a few weeks after this memorable scene that the real murderer was discovered. Every part of this story was extraordinary. The real murderer was Hawkins. He was found with his son, under a feigned name, at a village about thirty miles distant, in want of all the necessaries of life. He had lived there, from the period of his flight, in so private a manner, that all the enquiries that had been set on foot, by the benevolence of Mr. Falkland, or the insatiable malice of Mr. Tyrrel, had been insufficient to discover him. The first thing that had led to the detection was a parcel of clothes covered with blood, that were found in a ditch, and that, when drawn out, were known by the people of the village to belong to this man. The murder of Mr. Tyrrel was not a circumstance that could be unknown, and suspicion was immediately roused. A diligent search being made, the rusty handle, with part of the blade of a knife, was found thrown in a corner of his lodging, which, being applied to a piece of the point of a knife that had been broken in the wound, appeared exactly to correspond. Upon further enquiry two rustics, who had been accidentally on the spot, remembered to have seen Hawkins and his son in the town that very evening and to have called after them, and received no answer, though they were sure of their persons. Upon this accumulated evidence both Hawkins and his son were tried, condemned, and afterwards executed. In the interval between the sentence and execution Hawkins confessed his guilt with many marks of compunction; though there are persons by whom this is denied; but I have taken some pains to enquire into the fact, and am persuaded that their disbelief is precipitate and groundless.

The cruel injustice that this man had suffered from his village-tyrant was not forgotten upon the present occasion. It was by a strange fatality that the barbarous proceedings of Mr. Tyrrel seemed never to fall short of their completion; and even his death served eventually to consummate the ruin of a man he hated; a circumstance which, if it could have come to his knowledge, would perhaps have in some measure consoled him for his untimely end. This poor Hawkins was surely entitled to some pity, since his being finally urged to desperation, and brought, together with his son, to an ignominious fate, was originally owing to the sturdiness of his virtue and independence. But the compassion of the public was in a great measure shut against him, as they thought it a piece of barbarous and unpardonable selfishness, that he had not rather come boldly forward to meet the consequences of his own conduct, than suffer a man of so much public worth as Mr. Falkland, and who had been so desirous of doing him good, to be exposed to the risk of being tried for a murder that he had committed.

From this time to the present Mr. Falkland has been nearly such as you at present see him. Though it be several years since these transactions, the impression they made is for ever fresh in the mind of our unfortunate patron. From thenceforward his habits became totally different. He had before been fond of public scenes, and acting a part in the midst of the people among whom he immediately resided. He now made himself a rigid recluse. He had no associates, no friends. Inconsolable himself, he yet wished to treat others with kindness. There was a solemn sadness in his manner, attended with the most perfect gentleness and humanity. Every body respects him, for his benevolence is unalterable; but there is a stately coldness and reserve in his behaviour, which makes it difficult for those about him to regard him with the familiarity of affection. These symptoms are uninterrupted, except at certain times when his sufferings become intolerable, and he displays the marks of a furious insanity. At those times his language is fearful and mysterious, and he seems to figure to himself by turns every sort of persecution and alarm, which may be supposed to attend upon an accusation of murder. But, sensible of his own weakness, he is anxious at such times to withdraw into solitude: and his domestics in general know nothing of him, but the uncommunicative and haughty, but mild, dejection that accompanies every thing he does."

END OF THE FIRST VOLUME

VOLUME THE SECOND

CHAPTER I

I HAVE stated the narrative of Mr. Collins, interspersed with such other information as I was able to collect, with all the exactness that my memory, assisted by certain memorandums I made at the time, will afford. I do not pretend to warrant the authenticity of any part of these memoirs, except so much as fell under my own knowledge, and that part shall be given with the same simplicity and accuracy, that I would observe towards a court which was to decide in the last resort upon every thing dear to me. The same scrupulous fidelity restrains me from altering the manner of Mr. Collins's narrative to adapt it to the precepts of my own taste; and it will soon be perceived how essential that narrative is to the elucidation of my history.

The intention of my friend in this communication was to give me ease; but he in reality added to my embarrassment. Hitherto I had had no intercourse with the world and its passions; and, though I was not totally unacquainted with them as they appear in books, this proved of little service to me when I came to witness them myself. The case seemed entirely altered, when the subject of those passions was continually before my eyes, and the events had happened but the other day as it were, in the very neighbourhood where I lived. There was a connection and progress in this narrative, which made it altogether unlike the little village incidents I had hitherto known. My feelings were successively interested for the different persons that were brought upon the scene. My veneration was excited for Mr. Clare, and my applause for the intrepidity of Mrs. Hammond. I was astonished that any human creature should be so shockingly perverted as Mr. Tyrrel. I paid the tribute of my tears to the memory of the artless Miss Melville. I found a thousand fresh reasons to admire and love Mr. Falkland.

At present I was satisfied with thus considering every incident in its obvious sense. But the story I had heard was for ever in my thoughts, and I was peculiarly interested to comprehend its full import. I turned it a thousand ways, and examined it in every point of view. In the original communication it appeared sufficiently distinct and satisfactory; but as I brooded over it, it gradually became mysterious. There was something strange in the character of Hawkins. So firm, so sturdily honest and just, as he appeared at first; all at once to become a murderer! His first behaviour under the prosecution, how accurately was it calculated to prepossess one in his favour! To be sure, if he were guilty, it was unpardonable in him to permit a man of so much dignity and worth as Mr. Falkland to suffer under the imputation of his crime! And yet I could not help bitterly compassionating the honest fellow, brought to the gallows, as he was, strictly speaking, by the machinations of that devil incarnate, Mr. Tyrrel. His son, too, that son for whom he voluntarily sacrificed his all, to die with him at the same tree; surely never was a story more affecting!

Was it possible, after all, that Mr. Falkland should be the murderer? The reader will scarcely believe, that the idea suggested itself to my mind that I would ask him. It was but a passing thought; but it serves to mark the simplicity of my character. Then I recollected the virtues of my master, almost too sublime for human nature; I thought of his sufferings so unexampled, so unmerited; and chid myself for the suspicion. The dying confession of Hawkins recurred to my mind; and I felt that there was no longer a possibility of doubting. And yet what was the meaning of all Mr. Falkland's agonies and terrors? In fine, the idea having once occurred to my mind, it was fixed there for ever. My thoughts fluctuated from conjecture to conjecture, but this was the centre about which they revolved. I determined to place myself as a watch upon my patron.

The instant I had chosen this employment for myself, I found a strange sort of pleasure in it. To do what is forbidden always has its charms, because we have an indistinct apprehension of something arbitrary and tyrannical in the prohibition. To be a spy upon Mr. Falkland! That there was danger in the employment, served to give an alluring pungency to the choice. I remembered the stern reprimand I had received, and his terrible looks; and the recollection gave a kind of tingling sensation, not altogether unallied to enjoyment. The further I advanced, the more the sensation was irresistible. I seemed to myself perpetually upon the brink of being countermined, and perpetually roused to guard my designs. The more impenetrable Mr. Falkland was determined to be, the more uncontrollable was my curiosity. Through the whole, my alarm and apprehension of personal danger had a large mixture of frankness and simplicity, conscious of meaning no ill, that made me continually ready to say every thing that was upon my mind, and would not suffer me to believe that, when things were brought to the test, any one could be seriously angry with me.

These reflections led gradually to a new state of my mind. When I had first removed into Mr. Falkland's family, the novelty of the scene rendered me cautious and reserved. The distant and solemn manners of my master seemed to have annihilated my constitutional gaiety. But the novelty by degrees wore off, and my constraint in the same degree diminished. The story I had now heard, and the curiosity it excited, restored to me activity, eagerness and courage. I had always had a propensity to communicate my thoughts; my age was, of course, inclined to talkativeness; and I ventured occasionally in a sort of hesitating way, as if questioning whether such a conduct might be allowed, to express my sentiments as they arose, in the presence of Mr. Falkland.

The first time I did so, he looked at me with an air of surprise, made me no answer, and presently took occasion to leave me. The experiment was soon after repeated. My master seemed half inclined to encourage me, and yet doubtful whether he might venture. He had long been a stranger to pleasure of every sort, and my artless and untaught remarks appeared to promise him some amusement. Could an amusement of this sort be dangerous?

In this uncertainty he could not probably find it in his heart to treat with severity my innocent effusions. I needed but little encouragement; for the perturbation of my mind stood in want of this relief. My simplicity, arising from my being a total stranger to the intercourse of the world, was accompanied with a mind in some degree cultivated with reading, and perhaps not altogether destitute of observation and talent. My remarks were therefore perpetually unexpected, at one time implying extreme ignorance, and at another some portion of acuteness, but at all times having an air of innocence, frankness, and courage. There was still an apparent want of design in the manner, even after I was excited accurately to compare my observations, and study the inferences to which they led; for the effect of old habit was more visible than that of a recently conceived purpose which was yet scarcely mature.

Mr. Falkland's situation was like that of a fish that plays with the bait employed to entrap him. By my manner he was in a certain degree encouraged to lay aside his usual reserve, and relax his stateliness; till some abrupt observation or interrogatory stung him into recollection, and brought back his alarm. Still it was evident that he bore about him a secret wound. Whenever the cause of his sorrows was touched, though in a manner the most indirect and remote, his countenance altered, his distemper returned, and it was with difficulty that he could suppress his emotions, sometimes conquering himself with painful effort, and sometimes bursting into a sort of paroxysm of insanity, and hastening to bury himself in solitude.

These appearances I too frequently interpreted into grounds of suspicion, though I might with equal probability and more liberality have ascribed them to the cruel mortifications he had encountered in the objects of his darling ambition. Mr. Collins had strongly urged me to secrecy; and Mr. Falkland, whenever my gesture or his consciousness impressed him with the idea of my knowing more than I expressed, looked at me with wistful earnestness, as questioning what was the degree of information I possessed, and how it was obtained. But again at our next interview the simple vivacity of my manner restored his tranquillity, obliterated the emotion of which I had been the cause, and placed things afresh in their former situation.

The longer this humble familiarity on my part had continued, the more effort it would require to suppress it; and Mr. Falkland was neither willing to mortify me by a severe prohibition of speech, nor even perhaps to make me of so much consequence, as that prohibition might seem to imply. Though I was curious, it must not be supposed that I had the object of my enquiry for ever in my mind, or that my questions and innuendoes were perpetually regulated with the cunning of a grey-headed inquisitor. The secret wound of Mr. Falkland's mind was much more uniformly present to his recollection than to mine; and a thousand times he applied the remarks that occurred in conversation; when I had not the remotest idea of such an application, till some singularity in his manner brought it back to my thoughts. The consciousness of this morbid sensibility, and the imagination that its influence might perhaps constitute the whole of the case, served probably to spur Mr. Falkland again to the charge, and connect a sentiment of shame, with every project that suggested itself for interrupting the freedom of our intercourse.

I will give a specimen of the conversations to which I allude; and, as it shall be selected from those which began upon topics the most general and remote, the reader will easily imagine the disturbance that was almost daily endured by a mind so tremblingly alive as that of my patron.

"Pray, sir," said I, one day, as I was assisting Mr. Falkland in arranging some papers, previously to their being transcribed into his collection, "how came Alexander of Macedon to be surnamed the Great?"

"How came it? Did you never read his history?"

"Yes, sir."

"Well, Williams, and could you find no reasons there?"

"Why, I do not know, sir. I could find reasons why he should be so famous; but every man that is talked of is not admired. Judges differ about the merits of Alexander. Doctor Prideaux says in his Connection, that he deserves only to be called the Great Cut-throat; and the author of Tom Jones has written a volume, to prove that he and all other conquerors ought to be classed with Jonathan Wild."[1]

Mr. Falkland reddened at these citations.

"Accursed blasphemy! Did these authors think that, by the coarseness of their ribaldry, they could destroy his well-earned

---

1   Humphrey Prideaux, the "clerical pedant" named below, wrote *The Old and New Testament Connected in the History of the Jews and Neighbouring Nations* (1716-18); Henry Fielding, the "Westminster justice" better known as author of *Tom Jones*, also wrote *The Life of Jonathan Wild the Great* (1743), a narrative account of one of the most famous of British thieves. See Book I, Chapter I, for the reference to Alexander.

fame? Are learning, sensibility, and taste, no securities to exempt their possessor from this vulgar abuse? Did you ever read, Williams, of a man more gallant, generous, and free? Was ever mortal so completely the reverse of every thing engrossing and selfish? He formed to himself a sublime image of excellence, and his only ambition was to realise it in his own story. Remember his giving away every thing when he set out upon his grand expedition, professedly reserving for himself nothing but hope. Recollect his heroic confidence in Philip the physician, and his entire and unalterable friendship for Ephestion. He treated the captive family of Darius with the most cordial urbanity and the venerable Sysigambis with all the tenderness and attention of a son to his mother.[1] Never take the judgment, Williams, upon such a subject, of a clerical pedant or a Westminster justice. Examine for yourself, and you will find in Alexander a model of honour, generosity, and disinterestedness, – a man who, for the cultivated liberality of his mind, and the unparalleled grandeur of his projects, must stand alone the spectacle and admiration of all ages of the world."

"Ah, sir! it is a fine thing for us to sit here and compose his panegyric. But shall I forget what a vast expense was bestowed in erecting the monument of his fame? Was not he the common disturber of mankind? Did not he over-run nations that would never have heard of him but for his devastations? How many hundred thousands of lives did he sacrifice in his career? What must I think of his cruelties; a whole tribe massacred for a crime committed by their ancestors one hundred and fifty years before; fifty thousand sold into slavery; two thousand crucified for their gallant defence of their country? Man is surely a strange sort of creature, who never praises any one more hearti-

---

1   These instances of the virtues of Alexander the Great (356-323 BC) come from Plutarch's account of his life. When Alexander was seriously ill (possibly from bathing in the cold waters of the Cydnus River), only Philip among his physicians was willing to attempt a cure. Despite receiving a letter accusing Philip of wishing to kill him, Alexander drank Philip's potion, giving Philip the letter to read as he did so. Alexander ordered great public mourning and undertook a memorial campaign when his friend Hephaestion died, and was praised by Plutarch for his benevolent treatment of Sisygambis, mother of King Darius, and her family when he captured them during his campaign against the Persian empire.

ly than him who has spread destruction and ruin over the face of nations!"

"The way of thinking you express, Williams, is natural enough, and I cannot blame you for it. But let me hope that you will become more liberal. The death of a hundred thousand men is at first sight very shocking; but what in reality are a hundred thousand such men, more than a hundred thousand sheep? It is mind, Williams, the generation of knowledge and virtue, that we ought to love. This was the project of Alexander; he set out in a great undertaking to civilise mankind; he delivered the vast continent of Asia from the stupidity and degradation of the Persian monarchy; and, though he was cut off in the midst of his career, we may easily perceive the vast effects of his project. Grecian literature and cultivation, the Seleucidae, the Antiochuses, and the Ptolemies followed, in nations which before had been sunk to the condition of brutes.[1] Alexander was the builder, as notoriously as the destroyer, of cities."

"And yet, sir, I am afraid that the pike and the battleaxe are not the right instruments for making men wise. Suppose it were admitted that the lives of men were to be sacrificed without remorse if a paramount good were to result, it seems to me as if murder and massacre were but a very left-handed way of producing civilisation and love. But pray, do not you think this great hero was a sort of a madman? What now will you say to his firing the palace of Persepolis, his weeping for other worlds to conquer, and his marching his whole army over the burning sands of Libya, merely to visit a temple, and persuade mankind that he was the son of Jupiter Ammon?"[2]

"Alexander, my boy, has been much misunderstood. Mankind have revenged themselves upon him by misrepresen-

---

1   These were among the dynasties that succeeded in control of parts of Alexander's empire after his death.
2   Instances from Plutarch of Alexander's arbitrary, stubborn, and self-glorifying behavior. He completely destroyed the palace of Persepolis after the city had surrendered to him, according to Plutarch, at the instigation of a courtesan at a banquet. He insisted upon visiting the temple of Jupiter Ammon to consult the oracle there despite the great danger of the journey.

tation, for having so far eclipsed the rest of his species. It was necessary to the realising his project, that he should pass for a god. It was the only way by which he could get a firm hold upon the veneration of the stupid and bigoted Persians. It was this, and not a mad vanity, that was the source of his proceeding. And how much had he to struggle with in this respect, in the unapprehending obstinacy of some of his Macedonians?"

"Why then, sir, at last Alexander did but employ means that all politicians profess to use, as well as he. He dragooned men into wisdom, and cheated them into the pursuit of their own happiness. But what is worse, sir, this Alexander, in the paroxysm of his headlong rage, spared neither friend nor foe. You will not pretend to justify the excesses of his ungovernable passion. It is impossible, sure, that a word can be said for a man whom a momentary provocation can hurry into the commission of murders –"

The instant I had uttered these words, I felt what it was that I had done. There was a magnetical sympathy between me and my patron, so that their effect was not sooner produced upon him, than my own mind reproached me with the inhumanity of the allusion. Our confusion was mutual. The blood forsook at once the transparent complexion of Mr. Falkland, and then rushed back again with rapidity and fierceness. I dared not utter a word, lest I should commit a new error worse than that into which I had just fallen. After a short, but severe struggle to continue the conversation, Mr. Falkland began with trepidation, but afterwards became calmer: –

"You are not candid – Alexander – You must learn more clemency – Alexander, I say, does not deserve this rigour. Do you remember his tears, his remorse, his determined abstinence from food, which he could scarcely be persuaded to relinquish? Did not that prove acute feeling and a rooted principle of equity? – Well, well, Alexander was a true and judicious lover of mankind, and his real merits have been little comprehended."

I know not how to make the state of my mind at that moment accurately understood. When one idea has got possession of the soul, it is scarcely possible to keep it from finding its way to the lips. Error, once committed, has a fascinating power, like that ascribed to the eyes of the rattlesnake, to draw us into a second error. It deprives us of that proud confidence in our own strength, to which we are indebted for so much of our virtue. Curiosity is a restless propensity, and often does but hurry us forward the more irresistibly, the greater is the danger that attends its indulgence.

"Clitus," said I, "was a man of very coarse and provoking manners, was he not?"[1]

Mr. Falkland felt the full force of this appeal. He gave me a penetrating look, as if he would see my very soul. His eyes were then in an instant withdrawn. I could perceive him seized with a convulsive shuddering which, though strongly counteracted, and therefore scarcely visible, had I know not what of terrible in it. He left his employment, strode about the room in anger, his visage gradually assumed an expression as of supernatural barbarity, he quitted the apartment abruptly, and flung the door with a violence that seemed to shake the house.

"Is this," said I, "the fruit of conscious guilt, or of the disgust that a man of honour conceives at guilt undeservedly imputed?"

---

1   Clitus was a soldier and friend of Alexander's who had once saved his life. Clitus's sarcastic comments about Alexander's despotic tendencies at a banquet where both were drunk so enraged Alexander that he killed Clitus with a spear, though he immediately regretted the act.

CHAPTER II

THE reader will feel how rapidly I was advancing to the brink of the precipice. I had a confused apprehension of what I was doing, but I could not stop myself. "Is it possible," said I, "that Mr. Falkland, who is thus overwhelmed with a sense of the unmerited dishonour that has been fastened upon him in the face of the world, will long endure the presence of a raw and unfriended youth, who is perpetually bringing back that dishonour to his recollection, and who seems himself the most forward to entertain the accusation?"

I felt indeed that Mr. Falkland would not hastily incline to dismiss me, for the same reason that restrained him from many other actions, which might seem to savour of a too tender and ambiguous sensibility. But this reflection was little adapted to comfort me. That he should cherish in his heart a growing hatred against me, and that he should think himself obliged to retain me a continual thorn in his side, was an idea by no means of favourable augury to my future peace.

It was some time after this that, in clearing out a case of drawers, I found a paper that, by some accident, had slipped behind one of the drawers, and been overlooked. At another time perhaps my curiosity might have given way to the laws of decorum, and I should have restored it unopened to my master, its owner. But my eagerness for information had been too much stimulated by the preceding incidents, to allow me at present to neglect any occasion of obtaining it. The paper proved to be a letter written by the elder Hawkins, and from its contents seemed to have been penned when he had first been upon the point of absconding from the persecutions of Mr. Tyrrel. It was as follows: –

"Honourable sir,

"I have waited some time in daily hope of your honour's return into these parts. Old Warnes and his dame, who are left to take care of your house, tell me they cannot say when that will be, nor justly in what part of England you are at present.

For my share, misfortune comes so thick upon me, that I must determine upon something (that is for certain), and out of hand. Our squire, who I must own at first used me kindly enough, though I am afraid that was partly out of spite to Squire Underwood, has since determined to be the ruin of me. Sir, I have been no craven; I fought it up stoutly; for after all, you know, God bless your honour! it is but a man to a man; but he has been too much for me.

"Perhaps if I were to ride over to the market-town and enquire of Munsle, your lawyer, he could tell me how to direct to you. But having hoped and waited o' this fashion, and all in vain, has put me upon other thoughts. I was in no hurry, sir, to apply to you; for I do not love to be a trouble to any body. I kept that for my last stake. Well, sir, and now that has failed me like, I am ashamed, as it were, to have thought of it. Have not I, thinks I, arms and legs as well as other people? I am driven out of house and home. Well, and what then? Sure I arn't a cabbage, that if you pull it out of the ground it must die. I am pennyless. True; and how many hundreds are there that live from hand to mouth all the days of their life? (Begging your honour's pardon) thinks I, if we little folks had but the wit to do for ourselves, the great folks would not be such maggotty changelings as they are. They would begin to look about them.

"But there is another thing that has swayed with me more than all the rest. I do not know how to tell you, sir, – My poor boy, my Leonard, the pride of my life, has been three weeks in the county jail. It is true indeed, sir. Squire Tyrrel put him there. Now, sir, every time that I lay my head upon my pillow under my own little roof, my heart smites me with the situation of my Leonard. I do not mean so much for the hardship; I do not so much matter that. I do not expect him to go through the world upon velvet! I am not such a fool. But who can tell what may hap in jail! I have been three times to see him; and there is one man in the same quarter of the prison that looks so wicked! I do not much fancy the looks of the rest. To be sure, Leonard is as good a lad as ever lived. I think he will not give his mind to such. But come what will, I am determined he shall not stay among them twelve hours longer. I am an obstinate old fool perhaps; but I have taken it into my head, and I will do it. Do not ask me what. But, if I were to write to your honour, and wait for your answer, it might take a week or ten days more. I must not think of it!

"Squire Tyrrel is very headstrong, and you, your honour, might be a little hottish, or so. No, I would not have any body quarrel for me. There has been mischief enough done already; and I will get myself out of the way. So I write this, your honour, merely to unload my mind. I feel myself equally as much bound to respect and love you, as if you had done every thing for me, that I believe you would have done if things had chanced differently. It is most likely you will never hear of me any more. If it should be so, set your worthy heart at rest. I know myself too well, ever to be tempted to do any thing that is really bad. I have now my fortune to seek in the world. I have been used ill enough, God knows. But I bear no malice; my heart is at peace with all mankind; and I forgive every body. It is like enough that poor Leonard and I may have hardship enough to undergo, among strangers, and being obliged to hide ourselves like housebreakers or highwaymen. But I defy all the malice of fortune to make us do an ill thing. That consolation we will always keep against all the crosses of a heart-breaking world.

"God bless you!

"So prays,

"Your honour's humble servant to command,

"Benjamin Hawkins."

I read this letter with considerable attention, and it occasioned me many reflections. To my way of thinking it contained a very interesting picture of a blunt, downright, honest mind. "It is a melancholy consideration," said I to myself; "but such is man! To have judged from appearances one would have said, this is a fellow to have taken fortune's buffets and rewards with an incorruptible mind. And yet see where it all ends! This man was capable of afterwards becoming a murderer, and finished his life at the gallows. O poverty! thou art indeed omnipotent! Thou grindest us into desperation; thou confoundest all our boasted and most deep-rooted principles; thou fillest us to the very brim with malice and revenge, and renderest us capable of acts of unknown horror! May I never be visited by thee in the fulness of thy power!"

Having satisfied my curiosity with respect to this paper, I took care to dispose of it in such a manner as that it should be found by Mr. Falkland; at the same time that, in obedience to the principle which at present governed me with absolute dominion, I was willing that the way in which it offered itself to his attention should suggest to him the idea that it had possibly passed through my hands. The next morning I saw him, and I exerted myself to lead the conversation, which by this time I well knew how to introduce, by insensible degrees to the point I desired. After several previous questions, remarks, and rejoinders, I continued: —

"Well, sir, after all, I cannot help feeling very uncomfortably as to my ideas of human nature, when I find that there is no dependence to be placed upon its perseverance, and that, at least among the illiterate, the most promising appearances may end in the foulest disgrace."

"You think, then, that literature and a cultivated mind are the only assurance for the constancy of our principles!"

"Humph! — why do you suppose, sir, that learning and ingenuity do not often serve people rather to hide their crimes than to restrain them from committing them? History tells us strange things in that respect."

"Williams," said Mr. Falkland, a little disturbed, "you are extremely given to censure and severity."

"I hope not. I am sure I am most fond of looking on the other side of the picture, and considering how many men have been aspersed, and even at some time or other almost torn to pieces by their fellow-creatures, whom, when properly understood, we find worthy of our reverence and love."

"Indeed," replied Mr. Falkland, with a sigh, "when I consider these things I do not wonder at the dying exclamation of

Brutus, 'O Virtue, I sought thee as a substance, but I find thee an empty name!'[1] I am too much inclined to be of his opinion."

"Why, to be sure, sir, innocence and guilt are too much confounded in human life. I remember an affecting story of a poor man in the reign of Queen Elizabeth, who would have infallibly been hanged for murder upon the strength of circumstantial evidence, if the person really concerned had not been himself upon the jury and prevented it."

In saying this I touched the spring that wakened madness in his mind. He came up to me with a ferocious countenance, as if determined to force me into a confession of my thoughts. A sudden pang however seemed to change his design! he drew back with trepidation, and exclaimed, "Detested be the universe, and the laws that govern it! Honour, justice, virtue are all the juggle of knaves! If it were in my power I would instantly crush the whole system into nothing!"

I replied; "Oh, sir! things are not so bad as you imagine. The world was made for men of sense to do what they will with. Its affairs cannot be better than in the direction of the genuine heroes; and as in the end they will be found the truest friends of the whole, so the multitude have nothing to do but to look on, be fashioned, and admire."

Mr. Falkland made a powerful effort to recover his tranquillity. "Williams," said he, "you instruct me well. You have a right notion of things, and I have great hopes of you. I will be more of a man; I will forget the past, and do better for the time to come. The future, the future is always our own."

"I am sorry, sir, that I have given you pain. I am afraid to say all that I think. But it is my opinion that mistakes will ultimately be cleared up, justice done, and the true state of things come to light, in spite of the false colours that may for a time obscure it."

---

1   The classical historian, Cassius Dio, describes Brutus at his death quoting this line from an otherwise unknown tragedy about Heracles (47.49.1-2). "O wretch Valour, thou wert but a name/And yet I worshipped thee as real indeed/But now, it seems, thou wert but Fortune's slave" (Loeb Library translation).

The idea I suggested did not give Mr. Falkland the proper degree of delight. He suffered a temporary relapse. "Justice!" – he muttered. "I do not know what is justice. My case is not within the reach of common remedies; perhaps of none. I only know that I am miserable. I began life with the best intentions and the most fervid philanthropy; and here I am – miserable – miserable beyond expression or endurance."

Having said this, he seemed suddenly to recollect himself, and re-assumed his accustomed dignity and command. "How came this conversation?" cried he. "Who gave you a right to be my confidant? Base, artful wretch that you are! learn to be more respectful! Are my passions to be wound and unwound by an insolent domestic? Do you think I will be an instrument to be played on at your pleasure, till you have extorted all the treasures of my soul? Begone, and fear lest you be made to pay for the temerity you have already committed!"

There was an energy and determination in the gestures with which these words were accompanied, that did not admit of their being disputed. My mouth was closed; I felt as if deprived of all share of activity, and was only able silently and passively to quit the apartment.

CHAPTER III

Two days subsequent to this conversation, Mr. Falkland ordered me to be called to him. [I shall continue to speak in my narrative of the silent, as well as the articulate part of the intercourse between us. His countenance was habitually animated and expressive, much beyond that of any other man I have seen. The curiosity which, as I have said, constituted my ruling passion, stimulated me to make it my perpetual study. It will also most probably happen, while I am thus employed in collecting the scattered incidents of my history, that I shall upon some occasions annex to appearances an explanation which I was far from possessing at the time, and was only suggested to me through the medium of subsequent events.]

When I entered the apartment, I remarked in Mr. Falkland's countenance an unwonted composure. This composure however did not seem to result from internal ease, but from an effort which, while he prepared himself for an interesting scene, was exerted to prevent his presence of mind, and power of voluntary action, from suffering any diminution.

"Williams," said he, "I am determined, whatever it may cost me, to have an explanation with you. You are a rash and inconsiderate boy, and have given me much disturbance. You ought to have known that, though I allow you to talk with me upon indifferent subjects, it is very improper in you to lead the conversation to any thing that relates to my personal concerns. You have said many things lately in a very mysterious way, and appear to know something more than I am aware of. I am equally at a loss to guess how you came by your knowledge, as of what it consists. But I think I perceive too much inclination on your part to trifle with my peace of mind. That ought not to be, nor have I deserved any such treatment from you. But, be that as it will, the guesses in which you oblige me to employ myself are too painful. It is a sort of sporting with my feelings, which, as a man of resolution, I am determined to bring to an end. I expect you therefore to lay aside all mystery and equivocation, and inform me explicitly what it is upon which your allusions are built. What is it you know? What is it you want? I have been too much exposed already to unparalleled mortification and hardship, and my wounds will not bear this perpetual tampering."

"I feel, sir," answered I, "how wrong I have been, and am ashamed that such a one as I should have given you all this trouble and displeasure. I felt it at the time; but I have been hurried along, I do not know how. I have always tried to stop myself, but the demon that possessed me was too strong for me. I know nothing, sir, but what Mr. Collins told me. He told me the story of Mr. Tyrrel and Miss Melville and Hawkins. I am sure, sir, he said nothing but what was to your honour, and proved you to be more an angel than a man."

"Well, sir: I found a letter written by that Hawkins the other day; did not that letter fall into your hands? Did not you read it?"

"For God's sake, sir, turn me out of your house. Punish me in some way or other, that I may forgive myself. I am a foolish, wicked, despicable wretch. I confess, sir, I did read the letter."

"And how dared you read it? It was indeed very wrong of you. But we will talk of that by and by. Well, and what did you say to the letter? You know, it seems, that Hawkins was hanged."

"I say, sir? why it went to my heart to read it. I say, as I said the day before yesterday, that when I see a man of so much principle afterwards deliberately proceeding to the very worst of crimes, I can scarcely bear to think of it."

"That is what you say? It seems too you know – accursed remembrance! – that I was accused of this crime?"

I was silent.

"Well, sir. You know too, perhaps, that from the hour the crime was committed – yes, sir, that was the date [and as he said this, there was somewhat frightful, I had almost said diabolical, in his countenance] – I have not had an hour's peace; I became changed from the happiest to the most miserable thing that lives; sleep has fled from my eyes; joy has been a stranger to my thoughts; and annihilation I should prefer a thousand times to the being that I am. As soon as I was capable of a choice, I chose honour and the esteem of mankind as a good I preferred to all others. You know, it seems, in how many ways my ambition has been disappointed, – I do not thank Collins for having been the historian of my disgrace, – would to God that night could be blotted from the memory of man! – But the scene of that night, instead of perishing, has been a source of ever new calamity to me, which must flow for ever! Am I then, thus miserable and ruined, a proper subject upon which for you to exercise your ingenuity, and improve your power of tormenting? Was it not enough that I was publicly dishonoured? that I was deprived, by the pestilential influence of some demon, of the opportunity of avenging my dishonour? No: in addition to this, I have been charged with having in this critical moment intercepted my own vengeance by the foulest of crimes. That trial is past. Misery itself has nothing worse in store for me, except what you have inflicted: the seeming to doubt of my innocence, which, after the fullest and most solemn examination has been completely established. You have forced me to this explanation. You have extorted from me a confidence which I had no inclination to make. But it is a part of the misery of my situation, that I am at the mercy of every creature, however little, who feels himself inclined to sport with my distress. Be content. You have brought me low enough."

"Oh, sir, I am not content; I cannot be content! I cannot bear to think what I have done. I shall never again be able to look in the face of the best of masters and the best of men. I beg of you, sir, to turn me out of your service. Let me go and hide myself where I may never see you more."

Mr. Falkland's countenance had indicated great severity through the whole of this conversation; but now it became more harsh and tempestuous than ever. "How now, rascal!" cried he. "You want to leave me, do you? Who told you that I wished to part with you? But you cannot bear to live with such a miserable wretch as I am! You are not disposed to put up with the caprices of a man so dissatisfied and unjust!"

"Oh, sir! do not talk to me thus! Do with me any thing you will. Kill me if you please."

"Kill you!" [Volumes could not describe the emotions with which this echo of my words was given and received.]

"Sir, I could die to serve you! I love you more than I can express. I worship you as a being of a superior nature. I am foolish, raw, inexperienced, – worse than any of these; – but never did a thought of disloyalty to your service enter into my heart."

Here our conversation ended; and the impression it made upon my youthful mind it is impossible to describe. I thought with astonishment, even with rapture, of the attention and kindness towards me I discovered in Mr. Falkland, through all the roughness of his manner. I could never enough wonder at finding myself, humble as I was by my birth, obscure as I had hitherto been, thus suddenly become of so much importance to the happiness of one of the most enlightened and accomplished men in England. But this consciousness attached me to my patron more eagerly than ever, and made me swear a thousand times, as I meditated upon my situation, that I would never prove unworthy of so generous a protector.

CHAPTER IV

Is it not unaccountable that, in the midst of all my increased veneration for my patron, the first tumult of my emotion was scarcely subsided, before the old question that had excited my conjectures recurred to my mind, Was he the murderer? It was a kind of fatal impulse, that seemed destined to hurry me to my destruction. I did not wonder at the disturbance that was given to Mr. Falkland by any allusion, however distant, to this fatal affair. That was as completely accounted for from the consideration of his excessive sensibility in matters of honour, as it would have been upon the supposition of the most atrocious guilt. Knowing, as he did, that such a charge had once been connected with his name, he would of course be perpetually uneasy, and suspect some latent insinuation at every possible opportunity. He would doubt and fear, lest every man with whom he conversed harboured the foulest suspicion against him. In my case he found that I was in possession of some information, more than he was aware of, without its being possible for him to decide to what it amounted, whether I had heard a just or unjust, a candid or calumniatory tale. He had also reason to suppose that I gave entertainment to thoughts derogatory to his honour, and that I did not form that favourable judgment, which the exquisite refinement of his ruling passion made indispensable to his peace. All these considerations would of course maintain in him a state of perpetual uneasiness. But, though I could find nothing that I could consider as justifying me in persisting in the shadow of a doubt, yet, as I have said, the uncertainty and restlessness of my contemplations would by no means depart from me.

The fluctuating state of my mind produced a contention of opposite principles, that by turns usurped dominion over my conduct. Sometimes I was influenced by the most complete veneration for my master; I placed an unreserved confidence in his integrity and his virtue, and implicitly surrendered my understanding for him to set it to what point he pleased. At other times the confidence, which had before flowed with the most plenteous tide, began to ebb; I was, as I had already been, watchful, inquisitive, suspicious, full of a thousand conjectures as to the meaning of the most indifferent actions. Mr. Falkland, who was most painfully alive to every thing that related to his honour, saw these variations, and betrayed his consciousness of them now in one manner, and now in another, frequently before I was myself aware, sometimes almost before they existed. The situation of both was distressing; we were each of us a plague to the other; and I often wondered, that the forbearance and benignity of my master was not at length exhausted, and that he did not determine to thrust from him for ever so incessant an observer. There was indeed one eminent difference between his share in the transaction and mine. I had some consolation in the midst of my restlessness. Curiosity is a principle that carries its pleasures, as well as its pains, along with it. The mind is urged by a perpetual stimulus; it seems as if it were continually approaching to the end of its race; and as the insatiable desire of satisfaction is its principle of conduct, so it promises itself in that satisfaction an unknown gratification, which seems as if it were capable of fully compensating any injuries that may be suffered in the career. But to Mr. Falkland there was no consolation. What he endured in the intercourse between us appeared to be gratuitous evil. He had only to wish that there was no such person as myself in the world, and to curse the hour when his humanity led him to rescue me from my obscurity, and place me in his service.

A consequence produced upon me by the extraordinary nature of my situation it is necessary to mention. The constant state of vigilance and suspicion in which my mind was retained, worked a very rapid change in my character. It seemed to have all the effect that might have been expected from years of observation and experience. The strictness with which I endeavoured to remark what passed in the mind of one man, and the variety of conjectures into which I was led, appeared, as it were, to render me a competent adept in the different modes in which the human intellect displays its secret workings. I no longer said to myself, as I had done in the beginning, "I will ask Mr. Falkland whether he were the murderer." On the contrary, after having carefully examined the

different kinds of evidence of which the subject was susceptible, and recollecting all that had already passed upon the subject, it was not without considerable pain, that I felt myself
unable to discover any way in which I could be perfectly and
unalterably satisfied of my patron's innocence. As to his guilt, I
could scarcely bring myself to doubt that in some way or other,
sooner or later, I should arrive at the knowledge of that, if it
really existed. But I could not endure to think, almost for a
moment, of that side of the alternative as true; and with all my
ungovernable suspicion arising from the mysteriousness of the
circumstances, and all the delight which a young and unfledged
mind receives from ideas that give scope to all that imagination
can picture of terrible or sublime, I could not yet bring myself
to consider Mr. Falkland's guilt as a supposition attended with
the remotest probability.

I hope the reader will forgive me for dwelling thus long on
preliminary circumstances. I shall come soon enough to the
story of my own misery. I have already said, that one of the
motives which induced me to the penning of this narrative, was
to console myself in my insupportable distress. I derive a
melancholy pleasure from dwelling upon the circumstances
which imperceptibly paved the way to my ruin. While I recollect or describe past scenes, which occurred in a more
favourable period of my life, my attention is called off for a
short interval, from the hopeless misfortune in which I am at
present involved. The man must indeed possess an uncommon
portion of hardness of heart, who can envy me so slight a relief.
– To proceed.

For some time after the explanation which had thus taken
place between me and Mr. Falkland, his melancholy, instead of
being in the slightest degree diminished by the lenient hand of
time, went on perpetually to increase. His fits of insanity – for
such I must denominate them for want of a distinct appellation,
though it is possible they might not fall under the definition
that either the faculty or the court of chancery appropriate to
the term – became stronger and more durable than ever. It was
no longer practicable wholly to conceal them from the family,
and even from the neighbourhood. He would sometimes,

without any previous notice, absent himself from his house for two or three days, unaccompanied by servant or attendant. This was the more extraordinary, as it was well known that he paid no visits, nor kept up any sort of intercourse with the gentlemen of the vicinity. But it was impossible that a man of Mr. Falkland's distinction and fortune should long continue in such a practice, without its being discovered what was become of him; though a considerable part of our county was among the wildest and most desolate districts that are to be found in South Britain. Mr. Falkland was sometimes seen climbing among the rocks, reclining motionless for hours together upon the edge of a precipice, or lulled into a kind of nameless lethargy of despair by the dashing of the torrents. He would remain for whole nights together under the naked cope of heaven, inattentive to the consideration either of place or time; insensible to the variations of the weather, or rather seeming to be delighted with that uproar of the elements, which partially called off his attention from the discord and dejection that occupied his own mind.

At first, when we received intelligence at any time of the place to which Mr. Falkland had withdrawn himself, some person of his household, Mr. Collins or myself, but most generally myself, as I was always at home, and always, in the received sense of the word, at leisure, went to him to persuade him to return. But, after a few experiments, we thought it advisable to desist, and leave him to prolong his absence, or to terminate it, as might happen to suit his own inclination. Mr. Collins, whose grey hairs and long services seemed to give him a sort of right to be importunate, sometimes succeeded; though even in that case there was nothing that could sit more uneasily upon Mr. Falkland than this insinuation as if he wanted a guardian to take care of him, or as if he were in, or in danger of falling into, a state in which he would be incapable of deliberately controlling his own words and actions. At one time he would suddenly yield to his humble, venerable friend, murmuring grievously at the constraint that was put upon him, but without spirit enough even to complain of it with energy. At another time, even though complying, he would suddenly burst out in a paroxysm of resentment. Upon these occasions there was something inconceivably, savagely terrible in his anger, that gave to the person against whom it was directed the most humiliating and insupportable sensations. Me he always treated, at these times, with fierceness, and drove me from him with a vehemence lofty, emphatical, and sustained, beyond any thing of which I should have thought human nature to be capable. These sallies seemed always to constitute a sort of crisis in his indisposition; and, whenever he was induced to such a premature return, he would fall immediately after into a state of the most melancholy inactivity, in which he usually continued for two or three days. It was by an obstinate fatality that, whenever I saw Mr. Falkland in these deplorable situations, and particularly when I lighted upon him after having sought him among the rocks and precipices, pale, emaciated, solitary, and haggard, the suggestion would continually recur to me, in spite of inclination, in spite of persuasion, and in spite of evidence, Surely this man is a murderer!

CHAPTER V

IT was in one of the lucid intervals, as I may term them, that occurred during this period, that a peasant was brought before him, in his character of a justice of peace, upon an accusation of having murdered his fellow. As Mr. Falkland had by this time acquired the repute of a melancholy valetudinarian, it is probable he would not have been called upon to act in his official character upon the present occasion, had it not been that two or three of the neighbouring justices were all of them from home at once, so that he was the only one to be found in a circuit of many miles. The reader however must not imagine, though I have employed the word insanity in describing Mr. Falkland's symptoms, that he was by any means reckoned for a madman by the generality of those who had occasion to observe him.

It is true that his behaviour, at certain times, was singular and unaccountable; but then, at other times, there was in it so much dignity, regularity, and economy; he knew so well how to command and make himself respected; his actions and carriage were so condescending, considerate and benevolent, that, far from having forfeited the esteem of the unfortunate or the many, they were loud and earnest in his praises.

I was present at the examination of this peasant. The moment I heard of the errand which had brought this rabble of visitors, a sudden thought struck me. I conceived the possibility of rendering the incident subordinate to the great enquiry which drank up all the currents of my soul. I said, this man is arraigned of murder, and murder is the master-key that wakes distemper in the mind of Mr. Falkland. I will watch him without remission. I will trace all the mazes of his thought. Surely at such a time his secret anguish must betray itself. Surely, if it be not my own fault, I shall now be able to discover the state of his plea before the tribunal of unerring justice.

I took my station in a manner most favourable to the object upon which my mind was intent. I could perceive in Mr. Falkland's features, as he entered, a strong reluctance to the business in which he was engaged; but there was no possibility of retreating. His countenance was embarrassed and anxious; he scarcely saw any body. The examination had not proceeded far before he chanced to turn his eye to the part of the room where I was. It happened in this as in some preceding instances – we exchanged a silent look, by which we told volumes to each other. Mr. Falkland's complexion turned from red to pale, and from pale to red. I perfectly understood his feelings, and would willingly have withdrawn myself. But it was impossible; my passions were too deeply engaged; I was rooted to the spot; though my own life, that of my master, or almost of a whole nation had been at stake, I had no power to change my position.

The first surprise however having subsided, Mr. Falkland assumed a look of determined constancy, and even seemed to increase in self-possession much beyond what could have been expected from his first entrance. This he could probably have maintained, had it not been that the scene, instead of being permanent, was in some sort perpetually changing. The man who was brought before him was vehemently accused by the brother of the deceased as having acted from the most rooted malice. He swore that there had been an old grudge between the parties, and related several instances of it. He affirmed that the murderer had sought the earliest opportunity of wreaking his revenge; had struck the first blow; and, though the contest was in appearance only a common boxing match, had watched the occasion of giving a fatal stroke, which was followed by the instant death of his antagonist.

While the accuser was giving in his evidence, the accused discovered every token of the most poignant sensibility. At one time his features were convulsed with anguish; tears unbidden trickled down his manly cheeks; and at another he started with apparent astonishment at the unfavourable turn that was given to the narrative, though without betraying any impatience to interrupt. I never saw a man less ferocious in his appearance. He was tall, well made, and comely. His countenance was ingenuous and benevolent, without folly. By his side stood a young woman, his sweetheart, extremely agreeable in her person, and her looks testifying how deeply she interested herself in the fate of her lover. The accidental spectators were divided, between indignation against the enormity of the supposed criminal, and compassion for the poor girl that accompanied him. They seemed to take little notice of the favourable appearances visible in the person of the accused, till, in the sequel, those appearances were more forcibly suggested to their attention. For Mr. Falkland, he was at one moment engrossed by curiosity and earnestness to investigate the tale, while at another he betrayed a sort of revulsion of sentiment, which made the investigation too painful for him to support.

When the accused was called upon for his defence, he readily owned the misunderstanding that had existed, and that the deceased was the worst enemy he had in the world. Indeed he was his only enemy, and he could not tell the reason that had made him so. He had employed every effort to overcome his animosity, but in vain. The deceased had upon all occasions sought to mortify him, and do him an ill turn; but he had resolved never to be engaged in a broil with him, and till this day he had succeeded. If he had met with a misfortune with any other man, people at least might have thought it accident; but now it would always be believed that he had acted from secret malice and a bad heart.

The fact was, that he and his sweetheart had gone to a neighbouring fair, where this man had met them. The man had often tried to affront him; and his passiveness, interpreted into cowardice, had perhaps encouraged the other to additional rudeness. Finding that he had endured trivial insults to himself with an even temper, the deceased now thought proper to turn his brutality upon the young woman that accompanied him. He pursued them; he endeavoured in various manners to harass and vex them; they had sought in vain to shake him off. The young woman was considerably terrified. The accused expostulated with their persecutor, and asked him how he could be so barbarous as to persist in frightening a woman? He replied with an insulting tone, "Then the woman should find some one able to protect her; people that encouraged and trusted to such a thief as that, deserved no better!" The accused tried every expedient he could invent; at length he could endure it no longer; he became exasperated, and challenged the assailant. The challenge was accepted; a ring was formed; he confided the care of his sweetheart to a bystander; and unfortunately the first blow he struck proved fatal.

The accused added, that he did not care what became of him. He had been anxious to go through the world in an inoffensive manner, and now he had the guilt of blood upon him. He did not know but it would be kindness in them to hang him out of the way; for his conscience would reproach him as long as he lived, and the figure of the deceased, as he had lain senseless and without motion at his feet, would perpetually haunt him. The thought of this man, at one moment full of life and vigour, and the next lifted a helpless corpse from the ground, and all owing to him, was a thought too dreadful to be endured. He had loved the poor maiden, who had been the innocent occasion of this, with all his heart; but from this time he should never support the sight of her. The sight would bring a tribe of fiends in its rear. One unlucky minute had poisoned all his hopes, and made life a burden to him. Saying this, his countenance fell, the muscles of his face trembled with agony, and he looked the statue of despair.

This was the story of which Mr. Falkland was called upon to be the auditor. Though the incidents were, for the most part, wide of those which belonged to the adventures of the preceding volume, and there had been much less policy and skill displayed on either part in this rustic encounter, yet there were many points which, to a man who bore the former strongly in his recollection, suggested a sufficient resemblance. In each case it was a human brute persisting in a course of hostility to a man of benevolent character, and suddenly and terribly cut off in the midst of his career. These points perpetually smote upon the heart of Mr. Falkland. He at one time started with astonishment, and at another shifted his posture, like a man who is unable longer to endure the sensations that press upon him. Then he new strung his nerves to stubborn patience. I could see, while his muscles preserved an inflexible steadiness, tears of anguish roll down his cheeks. He dared not trust his eyes to glance towards the side of the room where I stood; and this gave an air of embarrassment to his whole figure. But when the accused came to speak of his feelings, to describe the depth of his compunction for an involuntary fault, he could endure it no longer. He suddenly rose, and with every mark of horror and despair rushed out of the room.

This circumstance made no material difference in the affair of the accused. The parties were detained about half an hour. Mr. Falkland had already heard the material parts of the evidence in person. At the expiration of that interval, he sent for Mr. Collins out of the room. The story of the culprit was confirmed by many witnesses who had seen the transaction. Word was brought that my master was indisposed; and, at the same time, the accused was ordered to be discharged. The vengeance of the brother however, as I afterwards found, did not rest here, and he met with a magistrate, more scrupulous or more despotic, by whom the culprit was committed for trial.

This affair was no sooner concluded, than I hastened into the garden, and plunged into the deepest of its thickets. My mind was full, almost to bursting. I no sooner conceived myself sufficiently removed from all observation, than my thoughts forced their way spontaneously to my tongue, and I exclaimed, in a fit of uncontrollable enthusiasm, "This is the murderer; the Hawkinses were innocent! I am sure of it! I will pledge my life for it! It is out! It is discovered! Guilty, upon my soul!"

While I thus proceeded with hasty steps along the most secret paths of the garden, and from time to time gave vent to the tumult of my thoughts in involuntary exclamations, I felt as if my animal system had undergone a total revolution. My blood boiled within me. I was conscious to a kind of rapture for which I could not account. I was solemn, yet full of rapid emotion, burning with indignation and energy. In the very tempest and hurricane of the passions, I seemed to enjoy the most soul-ravishing calm. I cannot better express the then state of my mind than by saying, I was never so perfectly alive as at that moment.

This state of mental elevation continued for several hours, but at length subsided, and gave place to more deliberate reflection. One of the first questions that then occurred was, What shall I do with the knowledge I have been so eager to acquire? I had no inclination to turn informer. I felt what I had had no previous conception of, that it was possible to love a murderer, and, as I then understood it, the worst of murderers. I conceived it to be in the highest degree absurd and iniquitous, to cut off a man qualified for the most essential and extensive utility, merely out of retrospect to an act which, whatever were its merits, could not be retrieved.

This thought led me to another, which had at first passed unnoticed. If I had been disposed to turn informer, what had occurred amounted to no evidence that was admissible in a court of justice. Well then, added I, if it be such as would not be admitted at a criminal tribunal, am I sure it is such as I ought to admit? There were twenty persons besides myself present at the scene from which I pretend to derive such entire conviction. Not one of them saw it in the light that I did. It either appeared to them a casual and unimportant circumstance, or they thought it sufficiently accounted for by Mr. Falkland's infirmity and misfortunes. Did it really contain such an extent of arguments and application, that nobody but I was discerning enough to see?

But all this reasoning produced no alteration in my way of thinking. For this time I could not get it out of my mind for a moment: "Mr. Falkland is the murderer! He is guilty! I see it! I feel it! I am sure of it!" Thus was I hurried along by an uncontrollable destiny. The state of my passions in their progressive career, the inquisitiveness and impatience of my thoughts, appeared to make this determination unavoidable.

An incident occurred while I was in the garden, that seemed to make no impression upon me at the time, but which I recollected when my thoughts were got into somewhat of a slower motion. In the midst of one of my paroxysms of exclamation, and when I thought myself most alone, the shadow of a man as avoiding me passed transiently by me at a small distance. Though I had scarcely caught a faint glimpse of his person, there was something in the occurrence that persuaded me it was Mr. Falkland. I shuddered at the possibility of his having overheard the words of my soliloquy. But this idea, alarming as it was, had not power immediately to suspend the career of my reflections. Subsequent circumstances however brought back the apprehension to my mind. I had scarcely a doubt of its reality, when dinner-time came, and Mr. Falkland was not to be found. Supper and bed-time passed in the same manner. The only conclusion made by his servants upon this circumstance was, that he was gone upon one of his accustomed melancholy rambles.

CHAPTER VI

THE period at which my story is now arrived seemed as if it were the very crisis of the fortune of Mr. Falkland. Incident followed upon incident, in a kind of breathless succession. About nine o'clock the next morning an alarm was given, that one of the chimneys of the house was on fire. No accident could be apparently more trivial; but presently it blazed with such fury as to make it clear that some beam of the house, which in the first building had been improperly placed, had been reached by the flames. Some danger was apprehended for the whole edifice. The confusion was the greater, in consequence of the absence of the master, as well as of Mr. Collins, the steward. While some of the domestics were employed in endeavouring to extinguish the flames, it was thought proper that others should busy themselves in removing the most valuable moveables to a lawn in the garden. I took some command in the affair, to which indeed my station in the family seemed to entitle me, and for which I was judged qualified by my understanding and mental resources.

Having given some general directions, I conceived, that it was not enough to stand by and superintend, but that I should contribute my personal labour in the public concern. I set out for that purpose; and my steps, by some mysterious fatality, were directed to the private apartment at the end of the library. Here, as I looked round, my eye was suddenly caught by the trunk mentioned in the first pages of my narrative.

My mind was already raised to its utmost pitch. In a window-seat of the room lay a number of chisels and other carpenter's tools. I know not what infatuation instantaneously seized me. The idea was too powerful to be resisted. I forgot the business upon which I came, the employment of the servants, and the urgency of general danger. I should have done the same if the flames that seemed to extend as they proceeded, and already surmounted the house, had reached this very apartment. I snatched a tool suitable for the purpose, threw myself upon the ground, and applied with eagerness to a magazine which inclosed all for which my heart panted. After two or three efforts, in which the energy of uncontrollable passion was added to my bodily strength, the fastenings gave way, the trunk opened, and all that I sought was at once within my reach.

I was in the act of lifting up the lid, when Mr. Falkland entered, wild, breathless, distracted in his looks! He had been brought home from a considerable distance by the sight of the flames. At the moment of his appearance the lid dropped down from my hand. He no sooner saw me than his eyes emitted sparks of rage. He ran with eagerness to a brace of loaded pistols which hung in the room, and, seizing one, presented it to my head. I saw his design, and sprang to avoid it; but, with the same rapidity with which he had formed his resolution, he changed it, and instantly went to the window, and flung the pistol into the court below. He bade me begone with his usual irresistible energy; and, overcome as I was already by the horror of the detection, I eagerly complied.

A moment after, a considerable part of the chimney tumbled with noise into the court below, and a voice exclaimed that the fire was more violent than ever. These circumstances seemed to produce a mechanical effect upon my patron, who, having first locked the closet, appeared on the outside of the house, ascended the roof, and was in a moment in every place where his presence was required. The flames were at length extinguished.

The reader can with difficulty form a conception of the state to which I was now reduced. My act was in some sort an act of insanity; but how undescribable are the feelings with which I looked back upon it! It was an instantaneous impulse, a short-lived and passing alienation of mind; but what must Mr. Falkland think of that alienation? To any man a person who had once shown himself capable of so wild a flight of the mind, must appear dangerous: how must he appear to a man under Mr. Falkland's circumstances? I had just had a pistol held to my head, by a man resolved to put a period to my existence. That indeed was past; but what was it that fate had yet in reserve for me! The insatiable vengeance of a Falkland, of a man whose hands were, to my apprehension, red with blood, and his thoughts familiar with cruelty and murder. How great were the resources of his mind, resources henceforth to be confederated for my destruction! This was the termination of an ungoverned curiosity, an impulse that I had represented to myself as so innocent or so venial.

In the high tide of boiling passion I had overlooked all consequences. It now appeared to me like a dream. Is it in man to leap from the high-raised precipice, or rush unconcerned into the midst of flames? Was it possible I could have forgotten for a moment the awe-creating manners of Falkland, and the inexorable fury I should awake in his soul? No thought of future security had reached my mind. I had acted upon no plan. I had conceived no means of concealing my deed, after it had once been effected. But it was over now. One short minute had effected a reverse in my situation, the suddenness of which the history of man, perhaps is unable to surpass.

I have always been at a loss to account for my having plunged thus headlong into an act so monstrous. There is something in it of unexplained and involuntary sympathy. One sentiment flows, by necessity of nature, into another sentiment of the same general character. This was the first instance in which I had witnessed a danger by fire. All was confusion around me, and all changed into hurricane within. The general situation, to my unpractised apprehension, appeared desperate, and I by contagion became alike desperate. At first I had been in some degree calm and collected, but that too was a desperate effort; and when it gave way, a kind of instant insanity became its successor.

I had now every thing to fear. And yet what was my fault? It proceeded from none of those errors which are justly held up to the aversion of mankind; my object had been neither wealth, nor the means of indulgence, nor the usurpation of power. No spark of malignity had harboured in my soul. I had always reverenced the sublime mind of Mr. Falkland; I reverenced it still. My offence had merely been a mistaken thirst of knowledge. Such however it was, as to admit neither of forgiveness nor remission. This epoch was the crisis of my fate, dividing what may be called the offensive part from the defensive, which has been the sole business of my remaining years. Alas! my offence was short, not aggravated by any sinister intention: but the reprisals I was to suffer are long, and can terminate only with my life!

In the state in which I found myself, when the recollection of what I had done flowed back upon my mind, I was incapable of any resolution. All was chaos and uncertainty within me. My thoughts were too full of horror to be susceptible of activity. I felt deserted of my intellectual powers, palsied in mind, and compelled to sit in speechless expectation of the misery to which I was destined. To my own conception I was like a man, who, though blasted with lightning, and deprived for ever of the power of motion, should yet retain the consciousness of his situation. Death-dealing despair was the only idea of which I was sensible.

I was still in this situation of mind when Mr. Falkland sent for me. His message roused me from my trance. In recovering, I felt those sickening and loathsome sensations, which a man may be supposed at first to endure who should return from the sleep of death. Gradually I recovered the power of arranging my ideas and directing my steps. I understood, that the minute the affair of the fire was over Mr. Falkland had retired to his own room. It was evening before he ordered me to be called.

I found in him every token of extreme distress, except that there was an air of solemn and sad composure that crowned the whole. For the present, all appearance of gloom, stateliness, and austerity was gone. As I entered he looked up, and seeing, who it was, ordered me to bolt the door. I obeyed. He went round the room, and examined its other avenues. He then returned to where I stood. I trembled in every joint of my frame. I exclaimed within myself, "What scene of death has Roscius now to act?"[1]

"Williams!" said he, in a tone which had more in it of sorrow than resentment, "I have attempted your life! I am a wretch devoted to the scorn and execration of mankind!" There he stopped.

"If there be one being on the whole earth that feels the

---

1   Shakespeare, 3 *Henry VI*, V.vi.10. Quintus Roscius (d. 62 BC) was the most celebrated Roman comic actor of his age.

scorn and execration due to such a wretch more strongly than another, it is myself. I have been kept in a state of perpetual torture and madness. But I can put an end to it and its consequences; and, so far at least as relates to you, I am determined to do it. I know the price, and – I will make the purchase.

"You must swear," said he. "You must attest every sacrament, divine and human, never to disclose what I am now to tell you." – He dictated the oath, and I repeated it with an aching heart. I had no power to offer a word of remark.

"This confidence," said he, "is of your seeking, not of mine. It is odious to me, and is dangerous to you."

Having thus prefaced the disclosure he had to make, he paused. He seemed to collect himself as for an effort of magnitude. He wiped his face with his handkerchief. The moisture that incommoded him appeared not to be tears, but sweat.

"Look at me. Observe me. Is it not strange that such a one as I should retain lineaments of a human creature? I am the blackest of villains. I am the murderer of Tyrrel. I am the assassin of the Hawkinses."

I started with terror, and was silent.

"What a story is mine! Insulted, disgraced, polluted in the face of hundreds, I was capable of any act of desperation. I watched my opportunity, followed Mr. Tyrrel from the rooms, seized a sharp-pointed knife that fell in my way, came behind him, and stabbed him to the heart. My gigantic oppressor rolled at my feet.

"All are but links of one chain. A blow! A murder! My next business was to defend myself, to tell so well-digested a lie as that all mankind should believe it true. Never was a task so harrowing and intolerable!

"Well, thus far fortune favoured me; she favoured me beyond my desire. The guilt was removed from me, and cast upon another; but this I was to endure. Whence came the circumstantial evidence against him, the broken knife and the blood, I am unable to tell. I suppose, by some miraculous accident, Hawkins was passing by, and endeavoured to assist his oppressor in the agonies of death. You have heard his story; you have read one of his letters. But you do not know the thousandth part of the proofs of his simple and unalterable rectitude that I have known. His son suffered with him; that son, for the sake of whose happiness and virtue he ruined himself, and would have died a hundred times. – I have had feelings, but I cannot describe them.

"This it is to be a gentleman! a man of honour! I was the fool of fame. My virtue, my honesty, my everlasting peace of mind, were cheap sacrifices to be made at the shrine of this divinity. But, what is worse, there is nothing that has happened that has in any degree contributed to my cure. I am as much the fool of fame as ever. I cling to it to my last breath. Though I be the blackest of villains, I will leave behind me a spotless and illustrious name. There is no crime so malignant, no scene of blood so horrible, in which that object cannot engage me. It is no matter that I regard these things at a distance with aversion; — I am sure of it; bring me to the test, and I shall yield. I despise myself, but thus I am; things are gone too far to be recalled.

"Why is it that I am compelled to this confidence? From the love of fame. I should tremble at the sight of every pistol or instrument of death that offered itself to my hands; and perhaps my next murder may not be so fortunate as those I have already committed. I had no alternative but to make you my confidant or my victim. It was better to trust you with the whole truth under every seal of secrecy, than to live in perpetual fear of your penetration or your rashness.

"Do you know what it is you have done? To gratify a foolishly inquisitive humour, you have sold yourself. You shall continue in my service, but can never share my affection. I will benefit you in respect of fortune, but I shall always hate you. If ever an unguarded word escape from your lips, if ever you excite my jealousy or suspicion, expect to pay for it by your death or worse. It is a dear bargain you have made. But it is too late to look back. I charge and adjure you by every thing that is sacred, and that is tremendous, preserve your faith!

"My tongue has now for the first time for several years spoken the language of my heart; and the intercourse from this hour shall be shut for ever. I want no pity. I desire no consolation. Surrounded as I am with horrors, I will at least preserve my fortitude to the last. If I had been reserved to a different destiny, I have qualities in that respect worthy of a better cause. I can be mad, miserable, and frantic; but even in frenzy I can preserve my presence of mind and discretion."

Such was the story I had been so desirous to know. Though my mind had brooded upon the subject for months, there was not a syllable of it that did not come to my ear with the most perfect sense of novelty. "Mr. Falkland is a murderer!" said I, as I retired from the conference. This dreadful appellative, "a murderer," made my very blood run cold within me. "He killed Mr. Tyrrel, for he could not control his resentment and anger: he sacrificed Hawkins the elder and Hawkins the younger, because he could upon no terms endure the public loss of honour: how can I expect that a man thus passionate and unrelenting will not sooner or later make me his victim?"

But, notwithstanding this terrible application of the story, an application to which perhaps in some form or other, mankind are indebted for nine tenths of their abhorrence against vice, I could not help occasionally recurring to reflections of an opposite nature. "Mr. Falkland is a murderer!" resumed I. "He might yet be a most excellent man, if he did but think so." It is the thinking ourselves vicious then, that principally contributes to make us vicious.

Amidst the shock I received from finding, what I had never suffered myself constantly to believe, that my suspicions were true, I still discovered new cause of admiration for my master. His menaces indeed were terrible. But, when I recollected the offence I had given, so contrary to every received principle of civilized society, so insolent and rude, so intolerable to a man of Mr. Falkland's elevation, and in Mr. Falkland's peculiarity of circumstances, I was astonished at his forbearance. There were indeed sufficiently obvious reasons why he might not choose to proceed to extremities with me. But how different from the fearful expectations I had conceived were the calmness of his behaviour, and the regulated mildness of his language! In this respect, I for a short time imagined that I was emancipated from the mischiefs which had appalled me; and that, in having to do with a man of Mr. Falkland's liberality, I had nothing rigorous to apprehend.

"It is a miserable prospect," said I, "that he holds up to me. He imagines that I am restrained by no principles, and deaf to the claims of personal excellence. But he shall find himself mistaken. I will never become an informer. I will never injure my patron; and therefore he will not be my enemy. With all his misfortunes and all his errors, I feel that my soul yearns for his welfare. If he have been criminal, that is owing to circumstances; the same qualities under other circumstances would have been, or rather were, sublimely beneficent."

My reasonings were, no doubt, infinitely more favourable to Mr. Falkland, than those which human beings are accustomed to make in the case of such as they style great criminals. This will not be wondered at, when it is considered that I had myself just been trampling on the established boundaries of obligation, and therefore might well have a fellow-feeling for other offenders. Add to which, I had known Mr. Falkland from the first as a beneficent divinity. I had observed at leisure, and with a minuteness which could not deceive me, the excellent qualities of his heart; and I found him possessed of a mind beyond comparison the most fertile and accomplished I had ever known. But though the terrors which had impressed me were considerably alleviated, my situation was notwithstanding sufficiently miserable. The ease and light-heartedness of my youth were for ever gone. The voice of an irresistible necessity had commanded me to "sleep no more."[1] I was tormented with a secret, of which I must never disburthen myself; and this consciousness was, at my age, a source of perpetual melancholy. I had made myself a prisoner, in the most intolerable sense of that term, for years – perhaps for the rest of my life. Though my prudence and discretion should be invariable, I must remember that I should have an overseer, vigilant from conscious guilt, full of resentment at the unjustifiable means by which I had extorted from him a confession, and whose lightest caprice might at any time decide upon every thing that was

1   Shakespeare, *Macbeth*, II.ii.35.

dear to me. The vigilance even of a public and systematical despotism is poor, compared with a vigilance which is thus goaded by the most anxious passions of the soul. Against this species of persecution I knew not how to invent a refuge. I dared neither fly from the observation of Mr. Falkland, nor continue exposed to its operation. I was at first indeed lulled in a certain degree to security upon the verge of the precipice. But it was not long before I found a thousand circumstances perpetually reminding me of my true situation. Those I am now to relate are among the most memorable.

CHAPTER VII

In no long time after the disclosure Mr. Falkland had made, Mr. Forester, his elder brother by the mother's side, came to reside for a short period in our family. This was a circumstance peculiarly adverse to my patron's habits and inclinations. He had broken off, as I have already said, all intercourse of visiting with his neighbours. He debarred himself every kind of amusement and relaxation. He shrunk from the society of his fellows, and thought he could never be sufficiently buried in obscurity and solitude. This principle was, in most cases, of no difficult execution to a man of firmness. But Mr. Falkland knew not how to avoid the visit of Mr. Forester. This gentleman was just returned from a residence of several years upon the continent; and his demand of an apartment in the house of his half-brother till his own house at the distance of thirty miles should be prepared for his reception, was made with an air of confidence that scarcely admitted of a refusal. Mr. Falkland could only allege, that the state of his health and spirits was such, that he feared a residence at his house would be little agreeable to his kinsman; and Mr. Forester conceived that this was a disqualification which would always augment in proportion as it was tolerated, and hoped that his society, by inducing Mr. Falkland to suspend his habits of seclusion, would be the means of essential benefit. Mr. Falkland opposed him no further. He would have been sorry to be thought unkind to a kinsman for whom he had a particular esteem; and the consciousness of not daring to assign the true reason, made him cautious of adhering to his objection.

The character of Mr. Forester was, in many respects, the reverse of that of my master. His very appearance indicated the singularity of his disposition. His figure was short and angular. His eyes were sunk far into his head, and were overhung with eye-brows, black, thick, and bushy. His complexion was swarthy, and his lineaments hard. He had seen much of the world; but, to judge of him from his appearance and manners, one would have thought that he had never moved from his fire-side.

His temper was acid, petulant, and harsh. He was easily offended by trifles, respecting which, previously to the offence, the persons with whom he had intercourse could have no suspicion of such a result. When offended, his customary behaviour was exceedingly rugged. He thought only of setting the delinquent right, and humbling him for his error; and, in his eagerness to do this, overlooked the sensibility of the sufferer, and the pains he inflicted. Remonstrance in such a case he regarded as the offspring of cowardice, which was to be extirpated with a steady and unshrinking hand, and not soothed with misjudging kindness and indulgence. As is usual in human character, he had formed a system of thinking to suit the current of his feelings. He held that the kindness we entertain for a man should be veiled and concealed, exerted in substantial benefits, but not disclosed, lest an undue advantage should be taken of it by its object.

With this rugged outside, Mr. Forester had a warm and generous heart. At first sight all men were deterred by his manner, and excited to give him an ill character. But the longer any one knew him, the more they approved him. His harshness was then only considered as habit; and strong sense and active benevolence were uppermost in the recollection of his familiar acquaintance. His conversation, when he condescended to lay aside his snappish, rude, and abrupt half-sentences, became flowing in diction, and uncommonly amusing with regard to its substance. He combined, with weightiness of expression, a dryness of characteristic humour, that demonstrated at once the vividness of his observation, and the force of his understanding.

The peculiarities of this gentleman's character were not undisplayed in the scene to which he was now introduced. Having much kindness in his disposition, he soon became deeply interested in the unhappiness of his relation. He did every thing in his power to remove it; but his attempts were rude and unskillful. With a mind so accomplished and a spirit so susceptible as that of Mr. Falkland, Mr. Forester did not venture to let loose his usual violence of manner; but, if he carefully abstained from harshness, he was however wholly incapable of that sweet and liquid eloquence of the soul, which would perhaps have stood the fairest chance of seducing Mr. Falkland for a moment to forget his anguish. He exhorted his host to rouse up his spirit, and defy the foul fiend; but the tone of his exhortations found no sympathetic chord in the mind of my patron. He had not the skill to carry conviction to an understanding so well fortified in error. In a word, after a thousand efforts of kindness to his entertainer, he drew off his forces, growling and dissatisfied with his own impotence, rather than angry at the obstinacy of Mr. Falkland. He felt no diminution of his affection for him, and was sincerely grieved to find that he was so little capable of serving him. Both parties in this case did justice to the merits of the other; at the same time that the disparity of their humours was such, as to prevent the stranger from being in any degree a dangerous companion to the master of the house. They had scarcely one point of contact in their characters. Mr. Forester was incapable of giving Mr. Falkland that degree either of pain or pleasure, which can raise the soul into a tumult, and deprive it for a while of tranquillity and self-command.

Our visitor was a man, notwithstanding appearances, of a peculiarly sociable disposition, and, where he was neither interrupted nor contradicted, considerably loquacious. He began to feel himself painfully out of his element upon the present occasion. Mr. Falkland was devoted to contemplation and solitude. He put upon himself some degree of restraint upon the arrival of his kinsman, though even then his darling habits would break out. But when they had seen each other a certain number of times, and it was sufficiently evident that the society of either would be a burthen rather than a pleasure to the other, they consented, by a sort of silent compact, that each should be at liberty to follow his own inclination. Mr. Falkland was, in a sense, the greater gainer by this. He returned to the habits of his choice, and acted as nearly as possible, just as he would have done if Mr. Forester had not been in existence. But the latter was wholly at a loss. He had all the disadvantages of retirement, without being able, as he might have done at his house, to bring his own associates or his own amusements about him.

In this situation he cast his eyes upon me. It was his principle to do every thing that his thoughts suggested, without caring for the forms of the world. He saw no reason why a peasant, with certain advantages of education and opportunity, might not be as eligible a companion as a lord; at the same time that he was deeply impressed with the venerableness of old institutions. Reduced as he was to a kind of last resort, he found me better qualified for his purpose than any other of Mr. Falkland's household.

The manner in which he began this sort of correspondence was sufficiently characteristical. It was abrupt; but it was strongly stamped with essential benevolence. It was blunt and humorous; but there was attractiveness, especially in a case of unequal intercourse, in that very rusticity by which he levelled himself with the mass of his species. He had to reconcile himself as well as to invite me; not to reconcile himself to the postponing an aristocratical vanity, for of that he had a very slender portion, but to the trouble of invitation, for he loved his ease. All this produced some irregularity and indecision in his own mind, and gave a whimsical impression to his behaviour.

On my part, I was by no means ungrateful for the distinction that was paid me. My mind had been relaxed into temporary dejection, but my reserve had no alloy of moroseness or insensibility. It did not long hold out against the condescending attentions of Mr. Forester. I became gradually heedful, encouraged, confiding. I had a most eager thirst for the knowledge of mankind; and though no person perhaps ever purchased so dearly the instructions he received in that school, the inclination was in no degree diminished. Mr. Forester was the second man I had seen uncommonly worthy of my analysis, and who seemed to my thoughts, arrived as I was at the end of my first essay, almost as much deserving to be studied as Mr. Falkland himself. I was glad to escape from the uneasiness of my reflections; and, while engaged with this new friend, I forgot the criticalness of the evils with which I was hourly menaced.

Stimulated by these feelings, I was what Mr. Forester wanted, a diligent and zealous hearer. I was strongly susceptible of impression; and the alternate impressions my mind received, visibly displayed themselves in my countenance and gestures.

The observations Mr. Forester had made in his travels, the set of opinions he had formed, all amused and interested me. His manner of telling a story, or explaining his thoughts, was forcible, perspicuous, and original: his style in conversation had an uncommon zest. Every thing he had to relate delighted me; while, in return, my sympathy, my eager curiosity, and my unsophisticated passions, rendered me to Mr. Forester a most desirable hearer. It is not to be wondered at, therefore, that every day rendered our intercourse more intimate and cordial.

Mr. Falkland was destined to be for ever unhappy; and it seemed as if no new incident could occur, from which he was not able to extract food for this imperious propensity. He was wearied with a perpetual repetition of similar impressions; and entertained an invincible disgust against all that was new. The visit of Mr. Forester he regarded with antipathy. He was scarcely able to look at him without shuddering; an emotion which his guest perceived, and pitied as the result of habit and disease, rather than of judgment. None of his actions passed unremarked; the most indifferent excited uneasiness and apprehension. The first overtures of intimacy between me and Mr. Forester probably gave birth to sentiments of jealousy in the mind of my master. The irregular, variable character of his visitor tended to heighten them, by producing an appearance of inexplicableness and mystery. At this time he intimated to me that it was not agreeable to him, that there should be much intercourse between me and this gentleman.

What could I do? Young as I was, could it be expected that I should play the philosopher, and put a perpetual curb upon my inclinations? Imprudent though I had been, could I voluntarily subject myself to an eternal penance, and estrangement from human society? Could I discourage a frankness so perfectly in consonance with my wishes, and receive in an ungracious way a kindness that stole away my heart?

Besides this, I was but ill prepared for the servile submission Mr. Falkland demanded. In early life I had been accustomed to be much my own master. When I first entered into Mr. Falkland's service, my personal habits were checked by the novelty of my situation, and my affections were gained by the high accomplishments of my patron. To novelty and its influence, curiosity had succeeded: curiosity, so long as it lasted, was a principle stronger in my bosom than even the love of independence. To that I would have sacrificed my liberty or my life; to gratify it, I would have submitted to the condition of a West Indian negro, or to the tortures inflicted by North American savages. But the turbulence of curiosity had now subsided.

As long as the threats of Mr. Falkland had been confined to generals, I endured it. I was conscious of the unbecoming action I had committed, and this rendered me humble. But, when he went further, and undertook to prescribe to every article of my conduct, my patience was at an end. My mind, before sufficiently sensible to the unfortunate situation to which my imprudence had reduced me, now took a nearer and a more alarming view of the circumstances of the case. Mr. Falkland was not an old man; he had in him the principles of vigour, however they might seem to be shaken; he might live as long as I should. I was his prisoner; and what a prisoner! All my actions observed; all my gestures marked. I could move neither to the right nor the left, but the eye of my keeper was upon me. He watched me; and his vigilance was a sickness to my heart. For me there was no more freedom, no more of hilarity, of thoughtlessness, or of youth. Was this the life upon which I had entered with such warm and sanguine expectation? Were my days to be wasted in this cheerless gloom; a galley-slave in the hands of the system of nature, whom death only, the death of myself or my inexorable superior, could free?

I had been adventurous in the gratification of an infantine and unreasonable curiosity; and I resolved not to be less adventurous, if need were, in the defence of every thing that can make life a blessing. I was prepared for an amicable adjustment of interests: I would undertake that Mr. Falkland should never sustain injury through my means; but I expected in return that I should suffer no encroachment, but be left to the direction of my own understanding.

I went on, then, to seek Mr. Forester's society with eagerness; and it is the nature of an intimacy that does not decline, progressively to increase. Mr. Falkland observed these symptoms with visible perturbation. Whenever I was conscious of their being perceived by him, I betrayed tokens of confusion: this did not tend to allay his uneasiness. One day he spoke to me alone; and, with a look of mysterious but terrible import, expressed himself thus: –

"Young man, take warning! Perhaps this is the last time you shall have an opportunity to take it! I will not always be the butt of your simplicity and inexperience, nor suffer your weakness to triumph over my strength! Why do you trifle with me? You little suspect the extent of my power. At this moment you are enclosed with the snares of my vengeance unseen by you, and, at the instant that you flatter yourself you are already beyond their reach, they will close upon you. You might as well think of escaping from the power of the omnipresent God, as from mine! If you could touch so much as my finger, you should expiate it in hours and months and years of a torment, of which as yet you have not the remotest idea. Remember! I am not talking at random! I do not utter a word, that, if you provoke me, shall not be executed to the severest letter!"

It may be supposed that these menaces were not without their effect. I withdrew in silence. My whole soul revolted against the treatment I endured, and yet I could not utter a word. Why could not I speak the expostulations of my heart, or propose the compromise I meditated? It was inexperience, and not want of strength, that awed me. Every act of Mr. Falkland contained something new, and I was unprepared to meet it. Perhaps it will be found that the greatest hero owes the propriety of his conduct to the habit of encountering difficulties, and calling out with promptness the energies of his mind.

I contemplated the proceedings of my patron with the deepest astonishment. Humanity and general kindness were fundamental parts of his character; but in relation to me they were sterile and inactive. His own interest required that he should purchase my kindness; but he preferred to govern me by terror, and watch me with unceasing anxiety. I ruminated with the most mournful sensations upon the nature of my calamity. I believed that no human being was ever placed in a situation so pitiable as mine. Every atom of my frame seemed to have a several existence, and to crawl within me. I had but too much reason to believe that Mr. Falkland's threats were not empty words. I knew his ability; I felt his ascendancy. If I encountered him, what chance had I of victory? If I were defeated, what was the penalty I had to suffer? Well then, the rest of my life must be devoted to slavish subjection. Miserable sentence! And, if it were, what security had I against the injustice of a man, vigilant, capricious, and criminal? I envied the condemned wretch upon the scaffold; I envied the victim of the inquisition in the midst of his torture. They know what they have to suffer. I had only to imagine every thing terrible, and then say, "The fate reserved for me is worse than this!"

It was well for me that these sensations were transient: human nature could not long support itself under what I then felt. By degrees my mind shook off its burthen. Indignation succeeded to emotions of terror. The hostility of Mr. Falkland excited hostility in me. I determined I would never calumniate him in matters of the most trivial import, much less betray the grand secret upon which every thing dear to him depended. But, totally abjuring the offensive, I resolved to stand firmly upon the defensive. The liberty of acting as I pleased I would preserve, whatever might be the risk. If I were worsted in the contest, I would at least have the consolation of reflecting that I had exerted myself with energy. In proportion as I thus determined, I drew off my forces from petty incursions, and felt the propriety of acting with premeditation and system. I ruminated incessantly upon plans of deliverance, but I was anxious that my choice should not be precipitately made.

It was during this period of my deliberation and uncertainty that Mr. Forester terminated his visit. He observed a strange distance in my behaviour, and, in his good-natured, rough way, reproached me for it. I could only answer with a gloomy look of mysterious import, and a mournful and expressive silence. He sought me for an explanation, but I was now as ingenious in avoiding as I had before been ardent to seek him; and he quitted our house, as he afterwards told me, with an impression, that there was some ill destiny that hung over it, which seemed fated to make all its inhabitants miserable, without its being possible for a by-stander to penetrate the reason.

CHAPTER VIII

MR. FORESTER had left us about three weeks, when Mr. Falkland sent me upon some business to an estate he possessed in a
neighbouring county, about fifty miles from his principal residence. The road led in a direction wholly wide of the habitation of our late visitor. I was upon my return from the place to
which I had been sent, when I began in fancy to take a survey
of the various circumstances of my condition, and by degrees
lost, in the profoundness of my contemplation, all attention to
the surrounding objects. The first determination of my mind
was to escape from the lynx-eyed jealousy and despotism of
Mr. Falkland; the second to provide, by every effort of prudence and deliberation I could devise, against the danger with
which I well knew my attempt must be accompanied.

Occupied with these meditations, I rode many miles before I
perceived that I had totally deviated from the right path. At
length I roused myself, and surveyed the horizon around me;
but I could observe nothing with which my organ was previously acquainted. On three sides, the heath stretched as far as
the eye could reach; on the fourth, I discovered at some distance a wood of no ordinary dimensions. Before me, scarcely a
single track could be found, to mark that any human being had
ever visited the spot. As the best expedient I could devise, I
bent my course towards the wood I have mentioned, and then
pursued, as well as I was able, the windings of the inclosure.
This led me, after some time, to the end of the heath; but I was
still as much at a loss as ever respecting the road I should pursue. The sun was hid from me by a grey and cloudy atmosphere; I was induced to continue along the skirts of the wood,
and surmounted with some difficulty the hedges and other
obstacles that from time to time presented themselves. My
thoughts were gloomy and disconsolate; the dreariness of the
day, and the solitude which surrounded me, seemed to communicate a sadness to my soul. I had proceeded a considerable way,
and was overcome with hunger and fatigue, when I discovered
a road and a little inn at no great distance. I made up to them,
and upon enquiry found that, instead of pursuing the proper
direction, I had taken one that led to Mr. Forester's rather than

to my own habitation. I alighted, and was entering the house, when the appearance of that gentleman struck my eyes.

Mr. Forester accosted me with kindness, invited me into the room where he had been sitting, and enquired what accident had brought me to that place. While he was speaking, I could not help recollecting the extraordinary manner in which we were thus once more brought together, and a train of ideas was by this means suggested to my mind. Some refreshment was, by Mr. Forester's order, prepared for me; I sat down, and partook of it. Still this thought dwelt upon my recollection: – "Mr. Falkland will never be made acquainted with our meeting; I have an opportunity thrown in my way, which if I do not improve, I shall deserve all the consequences that may result. I can now converse with a friend, and a powerful friend, without fear of being watched and overlooked." What wonder that I was tempted to disclose, not Mr. Falkland's secret, but my own situation, and receive the advice of a man of worth and experience, which might perhaps be adequately done without entering into any detail injurious to my patron?

Mr. Forester, on his part, expressed a desire to learn why it was I thought myself unhappy, and why I had avoided him during the latter part of his residence under the same roof, as evidently as I had before taken pleasure in his communications. I replied, that I could give him but an imperfect satisfaction upon these points; but what I could, I would willingly explain. The fact, I proceeded, was, that there were reasons which rendered it impossible for me to have a tranquil moment under the roof of Mr. Falkland. I had revolved the matter again and again in my mind, and was finally convinced that I owed it to myself to withdraw from his service. I added, that I was sensible, by this half-confidence, I might rather seem to merit the disapprobation of Mr. Forester than his countenance; but I declared my persuasion that, if he could be acquainted with the whole affair, however strange my behaviour might at present appear, he would applaud my reserve.

He appeared to muse for a moment upon what I had said, and then asked what reason I could have to complain of Mr. Falkland? I replied, that I entertained the deepest reverence for my patron; I admired his abilities, and considered him as formed for the benefit of his species. I should in my own opinion be the vilest of miscreants, if I uttered a whisper to his disadvantage. But this did not avail: I was not fit for him; perhaps I was not good enough for him; at all events, I must be perpetually miserable so long as I continued to live with him.

I observed Mr. Forester gaze upon me eagerly with curiosity and surprise; but this circumstance I did not think proper to notice. Having recovered himself, he enquired, why then, that being the case, I did not quit his service? I answered, what he now touched upon was that which most of all contributed to my misfortune. Mr. Falkland was not ignorant of my dislike to my present situation; perhaps he thought it unreasonable, unjust; but I knew that he would never be brought to consent to my giving way to it.

Here Mr. Forester interrupted me, and, smiling, said, I magnified obstacles, and overrated my own importance; adding, that he would undertake to remove that difficulty, as well as to provide me with a more agreeable appointment. This suggestion produced in me a serious alarm. I replied, that I must entreat him upon no account to think of applying to Mr. Falkland upon the subject. I added, that perhaps I was only betraying my imbecility; but in reality, unacquainted as I was with experience and the world, I was afraid, though disgusted with my present residence, to expose myself upon a mere project of my own, to the resentment of so considerable a man as Mr. Falkland. If he would favour me with his advice upon the subject, or if he would only give me leave to hope for his protection in case of any unforeseen accident, this was all I presumed to request; and, thus encouraged, I would venture to obey the dictates of my inclination, and fly in pursuit of my lost tranquillity.

Having thus opened myself to this generous friend, as far as I could do it with propriety and safety, he sat for some time silent, with an air of deep reflection. At length, with a countenance of unusual severity, and a characteristic fierceness of manner and voice, he thus addressed me: "Young man, perhaps you are ignorant of the nature of the conduct you at present hold. May be, you do not know that where there is mystery, there is always something at bottom that will not bear the telling. Is this the way to obtain the favour of a man of consequence and respectability? To pretend to make a confidence, and then tell him a disjointed story that has not common sense in it!"

I answered, that, whatever were the amount of that prejudice, I must submit. I placed my hope of a candid construction, in the present instance, in the rectitude of his nature.

He went on: "You do so; do you? I tell you, sir, the rectitude of my nature is an enemy to disguise. Come, boy, you must know that I understand these things better than you. Tell all, or expect nothing from me but censure and contempt."

"Sir," replied I, "I have spoken from deliberation; I have told you my choice, and, whatever be the result, I must abide by it. If in this misfortune you refuse me your assistance, here I must end, having gained by the communication only your ill opinion and displeasure."

He looked hard at me, as if he would see me through. At length he relaxed his features, and softened his manner. "You are a foolish, headstrong boy," said he, "and I shall have an eye upon you. I shall never place in you the confidence I have done. But – I will not desert you. At present, the balance between approbation and dislike is in your favour. How long it will last, I cannot tell; I engage for nothing. But it is my rule to act as I feel. I will for this time do as you require; – and, pray God, it may answer. I will receive you, either now or hereafter, under my roof, trusting that I shall have no reason to repent, and that appearances will terminate as favourably as I wish, though I scarcely know how to hope it."

We were engaged in the earnest discussion of subjects thus interesting to my peace, when we were interrupted by an event the most earnestly to have been deprecated. Without the smallest notice, and as if he had dropped upon us from the clouds, Mr. Falkland burst into the room. I found afterwards that Mr. Forester had come thus far upon an appointment to meet Mr. Falkland, and that the place of their intended rendezvous was at the next stage. Mr. Forester was detained at the inn where we now were by our accidental rencounter, and in reality had for the moment forgotten his appointment; while Mr. Falkland, not finding him where he expected, proceeded thus far towards the house of his kinsman. To me the meeting was the most unaccountable in the world.

I instantly foresaw the dreadful complication of misfortune that was included in this event. To Mr. Falkland, the meeting between me and his relation must appear not accidental, but, on my part at least the result of design. I was totally out of the road I had been travelling by his direction; I was in a road that led directly to the house of Mr. Forester. What must he think of this? How must he suppose I came to that place? The truth, if told, that I came there without design, and purely in consequence of having lost my way, must appear to be the most palpable lie that ever was devised.

Here then I stood detected in the fact of that intercourse which had been so severely forbidden. But in this instance it was infinitely worse than in those which had already given so much disturbance to Mr. Falkland. It was then frank and unconcealed; and therefore the presumption was, that it was for purposes that required no concealment. But the present interview, if concerted, was in the most emphatical degree clandestine. Nor was it less perilous than it was clandestine: it had been forbidden with the most dreadful menaces; and Mr. Falkland was not ignorant how deep an impression those menaces had made upon my imagination. Such a meeting therefore could not have been concerted under such circumstances, for a trivial purpose, or for any purpose that his heart did not ache to think of. Such was the amount of my crime, such was the agony my appearance was calculated to inspire; and it was reasonable to suppose that the penalty I had to expect would be proportionable. The threats of Mr. Falkland still sounded in my ears, and I was in a transport of terror.

The conduct of the same man in different circumstances, is often so various as to render it very difficult to be accounted for. Mr. Falkland, in this to him, terrible crisis, did not seem to be in any degree hurried away by passion. For a moment he was dumb; his eyes glared with astonishment; and the next moment, as it were, he had the most perfect calmness and self-command. Had it been otherwise, I have no doubt that I should instantly have entered into an explanation of the manner in which I came there, the ingenuousness and consistency of which could not but have been in some degree attended with a favourable event. But, as it was, I suffered myself to be overcome; I yielded, as in a former instance, to the discomfiting influence of surprise. I dared scarcely breathe; I observed the appearances with equal anxiety and surprise. Mr. Falkland quietly ordered me to return home, and take along with me the groom he had brought with him. I obeyed in silence.

I afterwards understood, that he enquired minutely of Mr. Forester the circumstances of our meeting; and that that gentleman, perceiving that the meeting itself was discovered, and guided by habits of frankness, which, when once rooted in a character, it is difficult to counteract, told Mr. Falkland every thing that had passed, together with the remarks it had suggested to his own mind. Mr. Falkland received the communication with an ambiguous and studied silence, which by no means operated to my advantage in the already poisoned mind of Mr. Forester. His silence was partly the direct consequence of a mind watchful, inquisitive, and doubting; and partly perhaps was adopted for the sake of the effect it was calculated to produce, Mr. Falkland not being unwilling to encourage prejudices against a character which might one day come in competition with his own.

As to me, I went home indeed, for this was not a moment to resist. Mr. Falkland, with a premeditation to which he had given the appearance of accident, had taken care to send with me a guard to attend upon his prisoner. I seemed as if conducting to one of those fortresses, famed in the history of despotism, from which the wretched victim is never known to come forth alive; and when I entered my chamber, I felt as if I were entering a dungeon. I reflected that I was at the mercy of a man, exasperated at my disobedience, and who was already formed to cruelty by successive murders. My prospects were now closed; I was cut off for ever from pursuits that I had meditated with ineffable delight; my death might be the event of a few hours. I was a victim at the shrine of conscious guilt, that knew neither rest nor satiety; I should be blotted from the catalogue of the living, and my fate remain eternally a secret; the man who added my murder to his former crimes, would show himself the next morning, and be hailed with the admiration and applause of his species.

In the midst of these terrible imaginations, one idea presented itself that alleviated my feelings. This was the recollection of the strange and unaccountable tranquillity which Mr. Falkland had manifested when he discovered me in company with Mr. Forester. I was not deceived by this. I knew that the calm was temporary, and would be succeeded by a tumult and whirlwind of the most dreadful sort. But a man under the power of such terrors as now occupied me catches at every reed. I said to myself, "This tranquillity is a period it is incumbent upon me to improve; the shorter its duration may be found, the more speedy am I obliged to be in the use of it." In a word, I took the resolution, because I already stood in fear of the vengeance of Mr. Falkland, to risk the possibility of provoking it in a degree still more inexpiable, and terminate at once my present state of uncertainty. I had now opened my case to Mr. Forester, and he had given me positive assurances of his protection. I determined immediately to address the following letter to Mr. Falkland. The consideration that, if he meditated any thing tragical, such a letter would only tend to confirm him, did not enter into the present feelings of my mind.

"Sir,
"I have conceived the intention of quitting your service. This is a measure we ought both of us to desire. I shall then be, what it is my duty to be, master of my own actions. You will be delivered from the presence of a person, whom you cannot prevail upon yourself to behold without unpleasing emotions.

"Why should you subject me to an eternal penance? Why should you consign my youthful hopes to suffering and despair? Consult the principles of humanity that have marked the general course of your proceedings, and do not let me, I entreat you, be made the subject of a useless severity. My heart is impressed with gratitude for your favours. I sincerely ask your forgiveness for the many errors of my conduct. I consider the treatment I have received under your roof, as one almost uninterrupted scene of kindness and generosity. I shall never forget my obligations to you, and will never betray them.

"I remain, Sir,

"Your most grateful, respectful, and dutiful servant,

"Caleb Williams."

Such was my employment of the evening of a day which will be ever memorable in the history of my life. Mr. Falkland not being yet returned, though expected every hour, I was induced to make use of the pretence of fatigue to avoid an interview. I went to bed. It may be imagined that my slumbers were neither deep nor refreshing.

The next morning I was informed that my patron did not come home till late; that he had enquired for me, and, being told that I was in bed, had said nothing further upon the subject. Satisfied in this respect, I went to the breakfasting parlour, and, though full of anxiety and trepidation, endeavoured to busy myself in arranging the books, and a few other little occupations, till Mr. Falkland should come down. After a short time I heard his step, which I perfectly well knew how to distinguish, in the passage. Presently he stopped, and, speaking to some one in a sort of deliberate, but smothered voice, I overheard him repeat my name as enquiring for me. In conformity to the plan I had persuaded myself to adopt, I now laid the letter I had written upon the table at which he usually sat, and made my exit at one door as Mr. Falkland entered at the other. This done, I withdrew, with flutterings and palpitation, to a private apartment, a sort of light closet at the end of the library, where I was accustomed not unfrequently to sit.

I had not been here three minutes, when I heard the voice of Mr. Falkland calling me. I went to him in the library. His manner was that of a man labouring with some dreadful thought, and endeavouring to give an air of carelessness and insensibility to his behaviour. Perhaps no carriage of any other sort could have produced a sensation of such inexplicable horror, or have excited, in the person who was its object, such anxious uncertainty about the event. – "That is your letter," said he, throwing it.

"My lad," continued he, "I believe now you have played all your tricks, and the farce is nearly at an end! With your apishness and absurdity however you have taught me one thing; and, whereas before I have winced at them with torture, I am now as tough as an elephant. I shall crush you in the end with the same indifference, that I would any other little insect that disturbed my serenity.

"I am unable to tell what brought about your meeting with Mr. Forester yesterday. It might be design; it might be accident. But, I shall not forget it. You write me here, that you are desirous to quit my service. To that I have a short answer: You never shall quit it with life. If you attempt it, you shall never cease to rue your folly as long as you exist. That is my will; and I will not have it resisted. The very next time you disobey me in that or any other article, there is an end of your vagaries for ever. Perhaps your situation may be a pitiable one; it is for you to look to that. I only know that it is in your power to prevent its growing worse; no time nor chance shall ever make it better.

"Do not imagine I am afraid of you! I wear an armour, against which all your weapons are impotent. I have dug a pit for you; and, whichever way you move, backward or forward, to the right or the left, it is ready to swallow you. Be still! If once you fall, call as loud as you will, no man on earth shall hear your cries; prepare a tale however plausible, or however true, the whole world shall execrate you for an impostor. Your innocence shall be of no service to you; I laugh at so feeble a defence. It is I that say it; you may believe what I tell you. – Do you not know, miserable wretch!" added he, suddenly altering his tone, and stamping upon the ground with fury, "that I have sworn to preserve my reputation, whatever be the expense; that I love it more than the whole world and its inhabitants taken together? And do you think that you shall wound it? Begone, miscreant! reptile! and cease to contend with insurmountable power!"

The part of my history which I am now relating is that which I reflect upon with the least complacency. Why was it, that I was once more totally overcome by the imperious carriage of Mr. Falkland, and unable to utter a word? The reader will be presented with many occasions in the sequel, in which I wanted neither facility in the invention of expedients, nor fortitude in entering upon my justification. Persecution at length gave firmness to my character, and taught me the better part of manhood. But in the present instance I was irresolute, overawed, and abashed.

The speech I had heard was the dictate of frenzy, and it created in me a similar frenzy. It determined me to do the very thing against which I was thus solemnly warned, and fly from my patron's house. I could not enter into parley with him; I could no longer endure the vile subjugation he imposed on me. It was in vain that my reason warned me of the rashness of a measure, to be taken without concert or preparation. I seemed to be in a state in which reason had no power. I felt as if I could coolly survey the several arguments of the case, perceive that they had prudence, truth, and common sense on their side; and then answer, I am under the guidance of a director more energetic than you.

I was not long in executing what I had thus rapidly determined. I fixed on the evening of that very day as the period of my evasion. Even in this short interval I had perhaps sufficient time for deliberation. But all opportunity was useless to me; my mind was fixed, and each succeeding moment only increased the unspeakable eagerness with which I meditated my escape. The hours usually observed by our family in this country residence were regular; and one in the morning was the time I selected for my undertaking.

In searching the apartment where I slept, I had formerly discovered a concealed door, which led to a small apartment of the most secret nature, not uncommon in houses so old as that of Mr. Falkland, and which had perhaps served as a refuge from persecution, or a security from the inveterate hostilities of a barbarous age. I believed no person was acquainted with this hiding-place but myself. I felt unaccountably impelled to remove into it the different articles of my personal property. I could not at present take them away with me. If I were never to recover them, I felt that it would be a gratification to my sentiment, that no trace of my existence should be found after my departure. Having completed their removal, and waited till the hour I had previously chosen, I stole down quietly from my chamber with a lamp in my hand. I went along a passage that led to a small door opening into the garden, and then crossed the garden, to a gate that intersected an elm-walk and a private horse-path on the outside.

I could scarcely believe my good fortune in having thus far executed my design without interruption. The terrible images Mr. Falkland's menaces had suggested to my mind, made me expect impediment and detection at every step; though the impassioned state of my mind impelled me to advance with desperate resolution. He probably however counted too securely upon the ascendancy of his sentiments, when imperiously pronounced, to think it necessary to take precautions against a sinister event. For myself, I drew a favourable omen as to the final result of my project, from the smoothness of success that attended it in the outset.

CHAPTER IX

THE first plan that had suggested itself to me was, to go to the nearest public road, and take the earliest stage for London. There I believed I should be most safe from discovery, if the vengeance of Mr. Falkland should prompt him to pursue me; and I did not doubt, among the multiplied resources of the metropolis, to find something which should suggest to me an eligible mode of disposing of my person and industry. I reserved Mr. Forester in my arrangement, as a last resource, not to be called forth unless for immediate protection from the hand of persecution and power. I was destitute of that experience of the world, which can alone render us fertile in resources, or enable us to institute a just comparison between the resources that offer themselves. I was like the fascinated animal, that is seized with the most terrible apprehensions, at the same time that he is incapable of adequately considering for his own safety.

The mode of my proceeding being digested, I traced, with a cheerful heart, the unfrequented path it was now necessary for me to pursue. The night was gloomy, and it drizzled with rain. But these were circumstances I had scarcely the power to perceive; all was sunshine and joy within me. I hardly felt the ground; I repeated to myself a thousand times, "I am free. What concern have I with danger and alarm? I feel that I am free; I feel that I will continue so. What power is able to hold in chains a mind ardent and determined? What power can cause that man to die, whose whole soul commands him to continue to live?" I looked back with abhorrence to the subjection in which I had been held. I did not hate the author of my misfortunes – truth and justice acquit me of that; I rather pitied the hard destiny to which he seemed condemned. But I thought with unspeakable loathing of those errors, in consequence of which every man is fated to be, more or less, the tyrant or the slave. I was astonished at the folly of my species, that they did not rise up as one man, and shake off chains so ignominious, and misery so insupportable. So far as related to myself, I resolved – and this resolution has never been entirely forgotten by me – to hold myself disengaged from this odious scene, and never fill the part either of the oppressor or the sufferer.

My mind continued in this enthusiastical state, full of confidence, and accessible only to such a portion of fear as served rather to keep up a state of pleasurable emotion than to generate anguish and distress, during the whole of this nocturnal expedition. After a walk of three hours, I arrived, without accident, at the village from which I hoped to have taken my passage for the metropolis. At this early hour every thing was quiet; no sound of any thing human saluted my ear. It was with difficulty that I gained admittance into the yard of the inn, where I found a single ostler taking care of some horses. From him I received the unwelcome tidings, that the coach was not expected till six o'clock in the morning of the day after tomorrow, its route through that town recurring only three times a week.

This intelligence gave the first check to the rapturous inebriation by which my mind had been possessed from the moment I quitted the habitation of Mr. Falkland. The whole of my fortune in ready cash consisted of about eleven guineas. I had about fifty more, that had fallen to me from the disposal of my property at the death of my father; but that was so vested as to preclude it from immediate use, and I even doubted whether it would not be found better ultimately to resign it, than, by claiming it, to risk the furnishing a clew to what I most of all dreaded, the persecution of Mr. Falkland. There was nothing I so ardently desired as the annihilation of all future intercourse between us, that he should not know there was such a person on the earth as myself, and that I should never more hear the repetition of a name which had been so fatal to my peace.

Thus circumstanced, I conceived frugality to be an object by no means unworthy of my attention, unable as I was to prognosticate what discouragements and delays might present themselves to the accomplishment of my wishes, after my arrival in London. For this and other reasons, I determined to adhere to my design of travelling by the stage; it only remaining for me to consider in what manner I should prevent the eventful delay of twenty-four hours from becoming, by any untoward event, a source of new calamity. It was by no means advisable to remain in the village where I now was during this interval; nor did I even think proper to employ it, in proceeding on foot along the great road. I therefore decided upon making a circuit, the direction of which should seem at first extremely wide of my intended route, and then, suddenly taking a different inclination, should enable me to arrive by the close of day at a market-town twelve miles nearer to the metropolis.

Having fixed the economy of the day, and persuaded myself that it was the best which, under the circumstances, could be adopted, I dismissed, for the most part, all further anxieties from my mind, and eagerly yielded myself up to the different amusements that arose. I rested and went forward at the impulse of the moment. At one time I reclined upon a bank immersed in contemplation, and at another exerted myself to analyse the prospects which succeeded each other. The haziness of the morning was followed by a spirit-stirring and beautiful day. With the ductility so characteristic of a youthful mind, I forgot the anguish which had lately been my continual guest, and occupied myself entirely in dreams of future novelty and felicity. I scarcely ever, in the whole course of my existence, spent a day of more various or exquisite gratification. It furnished a strong and perhaps not an unsalutary contrast, to the terrors which had preceded, and the dreadful scenes that awaited me.

In the evening I arrived at the place of my destination, and enquired for the inn at which the coach was accustomed to call. A circumstance however had previously excited my attention, and reproduced in me a state of alarm.

Though it was already dark before I reached the town, my observation had been attracted by a man, who passed me on horseback in the opposite direction, about half a mile on the other side of the town. There was an inquisitiveness in his gesture that I did not like; and, as far as I could discern his figure, I pronounced him an ill-looking man. He had not passed me more than two minutes before I heard the sound of a horse advancing slowly behind me. These circumstances impressed some degree of uneasy sensation upon my mind. I first mended my pace; and, this not appearing to answer the purpose, I afterwards loitered, that the horseman might pass me. He did so;

and, as I glanced at him, I thought I saw that it was the same man. He now put his horse into a trot, and entered the town. I followed; and it was not long before I perceived him at the door of an alehouse, drinking a mug of beer. This however the darkness prevented me from discovering, till I was in a manner upon him. I pushed forward, and saw him no more, till, as I entered the yard of the inn where I intended to sleep, the same man suddenly rode up to me, and asked if my name were Williams.

This adventure, while it had been passing, expelled the gaiety of my mind, and filled me with anxiety. The apprehension however that I felt, appeared to me groundless: if I were pursued, I took it for granted it would be by some of Mr. Falkland's people, and not by a stranger. The darkness took from me some of the simplest expedients of precaution. I determined at least to proceed to the inn, and make the necessary enquiries.

I no sooner heard the sound of the horse as I entered the yard, and the question proposed to me by the rider, than the dreadful certainty of what I feared instantly took possession of my mind. Every incident connected with my late abhorred situation was calculated to impress me with the deepest alarm. My first thought was, to betake myself to the fields, and trust to the swiftness of my flight for safety. But this was scarcely practicable: I remarked that my enemy was alone; and I believed that, man to man, I might reasonably hope to get the better of him, either by the firmness of my determination, or the subtlety of my invention.

Thus resolved, I replied in an impetuous and peremptory tone, that I was the man he took me for; adding, "I guess your errand; but it is to no purpose. You come to conduct me back to Falkland House; but no force shall ever drag me to that place alive. I have not taken my resolution without strong reasons; and all the world shall not persuade me to alter it. I am an Englishman, and it is the privilege of an Englishman to be sole judge and master of his own actions."

"You are in the devil of a hurry," replied the man, "to guess my intentions, and tell your own. But your guess is right; and mayhap you may have reason to be thankful that my errand is

not something worse. Sure enough the squire expects you; –
but I have a letter, and when you have read that, I suppose you
will come off a little of your stoutness. If that does not answer,
it will then be time to think what is to be done next."

Thus saying, he gave me his letter, which was from Mr.
Forester, whom, as he told me, he had left at Mr. Falkland's
house. I went into a room of the inn for the purpose of reading
it, and was followed by the bearer. The letter was as follows: –

"Williams,
"My brother Falkland has sent the bearer in pursuit of you. He
expects that, if found, you will return with him: I expect it too.
It is of the utmost consequence to your future honour and
character. After reading these lines, if you are a villain and a rascal, you will perhaps endeavour to fly; if your conscience tells
you, 'You are innocent,' you will, out of all doubt, come back.
Show me then whether I have been your dupe; and, while I
was won over by your seeming ingenuousness, have suffered
myself to be made the tool of a designing knave. If you come, I
pledge myself that, if you clear your reputation, you shall not
only be free to go wherever you please, but shall receive every
assistance in my power to give. Remember, I engage for nothing further than that.
                                        "Valentine Forester"

What a letter was this! To a mind like mine, glowing with
the love of virtue, such an address was strong enough to draw
the person to whom it was addressed from one end of the earth
to the other. My mind was full of confidence and energy. I felt
my own innocence, and was determined to assert it. I was willing to be driven out a fugitive; I even rejoiced in my escape,
and cheerfully went out into the world destitute of every provision, and depending for my future prospects upon my own
ingenuity.

Thus much, said I, Falkland! you may do. Dispose of me as
you please with respect to the goods of fortune; but you shall
neither make prize of my liberty, nor sully the whiteness of my
name. I repassed in my thoughts every memorable incident that

had happened to me under his roof. I could recollect nothing, except the affair of the mysterious trunk, out of which the shadow of a criminal accusation could be extorted. In that instance my conduct had been highly reprehensible, and I had never looked back upon it without remorse and self-condemnation. But I did not believe that it was of the nature of those actions which can be brought under legal censure. I could still less persuade myself that Mr. Falkland, who shuddered at the very possibility of detection, and who considered himself as completely in my power, would dare to bring forward a subject so closely connected with the internal agony of his soul. In a word, the more I reflected on the phrases of Mr. Forester's billet, the less could I imagine the nature of those scenes to which they were to serve as a prelude.

The inscrutableness however of the mystery they contained, did not suffice to overwhelm my courage. My mind seemed to undergo an entire revolution. Timid and embarrassed as I had felt myself, when I regarded Mr. Falkland as my clandestine and domestic foe, I now conceived that the case was entirely altered.

"Meet me," said I, "as an open accuser: if we must contend, let us contend in the face of day; and then, unparalleled as your resources may be, I will not fear you." Innocence and guilt were, in my apprehension, the things in the whole world the most opposite to each other. I would not suffer myself to believe, that the former could be confounded with the latter, unless the innocent man first allowed himself to be subdued in mind, before he was defrauded of the good opinion of mankind. Virtue rising superior to every calamity, defeating by a plain unvarnished tale all the stratagems of Vice, and throwing back upon her adversary the confusion with which he had hoped to overwhelm her, was one of the favourite subjects of my youthful reveries. I determined never to prove an instrument of destruction to Mr. Falkland; but I was not less resolute to obtain justice to myself.

The issue of all these confident hopes I shall immediately have occasion to relate. It was thus, with the most generous and undoubting spirit, that I rushed upon irretrievable ruin.

"Friend," said I to the bearer, after a considerable interval of silence, "you are right. This is, indeed, an extraordinary letter you have brought me; but it answers its purpose. I will certainly go with you now, whatever be the consequence. No person shall ever impute blame to me, so long as I have it in my power to clear myself."

I felt, in the circumstances in which I was placed by Mr. Forester's letter, not merely a willingness, but an alacrity and impatience to return. We procured a second horse. We proceeded on our journey in silence. My mind was occupied again in endeavouring to account for Mr. Forester's letter. I knew the inflexibility and sternness of Mr. Falkland's mind in accomplishing the purposes he had at heart; but I also knew that every virtuous and magnanimous principle was congenial to his character.

When we arrived, midnight was already past, and we were obliged to waken one of the servants to give us admittance. I found that Mr. Forester had left a message for me, in consideration of the possibility of my arrival during the night, directing me immediately to go to bed, and to take care that I did not come weary and exhausted to the business of the following day. I endeavoured to take his advice; but my slumbers were unrefreshing and disturbed. I suffered however no reduction of courage: the singularity of my situation, my conjectures with respect to the present, my eagerness for the future, did not allow me to sink into a languid and inactive state.

Next morning the first person I saw was Mr. Forester. He told me that he did not yet know what Mr. Falkland had to allege against me, for that he had refused to know. He had arrived at the house of his brother by appointment on the preceding day to settle some indispensable business, his intention having been to depart the moment the business was finished, as he knew that conduct on his part would be most agreeable to Mr. Falkland. But he was no sooner come, than he found the whole house in confusion, the alarm of my elopement having been given a few hours before. Mr. Falkland had despatched servants in all directions in pursuit of me; and the servant from the market-town arrived at the same moment with Mr.

Forester, with intelligence that a person answering the description he gave, had been there very early in the morning enquiring respecting the stage to London.

Mr. Falkland seemed extremely disturbed at this information, and exclaimed on me with acrimony, as an unthankful and unnatural villain.

Mr. Forester replied, "Have more command of yourself, sir! Villain is a serious appellation, and must not be trifled with. Englishmen are free; and no man is to be charged with villainy, because he changes one source of subsistence for another."

Mr. Falkland shook his head, and with a smile, expressive of acute sensibility said, "Brother, brother, you are the dupe of his art. I always considered him with an eye of suspicion, and was aware of his depravity. But I have just discovered – "

"Stop sir!" interrupted Mr. Forester. "I own I thought that, in a moment of acrimony, you might be employing harsh epithets in a sort of random style. But if you have a serious accusation to state, we must not be told of that, till it is known whether the lad is within reach of a hearing. I am indifferent myself about the good opinion of others. It is what the world bestows and retracts with so little thought, that I can make no account of its decision. But that does not authorise me lightly to entertain an ill opinion of another. The slenderest allowance I think I can make to such as I consign to be the example and terror of their species, is that of being heard in their own defence. It is a wise principle that requires the judge to come into court uninformed of the merits of the cause he is to try; and to that principle I am determined to conform as an individual. I shall always think it right to be severe and inflexible in my treatment of offenders; but the severity I exercise in the sequel, must be accompanied with impartiality and caution in what is preliminary."

While Mr. Forester related to me these particulars, he observed me ready to break out into some of the expressions which the narrative suggested; but he would not suffer me to speak. "No," said he; "I would not hear Mr. Falkland against you; and I cannot hear you in your defence. I come to you at present to speak, and not to hear. I thought it right to warn you of your danger, but I have nothing more to do now. Reserve what you have to say to the proper time. Make the best story you can for yourself – true, if truth, as I hope, will serve your purpose; but, if not, the most plausible and ingenious you can invent. That is what self-defence requires from every man, where, as it always happens to a man upon his trial, he has the whole world against him, and has his own battle to fight against the world. Farewell; and God send you a good deliverance! If Mr. Falkland's accusation, whatever it be, shall appear premature, depend upon having me more zealously your friend than ever. If not, this is the last act of friendship you will ever receive from me!"

It may be believed that this address, so singular, so solemn, so big with conditional menace, did not greatly tend to encourage me. I was totally ignorant of the charge to be advanced against me; and not a little astonished, when it was in my power to be in the most formidable degree the accuser of Mr. Falkland, to find the principles of equity so completely reversed, as for the innocent but instructed individual to be the party accused and suffering, instead of having, as was natural, the real criminal at his mercy. I was still more astonished at the superhuman power Mr. Falkland seemed to possess, of bringing the object of his persecution within the sphere of his authority; a reflection attended with some check to that eagerness and boldness of spirit, which now constituted the ruling passion of my mind.

But this was no time for meditation. To the sufferer the course of events is taken out of his direction, and he is hurried along with an irresistible force, without finding it within the compass of his efforts to check their rapidity. I was allowed only a short time to recollect myself, when my trial commenced. I was conducted to the library, where I had passed so many happy and so many contemplative hours, and found there Mr. Forester and three or four of the servants already assembled, in expectation of me and my accuser. Every thing was calculated to suggest to me that I must trust only in the justice of the parties concerned, and had nothing to hope from their indulgence. Mr. Falkland entered at one door, almost as soon as I entered at the other.

CHAPTER X

HE began: "It has been the principle of my life, never to inflict a wilful injury upon any thing that lives; I need not express my regret, when I find myself obliged to be the promulgator of a criminal charge. How gladly would I pass unnoticed the evil I have sustained; but I owe it to society to detect an offender, and prevent other men from being imposed upon, as I have been, by an appearance of integrity."

"It would be better," interrupted Mr. Forester, "to speak directly to the point. We ought not, though unwarily, by apologising for ourselves, to create at such a time a prejudice against an individual, against whom a criminal accusation will always be prejudice enough."

"I strongly suspect," continued Mr. Falkland, "this young man, who has been peculiarly the object of my kindness, of having robbed me to a considerable amount."

"What," replied Mr. Forester, "are the grounds of your suspicion?"

"The first of them is the actual loss I have sustained, in notes, jewels, and plate. I have missed banknotes to the amount of nine hundred pounds, three gold repeaters of considerable value, a complete set of diamonds, the property of my late mother and several other articles."

"And why," continued my arbitrator, astonishment, grief, and a desire to retain his self-possession, strongly contending in his countenance and voice, "do you fix on this young man as the instrument of the depredation?"

"I found him, on my coming home, upon the day when every thing was in disorder from the alarm of fire, in the very act of quitting the private apartment where these articles were deposited. He was confounded at seeing me, and hastened to withdraw as soon as he possibly could."

"Did you say nothing to him – take no notice of the confusion your sudden appearance produced?"

"I asked what was his errand in that place. He was at first so terrified and overcome, that he could not answer me. Afterwards, with a good deal of faltering, he said that, when all the

servants were engaged in endeavouring to save the most valuable part of my property, he had come hither with the same
view; but that he had as yet removed nothing."

"Did you immediately examine to see that every thing was
safe?"

"No. I was accustomed to confide in his honesty; and I was
suddenly called away, in the present instance, to attend to the
increasing progress of the flames. I therefore only took out the
key from the door of the apartment, having first locked it, and,
putting it in my pocket, hastened to go where my presence
seemed indispensably necessary."

"How long was it before you missed your property?"

"The same evening. The hurry of the scene had driven the
circumstance entirely out of my mind, till, going by accident
near the apartment, the whole affair, together with the singular
and equivocal behaviour of Williams, rushed at once upon my
recollection. I immediately entered, examined the trunk in
which these things were contained, and, to my astonishment,
found the locks broken, and the property gone."

"What steps did you take upon this discovery?"

"I sent for Williams, and talked to him very seriously upon
the subject. But he had now perfectly recovered his self-
command, and calmly and stoutly denied all knowledge of the
matter. I urged him with the enormousness of the offence, but
I made no impression. He did not discover either the surprise
and indignation one would have expected from a person
entirely innocent, or the uneasiness that generally attends upon
guilt. He was rather silent and reserved. I then informed him,
that I should proceed in a manner different from what he
might perhaps expect. I would not, as is too frequent in such
cases, make a general search; for I had rather lose my property
for ever without redress, than expose a multitude of innocent
persons to anxiety and injustice. My suspicion, for the present,
unavoidably fixed upon him. But, in a matter of so great consequence, I was determined not to act upon suspicion. I would
neither incur the possibility of ruining him, being innocent,
nor be the instrument of exposing others to his depredations, if
guilty. I should therefore merely insist upon his continuing in

my service. He might depend upon it he should be well watched, and I trusted the whole truth would eventually appear. Since he avoided confession now, I advised him to consider how far it was likely he would come off with impunity at last. This I determined on, that the moment he attempted an escape, I would consider that as an indication of guilt, and proceed accordingly."

"What circumstances have occurred from that time to the present?"

"None upon which I can infer a certainty of guilt; several that agree to favour a suspicion. From that time Williams was perpetually uneasy in his situation, always desirous, as it now appears, to escape, but afraid to adopt such a measure without certain precautions. It was not long after, that you, Mr. Forester, became my visitor. I observed, with dissatisfaction, the growing intercourse between you, reflecting on the equivocalness of his character, and the attempt he would probably make to render you the dupe of his hypocrisy. I accordingly threatened him severely; and I believe you observed the change that presently after occurred in his behaviour with relation to you."

"I did, and it appeared at that time mysterious and extraordinary."

"Some time after, as you well know, a rencounter took place between you, whether accidental or intentional on his part I am not able to say, when he confessed to you the uneasiness of his mind, without discovering the cause, and openly proposed to you to assist him in his flight, and stand, in case of necessity, between him and my resentment. You offered, it seems, to take him into your service; but nothing, as he acknowledged, would answer his purpose, that did not place his retreat wholly out of my power to discover."

"Did it not appear extraordinary to you, that he should hope for any effectual protection from me, while it remained perpetually in your power to satisfy me of his unworthiness?"

"Perhaps he had hopes that I should not proceed to that step, at least so long as the place of his retreat should be unknown to me, and of consequence the event of my proceeding dubious. Perhaps he confided in his own powers, which are far from contemptible, to construct a plausible tale, especially as he had taken care to have the first impression in his favour. After all, this protection, on your part, was merely reserved in case all other expedients failed. He does not appear to have had any other sentiment upon the subject, than that, if he were defeated in his projects for placing himself beyond the reach of justice, it was better to have bespoken a place in your patronage than to be destitute of every resource."

Mr. Falkland having thus finished his evidence, called upon Robert, the valet, to confirm that part of it which related to the day of the fire.

Robert stated, that he happened to be coming through the library that day, a few minutes after Mr. Falkland's being brought home by the sight of the fire; that he had found me standing there with every mark of perturbation and fright; that he could not help stopping to notice it; that he had spoken to me two or three times before he could obtain an answer; and that all he could get from me at last was, that I was the most miserable creature alive.

He further said, that in the evening of the same day Mr. Falkland called him into the private apartment adjoining to the library, and bid him bring a hammer and some nails. He then showed him a trunk standing in the apartment with its locks and fastenings broken, and ordered him to observe and remember what he saw, but not to mention it to any one. Robert did not at that time know what Mr. Falkland intended by these directions, which were given in a manner uncommonly solemn and significant; but he entertained no doubt, that the fastenings were broken and wrenched by the application of a chisel or such-like instrument, with the intention of forcibly opening the trunk.

Mr. Forester observed upon this evidence, that as much of it as related to the day of the fire seemed indeed to afford powerful reasons for suspicion; and that the circumstances that had occurred since strangely concurred to fortify that suspicion. Meantime, that nothing proper to be done might be omitted, he asked whether in my flight I had removed my boxes, to see whether by that means any trace could be discovered to confirm the imputation. Mr. Falkland treated this suggestion slightly, saying, that if I were the thief, I had no doubt taken the precaution to obviate so palpable a means of detection. To this Mr. Forester only replied, that conjecture, however skilfully formed, was not always realised in the actions and behaviour of mankind; and ordered that my boxes and trunks, if found, should be brought into the library. I listened to this suggestion with pleasure; and, uneasy and confounded as I was at the appearances combined against me, I trusted in this appeal to give a new face to my cause. I was eager to declare the place where my property was deposited; and the servants, guided by my direction, presently produced what was enquired for.

The two boxes that were first opened, contained nothing to confirm the accusation against me; in the third were found a watch and several jewels, that were immediately known to be the property of Mr. Falkland. The production of this seemingly decisive evidence excited emotions of astonishment and concern; but no person's astonishment appeared to be greater than that of Mr. Falkland. That I should have left the stolen goods behind me, would of itself have appeared incredible; but when it was considered what a secure place of concealment I had found for them, the wonder diminished; and Mr. Forester observed, that it was by no means impossible I might conceive it easier to obtain possession of them afterwards, than to remove them at the period of my precipitate flight.

Here however I thought it necessary to interfere. I fervently urged my right to a fair and impartial construction. I asked Mr. Forester whether it were probable, if I had stolen these things, that I should not have contrived, at least to remove them along with me? And again, whether, if I had been conscious they would be found among my property, I should myself have indicated the place where I had concealed it?

The insinuation I conveyed against Mr. Forester's impartiality overspread his whole countenance, for an instant, with the flush of anger.

"Impartiality, young man! Yes, be sure, from me you shall experience an impartial treatment! God send that may answer your purpose. Presently you shall be heard at full in your own defence.

"You expect us to believe you innocent, because you did not

remove these things along with you. The money is removed. Where, sir, is that? We cannot answer for the inconsistencies and oversights of any human mind, and, least of all, if that mind should appear to be disturbed with the consciousness of guilt.

"You observe that it was by your own direction these boxes and trunks have been found: that is indeed extraordinary. It appears little less than infatuation. But to what purpose appeal to probabilities and conjecture, in the face of incontestable facts? There, sir, are the boxes. You alone knew where they were to be found; you alone had the keys: tell us then how this watch and these jewels came to be contained in them?"

I was silent.

To the rest of the persons present I seemed to be merely the subject of detection; but in reality I was, of all the spectators, that individual who was most at a loss to conceive, through every stage of the scene, what would come next, and who listened to every word that was uttered with the most uncontrollable amazement. Amazement however alternately yielded to indignation and horror. At first I could not refrain from repeatedly attempting to interrupt; but I was checked in these attempts by Mr. Forester; and I presently felt how necessary it was to my future peace, that I should collect the whole energy of my mind to repel the charge, and assert my innocence.

Every thing being now produced that could be produced against me, Mr. Forester turned to me with a look of concern and pity, and told me that now was the time, if I chose to allege any thing in my defence. In reply to this invitation, I spoke nearly as follows: –

"I am innocent. It is in vain that circumstances are accumulated against me; there is not a person upon earth less capable than I of the things of which I am accused. I appeal to my heart – I appeal to my looks – I appeal to every sentiment my tongue ever uttered."

I could perceive that the fervour with which I spoke made some impression upon every one that heard me. But in a moment their eyes were turned upon the property that lay before them, and their countenances changed. I proceeded: –

"One thing more I must aver; – Mr. Falkland is not

deceived; he perfectly knows that I am innocent."

I had no sooner uttered these words, than an involuntary cry of indignation burst from every person in the room. Mr. Forester turned to me with a look of extreme severity, and said –

"Young man, consider well what you are doing! It is the privilege of the party accused to say whatever he thinks proper; and I will take care that you shall enjoy that privilege in its utmost extent. But do you think it will conduce in any respect to your benefit, to throw out such insolent and intolerable insinuations?"

"I thank you most sincerely," replied I, "for your caution; but I well know what it is I am doing. I make this declaration, not merely because it is solemnly true, but because it is inseparably connected with my vindication. I am the party accused, and I shall be told that I am not to be believed in my own defence. I can produce no other witnesses of my innocence; I therefore call upon Mr. Falkland to be my evidence. I ask him –

"Did you never boast to me in private of your power to ruin me? Did you never say that, if once I brought on myself the weight of your displeasure, my fall should be irreparable? Did you not tell me that, though I should prepare in that case a tale however plausible or however true, you would take care that the whole world should execrate me as an impostor? Were not those your very words? Did you not add, that my innocence should be of no service to me, and that you laughed at so feeble a defence? I ask you further, – Did you not receive a letter from me the morning of the day on which I departed, requesting your consent to my departure? Should I have done that if my flight had been that of a thief? I challenge any man to reconcile the expressions of that letter with this accusation. Should I have begun with stating that I had conceived a desire to quit your service, if my desire and the reasons for it, had been of the nature that is now alleged? Should I have dared to ask for what reason I was thus subjected to an eternal penance?"

Saying this, I took out a copy of my letter, and laid it open upon the table.

Mr. Falkland returned no immediate answer to my interrogations. Mr. Forester turned to him and said, "Well sir, what is your reply to this challenge of your servant?"

Mr. Falkland answered, "Such a mode of defence scarcely calls for a reply. But I answer, I held no such conversation; I never used such words; I received no such letter. Surely it is no sufficient refutation of a criminal charge, that the criminal repels what is alleged against him with volubility of speech, and intrepidity of manner."

Mr. Forester then turned to me: "If," said he, "you trust your vindication to the plausibility of your tale, you must take care to render it consistent and complete. You have not told us what was the cause of the confusion and anxiety in which Robert professes to have found you, why you were so impatient to quit the service of Mr. Falkland, or how you account for certain articles of his property being found in your possession."

"All that, sir," answered I, "is true. There are certain parts of my story that I have not told. If they were told they would not conduce to my disadvantage, and they would make the present accusation appear still more astonishing. But I cannot, as yet at least, prevail upon myself to tell them. Is it necessary to give any particular and precise reasons why I should wish to change the place of my residence? You all of you know the unfortunate state of Mr. Falkland's mind. You know the sternness, reservedness, and distance of his manners. If I had no other reasons, surely it would afford small presumption of criminality that I should wish to change his service for another.

"The question of how these articles of Mr. Falkland's property came to be found in my possession is more material. It is a question I am wholly unable to answer. Their being found there, was at least as unexpected to me as to any one of the persons now present. I only know that, as I have the most perfect assurance of Mr. Falkland's being conscious of my innocence – for, observe! I do not shrink from that assertion; I reiterate it with new confidence – I therefore firmly and from my soul believe, that their being there is of Mr. Falkland's contrivance."

I no sooner said this, than I was again interrupted by an involuntary exclamation from every one present. They looked at me with furious glances, as if they could have torn me to pieces. I proceeded: –

"I have now answered every thing that is alleged against me.

"Mr. Forester, you are a lover of justice; I conjure you not to violate it in my person. You are a man of penetration; look at me! do you see any of the marks of guilt? Recollect all that has ever passed under your observation; is it compatible with a mind capable of what is now alleged against me? Could a real criminal have shown himself so unabashed, composed, and firm as I have now done?

"Fellow-servants! Mr. Falkland is a man of rank and fortune; he is your master. I am a poor country lad, without a friend in the world. That is a ground of real difference to a certain extent; but it is not a sufficient ground for the subversion of justice. Remember, that I am in a situation that is not to be trifled with; that a decision given against me now, in a case in which I solemnly assure you I am innocent, will for ever deprive me of reputation and peace of mind, combine the whole world in a league against me, and determine perhaps upon my liberty and my life. If you believe – if you see – if you know, that I am innocent, speak for me. Do not suffer a pusil-lanimous timidity to prevent you from saving a fellow-creature from destruction, who does not deserve to have a human being for his enemy. Why have we the power of speech, but to com-municate our thoughts? I will never believe that a man, con-scious of innocence, cannot make other men perceive that he has that thought. Do not you feel that my whole heart tells me, I am not guilty of what is imputed to me?

"To you, Mr. Falkland, I have nothing to say: I know you, and know that you are impenetrable. At the very moment that you are urging such odious charges against me, you admire my resolution and forbearance. But I have nothing to hope from you. You can look upon my ruin without pity or remorse. I am most unfortunate indeed in having to do with such an adver-sary. You oblige me to say ill things of you; but I appeal to your own heart, whether my language is that of exaggeration or revenge."

Every thing that could be alleged on either side being now concluded, Mr. Forester undertook to make some remarks upon the whole.

"Williams," said he, "the charge against you is heavy; the

direct evidence strong; the corroborating circumstances numerous and striking. I grant that you have shown considerable dexterity in your answers; but you will learn, young man, to your cost, that dexterity, however powerful it may be in certain cases, will avail little against the stubbornness of truth. It is fortunate for mankind that the empire of talents has its limitations, and that it is not in the power of ingenuity to subvert the distinctions of right and wrong. Take my word for it, that the true merits of the case against you will be too strong for sophistry to overturn; that justice will prevail, and impotent malice be defeated.

"To you, Mr. Falkland, society is obliged for having placed this black affair in its true light. Do not suffer the malignant aspersions of the criminal to give you uneasiness. Depend upon it that they will be found of no weight. I have no doubt that your character, in the judgment of every person that has heard them, stands higher than ever. We feel for your misfortune, in being obliged to hear such calumnies from a person who has injured you so grossly. But you must be considered in that respect as a martyr in the public cause. The purity of your motives and dispositions is beyond the reach of malice; and truth and equity will not fail to award, to your calumniator infamy, and to you the love and approbation of mankind.

"I have now told you, Williams, what I think of your case. But I have no right to assume to be your ultimate judge. Desperate as it appears to me, I will give you one piece of advice, as if I were retained as a counsel to assist you. Leave out of it whatever tends to the disadvantage of Mr. Falkland. Defend yourself as well as you can, but do not attack your master. It is your business to create in those who hear you a prepossession in your favour. But the recrimination you have been now practising, will always create indignation. Dishonesty will admit of some palliation. The deliberate malice you have now been showing is a thousand times more atrocious. It proves you to have the mind of a demon, rather than of a felon. Wherever you shall repeat it, those who hear you will pronounce you guilty upon that, even if the proper evidence against you were glaringly defective. If therefore you would consult your interest, which seems to be your only consideration, it is incumbent upon you by all means immediately to retract that. If you desire to be believed honest, you must in the first place show that you have a due sense of merit in others. You cannot better serve your cause than by begging pardon of your master, and doing homage to rectitude and worth, even when they are employed in vengeance against you."

It is easy to conceive that my mind sustained an extreme shock from the decision of Mr. Forester; but his call upon me to retract and humble myself before my accuser penetrated my whole soul with indignation. I answered: –

"I have already told you I am innocent. I believe that I could not endure the effort of inventing a plausible defence, if it were otherwise. You have just affirmed that it is not in the power of ingenuity to subvert the distinctions of right and wrong, and in that very instant I find them subverted. This is indeed to me a very awful moment. New to the world, I know nothing of its affairs but what has reached me by rumour, or is recorded in books. I have come into it with all the ardour and confidence inseparable from my years. In every fellow-being I expected to find a friend. I am unpractised in its wiles, and have even no acquaintance with its injustice. I have done nothing to deserve the animosity of mankind; but, if I may judge from the present scene, I am henceforth to be deprived of the benefits of integrity and honour. I am to forfeit the friendship of every one I have hitherto known, and to be precluded from the power of acquiring that of others. I must therefore be reduced to derive my satisfaction from myself. Depend upon it, I will not begin that career by dishonourable concessions. If I am to despair of the good-will of other men, I will at least maintain the independence of my own mind. Mr. Falkland is my implacable enemy. Whatever may be his merits in other respects, he is acting towards me without humanity, without remorse, and without principle. Do you think I will ever make submissions to a man by whom I am thus treated, that I will fall down at the feet of one who is to me a devil, or kiss the hand that is red with my blood?"

"In that respect," answered Mr. Forester, "do as you shall think proper. I must confess that your firmness and consistency astonish me. They add something to what I had conceived of human powers. Perhaps you have chosen the part which, all things considered, may serve your purpose best; though I think more moderation would be more conciliating. The exterior of innocence will, I grant, stagger the persons who may have the direction of your fate, but it will never be able to prevail against plain and incontrovertible facts. But I have done with you. I see in you a new instance of that abuse which is so generally made of talents, the admiration of an undiscerning public. I regard you with horror. All that remains, is that I should discharge my duty, in consigning you, as a monster of depravity, to the justice of your country."

"No," rejoined Mr. Falkland, "to that I can never consent. I have put a restraint upon myself thus far, because it was right that evidence and enquiry should take their course. I have suppressed all my habits and sentiments, because it seemed due to the public that hypocrisy should be unmasked. But I can suffer this violence no longer. I have through my whole life interfered to protect, not overbear, the sufferer; and I must do so now. I feel not the smallest resentment of his impotent attacks upon my character; I smile at their malice; and they make no diminution in my benevolence to their author. Let him say what he pleases; he cannot hurt me. It was proper that he should be brought to public shame, that other people might not be deceived by him as we have been. But there is no necessity for proceeding further; and I must insist upon it that he be permitted to depart wherever he pleases. I am sorry that public interest affords so gloomy a prospect for his future happiness."

"Mr. Falkland," answered Mr. Forester, "these sentiments do honour to your humanity; but I must not give way to them. They only serve to set in a stronger light the venom of this serpent, this monster of ingratitude, who first robs his benefactor, and then reviles him. Wretch that you are, will nothing move you? Are you inaccessible to remorse? Are you not struck to the heart with the unmerited goodness of your master? Vile calumniator! you are the abhorrence of nature, the opprobrium of the human species, and the earth can only be freed from an insupportable burthen by your being exterminated! Recollect, sir, that this monster, at the very moment that you are exercising such unexampled forbearance in his behalf, has the presumption to charge you with prosecuting a crime of which you know him to be innocent, nay, with having conveyed the pretended stolen goods among his property, for the express purpose of ruining him. By this unexampled villainy, he makes it your duty to free the world from such a pest, and your interest to admit no relaxing in your pursuit of him, lest the world should be persuaded by your clemency to credit his vile insinuations."

"I care not for the consequences," replied Mr. Falkland; "I will obey the dictates of my own mind. I will never lend my assistance to the reforming mankind by axes and gibbets. I am sure things will never be as they ought, till honour, and not law, be the dictator of mankind, till vice be taught to shrink before the resistless might of inborn dignity, and not before the cold formality of statutes. If my calumniator were worthy of my resentment, I would chastise him with my own sword, and not that of the magistrate; but in the present case I smile at his malice, and resolve to spare him, as the generous lord of the forest spares the insect that would disturb his repose."

"The language you now hold," said Mr. Forester, "is that of romance, and not of reason. Yet I cannot but be struck with the contrast exhibited before me, of the magnanimity of virtue, and the obstinate impenetrable injustice of guilt. While your mind overflows with goodness, nothing can touch the heart of this thrice-refined villain. I shall never forgive myself for having once been entrapped by his detestable arts. This is no time for us to settle the question between chivalry and law. I shall therefore simply insist as a magistrate, having taken the evidence in this felony, upon my right and duty of following the course of justice, and committing the accused to the county jail."

After some further contest Mr. Falkland, finding Mr. Forester obstinate and impracticable, withdrew his opposition. Accordingly a proper officer was summoned from the neighbouring village, a mittimus[1] made out, and one of Mr. Falkland's carriages prepared to conduct me to the place of custody.

---

1 A warrant ordering the keeper of a prison to keep the person named in the warrant in custody.

It will easily be imagined that this sudden reverse was very painfully felt by me. I looked round on the servants who had been the spectators of my examination, but not one of them, either by word or gesture, expressed compassion for my calamity. The robbery of which I was accused appeared to them atrocious from its magnitude; and whatever sparks of compassion might otherwise have sprung up in their ingenuous and undisciplined minds, were totally obliterated by indignation at my supposed profligacy in recriminating upon their worthy and excellent master. My fate being already determined, and one of the servants despatched for the officer, Mr. Forester and Mr. Falkland withdrew, and left me in the custody of two others.

One of these was the son of a farmer at no great distance, who had been in habits of long established intimacy with my late father. I was willing accurately to discover the state of mind of those who had been witnesses of this scene, and who had had some previous opportunity of observing my character and manners. I, therefore, endeavoured to open a conversation with him. "Well, my good Thomas," said I, in a querulous tone, and with a hesitating manner, "am I not a most miserable creature?"

"Do not speak to me, Master Williams! You have given me a shock that I shall not get the better of for one while. You were hatched by a hen, as the saying is, but you came of the spawn of a cockatrice. I am glad to my heart that honest farmer Williams is dead; your villainy would else have made him curse the day that ever he was born."

"Thomas, I am innocent! I swear by the great God that shall judge me another day, I am innocent!"

"Pray, do not swear! for goodness' sake, do not swear! your poor soul is damned enough without that. For your sake, lad, I will never take any body's word, nor trust to appearances, thof it should be an angel. Lord bless us! how smoothly you palavered it over, for all the world, as if you had been as fair as a new-born babe! But it will not do; you will never be able to persuade people that black is white. For my own part, I have done with you. I loved you yesterday, all one as if you had been my own brother. To-day I love you so well, that I would go ten miles with all the pleasure in life to see you hanged."

"Good God, Thomas! have you the heart? What a change! I call God to witness, I have done nothing to deserve it! What a world do we live in!"

"Hold your tongue, boy! It makes my very heart sick to hear you! I would not lie a night under the same roof with you for all the world! I should expect the house to fall and crush such wickedness! I admire that the earth does not open and swallow you alive! It is poison so much as to look at you! If you go on at this hardened rate, I believe from my soul that the people you talk to will tear you to pieces, and you will never live to come to the gallows. Oh, yes, you do well to pity yourself; poor tender thing! that spit venom all round you like a toad, and leave the very ground upon which you crawl infected with your slime."

Finding the person with whom I talked thus impenetrable to all I could say, and considering that the advantage to be gained was small, even if I could overcome his prepossession, I took his advice, and was silent. It was not much longer before every thing was prepared for my departure, and I was conducted to the same prison which had so lately enclosed the wretched and innocent Hawkinses. They too had been the victims of Mr. Falkland. He exhibited, upon a contracted scale indeed, but in which the truth of delineation was faithfully sustained, a copy of what monarchs are, who reckon among the instruments of their power prisons of state.

FOR my own part, I had never seen a prison, and, like the majority of my brethren, had given myself little concern to enquire what was the condition of those who committed offence against, or became obnoxious to suspicion from, the community. Oh, how enviable is the most tottering shed under which the labourer retires to rest, compared with the residence of these walls!

To me every thing was new, – the massy doors, the resounding locks, the gloomy passages, the grated windows, and the characteristic looks of the keepers, accustomed to reject every petition, and to steel their hearts against feeling and pity. Curiosity, and a sense of my situation, induced me to fix my eyes on the faces of these men; but in a few minutes I drew them away with unconquerable loathing. It is impossible to describe the sort of squalidness and filth with which these mansions are distinguished. I have seen dirty faces in dirty apartments, which have nevertheless borne the impression of health, and spoke carelessness and levity rather than distress. But the dirt of a prison speaks sadness to the heart, and appears to be already in a state of putridity and infection.

I was detained for more than an hour in the apartment of the keeper, one turnkey after another coming in, that they might make themselves familiar with my person. As I was already considered as guilty of felony to a considerable amount, I underwent a rigorous search, and they took from me a penknife, a pair of scissors, and that part of my money which was in gold. It was debated whether or not these should be sealed up, to be returned to me, as they said, as soon as I should be acquitted; and had I not displayed an unexpected firmness of manner and vigour of expostulation, such was probably the conduct that would have been pursued. Having undergone these ceremonies, I was thrust into a day-room, in which all the persons then under confinement for felony were assembled, to the number of eleven. Each of them was too much engaged in his own reflections, to take notice of me. Of these, two were imprisoned for horse-stealing, and three for having stolen a sheep, one for shop-lifting, one for coining, two for highway-robbery, and two for burglary.

The horse-stealers were engaged in a game at cards, which was presently interrupted by a difference of opinion, attended with great vociferation, – they calling upon one and another to decide it, to no purpose; one paying no attention to their summons, and another leaving them in the midst of their story, being no longer able to endure his own internal anguish, in the midst of their mummery.

It is a custom among thieves to constitute a sort of mock tribunal of their own body, from whose decision every one is informed whether he shall be acquitted, respited, or pardoned, as well as respecting the supposed most skilful way of conducting his defence. One of the house-breakers, who had already passed this ordeal, and was stalking up and down the room with a forced bravery, exclaimed to his companion, that he was as rich as the Duke of Bedford himself. He had five guineas and a half, which was as much as he could possibly spend in the course of the ensuing month; and what happened after that, it was Jack Ketch's business to see to, not his.[1] As he uttered these words, he threw himself abruptly upon a bench that was near him, and seemed to be asleep in a moment. But his sleep was uneasy and disturbed, his breathing was hard, and, at intervals, had rather the nature of a groan. A young fellow from the other side of the room came softly to the place where he lay, with a large knife in his hand; and pressed the back of it with such violence upon his neck, the head hanging over the side of the bench, that it was not till after several efforts that he was able to rise. "Oh Jack!" cried this manual jester, "I had almost done your business for you!" The other expressed no marks of resentment, but sullenly answered, "Damn you, why did not you take the edge? It would have been the best thing you have done this many a day!"[2]

The case of one of the persons committed for highway-

---

1 Jack Ketch was a proverbial name for an executioner, taken from a seventeenth-century hangman noted for barbarity.

2 An incident exactly similar to this was witnessed by a friend of the author, a few years since, in a visit to the prison of Newgate. [Godwin's note]

robbery was not a little extraordinary. He was a common soldier of a most engaging physiognomy, and two-and-twenty years of age. The prosecutor, who had been robbed one evening, as he returned late from the alehouse of the sum of three shillings, swore positively to his person. The character of the prisoner was such as has seldom been equalled. He had been ardent in the pursuit of intellectual cultivation, and was accustomed to draw his favourite amusement from the works of Virgil and Horace. The humbleness of his situation, combined with his ardour for literature, only served to give an inexpressible heightening to the interestingness of his character. He was plain and unaffected; he assumed nothing; he was capable, when occasion demanded, of firmness, but, in his ordinary deportment, he seemed unarmed and unresisting, unsuspicious of guile in others, as he was totally free from guile in himself. His integrity was proverbially great. In one instance he had been intrusted by a lady to convey a sum of a thousand pounds to a person at some miles distance; in another, he was employed by a gentleman, during his absence, in the care of his house and furniture, to the value of at least five times that sum. His habits of thinking were strictly his own, full of justice, simplicity, and wisdom. He from time to time earned money of his officers, by his peculiar excellence in furbishing arms; but he declined offers that had been made to him to become a serjeant or a corporal, saying that he did not want money, and that in a new situation he should have less leisure for study. He was equally constant in refusing presents that were offered him by persons who had been struck with his merit; not that he was under the influence of false delicacy and pride, but that he had no inclination to accept that, the want of which he did not feel to be an evil. This man died while I was in prison. I received his last breath.[1]

The whole day I was obliged to spend in the company of these men, some of them having really committed the actions laid to their charge, others whom their ill fortune had rendered the victims of suspicion. The whole was a scene of misery, such

---

1   A story extremely similar to this is to be found in the Newgate Calendar, vol. i. p. 382. [Godwin's note]

as nothing short of actual observation can suggest to the mind. Some were noisy and obstreperous, endeavouring by a false bravery to keep at bay the remembrance of their condition; while others, incapable even of this effort, had the torment of their thoughts aggravated by the perpetual noise and confusion that prevailed around them. In the faces of those who assumed the most courage, you might trace the furrows of anxious care; and in the midst of their laboured hilarity dreadful ideas would ever and anon intrude, convulsing their features, and working every line into an expression of the keenest agony. To these men the sun brought no return of joy. Day after day rolled on, but their state was immutable. Existence was to them a scene of invariable melancholy; every moment was a moment of anguish; yet did they wish to prolong that moment, fearful that the coming period would bring a severer fate. They thought of the past with insupportable repentance, each man contented to give his right hand to have again the choice of that peace and liberty, which he had unthinkingly bartered away. We talk of instruments of torture; Englishmen take credit to themselves for having banished the use of them from their happy shore! Alas! he that has observed the secrets of a prison, well knows that there is more torture in the lingering existence of a criminal, in the silent intolerable minutes that he spends, than in the tangible misery of whips and racks!

Such were our days. At sunset our jailors appeared, and ordered each man to come away, and be locked into his dungeon. It was a bitter aggravation of our fate, to be under the arbitrary control of these fellows. They felt no man's sorrow; they were of all men least capable of any sort of feeling. They had a barbarous and sullen pleasure in issuing their detested mandates, and observing the mournful reluctance with which they were obeyed. Whatever they directed, it was in vain to expostulate; fetters, and bread and water were the sure consequences of resistance. Their tyranny had no other limit than their own caprice. To whom shall the unfortunate felon appeal? To what purpose complain, when his complaints are sure to be received with incredulity? A tale of mutiny and necessary precaution is the unfailing refuge of the keeper, and this tale is an everlasting bar against redress.

Our dungeons were cells, 7 feet by 6, below the surface of the ground, damp, without window, light, or air, except from a few holes worked for that purpose in the door. In some of these miserable receptacles three persons were put to sleep together.[1] I was fortunate enough to have one to myself. It was now the approach of winter. We were not allowed to have candles, and, as I have already said, were thrust in here at sunset, and not liberated till the returning day. This was our situation for fourteen or fifteen hours out of the four-and-twenty. I had never been accustomed to sleep more than six or seven hours, and my inclination to sleep was now less than ever. Thus was I reduced to spend half my day in this dreary abode, and in complete darkness. This was no trifling aggravation of my lot.

Among my melancholy reflections I tasked my memory, and counted over the doors, the locks, the bolts, the chains, the massy walls, and grated windows, that were between me and liberty. "These," said I, "are the engines that tyranny sits down in cold and serious meditation to invent. This is the empire that man exercises over man. Thus is a being, formed to expatiate, to act, to smile, and enjoy, restricted and benumbed. How great must be his depravity or heedlessness, who vindicates this scheme for changing health and gaiety and serenity, into the wanness of a dungeon, and the deep furrows of agony and despair!"

"Thank God," exclaims the Englishman, "we have no Bastile! Thank God, with us no man can be punished without a crime!" Unthinking wretch! Is that a country of liberty, where thousands languish in dungeons and fetters? Go, go, ignorant fool! and visit the scenes of our prisons! witness their unwholesomeness, their filth, the tyranny of their governors, the misery of their inmates! After that, show me the man shameless enough to triumph, and say, England has no Bastile! Is there any charge so frivolous, upon which men are not consigned to those detested abodes? Is there any villainy that is not practised by justices and prosecutors? But against all this perhaps you

---

1   See Howard on prisons. [Godwin's note; an extract from Howard's volume can be found in Appendix C.]

have been told there is redress. Yes; a redress, that it is the consummation of insult so much as to name! Where shall the poor wretch reduced to the last despair, and to whom acquittal perhaps comes just time enough to save him from perishing, – where shall this man find leisure, and much less money, to fee counsel and officers, and purchase the tedious dear-bought remedy of the law? No; he is too happy to leave his dungeon, and the memory of his dungeon, behind him; and the same tyranny and wanton oppression become the inheritance of his successor.

For myself, I looked round upon my walls, and forward upon the premature death I had too much reason to expect: I consulted my own heart, that whispered nothing but innocence; and I said, "This is society. This is the object, the distribution of justice, which is the end of human reason. For this sages have toiled, and midnight oil has been wasted. This!"

The reader will forgive this digression from the immediate subject of my story. If it should be said these are general remarks, let it be remembered that they are the dear-bought result of experience. It is from the fullness of a bursting heart that reproach thus flows to my pen. These are not the declamations of a man desirous to be eloquent. I have felt the iron of slavery grating upon my soul.

I believed that misery, more pure than that which I now endured, had never fallen to the lot of a human being. I recollected with astonishment my puerile eagerness to be brought to the test, and have my innocence examined. I execrated it, as the vilest and most insufferable pedantry. I exclaimed, in the bitterness of my heart, "Of what value is a fair fame? It is the jewel of men formed to be amused with baubles. Without it, I might have had serenity of heart and cheerfulness of occupation, peace and liberty; why should I consign my happiness to other men's arbitration? But, if a fair fame were of the most inexpressible value, is this the method which common sense would prescribe to retrieve it? The language which these institutions hold out to the unfortunate is, Come, and be shut out from the light of day; be the associate of those whom society has marked out for her abhorrence, be the slave of jailers, be loaded with fetters; thus shall you be cleared from every unworthy aspersion, and restored to reputation and honour! This is the consolation she affords to those whom malignity or folly, private pique or unfounded positiveness, have, without the smallest foundation, loaded with calumny. For myself, I felt my own innocence; and I soon found, upon enquiry, that three fourths of those who are regularly subjected to a similar treatment, are persons whom, even with all the superciliousness and precipitation of our courts of justice, no evidence can be found sufficient to convict. How slender then must be that man's portion of information and discernment, who is willing to commit his character and welfare to such guardianship!

But my case was even worse than this. I intimately felt that a trial, such as our institutions have hitherto been able to make it, is only the worthy sequel of such a beginning. What chance was there after the purgation I was now suffering, that I should come out acquitted at last? What probability was there that the trial I had endured in the house of Mr. Falkland was not just as fair as any that might be expected to follow? No; I anticipated my own condemnation.

Thus was I cut off, for ever from all that existence has to bestow – from all the high hopes I had so often conceived – from all the future excellence my soul so much delighted to imagine, – to spend a few weeks in a miserable prison, and then to perish by the hand of the public executioner. No language can do justice to the indignant and soul-sickening loathing that these ideas excited. My resentment was not restricted to my prosecutor, but extended itself to the whole machine of society. I could never believe that all this was the fair result of institutions inseparable from the general good. I regarded the whole human species as so many hangmen and torturers; I considered them as confederated to tear me to pieces; and this wide scene of inexorable persecution inflicted upon me inexpressible agony. I looked on this side and on that: I was innocent; I had a right to expect assistance; but every heart was steeled against me; every hand was ready to lend its force to make my ruin secure. No man that has not felt, in his own most momentous concerns, justice, eternal truth, unalterable equity engaged in his behalf, and on the other side brute force, impenetrable obstinacy, and unfeeling insolence, can imagine the sensations that then passed through my mind. I saw treachery triumphant and enthroned; I saw the sinews of innocence crumbled into dust by the gripe of almighty guilt.

What relief had I from these sensations? Was it relief, that I spent the day in the midst of profligacy and execrations – that I saw reflected from every countenance agonies only inferior to my own? He that would form a lively idea of the regions of the damned, need only to witness, for six hours, a scene to which I was confined for many months. Not for one hour could I withdraw myself from this complexity of horrors, or take refuge in the calmness of meditation. Air, exercise, series, contrast, those grand enliveners of the human frame, I was for ever debarred from, by the inexorable tyranny under which I was fallen. Nor did I find the solitude of my nightly dungeon less insupportable. Its only furniture was the straw that served me for my repose. It was narrow, damp and unwholesome. The slumbers of a mind, wearied, like mine, with the most detestable uniformity, to whom neither amusement nor occupation ever offered themselves to beguile the painful hours, were short, disturbed, and unrefreshing. My sleeping, still more than my waking thoughts, were full of perplexity, deformity, and disorder. To these slumbers succeeded the hours which, by the regulations of our prison, I was obliged, though awake, to spend in solitary and cheerless darkness. Here I had neither books nor pens, nor any thing upon which to engage my attention; all was a sightless blank. How was a mind, active and indefatigable like mine, to endure this misery? I could not sink it in lethargy; I could not forget my woes: they haunted me with unintermitted and demoniac malice. Cruel, inexorable policy of human affairs, that condemns a man to torture like this; that sanctions it, and knows not what is done under its sanction; that is too supine and unfeeling to enquire into these petty details; that calls this the ordeal of innocence, and the protector of freedom! A thousand times I could have dashed my brains against the walls of my dungeon; a thousand times I longed for death, and wished, with inexpressible ardour, for an end to

what I suffered; a thousand times I meditated suicide, and ruminated, in the bitterness of my soul, upon the different means of
escaping from the load of existence. What had I to do with life?
I had seen enough to make me regard it with detestation. Why
should I wait the lingering process of legal despotism, and not
dare so much as to die, but when and how its instruments
decreed? Still some inexplicable suggestion withheld my hand.
I clung with desperate fondness to this shadow of existence, its
mysterious attractions, and its hopeless prospects.

CHAPTER XII

SUCH were the reflections that haunted the first days of my imprisonment, in consequence of which they were spent in perpetual anguish. But, after a time nature, wearied with distress, would no longer stoop to the burthen; thought, which is incessantly varying, introduced a series of reflections totally different.

My fortitude revived. I had always been accustomed to cheerfulness, good humour, and serenity; and this habit now returned to visit me at the bottom of my dungeon. No sooner did my contemplations take this turn, than I saw the reasonableness and possibility of tranquillity and peace; and my mind whispered to me the propriety of showing, in this forlorn condition, that I was superior to all my persecutors. Blessed state of innocence and self-approbation! The sunshine of conscious integrity pierced through all the barriers of my cell, and spoke ten thousand times more joy to my heart, than the accumulated splendours of nature and art can communicate to the slaves of vice.

I found out the secret of employing my mind. I said, "I am shut up for half the day in total darkness, without any external source of amusement; the other half I spend in the midst of noise, turbulence, and confusion. What then? Can I not draw amusement from the stores of my own mind? Is it not freighted with various knowledge? Have I not been employed from my infancy in gratifying an insatiable curiosity? When should I derive benefit from these superior advantages, if not at present?" Accordingly I tasked the stores of my memory, and my powers of invention. I amused myself with recollecting the history of my life. By degrees I called to mind a number of minute circumstances, which, but for this exercise, would have been for ever forgotten. I repassed in my thoughts whole conversations, I recollected their subjects, their arrangement, their incidents, frequently their very words. I mused upon these ideas, till I was totally absorbed in thought. I repeated them, till my mind glowed with enthusiasm. I had my different employments, fitted for the solitude of the night, in which I could give full scope to the impulses of my mind; and for the uproar of the day, in which my chief object was, to be insensible to the disorder with which I was surrounded.

By degrees I quitted my own story, and employed myself in imaginary adventures. I figured to myself every situation in which I could be placed, and conceived the conduct to be observed in each. Thus scenes of insult and danger, of tenderness and oppression, became familiar to me. In fancy I often passed the awful hour of dissolving nature. In some of my reveries I boiled with impetuous indignation, and in others patiently collected the whole force of my mind for some fearful encounter. I cultivated the powers of oratory suited to these different states, and improved more in eloquence in the solitude of my dungeon, than perhaps I should have done in the busiest and most crowded scenes.

At length I proceeded to as regular a disposition of my time, as the man in his study, who passes from mathematics to poetry, and from poetry to the law of nations, in the different parts of each single day; and I as seldom infringed upon my plan. Nor were my subjects of disquisition less numerous than his. I went over, by the assistance of memory only, a considerable part of Euclid during my confinement, and revived, day after day, the series of facts and incidents in some of the most celebrated historians. I became myself a poet; and, while I described the sentiments cherished by the view of natural objects, recorded the characters and passions of men, and partook with a burning zeal in the generosity of their determinations, I eluded the squalid solitude of my dungeon, and wandered in idea through all the varieties of human society. I easily found expedients, such as the mind seems always to require, and which books and pens supply to the man at large, to record from time to time the progress that had been made.

While I was thus employed, I reflected with exultation upon the degree in which man is independent of the smiles and frowns of fortune. I was beyond her reach, for I could fall no lower. To an ordinary eye I might seem destitute and miserable, but in reality I wanted for nothing. My fare was coarse; but I was in health. My dungeon was noisome; but I felt no inconvenience. I was shut up from the usual means of exercise and air; but I found the method of exercising myself even to perspiration in my dungeon. I had no power of withdrawing my person from disgustful society, in the most cheerful and valuable part of the day; but I soon brought to perfection the art of withdrawing my thoughts, and saw and heard the people about me, for just as short a time, and as seldom, as I pleased.

Such is man in himself considered; so simple his nature; so few his wants. How different from the man of artificial society! Palaces are built for his reception, a thousand vehicles provided for his exercise, provinces are ransacked for the gratification of his appetite, and the whole world traversed to supply him with apparel and furniture. Thus vast is his expenditure, and the purchase slavery. He is dependent on a thousand accidents for tranquillity and health, and his body and soul are at the devotion of whoever will satisfy his imperious cravings.

In addition to the disadvantages of my present situation, I was reserved for an ignominious death. What then? Every man must die. No man knows how soon. It surely is not worse to encounter the king of terrors, in health, and with every advantage for the collection of fortitude, than to encounter him, already half subdued by sickness and suffering. I was resolved at least fully to possess the days I had to live; and this is peculiarly in the power of the man who preserves his health to the last moment of his existence. Why should I suffer my mind to be invaded by unavailing regrets? Every sentiment of vanity, or rather of independence and justice within me, instigated me to say to my persecutor, "You may cut off my existence, but you cannot disturb my serenity."

CHAPTER XIII

IN the midst of these reflections, another thought, which had not before struck me, occurred to my mind. "I exult," said I, "and reasonably, over the impotence of my persecutor. Is not that impotence greater than I have yet imagined? I say, he may cut off my existence, but cannot disturb my serenity. It is true: my mind, the clearness of my spirit, the firmness of my temper, are beyond his reach; is not my life equally so, if I please? What are the material obstacles, that man never subdued? What is the undertaking so arduous, that by some has not been accomplished? And if by others, why not by me? Had they stronger motives than I? Was existence more variously endeared to them? or had they more numerous methods by which to animate and adorn it? Many of those who have exerted most perseverance and intrepidity, were obviously my inferiors in that respect. Why should not I be as daring as they? Adamant and steel have a ductility like water, to a mind sufficiently bold and contemplative. The mind is master of itself and is endowed with powers that might enable it to laugh at the tyrant's vigilance." I passed and repassed these ideas in my mind; and, heated with the contemplation, I said, "No, I will not die!"

My reading, in early youth, had been extremely miscellaneous. I had read of housebreakers to whom locks and bolts were a jest, and who, vain of their art, exhibited the experiment of entering a house the most strongly barricaded, with as little noise, and almost as little trouble, as other men would lift up a latch. There is nothing so interesting to the juvenile mind, as the wonderful; there is no power that it so eagerly covets, as that of astonishing spectators by its miraculous exertions. Mind appeared, to my untutored reflections, vague, airy, and unfettered, the susceptible perceiver of reasons, but never intended by nature to be the slave of force. Why should it be in the power of man to overtake and hold me by violence? Why, when I choose to withdraw myself, should I not be capable of eluding the most vigilant search? These limbs, and this trunk, are a cumbrous and unfortunate load for the power of thinking to drag along with it; but why should not the power of thinking be able to lighten the load, till it shall be no longer felt? – These early modes of reflection were by no means indifferent to my present enquiries.

Our next-door neighbour at my father's house had been a carpenter. Fresh from the sort of reading I have mentioned, I was eager to examine his tools, their powers and their uses. This carpenter was a man of strong and vigorous mind; and, his faculties having been chiefly confined to the range of his profession, he was fertile in experiments, and ingenious in reasoning upon these particular topics. I therefore obtained from him considerable satisfaction; and, my mind being set in action, I sometimes even improved upon the hints he furnished. His conversation was particularly agreeable to me; I at first worked with him sometimes for my amusement, and afterwards occasionally for a short time as his journeyman. I was constitutionally vigorous; and, by the experience thus attained, I added to the abstract possession of power, the skill of applying it, when I pleased, in such a manner as that no part should be inefficient.

It is a strange, but no uncommon feature in the human mind, that the very resource of which we stand in greatest need in a critical situation, though already accumulated, it may be, by preceding industry, fails to present itself at the time when it should be called into action. Thus my mind had passed through two very different stages since my imprisonment, before this means of liberation suggested itself. My faculties were overwhelmed in the first instance, and raised to a pitch of enthusiasm in the second; while in both I took it for granted in a manner, that I must passively submit to the good pleasure of my persecutors.

During the period in which my mind had been thus undecided, and when I had been little more than a month in durance, the assizes, which were held twice a year in the town in which I was a prisoner, came on. Upon this occasion my case was not brought forward, but was suffered to stand over six months longer. It would have been just the same, if I had had as strong reason to expect acquittal as I had conviction. If I had been apprehended upon the most frivolous reasons upon which any justice of the peace ever thought proper to commit a naked beggar for trial, I must still have waited about two hundred and seventeen days before my innocence could be cleared. So imperfect are the effects of the boasted laws of a country, whose legislators hold their assembly from four to six months in every year! I could never discover with certainty, whether this delay were owing to any interference on the part of my prosecutor, or whether it fell out in the regular administration of justice, which is too solemn and dignified to accommodate itself to the rights or benefit of an insignificant individual.

But this was not the only incident that occurred to me during my confinement for which I could find no satisfactory solution. It was nearly at the same time, that the keeper began to alter his behaviour to me. He sent for me one morning into the part of the building which was appropriated for his own use, and, after some hesitation, told me he was sorry my accommodations had been so indifferent, and asked whether I should like to have a chamber in his family? I was struck with the unexpectedness of this question, and desired to know whether any body had employed him to ask it. No, he replied; but, now the assizes were over, he had fewer felons on his hands, and more time to look about him. He believed I was a good kind of a young man, and he had taken a sort of a liking to me. I fixed my eye upon his countenance as he said this. I could discover none of the usual symptoms of kindness; he appeared to me to be acting a part, unnatural, and that sat with awkwardness upon him. He went on however to offer me the liberty of eating at his table; which, if I chose it, he said, would make no difference to him, and he should not think of charging me any thing for it. He had always indeed as much upon his hands as one person could see to; but his wife and his daughter Peggy would be woundily pleased to hear a person of learning talk, as he understood I was; and perhaps I might not feel myself unpleasantly circumstanced in their company.

I reflected on this proposal, and had little doubt, notwithstanding what the keeper had affirmed to the contrary, that it did not proceed from any spontaneous humanity in him, but that he had, to speak the language of persons of his cast, good reasons for what he did. I busied myself in conjectures as to who could be the author of this sort of indulgence and attention. The two most likely persons were Mr. Falkland and Mr. Forester. The latter I knew to be a man austere and inexorable towards those whom he deemed vicious. He piqued himself upon being insensible to those softer emotions, which, he believed, answered no other purpose than to seduce us from our duty. Mr. Falkland, on the contrary, was a man of the acutest sensibility; hence arose his pleasures and his pains, his virtues and his vices. Though he were the bitterest enemy to whom I could possibly be exposed, and though no sentiments of humanity could divert or control the bent of his mind, I yet persuaded myself, that he was more likely than his kinsman, to visit in idea the scene of my dungeon, and to feel impelled to alleviate my sufferings.

This conjecture was by no means calculated to serve as balm to my mind. My thoughts were full of irritation against my persecutor. How could I think kindly of a man, in competition with the gratification of whose ruling passion my good name or my life was deemed of no consideration? I saw him crushing the one, and bringing the other into jeopardy, with a quietness and composure on his part that I could not recollect without horror. I knew not what were his plans respecting me. I knew not whether he troubled himself so much as to form a barren wish for the preservation of one whose future prospects he had so iniquitously tarnished. I had hitherto been silent as to my principal topic of recrimination. But I was by no means certain, that I should consent to go out of the world in silence, the victim of this man's obduracy and art. In every view I felt my heart ulcerated with a sense of his injustice; and my very soul spurned these pitiful indulgences, at a time that he was grinding me into dust with the inexorableness of his vengeance.

I was influenced by these sentiments in my reply to the jailor; and I found a secret pleasure in pronouncing them in all their bitterness. I viewed him with a sarcastic smile, and said, I was glad to find him of a sudden become so humane: I was not however without some penetration as to the humanity of a jailor, and could guess at the circumstances by which it was produced. But he might tell his employer, that his cares were fruitless: I would accept no favours from a man that held a halter about my neck; and had courage enough to endure the worst both in time to come and now. – The jailor looked at me with astonishment, and turning upon his heel, exclaimed, "Well done, my cock! You have not had your learning for nothing, I see. You are set upon not dying dunghill. But that is to come, lad; you had better by half keep your courage till you shall find it wanted."

The assizes, which passed over without influence to me, produced a great revolution among my fellow-prisoners. I lived long enough in the jail to witness a general mutation of its inhabitants. One of the housebreakers (the rival of the Duke of Bedford), and the coiner, were hanged. Two more were cast for transportation, and the rest acquitted. The transports remained with us; and, though the prison was thus lightened of nine of its inhabitants, there were, at the next half-yearly period of assizes, as many persons on the felons' side, within three, as I had found on my first arrival.

The soldier, whose story I have already recorded, died on the evening of the very day on which the judges arrived, of a disease the consequence of his confinement. Such was the justice, that resulted from the laws of his country to an individual who would have been the ornament of any age; one who, of all the men I ever knew, was perhaps the kindest, of the most feeling heart, of the most engaging and unaffected manners, and the most unblemished life. The name of this man was Brightwel. Were it possible for my pen to consecrate him to never-dying fame, I could undertake no task more grateful to my heart. His judgment was penetrating and manly, totally unmixed with imbecility and confusion, while at the same time there was such an uncontending frankness in his countenance, that a superficial observer would have supposed he must have been the prey of the first plausible knavery that was practised against him. Great reason have I to remember him with affection! He was the most ardent, I had almost said the last, of my friends. Nor did I remain in this respect in his debt. There was indeed a great congeniality, if I may presume to say so, in our characters, except that I cannot pretend to rival the originality and self-created vigour of his mind, or to compare with, what the world has scarcely surpassed, the correctness and untainted purity of his conduct. He heard my story, as far as I thought proper to disclose it, with interest; he examined it with sincere impartiality; and if, at first, any doubt remained upon his mind, a frequent observation of me in my most unguarded moments taught him in no long time to place an unreserved confidence in my innocence.

He talked of the injustice of which we were mutual victims without bitterness; and delighted to believe that the time would come, when the possibility of such intolerable oppression would be extirpated. But this, he said, was a happiness reserved for posterity; it was too late for us to reap the benefit of it. It was some consolation to him, that he could not tell the period in his past life, which the best judgment of which he was capable would teach him to spend better. He could say, with as much reason as most men, he had discharged his duty. But he foresaw that he should not survive his present calamity. This was his prediction, while yet in health. He might be said, in a certain sense, to have a broken heart. But, if that phrase were in any way applicable to him, sure never was despair more calm, more full of resignation and serenity.

At no time in the whole course of my adventures was I exposed to a shock more severe, than I received from this man's death. The circumstances of his fate presented themselves to my mind in their full complication of iniquity. From him, and the execrations with which I loaded the government that could be the instrument of this tragedy, I turned to myself. I beheld the catastrophe of Brightwel with envy. A thousand times I longed that my corse had lain in death, instead of his. I was only reserved, as I persuaded myself, for unutterable woe. In a few days he would have been acquitted; his liberty, his reputation restored; mankind perhaps, struck with the injustice he had suffered, would have shown themselves eager to balance his misfortunes, and obliterate his disgrace. But this man died; and I remained alive! I, who, though not less wrongfully treated than he, had no hope of reparation, must be marked as long as I lived for a villain, and in my death probably held up to the scorn and detestation of my species!

Such were some of the immediate reflections which the fate

of this unfortunate martyr produced in my mind. Yet my intercourse with Brightwel was not, in the review, without its portion of comfort. I said, "This man has seen through the veil of calumny that overshades me: he has understood, and has loved me. Why should I despair? May I not meet hereafter with men ingenuous like him, who shall do me justice, and sympathise with my calamity? With that consolation I will be satisfied. I will rest in the arms of friendship, and forget the malignity of the world. Henceforth I will be contented with tranquil obscurity, with the cultivation of sentiment and wisdom, and the exercise of benevolence within a narrow circle." It was thus that my mind became excited to the project I was about to undertake.

I had no sooner meditated the idea of an escape, than I determined upon the following method of facilitating the preparations for it. I undertook to ingratiate myself with my keeper. In the world I have generally found such persons as had been acquainted with the outline of my story, regarding me with a sort of loathing and abhorrence, which made them avoid me with as much care as if I had been spotted with the plague. The idea of my having first robbed my patron, and then endeavouring to clear myself by charging him with subornation against me, placed me in a class distinct from, and infinitely more guilty than that of common felons. But this man was too good a master of his profession to entertain aversion against a fellow-creature upon that score. He considered the persons committed to his custody, merely as so many human bodies, for whom he was responsible that they should be forthcoming in time and place; and the difference of innocence and guilt he looked down upon as an affair beneath his attention. I had not therefore the prejudices to encounter in recommending myself to him, that I have found so peculiarly obstinate in other cases. Add to which, the same motive, whatever it was, that had made him so profuse in his offers a little before, had probably its influence on the present occasion.

I informed him of my skill in the profession of a joiner, and offered to make him half a dozen handsome chairs, if he would facilitate my obtaining the tools necessary for carrying on my profession in my present confinement; for, without his consent previously obtained, it would have been in vain for me to expect that I could quietly exert an industry of this kind, even if my existence had depended upon it. He looked at me first, as asking himself what he was to understand by this novel proposal; and then, his countenance most graciously relaxing, said, he was glad I was come off a little of my high notions and my buckram, and he would see what he could do. Two days after, he signified his compliance. He said that, as to the matter of the present I had offered him, he thought nothing of that; I might do as I pleased in it; but I might depend upon every civility from him that he could show with safety to himself, if so be as, when he was civil, I did not offer a second time for to snap and take him up short.

Having thus gained my preliminary, I gradually accumulated tools of various sorts – gimlets, piercers, chisels, et cetera. I immediately set myself to work. The nights were long, and the sordid eagerness of my keeper, notwithstanding his ostentatious generosity, was great; I therefore petitioned for, and was indulged with, a bit of candle, that I might amuse myself for an hour or two with my work after I was locked up in my dungeon. I did not however by any means apply constantly to the work I had undertaken, and my jailor betrayed various tokens of impatience. Perhaps he was afraid I should not have finished it, before I was hanged. I however insisted upon working at my leisure as I pleased; and this he did not venture expressly to dispute. In addition to the advantages thus obtained, I procured secretly from Miss Peggy, who now and then came into the jail to make her observations of the prisoners, and who seemed to have conceived some partiality for my person, the implement of an iron crow.

In these proceedings it is easy to trace the vice and duplicity that must be expected to grow out of injustice. I know not whether my readers will pardon the sinister advantage I extracted from the mysterious concessions of my keeper. But I must acknowledge my weakness in that respect; I am writing my adventures, and not my apology; and I was not prepared to maintain the unvaried sincerity of my manners, at the expense of a speedy close of my existence.

My plan was now digested. I believed that, by means of the

crow, I could easily, and without much noise, force the door of my dungeon from its hinges, or if not, that I could, in case of necessity, cut away the lock. This door led into a narrow passage, bounded on one side by the range of dungeons, and on the other by the jailor's and turnkeys' apartments, through which was the usual entrance from the street. This outlet I dared not attempt, for fear of disturbing the persons close to whose very door I should in that case have found it necessary to pass. I determined therefore upon another door at the further end of the passage, which was well barricaded, and which led to a sort of garden in the occupation of the keeper. This garden I had never entered, but I had had an opportunity of observing it from the window of the felons' day-room, which looked that way, the room itself being immediately over the range of dungeons. I perceived that it was bounded by a wall of considerable height, which I was told by my fellow-prisoners was the extremity of the jail on that side, and beyond which was a back-lane of some length, that terminated in the skirts of the town. Upon an accurate observation, and much reflection upon the subject, I found I should be able, if once I got into the garden, with my gimlets and piercers inserted at proper distances to make a sort of ladder, by means of which I could clear the wall, and once more take possession of the sweets of liberty. I preferred this wall to that which immediately skirted my dungeon, on the other side of which was a populous street. I suffered about two days to elapse from the period at which I had thoroughly digested my project, and then in the very middle of the night began to set about its execution. The first door was attended with considerable difficulty; but at length this obstacle was happily removed. The second door was fastened on the inside. I was therefore able with perfect ease to push back the bolts. But the lock, which of course was depended upon for the principal security, and was therefore strong, was double-shot, and the key taken away. I endeavoured with my chisel to force back the bolt of the lock, but to no purpose. I then unscrewed the box of the lock; and, that being taken away, the door was no longer opposed to my wishes.

Thus far I had proceeded with the happiest success; but close on the other side of the door there was a kennel with a large mastiff dog, of which I had not the smallest previous knowledge. Though I stepped along in the most careful manner, this animal was disturbed, and began to bark. I was extremely disconcerted, but immediately applied myself to soothe the animal, in which I presently succeeded. I then returned along the passage to listen whether any body had been disturbed by the noise of the dog; resolved, if that had been the case, that I would return to my dungeon, and endeavour to replace every thing in its former state. But the whole appeared perfectly quiet, and I was encouraged to proceed in my operation.

I now got to the wall, and had nearly gained half the ascent, when I heard a voice at the garden-door, crying, "Holloa! who is there? who opened the door?" The man received no answer, and the night was too dark for him to distinguish objects at any distance. He therefore returned, as I judged, into the house for a light. Meantime the dog, understanding the key in which these interrogations were uttered, began barking again more violently than ever. I had now no possibility of retreat, and I was not without hopes that I might yet accomplish my object, and clear the wall. Meanwhile, a second man came out while the other was getting his lantern, and by the time I had got to the top of the wall was able to perceive me. He immediately set up a shout, and threw a large stone, which grazed me in its flight. Alarmed at my situation, I was obliged to descend on the other side without taking the necessary precautions, and in my fall nearly dislocated my ankle.

There was a door in the wall, of which I was not previously apprised; and, this being opened, the two men with the lantern were on the other side in an instant. They had then nothing to do but to run along the lane to the place from which I had descended. I endeavoured to rise after my fall; but the pain was so intense, that I was scarcely able to stand, and, after having limped a few paces, I twisted my foot under me, and fell down again. I had now no remedy, and quietly suffered myself to be retaken.

CHAPTER XIV

I WAS conducted to the keeper's room for that night, and the two men sat up with me. I was accosted with many interrogatories, to which I gave little answer, but complained of the hurt in my leg. To this I could obtain no reply, except "Curse you, my lad! if that be all, we will give you some ointment for that; we will anoint it with a little cold iron." They were indeed excessively sulky with me, for having broken their night's rest, and given them all this trouble. In the morning they were as good as their word, fixing a pair of fetters upon both my legs, regardless of the ankle which was now swelled to a considerable size, and then fastening me, with a padlock, to a staple in the floor of my dungeon. I expostulated with warmth upon this treatment, and told them, that I was a man upon whom the law as yet had passed no censure, and who therefore, in the eye of the law, was innocent. But they bid me keep such fudge for people who knew no better; they knew what they did, and would answer it to any court in England.

The pain of the fetter was intolerable. I endeavoured in various ways to relieve it, and even privily to free my leg; but the more it was swelled, the more was this rendered impossible. I then resolved to bear it with patience: still, the longer it continued, the worse it grew. After two days and two nights, I entreated the turnkey to go and ask the surgeon, who usually attended the prison, to look at it, for, if it continued longer as it was, I was convinced it would mortify. But he glared surlily at me, and said, "Damn my blood! I should like to see that day. To die of a mortification is too good an end for such a rascal!" At the time that he thus addressed me, the whole mass of my blood was already fevered by the anguish I had undergone, my patience was wholly exhausted, and I was silly enough to be irritated beyond bearing, by his impertinence and vulgarity: "Look, you, Mr. Turnkey," said I, "there is one thing that such fellows as you are set over us for, and another thing that you are not. You are to take care we do not escape; but it is no part of your office to call us names and abuse us. If I were not chained to the floor, you dare as well eat your fingers as use such language; and, take my word for it, you shall yet live to repent of your insolence."

While I thus spoke, the man stared at me with astonishment. He was so little accustomed to such reports, that, at first, he could scarcely believe his ears; and such was the firmness of my manner, that he seemed to forget for a moment that I was not at large. But, as soon as he had time to recollect himself, he did not deign to be angry. His face relaxed into a smile of contempt; he snapped his fingers at me, and, turning upon his heel, exclaimed, "Well said, my cock! crow away! Have a care you do not burst!" and, as he shut the door upon me, mimicked the voice of the animal he mentioned.

This rejoinder brought me to myself in a moment, and showed me the impotence of the resentment I was expressing. But, though he thus put an end to the violence of my speech, the torture of my body continued as great as ever. I was determined to change my mode of attack. The same turnkey returned in a few minutes; and, as he approached me, to put down some food he had brought, I slipped a shilling into his hand, saying at the same time, "My good fellow, for God's sake, go to the surgeon; I am sure you do not wish me to perish for want of assistance." The fellow put the shilling into his pocket, looked hard at me, and then with one nod of his head, and without uttering a single word, went away. The surgeon presently after made his appearance; and, finding the part in a high state of inflammation, ordered certain applications, and gave peremptory directions that the fetter should not be replaced upon that leg, till a cure had been effected. It was a full month before the leg was perfectly healed, and made equally strong and flexible with the other.

The condition in which I was now placed, was totally different from that which had preceded this attempt. I was chained all day in my dungeon, with no other mitigation, except that the door was regularly opened for a few hours in an afternoon, at which time some of the prisoners occasionally came and spoke to me, particularly one, who, though he could ill replace my benevolent Brightwel, was not deficient in excellent qualities. This was no other than the individual whom Mr. Falkland had, some months before, dismissed upon an accusation of murder. His courage was gone, his garb was squalid, and the comeliness and clearness of his countenance was utterly obliterated. He also was innocent, worthy, brave, and benevolent. He was, I believe, afterwards acquitted, and turned loose, to wander a desolate and perturbed spectre through the world. My manual labours were now at an end; my dungeon was searched every night, and every kind of tool carefully kept from me. The straw, which had been hitherto allowed me, was removed, under pretence that it was adapted for concealment; and the only conveniences with which I was indulged, were a chair and a blanket.

A prospect of some alleviation in no long time opened upon me; but this my usual ill fortune rendered abortive. The keeper once more made his appearance, and with his former constitutional and ambiguous humanity. He pretended to be surprised at my want of every accommodation. He reprehended in strong terms my attempt to escape, and observed, that there must be an end of civility from people in his situation, if gentlemen, after all, would not know when they were well. It was necessary, in cases the like of this, to let the law take its course; and it would be ridiculous in me to complain, if, after a regular trial, things should go hard with me. He was desirous of being in every respect my friend, if I would let him. In the midst of this circumlocution and preamble, he was called away from me, for something relating to the business of his office. In the mean time I ruminated upon his overtures; and, detesting as I did the source from which I conceived them to flow, I could not help reflecting how far it would be possible to extract from them the means of escape. But my meditations in this case were vain. The keeper returned no more during the remainder of that day, and, on the next, an incident occurred which put an end to all expectations from his kindness.

An active mind, which has once been forced into any particular train, can scarcely be persuaded to desert it as hopeless. I had studied my chains, during the extreme anguish that I endured from the pressure of the fetter upon the ankle which had been sprained; and though, from the swelling and acute sensibility of the part, I had found all attempts at relief, in that instance, impracticable, I obtained, from the coolness of my investigation, another and apparently superior advantage. During the night, my dungeon was in a complete state of darkness; but, when the door was open, the case was somewhat different. The passage indeed into which it opened, was so narrow, and the opposite dead wall so near, that it was but a glimmering and melancholy light that entered my apartment, even at full noon, and when the door was at its widest extent. But my eyes, after a practice of two or three weeks, accommodated themselves to this circumstance, and I learned to distinguish the minutest object. One day, as I was alternately meditating and examining the objects around me, I chanced to observe a nail trodden into the mud-floor at no great distance from me. I immediately conceived the desire of possessing myself of this implement; but, for fear of surprise, people passing perpetually to and fro, I contented myself, for the present, with remarking its situation so accurately, that I might easily find it again in the dark. Accordingly, as soon as my door was shut, I seized upon this new treasure, and, having contrived to fashion it to my purpose, found that I could unlock with it the padlock that fastened me to the staple in the floor. This I regarded as no inconsiderable advantage, separately from the use I might derive from it in relation to my principal object. My chain permitted me to move only about eighteen inches to the right or left; and, having borne this confinement for several weeks, my very heart leaped at the pitiful consolation of being able to range, without constraint, the miserable coop in which I was immured. This incident had occurred several days previously to the last visit of my keeper.

From this time it had been my constant practice to liberate myself every night, and not to replace things in their former situation till I awoke in the morning, and expected shortly to perceive the entrance of the turnkey. Security breeds negligence. On the morning succeeding my conference with the jailor, it so happened, whether I overslept myself, or the turnkey went his round earlier than usual, that I was roused from my sleep by the noise he made in opening the cell next to my own; and though I exerted the utmost diligence, yet having to grope for my materials in the dark, I was unable to fasten the chain to the staple, before he entered, as usual, with his lantern. He was extremely surprised to find me disengaged, and immediately summoned the principal keeper. I was questioned respecting my method of proceeding; and, as I believed concealment could lead to nothing but a severer search, and a more accurate watch, I readily acquainted them with the exact truth. The illustrious personage, whose functions it was to control the inhabitants of these walls, was, by this last instance, completely exasperated against me. Artifice and fair speaking were at an end. His eyes sparkled with fury; he exclaimed, that he was now convinced of the folly of showing kindness to rascals, the scum of the earth, such as I was; and, damn him, if any body should catch him at that again towards any one. I had cured him effectually! He was astonished that the laws had not provided some terrible retaliation for thieves that attempted to deceive their jailors. Hanging was a thousand times too good for me!

Having vented his indignation, he proceeded to give such orders as the united instigations of anger and alarm suggested to his mind. My apartment was changed. I was conducted to a room called the strong room, the door of which opened into the middle cell of the range of dungeons. It was underground, as they were, and had also the day-room for felons, already described, immediately over it. It was spacious and dreary. The door had not been opened for years; the air was putrid; and the walls hung round with damps and mildew. The fetters, the padlock, and the staple, were employed, as in the former case, in addition to which they put on me a pair of handcuffs. For my first provision, the keeper sent me nothing but a bit of bread, mouldy and black, and some dirty and stinking water. I know not indeed whether this is to be regarded as gratuitous tyranny on the part of the jailor; the law having providently directed, in certain cases, that the water to be administered to the prisoners shall be taken from "the next sink or puddle nearest to the jail."[1] It was further ordered, that one of the turnkeys should

---

1   In the case of the *peine forte et dure*. See State Trials, Vol. I, anno 1615. [Godwin's note refers to the trial of Richard Weston who, when he refused to enter a plea at his trial for murder, was told by the judge that unless he did plead innocent or

sleep in the cell that formed a sort of anti-chamber to my apartment. Though every convenience was provided, to render this chamber fit for the reception of a personage of a dignity so superior to the felon he was appointed to guard, he expressed much dissatisfaction at the mandate: but there was no alternative.

The situation to which I was thus removed was, apparently, the most undesirable that could be imagined; but I was not discouraged; I had for some time learned not to judge by appearances. The apartment was dark and unwholesome; but I had acquired the secret of counteracting these influences. My door was kept continually shut, and the other prisoners were debarred access to me; but if the intercourse of our fellow-men has its pleasure, solitude, on the other hand, is not without its advantages. In solitude we can pursue our own thoughts undisturbed; and I was able to call up at will the most pleasing avocations. Besides which, to one who meditated such designs as now filled my mind, solitude had peculiar recommendations. I was scarcely left to myself before I tried an experiment, the idea of which I conceived, while they were fixing my handcuffs; and, with my teeth only, disengaged myself from this restraint. The hours at which I was visited by the keepers were regular, and I took care to be provided for them. Add to which, I had a narrow grated window near the ceiling, about nine inches in perpendicular, and a foot and a half horizontally, which, though small, admitted a much stronger light than that to which I had been accustomed for several weeks. Thus circumstanced, I scarcely ever found myself in total darkness, and was better provided against surprises than I had been in my preceding situation. Such were the sentiments which this change of abode immediately suggested.

I had been a very little time removed, when I received an unexpected visit from Thomas, Mr. Falkland's footman, whom I have already mentioned in the course of my narrative. A servant of Mr. Forester happened to come to the town where I

---

guilty he would suffer the "heavy and harsh punishment" of increasingly heavy chains, naked exposure to the open air, and a meager diet of bread and standing water.]

was imprisoned, a few weeks before, while I was confined with the hurt in my ankle, and had called in to see me. The account he gave of what he observed had been the source of many an uneasy sensation to Thomas. The former visit was a matter of mere curiosity; but Thomas was of the better order of servants. He was considerably struck at the sight of me. Though my mind was now serene, and my health sufficiently good, yet the floridness of my complexion was gone, and there was a rudeness in my physiognomy, the consequence of hardship and fortitude, extremely unlike the sleekness of my better days. Thomas looked alternately in my face, at my hands, and my feet; and then fetched a deep sigh. After a pause,

"Lord bless us!" said he, in a voice in which commiseration was sufficiently perceptible, "is this you?"

"Why not, Thomas? You knew I was sent to prison, did not you?"

"Prison! and must people in prison be shackled and bound of that fashion? – and where do you lay of nights?"

"Here."

"Here? Why there is no bed!"

"No, Thomas, I am not allowed a bed. I had straw formerly, but that is taken away."

"And do they take off them there things of nights?"

"No; I am expected to sleep just as you see."

"Sleep! Why I thought this was a Christian country, but this usage is too bad for a dog."

"You must not say so, Thomas; it is what the wisdom of government has thought fit to provide."

"Zounds, how I have been deceived! They told me what a fine thing it was to be an Englishman, and about liberty and property, and all that there; and I find it is all a flam. Lord, what fools we be! Things are done under our very noses, and we know nothing of the matter; and a parcel of fellows with grave faces swear to us, that such things never happen but in France, and other countries the like of that. Why, you ha'n't been tried, ha' you?"

"No."

"And what signifies being tried, when they do worse than hang a man, and all beforehand? Well, master Williams, you have been very wicked to be sure, and I thought it would have done me good to see you hanged. But, I do not know how it is, one's heart melts, and pity comes over one, if we take time to cool. I know that ought not to be; but, damn it, when I talked of your being hanged, I did not think of your suffering all this into the bargain."

Soon after this conversation Thomas left me. The idea of the long connection of our families rushed upon his memory, and he felt more for my sufferings, at the moment, than I did for myself. In the afternoon I was surprised to see him again. He said that he could not get the thought of me out of his mind, and therefore he hoped I would not be displeased at his coming once more to take leave of me. I could perceive that he had something upon his mind, which he did not know how to discharge. One of the turnkeys had each time come into the room with him, and continued as long as he stayed. Upon some avocation however – a noise, I believe, in the passage–the turnkey went as far as the door to satisfy his curiosity; and Thomas, watching the opportunity, slipped into my hand a chisel, a file, and a saw, exclaiming at the same time with a sorrowful tone, "I know I am doing wrong; but, if they hang me too, I cannot help it; I cannot do no other. For Christ's sake, get out of this place; I cannot bear the thoughts of it!" I received the implements with great joy, and thrust them into my bosom; and, as soon as he was gone, concealed them in the rushes of my chair. For himself he had accomplished the object for which he came, and presently after bade me farewell.

The next day, the keepers, I know not for what reason, were more than usually industrious in their search, saying, though without assigning any ground for their suspicion, that they were sure I had some tool in my possession that I ought not; but the depository I had chosen escaped them.

I waited from this time the greater part of a week, that I might have the benefit of a bright moonlight. It was necessary that I should work in the night; it was necessary that my operations should be performed between the last visit of the keepers at night and their first in the morning, that is, between nine in the evening and seven. In my dungeon, as I have already said, I passed fourteen or sixteen hours of the four-and-twenty undisturbed; but since I had acquired a character for mechanical ingenuity, a particular exception with respect to me was made from the general rules of the prison.

It was ten o'clock when I entered on my undertaking. The room in which I was confined was secured with a double door. This was totally superfluous for the purpose of my detention, since there was a sentinel planted on the outside. But it was very fortunate for my plan; because these doors prevented the easy communication of sound, and afforded me tolerable satisfaction that, with a little care in my mode of proceeding, I might be secure against the danger of being overheard. I first took off my hand-cuffs. I then filed through my fetters; and next performed the same service to three of the iron bars that secured my window, to which I climbed, partly by the assistance of my chair, and partly by means of certain irregularities in the wall. All this was the work of more than two hours. When the bars were filed through, I easily forced them a little from the perpendicular, and then drew them, one by one, out of the wall, into which they were sunk about three inches perfectly straight, and without any precaution to prevent their being removed. But the space thus obtained was by no means wide enough to admit the passing of my body. I therefore applied myself, partly with my chisel, and partly with one of the iron bars, to the loosening the brick-work; and when I had thus disengaged four or five bricks, I got down and piled them upon the floor. This operation I repeated three or four times. The space was now sufficient for my purpose; and, having crept through the opening, I stepped upon a shed on the outside.

I was now in a kind of rude area between two dead walls, that south of the felons' day-room (the windows of which were at the east end) and the wall of the prison. But I had not, as formerly, any instruments to assist me in scaling the wall, which was of considerable height. There was, of consequence, no resource for me but that of effecting a practicable breach in the lower part of the wall, which was of no contemptible strength, being of stone on the outside, with a facing of brick within. The rooms for the debtors were at right angles with the building from which I had just escaped; and, as the night was extremely bright, I was in momentary danger, particularly in case of the least noise, of being discovered by them, several of their windows commanding this area. Thus circumstanced, I determined to make the shed answer the purpose of conceal- ment. It was locked; but, with the broken link of my fetters, which I had had the precaution to bring with me, I found no great difficulty in opening the lock. I had now got a sufficient means of hiding my person while I proceeded in my work, attended with no other disadvantage than that of being obliged to leave the door, through which I had thus broken, a little open for the sake of light. After some time, I had removed a considerable part of the brick-work of the outer wall; but, when I came to the stone, I found the undertaking infinitely more difficult. The mortar which bound together the building was, by length of time, nearly petrified, and appeared to my first efforts one solid rock of the hardest adamant. I had now been six hours incessantly engaged in incredible labour: my chisel broke in the first attempt upon this new obstacle; and between fatigue already endured, and the seemingly invincible difficulty before me, I concluded that I must remain where I was, and gave up the idea of further effort as useless. At the same time the moon, whose light had till now been of the greatest use to me, set, and I was left in total darkness.

After a respite of ten minutes however, I returned to the attack with new vigour. It could not be less than two hours before the first stone was loosened from the edifice. In one hour more, the space was sufficient to admit of my escape. The pile of bricks I had left in the strong room was considerable. But it was a mole-hill compared with the ruins I had forced from the outer wall. I am fully assured that the work I had thus performed would have been to a common labourer, with every advantage of tools, the business of two or three days.

But my difficulties, instead of being ended, seemed to be only begun. The day broke, before I had completed the open- ing, and in ten minutes more the keepers would probably enter my apartment, and perceive the devastation I had left. The lane, which connected the side of the prison through which I had escaped with the adjacent country, was formed chiefly by two dead walls, with here and there a stable, a few warehouses, and some mean habitations, tenanted by the lower order of people. My best security lay in clearing the town as soon as possible, and depending upon the open country for protection. My arms were intolerably swelled and bruised with my labour, and my strength seemed wholly exhausted with fatigue. Speed I was nearly unable to exert for any continuance; and, if I could, with the enemy so close at my heels, speed would too probably have been useless. It appeared as if I were now in almost the same situation as that in which I had been placed five or six weeks before, in which, after having completed my escape, I was obliged to yield myself up, without resistance, to my pursuers. I was not however disabled as then; I was capable of exertion, to what precise extent I could not ascertain; and I was well aware, that every instance in which I should fail of my purpose would contribute to enhance the difficulty of any future attempt. Such were the considerations that presented themselves in relation to my escape; and, even if that were effected, I had to reckon among my difficulties, that, at the time I quitted my prison, I was destitute of every resource, and had not a shilling remaining in the world.

END OF THE SECOND VOLUME

VOLUME THE THIRD

CHAPTER I

I PASSED along the lane I have described, without perceiving or being observed by a human being. The doors were shut, the window-shutters closed, and all was still as night. I reached the extremity of the lane unmolested. My pursuers, if they immediately followed, would know that the likelihood was small, of my having in the interval found shelter in this place; and would proceed without hesitation, as I on my part was obliged to do, from the end nearest to the prison to its furthest termination.

The face of the country, in the spot to which I had thus opened myself a passage, was rude and uncultivated. It was overgrown with brushwood and furze; the soil was for the most part of a loose sand; and the surface extremely irregular. I climbed a small eminence, and could perceive, not very remote in the distance, a few cottages thinly scattered. This prospect did not altogether please me; I conceived that my safety would, for the present, be extremely assisted, by keeping myself from the view of any human being.

I therefore came down again into the valley, and upon a careful examination perceived that it was interspersed with cavities, some deeper than others, but all of them so shallow, as neither to be capable of hiding a man, nor of exciting suspicion as places of possible concealment. Meanwhile the day had but just begun to dawn; the morning was lowring and drizzly; and, though the depth of these caverns was of course well known to the neighbouring inhabitants, the shadows they cast were so black and impenetrable, as might well have produced wider expectations in the mind of a stranger. Poor therefore as was the protection they were able to afford, I thought it right to have recourse to it for the moment, as the best the emergency would supply. It was for my life; and, the greater was the jeopardy to which it was exposed, the more dear did that life seem to become to my affections. The recess I chose, as most secure, was within little more than a hundred yards of the end of the lane, and the extreme buildings of the town.

I had not stood up in this manner two minutes, before I heard the sound of feet, and presently saw the ordinary turnkey and another pass the place of my retreat. They were so close to me that, if I had stretched out my hand, I believe I could have caught hold of their clothes, without so much as changing my posture. As no part of the overhanging earth intervened between me and them, I could see them entire, though the deepness of the shade rendered me almost completely invisible. I heard them say to each other in tones of vehement asperity, "Curse the rascal! which way can he be gone?" The reply was, "Damn him! I wish we had him but safe once again!" – "Never fear!" rejoined the first; "he cannot have above half a mile the start of us." They were presently out of hearing; for, as to sight, I dared not advance my body, so much as an inch, to look after them, lest I should be discovered by my pursuers in some other direction. From the very short time that elapsed, between my escape and the appearance of these men, I concluded that they had made their way through the same outlet as I had done, it being impossible that they could have had time to come, from the gate of the prison, and so round a considerable part of the town, as they must otherwise have done.

I was so alarmed at this instance of diligence on the part of the enemy, that, for some time, I scarcely ventured to proceed an inch from my place of concealment, or almost to change my posture. The morning, which had been bleak and drizzly, was succeeded by a day of heavy and incessant rain; and the gloomy state of the air and surrounding objects, together with the extreme nearness of my prison, and a total want of food, caused me to pass the hours in no very agreeable sensations. This inclemency of the weather however, which generated a feeling of stillness and solitude, encouraged me by degrees to change my retreat, for another of the same nature, but of somewhat greater security. I hovered with little variation about a single spot, as long as the sun continued above the horizon.

Towards evening, the clouds began to disperse, and the moon shone, as on the preceding night, in full brightness. I had perceived no human creature during the whole day, except in the instance already mentioned. This had perhaps been owing to the nature of the day; at all events I considered it as too hazardous an experiment, to venture from my hiding-place in so clear and fine a night. I was therefore obliged to wait for the setting of this luminary, which was not till near five o'clock in the morning. My only relief during this interval was to allow myself to sink to the bottom of my cavern, it being scarcely possible for me to continue any longer on my feet. Here I fell into an interrupted and unrefreshing doze, the consequence of a laborious night, and a tedious, melancholy day; though I rather sought to avoid sleep, which, co-operating with the coldness of the season, would tend more to injury than advantage.

The period of darkness, which I had determined to use for the purpose of removing to a greater distance from my prison, was, in its whole duration, something less than three hours. When I rose from my seat, I was weak with hunger and fatigue, and, which was worse, I seemed, between the dampness of the preceding day and the sharp, clear frost of the night, to have lost the command of my limbs. I stood up and shook myself; I leaned against the side of the hill, impelling in different directions the muscles of the extremities; and at length recovered in some degree the sense of feeling. This operation was attended with an incredible aching pain, and required no common share of resolution to encounter and prosecute it. Having quitted my retreat, I at first advanced with weak and tottering steps; but, as I proceeded, increased my pace. The barren heath, which reached to the edge of the town, was, at least on this side, without a path; but the stars shone, and, guiding myself by them, I determined to steer as far as possible from the hateful scene where I had been so long confined. The line I pursued was of irregular surface, sometimes obliging me to climb a steep ascent, and at others to go down into a dark and impenetrable dell. I was often compelled, by the dangerousness of the way, to deviate considerably from the direction I wished to pursue. In the mean time I advanced with as much rapidity as these and similar obstacles would permit me to do. The swiftness of the motion, and the thinness of the air, restored to me my alacrity. I forgot the inconveniences under which I laboured, and my mind became lively, spirited, and enthusiastic.

I had now reached the border of the heath, and entered

upon what is usually termed the forest. Strange as it may seem, it is nevertheless true, that, in this conjuncture, exhausted with hunger, destitute of all provision for the future, and surrounded with the most alarming dangers, my mind suddenly became glowing, animated, and cheerful. I thought that, by this time, the most formidable difficulties of my undertaking were surmounted; and I could not believe that, after having effected so much, I should find any thing invincible in what remained to be done. I recollected the confinement I had undergone, and the fate that had impended over me, with horror. Never did man feel more vividly, than I felt at that moment, the sweets of liberty. Never did man more strenuously prefer poverty with independence, to the artificial allurements of a life of slavery. I stretched forth my arms with rapture; I clapped my hands one upon the other, and exclaimed, "Ah, this is indeed to be a man! These wrists were lately galled with fetters; all my motions, whether I rose up or sat down, were echoed to with the clanking of chains; I was tied down like a wild beast, and could not move but in a circle of a few feet in circumference. Now I can run fleet as a greyhound, and leap like a young roe upon the mountains. Oh, God! (if God there be that condescends to record the lonely beatings of an anxious heart) thou only canst tell with what delight a prisoner, just broke forth from his dungeon, hugs the blessings of new-found liberty! Sacred and indescribable moment, when man regains his rights! But lately I held my life in jeopardy, because one man was unprincipled enough to assert what he knew to be false; I was destined to suffer an early and inexorable death from the hands of others, because none of them had penetration enough to distinguish from falsehood, what I uttered with the entire conviction of a full-fraught heart! Strange, that men, from age to age, should consent to hold their lives at the breath of another, merely that each in his turn may have a power of acting the tyrant according to law! Oh, God! give me poverty! shower upon me all the imaginary hardships of human life! I will receive them all with thankfulness. Turn me a prey to the wild beasts of the desert, so I be never again the victim of man, dressed in the gore-dripping robes of authority! Suffer me at least to call life, and the pursuits of life, my own! Let me hold it at the mercy of the elements, of the hunger of beasts, or the revenge of barbarians, but not of the cold-blooded prudence of monopolists and kings!" – How enviable was the enthusiasm which could thus furnish me with energy, in the midst of hunger, poverty, and universal desertion!

I had now walked at least six miles. At first I carefully avoided the habitations that lay in my way, and feared to be seen by any of the persons to whom they belonged, lest it should in any degree furnish a clue to the researches of my pursuers. As I went forward, I conceived it might be proper to relax a part of my precaution. At this time I perceived several persons coming out of a thicket close to me. I immediately considered this circumstance as rather favourable than the contrary. It was necessary for me to avoid entering any of the towns and villages in the vicinity. It was however full time that I should procure for myself some species of refreshment, and by no means improbable that these men might be in some way assisting to me in that respect. In my situation it appeared to me indifferent what might be their employment or profession. I had little to apprehend from thieves, and I believed that they, as well as honest men, could not fail to have some compassion for a person under my circumstances. I therefore rather threw myself in their way than avoided them.

They were thieves. One of the company cried out, "Who goes there? stand!" I accosted them; "Gentlemen," said I, "I am a poor traveller, almost" — While I spoke, they came round me; and he that had first hailed me said, "Damn me, tip us none of your palaver; we have heard that story of a poor traveller any time these five years. Come, down with your dust! let us see what you have got!" – "Sir," I replied, "I have not a shilling in the world, and am more than half starved beside." – "Not a shilling!" answered my assailant, "what, I suppose you are as poor as a thief? But, if you have not money, you have clothes, and those you must resign."

"My clothes!" rejoined I with indignation, "you cannot desire such a thing. Is it not enough that I am pennyless? I have been all night upon the open heath. It is now the second day that I have not eaten a morsel of bread. Would you strip me naked to the weather in the midst of this depopulated forest? No, no, you are men! The same hatred of oppression, that arms you against the insolence of wealth, will teach you to relieve those who are perishing like me. For God's sake, give me food! do not strip me of the comforts I still possess!"

While I uttered this apostrophe, the unpremeditated eloquence of sentiment, I could perceive by their gestures, though the day had not yet begun to dawn, that the feelings of one or two of the company appeared to take my part. The man, who had already undertaken to be their spokesman, perceived the same thing; and, excited either by the brutality of his temper or the love of command, hastened to anticipate the disgrace of a defeat. He brushed suddenly up to me, and by main force pushed me several feet from the place where I stood. The shock I received drove me upon a second of the gang, not one of those who had listened to my expostulation; and he repeated the brutality. My indignation was strongly excited by this treatment; and, after being thrust backward and forward two or three times in this manner, I broke through my assailants, and turned round to defend myself. The first that advanced within my reach, was my original enemy. In the present moment I listened to nothing but the dictates of passion, and I laid him at his length on the earth. I was immediately assailed with sticks and bludgeons on all sides, and presently received a blow that almost deprived me of my senses. The man I had knocked down was now upon his feet again, and aimed a stroke at me with a cutlass as I fell, which took place in a deep wound upon my neck and shoulder. He was going to repeat his blow. The two who had seemed to waver at first in their animosity, afterwards appeared to me to join in the attack, urged either by animal sympathy or the spirit of imitation. One of them however, as I afterwards understood, seized the arm of the man who was going to strike me a second time with his cutlass, and who would otherwise probably have put an end to my existence. I could hear the words, "Damn it, enough, enough! that is too bad, Gines!" – "How so?" replied a second voice; "he will but pine here upon the forest, and die by inches: it will be an act of charity to put him out of his pain." – It will be imagined that I was not uninterested in this sort of debate. I made an effort to speak; my voice failed me. I stretched out one hand with a gesture of entreaty. "You shall not strike, by God!" said one of the voices; "why should we be murderers?" – The side of forbearance at length prevailed. They therefore contented themselves with stripping me of my coat and waistcoat, and rolling me into a dry ditch. They then left me totally regardless of my distressed condition, and the plentiful effusion of blood, which streamed from my wound.

CHAPTER II

In this woeful situation, though extremely weak, I was not deprived of sense. I tore my shirt from my naked body, and endeavoured, with some success, to make of it a bandage to staunch the flowing of the blood. I then exerted myself to crawl up the side of the ditch. I had scarcely effected the latter, when, with equal surprise and joy, I perceived a man advancing at no great distance. I called for help as well as I could. The man came towards me with evident signs of compassion, and the appearance I exhibited was indeed sufficiently calculated to excite it. I had no hat. My hair was dishevelled, and the ends of the locks clotted with blood. My shirt was wrapped about my neck and shoulders, and was plentifully stained with red. My body, which was naked to my middle, was variegated with streams of blood; nor had my lower garments, which were white, by any means escaped.

"For God's sake, my good fellow!" said he, with a tone of the greatest imaginable kindness, "how came you thus?" and, saying this, he lifted me up, and set me on my feet. "Can you stand?" added he, doubtfully. "Oh, yes, very well," I replied. Having received this answer, he quitted me, and began to take off his own coat, that he might cover me from the cold. I had however over-rated my strength, and was no sooner left to myself than I reeled, and fell almost at my length upon the ground. But I broke my fall by stretching out my sound arm, and again raised myself upon my knees. My benefactor now covered me, raised me, and, bidding me lean upon him, told me he would presently conduct me to a place where I should be taken care of. Courage is a capricious property; and, though while I had no one to depend upon but myself, I possessed a mine of seemingly inexhaustible fortitude, yet no sooner did I find this unexpected sympathy on the part of another, than my resolution appeared to give way, and I felt ready to faint. My charitable conductor perceived this, and every now and then encouraged me, in a manner so cheerful, so good humoured and benevolent, equally free from the torture of droning expostulation, and the weakness of indulgence, that I thought myself under the conduct of an angel rather than a man. I could perceive that his behaviour had in it nothing of boorishness, and that he was thoroughly imbued with the principles of affectionate civility.

We walked about three quarters of a mile, and that not towards the open, but the most uncouth and unfrequented part of the forest. We crossed a place which had once been a moat, but which was now in some parts dry, and in others contained a little muddy and stagnated water. Within the enclosure of this moat, I could only discover a pile of ruins, and several walls, the upper part of which seemed to overhang their foundations, and to totter to their ruin. After having entered however with my conductor through an archway, and passed along a winding passage that was perfectly dark, we came to a stand.

At the upper end of this passage was a door, which I was unable to perceive. My conductor knocked at the door, and was answered by a voice from within, which, for body and force, might have been the voice of a man, but with a sort of female sharpness and acidity, enquiring, "Who is there?" Satisfaction was no sooner given on this point, than I heard two bolts pushed back, and the door unlocked. The apartment opened, and we entered. The interior of this habitation by no means corresponded with the appearance of my protector, but, on the contrary, wore the face of discomfort, carelessness, and dirt. The only person I saw within was a woman, rather advanced in life, and whose person had I know not what of extraordinary and loathsome. Her eyes were red and blood-shot; her hair was pendent in matted and shaggy tresses about her shoulders; her complexion swarthy, and of the consistency of parchment; her form spare, and her whole body, her arms in particular, uncommonly vigorous and muscular. Not the milk of human kindness, but the feverous blood of savage ferocity, seemed to flow from her heart; and her whole figure suggested an idea of unmitigable energy, and an appetite gorged in malevolence. This infernal Thalestris[1] had no sooner cast her

---

1 Mythological queen of the Amazons. Legend had it that in 330 BC she and 300 of her Amazons met Alexander the Great and asked that they be allowed to bear children by him and his troops.

eyes upon us as we entered, than she exclaimed in a discordant and discontented voice, "What have we got here? this is not one of our people!" My conductor, without answering this apostrophe, bade her push an easy chair which stood in one corner, and set it directly before the fire. This she did with apparent reluctance, murmuring, "Ah! you are at your old tricks; I wonder what such folks as we have to do with charity! It will be the ruin of us at last, I can see that!" – "Hold your tongue, beldam!" said he, with a stern significance of manner, "and fetch one of my best shirts, a waistcoat, and some dressings." Saying this, he at the same time put into her hand a small bunch of keys. In a word, he treated me with as much kindness as if he had been my father. He examined my wound, washed and dressed it; at the same time that the old woman, by his express order, prepared for me such nourishment as he thought most suitable to my weak and languid condition.

These operations were no sooner completed than my benefactor recommended to me to retire to rest, and preparations were making for that purpose, when suddenly a trampling of feet was heard, succeeded by a knock at the door. The old woman opened the door with the same precautions as had been employed upon our arrival, and immediately six or seven persons tumultuously entered the apartment. Their appearance was different, some having the air of mere rustics, and others that of a tarnished sort of gentry. All had a feature of boldness, inquietude, and disorder, extremely unlike any thing I had before observed in such a group. But my astonishment was still increased, when upon a second glance I perceived something in the general air of several of them, and of one in particular, that persuaded me they were the gang from which I had just escaped, and this one the antagonist by whose animosity I was so near having been finally destroyed. I imagined they had entered the hovel with a hostile intention, that my benefactor was upon the point of being robbed, and I probably murdered.

This suspicion however was soon removed. They addressed my conductor with respect, under the appellation of captain. They were boisterous and noisy in their remarks and exclamations, but their turbulence was tempered by a certain deference to his opinion and authority. I could observe in the person who had been my active opponent some awkwardness and irresolution as he first perceived me, which he dismissed with a sort of effort, exclaiming, "Who the devil is here?" There was something in the tone of this apostrophe that roused the attention of my protector. He looked at the speaker with a fixed and penetrating glance, and then said, "Nay, Gines, do you know? Did you ever see the person before?" – "Curse it, Gines!" interrupted a third, "you are damnably out of luck. They say dead men walk, and you see there is some truth in it." – "Truce with your impertinence, Jeckols!" replied my protector: "this is no proper occasion for a joke. Answer me, Gines, were you the cause of this young man being left naked and wounded this bitter morning upon the forest?"

"Mayhap I was. What then?"

"What provocation could induce you to so cruel a treatment?"

"Provocation enough. He had no money."

"What, did you use him thus, without so much as being irritated by any resistance on his part?"

"Yes, he did resist. I only hustled him, and he had the impudence to strike me."

"Gines! you are an incorrigible fellow."

"Pooh, what signifies what I am? You, with your compassion, and your fine feelings, will bring us all to the gallows."

"I have nothing to say to you; I have no hopes of you! Comrades, it is for you to decide upon the conduct of this man as you think proper. You know how repeated his offences have been; you know what pains I have taken to mend him. Our profession is the profession of justice." [It is thus that the prejudices of men universally teach them to colour the most desperate cause to which they have determined to adhere.] "We, who are thieves without a licence, are at open war with another set of men who are thieves according to law. With such a cause then to bear us out, shall we stain it with cruelty, malice, and revenge? A thief is, of course, a man living among his equals; I do not pretend therefore to assume any authority among you; act as you think proper; but, so far as relates to myself,

I vote that Gines be expelled from among us as a disgrace to our society."

This proposition seemed to meet the general sense. It was easy to perceive that the opinion of the rest coincided with that of their leader; notwithstanding which a few of them hesitated as to the conduct to be pursued. In the mean time Gines muttered something in a surly and irresolute way, about taking care how they provoked him. This insinuation instantly roused the courage of my protector, and his eyes flashed with contempt.

"Rascal!" said he, "do you menace us? Do you think we will be your slaves? No, no, do your worst! Go to the next justice of the peace, and impeach us; I can easily believe you are capable of it. Sir, when we entered into this gang, we were not such fools as not to know that we entered upon a service of danger. One of its dangers consists in the treachery of fellows like you. But we did not enter at first to flinch now. Did you believe that we would live in hourly fear of you, tremble at your threats, and compromise, whenever you should so please, with your insolence? That would be a blessed life indeed! I would rather see my flesh torn piecemeal from my bones! Go, sir! I defy you! You dare not do it! You dare not sacrifice these gallant fellows to your rage, and publish yourself to all the world a traitor and a scoundrel! If you do, you will punish yourself, not us! Begone!"

The intrepidity of the leader communicated itself to the rest of the company. Gines easily saw that there was no hope of bringing them over to a contrary sentiment. After a short pause, he answered, "I did not mean – No, damn it! I will not snivel neither. I was always true to my principles, and a friend to you all. But since you are resolved to turn me out, why – good bye to you!"

The expulsion of this man produced a remarkable improvement in the whole gang. Those who were before inclined to humanity, assumed new energy in proportion as they saw such sentiments likely to prevail. They had before suffered themselves to be overborne by the boisterous insolence of their antagonist; but now they adopted, and with success, a different conduct. Those who envied the ascendancy of their comrade, and therefore imitated his conduct, began to hesitate in their career. Stories were brought forward of the cruelty and brutality of Gines both to men and animals, which had never before reached the ear of the leader. The stories I shall not repeat. They could excite only emotions of abhorrence and disgust; and some of them argued a mind of such a stretch of depravity, as to many readers would appear utterly incredible; and yet this man had his virtues. He was enterprising, persevering, and faithful.

His removal was a considerable benefit to me. It would have been no small hardship to have been turned adrift immediately under my unfavourable circumstances, with the additional disadvantage of the wound I had received; and yet I could scarcely have ventured to remain under the same roof with a man, to whom my appearance was as a guilty conscience, perpetually reminding him of his own offence, and the displeasure of his leader. His profession accustomed him to a certain degree of indifference to consequences, and indulgence to the sallies of passion; and he might easily have found his opportunity to insult or injure me, when I should have had nothing but my own debilitated exertions to protect me.

Freed from this danger, I found my situation sufficiently fortunate for a man under my circumstances. It was attended with all the advantages for concealment my fondest imagination could have hoped; and it was by no means destitute of the benefits which arise from kindness and humanity. Nothing could be more unlike than the thieves I had seen in — jail, and the thieves of my new residence. The latter were generally full of cheerfulness and merriment. They could expatiate freely wherever they thought proper. They could form plans and execute them. They consulted their inclinations. They did not impose upon themselves the task, as is too often the case in human society, of seeming tacitly to approve that from which they suffered most; or, which is worse, of persuading themselves that all the wrongs they suffered were right; but were at open war with their oppressors. On the contrary, the imprisoned felons I had lately seen were shut up like wild beasts in a cage, deprived of activity, and palsied with indolence. The occasional demonstrations that still remained of their former enterprising life were the starts and convulsions of disease, not the meditated and consistent exertions of a mind in health. They had no more of hope, of project, of golden and animated dreams, but were reserved to the most dismal prospects, and forbidden to think upon any other topic. It is true, that these two scenes were parts of one whole, the one the consummation, the hourly to be expected successor of the other. But the men I now saw were wholly inattentive to this, and in that respect appeared to hold no commerce with reflection or reason.

I might in one view, as I have said, congratulate myself upon my present residence; it answered completely the purposes of concealment. It was the seat of merriment and hilarity; but the hilarity that characterised it produced no correspondent feelings in my bosom. The persons who composed this society had each of them cast off all control from established principle; their trade was terror, and their constant object to elude the vigilance of the community. The influence of these circumstances was visible in their character. I found among them benevolence and kindness: they were strongly susceptible of emotions of generosity. But, as their situation was precarious, their dispositions were proportionably fluctuating. Inured to the animosity of their species, they were irritable and passionate. Accustomed to exercise harshness towards the subject of their depredations, they did not always confine their brutality within that scope. They were habituated to consider wounds and bludgeons and stabbing as the obvious mode of surmounting every difficulty. Uninvolved in the debilitating routine of human affairs, they frequently displayed an energy which, from every impartial observer, would have extorted veneration. Energy is perhaps of all qualities the most valuable; and a just political system would possess the means of extracting from it, thus circumstanced, its beneficial qualities, instead of consigning it, as now, to indiscriminate destruction. We act like the chemist, who should reject the finest ore, and employ none but what was sufficiently debased to fit it immediately for the vilest uses. But the energy of these men, such as I beheld it, was in the highest degree misapplied, unassisted by liberal and enlightened views, and directed only to the most narrow and contemptible purposes.

The residence I have been describing might to many persons have appeared attended with intolerable inconveniences. But, exclusively of its advantages as a field for speculation, it was Elysium, compared with that from which I had just escaped. Displeasing company, incommodious apartments, filthiness, and riot, lost the circumstance by which they could most effectually disgust, when I was not compelled to remain with them. All hardships I could patiently endure, in comparison with the menace of a violent and untimely death. There was no suffering that I could not persuade myself to consider as trivial, except that which flowed from the tyranny, the frigid precaution, or the inhuman revenge of my own species.

My recovery advanced in the most favourable manner. The attention and kindness of my protector were incessant, and the rest caught the spirit from his example. The old woman who superintended the household still retained her animosity. She considered me as the cause of the expulsion of Gines from the fraternity. Gines had been the object of her particular partiality; and, zealous as she was for the public concern, she thought an old and experienced sinner for a raw probationer but an ill exchange. Add to which, that her habits inclined her to moroseness and discontent, and that persons of her complexion seem unable to exist without some object upon which to pour out the superfluity of their gall. She lost no opportunity, upon the most trifling occasion, of displaying her animosity; and ever and anon eyed me with a furious glance of canine hunger for my destruction. Nothing was more evidently mortifying to her, than the procrastination of her malice; nor could she bear to think that a fierceness so gigantic and uncontrollable should show itself in nothing more terrific than the pigmy spite of a chambermaid. For myself, I had been accustomed to the warfare of formidable adversaries, and the encounter of alarming dangers, and what I saw of her spleen had not power sufficient to disturb my tranquillity.

As I recovered, I told my story, except so far as related to the detection of Mr. Falkland's eventful secret, to my protector. That particular I could not, as yet, prevail upon myself to disclose, even in a situation like this, which seemed to preclude the possibility of its being made use of to the disadvantage of my persecutor. My present auditor however, whose habits of thinking were extremely opposite to those of Mr. Forester, did not, from the obscurity which flowed from this reserve, deduce any unfavourable conclusion. His penetration was such, as to afford little room for an impostor to hope to mislead him by a fictitious statement, and he confided in that penetration. So confiding, the simplicity and integrity of my manner carried conviction to his mind, and insured his good opinion and friendship.

He listened to my story with eagerness, and commented on the several parts as I related them. He said, that this was only one fresh instance of the tyranny and perfidiousness exercised by the powerful members of the community, against those who were less privileged than themselves. Nothing could be more clear, than their readiness to sacrifice the human species at large to their meanest interest or wildest caprice. Who that saw the situation in its true light would wait till their oppressors thought fit to decree their destruction, and not take arms in their defence while it was yet in their power? Which was most meritorious, the unresisting and dastardly submission of a slave, or the enterprise and gallantry of the man who dared to assert his claims? Since, by the partial administration of our laws, innocence, when power was armed against it, had nothing better to hope for than guilt, what man of true courage would fail to set these laws at defiance, and, if he must suffer by their injustice, at least take care that he had first shown his contempt of their yoke? For himself, he should certainly never have embraced his present calling, had he not been stimulated to it by these cogent and irresistible reasons; and he hoped, as experience had so forcibly brought a conviction of this sort to my mind, that he should for the future have the happiness to associate me to his pursuits. – It will presently be seen with what event these hopes were attended.

Numerous were the precautions exercised by the gang of thieves with whom I now resided, to elude the vigilance of the satellites of justice. It was one of their rules to commit no depredations but at a considerable distance from the place of their residence; and Gines had transgressed this regulation in the attack to which I was indebted for my present asylum. After having possessed themselves of any booty, they took care, in the sight of the persons whom they had robbed, to pursue a route as nearly as possible opposite to that which led to their true haunts. The appearance of their place of residence, together with its environs, was peculiarly desolate and forlorn, and it had the reputation of being haunted. The old woman I have described had long been its inhabitant, and was commonly supposed to be its only inhabitant; and her person well accorded with the rural ideas of a witch. Her lodgers never went out or came in but with the utmost circumspection, and generally by night. The lights which were occasionally seen from various parts of her habitation, were, by the country people, regarded with horror as supernatural; and if the noise of revelry at any time saluted their ears, it was imagined to proceed from a carnival of devils. With all these advantages, the thieves did not venture to reside here but by intervals: they frequently absented themselves for months, and removed to a different part of the country. The old woman sometimes attended them in these transportations, and sometimes remained; but in all cases her decampment took place either sooner or later than theirs, so that the nicest observer could scarcely have traced any connection between her reappearance, and the alarms of depredation that were frequently given; and the festival of demons seemed, to the terrified rustics, indifferently to take place whether she were present or absent.

CHAPTER III

ONE day, while I continued in this situation, a circumstance occurred which involuntarily attracted my attention. Two of our people had been sent to a town at some distance, for the purpose of procuring us the things of which we were in want. After having delivered these to our landlady, they retired to one corner of the room; and, one of them pulling a printed paper from his pocket, they mutually occupied themselves in examining its contents. I was sitting in an easy chair by the fire, being considerably better than I had been, though still in a weak and languid state. Having read for a considerable time, they looked at me, and then at the paper, and then at me again. They then went out of the room together, as if to consult without interruption upon something which that paper suggested to them. Some time after they returned; and my protector, who had been absent upon the former occasion, entered the room at the same instant.

"Captain!" said one of them with an air of pleasure, "look here! we have found a prize! I believe it is as good as a bank-note of a hundred guineas."

Mr. Raymond (that was his name) took the paper, and read. He paused for a moment. He then crushed the paper in his hand; and, turning to the person from whom he had received it, said, with the tone of a man confident in the success of his reasons, –

"What use have you for these hundred guineas? Are you in want? Are you in distress? Can you be contented to purchase them at the price of treachery – of violating the laws of hospitality?"

"Faith, captain, I do not very well know. After having violated other laws, I do not see why we should be frightened at an old saw. We pretend to judge for ourselves, and ought to be above shrinking from a bugbear of a proverb. Beside, this is a good deed, and I should think no more harm of being the ruin of such a thief than of getting my dinner."

"A thief! You talk of thieves!"

"Not so fast, captain. God defend that I should say a word against thieving as a general occupation! But one man steals in one way, and another in another. For my part, I go upon the highway, and take from any stranger I meet what, it is a hundred to one, he can very well spare. I see nothing to be found fault with in that. But I have as much conscience as another man. Because I laugh at assizes, and great wigs, and the gallows, and because I will not be frightened from an innocent action when the lawyers say me nay, does it follow that I am to have a fellow-feeling for pilferers, and rascally servants, and people that have neither justice nor principle? No; I have too much respect for the trade not to be a foe to interlopers, and people that so much the more deserve my hatred, because the world calls them by my name."

"You are wrong, Larkins! You certainly ought not to employ against people that you hate, supposing your hatred to be reasonable, the instrumentality of that law which in your practice you defy. Be consistent. Either be the friend of the law, or its adversary. Depend upon it that, wherever there are laws at all, there will be laws against such people as you and me. Either therefore we all of us deserve the vengeance of the law, or law is not the proper instrument for correcting the misdeeds of mankind. I tell you this, because I would fain have you aware, that an informer or a king's evidence, a man who takes advantage of the confidence of another in order to betray him, who sells the life of his neighbour for money, or, coward-like, upon any pretence calls in the law to do that for him which he cannot or dares not do for himself, is the vilest of rascals. But in the present case, if your reasons were the best in the world, they do not apply."

While Mr. Raymond was speaking, the rest of the gang came into the room. He immediately turned to them, and said, –

"My friends, here is a piece of intelligence that Larkins has just brought in which, with his leave, I will lay before you."

Then unfolding the paper he had received, he continued: "This is the description of a felon, with the offer of a hundred guineas for his apprehension. Larkins picked it up at ——. By the time and other circumstances, but particularly by the minute description of his person, there can be no doubt but the object of it is our young friend, whose life I was a while ago the instrument of saving. He is charged here with having taken advantage of the confidence of his patron and benefactor to rob him of property to a large amount. Upon this charge he was committed to the county jail, from whence he made his escape about a fortnight ago, without venturing to stand his trial; a circumstance which is stated by the advertiser as tantamount to a confession of his guilt.

"My friends, I was acquainted with the particulars of this story some time before. This lad let me into his history, at a time that he could not possibly foresee that he should stand in need of that precaution as an antidote against danger. He is not guilty of what is laid to his charge. Which of you is so ignorant as to suppose, that his escape is any confirmation of his guilt? Who ever thinks, when he is apprehended for trial, of his innocence or guilt as being at all material to the issue? Who ever was fool enough to volunteer a trial, where those who are to decide think more of the horror of the thing of which he is accused, than whether he were the person that did it; and where the nature of our motives is to be collected from a set of ignorant witnesses, that no wise man would trust for a fair representation of the most indifferent action of his life?

"The poor lad's story is a long one, and I will not trouble you with it now. But from that story it is as clear as the day, that, because he wished to leave the service of his master, because he had been perhaps a little too inquisitive in his master's concerns, and because, as I suspect, he had been trusted with some important secrets, his master conceived an antipathy against him. The antipathy gradually proceeded to such a length, as to induce the master to forge this vile accusation. He seemed willing to hang the lad out of the way, rather than suffer him to go where he pleased, or get beyond the reach of his power. Williams has told me the story with such ingenuousness, that I am as sure that he is guiltless of what they lay to his charge, as that I am so myself. Nevertheless the man's servants who were called in to hear the accusation, and his relation, who as justice of the peace made out the mittimus, and who had the folly to think he could be impartial, gave it on his side with one voice, and thus afforded Williams a sample of what he had to expect in the sequel.

"Larkins, who when he received this paper had no previous knowledge of particulars, was for taking advantage of it for the purpose of earning the hundred guineas. Are you of that mind now you have heard them? Will you for so paltry a considera-tion deliver up the lamb into the jaws of the wolf? Will you abet the purposes of this sanguinary rascal, who, not contented with driving his late dependent from house and home, depriv-ing him of character and all the ordinary means of subsistence, and leaving him almost without a refuge, still thirsts for his blood? If no other person have the courage to set limits to the tyranny of courts of justice, shall not we? Shall we, who earn our livelihood by generous daring, be indebted for a penny to the vile artifices of the informer? Shall we, against whom the whole species is in arms, refuse our protection to an individual, more exposed to, but still less deserving of, their persecution than ourselves?"

The representation of the captain produced an instant effect upon the whole company. They all exclaimed, "Betray him! No, not for worlds! He is safe. We will protect him at the haz-ard of our lives. If fidelity and honour be banished from thieves, where shall they find refuge upon the face of the earth?" Larkins in particular thanked the captain for his inter-ference, and swore that he would rather part with his right hand than injure so worthy a lad or assist such an unheard-of villainy. Saying this, he took me by the hand and bade me fear nothing. Under their roof no harm should ever befall me; and, even if the understrappers of the law should discover my retreat, they would to a man die in my defence, sooner than a hair of my head should be hurt. I thanked him most sincerely for his good-will; but I was principally struck with the fervent benevolence of my benefactor. I told them, I found that my enemies were inexorable, and would never be appeased but with my blood; and I assured them with the most solemn and

earnest veracity, that I had done nothing to deserve the persecution which was exercised against me.

The spirit and energy of Mr. Raymond had been such as to
leave no part for me to perform in repelling this unlooked-for
danger. Nevertheless, it left a very serious impression upon my
mind. I had always placed some confidence in the returning
equity of Mr. Falkland. Though he persecuted me with bitterness, I could not help believing that he did it unwillingly, and I
was persuaded it would not be for ever. A man, whose original
principles had been so full of rectitude and honour, could not
fail at some time to recollect the injustice of his conduct, and to
remit his asperity. This idea had been always present to me, and
had in no small degree conspired to instigate my exertions. I
said, "I will convince my persecutor that I am of more value
than that I should be sacrificed purely by way of precaution."
These expectations on my part had been encouraged by Mr.
Falkland's behaviour upon the question of my imprisonment,
and by various particulars which had occurred since.

But this new incident gave the subject a totally different
appearance. I saw him, not contented with blasting my reputation, confining me for a period in jail, and reducing me to the
situation of a houseless vagabond, still continuing his pursuit
under these forlorn circumstances with unmitigable cruelty.
Indignation and resentment seemed now for the first time to
penetrate my mind. I knew his misery so well, I was so fully
acquainted with its cause, and strongly impressed with the idea
of its being unmerited, that, while I suffered deeply, I still continued to pity, rather than hate my persecutor. But this incident
introduced some change into my feelings. I said, "Surely he
might now believe that he has sufficiently disarmed me, and
might at length suffer me to be at peace. At least, ought he not
to be contented to leave me to my fate, the perilous and uncertain condition of an escaped felon, instead of thus whetting the
animosity and vigilance of my countrymen against me? Were
his interference on my behalf in opposition to the stern severity of Mr. Forester, and his various acts of kindness since, a mere
part that he played in order to lull me into patience? Was he

perpetually haunted with the fear of an ample retaliation, and for that purpose did he personate remorse, at the very moment that he was secretly keeping every engine at play that could secure my destruction?" The very suspicion of such a fact filled me with inexpressible horror, and struck a sudden chill through every fibre of my frame.

My wound was by this time completely healed, and it became absolutely necessary that I should form some determination respecting the future. My habits of thinking were such as gave me an uncontrollable repugnance to the vocation of my hosts. I did not indeed feel that aversion and abhorrence to the men which are commonly entertained. I saw and respected their good qualities and their virtues. I was by no means inclined to believe them worse men, or more hostile in their dispositions to the welfare of their species, than the generality of those that look down upon them with most censure. But, though I did not cease to love them as individuals, my eyes were perfectly open to their mistakes. If I should otherwise have been in danger of being misled, it was my fortune to have studied felons in a jail before I studied them in their state of comparative prosperity; and this was an infallible antidote to the poison. I saw that in this profession were exerted uncommon energy, ingenuity, and fortitude, and I could not help recollecting how admirably beneficial such qualities might be made in the great theatre of human affairs; while, in their present direction, they were thrown away upon purposes diametrically at war with the first interests of human society. Nor were their proceedings less injurious to their own interest than incompatible with the general welfare. The man who risks or sacrifices his life for the public cause, is rewarded with the testimony of an approving conscience; but persons who wantonly defy the necessary, though atrociously exaggerated precautions of government in the matter of property, at the same time that they commit an alarming hostility against the whole, are, as to their own concerns, scarcely less absurd and self-neglectful than the man who should set himself up as a mark for a file of musqueteers to shoot at.

Viewing the subject in this light, I not only determined that I would have no share in their occupation myself, but thought I could not do less, in return for the benefits I had received from them, than endeavour to dissuade them from an employment in which they must themselves be the greatest sufferers. My expostulation met with a various reception. All the persons to whom it was addressed had been tolerably successful in persuading themselves of the innocence of their calling; and what remained of doubt in their mind was smothered, and, so to speak, laboriously forgotten. Some of them laughed at my arguments, as a ridiculous piece of missionary quixotism. Others, and particularly our captain, repelled them with the boldness of a man that knows he has got the strongest side. But this sentiment of ease and self-satisfaction did not long remain. They had been used to arguments derived from religion and the sacredness of law. They had long ago shaken these from them as so many prejudices. But my view of the subject appealed to principles which they could not contest, and had by no means the air of that customary reproof which is for ever dinned in our ears without finding one responsive chord in our hearts. Urged, as they now were, with objections unexpected and cogent, some of those to whom I addressed them began to grow peevish and impatient of the intrusive remonstrance. But this was by no means the case with Mr. Raymond. He was possessed of a candour that I have seldom seen equalled. He was surprised to hear objections so powerful to that which, as a matter of speculation, he believed he had examined on all sides. He revolved them with impartiality and care. He admitted them slowly, but he at length fully admitted them. He had now but one rejoinder in reserve.

"Alas! Williams," said he, "it would have been fortunate for me if these views had been presented to me previously to my embracing my present profession. It is now too late. Those very laws which, by a perception of their iniquity, drove me to what I am, preclude my return. God, we are told, judges of men by what they are at the period of arraignment, and whatever be their crimes, if they have seen and abjured the folly of those crimes, receives them to favour. But the institutions of countries that profess to worship this God admit no such distinctions. They leave no room for amendment, and seem to have a brutal delight in confounding the demerits of offenders. It signifies not what is the character of the individual at the hour of trial. How changed, how spotless, and how useful, avails him nothing. If they discover at the distance of fourteen[1] or of forty[2] years an action for which the law ordains that his life shall be the forfeit, though the interval should have been spent with the purity of a saint and the devotedness of a patriot, they disdain to enquire into it. What then can I do? Am I not compelled to go on in folly, having once begun?"

---

1 Eugene Aram. See Annual Register for 1759. [Godwin's note refers to the case of Eugene Aram (1704–59), a teacher who in 1745 murdered a friend whom he felt had committed adultery with his wife. Aram subsequently led a blameless life until the crime was discovered in 1759. When arrested, he confessed and was executed. Edward Bulwer Lytton wrote an 1832 novel about the case and may well have heard about it first from Godwin.]

2 William Andrew Horne. Ibid. [Godwin's note refers to a figure who committed multiple crimes of a sexual nature in the earlier part of his life, including contributing to the death of a child born of an incestuous relation with one of his sisters. When the crime was uncovered thirty-five years later, in 1759, he was tried and executed.]

CHAPTER IV

I was extremely affected by this plea. I could only answer, that Mr. Raymond must himself be the best judge of the course it became him to hold; I trusted the case was not so desperate as he imagined.

This subject was pursued no further, and was in some degree driven from my thoughts by an incident of a very extraordinary nature.

I have already mentioned the animosity that was entertained against me by the infernal portress of this solitary mansion. Gines, the expelled member of the gang, had been her particular favourite. She submitted to his exile indeed, because her genius felt subdued by the energy and inherent superiority of Mr. Raymond; but she submitted with murmuring and discontent. Not daring to resent the conduct of the principal in this affair, she collected all the bitterness of her spirit against me.

To the unpardonable offence I had thus committed in the first instance, were added the reasonings I had lately offered against the profession of robbery. Robbery was a fundamental article in the creed of this hoary veteran, and she listened to my objections with the same unaffected astonishment and horror that an old woman of other habits would listen to one who objected to the agonies and dissolution of the Creator of the world, or to the garment of imputed righteousness prepared to envelope the souls of the elect. Like the religious bigot, she was sufficiently disposed to avenge a hostility against her opinions with the weapons of sublunary warfare.

Meanwhile I had smiled at the impotence of her malice, as an object of contempt rather than alarm. She perceived, as I imagined, the slight estimation in which I held her, and this did not a little increase the perturbation of her thoughts.

One day I was left alone, with no other person in the house than this swarthy sybil. The thieves had set out upon an expedition about two hours after sunset on the preceding evening, and had not returned, as they were accustomed to do, before day-break the next morning. This was a circumstance that sometimes occurred, and therefore did not produce any extraordinary alarm. At one time the scent of prey would lead them beyond the bounds they had prescribed themselves, and at another the fear of pursuit: the life of a thief is always uncertain. The old woman had been preparing during the night for the meal to which they would expect to sit down as soon as might be after their return.

For myself, I had learned from their habits to be indifferent to the regular return of the different parts of the day, and in some degree to turn day into night, and night into day. I had been now several weeks in this residence, and the season was considerably advanced. I had passed some hours during the night in ruminating on my situation. The character and manners of the men among whom I lived were disgusting to me. Their brutal ignorance, their ferocious habits, and their coarse behaviour, instead of becoming more tolerable by custom, hourly added force to my original aversion. The uncommon vigour of their minds, and acuteness of their invention in the business they pursued, compared with the odiousness of that business and their habitual depravity, awakened in me sensations too painful to be endured. Moral disapprobation, at least in a mind unsubdued by philosophy, I found to be one of the most fertile sources of disquiet and uneasiness. From this pain the society of Mr. Raymond by no means relieved me. He was indeed eminently superior to the vices of the rest; but I did not less exquisitely feel how much he was out of his place, how disproportionably associated, or how contemptibly employed. I had attempted to counteract the errors under which he and his companions laboured; but I had found the obstacles that presented themselves greater than I had imagined.

What was I to do? Was I to wait the issue of this my missionary undertaking, or was I to withdraw myself immediately? When I withdrew, ought that to be done privately, or with an open avowal of my design, and an endeavour to supply by the force of example what was deficient in my arguments? It was certainly improper, as I declined all participation in the pursuits of these men, did not pay my contribution of hazard to the means by which they subsisted, and had no congeniality with their habits, that I should continue to reside with them longer than was absolutely necessary. There was one circumstance that rendered this deliberation particularly pressing. They intended in a few days removing from their present habitation, to a haunt to which they were accustomed, in a distant county. If I did not propose to continue with them, it would perhaps be wrong to accompany them in this removal. The state of calamity to which my inexorable prosecutor had reduced me, had made the encounter even of a den of robbers a fortunate adventure. But the time that had since elapsed, had probably been sufficient to relax the keenness of the quest that was made after me. I sighed for that solitude and obscurity, that retreat from the vexations of the world and the voice even of common fame, which I had proposed to myself when I broke my prison.

Such were the meditations which now occupied my mind. At length I grew fatigued with continual contemplation, and to relieve myself pulled out a pocket Horace, the legacy of my beloved Brightwel! I read with avidity the epistle in which he so beautifully describes to Fuscus, the grammarian, the pleasures of rural tranquillity and independence.[1] By this time the sun rose from behind the eastern hills, and I opened my casement to contemplate it. The day commenced with peculiar brilliancy, and was accompanied with all those charms which the poets of nature, as they have been styled, have so much delighted to describe. There was something in this scene, particularly as succeeding to the active exertions of intellect, that soothed the mind to composure. Insensibly a confused reverie invaded my faculties; I withdrew from the window, threw myself upon the bed, and fell asleep.

I do not recollect the precise images which in this situation passed through my thoughts, but I know that they concluded with the idea of some person, the agent of Mr. Falkland, approaching to assassinate me. This thought had probably been suggested by the project I meditated of entering once again into the world, and throwing myself within the sphere of his possible vengeance. I imagined that the design of the murderer was to come upon me by surprise, that I was aware of his

---

1   Horace, *Epistles*, Book I, x.

design, and yet, by some fascination, had no thought of evading it. I heard the steps of the murderer as he cautiously approached. I seemed to listen to his constrained yet audible breathings. He came up to the corner where I was placed, and then stopped.

The idea became too terrible; I started, opened my eyes, and beheld the execrable hag before mentioned standing over me with a butcher's cleaver. I shifted my situation with a speed that seemed too swift for volition, and the blow already aimed at my skull sunk impotent upon the bed. Before she could wholly recover her posture, I sprung upon her, seized hold of the weapon, and had nearly wrested it from her. But in a moment she resumed her strength and her desperate purpose, and we had a furious struggle – she impelled by inveterate malice, and I resisting for my life. Her vigour was truly Amazonian, and at no time had I ever occasion to contend with a more formidable opponent. Her glance was rapid and exact, and the shock with which from time to time she impelled her whole frame inconceivably vehement. At length I was victorious, took from her the instrument of death, and threw her upon the ground. Till now the earnestness of her exertions had curbed her rage; but now she gnashed with her teeth, her eyes seemed as if starting from their sockets, and her body heaved with uncontrollable insanity.

"Rascal! devil!" she exclaimed, "what do you mean to do to me?"

Till now the scene had passed uninterrupted by a single word.

"Nothing," I replied: "begone, infernal witch! and leave me to myself."

"Leave you! No: I will thrust my fingers through your ribs, and drink your blood! – You conquer me? – Ha, ha! – Yes, yes; you shall! – I will sit upon you, and press you to hell! I will roast you with brimstone, and dash your entrails into your eyes! Ha, ha! – ha!"

Saying this, she sprung up, and prepared to attack me with redoubled fury. I seized her hands, and compelled her to sit upon the bed. Thus restrained, she continued to express the tumult of her thoughts by grinning, by certain furious motions of her head, and by occasional vehement efforts to disengage herself from my grasp. These contortions and starts were of the nature of those fits in which the patients are commonly supposed to need three or four persons to hold them. But I found by experience that, under the circumstances in which I was placed, my single strength was sufficient. The spectacle of her emotions was inconceivably frightful. Her violence at length however began to abate, and she became convinced of the hopelessness of the contest.

"Let me go!" said she. "Why do you hold me? I will not be held."

"I wanted you gone from the first," replied I. "Are you contented to go now?"

"Yes, I tell you, misbegotten villain! Yes, rascal!".

I immediately loosed my hold. She flew to the door, and, holding it in her hand, said, "I will be the death of you yet: you shall not be your own man twenty-four hours longer!" With these words she shut the door, and locked it upon me. An action so totally unexpected startled me. Whither was she gone? What was it she intended? To perish by the machinations of such a hag as this was a thought not to be endured. Death in any form brought upon us by surprise, and for which the mind has had no time to prepare, is inexpressibly terrible. My thoughts wandered in breathless horror and confusion, and all within was uproar. I endeavoured to break the door, but in vain. I went round the room in search of some tool to assist me. At length I rushed against it with a desperate effort, to which it yielded, and had nearly thrown me from the top of the stairs to the bottom.

I descended with all possible caution and vigilance. I entered the room which served us for a kitchen, but it was deserted. I searched every other apartment in vain. I went out among the ruins; still I discovered nothing of my late assailant. It was extraordinary: what could be become of her? what was I to conclude from her disappearance! I reflected on her parting menace, — "I should not be my own man twenty-four hours longer." It was mysterious! it did not seem to be the menace of assassination.

Suddenly the recollection of the hand-bill brought to us by Larkins rushed upon my memory. Was it possible that she alluded to that in her parting words? Would she set out upon such an expedition by herself? Was it not dangerous to the whole fraternity, if, without the smallest precaution, she should bring the officers of justice in the midst of them? It was perhaps improbable she would engage in an undertaking thus desperate. It was not however easy to answer for the conduct of a person in her state of mind. Should I wait, and risk the preservation of my liberty upon the issue?

To this question I returned an immediate negative. I had resolved in a short time to quit my present situation, and the difference of a little sooner or a little later could not be very material. It promised to be neither agreeable nor prudent for me to remain under the same roof with a person who had manifested such a fierce and inexpiable hostility. But the consideration which had inexpressibly the most weight with me, belonged to the ideas of imprisonment, trial, and death. The longer they had formed the subject of my contemplation, the more forcibly was I impelled to avoid them. I had entered upon a system of action for that purpose; I had already made many sacrifices; and I believed that I would never miscarry in this project through any neglect of mine. The thought of what was reserved for me by my persecutors sickened my very soul; and the more intimately I was acquainted with oppression and injustice, the more deeply was I penetrated with the abhorrence to which they are entitled.

Such were the reasons that determined me instantly, abruptly, without leave-taking, or acknowledgment for the peculiar and repeated favours I had received, to quit a habitation to which, for six weeks, I had apparently been indebted for protection from trial, conviction, and an ignominious death. I had come hither pennyless; I quitted my abode with the sum of a few guineas in my possession, Mr. Raymond having insisted upon my taking a share at the time that each man received his dividend from the common stock. Though I had reason to suppose that the heat of the pursuit against me would be somewhat remitted by the time that had elapsed, the magnitude of the mischief that, in an unfavourable event, might fall on me, determined me to neglect no imaginable precaution. I recollected the hand-bill which was the source of my present alarm, and conceived that one of the principal dangers which threatened me was the recognition of my person, either by such as had previously known me, or even by strangers. It seemed prudent therefore to disguise it as effectually as I could. For this purpose I had recourse to a parcel of tattered garments, that lay in a neglected corner of our habitation. The disguise I chose was that of a beggar. Upon this plan, I threw off my shirt; I tied a handkerchief about my head, with which I took care to cover one of my eyes; over this I drew a piece of an old woollen nightcap. I selected the worst apparel I could find; and this I reduced to a still more deplorable condition, by rents that I purposely made in various places. Thus equipped, I surveyed myself in a looking-glass. I had rendered my appearance complete; nor would any one have suspected that I was not one of the fraternity to which I assumed to belong. I said, "This is the form in which tyranny and injustice oblige me to seek for refuge: but better, a thousand times better is it, thus to incur contempt with the dregs of mankind, than trust to the tender mercies of our superiors!"

CHAPTER V

THE only rule that I laid down to myself in traversing the forest, was to take a direction as opposite as possible to that which led to the scene of my late imprisonment. After about two hours walking I arrived at the termination of this ruder scene, and reached that part of the country which is inclosed and cultivated. Here I sat down by the side of a brook, and, pulling out a crust of bread which I had brought away with me, rested and refreshed myself. While I continued in this place, I began to ruminate upon the plan I should lay down for my future proceedings; and my propensity now led me, as it had done in a former instance, to fix upon the capital, which I believed, besides its other recommendations, would prove the safest place for concealment. During these thoughts I saw a couple of peasants passing at a small distance, and enquired of them respecting the London road. By their description I understood that the most immediate way would be to repass a part of the forest, and that it would be necessary to approach considerably nearer to the county-town than I was at the spot which I had at present reached. I did not imagine that this could be a circumstance of considerable importance. My disguise appeared to be a sufficient security against momentary danger; and I therefore took a path, though not the most direct one, which led towards the point they suggested.

Some of the occurrences of the day are deserving to be mentioned. As I passed along a road which lay in my way for a few miles, I saw a carriage advancing in the opposite direction. I debated with myself for a moment, whether I should pass it without notice, or should take this occasion, by voice or gesture, of making an essay of my trade. This idle disquisition was however speedily driven from my mind when I perceived that the carriage was Mr. Falkland's. The suddenness of the encounter struck me with terror, though perhaps it would have been difficult for calm reflection to have discovered any considerable danger. I withdrew from the road, and skulked behind a hedge till it should have completely gone by. I was too much occupied with my own feelings, to venture to examine whether or no the terrible adversary of my peace were in the carriage. I persuaded myself that he was. I looked after the equipage, and exclaimed, "There you may see the luxurious accommodations and appendages of guilt, and here the forlorn-ness that awaits upon innocence!" – I was to blame to imagine that my case was singular in that respect. I only mention it to show how the most trivial circumstance contributes to embit-ter the cup to the man of adversity. The thought however was a transient one. I had learned this lesson from my sufferings, not to indulge in the luxury of discontent. As my mind recovered its tranquillity, I began to enquire whether the phenomenon I had just seen could have any relation to myself. But though my mind was extremely inquisitive and versatile in this respect, I could discover no sufficient ground upon which to build a judgment.

At night I entered a little public-house at the extremity of a village, and, seating myself in a corner of the kitchen, asked for some bread and cheese. While I was sitting at my repast, three or four labourers came in for a little refreshment after their work. Ideas respecting the inequality of rank pervade every order in society; and, as my appearance was meaner and more contemptible than theirs, I found it expedient to give way to these gentry of a village alehouse, and remove to an obscurer station. I was surprised, and not a little startled, to find them fall almost immediately into conversation about my history, whom, with a slight variation of circumstances, they styled the notori-ous housebreaker, Kit Williams.

"Damn the fellow," said one of them, "one never hears of any thing else. O' my life, I think he makes talk for the whole country."

"That is very true," replied another. "I was at the market-town today to sell some oats for my master, and there was a hue and cry, some of them thought they had got him, but it was a false alarm."

"That hundred guineas is a fine thing," rejoined the first. "I should be glad if so be as how it fell in my way."

"For the matter of that," said his companion, "I should like a hundred guineas as well as another. But I cannot be of your mind for all that. I should never think money would do me any good that had been the means of bringing a Christian creature to the gallows."

"Poh, that is all my granny! Some folks must be hanged, to keep the wheels of our state-folks a-going. Besides, I could forgive the fellow all his other robberies, but that he should have been so hardened as to break the house of his own master at last, that is too bad."

"Lord! lord!" replied the other, "I see you know nothing of the matter! I will tell you how it was, as I learned it at the town. I question whether he ever robbed his master at all. But, hark you! you must know as how that Squire Falkland was once tried for murder" –

"Yes, yes, we know that."

"Well, he was as innocent as the child unborn. But I supposes as how he is a little soft or so. And so Kit Williams – Kit is a devilish cunning fellow, you may judge that from his breaking prison no less than five times, – so, I say, he threatened to bring his master to trial at 'size all over again, and so frightened him, and got money from him at divers times. Till at last one Squire Forester, a relation of t' other, found it all out. And he made the hell of a rumpus, and sent away Kit to prison in a twinky; and I believe he would have been hanged: for when two squires lay their heads together, they do not much matter law, you know; or else they twist the law to their own ends, I cannot exactly say which; but it is much at one when the poor fellow's breath is out of his body."

Though this story was very circumstantially told, and with a sufficient detail of particulars, it did not pass unquestioned. Each man maintained the justness of his own statement, and the dispute was long and obstinately pursued. Historians and commentators at length withdrew together. The terrors with which I was seized when this conversation began, were extreme. I stole a sidelong glance to one quarter and another, to observe if any man's attention was turned upon me. I trembled as if in an ague-fit; and, at first, felt continual impulses to quit the house, and take to my heels. I drew closer to my corner, held aside my head, and seemed from time to time to undergo a total revolution of the animal economy.

At length the tide of ideas turned. Perceiving they paid no

attention to me, the recollection of the full security my disguise afforded recurred strongly to my thoughts; and I began inwardly to exult, though I did not venture to obtrude myself to examination. By degrees I began to be amused at the absurdity of their tales, and the variety of the falsehoods I heard asserted around me. My soul seemed to expand; I felt a pride in the self-possession and lightness of heart with which I could listen to the scene; and I determined to prolong and heighten the enjoyment. Accordingly, when they were withdrawn, I addressed myself to our hostess, a buxom, bluff, good-humoured widow, and asked what sort of a man this Kit Williams might be? She replied that, as she was informed, he was as handsome, likely a lad, as any in four counties round; and that she loved him for his cleverness, by which he outwitted all the keepers they could set over him, and made his way through stone walls as if they were so many cobwebs. I observed, that the country was so thoroughly alarmed, that I did not think it possible he should escape the pursuit that was set up after him. This idea excited her immediate indignation: she said, she hoped he was far enough away by this time; but if not, she wished the curse of God might light on them that betrayed so noble a fellow to an ignominious end! – Though she little thought that the person of whom she spoke was so near her, yet the sincere and generous warmth with which she interested herself in my behalf gave me considerable pleasure. With this sensation to sweeten the fatigues of the day and the calamities of my situation, I retired from the kitchen to a neighbouring barn, laid myself down upon some straw, and fell into a profound sleep.

The next day about noon, as I was pursuing my journey, I was overtaken by two men on horseback, who stopped me, to enquire respecting a person that they supposed might have passed along that road. As they proceeded in their description, I perceived, with astonishment and terror, that I was myself the person to whom their questions related. They entered into a tolerably accurate detail of the various characteristics by which my person might best be distinguished. They said, they had good reason to believe that I had been seen at a place in that county the very day before. While they were speaking a third person, who had fallen behind, came up; and my alarm was greatly increased upon seeing that this person was the servant of Mr. Forester, who had visited me in prison about a fortnight before my escape. My best resource in this crisis was composure and apparent indifference. It was fortunate for me that my disguise was so complete, that the eye of Mr. Falkland itself could scarcely have penetrated it. I had been aware for some time before that this was a refuge which events might make necessary, and had endeavoured to arrange and methodise my ideas upon the subject. From my youth I had possessed a considerable facility in the art of imitation; and when I quitted my retreat in the habitation of Mr. Raymond, I adopted, along with my beggar's attire a peculiar, slouching and clownish gait, to be used whenever there should appear the least chance of my being observed, together with an Irish brogue which I had had an opportunity of studying in my prison. Such are the miserable expedients, and so great the studied artifice, which man, who never deserves the name of manhood but in proportion as he is erect and independent, may find it necessary to employ, for the purpose of eluding the inexorable animosity and unfeeling tyranny of his fellow man! I had made use of this brogue, though I have not thought it necessary to write it down in my narrative, in the conversation of the village alehouse. Mr. Forester's servant, as he came up, observed that his companions were engaged in conversation with me; and, guessing at the subject, asked whether they had gained any intelligence. He added to the information at which they had already hinted, that a resolution was taken to spare neither diligence nor expense for my discovery and apprehension, and that they were satisfied, if I were above ground and in the kingdom, it would be impossible for me to escape them.

Every new incident that had occurred to me tended to impress upon my mind the extreme danger to which I was exposed. I could almost have imagined that I was the sole subject of general attention, and that the whole world was in arms to exterminate me. The very idea tingled through every fibre of my frame. But, terrible as it appeared to my imagination, it did but give new energy to my purpose; and I determined that I would not voluntarily resign the field, that is, literally speaking, my neck to the cord of the executioner, notwithstanding the greatest superiority in my assailants. But the incidents which had befallen me, though they did not change my purpose, induced me to examine over again the means by which it might be effected. The consequence of this revisal was, to determine me to bend my course to the nearest sea-port on the west side of the island, and transport myself to Ireland. I cannot now tell what it was that inclined me to prefer this scheme to that which I had originally formed. Perhaps the latter, which had been for some time present to my imagination, for that reason appeared the more obvious of the two; and I found an appearance of complexity, which the mind did not stay to explain, in substituting the other in its stead.

I arrived without further impediment at the place from which I intended to sail, enquired for a vessel, which I found ready to put to sea in a few hours, and agreed with the captain for my passage. Ireland had to me the disadvantage of being a dependency of the British government, and therefore a place of less security than most other countries which are divided from it by the ocean. To judge from the diligence with which I seemed to be pursued in England, it was not improbable that the zeal of my persecutors might follow me to the other side of the channel. It was however sufficiently agreeable to my mind, that I was upon the point of being removed one step further from the danger which was so grievous to my imagination.

Could there be any peril in the short interval that was to elapse, before the vessel was to weigh anchor and quit the English shore? Probably not. A very short time had intervened between my determination for the sea and my arrival at this place; and if any new alarm had been given to my prosecutors, it proceeded from the old woman a very few days before. I hoped I had anticipated their diligence. Meanwhile, that I might neglect no reasonable precaution, I went instantly on board, resolved that I would not unnecessarily, by walking the streets of the town, expose myself to any untoward accident. This was the first time I had, upon any occasion, taken leave of my native country.

CHAPTER VI

THE time was now nearly elapsed that was prescribed for our stay, and orders for weighing anchor were every moment expected, when we were hailed by a boat from the shore, with two other men in it besides those that rowed. They entered our vessel in an instant. They were officers of justice. The passengers, five persons besides myself, were ordered upon deck for examination. I was inexpressibly disturbed at the occurrence of such a circumstance in so unseasonable a moment. I took it for granted that it was of me they were in search. Was it possible that, by any unaccountable accident, they should have got an intimation of my disguise? It was infinitely more distressing to encounter them upon this narrow stage, and under these pointed circumstances, than, as I had before encountered my pursuers, under the appearance of an indifferent person. My recollection however did not forsake me. I confided in my conscious disguise and my Irish brogue, as a rock of dependence against all accidents.

No sooner did we appear upon deck than, to my great consternation, I could observe the attention of our guests principally turned upon me. They asked a few frivolous questions of such of my fellow passengers as happened to be nearest to them; and then, turning to me, enquired my name, who I was, whence I came, and what had brought me there? I had scarcely opened my mouth to reply, when, with one consent, they laid hold of me, said I was their prisoner, and declared that my accent, together with the correspondence of my person, would be sufficient to convict me before any court in England. I was hurried out of the vessel into the boat in which they came, and seated between them, as if by way of precaution, lest I should spring overboard, and by any means escape them.

I now took it for granted that I was once more in the power of Mr. Falkland; and the idea was insupportably mortifying and oppressive to my imagination. Escape from his pursuit, freedom from his tyranny, were objects upon which my whole soul was bent. Could no human ingenuity and exertion effect them? Did his power reach through all space, and his eye penetrate every concealment? Was he like that mysterious being, to protect us from whose fierce revenge mountains and hills, we are told, might fall on us in vain? No idea is more heart-sickening and tremendous than this. But, in my case, it was not a subject of reasoning or of faith; I could derive no comfort, either directly from the unbelief which, upon religious subjects, some men avow to their own minds; or secretly from the remoteness and incomprehensibility of the conception: it was an affair of sense; I felt the fangs of the tiger striking deep into my heart.

But though this impression was at first exceedingly strong, and accompanied with its usual attendants of dejection and pusillanimity, my mind soon began, as it were mechanically, to turn upon the consideration of the distance between this seaport and my county prison, and various opportunities of escape that might offer themselves in the interval. My first duty was to avoid betraying myself, more than it might afterwards appear I was betrayed already. It was possible that, though apprehended, my apprehension might have been determined on upon some slight score, and that, by my dexterity, I might render my dismission as sudden as my arrest had been. It was even possible that I had been seized through a mistake, and that the present measure might have no connection with Mr. Falkland's affair. Upon every supposition, it was my business to gain information. In my passage from the ship to the town I did not utter a word. My conductors commented on my sulkiness; but remarked that it would avail me nothing – I should infallibly swing, as it was never known that any body got off who was tried for robbing his majesty's mail. It is difficult to conceive the lightness of heart which was communicated to me by these words: I persisted however in the silence I had meditated. From the rest of their conversation, which was sufficiently voluble, I learned that the mail from Edinburgh to London had been robbed about ten days before by two Irishmen, that one of them was already secured, and that I was taken up upon suspicion of being the other. They had a description of his person, which, though, as I afterwards found, it disagreed from mine in several material articles, appeared to them to tally to the minutest tittle. The intelligence that the whole proceeding against me was founded in a mistake, took an oppressive load from my mind. I believed that I should immediately be able to establish my innocence, to the satisfaction of any magistrate in the kingdom; and though crossed in my plans, and thwarted in my design of quitting the island, even after I was already at sea, this was but a trifling inconvenience compared with what I had had but too much reason to fear.

As soon as we came ashore, I was conducted to the house of a justice of peace, a man who had formerly been the captain of a collier, but who, having been successful in the world, had quitted this wandering life, and for some years had had the honour to represent his majesty's person. We were detained for some time in a sort of anti-room, waiting his reverence's leisure. The persons by whom I had been taken up were experienced in their trade, and insisted upon employing this interval in searching me, in presence of two of his worship's servants. They found upon me fifteen guineas and some silver. They required me to strip myself perfectly naked, that they might examine whether I had bank-notes concealed any where about my person. They took up the detached parcels of my miserable attire as I threw it from me, and felt them one by one, to discover whether the articles of which they were in search might by any device be sewn up in them. To all this I submitted without murmuring. It might probably come to the same thing at last; and summary justice was sufficiently coincident with my views, my principal object being to get as soon as possible out of the clutches of the respectable persons who now had me in custody.

This operation was scarcely completed, before we were directed to be ushered into his worship's apartment. My accusers opened the charge, and told him they had been ordered to this town, upon an intimation that one of the persons who robbed the Edinburgh mail was to be found here; and that they had taken me on board a vessel which was by this time under sail for Ireland. "Well," says his worship, "that is your story; now let us hear what account the gentleman gives of himself. What is your name – ha, sirrah? and from what part of Tipperary are you pleased to come?" I had already taken my determination upon this article; and the moment I learned the particulars of the charge against me, resolved, for the present at least, to lay aside my Irish accent, and speak my native tongue. This I had done in the very few words I had spoken to my conductors in the anti-room: they started at the metamorphosis; but they had gone too far for it to be possible they should retract, in consistence with their honour. I now told the justice that I was no Irishman, nor had ever been in that country: I was a native of England. This occasioned a consulting of the deposition in which my person was supposed to be described, and which my conductors had brought with them for their direction. To be sure, that required that the offender should be an Irishman.

Observing his worship hesitate, I thought this was the time to push the matter a little further. I referred to the paper, and showed that the description neither tallied as to height nor complexion. But then it did as to years and the colour of the hair; and it was not this gentleman's habit, as he informed me, to squabble about trifles, or to let a man's neck out of the halter for a pretended flaw of a few inches in his stature. "If a man were too short," he said, "there was no remedy like a little stretching." The miscalculation in my case happened to be the opposite way, but his reverence did not think proper to lose his jest. Upon the whole, he was somewhat at a loss how to proceed.

My conductors observed this, and began to tremble for the reward, which, two hours ago, they thought as good as in their own pocket. To retain me in custody they judged to be a safe speculation; if it turned out a mistake at last, they felt little apprehension of a suit for false imprisonment from a poor man, accoutred as I was, in rags. They therefore urged his worship to comply with their views. They told him that to be sure the evidence against me did not prove so strong as for their part they heartily wished it had, but that there were a number of suspicious circumstances respecting me. When I was brought up to them upon the deck of the vessel, I spoke as fine an Irish brogue as one shall hear in a summer's day; and now, all at once, there was not the least particle of it left. In searching me they had found upon me fifteen guineas, how should a poor beggar lad, such as I appeared, come honestly by fifteen guineas? Besides, when they had stripped me naked, though my dress was so shabby; my skin had all the sleekness of a gentleman. In fine, for what purpose could a poor beggar, who had never been in Ireland in his life, want to transport himself to that country? It was as clear as the sun that I was no better than I should be. This reasoning, together with some significant winks and gestures between the justice and the plaintiffs, brought him over to their way of thinking. He said, I must go to Warwick, where it seems the other robber was at present in custody, and be confronted with him; and if then every thing appeared fair and satisfactory, I should be discharged.

No intelligence could be more terrible than that which was contained in these words. That I, who had found the whole country in arms against me, who was exposed to a pursuit so peculiarly vigilant and penetrating, should now be dragged to the very centre of the kingdom, without power of accommodating myself to circumstances, and under the immediate custody of the officers of justice, seemed to my ears almost the same thing as if he had pronounced upon me a sentence of death! I strenuously urged the injustice of this proceeding. I observed to the magistrate, that it was impossible I should be the person at whom the description pointed. It required an Irishman; I was no Irishman. It described a person shorter than I; a circumstance of all others the least capable of being counterfeited. There was not the slightest reason for detaining me in custody. I had been already disappointed of my voyage, and lost the money I had paid down, through the officiousness of these gentlemen in apprehending me. I assured his worship, that every delay, under my circumstances, was of the utmost importance to me. It was impossible to devise a greater injury to be inflicted on me, than the proposal that, instead of being permitted to proceed upon my voyage, I should be sent, under arrest, into the heart of the kingdom.

My remonstrances were vain. The justice was by no means inclined to digest the being expostulated with in this manner by a person in the habiliments of a beggar. In the midst of my address he would have silenced me for my impertinence, but that I spoke with an earnestness with which he was wholly unable to contend. When I had finished, he told me it was all to no purpose, and that it might have been better for me, if I had shown myself less insolent. It was clear that I was a vagabond and a suspicious person. The more earnest I showed myself to get off, the more reason there was he should keep me fast. Perhaps, after all, I should turn out to be the felon in question. But, if I was not that, he had no doubt I was worse; a poacher, or, for what he knew, a murderer. He had a kind of a notion that he had seen my face before about some such affair; out of all doubt I was an old offender. He had it in his choice to send me to hard labour as a vagrant, upon the strength of my appearance and the contradictions in my story, or to order me to Warwick; and, out of the spontaneous goodness of his disposition, he chose the milder side of the alternative. He could assure me I should not slip through his fingers. It was of more benefit to his majesty's government to hang one such fellow as he suspected me to be, than, out of mistaken tenderness, to concern one's self for the good of all the beggars in the nation.

Finding it was impossible to work, in the way I desired, on a man so fully impressed with his own dignity and importance and my utter insignificance, I claimed that, at least, the money taken from my person should be restored to me. This was granted. His worship perhaps suspected that he had stretched a point in what he had already done, and was therefore the less unwilling to relax in this incidental circumstance. My conductors did not oppose themselves to this indulgence, for a reason that will appear in the sequel. The justice however enlarged upon his clemency in this proceeding. He did not know whether he was not exceeding the spirit of his commission in complying with my demand. So much money in my possession could not be honestly come by. But it was his temper to soften, as far as could be done with propriety, the strict letter of the law.

There were cogent reasons why the gentlemen who had originally taken me into custody, chose that I should continue in their custody when my examination was over. Every man is, in his different mode, susceptible to a sense of honour; and they did not choose to encounter the disgrace that would accrue to them, if justice had been done. Every man is in some degree influenced by the love of power; and they were willing I should owe any benefit I received, to their sovereign grace and benignity, and not to the mere reason of the case. It was not however an unsubstantial honour and barren power that formed the objects of their pursuit: no, their views were deeper than that. In a word, though they chose that I should retire from the seat of justice, as I had come before it, a prisoner, yet the tenor of my examination had obliged them, in spite of themselves, to suspect that I was innocent of the charge alleged against me. Apprehensive therefore that the hundred guineas which had been offered as a reward for taking the robber was completely out of the question in the present business, they were contented to strike at smaller game. Having conducted me to an inn, and given directions respecting a vehicle for the journey, they took me aside, while one of them addressed me in the following manner: —

"You see, my lad, how the case stands: hey for Warwick is the word! and when we are got there, what may happen then I will not pretend for to say. Whether you are innocent or no is no business of mine; but you are not such a chicken as to suppose, if so be as you are innocent, that that will make your game altogether sure. You say your business calls you another way, and as how you are in haste: I scorns to cross any man in his concerns, if I can help it. If therefore you will give us them there fifteen shiners, why snug is the word. They are of no use to you; a beggar, you know, is always at home. For the matter of that, we could have had them in the way of business, as you saw, at the justice's. But I am a man of principle; I loves to do things above board, and scorns to extort a shilling from any man."

He who is tinctured with principles of moral discrimination is apt upon occasion to be run away with by his feelings in that respect, and to forget the immediate interest of the moment. I confess, that the first sentiment excited in my mind by this overture was that of indignation. I was irresistibly impelled to give utterance to this feeling, and postpone for a moment the consideration of the future. I replied with the severity which so base a proceeding appeared to deserve. My bear-leaders were considerably surprised with my firmness, but seemed to think it beneath them to contest with me the principles I delivered. He who had made the overture contented himself with replying, "Well, well, my lad, do as you will; you are not the first man that has been hanged rather than part with a few guineas." His words did not pass unheeded by me. They were strikingly applicable to my situation, and I was determined not to suffer the occasion to escape me unimproved.

The pride of these gentlemen however was too great to admit of further parley for the present. They left me abruptly, having first ordered an old man, the father of the landlady, to stay in the room with me while they were absent. The old man they ordered, for security, to lock the door, and put the key in his pocket; at the same time mentioning below stairs the station in which they had left me, that the people of the house might have an eye upon what went forward, and not suffer me to escape. What was the intention of this manoeuvre I am unable certainly to pronounce. Probably it was a sort of compromise between their pride and their avarice; being desirous, for some reason or other, to drop me as soon as convenient, and therefore determining to wait the result of my private meditations on the proposal they had made.

CHAPTER VII

THEY were no sooner withdrawn than I cast my eye upon the old man, and found something extremely venerable and interesting in his appearance. His form was above the middle size. It indicated that his strength had been once considerable; nor was it at this time by any means annihilated. His hair was in considerable quantity, and was as white as the drifted snow. His complexion was healthful and ruddy, at the same time that his face was furrowed with wrinkles. In his eye there was remarkable vivacity, and his whole countenance was strongly expressive of good-nature. The boorishness of his rank in society was lost in the cultivation his mind had derived from habits of sensibility and benevolence.

The view of his figure immediately introduced a train of ideas into my mind, respecting the advantage to be drawn from the presence of such a person. The attempt to take any step without his consent was hopeless; for, though I should succeed with regard to him, he could easily give the alarm to other persons, who would, no doubt, be within call. Add to which, I could scarcely have prevailed on myself to offer any offence to a person whose first appearance so strongly engaged my affection and esteem. In reality my thoughts were turned into a different channel. I was impressed with an ardent wish to be able to call this man my benefactor. Pursued by a train of ill fortune, I could no longer consider myself as a member of society. I was a solitary being, cut off from the expectation of sympathy, kindness, and the good-will of mankind. I was strongly impelled, by the situation in which the present moment placed me, to indulge in a luxury which my destiny seemed to have denied. I could not conceive the smallest comparison between the idea of deriving my liberty from the spontaneous kindness of a worthy and excellent mind, and that of being indebted for it to the selfishness and baseness of the worst members of society. It was thus that I allowed myself in the wantonness of refinement, even in the midst of destruction.

Guided by these sentiments, I requested his attention to the circumstances by which I had been brought into my present situation. He immediately signified his assent, and said he would cheerfully listen to any thing I thought proper to communicate. I told him, the persons who had just left me in charge with him had come to this town for the purpose of apprehending some person who had been guilty of robbing the mail; that they had chosen to take me up under this warrant, and had conducted me before a justice of the peace; that they had soon detected their mistake, the person in question being an Irishman, and differing from me both in country and stature; but that, by collusion between them and the justice, they were permitted to retain me in custody, and pretended to undertake to conduct me to Warwick to confront me with my accomplice; that, in searching me at the justice's, they had found a sum of money in my possession which excited their cupidity, and that they had just been proposing to me to give me my liberty upon condition of my surrendering this sum into their hands. Under these circumstances, I requested him to consider, whether he would wish to render himself the instrument of their extortion. I put myself into his hands, and solemnly averred the truth of the facts I had just stated. If he would assist me in my escape, it could have no other effect than to disappoint the base passions of my conductors. I would upon no account expose him to any real inconvenience; but I was well assured that the same generosity that should prompt him to a good deed, would enable him effectually to vindicate it when done; and that those who detained me, when they had lost sight of their prey, would feel covered with confusion, and not dare to take another step in the affair.

The old man listened to what I related with curiosity and interest. He said that he had always felt an abhorrence to the sort of people who had me in their hands; that he had an aversion to the task they had just imposed upon him, but that he could not refuse some little disagreeable offices to oblige his daughter and son-in-law. He had no doubt, from my countenance and manner, of the truth of what I had asserted to him. It was an extraordinary request I had made, and he did not know what had induced me to think him the sort of person to whom, with any prospect of success, it might be made. In reality however his habits of thinking were uncommon, and he felt more than half inclined to act as I desired. One thing at least he would ask of me in return, which was to be faithfully informed in some degree respecting the person he was desired to oblige. What was my name?

The question came upon me unprepared. But, whatever might be the consequence, I could not bear to deceive the person by whom it was put, and in the circumstances under which it was put. The practice of perpetual falsehood is too painful a task. I replied, that my name was Williams.

He paused. His eye was fixed upon me. I saw his complexion alter at the repetition of that word. He proceeded with visible anxiety.

My Christian name?

Caleb.

Good God! it could not be ——? He conjured me by every thing that was sacred to answer him faithfully to one question more. I was not – no, it was impossible – the person who had – formerly lived servant with Mr. Falkland, of ——?

I told him that, whatever might be the meaning of his question, I would answer him truly. I was the individual he mentioned.

As I uttered these words the old man rose from his seat. He was sorry that fortune had been so unpropitious to him, as for him ever to have set eyes upon me! I was a monster with whom the very earth groaned!

I entreated that he would suffer me to explain this new misapprehension, as he had done in the former instance. I had no doubt that I should do it equally to his satisfaction.

No! no! no! he would upon no consideration admit, that his ears should suffer such contamination. This case and the other were very different. There was no criminal upon the face of the earth, no murderer, half so detestable as the person who could prevail upon himself to utter the charges I had done, by way of recrimination, against so generous a master. – The old man was in a perfect agony with the recollection.

At length he calmed himself enough to say, he should never cease to grieve that he had held a moment's parley with me.

He did not know what was the conduct severe justice required of him; but, since he had come into the knowledge of who I was only by my own confession, it was irreconcilably repugnant to his feelings to make use of that knowledge to my injury. Here therefore all relation between us ceased; as indeed it would be an abuse of words to consider me in the light of a human creature. He would do me no mischief but, on the other hand, he would not, for the world, be in any way assisting and abetting me.

I was inexpressibly affected at the abhorrence this good and benevolent creature expressed against me. I could not be silent; I endeavoured once and again to prevail upon him to hear me. But his determination was unalterable. Our contest lasted for some time, and he at length terminated it by ringing the bell, and calling up the waiter. A very little while after, my conductors entered, and the other persons withdrew.

It was a part of the singularity of my fate that it hurried me from one species of anxiety and distress to another, too rapidly to suffer any one of them to sink deeply into my mind. I am apt to believe, in the retrospect, that half the calamities I was destined to endure would infallibly have overwhelmed and destroyed me. But, as it was, I had no leisure to chew the cud upon misfortunes as they befell me, but was under the necessity of forgetting them, to guard against peril that the next moment seemed ready to crush me.

The behaviour of this incomparable and amiable old man cut me to the heart. It was a dreadful prognostic for all my future life. But, as I have just observed, my conductors entered, and another subject called imperiously upon my attention. I could have been content, mortified as I was at this instant, to have been shut up in some impenetrable solitude, and to have wrapped myself in inconsolable misery. But the grief I endured had not such power over me as that I could be content to risk the being led to the gallows. The love of life, and still more a hatred against oppression, steeled my heart against that species of inertness. In the scene that had just passed I had indulged, as I have said, in a wantonness and luxury of refinement. It was time that indulgence should be brought to a period. It was dangerous to trifle any more upon the brink of fate; and, penetrated as I was with sadness by the result of my last attempt, I was little disposed to unnecessary circumambulation.

I was exactly in the temper in which the gentlemen who had me in their power would have desired to find me. Accordingly we entered immediately upon business; and, after some chaffering, they agreed to accept eleven guineas as the price of my freedom. To preserve however the chariness of their reputation, they insisted upon conducting me with them for a few miles on the outside of a stage-coach. They then pretended that the road they had to travel lay in a crosscountry direction; and, having quitted the vehicle, they suffered me, almost as soon as it was out of sight, to shake off this troublesome association, and follow my own inclinations. It may be worth remarking by the way, that these fellows outwitted themselves at their own trade. They had laid hold of me at first under the idea of a prize of a hundred guineas; they had since been glad to accept a composition of eleven: but if they had retained me a little longer in their possession, they would have found the possibility of acquiring the sum that had originally excited their pursuit, upon a different score.

The mischances that had befallen me, in my late attempt to escape from my pursuers by sea, deterred me from the thought of repeating that experiment. I therefore once more returned to the suggestion of hiding myself, at least for the present, amongst the crowds of the metropolis. Meanwhile, I by no means thought proper to venture by the direct route, and the less so, as that was the course which would be steered by my late conductors; but took my road along the borders of Wales. The only incident worth relating in this place occurred in an attempt to cross the Severn in a particular point. The mode was by a ferry; but, by some strange inadvertence, I lost my way so completely as to be wholly unable that night to reach the ferry, and arrive at the town which I had destined for my repose.

This may seem a petty disappointment, in the midst of the overwhelming considerations that might have been expected to engross every thought of my mind. Yet it was borne by me with singular impatience. I was that day uncommonly fatigued. Previously to the time that I mistook, or at least was aware of the mistake of the road, the sky had become black and lowering, and soon after the clouds burst down in sheets of rain. I was in the midst of a heath, without a tree or covering of any sort to shelter me. I was thoroughly drenched in a moment. I pushed on with a sort of sullen determination. By and by the rain gave place to a storm of hail. The hail-stones were large and frequent. I was ill defended by the miserable covering I wore, and they seemed to cut me in a thousand directions. The hail-storm subsided, and was again succeeded by a heavy rain. By this time it was that I had perceived I was wholly out of my road. I could discover neither man nor beast, nor habitation of any kind. I walked on, measuring at every turn the path it would be proper to pursue, but in no instance finding a sufficient reason to reject one or prefer another. My mind was bursting with depression and anguish. I muttered imprecations and murmuring as I passed along. I was full of loathing and abhorrence of life, and all that life carries in its train. After wandering without any certain direction for two hours, I was overtaken by the night. The scene was nearly pathless, and it was vain to think of proceeding any farther.

Here I was, without comfort, without shelter, and without food. There was not a particle of my covering that was not as wet as if it had been fished from the bottom of the ocean. My teeth chattered. I trembled in every limb. My heart burned with universal fury. At one moment I stumbled and fell over some unseen obstacle; at another I was turned back by an impediment I could not overcome.

There was no strict connection between these casual inconveniences and the persecution under which I laboured. But my distempered thoughts confounded them together. I cursed the whole system of human existence. I said, "Here I am, an outcast, destined to perish with hunger and cold. All men desert me. All men hate me. I am driven with mortal threats from the sources of comfort and existence. Accursed world! that hates without a cause, that overwhelms innocence with calamities which ought to be spared even to guilt! Accursed world! dead to every manly sympathy; with eyes of horn, and hearts of steel! Why do I consent to live any longer? Why do I seek to drag on an existence, which, if protracted, must be protracted amidst the lairs of these human tigers?"

This paroxysm at length exhausted itself. Presently after, I discovered a solitary shed, which I was contented to resort to for shelter. In a corner of the shed I found some clean straw. I threw off my rags, placed them in a situation where they would best be dried, and buried myself amidst this friendly warmth. Here I forgot by degrees the anguish that had racked me. A wholesome shed and fresh straw may seem but scanty benefits; but they offered themselves when least expected, and my whole heart was lightened by the encounter. Through fatigue of mind and body, it happened in this instance, though in general my repose was remarkably short, that I slept till almost noon of the next day. When I rose, I found that I was at no great distance from the ferry, which I crossed, and entered the town where I intended to have rested the preceding night.

It was market-day. As I passed near the cross, I observed two people look at me with great earnestness: after which one of them exclaimed, "I will be damned if I do not think that this is the very fellow those men were enquiring for who set off an hour ago by the coach for —." I was extremely alarmed at this information; and, quickening my pace, turned sharp down a narrow lane. The moment I was out of sight I ran with all the speed I could exert, and did not think myself safe till I was several miles distant from the place where this information had reached my ears. I have always believed that the men to whom it related were the very persons who had apprehended me on board the ship in which I had embarked for Ireland; that, by some accident, they had met with the description of my person as published on the part of Mr. Falkland; and that, from putting together the circumstances, they had been led to believe that this was the very individual who had lately been in their custody. Indeed it was a piece of infatuation in me, for which I am now unable to account, that, after the various indications which had occurred in that affair, proving to them that I was a man in critical and peculiar circumstances, I should have persisted in wearing the same disguise without the smallest alteration. My escape in the present case was eminently fortunate. If I had not lost my way in consequence of the hail-storm on the preceding night, or if I had not so greatly overslept myself this very morning, I must almost infallibly have fallen into the hands of these infernal blood-hunters.

The town they had chosen for their next stage, the name of which I had thus caught in the market-place, was the town to which, but for this intimation, I should have immediately proceeded. As it was, I determined to take a road as wide of it as possible. In the first place to which I came, in which it was practicable to do so, I bought a great coat, which I drew over my beggar's weeds, and a better hat. The hat I slouched over my face, and covered one of my eyes with a green-silk shade. The handkerchief, which I had hitherto worn about my head, I now tied about the lower part of my visage, so as to cover my mouth. By degrees I discarded every part of my former dress, and wore for my upper garment a kind of carman's frock, which, being of the better sort, made me look like the son of a reputable farmer of the lower class. Thus equipped, I proceeded on my journey, and, after a thousand alarms, precautions, and circuitous deviations from the direct path, arrived safely in London.

CHAPTER VIII

HERE then was the termination of an immense series of labours, upon which no man could have looked back without astonishment, or forward without a sentiment bordering on despair. It was at a price which defies estimation that I had purchased this resting-place; whether we consider the efforts it had cost me to escape from the walls of my prison, or the dangers and anxieties to which I had been a prey, from that hour to the present.

But why do I call the point at which I was now arrived at a resting-place? Alas, it was diametrically the reverse! It was my first and immediate business to review all the projects of disguise I had hitherto conceived, to derive every improvement I could invent from the practice to which I had been subjected, and to manufacture a veil of concealment more impenetrable than ever. This was an effort to which I could see no end. In ordinary cases the hue and cry after a supposed offender is a matter of temporary operation; but ordinary cases formed no standard for the colossal intelligence of Mr. Falkland. For the same reason, London, which appears an inexhaustible reservoir of concealment to the majority of mankind, brought no such consolatory sentiment to my mind. Whether life were worth accepting on such terms I cannot pronounce. I only know that I persisted in this exertion of my faculties, through a sort of parental love that men are accustomed to entertain for their intellectual offspring; the more thought I had expended in rearing it to its present perfection, the less did I find myself disposed to abandon it. Another motive, not less strenuously exciting me to perseverance, was the ever-growing repugnance I felt to injustice and arbitrary power.

The first evening of my arrival in town I slept at an obscure inn in the borough of Southwark, choosing that side of the metropolis, on account of its lying entirely wide of the part of England from which I came. I entered the inn in the evening in my countryman's frock; and, having paid for my lodging before I went to bed, equipped myself next morning as differently as my wardrobe would allow, and left the house before day. The frock I made up into a small packet, and, having carried it to a distance as great as I thought necessary, I dropped it in the corner of an alley through which I passed. My next care was to furnish myself with another suit of apparel, totally different from any to which I had hitherto had recourse. The exterior which I was now induced to assume was that of a Jew. One of the gang of thieves upon — forest, had been of that race; and by the talent of mimicry, which I have already stated myself to possess, I could copy their pronunciation of the English language, sufficiently to answer such occasions as were likely to present themselves. One of the preliminaries I adopted, was to repair to a quarter of the town in which great numbers of this people reside, and study their complexion and countenance. Having made such provision as my prudence suggested to me, I retired for that night to an inn in the midway between Mileend and Wapping. Here I accoutred myself in my new habiliments; and, having employed the same precautions as before, retired from my lodging at a time least exposed to observation. It is unnecessary to describe the particulars of my new equipage; suffice it to say, that one of my cares was to discolour my complexion, and give it the dun and sallow hue which is in most instances characteristic of the tribe to which I assumed to belong; and that when my metamorphosis was finished, I could not, upon the strictest examination, conceive that any one could have traced out the person of Caleb Williams in this new disguise.

Thus far advanced in the execution of my project, I deemed it advisable to procure a lodging, and change my late wandering life for a stationary one. In this lodging I constantly secluded myself from the rising to the setting of the sun; the periods I allowed for exercise and air were few, and those few by night. I was even cautious of so much as approaching the window of my apartment, though upon the attic story; a principle I laid down to myself was, not wantonly and unnecessarily to expose myself to risk, however slight that risk might appear.

Here let me pause for a moment, to bring before the reader, in the way in which it was impressed upon my mind, the nature of my situation. I was born free: I was born healthy, vigorous, and active, complete in all the lineaments and members of a human body. I was not born indeed to the possession of hereditary wealth; but I had a better inheritance, an enterprising mind, an inquisitive spirit, a liberal ambition. In a word, I accepted my lot with willingness and content; I did not fear but I should make my cause good in the lists of existence. I was satisfied to aim at small things; I was pleased to play at first for a slender stake; I was more willing to grow than to descend in my individual significance.

The free spirit and the firm heart with which I commenced, one circumstance was sufficient to blast. I was ignorant of the power which the institutions of society give to one man over others; I had fallen unwarily into the hands of a person who held it as his fondest wish to oppress and destroy me.

I found myself subjected, undeservedly on my part, to all the disadvantages which mankind, if they reflected upon them, would hesitate to impose on acknowledged guilt. In every human countenance I feared to find the countenance of an enemy. I shrunk from the vigilance of every human eye. I dared not open my heart to the best affections of our nature. I was shut up, a deserted, solitary wretch, in the midst of my species. I dared not look for the consolations of friendship; but, instead of seeking to identify myself with the joys and sorrows of others, and exchanging the delicious gifts of confidence and sympathy, was compelled to centre my thoughts and my vigilance in myself. My life was all a lie. I had a counterfeit character to support. I had counterfeit manners to assume. My gait, my gestures, my accents, were all of them to be studied. I was not free to indulge, no not one, honest sally of the soul. Attended with these disadvantages, I was to procure myself a subsistence, a subsistence to be acquired with infinite precautions, and to be consumed without the hope of enjoyment.

This, even this, I was determined to endure; to put my shoulder to the burthen, and support it with unshrinking firmness. Let it not however be supposed that I endured it without repining and abhorrence. My time was divided between the terrors of an animal that skulks from its pursuers, the obstinacy of unshrinking firmness, and that elastic revulsion that from time to time seems to shrivel the very hearts of the miserable. If at some moments I fiercely defied all the rigours of my fate, at others, and those of frequent recurrence, I sunk into helpless despondence. I looked forward without hope through the series of my existence, tears of anguish rushed from my eyes, my courage became extinct, and I cursed the conscious life that was reproduced with every returning day.

"Why," upon such occasions I was accustomed to exclaim, "why am I overwhelmed with the load of existence? Why are all these engines at work to torment me? I am no murderer; yet, if I were, what worse could I be fated to suffer? How vile, squalid, and disgraceful is the state to which I am condemned! This is not my place in the roll of existence, the place for which either my temper or my understanding has prepared me! To what purpose serve the restless aspirations of my soul, but to make me, like a frighted bird, beat myself in vain against the enclosure of my cage? Nature, barbarous nature! to me thou hast proved indeed the worst of step-mothers; endowed me with wishes insatiate, and sunk me in never-ending degradation!"

I might have thought myself more secure if I had been in possession of money upon which to subsist. The necessity of earning for myself the means of existence, evidently tended to thwart the plan of secrecy to which I was condemned. Whatever labour I adopted, or deemed myself qualified to discharge, it was first to be considered how I was to be provided with employment, and where I was to find an employer or purchaser for my commodities. In the mean time I had no alternative. The little money with which I had escaped from the bloodhunters was almost expended.

After the minutest consideration I was able to bestow upon this question, I determined that literature should be the field of my first experiment. I had read of money being acquired in this way, and of prices given by the speculators in this sort of ware to its proper manufacturers. My qualifications I esteemed at a slender valuation. I was not without a conviction that experience and practice must pave the way to excellent production. But, though of these I was utterly destitute, my propensities had always led me in this direction; and my early thirst of knowledge had conducted me to a more intimate acquaintance with books, than could perhaps have been expected under my circumstances. If my literary pretensions were slight, the demand I intended to make upon them was not great. All I asked was a subsistence; and I was persuaded few persons could subsist upon slenderer means than myself. I also considered this as a temporary expedient, and hoped that accident or time might hereafter place me in a less precarious situation. The reasons that principally determined my choice were, that this employment called upon me for the least preparation, and could, as I thought, be exercised with least observation.

There was a solitary woman, of middle age, who tenanted a chamber in this house, upon the same floor with my own. I had no sooner determined upon the destination of my industry than I cast my eye upon her as the possible instrument for disposing of my productions. Excluded as I was from all intercourse with my species in general, I found pleasure in the occasional exchange of a few words with this inoffensive and good-humoured creature, who was already of an age to preclude scandal. She lived upon a very small annuity, allowed her by a distant relation, a woman of quality, who, possessed of thousands herself, had no other anxiety with respect to this person than that she should not contaminate her alliance by the exertion of honest industry. This humble creature was of a uniformly cheerful and active disposition, unacquainted alike with the cares of wealth and the pressure of misfortune. Though her pretensions were small, and her information slender, she was by no means deficient in penetration. She remarked the faults and follies of mankind with no contemptible discernment; but her temper was of so mild and forgiving a cast, as would have induced most persons to believe that she perceived nothing of the matter. Her heart overflowed with the milk of kindness. She was sincere and ardent in her attachments, and never did she omit a service which she perceived herself able to render to a human being.

Had it not been for these qualifications of temper, I should probably have found that my appearance, that of a deserted, solitary lad, of Jewish extraction, effectually precluded my demands upon her kindness. But I speedily perceived, from her manner of receiving and returning civilities of an indifferent sort, that her heart was too noble to have its effusions checked by any base and unworthy considerations. Encouraged by these preliminaries, I determined to select her as my agent. I found her willing and alert in the business I proposed to her. That I might anticipate occasions of suspicion, I frankly told her that, for reasons which I wished to be excused from relating, but which, if related, I was sure would not deprive me of her good opinion, I found it necessary, for the present, to keep myself private. With this statement she readily acquiesced, and told me that she had no desire for any further information than I found it expedient to give.

My first productions were of the poetical kind. After having finished two or three, I directed this generous creature to take them to the office of a newspaper; but they were rejected with contempt by the Aristarchus[1] of that place, who, having bestowed on them a superficial glance, told her that such matters were not in his way. I cannot help mentioning in this place, that the countenance of Mrs. Marney (this was the name of my ambassadress) was in all cases a perfect indication of her success, and rendered explanation by words wholly unnecessary. She interested herself so unreservedly in what she undertook, that she felt either miscarriage or good fortune much more exquisitely than I did. I had an unhesitating confidence in my own resources, and, occupied as I was in meditations more interesting and more painful, I regarded these matters as altogether trivial.

I quietly took the pieces back, and laid them upon my table. Upon revisal, I altered and transcribed one of them, and, joining it with two others, despatched them together to the editor of a magazine. He desired they might be left with him till the day after tomorrow. When that day came he told my friend they should be inserted; but, Mrs. Marney asking respecting the

---

1   Greek grammarian (*c.* 156 BC), known for editing the Homeric poems. He devised the still-current arrangement of both the *Iliad* and the *Odyssey* into twenty-four books.

price, he replied, it was their constant rule to give nothing for poetical compositions, the letter-box being always full of writings of that sort; but if the gentleman would try his hand in prose, a short essay or a tale, he would see what he could do for him.

With the requisition of my literary dictator I immediately complied. I attempted a paper in the style of Addison's Spectators,[1] which was accepted. In a short time I was upon an established footing in this quarter. I however distrusted my resources in the way of moral disquisition, and soon turned my thoughts to his other suggestion, a tale. His demands upon me were now frequent, and, to facilitate my labours, I bethought myself of the resource of translation. I had scarcely any convenience with respect to the procuring of books; but, as my memory was retentive, I frequently translated or modelled my narrative upon a reading of some years before. By a fatality, for which I did not exactly know how to account, my thoughts frequently led me to the histories of celebrated robbers; and I related, from time to time, incidents and anecdotes of Cartouche, Gusman d'Alfarache, and other memorable worthies, whose career was terminated upon the gallows or the scaffold.[2]

In the mean time a retrospect to my own situation rendered a perseverance even in this industry difficult to be maintained. I often threw down my pen in an ecstasy of despair. Sometimes for whole days together I was incapable of action, and sunk into a sort of partial stupor, too wretched to be described. Youth and health however enabled me, from time to time, to get the better of my dejection, and to rouse myself to something like a gaiety, which, if it had been permanent, might have made this interval of my story tolerable to my reflections.

---

1   Joseph Addison (1672-1719) founded and largely wrote the material for *The Spectator* (1711-14), which published essays on politics and on social life and manners, as well as serial critical essays on aesthetic topics.

2   Louis Dominique Cartouche was leader of a band of French thieves; he was captured and broken on the wheel. Guzmán de Alfarache was the title character of an influential Spanish picaresque novel by Mateo Alemán (1547-1614), published in 1599 and quickly translated into other European languages. An excerpt from the 1622 English translation is included in Appendix D.

CHAPTER IX

W<small>HILE</small> I was thus endeavouring to occupy and provide for the intermediate period, till the violence of the pursuit after me might be abated, a new source of danger opened upon me of which I had no previous suspicion.

Gines, the thief who had been expelled from Captain Raymond's gang, had fluctuated, during the last years of his life, between the two professions of a violator of the laws and a retainer to their administration. He had originally devoted himself to the first; and probably his initiation in the mysteries of thieving qualified him to be peculiarly expert in the profession of a thief-taker – a profession he had adopted, not from choice, but necessity. In this employment his reputation was great, though perhaps not equal to his merits; for it happens here as in other departments of human society, that, however the subalterns may furnish wisdom and skill, the principals exclusively possess the *éclat*. He was exercising this art in a very prosperous manner, when it happened, by some accident, that one or two of his achievements previous to his having shaken off the dregs of unlicensed depredation were in danger of becoming subjects of public attention. Having had repeated intimations of this, he thought it prudent to decamp; and it was during this period of his retreat that he entered into the —— gang.

Such was the history of this man antecedently to his being placed in the situation in which I had first encountered him. At the time of that encounter he was a veteran of Captain Raymond's gang; for thieves being a short-lived race, the character of veteran costs the less time in acquiring. Upon his expulsion from this community he returned once more to his lawful profession, and by his old comrades was received with congratulation as a lost sheep. In the vulgar classes of society no length of time is sufficient to expiate a crime; but among the honourable fraternity of thief-takers it is a rule never to bring one of their own brethren to a reckoning when it can with any decency be avoided. They are probably reluctant to fix an unnecessary stain upon the ermine of their profession. Another rule observed by those who have passed through the same gradation as Gines had done, and which was adopted by Gines himself, is always to reserve such as have been the accomplices of their depredations to the last, and on no account to assail them without great necessity or powerful temptation. For this reason, according to Gines's system of tactics, Captain Raymond and his confederates were, as he would have termed it, safe from his retaliation.

But, though Gines was, in this sense of the term, a man of strict honour, my case unfortunately did not fall within the laws of honour he acknowledged. Misfortune had overtaken me, and I was on all sides without protection or shelter. The persecution to which I was exposed was founded upon the supposition of my having committed felony to an immense amount. But in this Gines had had no participation; he was careless whether the supposition were true or false, and hated me as much as if my innocence had been established beyond the reach of suspicion.

The blood-hunters who had taken me into custody at —, related, as usual among their fraternity, a part of their adventure, and told of the reason which inclined them to suppose, that the individual who had passed through their custody, was the very Caleb Williams for whose apprehension a reward had been offered of a hundred guineas. Gines, whose acuteness was eminent in the way of his profession, by comparing facts and dates, was induced to suspect in his own mind, that Caleb Williams was the person he had hustled and wounded upon — forest. Against that person he entertained the bitterest aversion. I had been the innocent occasion of his being expelled with disgrace from Captain Raymond's gang; and Gines, as I afterwards understood, was intimately persuaded that there was no comparison between the liberal and manly profession of a robber from which I had driven him, and the sordid and mechanical occupation of a blood-hunter, to which he was obliged to return. He no sooner received the information I have mentioned than he vowed revenge. He determined to leave all other objects, and consecrate every faculty of his mind to the unkennelling me from my hiding-place. The offered reward, which his vanity made him consider as assuredly his own, appeared as the complete indemnification of his labour and expense. Thus I had to encounter the sagacity he possessed in the way of his profession, whetted and stimulated by a sentiment of vengeance, in a mind that knew no restraint from conscience or humanity.

When I drew to myself a picture of my situation soon after having fixed on my present abode, I foolishly thought, as the unhappy are accustomed to do, that my calamity would admit of no aggravation. The aggravation which, unknown to me, at this time occurred was the most fearful that any imagination could have devised. Nothing could have happened more critically hostile to my future peace, than my fatal encounter with Gines upon — forest. By this means, as it now appears, I had fastened upon myself a second enemy, of that singular and dreadful sort that is determined never to dismiss its animosity as long as life shall endure. While Falkland was the hungry lion whose roarings astonished and appalled me, Gines was a noxious insect, scarcely less formidable and tremendous, that hovered about my goings, and perpetually menaced me with the poison of his sting.

The first step pursued by him in execution of his project, was to set out for the sea-port town where I had formerly been apprehended. From thence he traced me to the banks of the Severn, and from the banks of the Severn to London. It is scarcely necessary to observe that this is always practicable, provided the pursuer have motives strong enough to excite him to perseverance, unless the precautions of the fugitive be, in the highest degree, both judicious in the conception, and fortunate in the execution. Gines indeed, in the course of his pursuit, was often obliged to double his steps; and, like the harrier, whenever he was at a fault, return to the place where he had last perceived the scent of the animal whose death he had decreed. He spared neither pains nor time in the gratification of the passion, which choice had made his ruling one.

Upon my arrival in town he for a moment lost all trace of me, London being a place in which, on account of the magnitude of its dimensions, it might well be supposed that an individual could remain hidden and unknown. But no difficulty could discourage this new adversary. He went from inn to inn (reasonably supposing that there was no private house to which I could immediately repair), till he found, by the description he gave, and the recollections he excited, that I had slept for one night in the borough of Southwark. But he could get no further information. The people of the inn had no knowledge what had become of me the next morning.

This however did but render him more eager in the pursuit. The describing me was now more difficult, on account of the partial change of dress I had made the second day of my being in town. But Gines at length overcame the obstacle from that quarter.

Having traced me to my second inn, he was here furnished with a more copious information. I had been a subject of speculation for the leisure hours of some of the persons belonging to this inn. An old woman, of a most curious and loquacious disposition, who lived opposite to it, and who that morning rose early to her washing, had espied me from her window, by the light of a large lamp which hung over the inn, as I issued from the gate. She had but a very imperfect view of me, but she thought there was something Jewish in my appearance. She was accustomed to hold a conference every morning with the landlady of the inn, some of the waiters and chambermaids occasionally assisting at it. In the course of the dialogue of this morning, she asked some questions about the Jew who had slept there the night before. No Jew had slept there. The curiosity of the landlady was excited in her turn. By the time of the morning it could be no other but me. It was very strange! They compared notes respecting my appearance and dress. No two things could be more dissimilar. The Jew Christian, upon any dearth of subjects of intelligence, repeatedly furnished matter for their discourse.

The information thus afforded to Gines appeared exceedingly material. But the performance did not for some time keep pace with the promise. He could not enter every private house into which lodgers were ever admitted, in the same manner that he had treated the inns. He walked the streets, and examined with a curious and inquisitive eye the countenance of every Jew about my stature; but in vain. He repaired to Duke's Place and the synagogues. It was not here that in reality he could calculate upon finding me; but he resorted to those means in despair, and as a last hope. He was more than once upon the point of giving up the pursuit; but he was recalled to it by an insatiable and restless appetite for revenge.

It was during this perturbed and fluctuating state of his mind, that he chanced to pay a visit to a brother of his, who was the head-workman of a printing-office. There was little inter-course between these two persons, their dispositions and habits of life being extremely dissimilar. The printer was industrious, sober, inclined to Methodism, and of a propensity to accumula-tion. He was extremely dissatisfied with the character and pur-suits of his brother, and had made some ineffectual attempts to reclaim him. But, though they by no means agreed in their habits of thinking, they sometimes saw each other. Gines loved to boast of as many of his achievements as he dared venture to mention; and his brother was one more hearer, in addition to the set of his usual associates. The printer was amused with the blunt sagacity of remark and novelty of incident that charac-terised Gines's conversation. He was secretly pleased, in spite of all his sober and church-going prejudices, that he was brother to a man of so much ingenuity and fortitude.

After having listened for some time upon this occasion to the wonderful stories which Gines, in his rugged way, conde-scended to tell, the printer felt an ambition to entertain his brother in his turn. He began to retail some of my stories of Cartouche and Gusman d'Alfarache. The attention of Gines was excited. His first emotion was wonder; his second was envy and aversion. Where did the printer get these stories? This question was answered. "I will tell you what," said the printer, "we none of us know what to make of the writer of these arti-cles. He writes poetry, and morality, and history: I am a printer, and corrector of the press, and may pretend without vanity to be a tolerably good judge of these matters: he writes them all to my mind extremely fine; and yet he is no more than a Jew." [To my honest printer this seemed as strange, as if they had been written by a Cherokee chieftain at the falls of the Mississippi.]

"A Jew! How do you know? Did you ever see him?"

"No; the matter is always brought to us by a woman. But my master hates mysteries; he likes to see his authors himself. So he plagues and plagues the old woman; but he can never get any thing out of her, except that one day she happened to drop that the young gentleman was a Jew."

A Jew! a young gentleman! a person who did every thing by proxy, and made a secret of all his motions! Here was abundant matter for the speculations and suspicions of Gines. He was confirmed in them, without adverting to the process of his own mind, by the subject of my lucubrations, – men who died by the hand of the executioner. He said little more to his brother, except asking, as if casually, what sort of an old woman this was? of what age she might be? and whether she often brought him materials of this kind? and soon after took occasion to leave him.

It was with vast pleasure that Gines had listened to this unhoped-for information. Having collected from his brother sufficient hints relative to the person and appearance of Mrs. Marney, and understanding that he expected to receive something from me the next day, Gines took his stand in the street early, that he might not risk miscarriage by negligence. He waited several hours, but not without success. Mrs. Marney came; he watched her into the house; and, after about twenty minutes delay, saw her return. He dogged her from street to street; observed her finally enter the door of a private house; and congratulated himself upon having at length arrived at the consummation of his labours.

The house she entered was not her own habitation. By a sort of miraculous accident she had observed Gines following her in the street. As she went home she saw a woman who had fallen down in a fainting fit. Moved by the compassion that was ever alive in her, she approached her in order to render her assistance. Presently a crowd collected round them. Mrs. Marney, having done what she was able, once more proceeded homewards. Observing the crowd round her, the idea of pick-pockets occurred to her mind; she put her hands to her sides, and at the same time looked round upon the populace. She had left the circle somewhat abruptly; and Gines, who had been obliged to come nearer, lest he should lose her in the confusion, was at that moment standing exactly opposite to her. His visage was of the most extraordinary kind; habit had written the characters of malignant cunning and dauntless effrontery in every line of his face; and Mrs. Marney, who was neither philosopher nor physiognomist, was nevertheless struck. This good woman, like most persons of her notable character, had a peculiar way of going home, not through the open streets, but by narrow lanes and alleys, with intricate insertions and sudden turnings. In one of these, by some accident, she once again caught a glance of her pursuer. This circumstance, together with the singularity of his appearance, awakened her conjectures. Could he be following her? It was the middle of the day, and she could have no fears for herself. But could this circumstance have any reference to me? She recollected the precautions and secrecy I practised, and had no doubt that I had reasons for what I did. She recollected that she had always been upon her guard respecting me; but had she been sufficiently so? She thought that, if she should be the means of any mischief to me, she should be miserable for ever. She determined therefore, by way of precaution in case of the worst, to call at a friend's house, and send me word of what had occurred. Having instructed her friend, she went out immediately upon a visit to a person in the exactly opposite direction, and desired her friend to proceed upon the errand to me, five minutes after she left the house. By this prudence she completely extricated me from the present danger.

Meantime the intelligence that was brought me by no means ascertained the greatness of the peril. For any thing I could discover in it the circumstance might be perfectly innocent, and the fear solely proceed from the over-caution and kindness of this benevolent and excellent woman. Yet, such was the misery of my situation, I had no choice. For this menace or no menace, I was obliged to desert my habitation at a minute's warning, taking with me nothing but what I could carry in my hand; to see my generous benefactress no more; to quit my little arrangements and provision; and to seek once again, in some forlorn retreat, new projects, and, if of that I could have any rational hope, a new friend. I descended into the street with a heavy, not an irresolute heart. It was broad day. I said, persons are at this moment supposed to be roaming the street in search of me: I must not trust to the chance of their pursuing one direction, and I another. I traversed half a dozen streets, and then dropped into an obscure house of entertainment for persons of small expense. In this house I took some refreshment, passed several hours of active but melancholy thinking, and at last procured a bed. As soon however as it was dark I went out (for this was indispensable) to purchase the materials of a new disguise. Having adjusted it as well as I could during the night, I left this asylum, with the same precautions that I had employed in former instances.

CHAPTER X

I PROCURED a new lodging. By some bias of the mind, it may be, gratifying itself with images of peril, I inclined to believe that Mrs. Marney's alarm had not been without foundation. I was however unable to conjecture through what means danger had approached me; and had therefore only the unsatisfactory remedy of redoubling my watch upon all my actions. Still I had the joint considerations pressing upon me of security and subsistence. I had some small remains of the produce of my former industry; but this was but small, for my employer was in arrear with me, and I did not choose in any method to apply to him for payment. The anxieties of my mind, in spite of all my struggles, preyed upon my health. I did not consider myself as in safety for an instant. My appearance was wasted to a shadow; and I started at every sound that was unexpected. Sometimes I was half tempted to resign myself into the hands of the law, and brave its worst; but resentment and indignation at those times speedily flowed back upon my mind, and re-animated my perseverance.

I knew no better resource with respect to subsistence than that I had employed in the former instance, of seeking some third person to stand between me and the disposal of my industry. I might find an individual ready to undertake this office in my behalf; but where should I find the benevolent soul of Mrs. Marney? The person I fixed upon was a Mr. Spurrel, a man who took in work from the watchmakers, and had an apartment upon our second floor. I examined him two or three times with irresolute glances, as we passed upon the stairs, before I would venture to accost him. He observed this, and at length kindly invited me into his apartment.

Being seated, he condoled with me upon my seeming bad health, and the solitary mode of my living, and wished to know whether he could be of any service to me. "From the first moment he saw me, he had conceived an affection for me." In my present disguise I appeared twisted and deformed, and in other respects by no means an object of attraction. But it seemed Mr. Spurrel had lost an only son about six months before, and I was "the very picture of him." If I had put off my counterfeited ugliness, I should probably have lost all hold upon his affections. "He was now an old man," as he observed, "just dropping into the grave, and his son had been his only consolation. The poor lad was always ailing, but he had been a nurse to him; and the more tending he required while he was alive, the more he missed him now he was dead. Now he had not a friend, nor any body that cared for him, in the whole world. If I pleased, I should be instead of that son to him, and he would treat me in all respects with the same attention and kindness."

I expressed my sense of these benevolent offers, but told him that I should be sorry to be in any way burthensome to him. My ideas at present led me to a private and solitary life, and my chief difficulty was to reconcile this with some mode of earning necessary subsistence. If he would condescend to lend me his assistance in smoothing this difficulty, it would be the greatest benefit he could confer on me. I added, "that my mind had always had a mechanical and industrious turn, and that I did not doubt of soon mastering any craft to which I seriously applied myself. I had not been brought up to any trade; but, if he would favour me with his instructions, I would work with him as long as he pleased for a bare subsistence. I knew that I was asking of him an extraordinary kindness; but I was urged on the one hand by the most extreme necessity, and encouraged on the other by the persuasiveness of his friendly professions."

The old man dropped some tears over my apparent distress, and readily consented to every thing I proposed. Our agreement was soon made, and I entered upon my functions accordingly. My new friend was a man of a singular turn of mind. Love of money, and a charitable officiousness of demeanour, were his leading characteristics. He lived in the most penurious manner, and denied himself every indulgence. I entitled myself almost immediately, as he frankly acknowledged, to some remuneration for my labours, and accordingly he insisted upon my being paid. He did not however, as some persons would have done under the circumstance, pay me the whole amount of my earnings, but professed to subtract from them twenty per cent, as an equitable consideration for instruction, and commission-money in procuring me a channel for my industry. Yet he frequently shed tears over me, was uneasy in every moment of our indispensable separation, and exhibited perpetual tokens of attachment and fondness. I found him a man of excellent mechanical contrivance, and received considerable pleasure from his communications. My own sources of information were various; and he frequently expressed his wonder and delight in the contemplation of my powers, as well of amusement as exertion.

Thus I appeared to have attained a situation not less eligible than in my connection with Mrs. Marney. I was however still more unhappy. My fits of despondence were deeper, and of more frequent recurrence. My health every day grew worse; and Mr. Spurrel was not without apprehensions that he should lose me, as he before lost his only son.

I had not been long however in this new situation, before an incident occurred which filled me with greater alarm and apprehension than ever. I was walking out one evening, after a long visitation of languor, for an hour's exercise and air, when my ears were struck with two or three casual sounds from the mouth of a hawker who was bawling his wares. I stood still to inform myself more exactly, when, to my utter astonishment and confusion, I heard him deliver himself nearly in these words: – *"Here you have the* MOST WONDERFUL AND SURPRISING HISTORY AND MIRACULOUS ADVENTURES OF CALEB WILLIAMS: *you are informed how he first robbed, and then brought false accusations against his master; as also of his attempting divers times to break out of prison, till at last he effected his escape in the most wonderful and uncredible manner; as also of his travelling the kingdom in various disguises, and the robberies he committed with a most desperate and daring gang of thieves; and of his coming up to London, where it is supposed he now lies concealed; with a true and faithful copy of the hue and cry printed and published by one of his Majesty's most principal secretaries of state, offering a reward of one hundred guineas for apprehending him. All for the price of one halfpenny."*

Petrified as I was at these amazing and dreadful sounds, I had the temerity to go up to the man and purchase one of his papers. I was desperately resolved to know the exact state of the fact, and what I had to depend upon. I carried it with me a little way, till, no longer able to endure the tumult of my impatience, I contrived to make out the chief part of its contents, by the help of a lamp, at the upper end of a narrow passage. I found it contained a greater number of circumstances than could have been expected in this species of publication. I was equalled to the most notorious housebreaker in the art of penetrating through walls and doors, and to the most accomplished swindler in plausibleness, duplicity, and disguise. The hand-bill which Larkins had first brought to us upon the forest was printed at length. All my disguises, previously to the last alarm that had been given me by the providence of Mrs. Marney, were faithfully enumerated; and the public were warned to be upon their watch against a person of an uncouth and extraordinary appearance, and who lived in a recluse and solitary manner. I also learned from this paper that my former lodgings had been searched on the very evening of my escape, and that Mrs. Marney had been sent to Newgate upon a charge of misprision of felony.[1] – This last circumstance affected me deeply. In the midst of my own sufferings my sympathies flowed undiminished. It was a most cruel and intolerable idea, if I were not only myself to be an object of unrelenting persecution, but my very touch were to be infectious, and every one that succoured me was to be involved in common ruin. My instant feeling was that of a willingness to undergo the utmost malice of my enemies, could I by that means have saved this excellent woman from alarm and peril. – I afterwards learned that Mrs. Marney was delivered from confinement, by the interposition of her noble relation.

My sympathy for Mrs. Marney however was at this moment a transient one. A more imperious and irresistible consideration demanded to be heard.

With what sensations did I ruminate upon this paper? Every word of it carried despair to my heart. The actual apprehension that I dreaded would perhaps have been less horrible. It would have put an end to that lingering terror to which I was a prey.

---

1   Newgate was the most famous of British criminal prisons. Misprision involves concealment of knowledge concerning the committing of a felony.

Disguise was no longer of use. A numerous class of individuals, through every department, almost every house of the metropolis, would be induced to look with a suspicious eye upon every stranger, especially every solitary stranger, that fell under their observation. The prize of one hundred guineas was held out to excite their avarice and sharpen their penetration. It was no longer Bow Street,[1] it was a million of men in arms against me. Neither had I the refuge, which few men have been so miserable as to want, of one single individual with whom to repose my alarms, and who might shelter me from the gaze of indiscriminate curiosity.

What could exceed the horrors of this situation? My heart knocked against my ribs, my bosom heaved, I gasped and panted for breath. "There is no end then," said I, "to my persecutors! My unwearied and long-continued labours lead to no termination! Termination! No; the lapse of time, that cures all other things, makes my case more desperate! Why then," exclaimed I, a new train of thought suddenly rushing into my mind, "why should I sustain the contest any longer? I can at least elude my persecutors in death. I can bury myself and the traces of my existence together in friendly oblivion; and thus bequeath eternal doubt, and ever new alarm, to those who have no peace but in pursuing me!"

In the midst of the horrors with which I was now impressed, this idea gave me pleasure; and I hastened to the Thames to put it in instant execution. Such was the paroxysm of my mind that my powers of vision became partially suspended. I was no longer conscious to the feebleness of disease, but rushed along with fervent impetuosity. I passed from street to street without observing what direction I pursued. After wandering I know not how long, I arrived at London Bridge. I hastened to the stairs, and saw the river covered with vessels.

"No human being must see me," said I, "at the instant that I vanish for ever." This thought required some consideration. A portion of time had elapsed since my first desperate purpose. My understanding began to return. The sight of the vessels

---

1   The street in London where the principal metropolitan police-court was located.

suggested to me the idea of once more attempting to leave my native country.

I enquired, and speedily found that the cheapest passage I could procure was in a vessel moored near the Tower, and which was to sail in a few days for Middleburgh in Holland. I would have gone instantly on board, and have endeavoured to prevail with the captain to let me remain there till he sailed; but unfortunately I had not money enough in my pocket to defray my passage.

It was worse than this. I had not money enough in the world. I however paid the captain half his demand, and promised to return with the rest. I knew not in what manner it was to be procured, but I believed that I should not fail in it. I had some idea of applying to Mr. Spurrel. Surely he would not refuse me? He appeared to love me with parental affection, and I thought I might trust myself for a moment in his hands.

I approached my place of residence with a heavy and fore-boding heart. Mr. Spurrel was not at home; and I was obliged to wait for his return. Worn out with fatigue, disappointment, and the ill state of my health, I sunk upon a chair. Speedily however I recollected myself. I had work of Mr. Spurrel's in my trunk, which had been delivered out to me that very morning, to five times the amount I wanted. I canvassed for a moment whether I should make use of this property as if it were my own; but I rejected the idea with disdain. I had never in the smallest degree merited the reproaches that were cast upon me; and I determined I never would merit them. I sat gasping, anxious, full of the blackest forebodings. My terrors appeared, even to my own mind, greater and more importunate than the circumstances authorised.

It was extraordinary that Mr. Spurrel should be abroad at this hour; I had never known it happen before. His bed-time was between nine and ten. Ten o'clock came, eleven o'clock, but not Mr. Spurrel. At midnight I heard his knock at the door. Every soul in the house was in bed. Mr. Spurrel, on account of his regular hours, was unprovided with a key to open for him-self. A gleam, a sickly gleam, of the social spirit came over my heart. I flew nimbly down stairs, and opened the door.

I could perceive, by the little taper in my hand, something extraordinary in his countenance. I had not time to speak, before I saw two other men follow him. At the first glance I was sufficiently assured what sort of persons they were. At the second, I perceived that one of them was no other than Gines himself. I had understood formerly that he had been of this profession, and I was not surprised to find him in it again. Though I had for three hours endeavoured, as it were, to prepare myself for the unavoidable necessity of falling once again into the hands of the officers of law, the sensation I felt at their entrance was indescribably agonising. I was besides not a little astonished at the time and manner of their entrance; and I felt anxious to know whether Mr. Spurrel could be base enough to have been their introducer.

I was not long held in perplexity. He no sooner saw his followers within the door, than he exclaimed, with convulsive eagerness, "There, there, that is your man! thank God! thank God!" Gines looked eagerly in my face, with a countenance expressive alternately of hope and doubt, and answered, "By God, and I do not know whether it be or no! I am afraid we are in the wrong box!" Then recollecting himself, "We will go into the house, and examine further however." We all went up stairs into Mr. Spurrel's room; I set down the candle upon the table. I had hitherto been silent; but I determined not to desert myself, and was a little encouraged to exertion by the scepticism of Gines. With a calm and deliberate manner therefore, in my feigned voice, one of the characteristics of which was lisping, I asked, "Pray, gentlemen, what may be your pleasure with me?" – "Why," said Gines, "our errand is with one Caleb Williams, and a precious rascal he is! I ought to know the chap well enough; but they say he has as many faces as there are days in the year. So you please to pull off your face; or, if you cannot do that, at least you can pull off your clothes, and let us see what your hump is made of."

I remonstrated, but in vain. I stood detected in part of my artifice; and Gines, though still uncertain, was every moment more and more confirmed in his suspicions. Mr. Spurrel perfectly gloated, with eyes that seemed ready to devour every thing that passed. As my imposture gradually appeared more palpable, he repeated his exclamation, "Thank God! thank God!" At last, tired with this scene of mummery, and disgusted beyond measure with the base and hypocritical figure I seemed to exhibit, I exclaimed, "Well, I am Caleb Williams; conduct me wherever you please! And now, Mr. Spurrel!" – He gave a violent start. The instant I declared myself his transport had been at the highest, and was, to any power he was able to exert, absolutely uncontrollable. But the unexpectedness of my address, and the tone in which I spoke, electrified him. — "Is it possible," continued I, "that you should have been the wretch to betray me? What have I done to deserve this treatment? Is this the kindness you professed? the affection that was perpetually in your mouth? to be the death of me!"

"My poor boy! my dear creature!" cried Spurrel, whimpering, and in a tone of the humblest expostulation, "indeed I could not help it! I would have helped it, if I could! I hope they will not hurt my darling! I am sure I shall die if they do!"

"Miserable driveller!" interrupted I, with a stern voice, "do you betray me into the remorseless fangs of the law, and then talk of my not being hurt? I know my sentence, and am prepared to meet it! You have fixed the halter upon my neck, and at the same price would have done so to your only son! Go, count your accursed guineas! My life would have been safer in the hands of one I had never seen than in yours, whose mouth and whose eyes for ever ran over with crocodile affection!"

I have always believed that my sickness, and, as he apprehended, approaching death, contributed its part to the treachery of Mr. Spurrel. He predicted to his own mind the time when I should no longer be able to work. He recollected with agony the expense that attended his son's illness and death. He determined to afford me no assistance of a similar kind. He feared however the reproach of deserting me. He feared the tenderness of his nature. He felt that I was growing upon his affections, and that in a short time he could not have deserted me. He was driven by a sort of implicit impulse, for the sake of avoiding one ungenerous action, to take refuge in another, the basest and most diabolical. This motive, conjoining with the prospect of the proffered reward, was an incitement too powerful for him to resist.

CHAPTER XI

HAVING given vent to my resentment, I left Mr. Spurrel motionless, and unable to utter a word. Gines and his companion attended me. It is unnecessary to repeat all the insolence of this man. He alternately triumphed in the completion of his revenge, and regretted the loss of the reward to the shrivelled old curmudgeon we had just quitted, whom however he swore he would cheat of it by one means or another. He claimed to himself the ingenuity of having devised the halfpenny legend, the thought of which was all his own, and was an expedient that was impossible to fail. There was neither law nor justice, he said, to be had, if Hunks who had done nothing were permitted to pocket the cash, and his merit were left undistinguished and pennyless.

I paid but little attention to his story. It struck upon my sense, and I was able to recollect it at my nearest leisure, though I thought not of it at the time. For the present I was busily employed, reflecting on my new situation, and the conduct to be observed in it. The thought of suicide had twice, in moments of uncommon despair, suggested itself to my mind; but it was far from my habitual meditations. At present, and in all cases where death was immediately threatened me from the injustice of others, I felt myself disposed to contend to the last.

My prospects were indeed sufficiently gloomy and discouraging. How much labour had I exerted, first to extricate myself from prison, and next to evade the diligence of my pursuers; and the result of all, to be brought back to the point from which I began! I had gained fame indeed, the miserable fame to have my story bawled forth by hawkers and ballad-mongers, to have my praises as an active and enterprising villain celebrated among footmen and chambermaids; but I was neither an Erostratus[1] nor an Alexander, to die contented with that species of eulogium. With respect to all that was solid, what chance could I find in new exertions of a similar nature? Never was a human creature pursued by enemies more inventive or envenomed. I

---

1   An Ephesian who set fire to a famous temple of Diana on the night that Alexander the Great was born in order to secure his own fame.

could have small hope that they would ever cease their persecution, or that my future attempts would be crowned with a more desirable issue.

They were considerations like these that dictated my resolution. My mind had been gradually weaning from Mr. Falkland, till its feeling rose to something like abhorrence. I had long cherished a reverence for him, which not even animosity and subornation on his part could utterly destroy. But I now ascribed a character so inhumanly sanguinary to his mind; I saw something so fiend-like in the thus hunting me round the world, and determining to be satisfied with nothing less than my blood, while at the same time he knew my innocence, my indisposition to mischief, nay, I might add, my virtues; that henceforth I trampled reverence and the recollection of former esteem under my feet. I lost all regard to his intellectual greatness, and all pity for the agonies of his soul. I also would abjure forbearance. I would show myself bitter and inflexible as he had done. Was it wise in him to drive me into extremity and madness? Had he no fears for his own secret and atrocious offences?

I had been obliged to spend the remainder of the night upon which I had been apprehended, in prison. During the interval I had thrown off every vestige of disguise, and appeared the next morning in my own person. I was of course easily identified; and, this being the whole with which the magistrates before whom I now stood thought themselves concerned, they were proceeding to make out an order for my being conducted back to my own county. I suspended the despatch of this measure by observing that I had something to disclose. This is an overture to which men appointed for the administration of criminal justice never fail to attend.

I went before the magistrates, to whose office Gines and his comrades conducted me, fully determined to publish those astonishing secrets of which I had hitherto been the faithful depository; and, once for all, to turn the tables upon my accuser. It was time that the real criminal should be the sufferer, and not that innocence should for ever labour under the oppression of guilt.

I said that "I had always protested my innocence, and must now repeat the protest."

"In that case," retorted the senior magistrate abruptly, "what can you have to disclose? If you are innocent, that is no business of ours! We act officially."

"I always declared," continued I, "that I was the perpetrator of no guilt, but that the guilt wholly belonged to my accuser. He privately conveyed these effects among my property, and then charged me with the robbery. I now declare more than that, that this man is a murderer, that I detected his criminality, and that, for that reason, he is determined to deprive me of life. I presume, gentlemen, that you do consider it as your business to take this declaration. I am persuaded you will be by no means disposed, actively or passively, to contribute to the atrocious injustice under which I suffer, to the imprisonment and condemnation of an innocent man, in order that a murderer may go free. I suppressed this story as long as I could. I was extremely averse to be the author of the unhappiness or the death of a human being. But all patience and submission have their limits."

"Give me leave, sir," rejoined the magistrate with an air of affected moderation, "to ask you two questions. Were you any way aiding, abetting, or contributing to this murder?"

"No."

"And pray, sir, who is this Mr. Falkland? and what may have been the nature of your connection with him?"

"Mr. Falkland is a gentleman of six thousand per annum. I lived with him as his secretary."

"In other words, you were his servant?"

"As you please."

"Very well, sir; that is quite enough for me. First, I have to tell you, as a magistrate, that I can have nothing to do with your declaration. If you had been concerned in the murder you talk of, that would alter the case. But it is out of all reasonable rule for a magistrate to take an information from a felon, except against his accomplices. Next, I think it right to observe to you, in my own proper person, that you appear to me to be the most impudent rascal I ever saw. Why, are you such an ass as to suppose, that the sort of story you have been telling, can be of any service to you, either here or at the assizes, or any where else? A fine time of it indeed it would be, if, when gentlemen of six thousand a year take up their servants for robbing them, those servants could trump up such accusations as these, and could get any magistrate or court of justice to listen to them! Whether or no the felony with which you stand charged would have brought you to the gallows, I will not pretend to say: but I am sure this story will. There would be a speedy end to all order and good government, if fellows that trample upon ranks and distinctions in this atrocious sort were upon any con- sideration suffered to get off."

"And do you refuse, sir, to attend to the particulars of the charge I allege?"

"Yes, sir, I do. – But, if I did not, pray what witnesses have you of the murder?"

This question staggered me.

"None. But I believe I can make out a circumstantial proof, of a nature to force attention from the most indifferent hearer."

"So I thought. – Officers, take him from the bar!"

Such was the success of this ultimate resort on my part, upon which I had built with such undoubting confidence. Till now, I had conceived that the unfavourable situation in which I was placed was prolonged by my own forbearance; and I had determined to endure all that human nature could support, rather than have recourse to this extreme recrimination. That idea secretly consoled me under all my calamities: it was a vol- untary sacrifice, and was cheerfully made. I thought myself allied to the army of martyrs and confessors; I applauded my fortitude and self-denial; and I pleased myself with the idea, that I had the power, though I hoped never to employ it, by an unrelenting display of my resources, to put an end at once to my sufferings and persecutions.

And this at last was the justice of mankind! A man, under certain circumstances, shall not be heard in the detection of a crime, because he has not been a participator of it! The story of a flagitious murder shall be listened to with indifference, while an innocent man is hunted, like a wild beast, to the furthest corners of the earth! Six thousand a year shall protect a man from accusation; and the validity of an impeachment shall be superseded, because the author of it is a servant!

I was conducted back to the very prison from which a few months before I had made my escape. With a bursting heart I entered those walls, compelled to feel that all my more than Herculean labours served for my own torture, and for no other end. Since my escape from prison I had acquired some knowledge of the world; I had learned by bitter experience, by how many links society had a hold upon me, and how closely the snares of despotism beset me. I no longer beheld the world, as my youthful fancy had once induced me to do, as a scene in which to hide or to appear, and to exhibit the freaks of a wanton vivacity. I saw my whole species as ready, in one mode or other, to be made the instruments of the tyrant. Hope died away in the bottom of my heart. Shut up for the first night in my dungeon, I was seized at intervals with temporary frenzy. From time to time, I rent the universal silence with the roarings of unsupportable despair. But this was a transient distraction. I soon returned to the sober recollection of myself and my miseries.

My prospects were more gloomy, and my situation apparently more irremediable than ever. I was exposed again, if that were of any account, to the insolence and tyranny that are uniformly exercised within those walls. Why should I repeat the loathsome tale of all that was endured by me, and is endured by every man who is unhappy enough to fall under the government of these consecrated ministers of national jurisprudence? The sufferings I had already experienced, my anxieties, my flight, the perpetual expectation of being discovered, worse than the discovery itself, would perhaps have been enough to satisfy the most insensible individual, in the court of his own conscience, if I had even been the felon I was pretended to be. But the law has neither eyes, nor ears, nor bowels of humanity; and it turns into marble the hearts of all those that are nursed in its principles.

I however once more recovered my spirit of determination. I resolved that, while I had life, I would never be deserted by this spirit. Oppressed, annihilated I might be; but, if I died, I would die resisting. What use, what advantage, what pleasurable sentiment, could arise from a tame surrender? There is no man that is ignorant, that to humble yourself at the feet of the law is a bootless task; in her courts there is no room for amendment and reformation.

My fortitude may to some persons appear above the standard of human nature. But if I draw back the veil from my heart they will readily confess their mistake. My heart bled at every pore. My resolution was not the calm sentiment of philosophy and reason. It was a gloomy and desperate purpose; the creature, not of hope, but of a mind austerely held to its design, that felt, as it were, satisfied with the naked effort, and prepared to give success or miscarriage to the winds. It was to this miserable condition, which might awaken sympathy in the most hardened bosom, that Mr. Falkland had reduced me.

In the mean time, strange as it may seem, here, in prison, subject to innumerable hardships, and in the assured expectation of a sentence of death, I recovered my health. I ascribe this to the state of my mind, which was now changed, from perpetual anxiety, terror, and alarm, the too frequent inmates of a prison, but which I upon this occasion did not seem to bring along with me, to a desperate firmness.

I anticipated the event of my trial. I determined once more to escape from my prison; nor did I doubt of my ability to effect at least this first step towards my future preservation. The assizes however were near, and there were certain considerations, unnecessary to be detailed, that persuaded me there might be benefit in waiting till my trial should actually be terminated, before I made my attempt.

It stood upon the list as one of the latest to be brought forward. I was therefore extremely surprised to find it called out of its order, early on the morning of the second day. But, if this were unexpected, how much greater was my astonishment, when my prosecutor was called, to find neither Mr. Falkland, nor Mr. Forester, nor a single individual of any description, appear against me! The recognizances into which my prosecutors had entered were declared to be forfeited; and I was dismissed without further impediment from the bar.

The effect which this incredible reverse produced upon my mind it is impossible to express. I, who had come to that bar with the sentence of death already in idea ringing in my ears, to be told that I was free to transport myself whithersoever I pleased! Was it for this that I had broken through so many locks and bolts, and the adamantine walls of my prison; that I had passed so many anxious days, and sleepless, spectre-haunted nights; that I had racked my invention for expedients of evasion and concealment; that my mind had been roused to an energy of which I could scarcely have believed it capable; that my existence had been enthralled to an ever-living torment, such as I could scarcely have supposed it in man to endure? Great God! what is man? Is he thus blind to the future, thus totally unsuspecting of what is to occur in the next moment of his existence? I have somewhere read, that heaven in mercy hides from us the future incidents of our life. My own experience does not well accord with this assertion. In this instance at least I should have been saved from insupportable labour and undescribable anguish, could I have foreseen the catastrophe of this most interesting transaction.

CHAPTER XII

IT was not long before I took my everlasting leave of this detested and miserable scene. My heart was for the present too full of astonishment and exultation in my unexpected deliverance, to admit of anxiety about the future. I withdrew from the town; I rambled with a slow and thoughtful pace, now bursting with exclamation, and now buried in profound and undefinable reverie. Accident led me towards the very heath which had first sheltered me, when, upon a former occasion, I broke out of my prison. I wandered among its cavities and its valleys. It was a forlorn and desolate solitude. I continued here I know not how long. Night at length overtook me unperceived, and I prepared to return for the present to the town I had quitted.

It was now perfectly dark, when two men, whom I had not previously observed, sprung upon me from behind. They seized me by the arms, and threw me upon the ground. I had no time for resistance or recollection. I could however perceive that one of them was the diabolical Gines. They blindfolded, gagged me, and hurried me I knew not whither. As we passed along in silence, I endeavoured to conjecture what could be the meaning of this extraordinary violence. I was strongly impressed with the idea, that, after the event of this morning, the most severe and painful part of my history was past; and, strange as it may seem, I could not persuade myself to regard with alarm this unexpected attack. It might however be some new project, suggested by the brutal temper and unrelenting animosity of Gines.

I presently found that we were returned into the town I had just quitted. They led me into a house, and, as soon as they had taken possession of a room, freed me from the restraints they had before imposed. Here Gines informed me with a malicious grin that no harm was intended me, and therefore I should show most sense in keeping myself quiet. I perceived that we were in an inn; I overheard company in a room at no great distance from us, and therefore was now as thoroughly aware as he could be, that there was at present little reason to stand in fear of any species of violence, and that it would be time enough to resist, when they attempted to conduct me from the inn in the same manner that they had brought me into it. I was not without some curiosity to see the conclusion that was to follow upon so extraordinary a commencement.

The preliminaries I have described were scarcely completed, before Mr. Falkland entered the room. I remember Collins, when he first communicated to me the particulars of our patron's history, observed that he was totally unlike the man he had once been. I had no means of ascertaining the truth of that observation. But it was strikingly applicable to the spectacle which now presented itself to my eyes, though, when I last beheld this unhappy man, he had been a victim to the same passions, a prey to the same undying remorse, as now. Misery was at that time inscribed in legible characters upon his countenance. But now he appeared like nothing that had ever been visible in human shape. His visage was haggard, emaciated, and fleshless. His complexion was a dun and tarnished red, the colour uniform through every region of the face, and suggested the idea of its being burnt and parched by the eternal fire that burned within him. His eyes were red, quick, wandering, full of suspicion and rage. His hair was neglected, ragged, and floating. His whole figure was thin, to a degree that suggested the idea rather of a skeleton than a person actually alive. Life seemed hardly to be the capable inhabitant of so woe-begone and ghost-like a figure. The taper of wholesome life was expired; but passion, and fierceness, and frenzy were able for the present to supply its place.

I was to the utmost degree astonished and shocked at the sight of him. – He sternly commanded my conductors to leave the room.

"Well, sir, I have this day successfully exerted myself to save your life from the gallows. A fortnight ago you did what you were able to bring my life to that ignominious close.

"Were you so stupid and undistinguishing as not to know that the preservation of your life was the uniform object of my exertions? Did not I maintain you in prison? Did not I endeavour to prevent your being sent thither? Could you mistake the bigoted and obstinate conduct of Forester, in offering a hundred guineas for your apprehension, for mine?

"I had my eye upon you in all your wanderings. You have taken no material step through their whole course with which I have not been acquainted. I meditated to do you good. I have spilt no blood but that of Tyrrel: that was in the moment of passion; and it has been the subject of my uninterrupted and hourly remorse. I have connived at no man's fate but that of the Hawkinses: they could no otherwise have been saved, than by my acknowledging myself a murderer. The rest of my life has been spent in acts of benevolence.

"I meditated to do you good. For that reason I was willing to prove you. You pretended to act towards me with consideration and forbearance. If you had persisted in that to the end, I would yet have found a way to reward you. I left you to your own discretion. You might show the impotent malignity of your own heart; but, in the circumstances in which you were then placed, I knew you could not hurt me. Your forbearance has proved, as I all along suspected, empty and treacherous. You have attempted to blast my reputation. You have sought to disclose the select and eternal secret of my soul. Because you have done that, I will never forgive you. I will remember it to my latest breath. The memory shall survive me, when my existence is no more. Do you think you are out of the reach of my power, because a court of justice has acquitted you?"

While Mr. Falkland was speaking a sudden distemper came over his countenance, his whole frame was shaken by an instantaneous convulsion, and he staggered to a chair. In about three minutes he recovered.

"Yes," said he, "I am still alive. I shall live for days, and months, and years; the power that made me, of whatever kind it be, can only determine how long. I live the guardian of my reputation. That, and to endure a misery such as man never endured, are the only ends to which I live. But, when I am no more, my fame shall still survive. My character shall be revered as spotless and unimpeachable by all posterity, as long as the name of Falkland shall be repeated in the most distant regions of the many-peopled globe."

Having said this, he returned to the discourse which more immediately related to my future condition and happiness.

"There is one condition," said he, "upon which you may

obtain some mitigation of your future calamity. It is for that purpose that I have sent for you. Listen to my proposal with deliberation and sobriety. Remember, that the insanity is not less to trifle with the resolved determination of my soul, than it would be to pull a mountain upon your head that hung trembling upon the edge of the mighty Apennine!

"I insist then upon your signing a paper, declaring, in the most solemn manner, that I am innocent of murder, and that the charge you alleged at the office in Bow Street is false, malicious and groundless. Perhaps you may scruple out of a regard to truth. Is truth then entitled to adoration for its own sake, and not for the sake of the happiness it is calculated to produce? Will a reasonable man sacrifice to barren truth, when benevolence, humanity, and every consideration that is dear to the human heart, require that it should be superseded? It is probable that I may never make use of this paper, but I require it, as the only practicable reparation to the honour you have assailed. This is what I had to propose. I expect your answer."

"Sir," answered I, "I have heard you to an end, and I stand in need of no deliberation to enable me to answer you in the negative. You took me up a raw and inexperienced boy, capable of being moulded to any form you pleased. But you have communicated to me volumes of experience in a very short period. I am no longer irresolute and pliable. What is the power you retain over my fate I am unable to discover. You may destroy me; but you cannot make me tremble. I am not concerned to enquire, whether what I have suffered flowed from you by design or otherwise; whether you were the author of my miseries, or only connived at them. This I know, that I have suffered too exquisitely on your account, for me to feel the least remaining claim on your part to my making any voluntary sacrifice.

"You say that benevolence and humanity require this sacrifice of me. No; it would only be a sacrifice to your mad and misguided love of fame, – to that passion which has been the source of all your miseries, of the most tragical calamities to others, and of every misfortune that has happened to me. I have no forbearance to exercise towards that passion. If you be not yet cured of this tremendous and sanguinary folly, at least I will do nothing to cherish it. I know not whether from my youth I was destined for a hero; but I may thank you for having taught me a lesson of insurmountable fortitude.

"What is it that you require of me? that I should sign away my own reputation for the better maintaining of yours. Where is the equality of that? What is it that casts me at such an immense distance below you, as to make every thing that relates to me wholly unworthy of consideration? You have been educated in the prejudice of birth. I abhor that prejudice. You have made me desperate, and I utter what that desperation suggests.

"You will tell me perhaps that I have no reputation to lose; that, while you are esteemed faultless and unblemished, I am universally reputed a thief, a suborner, and a calumniator. Be it so. I will never do any thing to countenance those imputations. The more I am destitute of the esteem of mankind, the more careful I will be to preserve my own. I will never from fear, or any other mistaken motive, do any thing of which I ought to be ashamed.

"You are determined to be for ever my enemy. I have in no degree deserved this eternal abhorrence. I have always esteemed and pitied you. For a considerable time I rather chose to expose myself to every kind of misfortune, than disclose the secret that was so dear to you. I was not deterred by your men-aces − (what could you make me suffer more than I actually suffered?) − but by the humanity of my own heart; in which, and not in means of violence, you ought to have reposed your confidence. What is the mysterious vengeance that you can yet execute against me? You menaced me before; you can menace no worse now. You are wearing out the springs of terror. Do with me as you please; you teach me to hear you with an unshrinking and desperate firmness. Recollect yourself! I did not proceed to the step with which you reproach me, till I was apparently urged to the very last extremity. I had suffered as much as human nature can suffer; I had lived in the midst of eternal alarm and unintermitted watchfulness; I had twice been driven to purposes of suicide. I am now sorry however, that the step of which you complain was ever adopted. But, urged to exasperation by an unintermitted rigour, I had no time to cool or to deliberate. Even at present I cherish no vengeance against you. All that is reasonable, all that can really contribute to your security, I will readily concede; but I will not be driven to an act repugnant to all reason, integrity, and justice."

Mr. Falkland listened to me with astonishment and impatience. He had entertained no previous conception of the firmness I displayed. Several times he was convulsed with the fury that laboured in his breast. Once and again he betrayed an intention to interrupt; but he was restrained by the collectedness of my manner, and perhaps by a desire to be acquainted with the entire state of my mind. Finding that I had concluded, he paused for a moment; his passion seemed gradually to enlarge, till it was no longer capable of control.

"It is well!" said he, gnashing his teeth, and stamping upon the ground. "You refuse the composition I offer! I have no power to persuade you to compliance! You defy me! At least I have a power respecting you, and that power I will exercise; a power that shall grind you into atoms. I condescend to no more expostulation. I know what I am, and what I can be. I know what you are, and what fate is reserved for you!"

Saying this he quitted the room.

Such were the particulars of this memorable scene. The impression it has left upon my understanding is indelible. The figure and appearance of Mr. Falkland, his death-like weakness and decay, his more than mortal energy and rage, the words that he spoke, the motives that animated him, produced one compounded effect upon my mind that nothing of the same nature could ever parallel. The idea of his misery thrilled through my frame. How weak in comparison of it is the imaginary hell, which the great enemy of mankind is represented as carrying every where about with him![1]

From this consideration, my mind presently turned to the menaces he had vented against myself. They were all mysterious and undefined. He had talked of power, but had given no

---

1   A reference to Satan's words in John Milton, *Paradise Lost*, IV.75. "Which way I fly is hell; myself am hell."

hint from which I could collect in what he imagined it to consist. He had talked of misery, but had not dropped a syllable respecting the nature of the misery to be inflicted.

I sat still for some time, ruminating on these thoughts. Neither Mr. Falkland nor any other person appeared to disturb my meditations. I rose, went out of the room, and from the inn into the street. No one offered to molest me. It was strange! What was the nature of this power, from which I was to apprehend so much, yet which seemed to leave me at perfect liberty? I began to imagine that all I had heard from this dreadful adversary was mere madness and extravagance, and that he was at length deprived of the use of reason, which had long served him only as a medium of torment. Yet was it likely in that case that he should be able to employ Gines and his associate, who had just been his instruments of violence upon my person?

I proceeded along the streets with considerable caution. I looked before me and behind me, as well as the darkness would allow me to do, that I might not again be hunted in sight by some men of stratagem and violence without my perceiving it. I went not, as before, beyond the limits of the town, but considered the streets, the houses, and the inhabitants, as affording some degree of security. I was still walking with my mind thus full of suspicion and forecast, when I discovered Thomas, that servant of Mr. Falkland whom I have already more than once had occasion to mention. He advanced towards me with an air so blunt and direct, as instantly to remove from me the idea of any thing insidious in his purpose; besides that I had always felt the character of Thomas, rustic and uncultivated as it was, to be entitled to a more than common portion of esteem.

"Thomas," said I, as he advanced, "I hope you are willing to give me joy, that I am at length delivered from the dreadful danger which for many months haunted me so unmercifully."

"No," rejoined Thomas, roughly; "I be not at all willing. I do not know what to make of myself in this affair. While you were in prison in that miserable fashion, I felt all at once almost as if I loved you: and now that that is over, and you are turned out loose in the world to do your worst, my blood rises at the very sight of you. To look at you, you are almost that very lad

Williams for whom I could with pleasure, as it were, have laid down my life; and yet, behind that smiling face there lie robbery, and lying, and every thing that is ungrateful and murderous. Your last action was worse than all the rest. How could you find in your heart to revive that cruel story about Mr. Tyrrel, which every body had agreed, out of regard to the squire, never to mention again, and of which I know, and you know, he is as innocent as the child unborn? There are causes and reasons, or else I could have wished from the bottom of my soul never to have set eyes on you again."

"And you still persist in your hard thoughts of me?"

"Worse! I think worse of you than ever! Before, I thought you as bad as man could be. I wonder from my soul what you are to do next. But you make good the old saying, 'Needs must go, that the devil drives.'"

"And so there is never to be an end of my misfortunes! What can Mr. Falkland contrive for me worse than the ill opinion and enmity of all mankind?"

"Mr. Falkland contrive! He is the best friend you have in the world, though you are the basest traitor to him. Poor man! it makes one's heart ache to look at him; he is the very image of grief. And it is not clear to me that it is not all owing to you. At least you have given the finishing lift to the misfortune that was already destroying him. There have been the devil and all to pay between him and Squire Forester. The squire is right raving mad with my master, for having outwitted him in the matter of the trial, and saved your life. He swears that you shall be taken up and tried all over again at the next assizes; but my master is resolute, and I believe will carry it his own way. He says indeed that the law will not allow Squire Forester to have his will in this. To see him ordering every thing for your benefit, and taking all your maliciousness as mild and innocent as a lamb, and to think of your vile proceedings against him, is a sight one shall not see again, go all the world over. For God's sake, repent of your reprobate doings, and make what little reparation is in your power! Think of your poor soul, before you awake, as to be sure one of these days you will, in fire and brimstone everlasting!"

Saying this, he held out his hand and took hold of mine. The action seemed strange; but I at first thought it the unpremeditated result of his solemn and well-intended adjuration. I felt however that he put something into my hand. The next moment he quitted his hold, and hastened from me with the swiftness of an arrow. What he had thus given me was a bank-note of twenty pounds. I had no doubt that he had been charged to deliver it to me from Mr. Falkland.

What was I to infer? what light did it throw upon the intentions of my inexorable persecutor? his animosity against me was as great as ever; that I had just had confirmed to me from his own mouth. Yet his animosity appeared to be still tempered with the remains of humanity. He prescribed to it a line, wide enough to embrace the gratification of his views, and within the boundaries of that line it stopped. But this discovery carried no consolation to my mind. I knew not what portion of calamity I was fated to endure, before his jealousy of dishonour, and inordinate thirst of fame would deem themselves satisfied.

Another question offered itself. Was I to receive the money which had just been put into my hands? the money of a man who had inflicted upon me injuries, less than those which he had entailed upon himself, but the greatest that one man can inflict upon another? who had blasted my youth, who had destroyed my peace, who had held me up to the abhorrence of mankind, and rendered me an outcast upon the face of the earth? who had forged the basest and most atrocious falsehoods, and urged them with a seriousness and perseverance which produced universal belief? who, an hour before, had vowed against me inexorable enmity, and sworn to entail upon me misery without end? Would not this conduct on my part betray a base and abject spirit, that crouched under tyranny, and kissed the hands that were imbrued in my blood?

If these reasons appeared strong, neither was the other side without reasons in reply. I wanted the money: not for any purpose of vice or superfluity, but for those purposes without which life cannot subsist. Man ought to be able, wherever placed, to find for himself the means of existence; but I was to open a new scene of life, to remove to some distant spot, to be prepared against all the ill-will of mankind, and the unexplored projects of hostility of a most accomplished foe. The actual means of existence are the property of all. What should hinder me from taking that of which I was really in want, when, in taking it, I risked no vengeance, and perpetrated no violence? The property in question will be beneficial to me, and the voluntary surrender of it is accompanied with no injury to its late proprietor; what other condition can be necessary to render the use of it on my part a duty? He that lately possessed it has injured me; does that alter its value as a medium of exchange? He will boast perhaps of the imaginary obligation he has conferred on me: surely to shrink from a thing in itself right from any such apprehension, can be the result only of pusillanimity and cowardice!

CHAPTER XIII

INFLUENCED by these reasonings, I determined to retain what had thus been put into my hands. My next care was in regard to the scene I should choose, as the retreat of that life which I had just saved from the grasp of the executioner. The danger to which I was exposed of forcible interruption in my pursuits, was probably, in some respects, less now than it had been previously to this crisis. Besides that, I was considerably influenced in this deliberation by the strong loathing I conceived for the situations in which I had lately been engaged. I knew not in what mode Mr. Falkland intended to exercise his vengeance against me; but I was seized with so unconquerable an aversion to disguise, and the idea of spending my life in personating a fictitious character, that I could not, for the present at least, reconcile my mind to any thing of that nature. The same kind of disgust I had conceived for the metropolis, where I had spent so many hours of artifice, sadness, and terror. I therefore decided in favour of the project which had formerly proved amusing to my imagination, of withdrawing to some distant, rural scene, a scene of calmness and obscurity, where for a few years at least, perhaps during the life of Mr. Falkland, I might be hidden from the world, recover the wounds my mind had received in this fatal connection, methodise and improve the experience which had been accumulated, cultivate the faculties I in any degree possessed, and employ the intervals of these occupations in simple industry, and the intercourse of guileless, uneducated, kind-intentioned minds. The menaces of my persecutor seemed to forebode the inevitable interruption of this system. But I deemed it wise to put these menaces out of my consideration. I compared them to death, which must infallibly overtake us we know not when; but the possibility of whose arrival next year, next week, to-morrow, must be left out of the calculation of him who would enter upon any important or well-concerted undertaking.

Such were the ideas that determined my choice. Thus did my youthful mind delineate the system of distant years, even when the threats of instant calamity still sounded in my ears. I was inured to the apprehension of mischief, till at last the hoarse roarings of the beginning tempest had lost their power of annihilating my peace. I however thought it necessary, while I was most palpably within the sphere of the enemy, to exert every practicable degree of vigilance. I was careful not to incur the hazards of darkness and solitude. When I left the town it was with the stage-coach, an obvious source of protection against glaring and enormous violence. Meanwhile I found myself no more exposed to molestation in my progress, than the man in the world who should have had the least reason for apprehensions of this nature. As the distance increased, I relaxed something in my precaution, though still awake to a sense of danger, and constantly pursued with the image of my foe. I fixed upon an obscure market-town in Wales as the chosen seat of my operations. This place recommended itself to my observation as I was wandering in quest of an abode. It was clean, cheerful, and of great simplicity of appearance. It was at a distance from any public and frequented road, and had nothing which could deserve the name of trade. The face of nature around it was agreeably diversified, being partly wild and romantic, and partly rich and abundant in production.

Here I solicited employment in two professions; the first, that of a watchmaker, in which though the instructions I had received were few, they were eked out and assisted by a mind fruitful in mechanical invention; the other, that of an instructor in mathematics and its practical application, geography, astronomy, land-surveying, and navigation. Neither of these was a very copious source of emolument in the obscure retreat I had chosen for myself; but, if my receipts were slender, my disbursements were still fewer. In this little town I became acquainted with the vicar, the apothecary, the lawyer, and the rest of the persons who, time out of mind, had been regarded as the top gentry of the place. Each of these centred in himself a variety of occupations. There was little in the appearance of the vicar that reminded you of his profession, except on the recurring Sunday. At other times he condescended, with his evangelical hand to guide the plough, or to drive the cows from the field to the farm-yard for the milking. The apothecary occasionally officiated as a barber, and the lawyer was the village school-master.

By all these persons I was received with kindness and hospitality. Among people thus remote from the bustle of human life there is an open spirit of confidence, by means of which a stranger easily finds access to their benevolence and good-will. My manners had never been greatly debauched from the simplicity of rural life by the scenes through which I had passed; and the hardships I had endured had given additional mildness to my character. In the theatre upon which I was now placed I had no rival. My mechanical occupation had hitherto been a non-resident; and the schoolmaster, who did not aspire to the sublime heights of science I professed to communicate, was willing to admit me as a partner in the task of civilising the unpolished manners of the inhabitants. For the parson, civilisation was no part of his trade; his business was with the things of a better life, not with the carnal concerns of this material scene; in truth, his thoughts were principally occupied with his oat-meal and his cows.

These however were not the only companions which this remote retirement afforded me. There was a family of a very different description, of which I gradually became the chosen intimate. The father was a shrewd, sensible, rational man, but who had turned his principal attention to subjects of agriculture. His wife was a truly admirable and extraordinary woman. She was the daughter of a Neapolitan nobleman who, after having visited, and made a considerable figure, in every country in Europe, had at length received the blow of fate in this village. He had been banished his country upon suspicion of religious and political heresy, and his estates confiscated. With this only child, like Prospero in the Tempest, he had withdrawn himself to one of the most obscure and uncultivated regions of the world.[1] Very soon however after his arrival in Wales he had been seized with a malignant fever, which carried him off in three days. He died possessed of no other property than a few

---

1 In Shakespeare's *The Tempest*, Prospero, the exiled Duke of Milan, lives with his only daugher, Miranda, on an island on which they have been shipwrecked.

jewels, and a bill of credit, to no considerable amount, upon an English banker.

Here then was the infant Laura, left in a foreign country, and without a single friend. The father of her present husband was led by motives of pure humanity to seek to mitigate the misfortunes of the dying Italian. Though a plain uninstructed man, with no extraordinary refinement of intellect, there was something in his countenance that determined the stranger in his present forlorn and melancholy situation, to make him his executor, and the guardian of his daughter. The Neapolitan understood enough of English to explain his wishes to this friendly attendant of his death-bed. As his circumstances were narrow, the servants of the stranger, two Italians, a male and a female, were sent back to their own country soon after the death of their master.

Laura was at this time eight years of age. At these tender years she had been susceptible of little direct instruction; and, as she grew up, even the memory of her father became, from year to year, more vague and indistinct in her mind. But there was something she derived from her father, whether along with the life he bestowed, or as the consequence of his instruction and manners, which no time could efface. Every added year of her life contributed to develop the fund of her accomplishments. She read, she observed, she reflected. Without instructors, she taught herself to draw, to sing, and to understand the more polite European languages. As she had no society in this remote situation but that of peasants, she had no idea of honour or superiority to be derived from her acquisitions; but pursued them from a secret taste, and as the sources of personal enjoyment.

A mutual attachment gradually arose between her and the only son of her guardian. His father led him, from early youth, to the labours and the sports of the field, and there was little congeniality between his pursuits and those of Laura. But this was a defect that she was slow to discover. She had never been accustomed to society in her chosen amusements, and habit at that time even made her conceive, that they were indebted to solitude for an additional relish. The youthful rustic had great integrity, great kindness of heart, and was a lad of excellent sense. He was florid, well-proportioned, and the goodness of his disposition made his manners amiable. Accomplishments greater than these she had never seen in human form, since the death of her father.

In fact, she is scarcely to be considered as a sufferer in this instance; since, in her forlorn and destitute condition, it is little probable, when we consider the habits and notions that now prevail, that her accomplishments, unassisted by fortune, would have procured her an equal alliance in marriage.

When she became a mother her heart opened to a new affection. The idea now presented itself, which had never occurred before, that in her children at least she might find the partners and companions of her favourite employments. She was, at the time of my arrival, mother of four, the eldest of which was a son. To all of them she had been a most assiduous instructor. It was well for her perhaps that she obtained this sphere for the exercise of her mind. It came just at the period when the charm which human life derives from novelty is beginning to wear off. It gave her new activity and animation. It is perhaps impossible that the refinements of which human nature is capable should not, after a time, subside into sluggishness, if they be not aided by the influence of society and affection.

The son of the Welsh farmer by this admirable woman was about seventeen years of age at the time of my settlement in their neighbourhood. His eldest sister was one year younger than himself. The whole family composed a group, with which a lover of tranquillity and virtue would have delighted to associate in any situation. It is easy therefore to conceive how much I rejoiced in their friendship, in this distant retirement, and suffering, as I felt myself, from the maltreatment and desertion of my species. The amiable Laura had a wonderful quickness of eye, and rapidity of apprehension; but this feature in her countenance was subdued by a sweetness of disposition, such as I never in any other instance saw expressed in the looks of a human being. She soon distinguished me by her kindness and friendship; for, living as she had done, though familiar with the written productions of a cultivated intellect, she had never seen the thing itself realised in a living being, except in the person of her father. She delighted to converse with me upon subjects of literature and taste, and she eagerly invited my assistance in the education of her children. The son, though young, had been so happily improved and instructed by his mother, that I found in him nearly all the most essential qualities we require in a friend. Engagement and inclination equally led me to pass a considerable part of every day in this agreeable society. Laura treated me as if I had been one of the family; and I sometimes flattered myself that I might one day become such in reality. What an enviable resting-place for me, who had known nothing but calamity, and had scarcely dared to look for sympathy and kindness in the countenance of a human being!

The sentiments of friendship which early disclosed themselves between me and the members of this amiable family daily became stronger. At every interview, the confidence reposed in me by the mother increased. While our familiarity gained in duration, it equally gained in that subtlety of communication by which it seemed to shoot forth its roots in every direction. There are a thousand little evanescent touches in the development of a growing friendship, that are neither thought of, nor would be understood, between common acquaintances. I honoured and esteemed the respectable Laura like a mother; for, though the difference of our ages was by no means sufficient to authorise the sentiment, it was irresistibly suggested to me by the fact of her always being presented to my observation under the maternal character. Her son was a lad of great understanding, generosity, and feeling, and of no contemptible acquirements; while his tender years, and the uncommon excellence of his mother, subtracted something from the independence of his judgment, and impressed him with a sort of religious deference for her will. In the eldest daughter I beheld the image of Laura; for that I felt attached to her for the present; and I sometimes conceived it probable that hereafter I might learn to love her for her own sake. – Alas, it was thus that I amused myself with the visions of distant years, while I stood in reality on the brink of the precipice!

It will perhaps be thought strange that I never once communicated the particulars of my story to this amiable matron, or to my young friend, for such I may also venture to call him, her son. But in truth I abhorred the memory of this story; I placed all my hopes of happiness in the prospect of its being consigned to oblivion. I fondly flattered myself that such would be the event: in the midst of my unlooked-for happiness, I scarcely recollected, or, recollecting, was disposed to yield but a small degree of credit to, the menaces of Mr. Falkland.

One day, that I was sitting alone with the accomplished Laura, she repeated his all-dreadful name. I started with astonishment, amazed that a woman like this, who knew nobody, who lived as it were alone in a corner of the universe, who had never in a single instance entered into any fashionable circle, this admirable and fascinating hermit, should, by some unaccountable accident, have become acquainted with this fatal and tremendous name. Astonishment however was not my only sensation. I became pale with terror; I rose from my seat; I attempted to sit down again; I reeled out of the room, and hastened to bury myself in solitude. The unexpectedness of the incident took from me all precaution, and overwhelmed my faculties. The penetrating Laura observed my behaviour; but nothing further occurred to excite her attention to it at that time; and, concluding from my manner that enquiry would be painful to me, she humanely suppressed her curiosity.

I afterwards found that Mr. Falkland had been known to the father of Laura; that he had been acquainted with the story of Count Malvesi, and with a number of other transactions redounding in the highest degree to the credit of the gallant Englishman. The Neapolitan had left letters in which these transactions were recorded, and which spoke of Mr. Falkland in the highest terms of panegyric. Laura had been used to regard every little relic of her father with a sort of religious veneration; and, by this accident, the name of Mr. Falkland was connected in her mind with the sentiments of unbounded esteem.

The scene by which I was surrounded was perhaps more grateful to me, than it would have been to most other persons with my degree of intellectual cultivation. Sore with persecution and distress, and bleeding at almost every vein, there was nothing I so much coveted as rest and tranquillity. It seemed as if my faculties were, at least for the time, exhausted by the late preternatural intensity of their exertions, and that they stood indispensably in need of a period of comparative suspension.

This was however but a temporary feeling. My mind had always been active, and I was probably indebted to the sufferings I had endured, and the exquisite and increased susceptibility they produced, for new energies. I soon felt the desire of some additional and vigorous pursuit. In this state of mind, I met by accident, in a neglected corner of the house of one of my neighbours, with a general dictionary of four of the northern languages. This incident gave a direction to my thoughts. In my youth I had not been inattentive to languages. I determined to attempt, at least for my own use, an etymological analysis of the English language. I easily perceived, that this pursuit had one advantage to a person in my situation, and that a small number of books, consulted with this view, would afford employment for a considerable time. I procured other dictionaries. In my incidental reading, I noted the manner in which words were used, and applied these remarks to the illustration of my general enquiry. I was unintermitted in my assiduity, and my collections promised to accumulate. Thus I was provided with sources both of industry and recreation, the more completely to divert my thoughts from the recollection of my past misfortunes.

In this state, so grateful to my feelings, week after week glided away without interruption and alarm. The situation in which I was now placed had some resemblance to that in which I had spent my earlier years, with the advantage of a more attractive society, and a riper judgment. I began to look back upon the intervening period as upon a distempered and tormenting dream; or rather perhaps my feelings were like those of a man recovered from an interval of raging delirium, from ideas of horror, confusion, flight, persecution, agony, and despair! When I recollected what I had undergone, it was not without satisfaction, as the recollection of a thing that was past; every day augmented my hope that it was never to return.

Surely the dark and terrific menaces of Mr. Falkland were rather the perturbed suggestions of his angry mind, than the final result of a deliberate and digested system! How happy should I feel, beyond the ordinary lot of man, if, after the terrors I had undergone, I should now find myself unexpectedly restored to the immunities of a human being!

While I was thus soothing my mind with fond imaginations, it happened that a few bricklayers and their labourers came over from a distance of five or six miles, to work upon some additions to one of the better sort of houses in the town, which had changed its tenant. No incident could be more trivial than this, had it not been for a strange coincidence of time between this circumstance, and a change which introduced itself into my situation. This first manifested itself in a sort of shyness with which I was treated, first by one person, and then another, of my new-formed acquaintance. They were backward to enter into conversation with me, and answered my enquiries with an awkward and embarrassed air. When they met me in the street or the field, their countenances contracted a cloud, and they endeavoured to shun me. My scholars quitted me one after another; and I had no longer any employment in my mechanical profession. It is impossible to describe the sensations, which the gradual but uninterrupted progress of this revolution produced in my mind. It seemed as if I had some contagious disease, from which every man shrunk with alarm, and left me to perish unassisted and alone. I asked one man and another to explain to me the meaning of these appearances; but every one avoided the task, and answered in an evasive and ambiguous manner. I sometimes supposed that it was all a delusion of the imagination; till the repetition of the sensation brought the reality too painfully home to my apprehension. There are few things that give a greater shock to the mind, than a phenomenon in the conduct of our fellow men, of great importance to our concerns, and for which we are unable to assign any plausible reason. At times I was half inclined to believe that the change was not in other men, but that some alienation of my own understanding generated the horrid vision. I endeavoured to awaken from my dream, and return to my former state of enjoyment and happiness; but in vain. To the same consideration it may be ascribed, that, unacquainted with the source of the evil, observing its perpetual increase, and finding it, so far as I could perceive, entirely arbitrary in its nature, I was unable to ascertain its limits, or the degree in which it would finally overwhelm me.

In the midst however of the wonderful and seemingly inexplicable nature of this scene, there was one idea that instantly obtruded itself, and that I could never after banish from my mind. It is Falkland! In vain I struggled against the seeming improbability of the supposition. In vain I said, "Mr. Falkland, wise as he is, and pregnant in resources, acts by human, not by supernatural means. He may overtake me by surprise, and in a manner of which I had no previous expectation; but he cannot produce a great and notorious effect without some visible agency, however difficult it may be to trace that agency to its absolute author. He cannot, like those invisible personages who are supposed from time to time to interfere in human affairs, ride in the whirlwind, shroud himself in clouds and impenetrable darkness, and scatter destruction upon the earth from his secret habitation." Thus it was that I bribed my imagination, and endeavoured to persuade myself that my present unhappiness originated in a different source from my former.

All evils appeared trivial to me, in comparison with the recollection and perpetuation of my parent misfortune. I felt like a man distracted, by the incoherence of my ideas to my present situation, excluding from it the machinations of Mr. Falkland, on the one hand; and on the other, by the horror I conceived at the bare possibility of again encountering his animosity, after a suspension of many weeks, a suspension as I had hoped for ever. An interval like this was an age to a person in the calamitous situation I had so long experienced. But, in spite of my efforts, I could not banish from my mind the dreadful idea. My original conceptions of the genius and perseverance of Mr. Falkland had been such, that I could with difficulty think any thing impossible to him. I knew not how to set up my own opinions of material causes and the powers of the human mind, as the limits of existence. Mr. Falkland had always been to my imagination an object of wonder, and that which excites our wonder we scarcely suppose ourselves competent to analyse.

It may well be conceived, that one of the first persons to whom I thought of applying for an explanation of this dreadful mystery was the accomplished Laura. My disappointment here cut me to the heart. I was not prepared for it. I recollected the ingenuousness of her nature, the frankness of her manners, the partiality with which she had honoured me. If I were mortified with the coldness, the ruggedness, and the cruel mistake of principles with which the village inhabitants repelled my enquiries, the mortification I suffered, only drove me more impetuously to seek the cure of my griefs from this object of my admiration. "In Laura," said I, "I am secure from these vulgar prejudices. I confide in her justice. I am sure she will not cast me off unheard, nor without strictly examining a question on all sides, in which every thing that is valuable to a person she once esteemed, may be involved."

Thus encouraging myself, I turned my steps to the place of her residence. As I passed along I called up all my recollection, I summoned my faculties. "I may be made miserable," said I, "but it shall not be for want of any exertion of mine, that promises to lead to happiness. I will be clear, collected, simple in narrative, ingenuous in communication. I will leave nothing unsaid that the case may require. I will not volunteer any thing that relates to my former transactions with Mr. Falkland; but, if I find that my present calamity is connected with those transactions, I will not fear but that by an honest explanation I shall remove it."

I knocked at the door. A servant appeared, and told me that her mistress hoped I would excuse her; she must really beg to dispense with my visit.

I was thunderstruck. I was rooted to the spot. I had been carefully preparing my mind for every thing that I supposed likely to happen, but this event had not entered into my calculations. I roused myself in a partial degree, and walked away without uttering a word.

I had not gone far before I perceived one of the workmen following me, who put into my hands a billet. The contents were these:

MR. WILLIAMS,

Let me see you no more. I have a right at least to expect your compliance with this requisition; and, upon that condition, I pardon the enormous impropriety and guilt with which you have conducted yourself to me and my family.

LAURA DENISON

The sensations with which I read these few lines are indescribable. I found in them a dreadful confirmation of the calamity that on all sides invaded me. But what I felt most was the unmoved coldness with which they appeared to be written. This coldness from Laura, my comforter, my friend, my mother! To dismiss, to cast me off for ever, without one thought of compunction!

I determined however, in spite of her requisition, and in spite of her coldness, to have an explanation with her. I did not despair of conquering the antipathy she harboured. I did not fear that I should rouse her from the vulgar and unworthy conception, of condemning a man, in points the most material to his happiness, without stating the accusations that are urged against him, and without hearing him in reply.

Though I had no doubt, by means of resolution, of gaining access to her in her house, yet I preferred taking her unprepared, and not warned against me by any previous contention. Accordingly, the next morning, at the time she usually devoted to half an hour's air and exercise, I hastened to her garden, leaped the paling, and concealed myself in an arbour. Presently I saw, from my retreat, the younger part of the family strolling through the garden, and from thence into the fields; but it was not my business to be seen by them. I looked after them however with earnestness, unobserved; and I could not help asking myself, with a deep and heartfelt sigh, whether it were possible that I saw them now for the last time?

They had not advanced far into the fields, before their mother made her appearance. I observed in her her usual serenity and sweetness of countenance. I could feel my heart knocking against my ribs. My whole frame was in a tumult. I stole out of the arbour; and, as I advanced nearer, my pace became quickened.

"For God's sake, madam," exclaimed I, "give me a hearing! Do not avoid me!"

She stood still. "No, sir," she replied, "I shall not avoid you. I wished you to dispense with this meeting; but since I cannot obtain that – I am conscious of no wrong; and therefore, though the meeting gives me pain, it inspires me with no fear."

"Oh, madam," answered I, "my Friend! the object of all my reverence! whom I once ventured to call my mother! can you wish not to hear me? Can you have no anxiety for my justification, whatever may be the unfavourable impression you may have received against me?"

"Not an atom. I have neither wish nor inclination to hear you. That tale which, in its plain and unadorned state, is destructive of the character of him to whom it relates, no colouring can make an honest one."

"Good God! Can you think of condemning a man when you have heard only one side of his story?"

"Indeed I can," replied she with dignity. "The maxim of hearing both sides may be very well in some cases; but it would be ridiculous to suppose that there are not cases, that, at the first mention, are too clear to admit the shadow of a doubt. By a well-concerted defence you may give me new reasons to admire your abilities; but I am acquainted with them already. I can admire your abilities, without tolerating your character."

"Madam! Amiable, exemplary Laura! whom, in the midst of all your harshness and inflexibility, I honour! I conjure you, by every thing that is sacred, to tell me what it is that has filled you with this sudden aversion to me."

"No, sir; that you shall never obtain from me. I have nothing to say to you. I stand still and hear you; because virtue disdains to appear abashed and confounded in the presence of vice.

Your conduct even at this moment, in my opinion, condemns you. True virtue refuses the drudgery of explanation and apology. True virtue shines by its own light, and needs no art to set it off. You have the first principles of morality as yet to learn."

"And can you imagine, that the most upright conduct is always superior to the danger of ambiguity?"

"Exactly so. Virtue, sir, consists in actions, and not in words. The good man and the bad are characters precisely opposite, not characters distinguished from each other by imperceptible shades. The Providence that rules us all, has not permitted us to be left without a clue in the most important of all questions. Eloquence may seek to confound it; but it shall be my care to avoid its deceptive influence. I do not wish to have my understanding perverted, and all the differences of things concealed from my apprehension."

"Madam, madam! it would be impossible for you to hold this language, if you had not always lived in this obscure retreat, if you had ever been conversant with the passions and institutions of men."

"It may be so. And, if that be the case, I have great reason to be thankful to my God, who has thus enabled me to preserve the innocence of my heart, and the integrity of my understanding."

"Can you believe then that ignorance is the only, or the safest, preservative of integrity?"

"Sir, I told you at first, and I repeat to you again, that all your declamation is in vain. I wish you would have saved me and yourself that pain which is the only thing that can possibly result from it. But let us suppose that virtue could ever be the equivocal thing you would have me believe. Is it possible, if you had been honest, that you would not have acquainted me with your story? Is it possible, that you would have left me to have been informed of it by a mere accident, and with all the shocking aggravations you well knew that accident would give it? Is it possible you should have violated the most sacred of all trusts, and have led me unknowingly to admit to the intercourse of my children a character, which if, as you pretend, it is substantially honest, you cannot deny to be blasted and branded in the face of the whole world? Go, sir; I despise you. You are a monster and not a man. I cannot tell whether my personal situation misleads me; but, to my thinking, this last action of yours is worse than all the rest. Nature has constituted me the protector of my children. I shall always remember and resent the indelible injury you have done them. You have wounded me to the very heart, and have taught me to what a pitch the villainy of man can extend."

"Madam, I can be silent no longer. I see that you have by some means come to a hearing of the story of Mr. Falkland."

"I have. I am astonished you have the effrontery to pronounce his name. That name has been a denomination, as far back as my memory can reach, for the most exalted of mortals, the wisest and most generous of men."

"Madam, I owe it to myself to set you right on this subject. Mr. Falkland. ——"

"Mr. Williams, I see my children returning from the fields, and coming this way. The basest action you ever did was the obtruding yourself upon them as an instructor. I insist that you see them no more. I command you to be silent. I command you to withdraw. If you persist in your absurd resolution of expostulating with me, you must take some other time."

I could continue no longer. I was in a manner heart-broken through the whole of this dialogue. I could not think of protracting the pain of this admirable woman, upon whom, though I was innocent of the crimes she imputed to me, I had inflicted so much pain already. I yielded to the imperiousness of her commands, and withdrew.

I hastened, without knowing why, from the presence of Laura to my own habitation. Upon entering the house, an apartment of which I occupied, I found it totally deserted of its usual inhabitants. The woman and her children were gone to enjoy the freshness of the breeze. The husband was engaged in his usual out-door occupations. The doors of persons of the lower order in this part of the country are secured, in the daytime, only with a latch. I entered, and went into the kitchen of the family. Here, as I looked round, my eyes accidentally glanced upon a paper lying in one corner, which, by some association I was unable to explain, roused in me a strong sensation of suspicion and curiosity. I eagerly went towards it, caught it up, and found it to be the very paper of the WONDERFUL AND SURPRISING HISTORY OF CALEB WILLIAMS, the discovery of which, towards the close of my residence in London, had produced in me such inexpressible anguish.

This encounter at once cleared up all the mystery that hung upon my late transactions. Abhorred and intolerable certainty succeeded to the doubts which had haunted my mind. It struck me with the rapidity of lightning. I felt a sudden torpor and sickness that pervaded every fibre of my frame.

Was there no hope that remained for me? Was acquittal useless? Was there no period, past or in prospect, that could give relief to my sufferings? Was the odious and atrocious falsehood that had been invented against me, to follow me wherever I went, to strip me of character, to deprive me of the sympathy and good-will of mankind, to wrest from me the very bread by which life must be sustained?

For the space perhaps of half an hour the agony I felt from this termination to my tranquillity, and the expectation it excited of the enmity which would follow me through every retreat, was such as to bereave me of all consistent thinking, much more of the power of coming to any resolution. As soon as this giddiness and horror of the mind subsided, and the deadly calm that invaded my faculties was no more, one stiff and master gale gained the ascendancy, and drove me to an instant desertion of this late cherished retreat. I had no patience to enter into further remonstrance and explanation with the inhabitants of my present residence. I believed that it was in vain to hope to recover the favourable prepossession and tranquillity I had lately enjoyed. In encountering the prejudices that were thus armed against me, I should have to deal with a variety of dispositions, and, though I might succeed with some, I could not expect to succeed with all. I had seen too much of the reign of triumphant falsehood, to have that sanguine confidence in the effects of my innocence, which would have suggested itself to the mind of any other person of my propensities and my age. The recent instance which had occurred in my conversation with Laura might well contribute to discourage me. I could not endure the thought of opposing the venom that was thus scattered against me, in detail and through its minuter particles. If ever it should be necessary to encounter it, if I were pursued like a wild beast, till I could no longer avoid turning upon my hunters, I would then turn upon the true author of this unprincipled attack; I would encounter the calumny in its strong hold; I would rouse myself to an exertion hitherto unessayed; and, by the firmness, intrepidity, and unalterable constancy I should display, would yet compel mankind to believe Mr. Falkland a suborner and a murderer!

CHAPTER XIV

I HASTEN to the conclusion of my melancholy story. I began to write soon after the period to which I have now conducted it. This was another resource that my mind, ever eager in inventing means to escape from my misery, suggested. In my haste to withdraw myself from the retreat in Wales, where first the certainty of Mr. Falkland's menaces was confirmed to me, I left behind me the apparatus of my etymological enquiries, and the papers I had written upon the subject. I have never been able to persuade myself to resume this pursuit. It is always discouraging, to begin over again a laborious task, and exert one's self to recover a position we had already occupied. I knew not how soon or how abruptly I might be driven from any new situation; the appendages of the study in which I had engaged were too cumbrous for this state of dependence and uncertainty; they only served to give new sharpness to the enmity of my foe, and new poignancy to my hourly-renewing distress.

But what was of greatest importance, and made the deepest impression upon my mind, was my separation from the family of Laura. Fool that I was, to imagine that there was any room for me in the abodes of friendship and tranquillity! It was now first, that I felt, with the most intolerable acuteness, how completely I was cut off from the whole human species. Other connections I had gained, comparatively without interest; and I saw them dissolved without the consummation of agony. I had never experienced the purest refinements of friendship, but in two instances, that of Collins, and this of the family of Laura. Solitude, separation, banishment! These are words often in the mouths of human beings; but few men except myself have felt the full latitude of their meaning. The pride of philosophy has taught us to treat man as an individual. He is no such thing. He holds necessarily, indispensably, to his species. He is like those twin-births, that have two heads indeed, and four hands; but, if you attempt to detach them from each other, they are inevitably subjected to miserable and lingering destruction.

It was this circumstance, more than all the rest, that gradually gorged my heart with abhorrence of Mr. Falkland. I could not think of his name but with a sickness and a loathing that seemed more than human. It was by his means that I suffered the loss of one consolation after another, of every thing that was happiness, or that had the resemblance of happiness.

The writing of these memoirs served me as a source of avocation for several years. For some time I had a melancholy satisfaction in it. I was better pleased to retrace the particulars of calamities that had formerly afflicted me, than to look forward, as at other times I was too apt to do, to those by which I might hereafter be overtaken. I conceived that my story, faithfully digested, would carry in it an impression of truth that few men would be able to resist; or, at worst, that, by leaving it behind me when I should no longer continue to exist, posterity might be induced to do me justice, and, seeing in my example what sort of evils are entailed upon mankind by society as it is at present constituted, might be inclined to turn their attention upon the fountain from which such bitter waters have been accustomed to flow. But these motives have diminished in their influence. I have contracted a disgust for life and all its appendages. Writing, which was at first a pleasure, is changed into a burthen. I shall compress into a small compass what remains to be told.

I discovered, not long after the period of which I am speaking, the precise cause of the reverse I had experienced in my residence in Wales, and, included in that cause, what it was I had to look for in my future adventures. Mr. Falkland had taken the infernal Gines into his pay, a man critically qualified for the service in which he was now engaged, by the unfeeling brutality of his temper, by his habits of mind at once audacious and artful, and by the peculiar animosity and vengeance he had conceived against me. The employment to which this man was hired, was that of following me from place to place, blasting my reputation, and preventing me from the chance, by continuing long in one residence, of acquiring a character for integrity, that should give new weight to any accusation I might at a future time be induced to prefer. He had come to the seat of my residence with the bricklayers and labourers I have mentioned; and, while he took care to keep out of sight so far as related to

me, was industrious in disseminating that which, in the eye of
the world, seemed to amount to a demonstration of the profligacy and detestableness of my character. It was no doubt from
him that the detested scroll had been procured, which I had
found in my habitation immediately prior to my quitting it. In
all this Mr. Falkland, reasoning upon his principles, was only
employing a necessary precaution. There was something in the
temper of his mind, that impressed him with aversion to the
idea of violently putting an end to my existence; at the same
time that unfortunately he could never deem himself sufficiently secured against my recrimination, so long as I remained alive.
As to the fact of Gines being retained by him for this tremendous purpose, he by no means desired that it should become
generally known; but neither did he look upon the possibility
of its being known with terror. It was already too notorious for
his wishes, that I had advanced the most odious charges against
him. If he regarded me with abhorrence as the adversary of his
fame, those persons who had had occasion to be in any degree
acquainted with our history, did not entertain less abhorrence
against me for my own sake. If they should at any time know
the pains he exerted in causing my evil reputation to follow
me, they would consider it as an act of impartial justice, perhaps
as a generous anxiety to prevent other men from being
imposed upon and injured, as he had been.

What expedient was I to employ for the purpose of counteracting the meditated and barbarous prudence, which was
thus destined, in all changes of scene, to deprive me of the
benefits and consolations of human society? There was one
expedient against which I was absolutely determined – disguise. I had experienced so many mortifications, and such
intolerable restraint, when I formerly had recourse to it; it was
associated in my memory with sensations of such acute anguish
that my mind was thus far entirely convinced: life was not
worth purchasing at so high a price! But, though in this respect
I was wholly resolved, there was another point that did not
appear so material, and in which therefore I was willing to
accommodate myself to circumstances. I was contented, if that
would insure my peace, to submit to the otherwise unmanly

expedient of passing by a different name.

But the change of my name, the abruptness with which I removed from place to place, the remoteness and the obscurity which I proposed to myself in the choice of my abode, were all insufficient to elude the sagacity of Gines, or the unrelenting constancy with which Mr. Falkland incited my tormentor to pursue me. Whithersoever I removed myself, it was not long before I had occasion to perceive this detested adversary in my rear. No words can enable me to do justice to the sensations which this circumstance produced in me. It was like what has been described of the eye of Omniscience, pursuing the guilty sinner, and darting a ray that awakens him to new sensibility, at the very moment that, otherwise, exhausted nature would lull him into a temporary oblivion of the reproaches of his conscience. Sleep fled from my eyes. No walls could hide me from the discernment of this hated foe. Every where his industry was unwearied to create for me new distress. Rest I had none; relief I had none: never could I count upon an instant's security; never could I wrap myself in the shroud of oblivion. The minutes in which I did not actually perceive him, were contaminated and blasted with the certain expectation of his speedy interference. In my first retreat I had passed a few weeks of delusive tranquillity, but never after was I happy enough to attain to so much as that shadowy gratification. I spent some years in this dreadful vicissitude of pain. My sensations at certain periods amounted to insanity.

I pursued in every succeeding instance the conduct I had adopted at first. I determined never to enter into a contest of accusation and defence with the execrable Gines. If I could have submitted to it in other respects, what purpose would it answer? I should have but an imperfect and mutilated story to tell. This story had succeeded with persons already prepossessed in my favour by personal intercourse; but could it succeed with strangers? It had succeeded so long as I was able to hide myself from my pursuers; but could it succeed now, that this appeared impracticable, and that they proceeded by arming against me a whole vicinity at once?

It is inconceivable the mischiefs that this kind of existence included. Why should I insist upon such aggravations as hunger, beggary, and external wretchedness? These were an inevitable consequence. It was by the desertion of mankind that, in each successive instance, I was made acquainted with my fate. Delay in such a moment served but to increase the evil; and when I fled, meagreness and penury were the ordinary attendants of my course. But this was a small consideration. Indignation at one time, and unconquerable perseverance at another, sustained me, where humanity, left to itself, would probably have sunk.

It has already appeared that I was not of a temper to endure calamity, without endeavouring, by every means I could devise, to elude and disarm it. Recollecting, as I was habituated to do, the various projects by which my situation could be meliorated, the question occurred to me, "Why should I be harassed by the pursuits of this Gines? Why, man to man, may I not, by the powers of my mind, attain the ascendancy over him? At present he appears to be the persecutor, and I the persecuted: is not this difference the mere creature of the imagination? May I not employ my ingenuity to vex him with difficulties, and laugh at the endless labour to which he will be condemned?"

Alas, this is a speculation for a mind at ease! It is not the persecution, but the catastrophe which is annexed to it, that makes the difference between the tyrant and the sufferer! In mere corporal exertion the hunter perhaps is upon a level with the miserable animal he pursues! But could it be forgotten by either of us, that at every stage Gines was to gratify his malignant passions, by disseminating charges of the most infamous nature, and exciting against me the abhorrence of every honest bosom, while I was to sustain the still-repeated annihilation of my peace, my character, and my bread? Could I, by any refinement of reason, convert this dreadful series into sport? I had no philosophy that qualified me for so extraordinary an effort. If, under other circumstances, I could even have entertained so strange an imagination, I was restrained in the present instance by the necessity of providing for myself the means of subsistence, and the fetters which, through that necessity, the forms of human society imposed upon my exertions.

In one of those changes of residence, to which my miserable fate repeatedly compelled me, I met, upon a road which I was obliged to traverse, the friend of my youth, my earliest and best beloved friend, the venerable Collins. It was one of those misfortunes which served to accumulate my distress, that this man had quitted the island of Great Britain only a very few weeks before that fatal reverse of fortune which had ever since pursued me with unrelenting eagerness. Mr. Falkland, in addition to the large estate he possessed in England, had a very valuable plantation in the West Indies. This property had been greatly mismanaged by the person who had the direction of it on the spot; and, after various promises and evasions on his part, which, however they might serve to beguile the patience of Mr. Falkland, had been attended with no salutary fruits, it was resolved that Mr. Collins should go over in person, to rectify the abuses which had so long prevailed. There had even been some idea of his residing several years, if not settling finally, upon the plantation. From that hour to the present I had never received the smallest intelligence respecting him.

I had always considered the circumstances of his critical absence as one of my severest misfortunes. Mr. Collins had been one of the first persons, even in the period of my infancy, to conceive hopes of me, as of something above the common standard; and had contributed more than any other to encourage and assist my juvenile studies. He had been the executor of the little property of my father, who had fixed upon him for that purpose in consideration of the mutual affection that existed between us; and I seemed, on every account, to have more claim upon his protection than upon that of any other human being. I had always believed that, had he been present in the crisis of my fortune, he would have felt a conviction of my innocence; and, convinced himself, would, by means of the venerableness and energy of his character, have interposed so effectually, as to have saved me the greater part of my subsequent misfortunes.

There was yet another idea in my mind relative to this subject, which had more weight with me, than even the substantial exertions of friendship I should have expected from him. The greatest aggravation of my present lot was, that I was cut off from the friendship of mankind. I can safely affirm, that poverty and hunger, that endless wanderings, that a blasted character and the curses that clung to my name, were all of them slight misfortunes compared to this. I endeavoured to sustain myself by the sense of my integrity, but the voice of no man upon earth echoed to the voice of my conscience. "I called aloud; but there was none to answer; there was none that regarded."[1] To me the whole world was unhearing as the tempest, and as cold as the torpedo. Sympathy, the magnetic virtue, the hidden essence of our life, was extinct. Nor was this the sum of my misery. This food, so essential to an intelligent existence, seemed perpetually renewing before me in its fairest colours, only the more effectually to elude my grasp, and to mock my hunger. From time to time I was prompted to unfold the affections of my soul, only to be repelled with the greater anguish, and to be baffled in a way the most intolerably mortifying.

No sight therefore could give me a purer delight than that which now presented itself to my eyes. It was some time however, before either of us recognised the person of the other. Ten years had elapsed since our last interview. Mr. Collins looked much older than he had done at that period; in addition to which, he was, in his present appearance, pale, sickly, and thin. These unfavourable effects had been produced by the change of climate, particularly trying to persons in an advanced period of life. Add to which, I supposed him to be at that moment in the West Indies. I was probably as much altered in the period that had elapsed as he had been. I was the first to recollect him. He was on horseback; I on foot. I had suffered him to pass me. In a moment the full idea of who he was rushed upon my mind; I ran; I called with an impetuous voice; I was unable to restrain the vehemence of my emotions.

The ardour of my feelings disguised my usual tone of speaking, which otherwise Mr. Collins would infallibly have recognized. His sight was already dim; he pulled up his horse till I

---

1   Job 30:20, the King James translation of which reads, "I cry to thee, and thou dost not hear me; I stand up, and thou regardest me *not*."

should overtake him; and then said, "Who are you? I do not know you."

"My father!" exclaimed I, embracing one of his knees with fervour and delight, "I am your son; once your little Caleb, whom you a thousand times loaded with your kindness!"

The unexpected repetition of my name gave a kind of shuddering emotion to my friend, which was however checked by his age, and the calm and benevolent philosophy that formed one of his most conspicuous habits.

"I did not expect to see you!" replied he: "I did not wish it!"

"My best, my oldest friend!" answered I, respect blending itself with my impatience, "do not say so! I have not a friend any where in the whole world but you! In you at least let me find sympathy and reciprocal affection! If you knew how anxiously I have thought of you during the whole period of your absence, you would not thus grievously disappoint me in your return!"

"How is it," said Mr. Collins, gravely, "that you have been reduced to this forlorn condition? Was it not the inevitable consequence of your own actions?"

"The actions of others, not mine! Does not your heart tell you that I am innocent?"

"No. My observation of your early character taught me that you would be extraordinary; but, unhappily, all extraordinary men are not good men: that seems to be a lottery, dependent on circumstances apparently the most trivial."

"Will you hear my justification? I am as sure as I am of my existence, that I can convince you of my purity."

"Certainly, if you require it, I will hear you. But that must not be just now. I could have been glad to decline it wholly. At my age I am not fit for the storm; and I am not so sanguine as you in my expectation of the result. Of what would you convince me? That Mr. Falkland is a suborner and murderer?"

I made no answer. My silence was an affirmative to the question.

"And what benefit will result from this conviction? I have known you a promising boy, whose character might turn to one side or the other as events should decide. I have known

Mr. Falkland in his maturer years, and have always admired him, as the living model of liberality and goodness. If you could change all my ideas, and show me that there was no criterion by which vice might be prevented from being mistaken for virtue, what benefit would arise from that? I must part with all my interior consolation, and all my external connections. And for what? What is it you propose? The death of Mr. Falkland by the hands of the hangman."

"No; I will not hurt a hair of his head, unless compelled to it by a principle of defence. But surely you owe me justice?"

"What justice? The justice of proclaiming your innocence? You know what consequences are annexed to that. But I do not believe I shall find you innocent. If you even succeed in perplexing my understanding, you will not succeed in enlightening it. Such is the state of mankind, that innocence, when involved in circumstances of suspicion, can scarcely ever make out a demonstration of its purity; and guilt can often make us feel an insurmountable reluctance to the pronouncing it guilt. Meanwhile, for the purchase of this uncertainty, I must sacrifice all the remaining comforts of my life. I believe Mr. Falkland to be virtuous; but I know him to be prejudiced. He would never forgive me even this accidental parley, if by any means he should come to be acquainted with it."

"Oh, argue not the consequences that are possible to result!" answered I, impatiently. "I have a right to your kindness; I have a right to your assistance!"

"You have them. You have them to a certain degree; and it is not likely that, by any process of examination, you can have them entire. You know my habits of thinking. I regard you as vicious; but I do not consider the vicious as proper objects of indignation and scorn. I consider you as a machine; you are not constituted, I am afraid, to be greatly useful to your fellow men: but you did not make yourself; you are just what circumstances irresistibly compelled you to be. I am sorry for your ill properties; but I entertain no enmity against you, nothing but benevolence. Considering you in the light in which I at present consider you, I am ready to contribute every thing in my power to your real advantage, and would gladly assist you, if I knew how, in detecting and extirpating the errors that have misled you. You have disappointed me, but I have no reproaches to utter: it is more necessary for me to feel compassion for you, than that I should accumulate your misfortune by my censures."

What could I say to such a man as this? Amiable, incomparable man! Never was my mind more painfully divided than at that moment. The more he excited my admiration, the more imperiously did my heart command me, whatever were the price it should cost, to extort his friendship. I was persuaded that severe duty required of him, that he should reject all personal considerations, that he should proceed resolutely to the investigation of the truth, and that, if he found the result terminating in my favour, he should resign all his advantages, and, deserted as I was by the world, make a common cause, and endeavour to compensate the general injustice. But was it for me to force this conduct upon him, if, now in his declining years, his own fortitude shrank from it? Alas, neither he nor I foresaw the dreadful catastrophe that was so closely impending! Otherwise, I am well assured that no tenderness for his remaining tranquillity would have withheld him from a compliance with my wishes! On the other hand, could I pretend to know what evils might result to him from his declaring himself my advocate? Might not his integrity be browbeaten and defeated, as mine had been? Did the imbecility of his grey hairs afford no advantage to my terrible adversary in the contest? Might not Mr. Falkland reduce him to a condition as wretched and low as mine? After all, was it not vice in me to desire to involve another man in my sufferings? If I regarded them as intolerable, this was still an additional reason why I should bear them alone.

Influenced by these considerations, I assented to his views. I assented to be thought hardly of by the man in the world whose esteem I most ardently desired, rather than involve him in possible calamity. I assented to the resigning what appeared to me at that moment as the last practicable comfort of my life; a comfort, upon the thought of which, while I surrendered it, my mind dwelt with undescribable longings. Mr. Collins was deeply affected with the apparent ingenuousness with which I expressed my feelings. The secret struggle of his mind was, "Can this be hypocrisy? The individual with whom I am conferring, if virtuous, is one of the most disinterestedly virtuous persons in the world." We tore ourselves from each other. Mr. Collins promised, as far as he was able, to have an eye upon my vicissitudes, and to assist me, in every respect that was consistent with a just recollection of consequences. Thus I parted as it were with the last expiring hope of my mind; and voluntarily consented, thus maimed and forlorn, to encounter all the evils that were yet in store for me.

This is the latest event which at present I think it necessary to record. I shall doubtless hereafter have further occasion to take up the pen. Great and unprecedented as my sufferings have been, I feel intimately persuaded that there are worse sufferings that await me. What mysterious cause is it that enables me to write this, and not to perish under the horrible apprehension!

CHAPTER XV

IT is as I foreboded. The presage with which I was visited was prophetic. I am now to record a new and terrible revolution of my fortune and my mind.

Having made experiment of various situations with one uniform result, I at length determined to remove myself, if possible, from the reach of my persecutor, by going into voluntary banishment from my native soil. This was my last resource for tranquillity, for honest fame, for those privileges to which human life is indebted for the whole of its value. "In some distant climate," said I, "surely I may find that security which is necessary to persevering pursuit; surely I may lift my head erect, associate with men upon the footing of a man, acquire connections, and preserve them!" It is inconceivable with what ardent reachings of the soul I aspired to this termination.

This last consolation was denied me by the inexorable Falkland.

At the time the project was formed I was at no great distance from the east coast of the island, and I resolved to take ship at Harwich, and pass immediately into Holland. I accordingly repaired to that place, and went, almost as soon as I arrived, to the port. But there was no vessel perfectly ready to sail. I left the port, and withdrew to an inn, where, after some time, I retired to a chamber. I was scarcely there before the door of the room was opened, and the man whose countenance was the most hateful to my eyes, Gines, entered the apartment. He shut the door as soon as he entered.

"Youngster," said he, "I have a little private intelligence to communicate to you. I come as a friend, and that I may save you a labour-in-vain trouble. If you consider what I have to say in that light, it will be the better for you. It is my business now, do you see, for want of a better, to see that you do not break out of bounds. Not that I much matter having one man for my employer, or dancing attendance after another's heels; but I have special kindness for you, for some good turns that you wot of, and therefore I do not stand upon ceremonies! You have led me a very pretty round already; and, out of the love I bear you, you shall lead me as much further, if you will. But beware the salt seas! They are out of my orders. You are a prisoner at present, and I believe all your life will remain so. Thanks to the milk-and-water softness of your former master! If I had the ordering of these things, it should go with you in another fashion. As long as you think proper, you are a prisoner within the rules; and the rules with which the soft-hearted squire indulges you, are all England, Scotland, and Wales. But you are not to go out of these climates. The squire is determined you shall never pass the reach of his disposal. He has therefore given orders that, whenever you attempt so to do, you shall be converted from a prisoner at large to a prisoner in good earnest. A friend of mine followed you just now to the harbour; I was within call; and, if there had been any appearance of your setting your foot from land, we should have been with you in a trice, and laid you fast by the heels. I would advise you, for the future, to keep at a proper distance from the sea, for fear of the worst. You see I tell you all this for your good. For my part, I should be better satisfied if you were in limbo, with a rope about your neck, and a comfortable bird's eye prospect to the gallows: but I do as I am directed; and so good night to you!"

The intelligence thus conveyed to me occasioned an instantaneous revolution in both my intellectual and animal system. I disdained to answer, or take the smallest notice of the fiend by whom it was delivered. It is now three days since I received it, and from that moment to the present my blood has been in a perpetual ferment. My thoughts wander from one idea of horror to another, with incredible rapidity. I have had no sleep. I have scarcely remained in one posture for a minute together. It has been with the utmost difficulty that I have been able to command myself far enough to add a few pages to my story. But, uncertain as I am of the events of each succeeding hour, I determined to force myself to the performance of this task. All is not right within me. How it will terminate, God knows. I sometimes fear that I shall be wholly deserted of my reason.

What – dark, mysterious, unfeeling, unrelenting tyrant! – is it come to this? When Nero and Caligula swayed the Roman sceptre, it was a fearful thing to offend these bloody rulers. The empire had already spread itself from climate to climate, and from sea to sea. If their unhappy victim fled to the rising of the sun, where the luminary of day seems to us first to ascend from the waves of the ocean, the power of the tyrant was still behind him. If he withdrew to the west, to Hesperian darkness, and the shores of barbarian Thule, still he was not safe from his gore-drenched foe.[1] – Falkland! art thou the offspring, in whom the lineaments of these tyrants are faithfully preserved? Was the world, with all its climates, made in vain for thy helpless unoffending victim?

Tremble!

Tyrants have trembled, surrounded with whole armies of their Janissaries![2] What should make thee inaccessible to my fury? No, I will use no daggers! I will unfold a tale! – I will show thee to the world for what thou art; and all the men that live, shall confess my truth! – Didst thou imagine that I was altogether passive, a mere worm, organised to feel sensations of pain, but no emotion of resentment? Didst thou imagine that there was no danger in inflicting on me pains however great, miseries however dreadful? Didst thou believe me impotent, imbecile, and idiot-like, with no understanding to contrive thy ruin, and no energy to perpetrate it?

I will tell a tale – ! The justice of the country shall hear me! The elements of nature in universal uproar shall not interrupt me! I will speak with a voice more fearful than thunder! – Why should I be supposed to speak from any dishonourable motive? I am under no prosecution now! I shall not now appear to be endeavouring to remove a criminal indictment from myself, by throwing it back on its author! – Shall I regret the ruin that will overwhelm thee? Too long have I been tender-hearted and forbearing! What benefit has ever resulted

---

1 The Hesperides were the goddesses in Greek mythology who guarded golden apples given to Hera by the Earth, Gaia, at her marriage to Zeus; they were said to live by the river Oceanus, in the far west. Thule was the name of an island regarded by the ancient Greeks as the most northerly point on the earth.
2 Turkish infantry responsible for guarding the Sultan.

from my mistaken clemency? There is no evil thou hast scrupled to accumulate upon me! Neither will I be more scrupulous! Thou hast shown no mercy; and thou shalt receive none! – I must be calm! bold as a lion, yet collected!

This is a moment pregnant with fate. I know – I think I know – that I will be triumphant, and crush my seemingly omnipotent foe. But, should it be otherwise, at least he shall not be every way successful. His fame shall not be immortal as he thinks. These papers shall preserve the truth; they shall one day be published, and then the world shall do justice on us both. Recollecting that, I shall not die wholly without consolation. It is not to be endured that falsehood and tyranny should reign for ever.

How impotent are the precautions of man against the eternally existing laws of the intellectual world! This Falkland has invented against me every species of foul accusation. He has hunted me from city to city. He has drawn his lines of circumvallation round me that I may not escape. He has kept his scenters of human prey for ever at my heels. He may hunt me out of the world. – In vain! With this engine, this little pen, I defeat all his machinations; I stab him in the very point he was most solicitous to defend!

Collins! I now address myself to you. I have consented that you should yield me no assistance in my present terrible situation. I am content to die rather than do any thing injurious to your tranquillity. But remember, you are my father still! I conjure you, by all the love you ever bore me, by the benefits you have conferred on me, by the forbearance and kindness towards you that now penetrates my soul, by my innocence – for, if these be the last words I shall ever write, I die protesting my innocence! – by all these, or whatever tie more sacred has influence on your soul, I conjure you, listen to my last request! Preserve these papers from destruction, and preserve them from Falkland! It is all I ask! I have taken care to provide a safe mode of conveying them into your possession: and I have a firm confidence, which I will not suffer to depart from me, that they will one day find their way to the public!

The pen lingers in my trembling fingers! Is there any thing I have left unsaid? – The contents of the fatal trunk, from which all my misfortunes originated, I have never been able to ascertain. I once thought it contained some murderous instrument or relic connected with the fate of the unhappy Tyrrel. I am now persuaded that the secret it encloses, is a faithful narrative of that and its concomitant transactions, written by Mr. Falkland, and reserved in case of the worst, that, if by any unforeseen event his guilt should come to be fully disclosed, it might contribute to redeem the wreck of his reputation. But the truth or the falsehood of this conjecture is of little moment. If Falkland shall never be detected to the satisfaction of the world, such a narrative will probably never see the light. In that case this story of mine may amply, severely perhaps, supply its place.

I know not what it is that renders me thus solemn. I have a secret foreboding, as if I should never again be master of myself. If I succeed in what I now meditate respecting Falkland, my precaution in the disposal of these papers will have been unnecessary; I shall no longer be reduced to artifice and evasion. If I fail, the precaution will appear to have been wisely chosen.

Postscript

All is over. I have carried into execution my meditated attempt. My situation is totally changed; I now sit down to give an account of it. For several weeks after the completion of this dreadful business, my mind was in too tumultuous a state to permit me to write. I think I shall now be able to arrange my thoughts sufficiently for that purpose. Great God! how wondrous, how terrible are the events that have intervened since I was last employed in a similar manner! It is no wonder that my thoughts were solemn, and my mind filled with horrible forebodings!

Having formed my resolution, I set out from Harwich, for the metropolitan town of the county in which Mr. Falkland resided. Gines, I well knew, was in my rear. That was of no consequence to me. He might wonder at the direction I pursued, but he could not tell with what purpose I pursued it. My design was a secret, carefully locked up in my own breast. It was not without a sentiment of terror that I entered a town which had been the scene of my long imprisonment. I proceeded to the house of the chief magistrate the instant I arrived, that I might give no time to my adversary to counterwork my proceeding.

I told him who I was, and that I was come from a distant part of the kingdom, for the purpose of rendering him the medium of a charge of murder against my former patron. My name was already familiar to him. He answered, that he could not take cognizance of my deposition; that I was an object of universal execration in that part of the world; and he was determined upon no account to be the vehicle of my depravity.

I warned him to consider well what he was doing. I called upon him for no favour; I only applied to him in the regular exercise of his function. Would he take upon him to say that he had a right, at his pleasure, to suppress a charge of this complicated nature? I had to accuse Mr. Falkland of repeated murders. The perpetrator knew that I was in possession of the truth upon the subject; and, knowing that, I went perpetually in danger of my life from his malice and revenge. I was resolved to go through with the business, if justice were to be obtained from any court in England. Upon what pretence did he refuse my deposition? I was in every respect a competent witness. I was of age to understand the nature of an oath; I was in my perfect senses; I was untarnished by the verdict of any jury, or the sentence of any judge. His private opinion of my character could not alter the law of the land. I demanded to be confronted with Mr. Falkland, and I was well assured I should substantiate the charge to the satisfaction of the whole world. If he did not think proper to apprehend him upon my single testimony, I should be satisfied if he only sent him notice of the charge, and summoned him to appear.

The magistrate, finding me thus resolute, thought proper a little to lower his tone. He no longer absolutely refused to comply with my requisition, but condescended to expostulate with me. He represented to me Mr. Falkland's health, which had for some years been exceedingly indifferent; his having been once already brought to the most solemn examination upon this charge; the diabolical malice in which alone my proceeding must have originated; and the ten-fold ruin it would bring down upon my head. To all these representations my answer was short. "I was determined to go on, and would abide the consequences." A summons was at length granted, and notice sent to Mr. Falkland of the charge preferred against him.

Three days elapsed before any further step could be taken in this business. This interval in no degree contributed to tranquillise my mind. The thought of preferring a capital accusation against, and hastening the death of, such a man as Mr. Falkland, was by no means an opiate to reflection. At one time I commended the action, either as just revenge (for the benevolence of my nature was in a great degree turned to gall), or as necessary self-defence, or as that which, in an impartial and philanthropical estimate, included the smallest evil. At another time I was haunted with doubts. But, in spite of these variations of sentiment, I uniformly determined to persist! I felt as if impelled by a tide of unconquerable impulse. The consequences were such as might well appall the stoutest heart. Either the ignominious execution of a man whom I had once so deeply venerated, and whom now I sometimes suspected not to be without his claims to veneration; or a confirmation, perhaps an increase, of the calamities I had so long endured. Yet these I preferred to a state of uncertainty. I desired to know the worst; to put an end to the hope, however faint, which had been so long my torment; and, above all, to exhaust and finish the catalogue of expedients that were at my disposition. My mind was worked up to a state little short of frenzy. My body was in a burning fever with the agitation of my thoughts. When I laid my hand upon my bosom or my head, it seemed to scorch them with the fervency of its heat. I could not sit still for a moment. I panted with incessant desire that the dreadful crisis I had so eagerly invoked, were come, and were over.

After an interval of three days, I met Mr. Falkland in the presence of the magistrate to whom I had applied upon the subject. I had only two hours' notice to prepare myself; Mr. Falkland seeming as eager as I to have the question brought to a crisis, and laid at rest for ever. I had an opportunity, before the examination, to learn that Mr. Forester was drawn by some business on an excursion on the continent; and that Collins, whose health when I saw him was in a very precarious state, was at this time confined with an alarming illness. His constitution had been wholly broken by his West Indian expedition. The audience I met at the house of the magistrate consisted of several gentlemen and others selected for the purpose; the plan being, in some respects, as in the former instance, to find a medium between the suspicious air of a private examination, and the indelicacy, as it was styled, of an examination exposed to the remark of every casual spectator.

I can conceive of no shock greater than that I received from the sight of Mr. Falkland. His appearance on the last occasion on which we met had been haggard, ghost-like, and wild, energy in his gestures, and frenzy in his aspect. It was now the appearance of a corpse. He was brought in in a chair, unable to stand, fatigued and almost destroyed by the journey he had just taken. His visage was colourless; his limbs destitute of motion, almost of life. His head reclined upon his bosom, except that now and then he lifted it up, and opened his eyes with a languid glance; immediately after which he sunk back into his former apparent insensibility. He seemed not to have three hours to live. He had kept his chamber for several weeks; but the summons of the magistrate had been delivered to him at his bed-side, his orders respecting letters and written papers being so peremptory that no one dared to disobey them. Upon reading the paper he was seized with a very dangerous fit; but, as soon as he recovered, he insisted upon being conveyed, with all practicable expedition, to the place of appointment. Falkland, in the most helpless state, was still Falkland, firm in command, and capable to extort obedience from every one that approached him.

What a sight was this to me! Till the moment that Falkland was presented to my view, my breast was steeled to pity. I thought that I had coolly entered into the reason of the case (passion, in a state of solemn and omnipotent vehemence, always appears to be coolness to him in whom it domineers), and that I had determined impartially and justly. I believed that, if Mr. Falkland were permitted to persist in his schemes, we must both of us be completely wretched. I believed that it was in my power, by the resolution I had formed, to throw my share of this wretchedness from me, and that his could scarcely be increased. It appeared therefore to my mind, to be a mere piece of equity and justice, such as an impartial spectator would desire, that one person should be miserable in preference to two; that one person rather than two should be incapacitated from acting his part, and contributing his share to the general welfare. I thought that in this business I had risen superior to personal considerations, and judged with a total neglect of the suggestions of self-regard. It is true, Mr. Falkland was mortal; but, notwithstanding his apparent decay, he might live long. Ought I to submit to waste the best years of my life in my present wretched situation? He had declared that his reputation should be for ever inviolate; this was his ruling passion, the thought that worked his soul to madness. He would probably therefore leave a legacy of persecution to be received by me from the hands of Gines, or some other villain equally atrocious, when he should himself be no more. Now or never was the time for me to redeem my future life from endless woe.

But all these fine-spun reasonings vanished before the object that was now presented to me. "Shall I trample upon a man thus dreadfully reduced? Shall I point my animosity against one, whom the system of nature has brought down to the grave? Shall I poison, with sounds the most intolerable to his ears, the last moments of a man like Falkland? It is impossible. There must have been some dreadful mistake in the train of argument that persuaded me to be the author of this hateful scene. There must have been a better and more magnanimous remedy to the evils under which I groaned."

It was too late: the mistake I had committed was now gone past all power of recall. Here was Falkland, solemnly brought before a magistrate to answer to a charge of murder. Here I stood, having already declared myself the author of the charge, gravely and sacredly pledged to support it. This was my situation; and, thus situated, I was called upon immediately to act. My whole frame shook. I would eagerly have consented that that moment should have been the last of my existence. I however believed, that the conduct now most indispensably incumbent on me was to lay the emotions of my soul naked before my hearers. I looked first at Mr. Falkland, and then at the magistrate and attendants, and then at Mr. Falkland again. My voice was suffocated with agony. I began: –

"Why cannot I recall the last four days of my life? How was it possible for me to be so eager, so obstinate, in a purpose so diabolical? Oh, that I had listened to the expostulations of the magistrate that hears me, or submitted to the well-meant despotism of his authority! Hitherto I have been only miserable; henceforth I shall account myself base! Hitherto, though hardly treated by mankind, I stood acquitted at the bar of my own conscience. I had not filled up the measure of my wretchedness!

"Would to God it were possible for me to retire from this scene without uttering another word! I would brave the consequences – I would submit to any imputation of cowardice, falsehood, and profligacy, rather than add to the weight of misfortune with which Mr. Falkland is overwhelmed. But the situation, and the demands of Mr. Falkland himself, forbid me. He, in compassion for whose fallen state I would willingly forget every interest of my own, would compel me to accuse, that he might enter upon his justification. I will confess every sentiment of my heart.

"No penitence, no anguish, can expiate the folly and the cruelty of this last act I have perpetrated. But Mr. Falkland well knows – I affirm it in his presence – how unwillingly I have proceeded to this extremity. I have reverenced him; he was worthy of reverence: I have loved him; he was endowed with qualities that partook of divine.

"From the first moment I saw him, I conceived the most ardent admiration. He condescended to encourage me; I attached myself to him with the fulness of my affection. He was unhappy; I exerted myself with youthful curiosity to discover the secret of his woe. This was the beginning of misfortune.

"What shall I say? – He was indeed the murderer of Tyrrel; he suffered the Hawkinses to be executed, knowing that they were innocent, and that he alone was guilty. After successive surmises, after various indiscretions on my part, and indications on his, he at length confided to me at full the fatal tale!

"Mr. Falkland! I most solemnly conjure you to recollect yourself! Did I ever prove myself unworthy of your confidence? The secret was a most painful burthen to me; it was the extremest folly that led me unthinkingly to gain possession of it; but I would have died a thousand deaths rather than betray it. It was the jealousy of your own thoughts, and the weight that hung upon your mind, that led you to watch my motions, and to conceive alarm from every particle of my conduct.

"You began in confidence; why did you not continue in confidence? The evil that resulted from my original imprudence would then have been comparatively little. You threatened me: did I then betray you? A word from my lips at that time would have freed me from your threats for ever. I bore them for a considerable period, and at last quitted your service, and threw myself a fugitive upon the world, in silence. Why did you not suffer me to depart? You brought me back by stratagem and violence, and wantonly accused me of an enormous felony! Did I then mention a syllable of the murder, the secret of which was in my possession?

"Where is the man that has suffered more from the injustice of society than I have done? I was accused of a villainy that my heart abhorred. I was sent to jail. I will not enumerate the horrors of my prison, the lightest of which would make the heart of humanity shudder. I looked forward to the gallows! Young, ambitious, fond of life, innocent as the child unborn, I looked forward to the gallows! I believed that one word of resolute accusation against my patron would deliver me; yet I was silent, I armed myself with patience, uncertain whether it were better to accuse or to die. Did this show me a man unworthy to be trusted?

"I determined to break out of prison. With infinite difficulty, and repeated miscarriages, I at length effected my purpose. Instantly, a proclamation with a hundred guineas reward, was issued for apprehending me. I was obliged to take shelter among the refuse of mankind, in the midst of a gang of thieves. I encountered the most imminent peril of my life when I entered this retreat, and when I quitted it. Immediately after, I travelled almost the whole length of the kingdom, in poverty and distress, in hourly danger of being retaken and manacled like a felon. I would have fled my country; I was prevented. I had recourse to various disguises; I was innocent, and yet was compelled to as many arts and subterfuges as could have been entailed on the worst of villains. In London I was as much harassed and as repeatedly alarmed as I had been in my flight through the country. Did all these persecutions persuade me to put an end to my silence? No: I suffered them with patience and submission; I did not make one attempt to retort them upon their author.

"I fell at last into the hands of the miscreants that are nourished with human blood. In this terrible situation I, for the first time, attempted, by turning informer, to throw the weight from myself. Happily for me, the London magistrate listened to my tale with insolent contempt.

"I soon, and long, repented of my rashness, and rejoiced in my miscarriage.

"I acknowledge that, in various ways, Mr. Falkland showed humanity towards me during this period. He would have prevented my going to prison at first; he contributed towards my subsistence, during my detention; he had no share in the pursuit that had been set on foot against me; he at length procured my discharge, when brought forward for trial. But a great part of his forbearance was unknown to me; I supposed him to be my unrelenting pursuer. I could not forget that, whoever heaped calamities on me in the sequel, they all originated in his forged accusation.

"The prosecution against me for felony was now at an end. Why were not my sufferings permitted to terminate then, and I allowed to hide my weary head in some obscure yet tranquil retreat? Had I not sufficiently proved my constancy and fidelity? Would not a compromise in this situation have been most wise and most secure? But the restless and jealous anxiety of Mr. Falkland would not permit him to repose the least atom of confidence. The only compromise that he proposed was that, with my own hand, I should sign myself a villain. I refused this proposal, and have ever since been driven from place to place, deprived of peace, of honest fame, even of bread. For a long time I persisted in the resolution that no emergency should convert me into the assailant. In an evil hour I at last listened to my resentment and impatience, and the hateful mistake into which I fell has produced the present scene.

"I now see that mistake in all its enormity. I am sure that if I had opened my heart to Mr. Falkland, if I had told to him privately the tale that I have now been telling, he could not have resisted my reasonable demand. After all his precautions, he must ultimately have depended upon my forbearance. Could he be sure that, if I were at last worked up to disclose every thing I knew, and to enforce it with all the energy I could exert, I should obtain no credit? If he must in every case be at my mercy, in which mode ought he to have sought his safety, in conciliation, or in inexorable cruelty?

"Mr. Falkland is of a noble nature. Yes; in spite of the catastrophe of Tyrrel, of the miserable end of the Hawkinses, and of all that I have myself suffered, I affirm that he has qualities of the most admirable kind. It is therefore impossible that he could have resisted a frank and fervent expostulation, the frankness and the fervour in which the whole soul is poured out. I despaired, while it was yet time to have made the just experiment; but my despair was criminal, was treason against the sovereignty of truth.

"I have told a plain and unadulterated tale. I came hither to curse, but I remain to bless. I came to accuse, but am compelled to applaud. I proclaim to all the world, that Mr. Falkland is a man worthy of affection and kindness, and that I am myself the basest and most odious of mankind! Never will I forgive myself the iniquity of this day. The memory will always haunt me, and embitter every hour of my existence. In thus acting I have been a murderer – a cool, deliberate, unfeeling murderer. – I have said what my accursed precipitation has obliged me to say. Do with me as you please! I ask no favour. Death would be a kindness, compared to what I feel!"

Such were the accents dictated by my remorse. I poured

them out with uncontrollable impetuosity; for my heart was pierced, and I was compelled to give vent to its anguish. Every one that heard me, was petrified with astonishment. Every one that heard me, was melted into tears. They could not resist the ardour with which I praised the great qualities of Falkland; they manifested their sympathy in the tokens of my penitence.

How shall I describe the feelings of this unfortunate man? Before I began, he seemed sunk and debilitated, incapable of any strenuous impression. When I mentioned the murder, I could perceive in him an involuntary shuddering, though it was counteracted partly by the feebleness of his frame, and partly by the energy of his mind. This was an allegation he expected, and he had endeavoured to prepare himself for it. But there was much of what I said, of which he had had no previous conception. When I expressed the anguish of my mind, he seemed at first startled and alarmed, lest this should be a new expedient to gain credit to my tale. His indignation against me was great for having retained all my resentment towards him, thus, as it might be, to the last hour of his existence. It was increased when he discovered me, as he supposed, using a pretence of liberality and sentiment to give new edge to my hostility. But as I went on he could no longer resist. He saw my sincerity; he was penetrated with my grief and compunction. He rose from his seat, supported by the attendants, and – to my infinite astonishment – threw himself into my arms!

"Williams," said he, "you have conquered! I see too late the greatness and elevation of your mind. I confess that it is to my fault and not yours, that it is to the excess of jealousy that was ever burning in my bosom, that I owe my ruin. I could have resisted any plan of malicious accusation you might have brought against me. But I see that the artless and manly story you have told, has carried conviction to every hearer. All my prospects are concluded. All that I most ardently desired, is for ever frustrated. I have spent a life of the basest cruelty, to cover one act of momentary vice, and to protect myself against the prejudices of my species. I stand now completely detected. My name will be consecrated to infamy, while your heroism, your patience, and your virtues will be for ever admired. You have inflicted on me the most fatal of all mischiefs; but I bless the hand that wounds me. And now, – turning to the magistrate – and now, do with me as you please. I am prepared to suffer all the vengeance of the law. You cannot inflict on me more than I deserve. You cannot hate me, more than I hate myself. I am the most execrable of all villains. I have for many years (I know not how long) dragged on a miserable existence in insupportable pain. I am at last, in recompense for all my labours and my crimes, dismissed from it with the disappointment of my only remaining hope, the destruction of that for the sake of which alone I consented to exist. It was worthy of such a life, that it should continue just long enough to witness this final overthrow. If however you wish to punish me, you must be speedy in your justice; for, as reputation was the blood that warmed my heart, so I feel that death and infamy must seize me together."

I record the praises bestowed on me by Falkland, not because I deserved them, but because they serve to aggravate the baseness of my cruelty. He survived this dreadful scene but three days. I have been his murderer. It was fit that he should praise my patience, who has fallen a victim, life and fame, to my precipitation! It would have been merciful in comparison, if I had planted a dagger in his heart. He would have thanked me for my kindness. But, atrocious, execrable wretch that I have been! I wantonly inflicted on him an anguish a thousand times worse than death. Meanwhile I endure the penalty of my crime. His figure is ever in imagination before me. Waking or sleeping, I still behold him. He seems mildly to expostulate with me for my unfeeling behaviour. I live the devoted victim of conscious reproach. Alas! I am the same Caleb Williams that, so short a time ago, boasted that, however great were the calamities I endured, I was still innocent.

Such has been the result of a project I formed, for delivering myself from the evil that had so long attended me. I thought that, if Falkland were dead, I should return once again to all that makes life worth possessing. I thought that, if the guilt of Falkland were established, fortune and the world would smile upon my efforts. Both these events are accomplished; and it is now only that I am truly miserable.

Why should my reflections perpetually centre upon myself?

– self, an overweening regard to which has been the source of my errors! Falkland, I will think only of thee, and from that thought will draw ever-fresh nourishment for my sorrows! One generous, one disinterested tear I will consecrate to thy ashes! A nobler spirit lived not among the sons of men. Thy intellectual powers were truly sublime, and thy bosom burned with a godlike ambition. But of what use are talents and sentiments in the corrupt wilderness of human society? It is a rank and rotten soil, from which every finer shrub draws poison as it grows. All that, in a happier field and a purer air, would expand into virtue and germinate into usefulness, is thus converted into henbane and deadly nightshade.

Falkland! thou enteredst upon thy career with the purest and most laudable intentions. But thou imbibedst the poison of chivalry with thy earliest youth; and the base and low-minded envy that met thee on thy return to thy native seats, operated with this poison to hurry thee into madness. Soon, too soon, by this fatal coincidence, were the blooming hopes of thy youth blasted for ever. From that moment thou only continuedst to live to the phantom of departed honour. From that moment thy benevolence was, in a great part, turned into rankling jealousy and inexorable precaution. Year after year didst thou spend in this miserable project of imposture; and only at last continuedst to live, long enough to see, by my misjudging and abhorred intervention, thy closing hope disappointed, and thy death accompanied with the foulest disgrace!

I began these memoirs with the idea of vindicating my character. I have now no character that I wish to vindicate: but I will finish them that thy story may be fully understood; and that, if those errors of thy life be known which thou so ardently desiredst to conceal, the world may at least not hear and repeat a half-told and mangled tale.

THE END

Appendix A: The Composition of the Novel

1. The Original Manuscript Ending of the Novel, from *Caleb Williams*. Ed. Pamela Clemit (London: Pickering & Chatto, 1992).

[Godwin's original ending for *Caleb Williams* was very different from the version familiar to readers of the text. Godwin's diary and other manuscript notes show that he finished the novel with its original ending on April 30, 1794. Four days later, however, he began writing a "new catastrophe" (as he called it), which became the ending published in the first and all subsequent editions. Two pages of what was originally a nine-page manuscript are no longer contained in Godwin's *Caleb Williams* manuscript (located in the Victoria and Albert Museum's Forster Collection) and must be presumed lost. The ending below begins at the point where Caleb sees an emaciated Falkland enter the courtroom in the novel's last scene. It follows directly after his observation that "Falkland, in the most helpless state, was still Falkland, firm in command, and capable to extort obedience from every one that approached him." (p. 426 of this edition).]

What a sight was this to me? It harmonised with the madness of my soul, and gave double vehemence to the tide of my fury. Could I allow my tongue to accuse a man thus deplorably circumstanced, and impel the stroke of death which was ready to fall on him? Yes: how knew I that this was not a new expedient of my hundred-handed foe, merely to evade the blow, and prolong my misery? Yes: he had declared that his reputation should be for ever inviolate, and therefore would probably leave a legacy of persecution to be received by me from the hand of Jones[1] or some other villain equally atrocious, whom his ingenious animosity could easily raise up against me. Yes: for I had no longer the liberty of choice. I must either suffer the penalties of

---

1   This was the name of the character Gines in the first edition, changed by Godwin for the second and all subsequent editions.

a false accuser; or go on, resolute and unaltered, in the prosecution I had begun.

As soon as I entered, the magistrate addressed me with a stern voice, and asked me, Whether what I saw there did not make me repent my villainy? Had I the heart under these circumstances to perpetrate the miserable scheme I had contrived? – The peculiarity of the scene before him deprived the magistrate of all power to control this burst of his indignation.

Mr. Falkland motioned to speak. His voice was inward, and with difficulty audible. He begged them upon no account to interpose and endeavour to alter my design. It was necessary to his vindication that I should be invited to say all that I had meditated. He was thankful that his life had been spared long enough to meet this last essay of the malice of his fate.

I collected myself for the awful minute that was now before me; and the sense of its inestimable importance seemed to put to instant flight the tumult of contending passions that had till then possessed me. In a moment I recovered from a state little short of frenzy, and found myself perfectly self-possessed. My mind reviewed with ease the successive parts of the transaction I had to explain. I was varied, perspicuous and forcible. My confidence every instant increased, till I felt all the satisfaction of undoubting certainty.

I described how much I was at present exempt from that state of retort and recrimination, which formerly, while I was myself under prosecution, had rendered my evidence, perhaps reasonably arguing upon general principles, though unjustly in my particular instance, a subject of suspicion. I now came forward voluntarily, when all was over; and was as well entitled to be heard as another man.

I expressed my sorrow for the apparent state of Mr. Falkland's health. I did not thirst for his blood. But I could no longer be easy to confine within my own bosom the knowledge I had upon this terrible subject.

I related to them a variety of particulars with which the reader is already acquainted. I entered with minuteness into some parts of the story. I depended for my success upon the consistency and probability of my narrative. In several places I pointed it expressly to Mr. Falkland, and I could perceive the shuddering which was partly counteracted by the firmness of his mind, and partly by the general relaxation of his frame incapable either to receive or to convey strong impressions. In several places I could discern in my audience feelings exactly such as I intended to excite. Upon the effect now to be produced depended my future character, my liberty and my peace. I remembered this. I spoke with energy, fervour and conscious truth.

When I had finished, Mr. Falkland begged leave to answer me. He appeared to bring out his words with great difficulty. He observed that he was not able, as he could have wished to have done, to follow me through the particulars of my story. He acknowledged that it was told with great artifice and appearance of consistency. To as much of it as related to Mr. Tyrrel he had already answered upon solemn occasion in the face of his country. This charge I had accumulated with the accusation of his being in the eye of reason the murderer also of the Hawkinses; and I had added to all the rest the unparalleled effrontery of pretending to have received a confession of these facts from his own mouth.

To these allegations he would offer under the present circumstances only one short answer. The character of neither of the parties, the accuser or the accused, was wholly unknown. He had lived in the face of his country and in the face of Europe. His life had been irreproachable; it had been more than this; he must say it, it had been uniformly benevolent and honourable. I also was known, notwithstanding the meanness of my origin, as extensively as he was. My history was notorious; first a thief; then a breaker of prisons; and last a consummate adept in every species of disguise. The question under discussion by its very nature depended upon the veracity of the parties. I affirmed that I had had the confession from his own mouth; he that he had made no such confession, for he had had no such confession to make. Which of the two would they believe? What credit was due to the palpable mockery of oaths and asseverations, when put into competition with a life of unimpeachable virtue?

He added that he might safely risk the question upon another issue. He would consent that they should believe every tittle of my deposition, if I could assign any probable reason for making it. I pretended that I did not thirst for his blood, and that I should be contented to drop the business in its present stage, if the facts to which I swore were fully admitted for true. What an absurd declaration? I said that my conscience was uneasy, and I was anxious to disburthen it. That sentiment, if it existed, would render me either desirous to see my deposition followed up by the exemplary punishment of the party accused, or would make me contented to relate what I knew, without being anxious as to the reception it experienced. No: it was plain that my motive was either revenge for his having brought me to shame, though he had generously remitted to me the penalty annexed; or a weak hope of retrieving my character by retaliating upon my prosecutor the disgrace I had suffered.

I listened with impatience to the animadversions of Mr. Falkland. They did not appear to my inflamed mind to have any considerable force; yet I was anxious to destroy their possible effect. The moment he ceased, I began again; without waiting till I was called upon, without waiting to see whether it was likely I should be called upon.

I said, I stood there for justice. I observed that it was of consequence, in a degree beyond any thing they could suspect, that justice should be done. I intreated them by every thing that was honourable, I conjured them by every thing that was tremendous, to deal impartially and truly. I spoke with a rapidity, perturbation and vehemence that were absolutely alarming to my hearers. I offered to produce witnesses of the symptoms of guilt which Mr. Falkland had long continued to display, of the early date of my accusations against him, and of the mischiefs I was every day suffering from his unremitting jealousy.

Having spoken for some time with incredible eagerness, and at length gasping and panting for breath, the magistrate sternly interposed. Be silent! said he. What is it you intend by thus continuing to intrude yourself? Do you believe you can overbear and intimidate us? We will hear none of your witnesses. We have heard you too long. Never was the dignity of administrative justice in any instance insulted with so bare faced and impudent a forgery!

Great God! with what an effect did these words....[1]

Postscript No. I

vicissitude of my fortune may be styled pleasure, in comparison with what I underwent in this situation. Wild and incoherent visions perpetually succeeded each other, dragged my attention this way and that, and allowed me not a moment's respite. I had no sleep; day and night it was still the same; the same torture and racking of the faculties. If at any time the pictures that glided along before my terrified imagination moved with a slower pace, the idea then occurred of mystery, of something which the understanding was incessantly anxious to penetrate, it turned it on this side and on that, it tried to enter by a thousand paths, but always returned empty, wearied, dissatisfied and unrewarded. His keeper is to a madman something infinitely terrible, a being that delights to thwart him, that endures no expostulation, and whose authority is uncontrollable and omnipotent. But Jones was no common keeper. He stood connected in my mind with other detestable associations, beside those which belonged to his present office. Jones also, habituated to cruelty and revenge, reserved all the refinement and luxury of these passions to be exercised on me. He would continue with me for hours still inventing new methods of exasperation. I have no distinct conception of what he practised on me during the period of my insanity; but I am persuaded that no distracted slave of superstition ever annexed such painful ideas to his dreaded Beelzebub, as I annexed to the figure and appearance of this man.

By what strange cause it has happened that under the discipline of this man I have ever recovered any portion of reason, I am unable to pronounce. How long I shall retain the degree of composure I at present feel, or what will be the fate of my remaining life, I have no materials to judge. It would be better at once to cease to exist, than remain for ever in this horrible

---

1 Two pages are missing in the manuscript at this point. We next see Caleb incarcerated in an "apartment" with Jones (Gines) as his "keeper."

situation. But hope still clings to my heart. I may escape. Why should I, who have broken fetters, and made my way through walls of stone, doubt of my deliverance from this new confinement? I dare not attempt this at present. It is my duty to wait till I can be more sure of my faculties, both that I may contrive more wisely the methods of escape, and that I may have less reason to fear the afterwards betraying myself through any sudden impulse of absurdity. At present I by no means find myself satisfied with the state of my intellects. I am subject to wanderings in which the imagination seems to refuse to obey the curb of judgment. I dare not attempt to think long and strenuously on any one subject. In writing these pages I obtain in the first place a means of essaying the force of my new found understanding; and I am able, writing them as I do, uncertainly and by short snatches, to proportion my essay to the strength of which I am conscious. Above all, I must reserve strength enough to counteract the malignity of Jones, and not suffer him again to irritate me into madness.

One of the thoughts that first presented itself to my mind with the dawn of returning reason, was that of recording these recent and tragical transactions which had occurred subsequently to my putting out of my possession the body of my memoirs. Surely, said I, such a story is worth recording! Surely incidents so extraordinary and so terrible cannot fail to be pregnant with instruction to mankind! It is not necessary that I should trouble the reader with a detail of the expedients by which I enabled myself to reduce this design into practice in my present forlorn situation. I have seen but two persons, Jones and a woman whose business it is to do the drudgery of my apartment. The woman I have seldom seen, it was intended I should have never seen, apart. But the man that watches his opportunity with a quick and eager eye, and who is ardently solicitous to accomplish his purpose, will seldom be long frustrated in an attempt of this sort. The woman has not a heart of flint.

I understand that Mr. Falkland contrary to all previous appearances still lives, nay, that he is considerably better in his health. Alas! alas! it too plainly appears in my history that persecution and tyranny can never die!

I am still in the highest degree perplexed, whenever it recurs to my mind, to account for the entire and ignominious miscarriage of my last solemn accusation before the chief magistrate at ——. Mr. Falkland to have so little to say! I so ardent, so impassioned, so full of my subject, so confident in the justice of my cause! It must surely have been with the persons that heard me an affair of the senses rather than the understanding. They were seduced by the forlorn and deplorable appearance of my adversary; yet how formidable [it is dishonour and madness so much as to think of that!] in the midst of ruin!

Am I not deceiving myself while I thus explain my defeat? Am I not applying an imaginary balm to the gaping wounds of my mind? Perhaps all men will reason upon my story as these men reasoned. Perhaps I am beguiling myself during all this time, merely for want of strength to put myself in the place of an unprepossessed auditor, and to conceive how the story will impress every one that hears it. My innocence will then die with me! The narrative I have taken the pains to digest will then only perpetuate my shame and spread more widely the persuasion of my nefarious guilt! How excruciating so much as to suspect the possibility of such an issue to the scene! This is the bitterest aggravation of all my sufferings! I cannot endure to think it!

I just now feel a sensation unexperienced before. During the whole of my restraint sleep has been a stranger to me; its visits have been rare and of short duration. I feel now a benumbing heaviness, that I conceive to have something in it more than natural. I have tried again and again to shake it off. I can scarcely hold my pen. Surely – surely there is no foul play in all this! My mind misgives me. I will send away these papers, while I am yet able to do so.

Postscript No. II

Dear Mr. Collins, I have a thousand things to tell you – I do not know what is the matter with me, but I am very ill – My head throbs, and my pulses flutter, and yet I am so heavy – Indeed, if you were to see me, you would pity me now – and you would not refuse to take my part as you did at a certain time! – Well, I had something to say – but I cannot think of it – and I cannot hold up my head.

There was once a poor traveller – he was very good natured – and very innocent – and meant no ill to any living soul – he met with a wild beast – the creature seemed to be in great distress, and moaned most piteously – I forget whether it had hurt itself – but the traveller came up to it, and asked it what it wanted, and would have assisted it – but the cries of the beast were only an imposition! – It was a CROCODILE!

I wonder how long I have slept – sometimes it seems to have been so long – and sometimes it seems a very little while – As soon as I eat, and drink, I fall asleep again – is not that strange?

I should like to recollect something – it would make an addition to my history – but it is all a BLANK! – sometimes it is day, and some times it is night – but nobody does any thing, and nobody says any thing – It would be an odd kind of a history!

Once I had an enemy – oh! two or three enemies! – and they drove me about, and menaced me, and tormented me! – and now nobody disturbs me – I am so quiet – I have not an enemy in the world – *nor a* FRIEND!

So you tell me Mr. Falkland is dead? – Very likely – it was high time – I believe – was not it?

They do nothing but tell me over and over again that Mr. Falkland is dead – What is that to me? – Heaven rest his soul! – I wonder who that Mr. Falkland was, for every body to think so much about him? Do you know?

If I could once again be thoroughly myself, I should tell such tales! – Some folks are afraid of that, do you see, and so – But I never shall – never – never! – I sit in a chair in a corner, and never move hand or foot – I am like a log – I know all that very well, but I cannot help it! – I wonder which is the man, I or my chair?

I have dreams – they are strange dreams – I never know what they are about – No, not while I am dreaming – they are about nothing at all – and yet there is one thing first, and then another thing, and there is so much of them, and it is all nothing – when I am awake it is just the same! – I used to have dreams of quite a different kind – and to talk in my dreams – and some folks said I disturbed them – and so, I believe they have given me something to quiet me.

Well, it is all one at last – I believe there was nothing in life worth making such a bustle about – no, nor in SECRETS – nor in MURDERS neither, for the matter of that – when people are dead, you know, one cannot bring them to life again! – dead folks tell no tales – ghosts do not walk these days – I never saw Mr. Tyrrel's – Only once!

Well then, – It is wisest to be quiet, it seems – Some people are ambitious – other people talk of sensibility – but it is all folly! – I am sure I am not one of those – was I ever? – True happiness lies in being like a stone – Nobody can complain of me – all day long I do nothing am a stone – a GRAVESTONE! – an obelisk to tell you, HERE LIES WHAT WAS ONCE A MAN!

2. Godwin's Account of the Composition of the Novel from the Preface to the "Standard Novels" Edition of *Fleetwood* (London: R. Bentley, 1832).

PREFACE
To the Present Edition

London, 20 November 1832

"CALEB WILLIAMS" has always been regarded by the public with an unusual degree of favour. The proprietor of "THE STANDARD NOVELS" has therefore imagined, that even an account of the concoction and mode of writing of the work would be viewed with some interest.

I finished the "Enquiry concerning Political Justice," the first work which may be considered as written by me in a certain degree in the maturity of my intellectual powers, and bearing my name, early in January, 1793; and about the middle of the following month the book was published. It was my fortune at that time to be obliged to consider my pen as the sole instrument for supplying my current expenses. By the liberality of my bookseller, Mr. George Robinson, of Paternoster Row, I was enabled then, and for nearly ten years before, to meet these expenses, while writing different things of obscure note, the names of which though innocent, and in some degree useful, I am rather inclined to suppress. In May, 1791, I projected this, my favourite work, and from that time gave up every other occupation that might interfere with it. My agreement with Robinson was, that he was to supply my wants at a specified rate, while the book was in the train of composition. Finally, I was very little beforehand with the world on the day of its publication, and was therefore obliged to look round and consider to what species of industry I should next devote myself.

I had always felt in myself some vocation towards the composition of a narrative of fictitious adventure; and among the things of obscure note, which I have above referred to, were two or three pieces of this nature. It is not therefore extraordinary that some project of the sort should have suggested itself on the present occasion.

But I stood now in a very different situation from that in which I had been placed at a former period. In past years, and even almost from boyhood, I was perpetually prone to exclaim with Cowley, –

"What shall I do to be for ever known,
And make the age to come my own?"[1]

But I had endeavoured for ten years, and was as far from approaching my object as ever. Every thing I wrote fell dead-born from the press. Very often I was disposed to quit the enterprise in despair. But still I felt ever and anon impelled to repeat my effort.

At length I conceived the plan of Political Justice. I was convinced that my object of building to myself a name would never be attained, by merely repeating and refining a little upon what other men had said, even though I should imagine that I delivered things of this sort with a more than usual point and elegance. The world, I believed, would accept nothing from me

---

1 Abraham Cowley, *Miscellanies*, "The Motto," II.1-2.

with distinguishing favour, that did not bear upon the face of it the undoubted stamp of originality. Having long ruminated upon the principles of Political Justice, I persuaded myself that I could offer to the public, in a treatise on this subject, things at once new, true and important. In the progress of the work I became more sanguine and confident. I talked over my ideas with a few familiar friends during its progress, and they gave me every generous encouragement. It happened that the fame of my book, in some inconsiderable degree, got before its publication, and a certain number of persons were prepared to receive it with favour. It would be false modesty in me to say, that its acceptance, when published, did not early come up to every thing that could soberly have been expected by me. In consequence of this, the tone of my mind, both during the period in which I was engaged in the work, and afterwards, acquired a certain elevation, and made me now unwilling to stoop to what was insignificant.

I formed a conception of a book of fictitious adventure, that should in some way be distinguished by a very powerful interest. Pursuing this idea, I invented first the third volume of my tale, then the second, and last of all the first. I bent myself to the conception of a series of adventures of flight and pursuit; the fugitive in perpetual apprehension of being overwhelmed with the worst calamities, and the pursuer, by his ingenuity and resources, keeping his victim in a state of the most fearful alarm. This was the project of my third volume.

I was next called upon to conceive a dramatic and impressive situation adequate to account for the impulse that the pursuer should feel, incessantly to alarm and harass his victim, with an inextinguishable resolution never to allow him the least interval of peace and security. This I apprehended could best be effected by a secret murder, to the investigation of which the innocent victim should be impelled by an unconquerable spirit of curiosity. The murderer would thus have a sufficient motive to persecute the unhappy discoverer, that he might deprive him of peace, character and credit, and have him for ever in his power. This constituted the outline of my second volume.

The subject of the first volume was still to be invented. To account for the fearful events of the third, it was necessary that the pursuer should be invested with every advantage of fortune, with a resolution that nothing could defeat or baffle, and with extraordinary resources of intellect. Nor could my purpose of giving an overpowering interest to my tale be answered, without his appearing to have been originally endowed with a mighty store of amiable dispositions and virtues, so that his being driven to the first act of murder should be judged worthy of the deepest regret, and should be seen in some measure to have arisen out of his virtues themselves. It was necessary to make him, so to speak, the tenant of an atmosphere of romance, so that every reader should feel prompted almost to worship him for his high qualities. Here were ample materials for a first volume.

I felt that I had a great advantage in thus carrying back my invention from the ultimate conclusion to the first commencement of the train of adventures upon which I purposed to employ my pen. An entire unity of plot would be the infallible result; and the unity of spirit and interest in a tale truly considered, gives it a powerful hold on the reader, which can scarcely be generated with equal success in any other way.

I devoted about two or three weeks to the imagining and putting down hints for my story, before I engaged seriously and methodically in its composition. In these hints I began with my third volume, then proceeded to my second, and last of all grappled with the first. I filled two or three sheets of demy writing-paper, folded in octavo, with these memorandums. They were put down with great brevity, yet explicitly enough to secure a perfect recollection of their meaning, within the time necessary for drawing out the story at full, in short paragraphs of two, three, four, five or six lines each.

I then sat down to write my story from the beginning. I wrote for the most part but a short portion in any single day. I wrote only when the afflatus was upon me. I held it for a maxim, that any portion that was written when I was not fully in the vein, told for considerably worse than nothing. Idleness was a thousand times better in this case, than industry against the grain. Idleness was only time lost; and the next day, it may be, was as promising as ever. It was merely a day perished from the calendar. But a passage written feebly, flatly, and in a wrong spirit, constituted an obstacle that it was next to impossible to correct and set right again. I wrote therefore by starts; sometimes for a week or ten days not a line. Yet all came to the same thing in the sequel. On an average, a volume of "Caleb Williams" cost me four months, neither less, nor more.

It must be admitted however, that, during the whole period, bating a few intervals, my mind was in a high state of excitement. I said to myself a thousand times, "I will write a tale, that shall constitute an epoch in the mind of the reader, that no one, after he has read it, shall ever be exactly the same man that he was before." – I put these things down just as they happened, and with the most entire frankness. I know that it will sound like the most pitiable degree of self-conceit. But such perhaps ought to be the state of mind of an author, when he does his best. At any rate, I have said nothing of my vain-glorious impulse for nearly forty years.

When I had written about seven-tenths of the first volume, I was prevailed upon by the extreme importunity of an old and intimate friend to allow him the perusal of my manuscript.[1] On the second day he returned it with a note to this purpose: "I return you your manuscript, because I promised to do so. If I had obeyed the impulse of my own mind, I should have thrust it in the fire. If you persist, the book will infallibly prove the grave of your literary fame."

I doubtless felt no implicit deference for the judgment of my friendly critic. Yet it cost me at least two days of deep anxiety, before I recovered the shock. Let the reader picture to himself my situation. I felt no implicit deference for the judgment of my friendly critic. But it was all I had for it. This was my first experiment of an unbiased decision. It stood in the place of all the world to me. I could not, and I did not feel disposed to, appeal any further. If I had, how could I tell that the second and third judgment would be more favourable than the first? Then what would have been the result? No; I had nothing for

---

1 James Marshall, a long-time friend of Godwin's from their school-days, who frequently read and commented upon Godwin's work during this period.

it but to wrap myself in my own integrity. By dint of resolution I became invulnerable. I resolved to go on to the end, trusting as I could to my own anticipations of the whole, and bidding the world wait its time, before it should be admitted to the consult.

I began my narrative, as is the more usual way, in the third person. But I speedily became dissatisfied. I then assumed the first person, making the hero of my tale his own historian; and in this mode I have persisted in all my subsequent attempts at works of fiction. It was infinitely the best adapted, at least, to my vein of delineation, where the thing in which my imagination revelled the most freely, was the analysis of the private and internal operations of the mind, employing my metaphysical dissecting knife in tracing and laying bare the involutions of motive, and recording the gradually accumulating impulses, which led the personages I had to describe primarily to adopt the particular way of proceeding in which they afterwards embarked.

When I had determined on the main purpose of my story, it was ever my method to get about me any productions of former authors that seemed to bear on my subject. I never entertained the fear, that in this way of proceeding I should be in danger of servilely copying my predecessors. I imagined that I had a vein of thinking that was properly my own, which would always preserve me from plagiarism. I read other authors, that I might see what they had done, or more properly, that I might forcibly hold my mind and occupy my thoughts in a particular train, I and my predecessors travelling in some sense to the same goal, at the same time that I struck out a path of my own, without ultimately heeding the direction they pursued, and disdaining to enquire whether by any chance it for a few steps coincided or did not coincide with mine.

Thus, in the instance of "Caleb Williams," I read over a little old book, entitled "The Adventures of Mademoiselle de St. Phale" a French Protestant in the times of the fiercest persecution of the Huguenots, who fled through France in the utmost terror, in the midst of eternal alarms and hair-breadth escapes, having her quarters perpetually beaten up, and by scarcely any chance finding a moment's interval of security.[1] I turned over the pages of a tremendous compilation, entitled "God's Revenge against Murder," where the beam of the eye of Omniscience was represented as perpetually pursuing the guilty, and laying open his most hidden retreats to the light of day. I was extremely conversant with the "Newgate Calendar," and the "Lives of the Pirates." In the mean time no works of fiction came amiss to me, provided they were written with energy. The authors were still employed upon the same mine as myself, however different was the vein they pursued: we were all of us engaged in exploring the entrails of mind and motive, and in tracing the various rencontres and clashes that may occur between man and man in the diversified scene of human life.

I rather amused myself with tracing a certain similitude between the story of Caleb Williams and the tale of Bluebeard, than derived any hints from that admirable specimen of the terrific. Falkland was my Bluebeard, who had perpetrated atrocious crimes, which if discovered, he might expect to have all the world roused to revenge against him. Caleb Williams was the wife, who in spite of warning, persisted in his attempts to discover the forbidden secret; and, when he had succeeded, struggled as fruitlessly to escape the consequences, as the wife of Bluebeard in washing the key of the ensanguined chamber, who, as often as she cleared the stain of blood from the one side, found it showing itself with frightful distinctness on the other.

When I had proceeded as far as the early pages of my third volume, I found myself completely at a stand. I rested on my arms from the 2d of January, 1794, to the 1st of April following, without getting forward in the smallest degree. It has ever been thus with me in works of any continuance. The bow will not be for ever bent.

"Opere in longo fas est obrepere somnum."[2]

---

1 See the editors' introduction for discussion of these and other sources mentioned here by Godwin.
2 "When a work is long, sleep inevitably creeps over it." Horace, *The Art of Poetry*, 1.360.

I endeavoured however to take my repose to myself in security, and not to inflict a set of crude and incoherent dreams upon my readers. In the mean time, when I revived, I revived in earnest, and in the course of that month carried on my work with unabated speed to the end.

Thus I have endeavoured to give a true history of the concoction and mode of writing of this mighty trifle. When I had done, I soon became sensible that I had done in a manner nothing. How many flat and insipid parts does the book contain! How terribly unequal does it appear to me! From time to time the author plainly reels to and fro like a drunken man. And, when I had done all, what had I done? Written a book to amuse boys and girls in their vacant hours, a story to be hastily gobbled up by them, swallowed in a pusillanimous and unanimated mood, without chewing and digestion. I was in this respect greatly impressed with the confession of one of the most accomplished readers and excellent critics that any author could have fallen in with (the unfortunate Joseph Gerald). He told me that he had received my book late one evening, and had read through the three volumes before he closed his eyes. Thus, what had cost me twelve months' labour, ceaseless heartaches and industry, now sinking in despair, and now roused and sustained in unusual energy, he went over in a few hours, shut the book, laid himself on his pillow, slept and was refreshed, and cried,

"To-morrow to fresh woods and pastures new."[1]

I had thought to have said something here respecting the concoction of "St Leon," and "Fleetwood." But all that occurs to me on the subject seems to be anticipated in the following.

3. Godwin's Account of the Novel's Aims, from the *British Critic* 6 (July 1795), 94-95.

[Godwin wrote this letter in response to the attack on the novel included in Appendix F.3 below.]

---

1   John Milton, "Lycidas," I.193.

To the Editor of the BRITISH CRITIC.

SIR,

I have just seen in your Review for April an attack by one of your correspondents on the novel of Caleb Williams. An author is perhaps the worst judge in the world what attacks it becomes him to notice, and what to pass over in silence. Where he observes sophistry and mistake, he is apt to suppose that every other reader will perceive them without his assistance. I have been told, however, that the remarks of your correspondent are so written as to have a superficial plausibility; and I yield my own judgment to this friendly suggestion, when I trouble you with a few lines in reply.

He supposes that my book was written "to throw an odium upon the laws of my country." But this is a mistake into which no attentive and clear-sighted reader could possibly fall. The object is of much greater magnitude. It is to expose the evils which arise out of the present system of civilized society; and, having exposed them, to lead the enquiring reader to examine whether they are, or are not, as has commonly been supposed, irremediable; in a word, to disengage the minds of men from prepossession, and launch them upon the sea of moral and political enquiry. Having formed this plan, I was obviously led to place my scene, and draw my instances from the country with which I was best acquainted – England. Not that I thought the laws of England worse than the laws of most other countries. Your correspondent comes nearer the point when he afterwards states my object to be, "the laws of this country, and the mode of their execution;" or rather, as he ought to have stated, the administration of justice and equity, with its consequences, as it exists in the world at large, and in Great Britain in particular.

This clue will immediately enable the reader to solve most of the objections proposed. It was not the business of such a work to enquire whether the law authorised a rich man to spoil the crop of a poor one, to poison his cattle, or to commit him to jail upon an absurd and sophistical charge of burglary. It was enough that oppressions of a similar nature, and of equal magnitude, are known to be perpetually practised with impunity; and your correspondent, if he have a taste for that amusement, may easily supply himself with volumes of facts in proof of this assertion: facts, the memory of which unfortunately, for want of collection, is suffered to perish, almost as rapidly as the facts themselves are produced. Your correspondent closes his remarks on the episode of Hawkins, with suggesting "a doubt, whether I have even taken a common and superficial view of the state of society in this country, instead of having surveyed it with the precision and sagacity of a philosopher." I am willing to abide by the test here proposed; and I ask any man, in the least degree informed as to the history of squires and their tenants in Great Britain, whether he can read this episode; and not recognise its counterpart in what he has himself heard and seen?

It is curious to observe, that your correspondent, who affects to be a great lawyer, does not hesitate to affirm that "it is certain, and universally known, that a verdict of acquittal upon a criminal charge, is a complete bar to any further trial for the same offence." Surely, Sir, a man who ventures to affirm in so peremptory a manner, and that in the very act of attempting to chastise another for ignorance or misrepresentation, ought first to have had the modesty to consult the Newgate Calendar, or any of the most common records, which would have given him repeated instances, not only of trials, but executions, in refutation of his *certain* assertion.[1]

I acknowledge that I am far from a consummate lawyer. I acknowledge that I do not bear that affection for the laws of my country which should lead me to study them farther than the pressure of immediate occasion may seem to demand. I went therefore no farther in pursuit of authorities for the second trial of Falkland than I have just stated, and consequently was, I believe, guilty of an oversight, which your correspondent, however, has not had the ingenuity to detect. I have since been told by professional lawyers, that such a second trial cannot take place, but upon an appeal from the relations of the deceased, which in my fiction I have neglected to provide. Whether this be so or not, I have not yet had leisure to examine.

---

1   Case of Christopher Slaughterford, 1708. Newgate Calendar, Vol. 1. P. 118. – Case of James Cluff, 1729. Lives of the Convicts, Vol. II. P. 199. [Godwin's note]

With the virulent and scurrilous epithets of your correspondent I have no concern. I trust no person tolerably impartial can peruse my writings, without perceiving, what I myself intimately feel, that I have no sentiment nearer my heart than a liberal and disinterested concern for the true welfare of my species. But the books must speak for themselves: if they will not obtain credit for the benevolence of their purposes, any professions of mine would be of little avail. Perhaps they will be thought honourable to the intentions of their author, when party animosities are forgotten; and then, if this attack could be remembered, the personalities that characterise it will be thought discreditable to its writer and not to me.

W. GODWIN.

June 7, 1795.

4. Godwin's Essay, "Of History and Romance" (1797), from
Political and Philosophical Writings, **vol. 5. Ed. Pamela Clemit**
(London: Pickering & Chatto, 1993).

[This essay is from a manuscript in the Abinger Collection of the Bodleian Library at Oxford. Godwin included on the page this note: "These Essays were written while the Enquirer was in the press, under the impression that the favour of the public might have demanded another volume." It was unpublished in Godwin's lifetime, first appearing in Maurice Hindle's 1987 Penguin edition of *Caleb Williams*.]

The study of history may well be ranked among those pursuits which are most worthy to be chosen by a rational being.

The study of history divides itself into two principal branches; the study of mankind in a mass, of the progress, the fluctuations, the interests and the vices of society; and the study of the individual.

The history of a nation might be written in the first of these senses, entirely in terms of abstraction, and without descending so much as to name one of those individuals of which the nation is composed.

It is curious, and it is important, to trace the progress of mankind from the savage to the civilised state; to observe the points of similitude between the savages of America and the savages of ancient Italy or Greece; to investigate the rise of property moveable to immoveable; and thus to ascertain the causes that operate universally upon masses of men under given circumstances, without being turned aside in their operation by the varying character of individuals.

The fundamental article in this branch of historical investigation, is the progress and varieties of civilisation. But there are many subordinate channels into which it has formed itself. We may study the history of eloquence or the history of philosophy. We may apply ourselves to the consideration of the arts of life, and the arts of refinement and pleasure. There lie before us the history of wealth and the history of commerce. We may study the progress of revenue and the arts of taxation. We may follow the varieties of climates, and trace their effect on the human body and the human mind. Nay, we may descend still lower; we may have our attention engrossed by the succession of archons and the adjustment of olympiads; or may apply ourselves entirely to the examination of medals and coins.

There are those who conceive that history, in one or all the kinds here enumerated, is the only species of history deserving a serious attention. They disdain the records of individuals. To interest our passions, or employ our thoughts about personal events, be they of patriots, of authors, of heroes or kings, they regard as a symptom of effeminacy. Their mighty minds cannot descend to be busied about any thing less than the condition of nations, and the collation and comparison of successive ages. Whatever would disturb by exciting our feelings the torpid tranquillity of the soul, they have in unspeakable abhorrence.

It is to be feared that one of the causes that have dictated the panegyric which has so often been pronounced upon this species of history, is its dry and repulsive nature. Men who by persevering exertions have conquered a subject in defiance of innumerable obstacles, will almost always be able to ascribe to it a disproportionate value. Men who have not done this, often imagine they shall acquire at a cheap rate among the ignorant the reputation of profound, by praising, in the style of an adept, that which few men venture so much as to approach. Difficulty has a tendency to magnify to almost all eyes the excellence of that which only through difficulty can be attained.

The mind of man does not love abstractions. Its genuine and native taste, as it discovers itself in children and uneducated persons, rests entirely in individualities. It is only by perseverance and custom that we are brought to have a relish for philosophy, mathematical, natural or moral. There was a time when the man, now most eagerly attached to them, shrunk with terror from their thorny path.

But the abstractions of philosophy, when we are grown familiar with them, often present to our minds a simplicity and precision, that may well supply the place of entire individuality. The abstractions of history are more cumbrous and unwieldy. In their own nature perhaps they are capable of simplicity. But this species of science is yet in its infancy. He who would study the history of nations abstracted from individuals whose passions and peculiarities are interesting to our minds, will find it a dry and frigid science. It will supply him with no clear ideas. The mass, as fast as he endeavours to cement and unite it, crumbles from his grasp, like a lump of sand. Those who study revenue or almost any other of the complex subjects above enumerated, are ordinarily found, with immense pains to have compiled a species of knowledge which is no sooner accumulated than it perishes, and rather to have confounded themselves with a labyrinth of particulars, than to have risen to the dignity of principles.

Let us proceed to the consideration of the second great branch of the study of history. In doing so, we shall be insensibly led to assign to the first branch its proper rank.

The study of individual man can never fail to be an object of the highest importance. It is only by comparison that we come to know any thing of mind or of ourselves. We go forth into the world; we see what man is; we enquire what he was; and when we return home and engage in the solemn act of self-investigation, our most useful employment is to produce the materials we have collected abroad, and, by a sort of magnetism, cause those particulars to start out to view in ourselves, which might otherwise have lain for ever undetected.

But the study of individual history has a higher use than

merely as it conduces to the elucidation of science. It is the most fruitful source of activity and motive. If a man were condemned to perfect solitude, he would probably sink into the deepest and most invariable lethargy of soul. If he only associate, as most individuals are destined to do, with ordinary men, he will be in danger of becoming such as they are. It is the contemplation of illustrious men, such as we find scattered through the long succession of ages, that kindles into a flame the hidden fire within us. The excellence indeed of sages, of patriots and poets, as we find it exhibited at the period of their maturity, is too apt to overwhelm and discourage us with its lustre. But history takes away the cause of our depression. It enables us to view minutely and in detail what to the uninstructed eye was too powerful to be gazed at; and, by tracing the progress of the virtuous and the wise from its first dawn to its meridian lustre, shows us that they were composed of materials merely human. It was the sight of the trophies of Mithrades, that recurred to break the infant slumbers of his more illustrious successor.[1] While we admire the poet and the hero, and sympathise with his generous ambition or his ardent exertions, we insensibly imbibe the same spirit, and burn with kindred fires.

But let us suppose that the genuine purpose of history, was to enable us to understand the machine of society, and to direct it to its best purposes. Even here individual history will perhaps be found in point of importance to take the lead of general. General history will furnish us precedents in abundance, will show us how that which happened in one country has been repeated in another, and may perhaps even instruct us how that which has occurred in the annals of mankind, may under similar circumstances be produced again. But, if the energy of our minds should lead us to aspire to something more animated and noble than dull repetition, if we love the happiness of mankind enough to feel ourselves impelled to explore new and untrod-

---

1 Probably a reference to Mithridates V, father of Mithridates VI, also known as Mithridates Eupator or Mithridates the Great (c. 131-63 BC). Both were kings of Pontus and fierce opponents of the Romans. Mithridates VI was finally defeated by Pompey and killed himself rather than fall into the hands of the Romans. The source of this particular story is unknown, though the fullest account of Mithridates' life is Appian's *Mithridatica*.

den paths, we must then not rest contented with considering society in a mass, but must analyse the materials of which it is composed. It will be necessary for us to scrutinise the nature of man, before we can pronounce what it is of which social man is capable. Laying aside the generalities of historical abstraction, we must mark the operation of human passions; must observe the empire of motives whether groveling or elevated; and must note the influence that one human being exercises over another, and the ascendancy of the daring and the wise over the vulgar multitude. It is thus, and thus only, that we shall be enabled to add, to the knowledge of the past, a sagacity that can penetrate into the depths of futurity. We shall not only understand those events as they arise, which are no better than old incidents under new names, but shall judge truly of such conjunctures and combinations, their sources and effects, as, though they have never yet occurred, are within the capacities of our nature. He that would prove the liberal and spirited benefactor of his species, must connect the two branches of history together, and regard the knowledge of the individual, as that which can alone give energy and utility to the records of our social existence.

From these considerations one inference may be deduced, which constitutes perhaps the most important rule that can be laid down respecting the study of history. This is, the wisdom of studying it in detail, and not in abridgement. The prolixity of dullness is indeed contemptible. But the copiousness of wisdom and genius is treasure inestimable. To read a history which, expanding itself through several volumes, treats only of a short period, is true economy. To read historical abridgements, in which each point of the subject is touched upon only, and immediately dismissed, is a wanton prodigality of time worthy only of folly or of madness.

The figures which present themselves in such a history, are like the groups that we sometimes see placed in the distance of a landscape, that are just sufficiently marked to distinguish the man from the brute, or the male from the female, but are totally unsusceptible of discrimination of form or expression of sentiment. The men I would study upon the canvas of history, are men worth the becoming intimately acquainted with.

It is in history, as it is in life. Superficial acquaintance is nothing. A scene incessantly floating, cannot instruct us; it can scarcely become a source of amusement to a cultivated mind. I would stop the flying figures, that I may mark them more clearly. There must be an exchange of real sentiments, or an investigation of subtle peculiarities, before improvement can be the result. There is a magnetical virtue in man; but there must be friction and heat, before the virtue will operate.

Pretenders indeed to universal science, who examine nothing, but imagine they understand every thing, are ready from the slightest glance to decypher the whole character. Not so the genuine scholar. His curiosity is never satiated. He is ever upon the watch for further, and still further, particulars. Trembling for his own fallibility and frailty, he employs every precaution to guard himself against them.

There are characters in history that may almost be said to be worth an eternal study. They are epitomes of the world, of its best and most exalted features, purified from their grossness. I am not contented to observe such a man upon the public stage, I would follow him into his closet. I would see the friend and the father of a family, as well as the patriot. I would read his works and his letters, if any remain to us. I would observe the turn of his thoughts and the character of his phraseology. I would study his public orations. I would collate his behaviour in prosperity with his behaviour in adversity. I should be glad to know the course of his studies, and the arrangement of his time. I should rejoice to have, or to be enabled to make, if that were possible, a journal of his ordinary and minutest actions. I believe I should be better employed in thus studying one man, than in perusing the abridgement of Universal History in sixty volumes. I would rather be acquainted with a few trivial particulars of the actions and dispositions of Virgil and Horace, than with the lives of many men, and the history of many nations.

This leads us to a second rule respecting the study of history. Those histories alone are worthy of attentive and persevering study, that treat of the development of great genius, or the exhibition of bold and masculine virtues. Modern history indeed we ought to peruse, because all that we wish must be connected with all that we are, and because it is incumbent upon us to explore the means by which the latter may be made, as it were, to slide into the former. But modern history, for the most part, is not to be perused for its own sake.

The ancients were giants, but we, their degenerate successors, are pygmies. There was something in the nature of the Greek and Roman republics that expanded and fired the soul. He that sees not this, if he have had an adequate opportunity to see it, must be destitute of some of the first principles of discrimination. He that feels not the comparative magnitude of their views, must be himself the partaker of a slow-working and unelevated soul.

To convince us of this, we need do no more than look into the biographical collection of Plutarch.[1] Plutarch is neither lucid in his arrangement, eloquent in his manner, nor powerful in his conceptions. The effect he produces upon us, is the effect of his subject, and is scarcely in any respect aided by the skill of the writer.

From Plutarch let us turn to the collections, in English, French and Italian, relative to the persons who in modern times have reflected most honour upon any of these nations. We sometimes no doubt admire; occasionally we sympathise. But the greatest personages there upon record, appear in the comparison encumbered with their rank. Their march is slow, weighed down as they are on every side with prejudices and precedents. They are disciplined to dull monotony. They are cast together in one uncharacteristic mould. There is something in the nature of modern governments and institutions, that seems to blight in the bud every grander and more ample development of the soul. When we attempt to display the agility or the grace, the capacity for which inheres in our nature, we resemble a vaulter or *figurante* that should undertake to dance in fetters.

The ancients on the other hand are men of a free and undaunted spirit. There is a conscious dignity in their mien that impresses us with awe. Whatever they undertake, they

---

1 Plutarch (AD 46-120) was a Roman biographer and philosopher. His *Parallel Lives* of prominent Greeks and Romans was the most widely read historical work in Europe well into the nineteenth century.

undertake with a full and undivided soul. They proceed to their object with an unerring aim, and do not lose themselves in dark, inexplicable windings. He that shall study their history with an unbiassed spirit, will almost imagine that he is reading of a different species. He will not be blind to their mistakes, their abuses and their crimes, but he will confess that their minds are of a more decisive character, and their virtues more attractive and sublime.

We are sometimes told that the remoteness of the object in this case misleads us, and that we admire the ancients for this reason merely, because they are ancients. But this solution will not account for the phenomenon. Read on the one hand Thucydides and Livy, and on the other Hume and Voltaire and Robertson.[1] When we admire the personages of the former, we simply enter into the feelings with which these authors recorded them. The latter neither experience such emotions nor excite them. The ancients were not ancients to their contemporaries. "Les anciens étaient contemporains de leurs historiens, et nous ont pourtant appris à les admirer. Assurément si la postérité jamais admire les nôtres, elle ne l'aura pas appris de nous." (Rousseau, *Nouvelle Héloïse*, Lettre XII)[2] No: the difference is intrinsic, and the emotions will be generated as long as history endures.

What sort of an object is the history of England? Till the extinction of the wars of York and Lancaster, it is one scene of barbarism and cruelty. Superstition rides triumphant upon the subject neck of princes and of people, intestine war of noble with noble, or of one pretender to the crown against another, is

---

1   Thucydides (460-395 BC) was an Athenian statesman and historian, whose *History of the Peloponnesian War* was a seminal work for European historiography. Livy (59 BC-17 AD) was one of the most prominent historians of Rome. David Hume (1711-76) was the Scottish philosopher, best known for his *A Treatise of Human Nature*, who also wrote an influential *History of England*. Voltaire was the pen name of François Marie Arouet (1694-1778), the most famous French Enlightenment philosopher and author of several historical tragedies. William Robertson (1721-93) was a Scottish Enlightenment historian.

2   "The ancients were the contemporaries of their historians, and yet have taught us to admire them. It is certain that if posterity ever admires ours, it will not have learned it from us." Jean Jacques Rousseau (1712-78) was the author of the novel, *La Nouvelle Héloïse* (1761).

almost incessant. The gallant champion is no sooner worsted, than he is led without form of law to the scaffold, or massacred in cold blood upon the field. In all these mighty struggles, scarcely a trace is to be found of a sense of the rights of men. They are combinations among the oppressors against him that would usurp their tyranny, or they are the result of an infatuated predilection for one despotic monster in preference to another. The period of the Tudors is a period of base and universal slavery. The reign of Elizabeth is splendid, but its far-famed worthies are in reality supple and servile courtiers, treacherous, undermining and unprincipled. The period of the Stuarts is the only portion of our history interesting to the heart of man. Yet its noblest virtues are obscured by the vile jargon of fanaticism and hypocrisy. From the moment that the grand contest excited under the Stuarts was quieted by the Revolution, our history assumes its most insipid and insufferable form. It is the history of negotiations and tricks; it is the history of revenues and debts; it is the history of corruption and political profligacy, but it is not the history of genuine, independent man.

Some persons, endowed with too much discernment and taste not to perceive the extreme disparity that subsists between the characters of ancient and of modern times, have observed that ancient history carries no other impression to their minds than that of exaggeration and fable.

It is not necessary here to enter into a detail of the evidence upon which our belief of ancient history is founded. Let us take it for granted that it is a fable. Are all fables unworthy of regard? Ancient history, says Rousseau, is a tissue of such fables, as have a moral perfectly adapted to the human heart. I ask not, as a principal point, whether it be true or false? My first enquiry is, Can I derive instruction from it? Is it a genuine praxis upon the nature of man? Is it pregnant with the most generous motives and the most fascinating examples? If so, I had rather be profoundly versed in this fable, than in all the genuine histories that ever existed.

It must be admitted indeed that all history bears too near a resemblance to fable. Nothing is more uncertain, more contradictory, more unsatisfying, than the evidence of facts. If this be the case in courts of justice, where truth is sometimes sifted with tenacious perseverance, how much more will it hold true of the historian? He can administer no oath; he cannot issue his precept, and summon his witnesses from distant provinces; he cannot arraign his personages, and compel them to put in their answer. He must take what they choose to tell; the broken fragments, and the scattered ruins of evidence.

That history which comes nearest to truth, is the mere chronicle of facts, places and dates. But this is in reality no history. He that knows only on what day the Bastille was taken, and on what spot Louis XVI perished, knows nothing. He possesses the mere skeleton of history. The muscles, the articulations, every thing in which the life emphatically resides, is absent.

Read Sallust.[1] To every action he assigns a motive. Rarely an uncertainty diversifies his page. He describes his characters with preciseness and decision. He seems to enter into the hearts of his personages, and unfolds their secret thoughts. Considered as fable, nothing can be more perfect. But neither is this history.

There is but one further mode of writing history, and this is the mode principally prevalent in modern times. In this mode, the narrator is sunk in the critic. The main body of the composition consists of a logical deduction and calculation of probabilities. This species of writing may be of use as a whetstone upon which to sharpen our faculty of discrimination; but it answers none of the legitimate purposes of history.

From these considerations it follows that the noblest and most excellent species of history, may be decided to be a composition in which, with a scanty substratum of facts and dates, the writer interweaves a number of happy, ingenious and instructive inventions, blending them into one continuous and indiscernible mass. It sufficiently corresponds with the denomination, under which abbé Prévost acquired considerable

---

1   Sallust (86-34 BC), Roman statesman and ally of Caesar, author of several works of Roman history.

applause, of historical romance.[1] Abbé Prévost differs from Sallust, inasmuch as he made a freer use of what may be styled, the *licentia historica.*

If then history be little better than romance under a graver name, it may not be foreign to the subject here treated, to enquire into the credit due to that species of literature, which bears the express stamp of invention, and calls itself romance or novel.

This sort of writing has been exposed to more obloquy and censure than any other.

The principal cause of this obloquy is sufficiently humorous and singular.

Novels, as an object of trade among booksellers, are of a peculiar cast. There are few by which immense sums of money can be expected to be gained. There is scarcely one by which some money is not gained. A class of readers, consisting of women and boys, and which is considerably numerous, requires a continual supply of books of this sort. The circulating libraries therefore must be furnished; while, in consequence of the discredit which has fallen upon romance, such works are rarely found to obtain a place in the collection of the gentleman or the scholar. An ingenious bookseller of the metropolis, speculating upon this circumstance, was accustomed to paste an advertisement in his window, to attract the eye of the curious passenger, and to fire his ambition, by informing him of a "want of novels for the ensuing season."

The critic and the moralist, in their estimate of romances, have borrowed the principle that regulates the speculations of trade. They have weighed novels by the great and taken into their view the whole scum and surcharge of the press. But surely this is not the way in which literature would teach us to consider the subject.

When we speak of poetry, we do not fear to commend this species of composition, regardless of the miserable trash that from month to month finds its way from the press under the

---

1 Antoine François Prévost d'Exiles (1697-1763), author of several influential historical romances including *Manon Lescaut* (1731).

appellation of poetry. The like may be said of history, or of books of philosophy, natural and intellectual. There is no species of literature that would stand this ordeal.

If I would estimate truly any head of composition, nothing can be more unreasonable, than for me to take into account every pretender to literature that has started in it. In poetry I do not consider those persons who merely know how to count their syllables and tag a rhyme; still less those who print their effusion in the form of verse without being adequate to either of these. I recollect those authors only who are endowed with some of the essentials of poetry, with its imagery, its enthusiasm, or its empire over the soul of man. Just so in the case before us, I should consider only those persons who had really written romance, not those who had vainly attempted it.

Romance then, strictly considered, may be pronounced to be one of the species of history. The difference between romance and what ordinarily bears the denomination of history, is this. The historian is confined to individual incident and individual man, and must hang upon that his invention or conjecture as he can. The writer of romance collects his materials from all sources, experience, report, and the records of human affairs; then generalises them; and finally selects, from their elements and the various combinations they afford, those instances which he is best qualified to portray, and which he judges most calculated to impress the heart and improve the faculties of his reader. In this point of view we should be apt to pronounce that romance was a nobler species of composition than history.

It has been affirmed by the critics that the species of composition which abbé Prévost and others have attempted, and according to which, upon a slight substratum of fact, all the license of romantic invention is to be engrafted, is contrary to the principles of a just taste. History is by this means debauched and corrupted. Real characters are wantonly misrepresented. The reader, who has been interested by a romance of this sort, scarcely knows how to dismiss it from his mind when he comes to consider the genuine annals of the period to which it relates. The reality and the fiction, like two substances of disagreeing natures, will never adequately blend with each other. The invention of the writer is much too wanton not to discolour and confound the facts with which he is concerned; while on the other hand, his imagination is fettered and checked at every turn by facts that will not wholly accommodate themselves to the colour of his piece, or the moral he would adduce from it.

These observations, which have been directed against the productions of historical romance, will be found not wholly inapplicable to those which assume the graver and more authentic name of history. The reader will be miserably deluded if, while he reads history, he suffers himself to imagine that he is reading facts. Profound scholars are so well aware of this, that, when they would study the history of any country, they pass over the historians that have adorned and decorated the facts, and proceed at once to the naked and scattered materials, out of which the historian constructed his work. This they do, that they may investigate the story for themselves; or, more accurately speaking, that each man, instead of resting in the inventions of another, may invent his history for himself, and possess his creed as he possesses his property, single and incommunicable.

Philosophers, we are told, have been accustomed by old prescription to blunder in the dark; but there is perhaps no darkness, if we consider the case maturely, so complete as that of the historian. It is a trite observation, to say that the true history of a public transaction is never known till many years after the event. The places, the dates, those things which immediately meet the eye of the spectator, are indeed as well known as they are ever likely to be. But the comments of the actors come out afterwards; to what are we the wiser? Whitlock and Clarendon, who lived upon the spot, differ as much in their view of the transactions, as Hume and the whig historians have since done.[1] Yet all are probably honest. If you be a superficial thinker, you will take up with one or other of their representations, as best suits your prejudices. But, if you are a profound one, you will

---

[1] Bulstrode Whitlocke (1605-75) and the Earl of Clarendon (1609-74) wrote opposed accounts of the Glorious Revolution, as Hume and the Whig historians later did.

see so many incongruities and absurdities in all, as deeply to impress you with the scepticism of history.

The man of taste and discrimination, who has properly weighed these causes, will be apt to exclaim, Dismiss me from the falsehood and impossibility of history, and deliver me over to the reality of romance.

The conjectures of the historian must be built upon a knowledge of the characters of his personages. But we never know any man's character. My most intimate and sagacious friend continually misapprehends my motives. He is in most cases a little worse judge of them than myself and I am perpetually mistaken. The materials are abundant for the history of Alexander, Caesar, Cicero and Queen Elizabeth. Yet how widely do the best informed persons differ respecting them? Perhaps by all their character is misrepresented. The conjectures therefore respecting their motives in each particular transaction must be eternally fallacious. The writer of romance stands in this respect upon higher ground. He must be permitted, we should naturally suppose, to understand the character which is the creature of his own fancy.

The writer of romance then is to be considered as the writer of real history; while he who was formerly called the historian, must be contented to step down into the place of his rival, with this disadvantage, that he is a romance writer, without the ardour, the enthusiasm, and the sublime licence of imagination, that belong to that species of composition. True history consists in a delineation of consistent, human character, in a display of the manner in which such a character acts under successive circumstances, in showing how character increases and assimilates new substances to its own, and how it decays, together with the catastrophe into which by its own gravity it naturally declines.

There is however, after all, a deduction to be made from this eulogium of the romance writer. To write romance is a task too great for the powers of man, and under which he must be expected to totter. No man can hold the rod so even, but that it will tremble and vary from its course. To sketch a few bold outlines of character is no desperate undertaking; but to tell precisely how such a person would act in a given situation, requires a sagacity scarcely less than divine. We never conceive a situation, or those minute shades in a character that would modify its conduct. Naturalists tell us that a single grain of sand more or less on the surface of the earth, would have altered its motion, and, in process of ages, have diversified its events. We have no reason to suppose in this respect, that what is true in matter, is false in morals.

Here then the historian in some degree, though imperfectly, seems to recover his advantage upon the writer of romance. He indeed does not understand the character he exhibits, but the events are taken out of his hands and determined by the system of the universe, and therefore, as far as his information extends, must be true. The romance writer, on the other hand, is continually straining at a foresight to which his faculties are incompetent, and continually fails. This is ludicrously illustrated in those few romances which attempt to exhibit the fictitious history of nations. That principle only, which holds the planets in their course, is competent to produce that majestic series of events which characterises flux, and successive multitudes.

The result of the whole, is that the sciences and the arts of man are alike imperfect, and almost infantine. He that will not examine the collections and the efforts of man, till absurdity and folly are extirpated from among them, must be contented to remain in ignorance, and wait for the state, where he expects that faith will give place to sight, and conjecture be swallowed up in knowledge.

Appendix B: The Foundations of the Novel: Godwin's Political Philosophy and England in the 1790s

1. British Responses to the French Revolution

i. From Edmund Burke, *Reflections on the Revolution in France* (1790)

From Section II, part 3. OF THE RIGHT OF THE PEOPLE TO FORM A GOVERNMENT FOR THEMSELVES

(a) *The Revolution of 1688 does not justify this interpretation*[1]
The third head of right, asserted by the pulpit of the Old Jewry, namely, the "right to form a government for ourselves,"[2] has, at least, as little countenance from anything done at the Revolution, either in precedent or principle, as the two first of their claims. The Revolution was made to preserve our ancient, indisputable laws and liberties and that ancient constitution of government which is our only security for law and liberty. If you are desirous of knowing the spirit of our constitution and the policy which predominated in that great period which has secured it to this hour, pray look for both in our histories, in our records, in our acts of parliament, and journals of parliament, and not in the sermons of the Old Jewry and the after-dinner toasts of the Revolution Society. In the former you will find other ideas and another language. Such a claim is as ill-suited to our temper and wishes as it is unsupported by any appearance of authority. The very idea of the fabrication of a new government is enough to fill us with disgust and horror. We wished at the period of the Revolution, and do now wish, to derive all we possess as *an inheritance from our forefathers.* Upon

---

1   In the "Glorious Revolution" of 1688, Protestant Whigs in England drove out the Catholic King James II and replaced him with his daughter Mary and her husband William, Prince of Orange (in the Netherlands), who re-established a Protestant monarchy.

2   Burke is referring to Richard Price's sermon of November 4, 1789. Richard Price (1723-91) was a prominent Dissenting minister, whose sermon in support of the French Revolution helped provoke Burke's *Reflections.*

that body and stock of inheritance we have taken care not to inoculate any scion alien to the nature of the original plant. All the reformations we have hitherto made have proceeded upon the principle of reverence to antiquity; and I hope, nay, I am persuaded, that all those which possibly may be made hereafter will be carefully formed upon analogical precedent, authority, and example.

Our oldest reformation is that of Magna Charta. You will see that Sir Edward Coke, that great oracle of our law, and indeed all the great men who follow him, to Blackstone, are industrious to prove the pedigree of our liberties. They endeavor to prove that the ancient charter, the Magna Charta of King John, was connected with another positive charter from Henry I and that both the one and the other were nothing more than a reaffirmance of the still more ancient standing law of the kingdom. In the matter of fact, for the greater part these authors appear to be in the right; perhaps not always; but if the lawyers mistake in some particulars, it proves my position still the more strongly, because it demonstrates the powerful prepossession toward antiquity, with which the minds of all our lawyers and legislators, and of all the people whom they wish to influence, have been always filled, and the stationary policy of this kingdom in considering their most sacred rights and franchises as *inheritance*....

(b) *British liberties closely linked with a hereditary monarchy are an old inheritance and a factor of social stability.*
You will observe that from Magna Charta to the Declaration of Right it has been the uniform policy of our constitution to claim and assert our liberties as an entailed inheritance derived to us from our forefathers, and to be transmitted to our posterity – as an estate specially belonging to the people of this kingdom, without any reference whatever to any other more general or prior right. By this means our constitution preserves a unity in so great a diversity of its parts. We have an inheritable crown, an inheritable peerage, and a House of Commons and a people inheriting privileges, franchises, and liberties from a long line of ancestors.

This policy appears to me to be the result of profound reflection, or rather the happy effect of following nature, which is wisdom without reflection, and above it. A spirit of innovation is generally the result of a selfish temper and confined views. People will not look forward to posterity, who never look backward to their ancestors. Besides, the people of England well know that the idea of inheritance furnishes a sure principle of conservation and a sure principle of transmission, without at all excluding a principle of improvement. It leaves acquisition free, but it secures what it acquires. Whatever advantages are obtained by a state proceeding on these maxims are locked fast as in a sort of family settlement, grasped as in a kind of mortmain forever. By a constitutional policy, working after the pattern of nature, we receive, we hold, we transmit our government and our privileges in the same manner in which we enjoy and transmit our property and our lives. The institutions of policy, the goods of fortune, the gifts of providence, are handed down to us, and from us, in the same course and order. Our political system is placed in a just correspondence and symmetry with the order of the world and with the mode of existence decreed to a permanent body composed of transitory parts, wherein, by the disposition of a stupendous wisdom, molding together the great mysterious incorporation of the human race, the whole, at one time, is never old or middle-aged or young, but, in a condition of unchangeable constancy, moves on through the varied tenor of perpetual decay, fall, renovation, and progression. Thus, by preserving the method of nature in the conduct of the state, in what we improve we are never wholly new; in what we retain we are never wholly obsolete. By adhering in this manner and on those principles to our forefathers, we are guided not by the superstition of antiquarians, but by the spirit of philosophic analogy. In this choice of inheritance we have given to our frame of polity the image of a relation in blood, binding up the constitution of our country with our dearest domestic ties, adopting our fundamental laws into the bosom of our family affections, keeping inseparable and cherishing with the warmth of all their combined and mutually reflected charities our state, our hearths, our sepulchres, and our altars.

(b) *The true concept of the rights of man*
Far am I from denying in theory, full as far is my heart from
withholding in practice (if I were of power to give or to withhold) the real rights of men. In denying their false claims of
right, I do not mean to injure those which are real, and are such
as their pretended rights would totally destroy. If civil society
be made for the advantage of man, all the advantages for which
it is made become his right. It is an institution of beneficence;
and law itself is only beneficence acting by a rule. Men have a
right to live by that rule; they have a right to do justice, as
between their fellows, whether their fellows are in public function or in ordinary occupation. They have a right to the fruits
of their industry and to the means of making their industry
fruitful. They have a right to the acquisitions of their parents,
to the nourishment and improvement of their offspring, to
instruction in life, and to consolation in death. Whatever each
man can separately do, without trespassing upon others, he has
a right to do for himself; and he has a right to a fair portion of
all which society, with all its combinations of skill and force,
can do in his favor. In this partnership all men have equal
rights, but not to equal things. He that has but five shillings in
the partnership has as good a right to it as he that has five hundred pounds has to his larger proportion. But he has not a right
to an equal dividend in the product of the joint stock; and as to
the share of power, authority, and direction which each individual ought to have in the management of the state, that I
must deny to be amongst the direct original rights of man in
civil society, for I have in my contemplation the civil social
man, and no other. It is a thing to be settled by convention.

If civil society be the offspring of convention, that convention must be its law. That convention must limit and modify all
the descriptions of constitution which are formed under it.
Every sort of legislative, judicial, or executory power are its
creatures. They can have no being in any other state of things;
and how can any man claim under the conventions of civil
society rights which do not so much as suppose its existence –

rights which are absolutely repugnant to it? One of the first motives to civil society, and which becomes one of its fundamental rules, *is that no man should be judge in his own cause.* By this each person has at once divested himself of the first fundamental right of uncovenanted man, that is, to judge for himself and to assert his own cause. He abdicates all right to be his own governor. He inclusively, in a great measure, abandons the right of self-defense, the first law of nature. Men cannot enjoy the rights of an uncivil and of a civil state together. That he may obtain justice, he gives up his right of determining what it is in points the most essential to him. That he may secure some liberty, he makes a surrender in trust of the whole of it.

(c) *The true nature of government*
Government is not made in virtue of natural rights, which may and do exist in total independence of it, and exist in much greater clearness and in a much greater degree of abstract perfection; but their abstract perfection is their practical defect. By having a right to everything they want everything. Government is a contrivance of human wisdom to provide for human wants. Men have a right that these wants should be provided for by this wisdom. Among these wants is to be reckoned the want, out of civil society, of a sufficient restraint upon their passions. Society requires not only that the passions of individuals should be subjected, but that even in the mass and body, as well as in the individuals, the inclinations of men should frequently be thwarted, their will controlled, and their passions brought into subjection. This can only be done by a power out of themselves, and not, in the exercise of its function, subject to that will and to those passions which it is its office to bridle and subdue. In this sense the restraints on men, as well as their liberties, are to be reckoned among their rights. But as the liberties and the restrictions vary with times and circumstances and admit to infinite modifications, they cannot be settled upon any abstract rule; and nothing is so foolish as to discuss them upon that principle.

The moment you abate anything from the full rights of men, each to govern himself, and suffer any artificial, positive limitation upon those rights, from that moment the whole organization of government becomes a consideration of convenience. This it is which makes the constitution of a state and the due distribution of its powers a matter of the most delicate and complicated skill. It requires a deep knowledge of human nature and human necessities, and of the things which facilitate or obstruct the various ends which are to be pursued by the mechanism of civil institutions. The state is to have recruits to its strength, and remedies to its distempers. What is the use of discussing a man's abstract right to food or medicine? The question is upon the method of procuring and administering them. In that deliberation I shall always advise to call in the aid of the farmer and the physician rather than the professor of metaphysics.

The science of constructing a commonwealth, or renovating it, or reforming it, is, like every other experimental science, not to be taught *a priori*. Nor is it a short experience that can instruct us in that practical science, because the real effects of moral causes are not always immediate; but that which in the first instance is prejudicial may be excellent in its remoter operation, and its excellence may arise even from the ill effects it produces in the beginning. The reverse also happens: and very plausible schemes, with very pleasing commencements, have often shameful and lamentable conclusions. In states there are often some obscure and almost latent causes, things which appear at first view of little moment, on which a very great part of its prosperity or adversity may most essentially depend. The science of government being therefore so practical in itself and intended for such practical purposes – a matter which requires experience, and even more experience than any person can gain in his whole life, however sagacious and observing he may be – it is with infinite caution that any man ought to venture upon pulling down an edifice which has answered in any tolerable degree for ages the common purposes of society, or on building it up again without having models and patterns of approved utility before his eyes.

From Section V, part 3. *THE OTHER (SOCIAL) REVOLU-TIONS THE ENLIGHTENMENT HAS BROUGHT ABOUT*

(a) *The age of chivalry is gone and sophisters, economists and calculators have taken over*
This mixed system of opinion and sentiment had its origin in the ancient chivalry; and the principle, though varied in its appearance by the varying state of human affairs, subsisted and influenced through a long succession of generations even to the time we live in. If it should ever be totally extinguished, the loss I fear will be great. It is this which has given its character to modern Europe. It is this which has distinguished it under all its forms of government, and distinguished it to its advantage, from the states of Asia and possibly from those states which flourished in the most brilliant periods of the antique world. It was this which, without confounding ranks, had produced the noble equality and handed it down through all the gradations of social life. It was this opinion which mitigated kings into companions and raised private men to be fellows with kings. Without force or opposition, it subdued the fierceness of pride and power, it obliged sovereigns to submit to the soft collar of social esteem, compelled stern authority to submit to elegance, and gave a dominating vanquisher of laws to be subdued by manners.

But now all is to be changed. All the pleasing illusions which made power gentle and obedience liberal, which harmonized the different shades of life, and which, by a bland assimilation, incorporated into politics the sentiments which beautify and soften private society, are to be dissolved by this new conquering empire of light and reason. All the decent drapery of life is to be rudely torn off. All the superadded ideas, furnished from the wardrobe of a moral imagination, which the heart owns and the understanding ratifies as necessary to cover the defects of our naked, shivering nature, and to raise it to dignity in our own estimation, are to be exploded as ridiculous, absurd, and antiquated fashion.

On this scheme of things, a king is but a man, a queen is but a woman; a woman is but an animal, and an animal not of the highest order. All homage paid to the sex in general as such, and without distinct views, is to be regarded as romance and folly. Regicide, and parricide, and sacrilege are but fictions of superstition, corrupting jurisprudence by destroying its simplicity. The murder of a king, or a queen, or a bishop, or a father are only common homicide; and if the people are by any chance or in any way gainers by it, a sort of homicide much the most pardonable, and into which we ought not to make too severe a scrutiny.

On the scheme of this barbarous philosophy, which is the offspring of cold hearts and muddy understandings, and which is as void of solid wisdom as it is destitute of all taste and elegance, laws are to be supported only by their own terrors and by the concern which each individual may find in them from his own private speculations or can spare to them from his own private interests. In the groves of their academy, at the end of every vista, you see nothing but the gallows. Nothing is left which engages the affections on the part of the commonwealth. On the principles of this mechanic philosophy, our institutions can never be embodied, if I may use the expression, in persons so as to create in us love, veneration, admiration, or attachment. But that sort of reason which banished the affections is incapable of filling their place. These public affections, combined with manners, are required sometimes as supplements, sometimes as correctives, always as aids to law. The precept given by a wise man, as well as a great critic, for the construction of poems is equally true as to states: – *Non satis est pulchra esse poemata, dulcia sunto.*[1]

From Section VI, part 2. THE SOCIAL FUNCTION OF JUST PREJUDICES

(a) *Through just prejudice a man's duty becomes a part of his nature*
You see, Sir, that in this enlightened age I am bold enough to confess that we are generally men of untaught feelings, that,

---

1 "It is not enough that poems be beautiful; they must also be affecting." Horace, *Ars Poetica* 99.

instead of casting away all our old prejudices, we cherish them to a very considerable degree, and, to take more shame to ourselves, we cherish them because they are prejudices; and the longer they have lasted and the more generally they have prevailed, the more we cherish them. We are afraid to put men to live and trade each on his own private stock of reason, because we suspect that this stock in each man is small, and that the individuals would do better to avail themselves of the general bank and capital of nations and of ages. Many of our men of speculation, instead of exploding general prejudices, employ their sagacity to discover the latent wisdom which prevails in them. If they find what they seek, and they seldom fail, they think it more wise to continue the prejudice, with the reason involved, than to cast away the coat of prejudice and to leave nothing but the naked reason; because prejudice, with its reason, has a motive to give action to that reason, and an affection which will give it permanence. Prejudice is of ready application in the emergency; it previously engages the mind in a steady course of wisdom and virtue and does not leave the man hesitating in the moment of decision skeptical, puzzled, and unresolved. Prejudice renders a man's virtue his habit, and not a series of unconnected acts. Through just prejudice, his duty becomes a part of his nature.

ii. From Thomas Paine, *Rights of Man* (1791)

AMONG the incivilities by which nations or individuals provoke and irritate each other, Mr. Burke's pamphlet on the French Revolution is an extraordinary instance. Neither the People of France, nor the National Assembly, were troubling themselves about the affairs of England, or the English Parliament; and why Mr. Burke should commence an unprovoked attack upon them, both in parliament and in public, is a conduct that cannot be pardoned on the score of manners, nor justified on that of policy.

There is scarcely an epithet of abuse to be found in the English language, with which Mr. Burke has not loaded the French Nation and the National Assembly. Everything which rancour, prejudice, ignorance, or knowledge could suggest, are poured forth in the copious fury of near four hundred pages. In the strain and on the plan Mr. Burke was writing, he might have written on to as many thousands. When the tongue or the pen is let loose in a frenzy of passion, it is the man, and not the subject, that becomes exhausted....

Not sufficiently content with abusing the National Assembly, a great part of his work is taken up with abusing Dr. Price (one of the best-hearted men that lives), and the two societies in England known by the name of the Revolution Society, and the Society for Constitutional Information.

Dr. Price had preached a sermon on the 4th of November 1789, being the anniversary of what is called in England, the Revolution which took place in 1688. Mr. Burke, speaking of this sermon, says, "The Political Divine proceeds dogmatically to assert, that, by the principles of the Revolution, the people of England have acquired three fundamental rights:

1. To choose our own governors.
2. To cashier them for misconduct.
3. To frame a government for ourselves."

Dr. Price does not say that the right to do these things exists in this or in that person, or in this or in that description of persons, but that it exists in the whole; that it is a right resident in the nation. – Mr. Burke, on the contrary, denies that such a right exists in the nation, either in whole or in part, or that it exists anywhere; and, what is still more strange and marvelous, he says, "that the people of England utterly disclaim such a right, and that they will resist the practical assertion of it with their lives and fortunes." That men should take up arms, and spend their lives and fortunes, not to maintain their rights, but to maintain they have not rights, is an entirely new species of discovery, and suited to the paradoxical genius of Mr. Burke....

As Mr. Burke occasionally applies the poison drawn from his horrid principles, not only to the English nation, but to the French Revolution and the National Assembly, and charges that august, illuminated and illuminating body of men with the epithet of *usurpers*, I shall, *sans ceremonie*, place another system of principles in opposition to his.

The English Parliament of 1688 did a certain thing, which, for themselves and their constituents, they had a right to do, and which it appeared right should be done: But, in addition to this right, which they possessed by delegation, *they set up another right by assumption*, that of binding and controlling posterity to the end of time. The case, therefore, divides itself into two parts; the right which they possessed by delegation, and the right which they set up by assumption. The first is admitted; but, with respect to the second, I reply –

There never did, there never will, and there never can exist a parliament, or any description of men, or any generation of men, in any country, possessed of the right or the power of binding and controlling posterity to the "*end of time*," or of commanding for ever how the world shall be governed, or who shall govern it; and therefore, all such clauses, acts or declarations, by which the makers of them attempt to do what they have neither the right nor the power to do, nor the power to execute, are in themselves null and void. – Every age and generation must be as free to act for itself, in all cases, as the ages and generations which preceded it. The vanity and presumption of governing beyond the grave, is the most ridiculous and insolent of all tyrannies. Man has no property in man; neither has any generation a property in the generations which are to follow. The parliament or the people of 1688, or of any other period, has no more right to dispose of the people of the present day, or to bind or to control them *in any shape whatever*, than the parliament of the people of the present day have to dispose of, bind or control those who are to live a hundred or a thousand years hence. Every generation is, and must be, competent to all the purposes which its occasions require. It is the living, and not the dead, that are to be accommodated. When man ceases to be, his power and his wants cease with him; and having no longer any participation in the concerns of this world, he has no longer any authority in directing who shall be its governors, or how is government shall be organized, or how administered.

I am not contending for nor against any form of government, nor for nor against any party here or elsewhere. That which a whole nation chooses to do, it has a right to do. Mr. Burke says, No. Where then *does* the right exist? I am contending for the rights of the *living*, and against their being willed away, and controlled and contracted for, by the manuscript assumed authority of the dead; and Mr. Burke is contending for the authority of the dead over the rights and freedom of the living. There was a time when kings disposed of their crowns by will upon their deathbeds, and consigned the people, like beasts of the field, to whatever successor they appointed. This is now so exploded as scarcely to be remembered, and so monstrous as hardly to be believed: But the parliamentary clauses upon which Mr. Burke builds his political church, are of the same nature....

We now come more particularly to the affairs of France. Mr. Burke's book has the appearance of being written as instruction to the French nation; but if I may permit myself the use of an extravagant metaphor, suited to the extravagance of the case, it is darkness attempting to illuminate light.

While I am writing this, there are accidentally before me some proposals for a declaration of rights by the Marquis de Lafayette (I ask his pardon for using his former address, and do it only for distinction's sake) to the National Assembly, on the 11th of July 1789, three days before the taking of the Bastille; and I cannot but remark with astonishment how opposite the sources are from which that Gentleman and Mr. Burke draw their principles. Instead of referring to musty records and mouldy parchments to prove that the rights of the living are lost, "renounced and abdicated for ever," by those who are now no more, as Mr. Burke has done, M. de Lafayette applies to the living world, and emphatically says, "Call to mind the sentiments which Nature has engraved in the heart of every citizen, and which take a new force when they are solemnly recognized by all: – For a nation to love liberty, it is sufficient that she knows it; and to be free, it is sufficient that she wills it." How dry, barren, and obscure is the source from which Mr. Burke labours! And how ineffectual, though gay with flowers, are all his declamation and his arguments, compared with these clear, concise, and soul-animating sentiments! Few and short as they are, they lead on to a vast field of generous and manly thinking, and do not finish, like Mr. Burke's periods, with music in the ear, and nothing in the heart....

But there are many points of view in which this revolution may be considered. When despotism has established itself for ages in a country, as in France, it is not in the person of the King only that it resides. It has the appearance of being so in show, and in nominal authority; but it is not so in practice, and in fact. It has its standard everywhere. Every office and department has its despotism, founded upon custom and usage. Every place has its Bastille, and every Bastille its despot. The original hereditary despotism resident in the person of the King, divides and subdivides itself into a thousand shapes and forms, till at last the whole of it is acted by deputation. This was the case in France; and against this species of despotism, proceeding on through an endless labyrinth of office till the source of it is scarcely perceptible, there is no mode of redress. It strengthens itself by assuming the appearance of duty, and tyrannizes under the pretence of obeying....

When we see a man dramatically lamenting in a publication intended to be believed, that, "*The age of chivalry is gone!*" that "*The glory of Europe is extinguished for ever!*" that "*The unbought grace of life*" (If any one knows what it is), "*the cheap defence of nations, the nurse of manly sentiment and heroic enterprise, is gone!*" and all this because the Quixote age of chivalry nonsense is gone, what opinion can we form of his judgment, or what regard can we pay to his facts? In the rhapsody of his judgement, he has discovered a world of windmills, and his sorrows are, that there are no Quixotes to attack them. But if the age of aristocracy, like that of chivalry, should fall, (and they had originally some connexion), Mr. Burke, the trumpeter of the Order, may continue his parody to the end, and finish with exclaiming, "Othello's occupation's gone!" ...

There is a general enigma running through the whole of Mr. Burke's book. He writes in a rage against the National Assembly; but what is he enraged about? ... It is not the Nation of France that Mr. Burke means, but the COURT; and every Court in Europe, dreading the same fate, is in mourning. He writes neither in the character of a Frenchman nor an Englishman, but in the fawning character of that creature known in all countries, and a friend to none, a COURTIER.

From the Conclusion

When we survey the wretched condition of man under the monarchical and hereditary systems of Government, dragged from his home by one power, or driven by another, and impoverished by taxes more than by enemies, it becomes evident that those systems are bad, and that a general revolution in the principle and construction of Governments is necessary.

What is government more than the management of the affairs of a Nation? It is not, and from its nature cannot be, the property of any particular man or family, but of the whole community, at whose expense it is supported; and though by force or contrivance it has been usurped into an inheritance, the usurpation cannot alter the right of things. Sovereignty, as a matter of right, appertains to the Nation only, and not to any individual; and a Nation has at all times an inherent indefeasible right to abolish any form of Government it finds inconvenient, and establish such as accords with its interest, disposition, and happiness. The romantic and barbarous distinction of men into Kings and subjects, though it may suit the condition of courtiers, cannot that of citizens; and is exploded by the principle upon which Governments are now founded. Every citizen is a member of the Sovereignty, and, as such, can acknowledge no personal subjection; and his obedience can be only to the laws.

When men think of what Government is, they must necessarily suppose it to possess a knowledge of all the objects and matters upon which its authority is to be exercised. In this view of Government, the republican system, as established by America and France, operates to embrace the whole of a Nation; and the knowledge necessary to the interest of all the parts, is to be found in the centre, which the parts by representation form: But the old Governments are on a construction that excludes knowledge as well as happiness; Government by monks, who know nothing of the world beyond the walls of a convent, is as consistent as government by Kings.

What were formerly called Revolutions, were little more than a change of persons, or an alteration of local circumstances. They rose and fell like things of course, and had nothing in their existence or their fate that could influence beyond the spot that produced them. But what we now see in the world, from the Revolutions of America and France, are a renovation of the natural order of things, a system of principles as universal as truth and the existence of man, and combining moral with political happiness and national prosperity.

I. *Men are born and always continue free, and equal in respect of their rights. Civil distinctions, therefore, can be founded only on public utility.*

II. *The end of all political associations is the preservation of the natural and imprescriptible rights of man; and these rights are liberty, property, security, and resistance of oppression.*

III. *The Nation is essentially the source of all Sovereignty; nor can any* INDIVIDUAL, *or* ANY BODY OF MEN, *be entitled to any authority which is not expressly derived from it.*

In these principles, there is nothing to throw a Nation into confusion by inflaming ambition. They are calculated to call forth wisdom and abilities, and to exercise them for the public good, and not for the emolument or aggrandizement of particular descriptions of men or families. Monarchical sovereignty, the enemy of mankind, and the source of misery, is abolished; and sovereignty itself is restored to its natural and original place, the Nation. Were this the case throughout Europe, the cause of wars would be taken away.

2. From William Godwin, *Enquiry Concerning Political Justice and its Influence on General Virtue and Happiness* (1793).

i. From Book I, Chapter V, "Influence of Political Institutions Exemplified"

A third disadvantage that is apt to connect poverty with discontent consists in the insolence and usurpation of the rich. If the poor man would in other respects compose himself in philosophic indifference, and, conscious that he possesses every thing that is truly honourable to man as fully as his rich neighbour, would look upon the rest as beneath his envy, his neighbour would not permit him to do so. He seems as if he could never be satisfied with his possessions unless he can make the spectacle of them grating to others; and that honest self-esteem, by which his inferior might otherwise arrive at apathy, is rendered the instrument of galling him with oppression and injustice. In many countries justice is avowedly made a subject of solicitation, and the man of the highest rank and most splendid connections almost infallibly carries his cause against the unprotected and friendless. In countries where this shameless practice is not established, justice is frequently a matter of expensive purchase, and the man with the longest purse is proverbially victorious. A consciousness of these facts must be expected to render the rich little cautious of offence in his dealings with the poor, and to inspire him with a temper overbearing, dictatorial and tyrannical. Nor does this indirect oppression satisfy his despotism. The rich are in all such countries directly or indirectly the legislators of the state; and of consequence are perpetually reducing oppression into a system, and depriving the poor of that little commonage of nature as it were, which might otherwise still have remained to them....

First then, legislation is in almost every country grossly the favourer of the rich against the poor. Such is the character of the game laws, by which the industrious rustic is forbidden to destroy the animal that preys upon the hopes of his future subsistence, or to supply himself with the food that unsought thrusts itself in his path. Such was the spirit of the late revenue laws of France, which in several of their provisions fell exclusively upon the humble and industrious, and exempted from their operation those who were best able to support it. Thus in England the land tax at this moment produces half a million less than it did a century ago, while the taxes on consumption have experienced an addition of thirteen millions per annum during the same period. This is an attempt, whether effectual or not, to throw the burthen from the rich upon the poor, and as such is an exhibition of the spirit of legislation. Upon the same principle robbery and other offences, which the wealthier part of the community have no temptation to commit, are treated as capital crimes, and attended with the most rigorous, often the most inhuman punishments. The rich are encouraged to associate for the execution of the most partial and oppressive positive laws. Monopolies and patents are lavishly dispensed to such as are able to purchase them. While the most vigilant policy is employed to prevent combinations of the poor to fix the price of labour, and they are deprived of the benefit of that prudence and judgment which would select the scene of their industry.

Secondly, the administration of law is not less iniquitous than the spirit in which it is framed. Under the late government of France the office of judge was a matter of purchase, partly by an open price advanced to the crown, and partly by a secret douceur paid to the minister. He, who knew best how to manage his market in the retail trade of justice, could afford to purchase the good will of its functions at the highest price. To the client justice was avowedly made an object of personal solicitation, and a powerful friend, a handsome woman, or a proper present, were articles of much greater value than a good cause. In England the criminal law is administered with tolerable impartiality so far as regards the trial itself; but the number of capital offences, and of consequence the frequency of pardons, open even here a wide door to favour and abuse. In causes relating to property the practice of law is arrived at such a pitch as to render all justice ineffectual. The length of our chancery suits, the multiplied appeals from court to court, the enormous fees of counsel, attorneys, secretaries, clerks, the drawing of briefs, bills, replications and rejoinders, and what has sometimes been called the "glorious uncertainty" of the law, render it frequently more advisable to resign a property than to contest it, and particularly exclude the impoverished claimant from the faintest hope of redress.

ii. From Book III, Chapter 6, "Of Obedience"

Having enquired into the just and legitimate source of authority, we will next turn our attention to what has usually been considered as its correlative, obedience. This has always been found a subject of peculiar difficulty, as well in relation to the measure and extent of obedience, as to the source of our obligation to obey.

The true solution will probably be found in the observation that obedience is by no means the proper correlative. The object of government, as has been already demonstrated, is the exertion of force. Now force can never be regarded as an appeal to understanding; and therefore obedience, which is an act of the understanding or will, can have no legitimate connection with it. I am bound to submit to justice and truth, because they approve themselves to my judgment. I am bound to co-operate with government, as far as it appears to me to coincide with these principles. But I submit to government when I think it erroneous, merely because I have no remedy.

No truth can be more simple, at the same time that no truth has been more darkened by the glosses of interested individuals, than that one man can in no case be bound to yield obedience to any other man or set of men upon earth.

iii. From Book IV, Chapter IV, "Of the Cultivation of Truth"

All these reasonings are calculated to persuade us that the most precious boon we can bestow upon others is virtue, that the highest employment of virtue is to propagate itself. But, as virtue is inseparably connected with knowledge in my own mind, so can it only by knowledge be communicated to others. How can the virtue we have just been contemplating be created, but by infusing comprehensive views and communicating energetic truths? Now that man alone is qualified to give these views, and communicate these truths, who is himself pervaded with them.

Let us suppose for a moment virtuous dispositions as existing without knowledge or outrunning knowledge, the last of which is certainly possible, and we shall presently find how little such virtue is worthy to be propagated. The most generous views will in such cases frequently lead to the most nefarious actions. A Calvin will burn Servetus, and a Digby generate the gunpowder treason.[1] But, to leave these extreme instances, in all cases where mistaken virtue leads to cruel and tyrannical actions, the mind will be soured and made putrescent by the actions it perpetrates. Truth, immortal and ever present truth, is so powerful, that, in spite of all his inveterate prejudices, the upright man will suspect himself, when he resolves upon an action that is at war with the plainest principles of morality. He will become melancholy, dissatisfied and anxious. His firmness will degenerate into obstinacy, and his justice into inexorable severity. The farther he pursues his system, the more erroneous will he become. The farther he pursues it, the less will he be satisfied with it. As truth is an endless source of tranquillity and delight, error will be a prolific fountain of new mistakes and discontent....

From the whole of the subject it seems to appear, that men of talents, even when they are erroneous, are not destitute of virtue, and that there is a degree of guilt of which they are incapable. There is no ingredient that so essentially contributes to a virtuous character as a sense of justice. Philanthropy, as contradistinguished to justice, is rather an unreflecting feeling, than a rational principle. It leads to an absurd indulgence, which is frequently more injurious than beneficial even to the individual it proposes to favour. It leads to a blind partiality,

---

1   Michael Servetus (1511-53) was a Spanish doctor and theologian, burned for heresy in 1553 in Geneva at the instigation of John Calvin (1509-64), the radical Protestant theologian. Sir Everard Digby (1578-1606) was one of the participants in the Gunpowder Treason plot to blow up King James I and the British Parliament on November 5, 1605.

inflicting calamity without remorse upon many perhaps, in order to promote the imagined interest of a few. But justice measures by one inflexible standard the claims of all, weighs their opposite pretensions, and seeks to diffuse happiness, because happiness is the fit and reasonable adjunct of a conscious being. Wherever therefore a strong sense of justice exists, it is common and reasonable to say, that in that mind exists considerable virtue, though the individual from an unfortunate concurrence of circumstances may with all his great qualities be the instrument of a very small portion of benefit. Can great intellectual energy exist without a strong sense of justice?

It has no doubt resulted from a train of speculation similar to this, that poetical readers have commonly remarked Milton's devil to be a being of considerable virtue. It must be admitted that his energies centred too much on personal regards. But why did he rebel against his maker? It was, as he himself informs us, because he saw no sufficient reason for that extreme inequality of rank and power which the creator assumed. It was because prescription and precedent form no adequate ground for implicit faith. After his fall, why did he still cherish the spirit of opposition? From a persuasion that he was hardly and injuriously treated. He was not discouraged by the apparent inequality of the contest: because a sense of reason and justice was stronger in his mind, than a sense of brute force: because he had much of the feelings of an Epictetus or a Cato,[1] and little of those of a slave. He bore his torments with fortitude, because he disdained to be subdued by despotic power. He sought revenge, because he could not think with tameness of the unexpostulating authority that assumed to dispose of him. How beneficial and illustrious might the temper from which these qualities flowed have proved with a small diversity of situation!

Let us descend from these imaginary existences to real history. We shall find that even Cæsar and Alexander had their virtues. There is great reason to believe that, however mistaken

---

1   Epictetus (*c.* AD 60-140) was a Stoic philosopher, Cato (234-149 BC) a Roman politician who committed suicide rather than fall into his enemies' hands.

was their system of conduct, they imagined it reconcileable and even conducive to the general good. If they had desired the general good more earnestly, they would have understood better how to promote it.

Upon the whole it appears, that great talents are great energies, and that great energies cannot flow but from a powerful sense of fitness and justice. A man of uncommon genius is a man of high passions and lofty design; and our passions will be found in the last analysis to have their surest foundation in a sentiment of justice. If a man be of an aspiring and ambitious temper, it is because at present he finds himself out of his place, and wishes to be in it. Even the lover imagines that his qualities or his passion give him a title superior to that of other men. If I accumulate wealth, it is because I think that the most rational plan of life cannot be secured without it; and, if I dedicate my energies to sensual pleasures, it is that I regard other pursuits as irrational and visionary. All our passions would die in the moment they were conceived were it not for this reinforcement. A man of quick resentment, of strong feelings, and who pertinaciously resists every thing that he regards as an unjust assumption, may be considered as having in him the seeds of eminence. Nor is it easily to be conceived that such a man should not proceed from a sense of justice to some degree of benevolence; as Milton's hero felt real compassion and sympathy for his partners in misfortune.

iv. From Book IV, Chapter VI, "Inferences from the Doctrine of Necessity"

First then it appears, that, in the emphatical and refined sense in which the word has sometimes been used, there is no such thing as action. Man is in no case strictly speaking the beginner of any event or series of events that takes place in the universe, but only the vehicle through which certain causes operate, which causes, if he were supposed not to exist, would cease to operate. Action however, in its more simple and obvious sense, is sufficiently real, and exists equally both in mind and in matter. When a ball upon a billiard board is struck by a person playing, and afterwards impinges upon a second ball, the ball which was first in motion, is said to act upon the second, though it operate in the strictest conformity to the impression it received, and the motion it communicates be precisely determined by the circumstances of the case. Exactly similar to this, upon the principles already explained, are the actions of the human mind. Mind is a real cause, an indispensible link in the great chain of the universe; but not, as has sometimes been supposed, a cause of that paramount description, as to supersede all necessities, and be itself subject to no laws and methods of operation....

Is this view of things incompatible with the existence of virtue?

If by virtue we understand, the operation of an intelligent being in the exercise of an optional power, so that under the same precise circumstances it might or might not have taken place, undoubtedly it will annihilate it.

But the doctrine of necessity does not overturn the nature of things. Happiness and misery, wisdom and error will still be distinct from each other, and there will still be a connexion between them. Wherever there is distinction, there is ground for preference and desire, or on the contrary for neglect and aversion. Benevolence and wisdom will be objects worthy to be desired, misery and error worthy to be disliked. If therefore by virtue we mean that principle which asserts the preference of the former over the latter, its reality will remain undiminished by the doctrine of necessity....

Correlative to the feelings of resentment, indignation and anger against the offences of others, are those of repentance, contrition and sorrow for our own. As long as we admit of an essential difference between virtue and vice, no doubt all erroneous conduct, whether of ourselves or others, will be regarded with disapprobation. But it will in both cases be considered, under the system of necessity, as a link in the great chain of events which could not have been otherwise than it is. We shall therefore no more be disposed to repent of our own faults than of the faults of others. It will be proper to view them both as actions injurious to the public good, and the repetition of which is to be deprecated. Amidst our present imperfections it will perhaps be useful to recollect what is the error by which we are most easily seduced. But, in proportion as our views extend, we shall find motives sufficient to the practice of virtue, without any partial retrospect to ourselves, or recollection of our own propensities and habits.

v. From Book VII, Chapter I, "Limitations of the Doctrine of Punishment which Result from the Principles of Morality"

The justice of punishment therefore, in the strict import of the word, can only be a deduction from the hypothesis of free-will, and must be false, if human actions are necessary. Mind, as was sufficiently apparent when we treated of that subject, is an agent, in no other sense than matter is an agent. It operates and is operated upon, and the nature, the force and line of direction of the first, is exactly in proportion to the nature, force and line of direction of the second. Morality in a rational and designing mind is not essentially different from morality in an inanimate substance. A man of certain intellectual habits is fitted to be an assassin, a dagger of a certain form is fitted to be his instrument. The one or the other excites a greater degree of disapproba-tion, in proportion as its fitness for mischievous purposes appear, to be more inherent and direct. I view a dagger on this account with more disapprobation than a knife, which is per-haps equally adapted for the purposes of the assassin; because the dagger has few or no beneficial uses to weigh against those that are hurtful, and because it has a tendency by means of asso-ciation to the exciting of evil thoughts. I view the assassin with more disapprobation than the dagger, because he is more to be feared, and it is more difficult to change his vicious structure or take from him his capacity to injure. The man is propelled to act by necessary causes and irresistible motives, which, having once occurred, are likely to occur again. The dagger has no quality adapted to the contraction of habits, and, though it have committed a thousand murders, is not at all more likely (unless so far as those murders, being known, may operate as a slight associated motive with the possessor) to commit murder again.

Except in the articles here specified, the two cases are exactly parallel. The assassin cannot help the murder he commits any more than the dagger.

vi. From Book VIII, Chapter II, "Benefits Arising from the Genuine System of Property"

Its first effect [of the established system of property] is that which we have already mentioned, a sense of dependence. It is true that courts are mean spirited, intriguing and servile, and that this disposition is transferred by contagion from them to all ranks of society. But property brings home a servile and truckling spirit by no circuitous method to every house in the nation. Observe the pauper fawning with abject vileness upon his rich benefactor, and speechless with sensations of gratitude for having received that which he ought to have claimed with an erect mien, and with a consciousness that his claim was irresistible. Observe the servants that follow in a rich man's train, watchful of his looks, anticipating his commands, not daring to reply to his insolence, all their time and their efforts under the direction of his caprice. Observe the tradesman, how he studies the passions of his customers, not to correct, but to pamper them, the vileness of his flattery and the systematical constancy with which he exaggerates the merit of his commodities. Observe the practices of a popular election, where the great mass are purchased by obsequiousness, by intemperance and bribery, or driven by unmanly threats of poverty and persecution. Indeed "the age of chivalry is" not "gone!"[1] The feudal spirit still survives, that reduced the great mass of mankind to the rank of slaves and cattle for the service of a few.

---

1   A reference to Section V, Part 3, of Edmund Burke's *Reflections on the Revolution in France*. See p. 474 of this edition.

3. From William Godwin, *Enquiry Concerning Political Justice* (1796).

i. From Book I, Chapter V, "The Voluntary Actions of Men Originate in Their Opinions"

"According to the ideas here delivered, men always proceed in their voluntary actions upon judgments extant to their understanding. Such judgments must be attended with consciousness; and, were this hypothesis a sound one, nothing could be more easy than for a man in all cases to assign the precise reason that induced him to any particular action. The human mind would then be a very simple machine, always aware of the grounds upon which it proceeded, and self-deception would be impossible. But this statement is completely in opposition to experience and history. Ask a man the reason why he puts on his clothes, why he eats his dinner, or performs any other ordinary action of his life. He immediately hesitates, endeavours to recollect himself, and often assigns a reason the most remote from what the true philosophy of motive would have led us to expect. Nothing is more clear, than that the moving cause of this action was not expressly present to his apprehension at the time he performed it. Self-deception is so far from impossible, that it is one of the most ordinary phenomena with which we are acquainted. Nothing is more usual than for a man to impute his actions to honourable motives, when it is nearly demonstrable that they flowed from some corrupt and contemptible source. On the other hand many persons suppose themselves to be worse, than an impartial spectator will find any good reason to believe them. A penetrating observer will frequently be able to convince his neighbour that upon such an occasion he was actuated by motives very different from what he imagined. Philosophers to this hour dispute whether human beings in their most virtuous exertions, are under the power of disinterested benevolence, or merely of an enlightened self-interest. Here then we are presented, in one or other of these sets of philosophers, with a striking instance of men's acting from motives diametrically opposite to those which they suppose to be the guides of their conduct. Self-examination is to a proverb one of the most arduous of those tasks which true virtue imposes." . . .

Perhaps no action of a man arrived at years of maturity is, in the sense above defined, perfectly voluntary; as there is no demonstration in the higher branches of the mathematics, which contains the whole of its proof within itself, and does not depend upon former propositions, the proofs of which are not present to the mind of the learner. The subtlety of the human mind in this respect is incredible. Many single actions, if carefully analysed and traced to their remotest source, would be found to be the complex result of different motives, to the amount perhaps of some hundreds.

In the mean time it is obvious to remark, that the perfection of the human character consists in approaching as nearly as possible to the perfectly voluntary state. We ought to be upon all occasions prepared to render a reason of our actions. We should remove ourselves to the farthest distance from the state of mere inanimate machines, acted upon by causes of which they have no understanding. We should be cautious of thinking it a sufficient reason for an action, that we are accustomed to perform it, and that we once thought it right. The human understanding has so powerful a tendency to improvement, that it is more than probable that, in many instances, the arguments which once appeared to us sufficient, would upon re-examination appear inadequate and futile. We should therefore subject them to perpetual revisal. In our speculative opinions and our practical principles we should never consider the book of enquiry as shut. We should accustom ourselves not to forget the reasons that produced our determination, but be ready upon all occasions clearly to announce and fully to enumerate them....

Let us attend for a moment to the general result of the preceding discussions. The tendency of the whole is, to ascertain an important principle in the science of the human mind. If the arguments here adduced be admitted to be valid, it necessarily follows, that whatever can be adequately brought home to the conviction of the understanding, may be depended upon as affording a secure hold upon the conduct. We are no longer at liberty to consider man as divided between two independent principles, or to imagine that his inclinations are in any case inaccessible through the medium of his reason. We find the thinking principle within us to be uniform and simple; in consequence of which we are entitled to conclude, that it is in every respect the proper subject of education and persuasion, and is susceptible of unlimited improvement. There is no conduct, in itself reasonable, which the refutation of error, and dissipating of uncertainty, will not make appear to be such. There is no conduct which can be shown to be reasonable, the reasons of which may not sooner or later be made impressive, irresistible, and matter of habitual recollection. Lastly, there is no conduct, the reasons of which are thus conclusive and thus communicated, which will not infallibly and uniformly be adopted by the man to whom they are communicated.

ii. From Book II, Chapter V, "Of Rights"

Morality is nothing else but that system, which teaches us to contribute upon all occasions, to the extent of our power, to the well-being and happiness of every intellectual and sensitive existence. But there is no action of our lives, which does not in some way affect that happiness. Our property, our time, and our faculties, may all of them be made to contribute to this end. The periods, which cannot be spent in the active production of happiness, may be spent in preparation. There is not one of our avocations or amusements, that does not, by its effects, render us more or less fit to contribute our quota to the general utility. If then every one of our actions fall within the province of morals, it follows that we have no rights in relation to the selecting them. No one will maintain, that we have a right to trespass upon the dictates of morality.

It has been observed by natural philosophers, that a single grain of sand more or less in the structure of the earth, would have produced an infinite variation in its history. If this be true in inanimate nature, it is much more so in morals. The encounter of two persons of opposite sexes, so as to lead to the relation of marriage, in many cases obviously depends upon the most trivial circumstances, any one of which being changed, the relation would not have taken place. Let the instance be the father and mother of Shakespear. If they had not been connected, Shakespear would never have been born. If any accident had happened to the wife during pregnancy, if she had on any day set her foot half an inch too far and fallen down a flight of stairs, if she had turned down one street instead of another, through which, it may be, some hideous object was passing along, Shakespear might never have come alive into the world. The determination of mind, in consequence of which the child contracts some of his earliest propensities, which call out his curiosity, industry and ambition, or on the other hand leave him unobserving, indolent and phlegmatic, is produced by circumstances so minute and subtle, as in few instances to have been made the subject of history. The events which afterwards produce his choice of a profession or pursuit, are not less precarious. Every one of these incidents, when it occurred, grew out of a series of incidents that had previously taken place. Every thing is connected in the universe. If any man asserted that, if Alexander had not bathed in the river Cydnus, Shakespear would never have written, it would be impossible to affirm that his assertion was untrue.

iii. From Book VIII, Chapter II, "Principles of Property"

The third degree of property, is that which occupies the most vigilant attention in the civilised states of Europe. It is a system, in whatever manner established, by which one man enters into the faculty of disposing of the produce of another man's industry. There is scarcely any species of wealth, expenditure or splendour, existing in any civilised country, that is not, in some way, produced, by the express manual labour, and corporeal industry, of the inhabitants of that country. The spontaneous productions of the earth are few, and contribute little to wealth, expenditure or splendour. Every man may calculate, in every glass of wine he drinks, and every ornament he annexes to his person, how many individuals have been condemned to slavery and sweat, incessant drudgery, unwholsome food, continual hardships, deplorable ignorance, and brutal insensibility, that he may be supplied with these luxuries. It is a gross imposition, that men are accustomed to put upon themselves, when they talk of the property bequeathed to them by their ancestors. The property is produced by the daily labour of men who are now in existence. All that their ancestors bequeathed to them, was a mouldy patent, which they show, as a title to extort from their neighbours what the labour of those neighbours has produced....

The most desirable state of human society would require, that the quantity of manual labour and corporal industry to be exerted, and particularly that part of it which is not the un-influenced choice of our own judgment, but is imposed upon each individual by the necessity of his affairs, should be reduced within as narrow limits as possible. For any man to enjoy the most trivial accommodation, while, at the same time, a similar accommodation is not accessible to every other member of the community, is, absolutely speaking, wrong. All refinements of luxury, every invention that tends to give employment to a great number of labouring hands, are directly adverse to the propagation of happiness. Every additional tax that is laid on, every new channel that is opened for the expenditure of the public money, unless it be compensated (which is scarcely ever the case) by an equivalent deduction from the luxuries of the rich, is so much added to the general stock of ignorance, drudgery and hardship.... Those who, by fraud or force, have usurped the power of buying and selling the labour of the great mass of the community, are sufficiently disposed to take care that they should never do more than subsist. An object of industry added to or taken from the general stock, produces a momentary difference, but things speedily fall back into their former state. If every labouring inhabitant of Great Britain were able and willing to-day to double the quantity of his industry, for a short time he would derive some advantage from the increased stock of commodities produced. But the rich would speedily discover the means of monopolising this produce, as they had done the former. A small part of it only, could consist in commodities essential to the simple and unadulterated subsistence of man, or be fairly distributed through the community. All that is luxury and superfluity, would increase the accommodations of the rich, and perhaps, by reducing the price of luxuries, augment the number of those to whom such accommodations were accessible. But it would afford no alleviation to the great mass of the community. Its more favoured members would give their inferiors no greater wages for twenty hours' labour, suppose, than they now do for ten....

Every man should be urged to the performance of his duty, as much as possible, by the instigations of reason alone. Compulsion to be exercised by one human being over another, whether individually, or in the name of the community, if in any case to be resorted to, is at least to be resorted to only in cases of indispensible urgency. It is not therefore to be called in, for the purpose of causing one individual to exert a little more, or another a little less, of productive industry. Neither is it to be called in, for the purpose of causing the industrious individual to make the precise distribution of his produce which he ought to make. Hence it follows that, while the present erroneous opinions and prejudices respecting accumulation continue, actual accumulation will, in some degree, take place.

For, let it be observed that, not only no well informed community will interfere with the quantity of any man's industry, or the disposal of its produce, but the members of every such well informed community will exert themselves, to turn aside the purpose of any man who shall be inclined, to dictate to, or restrain, his neighbour in this respect.

The most destructive of all excesses, is that, where one man shall dictate to another, or undertake to compel him to do, or refrain from doing, any thing (except, as was before stated, in cases of the most indispensible urgency), otherwise than with his own consent. Hence it follows that the distribution of wealth in every community, must be left to depend upon the sentiments of the individuals of that community. If, in any society, wealth be estimated at its true value, and accumulation and monopoly be regarded as the seals of mischief, injustice and dishonour, instead of being treated as titles to attention and deference, in that society the accommodations of human life will tend to their level, and the inequality of conditions will be destroyed. A revolution of opinions is the only means of attaining to this inestimable benefit. Every attempt to effect this purpose by means of regulation, will probably be found ill conceived and abortive. Be this as it will, every attempt to correct the distribution of wealth by individual violence, is certainly to be regarded as hostile to the first principles of public security....

It will not be difficult to find the instances, in every polished country of Europe, in which civil institution, instead of granting, to the inequalities of accumulation, only what could not prudently be withheld, has exerted itself, for the express purpose of rendering these inequalities greater and more oppressive. Such instances are, the feudal system, and the system of ranks, seignorial duties, fines, conveyances, entails, the distinction, in landed property, of freehold, copyhold and manor, the establishment of vassalage, and the claim of primogeniture. We here distinctly recognise the policy of men who, having first gained a superiority, by means of the inevitable openings before cited, have made use of this superiority, for the purpose of conspiring to monopolise whatever their rapacity could seize, in direct opposition to every dictate of the general interest. These articles fall under the distinction, brought forward in the outset, of laws or practices not common to all civilised communities, but peculiar to certain ages and countries.

It should seem therefore that these are institutions, the abolition of which is not to be entirely trusted to the silent hostility of opinion, but that they are to be abrogated by the express and positive decision of the community.

4. From Godwin's Correspondence.

i. Letter from "Mucius" addressed to John Reeves, on Thomas Paine and the English Constitution, from the *Morning Chronicle*, February 8, 1793.

To Mr. REEVES, Chairman of the Society for protecting Liberty and Property against Republicans and Levellers.

Sir,

You have conceived or professed an alarm for the safety of your country. Some of the grounds of that alarm are as follows: Associations have been entered into in various parts of the kingdom, for the purpose of diffusing opinions and concentrating exertions among the middling and lower orders of the community. Pamphlets, tending to produce rancour and dissension, have been both sold at a trivial price, and distributed gratis. Hand-bills have been pasted upon the walls and dispersed in the streets. Absurd and barbarous inscriptions have been scribbled on the outside of the churches and other buildings.

Sir, I agree with you that these things are unseemly and injurious. I am no friend to force either on the part of the Populace or of Government: but, if you had employed none but the regular and moderate interference of coercion to suppress them, you would certainly never have heard from me upon the present occasion. Your exertions have been indefatigable. – The Associations are silent; the pamphlets are no longer sold; the walls have ceased to be made the instruments of disloyalty. If you had stopped here, you might have passed for an honest man. But your next step brands you and your party (except those who blindly follow your insidious guidance) for the most ignominious of cowards.

You deprive the intemperate advocates of Reform of the instruments they were so forward to employ. You tell them, and you tell them true, that such instruments are disgraceful to a civilised community. – And what is the next thing you do? Will any one, not a witness to the transaction, believe me when I affirm, that a man of liberal education, a writer of repute upon the History of English Law, could forget himself so far as, having wrested these weapons from his antagonists, instead of dashing them indignantly to the earth, to employ them himself for the purpose of wounding those he had already disarmed?

Sir, you may boldly challenge all the annals of despotism and injustice to match this iniquity. You have all the honours of originality. Dionysius and Nero would have scorned so base a proceeding. You must have the credit of adding a new phenomena to the philosophy of the human mind. There is no instance upon record of a man, avowedly and in the face of a great nation, silencing his antagonist that he only might be heard; and coming forward gravely with this maxim, "Hear one side only, that you may be able to judge."

Good God! what species of monster is this Thomas Paine, that all the rules of equity cease to be rules the moment he is the subject of animadversion? I was myself present at the trial of this man. We all know by what means a verdict was procured: by repeated proclamations, by all the force, and all the fears of the kingdom being artfully turned against one man. As I came out of court, I saw hand-bills, in the most vulgar and illiberal styled distributed, entitled, The Confession of Thomas Paine. I had not walked three streets, before I was encountered by ballad singers, roaring in cadence rude, a miserable set of scurrilous stanzas upon his private life. You know best, Sir, what concern you had in these things. But the people of England will need very strong evidence to convince them of your innocence. Other parts of the transaction you openly boast. No sooner were the cheap pamphlets of Mr. Paine, and the hand-bills of his partisans suppressed, than pamphlets, printed sheets, and hand-bills without number issued from the press in answer to his reasonings.

You may imagine, Sir, that you shall escape the detestation annexed to such proceedings: but you are mistaken. An infatuated people may, for the present, even applaud them. But you shall be recorded to the latest posterity for shameless injustice and effrontery unparalleled. If it were possible that such machinations should be crowned with success, you should be inscribed, not perhaps on your tomb, but on the deathless page of history – "Reeves, the assassin of the Liberties of Englishmen."

What is there in these instruments of hand-bills, ballads, and pamphlets, that should render them, thought before profane, sacred the moment they come into your hands? If Mr. Paine may not inflame the vulgar against the House of Brunswick, by what right do you excite them; for that is the direct tendency of your proceedings, to pull down the houses and destroy the property of Dissenters? Sir, a liberal, a manly, and an honest mind, would not point the animosities of the populace against any man, as little against the obscurest individual, as against the Princes upon the throne. What is more clear than that you ought, in the outset of this business, to have chosen your alternative; either to have met these Republicans at their own weapons, or to have proscribed all such irregular and ungenerous warfare? But you resolved to engross to yourself all the advantages of both plans; and, having power on your side, to make that serve you instead of argument, decency, and truth.

I said, in my former letter, that I was educated in a respect for the English Constitution. You have done more, Sir, to annihilate that respect in the breasts of your countrymen, than any Englishman in this inglorious reign. Is it possible for me to value any thing that I do not deem consonant to truth? Is it possible for me to be the champion of a system that will not stand the test of argument? What sort of Constitution is it that you pretend to recommend to our reverence? A Constitution that can be defended only by your declarations, while your antagonists are silenced – a Constitution that must always be applauded, and never examined: a Constitution that can only be supported by hand-bills, ballads, and misrepresentation, that exists by the shouts of a mob, and the burning of an effigy. Sir, you are the most virulent of all libellers. One column of your hand-bills is as effectual to excite serious doubts in the dispassionate mind against the English Constitution, as all Mr. Paine's pamphlets. I impeach you at the bar of my country as a conspirator against its liberties.

But you, Sir, are an insignificant individual; it is only your vices and your impudence that exalt you into notice. I turn therefore from you to the Public at large. I call upon my countrymen to consider whether this character, which your proceedings have fixed upon the English Constitution, be that to which it is truly entitled; if it be, for God's sake let it be fairly known, that every man of honour may set his face against the Constitution. It is the worst feature of the worst governments that they may not be written or spoken against. What should Englishmen fear? If our Constitution be truly good, it will pass every ordeal, and come out the purer for the scrutiny to which it shall have been subjected. Every sincere advocate for the Constitution will wish for no better than a fair and tranquil field of debate, and an honourable surrender on both sides of all the means of inflammation. He would think that he betrayed his sentiments and blasted his cause, the moment he had recourse to one illiberal and insidious weapon.

Sir, I affirm, without the shadow of hesitation, that you are not a sincere adherent of the English Constitution. I appeal to your own evidence to prove my assertion. Every disputant that breaks out into rage, scurrility, and violence, proves that he has no confidence in the strength of his arguments. If you believed what you pretend to believe, you would scorn to take advantages; you would not fear for the event of the contest. I affirm more than this, that you have formed a plan for the destruction of the Constitution. Can you be a friend to the Revolution of 1688? Can you be a friend to the Bill of Rights? I appeal to every article of your proceedings. You employ the vulgar artifice of raising a cry against Democrats and Levellers, and then hope, under favour of this cry, to strip us of every one of our privileges. But you shall be disappointed. A very few months only shall elapse, before multitudes of your present followers will be astonished at the first success of your deception, and will execrate the deceiver. It is not in the nature of Englishmen to be juggled by so paltry and palpable a device out of every thing that is dear to them.

MUCIUS.

ii. Letter from Mucius "To Such Persons As May Be Appointed to Serve Upon Juries for the Trial of Seditious and Treasonable Words," on the Trial of Daniel Crichton, from the *Morning Chronicle*, March 30, 1793.

Gentlemen,
The importance of your situation is so great as to impress me with considerable awe when I undertake to address you. It is out of all comparison superior to that which you would be called on to fill, if you were individually Members of the British House of Commons. There, with the best intentions

and the most constant resolution, you might be overpowered by influence or by numbers. In your situation as jurymen this is impossible. You have to expostulate with a small number of your countrymen, untramelled in the mysteries of political corruption, and who from education are more open than their more learned and self-satisfied countrymen to the voice of conviction. The very circumstance of the unanimity which the law requires from them, renders them tractable. It is impossible that one juryman, fully possessed of the reason of the case, and endowed with moderation, intrepidity, and benevolence, should not bring over the whole pannel to his side....

Great God, what honours might not a just and intrepid juryman deserve in times of clamour and alarm like these! How I envy you the patriotism of which your situation is capable! One upright and intelligent juryman might put a close to that scene of persecution which is the disgrace of Britain. Let us figure this man to ourselves, contending with the prejudices and passions of his colleagues. Let us figure his mildness and equanimity in the midst of their impatience, and perhaps their scurrility. Let us figure to ourselves that clear, simple, unornamented understanding, which furnishes him with a plain and undeniable answer to all their objections. Let us suppose truth by his instrumentality victorious, not merely over the passions, but over the understanding of united numbers. Let us follow him from the apartment in which the jury was inclosed, back to the presence of the judge. Let us suppose it possible that a judge should be found, the slave of a court, the unrelenting adversary of the prosecuted party, who shall undertake to brow beat, to insult, and to compel the jury into a desertion of their duty. Let us figure to ourselves this juryman defeating by plain good sense and determined honesty, the practised wiles of a hoary lawyer invested with the symbols of authority. Let us farther conceive him attacked by the venal pens of prostituted writers as turbulent and factious; and let him show by a frank and simple tale, that he is the true friend of order and peace, and that his pannel by their verdict have redeemed their country.

Is there no such man? Oh, for a man like this, to suspend the torrent of absolute power, and prove that I am not fallen upon an age of savage barbarism and ignorance! Oh, for a man like this, to inscribe his name upon the pages of history, and eclipse with its lustre the renown of Hampden and Russel!

Integrity never appears more divine in human form, than when it bursts forth from obscurity: than when it appears, unornamented by rank, unassisted by learning, invincible, though alone; than when it disdains circumlocution, tells a plain and artless tale, and shows that all the powers of sophistry and intimidation are impotent, when set in opposition to it....

Your duty is so plain in the present case, that nothing can be more astonishing than the universal consent with which all late juries in such questions have neglected it.... The character required in the present case, is so simple and moderate, that the most shameless government would scarcely venture to pro-scribe it.

He need not be the enemy, but on the contrary, may be the warmest friend of the English Constitution. He has only to bear in mind one plain principle, and to say, "This man, though he differs from me, may yet be honest." Liberty does not consist in giving a favourable verdict when we think the accused party has delivered the exact truth. It consists in allowing every man, in the way of enquiry and argument, to speak what he thinks. It consists in delivering us from the empire of spies and inform-ers in not subjecting us to perpetual watchfulness and reserve, in not putting an instrument of vengeance into the hands of every man who many think proper to quarrel with it.

Good God! what had this poor tallow-chandler, this Crich-ton done, that ought to have rendered him amenable to the jus-tice of his country? Was he to overturn the government of his country? Was he engaged in any conspiracy for that purpose? Nothing of the kind is alledged against him. He merely got drunk, and then talked idly, as men when they are drunk usual-ly do. Is the fabric of our law in danger from the ramblings of an intoxicated journeyman? No, he has not overturned the constitution of his country; but the constitution of his country is to be overturned by prosecuting him. Do you know how much injury this man may sustain from his sentence? Do you know what miserable wretches the people of England become, if they live in hourly fear of such prosecutions? There is not one of us, however sober and loyal, that is not obnoxious to them. Where is the man that was never intoxicated? Who will answer for himself, that, when intoxicated, he may not be played upon by some spy, some treasury runner, some mercenary informer, some malignant enemy, and provoked to say, "Damn the King!" Would to Heaven it were practicable for this cause to be tried over again, and that the laws of my country would permit me, who am no lawyer, to plead it. It would be impossible for any jury to refill the clear justice and the strong reason with which it might be pleaded. It might be brought home to every one of them. They might be shown that such a prosecution could lead only to slavery in its most atrocious form, and that none but the foulest traitors (had the reason of the case been fully and powerfully exhibited to them) could bring in a verdict of guilty.

iii. Letter to Joseph Gerrald on the eve of his trial for sedition, January 23, 1794, from Charles Kegan Paul, *William Godwin, his Friends and Contemporaries* (London, 1876), vol. I, 125-28.

I cannot recollect the situation in which you are in a few days to be placed without emotions of respect, and I had almost said of envy. For myself I will never adopt any conduct for the express purpose of being put upon my trial, but if I be ever so put, I will consider that day as a day of triumph.

Your trial, if you so please, may be a day such as England, and I believe the world, never saw. It may be the means of converting thousands, and, progressively, millions, to the cause of reason and public justice. You have a great stake, you place your fortune, your youth, your liberty, and your talents on a single throw. If you must suffer, do not, I conjure you, suffer without making use of this opportunity of telling a tale upon which the happiness of nations depends. Spare none of the resources of your powerful mind. Is this a day of reserve, a day to be slurred over in neglect – the day that constitutes the very crisis of your fate?

Never forget that juries are men, and that men are made of

penetrable stuff: probe all the recesses of their souls. Do not spend your strength in vain defiance and empty vaunting. Let every syllable you utter be fraught with persuasion. What an event would it be for England and mankind if you could gain an acquittal! Is not such an event worth striving for? It is in man, I am sure it is, to effect that event. Gerrald, you are that man. Fertile in genius, strong in moral feeling, prepared with every accomplishment that literature and reflection can give. Stand up to the situation – be wholly yourself. "I know," I would say to this jury, "that you are packed, you are picked and culled from all the land by the persons who have at present the direction of public affairs, as men upon whom they can depend; but I do not fear the event; I do not believe you will be slaves. I do not believe that you will be inaccessible to considerations irresistible in argument, and which speak to all the genuine feelings of the human heart. I have been told that there are men upon whom truth, truth fully and adequately stated, will make no impression. It is a vile and groundless calumny upon the character of the human mind. This is my theory, and I now come before *you* for the practice."

If you should fail of a verdict – but why should I suppose it? – this manner of stating your defence is best calculated to persuade the whole audience, and the whole world, for the same reason that it is best calculated to persuade a jury....

You stand on as clear ground as man can stand on. You are brought there for meeting in convention to deliberate on grievances. Do not fritter away your defence by anxiety about little things; do not perplex the jury by dividing their attention. Depend upon it, that if you can establish to their full conviction the one great point – the lawfulness of your meeting – you will obtain a verdict....

Above all, let me entreat you to abstain from harsh epithets and bitter invective. Show that you are not terrible but kind, and anxious for the good of all. Truth will lose nothing by this. Truth can never gain by passion, violence, and resentment. It is never so strong as in the firm, fixed mind, that yields to the emotions neither of rage nor fear. It is by calm and recollected boldness that we can shake the pillars of the vault of heaven.

How great will you appear if you show that all the injustice with which you are treated cannot move you: that you are too great to be wounded by their arrows; that you still hold the steadfast course that becomes the friend of man, and that while you expose their rottenness you harbour no revenge. The public want men of this unaltered spirit, whom no persecution can embitter. The jury, the world will feel your value, if you show yourself such a man: let no human ferment mix in the sacred work.

Farewell; my whole soul goes with you. You represent us all.

Appendix C: Criminal Lives and the State of the Prisons

1. From the Account of Jack Sheppard, in *The Malefactor's Register; or the Newgate Calendar* (1779).

ALTHOUGH only in the twenty-third year of his age when he was executed at Tyburn, on the 16th of November, 1724, Jack Sheppard had become so notorious as a housebreaker and prison-breaker that his exploits were the talk of all ranks of society. A great warrior could not have received greater attention than this famous criminal. Books and pamphlets were written about him; a pantomime at Drury lane, called *Harlequin Sheppard*, was based on the story of his adventures, and so was a three-act farce, called *The Prison-Breaker*. Dozens of songs and glees referred to his prowess, and clergymen preached sermons about him. Sir James Thornhill, the celebrated painter who decorated the dome of St Paul's Cathedral, painted his portrait, from which engravings in mezzotinto were made....

John Sheppard was born in Spitalfields in the year 1702. His father, who was a carpenter, bore the character of an honest man; yet he had another son, named Thomas, who, as well as Jack, turned out a thief. The father dying while the boys were very young, they were left to the care of the mother, who placed Jack at a school in Bishopsgate Street, where he remained two years, and was then put apprentice to a carpenter. He behaved with decency in this place for about four years, when, frequenting the Black Lion alehouse, in Drury Lane, he became acquainted with some abandoned women, among whom the principal was Elizabeth Lyon, otherwise called "Edgworth Bess," from the town of Edgworth, where she was born.

While he continued to work as a carpenter, he often committed robberies in the houses where he was employed, stealing tankards, spoons and other articles, which he carried to Edgworth Bess; but not being suspected of having committed these robberies, he at length resolved to commence housebreaking....

Sheppard's master seemed willing to think well of him, and he remained some time longer in the family; but after associating himself with the worst of company, and frequently staying out the whole night, his master and he quarrelled, and the headstrong youth totally absconded in the last year of his apprenticeship and became connected with a set of villains of Jonathan Wild's gang....

Not long after this Edgworth Bess was apprehended and lodged in the roundhouse of the parish of St Giles's, where Sheppard went to visit her, and the beadle refusing to admit him he knocked him down, broke open the door, and carried her off in triumph – an exploit which acquired him a high degree of credit with the women of abandoned character....

Within a short time after this, as Sheppard and an associate named Benson were crossing Leicester Fields, the latter endeavoured to pick a gentleman's pocket of his watch, but, failing in the attempt, the gentleman called out: "A pickpocket!" – on which Sheppard was taken and lodged in St Ann's Roundhouse, where he was visited by Edgworth Bess, who was detained on suspicion of being one of his accomplices.

On the following day they were carried before a magistrate, and, some persons appearing who charged them with felonies, they were committed to New Prison; and as they passed for husband and wife they were permitted to lodge together in a room known by the name of Newgate Ward.

Sheppard being visited by several of his acquaintances, some of them furnished him with implements to make his escape, and early in the morning, a few days after his commitment, he filed off his fetters and, having made a hole in the wall, he took an iron bar and a wooden one out of the window; but as the height from which he was to descend was twenty-five feet he tied a blanket and sheet together, and, making one of them fast to a bar in the window Edgworth Bess first descended, and Jack followed her.

Having reached the yard, they had still a wall of twenty-two feet high to scale; but climbing up by the locks and bolts of the great gate, they got quite out of the prison, and effected a perfect escape....

At the sessions held at the Old Bailey, in August, 1724, he was indicted for several offences, and among the rest for breaking and entering the house of William Kneebone and stealing one hundred and eight yards of woollen cloth and other articles; and, being capitally convicted, received sentence of death.... On Monday, the 30th of August, 1724, a warrant was sent to Newgate for the execution of Sheppard, with other convicts under sentence of death.

It is proper to observe that in the old jail of Newgate there was within the lodge a hatch, with large iron spikes, which hatch opened into a dark passage, whence there were a few steps into the condemned hold. The prisoners being permitted to come down to the hatch to speak with their friends, Sheppard, having been supplied with instruments, took an opportunity of cutting one of the spikes in such a manner that it might be easily broken off.

On the evening of the above-mentioned 30th of August, two women of Sheppard's acquaintance going to visit him, he broke off the spike and, thrusting his head and shoulders through the space, the women pulled him down, and he effected his escape, notwithstanding some of the keepers were at that time drinking at the other end of the lodge....

Some of Sheppard's old acquaintances informing him that strict search was being made for him, he and Page retired to Finchley, in the hope of lying there concealed till the diligence of the jail-keepers should relax; but the keepers of Newgate, having intelligence of their retreat, took Sheppard into custody and conveyed him to his old lodgings.

Such steps were now taken as were thought would be effectual to prevent his future escape. He was put into a strong-room called the "Castle," handcuffed, loaded with a heavy pair of irons, and chained to a staple fixed in the floor. The curiosity of the public being greatly excited by his former escape, he was visited by great numbers of people of all ranks, and scarce anyone left him without making him a present in money, though he would have more gladly received a file, a hammer, or a chisel; but the utmost care was taken that none of his visitors should furnish him with such implements.

Notwithstanding this disadvantageous situation, Sheppard was continually employing his thoughts on the means of another escape. On the 14th of October the sessions began at the Old Bailey, and, the keepers being much engaged in attending the court, he thought they would have little time to visit him, and therefore the present juncture would be the most favourable to carry his plan into execution.

About two o'clock on the afternoon of the following day one of the keepers carried him his dinner, and having carefully examined his irons and found them fast, he left him for the day. Some days before this Jack had found a small nail in the room, with which he could, at pleasure, unlock the padlock that went from the chain to the staple in the floor; and in his own account of this transaction he says that he was frequently about the room, and had several times slept on the barracks when the keepers imagined he had not been out of his chair.

The keeper had not left him more than an hour when he began his operations. He first took off his handcuffs and then opened the padlock that fastened the chain to the staple. He next, by mere strength, twisted asunder a small link of the chain between his legs, and then drawing up his fetters as high as he could he made them fast with his garters.

He then attempted to get up the chimney, but had not advanced far before he was stopped by an iron bar that went across it; on which he descended, and with a piece of his broken chain picked out the mortar, and moving a small stone or two, about six feet from the floor, he got out the iron bar, which was three feet long and an inch square, and proved very serviceable to him in his future proceedings.

He in a short time made such a breach as to enable him to get into the red room over the "castle"; and here he found a large nail, which he made use of in his further operations. It was seven years since the door of this red room had been opened, but Sheppard wrenched off the lock in less than seven minutes, and got into the passage leading to the chapel. In this place he found a door which was bolted on the opposite side, but making a hole through the wall he pushed the bolt back, and opened the door.

Arriving at the door of the chapel, he broke off one of the iron spikes, and keeping this for his further use got into an entry between the chapel and the lower leads. The door of this entry was remarkably strong, and fastened with a large lock, and, night coming on, Sheppard was obliged to work in the dark. Notwithstanding this disadvantage he in half-an-hour forced open the box of the lock and opened the door; but this led him to another room still more difficult, for it was barred and bolted as well as locked; however he wrenched the fillet from the main post of the door, and the box and staples came off with it.

It was now eight o'clock, and Sheppard found no further obstruction to his proceedings, for he had only one other door to open, which, being bolted on the inside, was opened without difficulty, and he got over a wall to the upper leads.

His next consideration was how he should descend with the greatest safety. Accordingly he found that the most convenient place for him to alight on would be the turner's house adjoining to Newgate, but as it would have been very dangerous to have jumped to such a depth he went back for the blanket with which he used to cover himself when he slept in the "Castle," and endeavoured to fasten his stocking to the blanket to ease his descent; but not being able to do so, he was compelled to use the blanket alone; wherefore he made it fast to the wall of Newgate with the spike that he took out of the chapel and, sliding down, dropped on the turner's lead just as the clock was striking nine. It happened that the door of the garret next the turner's leads was open, on which he stole softly down two pair of stairs, and heard some company talking in a room. His irons clinking, a woman cried, "What noise is that?" and a man answered, "Perhaps the dog or cat."

Sheppard, who was exceedingly fatigued, returned to the garret and lay down for more than two hours; after which he crept down once more as far as the room where the company were, when he heard a gentleman taking leave of the family, and saw the maid light him downstairs. As soon as the maid returned he resolved to venture all hazards, but in stealing down the stairs he stumbled against a chamber door; but instantly recovering himself, he got into the street.

By this time it was after twelve o'clock, and passing by the watch-house of St Sepulchre he bid the watchman good-morrow; then going up Holborn he turned down Gray's Inn Lane, and about two in the morning got into the fields near Tottenham Court, where he took shelter in a place that had been a cowhouse, and slept soundly about three hours. His fetters being still on, his legs were greatly bruised and swelled, and he dreaded the approach of daylight, lest he should be discovered. He had now above forty shillings in his possession, but was afraid to send to any person for assistance.

At seven in the morning it began to rain hard, and continued to do so all day, so that no person appeared in the fields; and during this melancholy day he would, to use his own expression, have given his right hand for "a hammer, a chisel and a punch." Night coming on, and being pressed by hunger, he ventured to a chandler's little shop in Tottenham Court Road, where he got a supply of bread and cheese, small-beer and some other necessaries, hiding his irons with a long greatcoat. He asked the woman of the house for a hammer, but she had no such utensil; on which he retired to the cowhouse, where he slept that night, and remained all the next day....

Soon after ... Sheppard saw a journeyman shoemaker, to whom he told the same story of the bastard child, and offered him twenty shillings if he would procure a smith's hammer and a punch. The poor man, tempted by the reward, procured them accordingly, and assisted him in getting rid of his irons, which work was completed by five o'clock in the evening.

When night came on, our adventurer tied a handkerchief about his head, tore his woollen cap in several places, and likewise tore his coat and stockings, so as to have the appearance of a beggar; and in this condition he went to a cellar near Charing Cross, where he supped on roast veal and listened to the conversation of the company, all of whom were talking of the escape of Sheppard.

On the Monday he sheltered himself at a public-house of

little trade in Rupert Street, and conversing with the landlady about Sheppard told her it was impossible for him to get out of the kingdom, and that the keepers would certainly have him again in a few days; on which the woman wished that a curse might fall on those who should betray him. Remaining in this place till evening, he went into the Haymarket, where a crowd of people were surrounding two ballad-singers and listening to a song made on his adventures and escape....

On the 31st of October he dined with two women at a public-house in Newgate Street.... Being now grown valiant through an excess of liquor he wandered from ale-houses to gin-shops in the neighbourhood till near twelve o'clock at night, when he was apprehended, in consequence of the information of an ale-house boy who knew him. When taken into custody he was quite senseless, from the quantity and variety of liquors he had drunk, and was conveyed to Newgate in a coach, without being capable of making the least resistance, though he had two pistols then in his possession.

His fame was now so much increased by his exploits that he was visited by great numbers of people, and some of them of the highest quality. He endeavoured to divert them by a recital of the particulars of many robberies in which he had been concerned; and when any nobleman came to see him he never failed to beg that they would intercede with the King for a pardon, to which he thought that his singular dexterity gave him some pretensions.

Having been already convicted, he was carried to the bar of the Court of King's Bench on the 10th of November, and the record of the conviction being read, and an affidavit being made that he was the same John Sheppard mentioned in the record, sentence of death was passed upon him by Mr Justice Powis, and a rule of court was made for his execution on the Monday following....

Even when the day of execution arrived Sheppard did not appear to have given over all expectations of eluding justice; for having been furnished with a penknife he put it in his pocket, with the view, when the melancholy procession came opposite Little Turnstile, of cutting the cord that bound his arms, and throwing himself out of the cart among the crowd, to run through the narrow passage where the sheriff's officers could not follow on horseback, and he had no doubt but that he should make his escape, with the assistance of the mob.

It is not impossible that this scheme might have succeeded; but before Sheppard left the press-yard one Watson, an officer, searching his pockets, found the knife, and was cut with it so as to occasion a great effusion of blood.

Sheppard had yet a further view to his preservation, even after execution; for he desired his acquaintances to put him into a warm bed as soon as he should be cut down and try to open a vein, which he had been told would restore him to life.

He behaved with great decency at the place of execution, and confessed having committed two robberies for which he had been tried and acquitted. He suffered in the twenty-third year of his age. He died with difficulty, and was much pitied by the surrounding multitude. When he was cut down his body was delivered to his friends, who carried him to a public-house in Long Acre, whence he was removed in the evening and buried in the churchyard of St Martin's-in-the-Fields.

2. From John Howard, *The State of the Prisons* (1777).

i. From "General View of Distress in Prisons"

There are prisons, into which whoever looks will, at first sight of the people confined, be convinced, that there is some great error in the management of them: their sallow meagre countenances declare, without words, that they are very miserable. Many who went in healthy, are in few months changed to emaciated dejected objects. Some are seen pining under diseases, "sick, and in prison"; expiring on the floors, in loathsome cells, of pestilential fevers, and the confluent smallpox; victims, I must not say to the cruelty, but I will say to the inattention, of sheriffs, and gentlemen in the commission of the peace.

The cause of this distress is, that many prisons are scantily supplied, and some almost totally destitute of the necessaries of life.

There are several bridewells[1] (to begin with them) in which prisoners have no allowance of food at all. In some, the keeper farms what little is allowed them: and where he engages to supply each prisoner with one or two pennyworth of bread a day, I have known this shrunk to half, sometimes less than half the quantity, cut or broken from his own loaf....

I have asked some keepers, since the late act for preserving the health of prisoners, why no care is taken of their sick: and have been answered, that the magistrates tell them the act does not extend to the bridewells.

In consequence of this, at the quarter sessions you see prisoners covered (hardly covered) with rags; almost famished; and sick of diseases, which the discharged spread where they go; and with which those who are sent to the county gaols infect these prisons.

The same complaint, want of food, is to be found in many county gaols. In above half these, debtors have no bread; although it is granted to the highwayman, the house-breaker, and the murderer: and medical assistance, which is provided for the latter, is withheld from the former. In many of these gaols, debtors who would work are not permitted to have any tools, lest they should furnish felons with them for escape or other mischief. I have often seen these prisoners eating their water-soup (bread boiled in mere water) and heard them say, "We are locked up and almost starved to death." ...

Many prisons have no water. This defect is frequent in bridewells, and town gaols. In the felons' courts of some county gaols there is no water: in some places where there is water, prisoners are always locked up within doors, and have no more than the keeper or his servants think fit to bring them: in one place they were limited to three pints a day each: a scanty provision for drink and cleanliness!...

From hence any one may judge of the probability there is against the health, and life, of prisoners crowded in close rooms, cells, and subterraneous dungeons, for fourteen or fifteen hours out of the four and twenty. In some of those caverns the floor is

---

1   English prisons, specifically houses of correction requiring forced labor, were often called "bridewells," after Bridewell Prison in London.

very damp: in others there is sometimes an inch or two of water: and the straw, or bedding is laid on such floors; seldom on barrack-bedsteads.... Some gaols have no sewers or vaults; and in those that have, if they be not properly attended to, they are, even to a visitant, offensive beyond expression: how noxious then to people constantly confined in those prisons....

In many gaols, and in most bridewells, there is no allowance of bedding or straw for prisoners to sleep on; and if by any means they get a little, it is not changed for months together, so that it is offensive and almost worn to dust. Some lie upon rags, others upon the bare floors. When I have complained of this to the keepers, their justification has been, "The county allows no straw; the prisoners have none but at my cost."

The evils mentioned hitherto affect the health and life of prisoners. I have now to complain of what is pernicious to their morals; and that is, the confining of all sorts of prisoners together: debtors and felons, men and women, the young beginner and the old offender; and with all these, in some counties, such as are guilty of misdemeanors only; who should have been committed to bridewell to be corrected, by diligence and labour; but for want of food, and the means of procuring it in those prisons, are in pity sent to such county gaols as afford these offenders prison-allowance.

Few prisons separate men and women in the daytime. In some counties the gaol is also the bridewell: in others those prisons are contiguous, and the courtyard common. There the petty offender is committed for instruction to the most profligate. In some gaols you see (and who can see it without sorrow) boys of twelve or fourteen eagerly listening to the stories told by practised and experienced criminals, of their adventures, successes, stratagems, and escapes....

I am ready to think, that none who give credit to what is contained in the foregoing pages, will wonder at the havoc made by the gaol-fever. From my own observations in 1773, 1774, and 1775, I was fully convinced that many more prisoners were destroyed by it, than were put to death by all the public executions in the kingdom. This frequent effect of confinement in prison seems generally understood, and shows how full of emphatical meaning is the curse of a severe creditor, who pronounces his debtor's doom to rot in gaol.

ii. From "Bad Customs in Prisons"

A cruel custom obtains in most of our gaols, which is that of the prisoners demanding of a new comer garnish, footing, or (as it is called in some London gaols) chummage. "Pay or strip," are the fatal words. I say fatal, for they are so to some; who having no money, are obliged to give up part of their scanty apparel; and then if they have no bedding or straw to sleep on, contract diseases, which I have known to prove mortal....

Loading prisoners with heavy irons, which make their walking, and even lying down to sleep, difficult and painful, is another custom which I cannot but condemn. In some county gaols and even bridewells the women do not escape this severity: but in London they do: and therefore it is not necessary in the country....

The distress occasioned by chains is increased by varying the towns where quarter-sessions and assizes are held: so that prisoners have to walk in irons ten or fifteen miles to their trial: and sometimes to towns that have no prison; where numbers of both sexes are shut up together for many days and nights in one room. This occasions such confusion and distress, and such shrieks and outcries, as can be better conceived than described. Surely prisoners ought to be conveyed in carts; or else committed at first to the town where the sessions or assizes are to be held. And in that town a proper prison ought to be built.

Gaol delivery is in some counties but once a year. What reparation can be made to a poor creature for the misery he has suffered, and the corruption of his morals, by confinement in a prison near twelve months before a trial, in which, perhaps he is at last to be declared by his country not guilty?

Appendix D: Literary Influences: Crime and Pursuit Narratives and Scenes of Confrontation

1. From Mateo Alemán, *Guzmán de Alfarache* (1599, 1602); from the English translation of James Mabbe, *The Rogue* (London, 1622).

[From the Seconde Booke, Chapter II. In this section, the *picaro* Guzman comes upon Alexandro Bentivoglio, who has stolen goods from him. He appeals first to Alexandro's father, a local dignitary, for restitution, then proceeds to take legal action.]

So that at last, we grew to this conclusion, that I, by a third person, should use some meanes, to have his father talkt withall, making him acquainted with the businesse, and the whole manner how it was carried, giving him a large account of every particular thing, remitting my selfe to his good will and pleasure, how he in his owne discretion should thinke meet I deserv'd to be dealt withall, and that he would not enforce mee (considering my faire manner of proceeding with him) to recover mine owne by rigour of Law, being there was *Evidentia facti*; besides many other pregnant proofes to be produced, that these goods were mine. And so I did, as we had devised; having made choice of a discreet person, who should secretly and with fitting language, deliver thus much unto him. But because Power is commonly accompanied with Pride, and Pride is still attended with Tyranny, he was so farre from compounding the businesse, that he made little reckoning of it, taking it ill at his hands that treated with him about it, wishing him that hee should speake no more of it, deeming it as an affront done unto his honour, and a meere defamation. He feigned him-selfe to be greatly wronged, though he knew well enough that I was he, that was injur'd; and without giving us either good hopes, or good words, he dispatcht my messenger.

When I receiv'd this answere, I hatched a thousand evill imaginations in my heart. But because I would not returne evill for evill, I resolved to talke with some one Lawyer or other of that University, that should be recommended unto me for the nimblenesse of his wit, and soundnesse of judgement ... Whereupon, I being very desirous, that a bill should be exhibited against him, he presently (according to my information) drew one out, which I forthwith presented to the *Auditore del Torrone*, who is there the Judge in all Causes Criminall. But, be it as it may be, whether it were immediately from the Judge him-selfe, or from the Notarie, I know not which, nor from whence, nor how it came to passe, but sure I am, that this businesse of mine was instantly over all the Towne, and particular notice was given thereof unto Alexandro's father. And for that he was a man of authoritie in that Towne, and carried a great hand there amongst them, he hyes him in all haste to the Judge, and there accusing me for this my bold attempt, and inconsiderate rashnesse, (as it pleased him to terme it) he formed a complaint against me, that I had defamed, and dishonoured his house, and that therefore he was of purpose come unto him to desire his lawfull favour, and that he would be pleased to doe him justice, to the end that I might be severely punished for this my presumption. I know not how, but the matter was so carried betweene them, that it had beene better for me, to have held my peace. He was a powerfull man in that Citie, and the Judge (it seemed) was very willing to pleasure him. I began now to feare, that occasions of quarrell would be pickt against me; mole-hils made mountaines; and this my losse, turne to my greater losse; making my undoing, an occasion of my farther undoing. For Love, Interest, and Hatred, are ever maine enemies to the Truth. And in many places, As a man is befriended, so his Cause is ended. But he that hath both money and friends, is sure to worke out his ends. Money is of no great thicknesse, yet it dulls the double edg'd sword of justice, if it but once offer to touch it. Gold, is a heavy mettall; and that makes the ballance of Justice so light....

Well; such was my hard fortune, that being not able to bring in my proofes in so short a time, it so fell out with me, that my Bill of Complaint, was throwne out of the Court, and held as a thing of no validitie or force in Law, and that of the adverse part, tooke place against me; declaring there in Court, that I by this my petition, had framed an infamous Libell against his sonne, by meanes whereof his House, and his honour was much defamed.... That I did it wittingly and willingly, impudently and malitiously, aggravating the matter against me with all the odious termes they could devise, that if I should set them downe one by one, they would take up a whole sheet of paper. Alleaging farther against me, that forasmuch as his sonne, was a quiet, honest, and peaceable Gentleman, and of a good both report, and life, I did deserve I know not what exemplarie punishment, hanging, burning, and drowning, all was too little, that I knew not what to make of it, nor what a Gods name, they would doe with me. Which things, when they were read unto me, I said to my selfe; These men may have healthy bodies, but I am sure they have sicke soules; They may have good purses, but I finde (to my cost) they have bad consciences. I was carelesse, (as one that was confident of a good cause) I never shrunke aside, and as I was afterwards going about my businesse, that my sute might not fall, for want of following, I was taken-up in the midst of the street by an Arrest, and presently carried away to prison, without any other information against me, save only the putting up of my petition, and acknowledging it to be mine.

There is no sword, that hath so keene and sharpe an edge, as Calumnie, and false Accusation: and then cuts deepest, when it is in the hand of a tyrannous Judge; whose force and power is such, that it is able to overthrow, and lay levell with the ground, the best grounded Justice that is, though it have never so sure, never so strong a foundation. Which it doth then most, and most easily, when a poore mans cause comes in his way, who suspects (Poore harmelesse soule) nothing lesse, then to receive hurt from him, to whom he flyes for helpe....

They punisht me, as an unmannerly man of my tongue, a lyar, and a lewd companion. I had spent my moneyes, lost my goods, put in prison, gyves clapt on my legs, treated with evill language, upbraiding mee with many foule and uncivill reproches, unworthy my person, without suffering me to open my mouth in mine owne defence. And when I would have answered their objections, and given them satisfaction by writing, when they saw how the world went with me, my Proctor forsooke me, my Solicitor would not come at me, my Advocate refused to plead for me, so that I only now remained in the power of the publike Notarie. The only comfort that I had, was the generall voice of my wrong, comforting me, that that terrible and fearefull day, would one day come, that the powerfull shall for all his power, be condemned to Hell, and that there, *your potentes, potenter punientur,* your mighty men shall be mightily punished; for that they are accursed of God for perverting of Justice.

2. From *The History of Madamoiselle de St. Phale, Giving a Full Account of The Miraculous Conversion of a Noble French Lady And her Daughter, to the Reformed Religion. With the Defeat of the Intriegues of a Jesuite their Confessor* **(1690), translated from the French (1691).**

[In this early confessional narrative, the speaker describes her childhood in seventeenth-century France as the daughter of a Huguenot (Protestant) father and a strictly Catholic mother. Because her parents have agreed to raise their sons as Protestants and their daughters as Catholics, Mlle. Justine de St. Phale shares her religion with her mother. Goaded by her confessor, her mother persuades Justine to attempt to win her brother over to the Catholic faith. But during their discussions, it is Justine who is convinced of the rightness of the Protestant faith. The excerpt that follows details the first of a series of adventures as Justine is tormented by her vengeful mother. It begins in Chapter IV just as the narrator's traitorous maid spies her writing a letter to her brother Ferdinand, asking for his protection from the wrath of their mother.]

I had left the Door of my Chamber open, and my Traitress seeing that I wrote, hid her self, to see what I would do after I had written, and seeing that I delivered a Billet to the Servant, who was ready to take Horse when I brought it him, she ran and acquainted my Mother with it, who sent after him immediately to stop and search him; but he was gone too far, so that 'twas to no purpose. When my Mother saw this, she doubted lest I had discovered some of her Designs, for which reason she lookt athwart on me for a long time without saying a word to me: She had also fresh Discourses with my Maid, who did such things in my Presence that I had but too much reason to suspect that I was just upon the brink of ruine. I spent this Day in a great deal of perplexity; foreseeing the Afflictions that were like to befall me, which made me imploy all my time in reading the Holy Scriptures and in Prayer.

About Sun-set my Mother sent for me into the Garden to speak with me there. This Message filled me with trembling and terrour, yet I went down to her. I found my Mother alone in one of the Alleys, as soon as she saw me, she looked on me with Eyes that seemed to sparkle with Indignation, yet said nothing to me as neither did I to her; so that for some time we both were silent. At length, your heart is very proud, Mademoiselle *Justine*, said she, to oblige me to speak first. Oh good God, (said I) what may this mean! is it my part, Mother, to speak before you? or not rather to expect your pleasure? She made no reply, but continued on her Walk, and I with her. But immediately I saw two Men enter the Garden, whom I knew not, (where of one seemed of a good Carriage.) as also my Maid with some other men, bringing with them such things as belonged to me.

I saw all these things without being able to guess what they meant, when my Mother asked them aloud, whether all things were ready? Yes, Madam answered the Gentilest, they are. Then my Mother turning to me, spake to me in such terms as were most bitter and cruel. Ingrateful and perfidious Daughter, said she, You have made it your business to deceive your Mother, the day is coming in which I'll revenge me on you, for all the Treasons which you and your Brother have acted against me, and hinder your damnable Projects. An Iron Grate shall secure you, and answer for all your actions during your life. Go, follow these Men, to whom I have given Orders what to do, unless you would have them dragg you to the place where I would have you be. The Passion that seized me on these last words, quite transported me. Drag me! said I, your Anger, Madam, hath blinded you; and lifting up my hand to Heaven, I said, I call God to witness of the perfidiousness and treachery which hath been acted against me, and I pray him to deliver me out of your hand, which I hope he will do. Farewell Madam, after this baseness the worst place in the World will be better to me than to be with you: And having said thus, I turned about, and gave my hand to the Gentilest of the two, and went out of the Garden by a Gate that led towards the High-way, where I found a Coach with four Horses, and four Troopers to guard it: I went into the Coach with my Maid and the two Men. It was above two hours after before I spoke one word; and I was so overwhelmed with weariness, vexation and rage against my Ravishers, that I did not concern my self to enquire who they were, nor what had obliged them to take my Mothers part, and become the Ministers of her Violence.

My Maid was grown so impudent, that she durst insult over my Miseries, laughing at my very face. Take Courage, Madamoiselle, (said she) your condition is not so bad as you imagine. 'Tis bad to extremity answered I coldly, in that I am obliged to have before my Eyes such a Traiteress as you are; and which it may be hath not her like in all the World. See (said she) what Persons get by doing their Duty! they are abused for doing good, you are only enraged against me because I opposed your Intentions, which would have ruined your Soul. If (said I) you make not this insolent Wretch hold her Tongue, I'll throw my self out of the coach though it cost my Life. Ah Madamoiselle, said she, you speak very loftily, as though you were still at *Ponsins*, it may be you would not do amiss to use your self to other Language. The insolence of these words made me turn pale with Anger, which one of the Men perceiving, imposed silence on *Soubrette*: If you hold not your Tongue, (said he to her) I shall find a means to force you to it, which you may repent of: This threatning stopt her mouth.

During this, the Night grew so dark, that in a Wood through which we were to pass, the Coachman mistook his way. The Troopers that guarded us called on all sides, to find some House where they might refresh themselves; but none answered their

Calls but the Eccho of the Wood: At length 'twas resolved to spend the Night where we were; the two men had the discretion to leave the Coach; after having shut it fast, rather to prevent my flight, than to secure me from the injuries of the Cold and Wind as they pretended. I had this day endured so many fatigues, and had taken so little rest some Nights before, that I slept very soundly till the Morning, when our Attendants were in a greater trouble than before, seeing themselves in an unknown Countrey in the midst of a vast Forrest, the Weather very misty, the ways exceedingly bad, without Guide or Victuals, and without hopes of being able to reach any other place.

They unharnassed the Horses of the Coach, and unbridled those of the Troopers, who were more happy than their Masters in that they had wherewith to fill their Bellies. This Accident rejoyced me exceedingly in my Troubles: Well, my Friend (said I) you have carried me away by force to kill me with hunger: I shall take my Death very patiently, for I desire nothing else but to have you keep me Company; this I am sure goes against the grain with you. My Maid was upon the point of despair; in the mean time I had the comfort of insulting over her in my turn. Wretch that thou art, said I, thou art the cause of my Death, but righteous Heaven will that thou dye with me; and whereas I shall receive Consolation and Joy, thou art to expect nothing else but the Torment due to thy Treasons.

These words filled her with Confusion and Despair, for she had not a word to answer. After some time we again set forward; but 'twas past Noon by my Watch, when we found our selves in the same place, and the mist was so thick that we could discern our way no better than in the Night. At length was resolved to send our four Troopers into four parts of the Wood to enquire the way, and to get us some Victuals. Three of them returned to us, after having rid a great way, and taken a great deal of Pains to no purpose, 'Twas then that I believed in earnest that we should be all starved; and having eaten but little for two days before, I was so very weak that I fainted, and they had a great deal of trouble to bring me to my self, though they threw abundance of water on my Face.

Just as I was recovered, the fourth Trooper returned and told us that about a League and half off, we should find a good Village; whereupon I went into the Coach again, but not having strength to sit upright, I was forced to lye along; those that kept me Company placed themselves as well as they could, that they might not incommode me; and at the end of some Hours we came to the Village, to the great joy of all our Company besides my self. In this Village we had some New Adventures, but you must give me leave to deferr the Relationship of them 'till another time.

3. From Daniel Defoe, *The History and Remarkable Life of the Truly Honourable Col. Jacque, Commonly Called Col. Jack* (1722).

[Although born a gentleman, "Colonel Jack" grows up on the streets of London, eventually falling among a gang of thieves. Here he describes some of his early adventures with his fellow thief, Will.]

WE had however in the mean time a great many other successful Enterprizes, some of one kind, some of another, and were never so much as in danger of being apprehended; but my Companion *Will*, who was now grown a Man, and encourag'd by these Advantages fell into quite another Vein of Wickedness, getting acquainted with a wretched Gang of Fellows, that turn'd their Hands to every Thing that was vile....

But come you are grown almost a Man now, and you shall not be always at play at Push-pin, I am got into better Business I assure you, and you shall come into it too, I'll bring you into a brave Gang *Jack, says he*, where you shall see we shall be all Gentlemen.

THEN he told me the Trade it self in short, which was with a Set of Fellows, that had two of the most desperate Works upon their Hands that belong'd to the whole Art of Thieving: *that is to say*, in the Evening they were Footpads, and in the Night they were House-breakers: *Will* told me so many plausible Stories, and talk'd of such great things, that in short, I who had been always us'd to do any thing he bid me do, went with him without any hesitation.

NOTHING is more certain, than that hitherto being partly from the gross Ignorance of my untaught Childhood, as I observ'd before, partly from the hardness, and wickedness of the Company I kept, and add to these, that it was the Business I might be said to be brought up to, I had, *I say*, all the way hitherto, no manner of thoughts about the Good or Evil of what I was embark'd in; consequently, I had no Sense of Conscience, no Reproaches upon my Mind for having done amiss.

YET I had something in me, by what secret Influence I knew not, kept me from the other degrees of Raking and Vice, and in short, from the general Wickedness of the rest of my Companions: For Example, I never us'd any ill Words, no Body ever heard me swear, nor was I given to drink, or to love strong drink. But from that time forward I never had the least Inclination to Swearing, or ill Words, and abhored it when I heard the other Boys do it; as to Drinking, I had no Opportunity, for I had nothing to Drink, but Water or small Beer, that any body gave me in Charity, for they seldom gave away strong Beer; and after I had Money, I neither desir'd strong Beer, or car'd to part with my Money to Buy it....

THEN as to Principle, 'tis true I had no Foundation lay'd in me by Education; and being early led by my fate into Evil, I had the less Sense of its being Evil left upon my Mind: But when I began to grow to an Age of understanding, and to know that I was a Thief, growing up in all manner of Villany, and ripening a-pace for the Gallows, it came often into my thoughts that I was going wrong, that I was in the high Road to the Devil, and several times would stop short, and ask my self, if this was the Life of a Gentleman?

BUT these little things wore off again, as often as they came on, and I follow'd the old Trade again; especially when *Will* came to prompt me as I have observ'd, for he was a kind of a Guide to me in all these things, and I had by Custom and Application, together with seeing his way, learnt to be as acute a Workman as my Master.

BUT to go back where I left off, *Will* came to me as I have said, and telling me how much better Business he was fallen into, would have me go along with him, and I should be a

Gentleman: *Will* it seems understood that Word in a quite differing manner from me; for his Gentleman was nothing more or less than a Gentleman Thief, a Villain of a higher Degree than a Pick-pocket; and one that might do something more Wicked, and better Entituling him to the Gallows, than could be done in our way: But my Gentleman that I had my Eye upon, was another thing quite, tho' I cou'd not really tell how to describe it neither.

HOWEVER the Word took with me, and I went with him; we were neither of us Old, *Will* was about 24, and as for me I was now about 18, and pretty Tall of my Age.

THE first time I went with him, he brought me into the Company only of two more young Fellows; we met at the lower part of *Grays-Inn-Lane*, about an Hour before Sun-set, and went out into the Fields toward a place call'd *Pindar of Wakefield*, where are abundance of Brick-Kilns: Here it was agreed to spread from the Field Path to the Road way, all the way towards *Pancrass Church*, to observe any Chance Game, which as they call'd it, they might shoot Flying: Upon the Path within the Bank, on the side of the Road going towards *Kentish Town*, two of our Gang, *Will*, and one of the other, met a single Gentleman walking a-pace towards the Town, being almost Dark: *Will* Cryed, *Mark ho*, which it seems was the Word, at which we were all to stand still at a distance, come in if he wanted help, and give a Signal if any thing appear'd that was Dangerous.

Will steps up to the Gentleman, stops him, and put the Question, that is, *Sir, your Money?* the Gentleman seeing he was alone, struck at him with his Cane, but *Will* a Nimble strong Fellow flew it upon him, and with Struggling, got him down, then he begg'd for his Life, *Will* having told him with an Oath, that he would Cut his Throat: In that Moment, while this was doing, comes a Hackney Coach along the Road; and the fourth Man who was that way, Crys, *Mark ho*, which was to intimate that it was a Prize, not a Surprize, and accordingly the next Man went up to assist him, where they stop'd the Coach, which had a Doctor of Physick and a Surgeon in it, who had been to Visit some considerable Patient; and I suppose had had considerable Fees; for here they got two good Purses, one with 11 or 12 Guineas, the other Six, with some Pocket Money, two Watches, one Diamond Ring, and the Surgeons Plaister-box, which was most of it full of Silver Instruments.

WHILE they were at this Work, *Will* kept the Man down, who was under him; and tho' he promis'd not to Kill him unless he offer'd to make a Noise, yet he would not let him stir till he heard the Noise of the Coach going on again, by which he knew the jobb was over on that Side: Then he Carried him a little out of the way, ty'd his Hands behind him, and bid him lye still and make no Noise, and he would come back in half an Hour and untie him upon his Word, but if he Cryed out he would come back and Kill him.

[Col. Jack continues the story of the night's adventures, which include robbing a woman who falls to her knees and begs the thieves not to take the only money she has in the world.]

BUT my Heart was full of the poor Woman's Case at *Kentish* Town, and I resolv'd, if possible to find her out, and give her her Money: With the abhorrence that fill'd my Mind at the Cruelty of that Act, there necessarily follow'd a little Distaste of the thing it self, and now it came into my Head with a double force, that this was the High Road to the Devil, and that certainly this was not the Life of a Gentleman!

Will and I parted for that time, but next Morning we met again, and *Will* was mighty Brisk and Merry; and now Col. *Jack, says he*, we shall be Rich very quickly; well, *says I*, and what shall we do, when we are Rich? do, *says he*, we will buy a Couple of good Horses, and go farther a Field; what do you mean by farther a Field, *said I*? why, *says he*, we will take the Highway like Gentlemen, and then we shall get a great deal of Money indeed; well, *says I*, what then? why then, *says he*, we shall live like Gentlemen.

BUT *Will, says I*, if we get a great deal of Money, shan't we leave this Trade off, and sit down, and be Safe and Quiet?

AY, *says Will*, when we have got a great Estate we shall be willing to lay it down; but where, *says I*, shall we be before that time comes, if we should drive on this cursed kind of Trade?

PRETHEE never think of that, *says Will*, if you think of those things, you will never be fit to be a Gentleman; he touch'd me there indeed, for it run much in my Mind still, that I was to be a Gentleman, and it made me Dumb for a while; but I came to my self after a little while, and *I said to him*, pretty Tartly, Why *Will*, do you call this way of Living the Life of a Gentleman?

WHY, *says Will*, why not?

WHY, *says I*, was it like a Gentleman for me to take that Two and Twenty Shillings from a poor antient Woman, when she beg'd of me upon her Knees not to take it, and told me it was all she had in the World to buy her Bread for her self and a sick Child which she had at home, do you think I could be so Cruel if you had not stood by, and made me do it? why, I cry'd at doing it, as much as the poor Woman did, tho' I did not let you see me.

YOU FOOL you, *says Will*, you will never be fit for our Business indeed, if you mind such things as those, I shall bring you off of those things quickly; why, if you will be fit for Business, you must learn to fight when they resist, and cut their Throats when they submit; you must learn to stop their Breath, that they may beg and pray no more; what signifies pity? prethee, who will pity us when we come to the *Old-Baily?* I warrant you that whining old Woman that beg'd so heartily for her Two and Twenty Shillings would let you, or I beg upon our Knees, and would not save our Lives by not coming in for an Evidence against us; did you ever see any of them cry when they see Gentlemen go to the Gallows?

WELL, *Will, says I*, you had better let us keep to the Business we were in before; there was no such cruel doings in that, and yet we got more Money by it, then I believe we shall get at this.

4. From Samuel Richardson, *Pamela, Or, Virtue Rewarded* (1740-41).

[Pamela is a young serving girl who writes to her parents at home about her efforts to avoid the relentless sexual advances of her employer, Mr. B. When he discovers that Pamela has told others of his advances, Mr. B. confronts her and attempts to bully her into submission.]

From Letters XV and XVI

My dear Mother,

I broke off abruptly my last letter; for I feared he was coming; and so it happened. I put the letter into my bosom, and took up my work, which lay by me; but I had so little of the *artful*, as he called it, that I looked as confused, as if I had been doing some great harm.

"Sit still, Pamela," said he, "and go on with your work, for all me. You don't tell me I am welcome home after my journey to Lincolnshire." "It would be hard, sir," said I, "if you were not always welcome to your honour's own house."

I would have gone; but he said, "Don't run away, I tell you. I have a word or two to say to you." O how my heart fluttered! "When I was a *little kind* to you," said he, "in the summer-house, and you behaved so *foolishly* upon it, as if I had intended to do you great harm, did I not tell you, you should take no notice of what passed to any creature? And yet you have made a common talk of the matter, not considering either my reputation, or your own." "I made a common talk of it, sir!" said I: "I have nobody to talk to, hardly—"

He interrupted me, "*Hardly*! you little equivocator! what do you mean by *hardly*? Let me ask you, Have you not told Mrs. Jervis for one?" "Pray your honour," said I, all in agitation, "let me go down; for it is not for *me* to hold an argument with your honour." "Equivocator, again!" and took my hand, why do you talk of an *argument*? Is it holding an argument with me, to answer a plain question? Answer me to what I asked." "O good sir," said I, "let me beg you will not urge me further, for fear I forget myself again, and be *saucy*."

"Answer me then, I bid you, Have you not told Mrs. Jervis? It will be *saucy* in you, if you don't directly answer my question." "Sir," said I (and fain would have pulled my hand from him), "perhaps I should be for answering you by another question, and that would not become me." "What is it you would say?" replied he; "speak out."

"Then, sir," said I, "why should your honour be so angry I should tell Mrs. Jervis, or any body else, what passed, if you intended no harm?"

"Well said, pretty *innocent* and *artless*! as Mrs. Jervis calls you," said he; "and is it thus, insolent as you are! you taunt and retort upon me! But still I will be answered directly to my question." "Why then, sir," said I, "I will not tell a lye for the world: I *did* tell Mrs. Jervis; for my heart was almost broken; but I opened not my mouth to any other." "Very well, bold-face," said he, "and equivocator again! You did not open your *mouth* to any other; but did you not *write* to some other?" "Why now, and please your honour," said I, (for I was quite courageous just then) "you could not have asked me this question, if you had not taken from me my letter to my father and mother, in which (I own it) I had broke my mind freely to them, and asked their advice, and poured forth my griefs!"

"And so I am to be exposed, am I," said he, "*in* my own house, and *out* of my house, to the whole world, by such a saucebox?" "No, good sir," said I, "and I pray your honour not to be angry with me; it is not *I* that expose you, if I say nothing but the truth." He was then very angry, and called me assurance; and bid me remember to whom I was talking.

"Pray, sir," said I, "of whom can a poor girl take advice, if it must not be of her father and mother, and such a good woman as Mrs. Jervis, who, for her sex-sake, should give it me when asked?" "Insolence!" he then called me, and stamped with his foot. I fell down on my knees, and said, "For heaven's sake, your honour, pity a poor creature, that knows nothing, but how to cherish her virtue and good name: I have nothing else to trust to; and though poor and friendless here, yet I have always been taught to value honesty about my life." "Honesty, foolish girl!" said he. "But is it not one part of honesty to be dutiful and grateful to your master?" "Indeed, sir," said I, "it is impossible I should be ungrateful to your honour, or disobedient, or deserve the names of boldface and insolent, which you are pleased to call me, but when your commands are contrary to that first duty, which shall ever be the principle of my life!"

He seemed to be moved, and rose up, and walked into the great chamber two or three turns, leaving me on my knees; and I threw my apron over my face, and laid my head on a chair, and cried as if my heart would break, but had no power to go from the place.

At last he came in again, but with mischief in his heart! and raising me up, he said, "Rise, Pamela, rise; you are your own enemy. Your perverse folly will be your ruin: I am very much displeased with the freedoms you have taken with my name to my house-keeper, as also to your father and mother; and you may as well have *real* cause to take these freedoms with me, as to make my name suffer for *imaginary* ones." And saying so, he lifted me up, and offered to set me on his knee.

O how I was terrified! I said, like as I had read in a book a night or two before, "Angels and saints, and all the host of heaven, defend me! And may I never survive one moment, that fatal one in which I shall forfeit my innocence!" "Pretty fool!" said he, "how will you forfeit your innocence, if you are oblig-ed to yield to a force you cannot withstand? Be easy, for let the worst happen that can, *you'll* have the merit, and *I* the blame; and it will be a good subject for letters to your father and mother, and a pretty tale moreover for Mrs. Jervis."

[Pamela manages to escape from Mr. B., but only to hear later that she has been commanded to appear before him again on the following day, as she reports in her next letter.]

Well! you may believe how uneasily I passed the time, till his appointed hour came. Every minute, as it grew nearer, my ter-rors increased; and sometimes I had great courage, and some-times none at all; and I thought I should faint, when it came to the time my master had dined. I could neither eat nor drink; and, do what I could, my eyes were swelled with crying.

At last he went up to the closet, which was my good lady's dressing-room; a room I once loved, but then dreaded.

Don't your heart ake for me? I am sure mine fluttered about like a new-caught bird in a cage. O Pamela, said I to myself, why art thou so fearful! Thou has done no harm! What, if thou fearest an unjust judge, when thou art innocent, wouldst thou do before a just one, if thou wert guilty? Have courage, Pamela, thou knowest the worst! Any how much happier a choice is poverty with honesty, than plenty with wickedness!

So I cheared myself; but yet my poor heart sunk, and my spirits were quite broken. Every thing that stirred, I thought was to call me to my account. I dreaded it, and yet I wished it to come.

Well, at last he rung the bell; O, thought I, that it was my passing-bell!

Mrs. Jervis went up, with a full heart enough, poor good woman! He said, "Where's Pamela? Let her come up, and do you come with her."

She came to me; I was ready to go with my feet, but my heart was with my dear father and mother, wishing to share your poverty and content. I went up, however.

O how can wicked men seem so steady and untouched, with such black hearts, while poor innocents stand like malefactors before them!

He looked so stern, that my heart failed me, and I wished myself any where but there, though I had before been summoning up all my courage. Good heaven, said I to myself, give me courage to stand before this naughty master! O soften him, or harden me!

"Come in, fool," said he, angrily, as soon as he saw me (and snatched my hand with a pull); "you may well be ashamed to see me, after your noise and nonsense, and exposing me as you have done."

I ashamed to see *you*! thought I: Very pretty indeed! But I said nothing.

"Mrs. Jervis," said he, "here you are both together: Do you sit down; but let her stand, if she will" (Ay, thought I, if I *can*; for my knees beat one against the other). "Did you not think, when you saw the girl in the way you found her in, that I had given her the greatest occasion for complaint, that could possibly be given to a woman; and that I had actually ruined her, as she calls it? Tell me, *could* you think any thing less?" "Indeed," said she, "I feared so at first." "Has she told you what I did to her, and *all* I did to her, to occasion the folly, by which my reputation might have suffered in your opinion, and in that of all the family? Inform me, what has she told you?"

She was a little too much frighted, as she owned afterwards, at his sternness; and said, "indeed she told me you *only* pulled her on your knee, and kissed her."

Then I plucked up my spirit a little. "*Only!* Mrs. Jervis," said I; "and was not that enough to shew me what I had to fear? When a master of his honour's degree demeans himself to be so free as that to such a poor servant as me, what is not to be apprehended? But your honour went further; and talked of Lucretia, and her hard fate. Your honour knows you went too far for a master to a servant, or even to his equal; and," bursting into tears, "I cannot bear it."

Mrs. Jervis began to excuse me, and to beg he would pity a poor maiden, who had such a value for her reputation. He said, "I speak it to her face, I think her pretty, and I thought her humble, and one that would not grow upon my favours, or the notice I took of her; but I abhor the thought of compelling her to any thing. I know better what belongs to myself; but I was bewitched by her, I think, to be freer than became me; though I had no intention to carry the jest farther."

What poor stuff was all this, my dear mother, from a man of his sense! But see how a bad cause, and bad actions, confound the greatest wits! It gave me a little more courage then; for innocence, I find, in a low fortune, and not strong mind, has many advantages over guilt, with all its riches and wisdom.

"Your honour," said I, "may call this jest or sport, or what you please; but indeed, sir, it is not a jest that becomes the distance between a master and a servant." "Do you hear, Mrs. Jervis?" said he, "do you hear the pertness of the creature? I had a good deal of this sort before in the summer-house, and yesterday too, which made me rougher with her than perhaps I had otherwise been."

"Pamela, don't be pert to his honour," said Mrs. Jervis; "you should know your distance; you see his honour was only in jest." "O dear Mrs. Jervis," said I, "don't *you* blame me too. It is very difficult for a servant to keep her distance to her master, when her master departs from his dignity to her."

"See again!" said he; "could you believe this of the young baggage, if you had not heard it?" "Good, your honour," said the well-meaning gentlewoman, "pity and forgive the poor girl: She is but a girl, and her virtue is very dear to her; and I will pawn my life for her, she will never be pert to your honour, if you'll be so good as not to molest her any more, nor frighten her again. You saw, sir, by her fits, the terror she was in: She could not help it; and though your honour intended her no harm, yet the apprehension was almost death to her; and I had much ado to bring her to herself."

"O the little hypocrite!" said he; "she has all the arts of her sex; they were *born* with her. I told you a while ago, you did not know her. But his was not the reason principally of my calling you before me together: I find I am likely to suffer in my reputation by the perverseness and folly of this girl. She has told you all, and perhaps more than all; nay, I make no doubt of it; and she has written letters (for I find she is a mighty letter writer!) to her father and mother, and to *others*, as far as I know; in which, representing herself as an angel of light, she makes her kind master and benefactor, a devil incarnate." (O how people will sometimes, thought I, call themselves by their right names!) "And all this," added he, "I won't bear; and so I am resolved she shall return to the condition she was taken from; and let her be careful how she uses my name with freedom when she is gone from me."

I brightened up at once at these welcome words; I threw myself upon my knees at his feet, with a most sincere, glad heart; and said, "May your honour be for ever blessed for your resolution! Now I shall be happy. And permit me, on my knees, to thank you for all the benefits and favours you have heaped upon me, for the opportunities I have had of improvement and learning, through my good lady's means, and yours. I will now forget all your honour has offered to me: and I promise you, that I will never let your name pass my lips, but with reverence and gratitude: And so God Almighty for ever bless your hon-our!"

Then rising, I went away with a much lighter heart than I came into his presence with: And fell to writing this letter.

5. From Thomas Holcroft, *Anna St. Ives* (1792).

[One of the first Jacobin novels, *Anna St. Ives* depicts as its heroine a young woman of unusual capabilities, who sees even marriage as a route to social reform. She chooses not to marry her ideal mate, Frank Henley, because this choice would dis-please her aristocratic family, and agrees instead to marry the haughty rake, Coke Clifton, the brother of her friend, Louisa. The two letters that follow convey Anna's and Coke's quite different agendas in a debate about marriage.]

Letter LXXXII

Anna Wenbourne St. Ives to Louisa Clifton
London, Grosvenor-Street

A FORTNIGHT has almost elapsed since I last wrote to my Louisa, till my heart begins to cry shame at the delay. Could I please no other excuse than the trifling occupations of a trifling world I must sign my own condemnation; but your brother has afforded me better employment. Our frequent conversations on many of the best and most dignified of moral enquiries, his acute remarks and objections, and the difficult problems he has occasionally given me to solve, have left me in no danger of being idle....

The course of our enquiries has several times forced us upon that great question, "the progress of the mind toward perfec-tion, and the different order of things which must inevitably be the result." Yesterday this theme again occurred. Frank was pre-sent; and his imagination, warm with the sublimity of the sub-ject, drew a bold and splendid picture of the felicity of that state of society when personal property no longer shall exist, when the whole torrent of mind shall unite in enquiry after the beautiful and the true, when it shall no longer be diverted by those insignificant pursuits to which the absurd follies that originate in our false wants give birth, when individual selfishness shall be unknown, and when all shall labour for the good of all!

A state so distant from present manners and opinions, and apparently so impossible, naturally gave rise to objections; and your brother put many shrewd and pertinent questions, which would have silenced a mind less informed and less comprehensive than that of our instructor.

At last a difficulty arose which to me wore a very serious form; and as what was said left a strong impression on my memory, I will relate that part of the conversation. Observe, Louisa, that Clifton and Frank were the chief speakers. Your brother began.

I confess, sir, you have removed many apparently unconquerable difficulties: but I have a further objection which I think unanswerable.

What is it?

Neither man nor woman in such a state can have any thing peculiar: the whole must be for the use and benefit of the whole?

As generally as practice will admit: and how very generally that may be, imperfect as its constitution was, Sparta remained during five hundred years a proof.

Then how will it be possible, when society shall be the general possessor, for any man to say – *This is my servant?*

He cannot: there will be no servants.

Well but – *This is my child?*

Neither can he do that: they will be the children of the state.

Indeed! – And what say you to – *This is my wife?* – Can appropriation more than for the minute the hour or the day exist? Or, among so disinterested a people, can a man say even of the woman he loves – *She is mine?*

[We paused – I own, Louisa, I found myself at a loss; but Frank soon gave a very satisfactory reply.]

You have started a question of infinite importance, which perhaps I am not fully prepared to answer. I doubt whether in that better state of human society, to which I look forward with such ardent aspiration, the intercourse of the sexes will be altogether promiscuous and unrestrained; or whether they will admit of something that may be denominated marriage. The former may perhaps be the truth: but it is at least certain that in the sense in which we understand marriage and the affirmation – *This is my wife* – neither the institution nor the claim can in such a state, or indeed in justice exist. Of all the regulations which were ever suggested to the mistaken tyranny of selfishness, none perhaps to this day have surpassed the despotism of those which undertake to bind not only body to body but soul to soul, to all futurity, in despite of every possible change which our vices and our virtues might effect, or however numerous the secret corporal or mental imperfections might prove which a more intimate acquaintance should bring to light!

Then you think that some stipulation or bargain between the sexes must take place, in the most virtuous ages?

In the most virtuous ages the word bargain, like the word promise, will be unintelligible – We cannot bargain to do what is wrong, nor can we, though there should be no bargain, forbear to do what is right, without being unjust.

Whence it results that marriage, as a civil institution, must ever be an evil?

Yes. It ought not to be a civil institution. It is the concern of the individuals who consent to this mutual association, and they ought not to be prevented from beginning, suspending, or terminating it as they please.

Clifton addressed himself to me – What say you to this doctrine, madam? Does it not shock, does it not terrify you?

As far as I have considered it, no. It appears to be founded on incontrovertible principles; and I ought not to be shocked that some of my prejudices are opposed, or at being reminded that men have not yet attained the true means of correcting their own vices.

Surely the consequences are alarming! The man who only studied the gratification of his desires would have a new wife each new day; and the unprotected fair would be abandoned to all the licentiousness of libertinism!

Frank again replied – Then you think the security of women would increase with their imagined increase of danger; and that an unprincipled man, who even at present if he be known is avoided and despised, would then find a more ready welcome, because as you suppose he would have more opportunities to injure?

I must own that the men fit to be trusted with so much power are in my opinion very few indeed.

You are imagining a society as perverse and vitiated as the present: I am supposing one wholly the contrary. I know too well that there are men who, because unjust laws and customs worthy of barbarians have condemned helpless women to infamy, for the loss of that which under better regulations and in ages of more wisdom has been and will again be guilt to keep, I know, sir, I say that the present world is infested by men, who make it the business and the glory of their lives to bring this infamy upon the very beings for whom they feign the deepest affection! – If ever patience can forsake me it will be at the recollection of these demons in the human form, who come tricked out in all the smiles of love, the protestations of loyalty, and the arts of hell, unrelentingly and causelessly to prey upon confiding innocence! Nothing but the malverse selfishness of man could give being or countenance to such a monster! Whatever is good, exquisite, or precious, we are individually taught to grasp at, and if possible to secure; but we have each a latent sense that this principle has rendered us a society of detestable misers, and therefore to rob each other seems almost like the sports of justice.

For which reason, sir, were I a father, I think I should shudder to hear you instructing my daughters in your doctrines.

I perceive you wholly misconceive me; and I very seriously request, pray observe, sir, I very seriously request you to remember that I would not teach any man's daughters so mad a doctrine as to indulge in sensual appetites, or foster a licentious imagination. I am not the apostle of depravity. While men shall be mad, foolish, and dishonest enough to be vain of bad principles, women may be allowed to seek such protection as bad laws can afford – It is an eternal truth that the wisdom of man is superior to the strength of lions; but I would not therefore turn an infant into a lion's den.

I am glad to be undeceived. I thought it was scarcely possible you should mean what your words seemed to imply – At present I understand you; and I again confess my surprise to find so much consistency, and so many powerful arguments on a question in favour of which I thought nothing rational could be advanced. You have afforded me food for reflection, and I thank you. I shall not easily forget what has been said.

Letter LXXXIII

Coke Clifton to Guy Fairfax
London, Dover Street

My intention was to keep my countenance, but to laugh at them in my heart most incontinently. However, I soon found my side of the question was not so perfectly beyond all doubt, nor theirs quite so ridiculous as I had imagined.

'Tis true, I went predetermined to be convinced, and to take all they should tell me for gospel. I had a conclusion of my own to draw, and if I could but lead to that, I cared not how much I granted.

I know not whether this predisposition in me was of any advantage to their argument, though I think it was not; for, so ready was the solution to every difficulty, I boldly ventured to state objections which I meant to have kept out of sight, lest I should myself overturn a system that suited my purpose. I perceived their eagerness, saw there was no danger that they should stop at trifles even if I should happen to throw them a bone to pick, and the readiness of each reply raised my curiosity. I fearlessly drew out my heavy artillery, which they with ease and safety as fearlessly dismounted. With a breath my strong holds were all puffed down, like so many houses of cards.

By this however my main business was done more effectually. We came to it by fair deduction. It was not abruptly introduced; it was major, minor, and consequent – All individual property is an evil – Marriage makes woman individual property – Therefore marriage is an evil – Could there be better logic?

As for his saving clause, that marriage in these times of prejudice and vice [I have the whole cant by rote, Fairfax.] is a necessary evil, leave me to do that away. What! Is she not a heroine? And can I not convince her that to act according to a bad system, when there is a better, were to descend to the ways of the vulgar? Can I not teach her how superior she is to the pretty misses who conform to such mistaken laws? Shall she want the courage and the generosity to set the first good example? How often have I seen her eyes sparkle, her bosom heave, and her zeal break forth in virtuous resolutions to encounter any peril to obtain a worthy purpose! And can there be a more worthy?

Curse upon these qualms of conscience! Never before did I feel any thing so teazing, so tormenting! And, knowing what I know, remembering what I never can forget, the sights, injuries, and insults I have received, how I came to feel them now is to me wholly inconceivable. She is acting it is true with what she calls the best and purest of intentions toward me; she believes them to be such; she sometimes almost obliges me to believe them such myself. She tortures me, by half constraining me to revere the virtues in favour of which she harangues so divinely. But shall I like a poor uxorious lackadaisy driveller sit down satisfied with a divided heart? – I! – Has she not with her own lips, under her own hand, avowed and signed her contumelious guilt, her audacious preference of a rival? – A mean, a base, a vulgar rival! – And after this shall my projects suffer impediment from cheesecurd compassion? – Shall the querulous voice of conscience arrest my avenging arm? – No, Fairfax! – It cannot be! Though my heart in its anger could not accuse her of a single crime beside, that alone, that damning preference would be all-sufficient! – The furies have no stings that equal this recollection!

Appendix E: The Influence of Caleb Williams

1. From George Colman, *The Iron Chest* (1796).

[Colman's unauthorized dramatization of *Caleb Williams* was first performed at Drury Lane on March 12, 1796, with Godwin in attendance. The play enjoyed a great success well into the early years of the nineteenth century as part of the repertory of the Haymarket Theatre, and also enjoyed a successful run in America. The excerpts below indicate Colman's Advertisement to the second published edition of the play in 1796. The early confrontation between master and servant from Act I, Scene iii follows. In the play Caleb is renamed "Wilford," Falkland "Sir Edward Mortimer," and Mr. Collins, "Adam Winterton."]

From the Advertisement to the Reader

I am indebted for the ground-work of this Play to a Novel, entitled "*Things as They Are, or the Adventures of Caleb Williams*; written by William Godwin." Much of Mr. Godwin's story I have omitted; much, which I have adopted, I have compress'd; much I have added; and much I have taken the liberty to alter.

All this I did that I might fit it, in the best of my judgment, to the stage.

I have cautiously avoided all tendency to that which, vulgarly, (and wrongly, in many instances,) is termed Politicks; with which, many have told me, *Caleb Williams* teems.

The stage has, now, no business with Politicks: and, should a Dramatick Author endeavour to dabble in them, it is the Lord Chamberlain's office to check his attempts, before they meet the eye of the Publick. I perused Mr. Godwin's book as a tale replete with interesting incident, ingenious in its arrangement, masterly in its delineation of character, and forcible in its language. I considered it as right of Common; and, by a title which custom has given to Dramatists, I enclosed it within my theatrical paling. However I may have till'd the land, I trust he discovers no intentional injury to him, in my proceeding....

The Piece is, now, printed as it was acted on the first night; that they who peruse it may decide whether, even in that shape, (with all the misfortunes, before enumerated, with which it was doomed to struggle) it should be, for ever, consigned to moulder on the shelf.

From Act I, Scene iii

[The scene is the Library in Sir Edward Mortimer's house; Mortimer (Falkland) is seated at a writing table, with his servant Adam Winterton (Mr. Collins) attending him. In the previous scene, Winterton tells Wilford (Caleb) about the secret in Mortimer's past, and Wilford has begun to suspect Mortimer of having murdered his enemy.]

Mort. Is Wilford waiting?
Wint. Wilford! mercy on me!
I tremble now to hear his name. He is —
Here in the hall, sir.
Mort. Send him in, prithee.
Wint. I shall, sir. Heaven bless you! heaven bless you! *(Exit.)*
Mort. Good morning, good old heart! This honest soul
Would fain look cheery in my house's gloom,
And, like a gay and sturdy ever-green,
Smiles in the midst of blast, and desolation,
Where all around him withers. Well, well — wither!
Perish this frail and fickle frame! — this clay,
That in it's dross-like compound, doth contain
The mind's pure ore and essence. — Oh! that mind!
That mind of man! that god-like spring of action!
That source, whence Learning, Virtue, Honour, flow! —
Which lifts us to the stars; which carries us
O'er the swoln waters of the angry deep,
As swallows skim the air. — That Fame's sole fountain!
That doth transmit a fair, and spotless name,
When the vile trunk is rotten: – Give me that!
Oh! give me but to live, in after-age,
Remember'd and unsullied! – Heaven and earth!

Let my pure flame of Honour shine in story,
When I am cold in death – and the slow fire,
That wears my vitals now, will no more move me
Than 'twould a corpse within a monument.
(A knock at the door of the library.)
 How now! Who's there? Come in.
(Enter Wilford.)
Wilford! is't you? You were not wont to knock.
Wilf. I fear'd I might surprise you, sir,
Mort. Surprise me!
Wilf. I mean – disturb you, sir: – yes – at your studies —
Disturb you at your studies.
Mort. Very strange!
You were not used to be so cautious.
Wilf. No —
I never used – but I – hum – I have learnt —
Mort. Learnt!
Wilf. Better manners, sir. I was quite raw,
When, in your bounty, you first shelter'd me:
But thanks to your great goodness, and the lessons
Of Mr. Winterton, I still improve,
And pick up something daily.
Mort. Aye, indeed!
Winterton! No he dare not. Hark you, sir.
(stepping up to him)
Wilf. Sir!
Mort. (retreating from him). What I am about!
 – Oh, honour, honour!
Thy pile should be so uniform, displace
One atom of thee, and the slightest breath
Of a rude peasant makes thy owner tremble
For his whole building. Reach me, from the shelf,
The volume I was busied in, last night.
Wilf. Last night, sir?
Mort. Aye; – it treats of Alexander.
Wilf. Oh, I remember, sir – of Macedon.
I made some extracts, by your order. *(goes to the Book Case)*
Mort. Books

(My only commerce, now,) will sometimes rouse me
Beyond my nature. I have been so warm'd,
So heated, by a well-turn'd rhapsody,
That I have seem'd the hero of the tale,
So glowingly described. Draw me a man
Struggling for Fame, attaining, keeping it,
Dead ages since, and the Historian
Decking his memory, in polish'd phrase,
And I can follow him through every turn,
Grow wild in his exploits, myself himself,
Until the thick pulsation of my heart
Wakes me, to ponder on the thing I am.
Wilf. (giving him the book)
To my poor thinking, this Alexander
Would scarcely rouse a man to follow him.
Mort. Indeed! why so lad? He is rekoned brave,
Wise, generous, learn'd by older heads than thine.
Wilf. I cannot tell, sir: – I have but a gleaning. –
He conquer'd all the world; but left unconquer'd
A world of his own passions – and they led him,
(It seems so there) on petty provocation,
Even to murder. *(Mortimer starts – Wilford and
he exchange looks – both confused.)*
I have touch'd the string –
'Twas unawares – I cannot help it. *(Aside.)*
 Mort. (attempting to recover himself.) Wilford
 — Wilford, I — you mistake the character –
I, mark you – he – death and eternal tortures!
(dashes the book on the floor, and seizes Wilford.)
Slave! I will crush thee! pulverise thy frame!
That no vile particle of prying nature
May — Ha, ha, ha! — I will not harm thee,
boy —
O, agony! *(Exit.)*
Wilf. Is this the high-flown honour, and delicate feeling, old
Winterton talked of, that cannot bear a glance at the trial? –
Delicate! had I been born under a throttling planet, I had never
survived this collaring. This may be guilt. If so — well, what

have I to do with the knowledge on't – what *could* I do? cut off my benefactor! who gives me bread! who is respected for his virtues, pitied for his misfortunes, loved by his family, blessed by the poor! Pooh! he is innocent. This is his pride and shame. He was acquitted – thousands witnessed it – thousands rejoiced at it – thousands — eh? the key left in the iron chest! Circumstance and mystery tempt me at every turn. Ought I – no matter. These are no common incitements, and I submit to the impulse. I heard him stride down the stairs. It opens with a spring, I see. I tremble in every joint. *(goes to the chest.)*

Enter Sir EDWARD MORTIMER.

Mort. I had forgot the key and — ha! by hell!

(Sees Wilford; snatches a pistol from the table, runs up to him, and holds it to his head. Wilford on his knees, claps down the lid of the trunk which he has just opened. After an apparent struggle of mind, Mortimer throws the pistol from him.)

Mort. Begone! — Come back. – Come hither to me.
Mark me – I see thou dost at every turn –
And I have noted thee, too. Thou hast found
(I know not how) some clue to my disgrace: –
Aye, my disgrace – we must not mince it now –
Public dishonour! – trod on! – buffeted!
Then tried as the foul demon who had foil'd
My manly means of vengeance. Anguish gnaws me:
Mountains of shame are piled upon me! – Me,
Who have made Fame my idol. 'Twas enough!
But something must be super-added. You, –
A worm, a viper I have warm'd, must plant,
In venom'd sport, your sting into my wounds,
Too tender e'en for tenderness to touch,
And work me into madness. Thou wouldst question
My very — slave! — my very innocence!
Ne'er doubted yet by judges nor arraigners.
Wretch! you have wrung this from me. Be content;
I am sunk low enough.
Wilf. (returning the key) Oh sir! I ever
Honour'd and lov'd you. But I merit all.
My passions hurried me I know not whither.

Do with me as you please, my kind, wrong'd master!
Discard me – thrust me forth – nay, kill me. —
Mort. Kill you!
Wilf. I know not what I say. – I know but this,
That I would die to serve you.
Enter a Servant.
Servant. Sir, your brother
Is just alighted at the gate.
Mort. My brother!
He could not time it worse. Wilford, remember.
Come, shew me to him. *(Exit with servant.)*

Wilf. Remember! I shall never while I live forget it: nay, I shall never while I live forgive myself. My knees knock together still; and the cold drops stand on my forehead, like rain-water on a pent-house.

2. From Mary Wollstonecraft, *The Wrongs of Woman: or, Maria* (*Posthumous Works*, London, 1798).

[As Godwin had composed *Caleb Williams* to illustrate his political philosophy, Mary Wollstonecraft spent the final months of her life trying to produce a novel that would illustrate the arguments of her *A Vindication of the Rights of Woman*. The novel remained unfinished at the time of Wollstonecraft's death in September 1797, but Godwin pieced together a makeshift ending from sketchy notes his wife had left and published it in a collection of her *Posthumous Works* in 1798. The novel's heroine is a severely abused wife who is imprisoned in a madhouse by her husband when she expresses her desire to end her marriage. In the passage below, Maria describes her first attempt to flee England. Her memoirs are composed as an address to her infant daughter.]

From Chapter XIV

"As my mind grew calmer, the visions of Italy again returned with their former glow of colouring; and I resolved on quitting the kingdom for a time, in search of the cheerfulness, that naturally results from a change of scene, unless we carry the barbed arrow with us, and only see what we feel.

"During the period necessary to prepare for a long absence, I sent a supply to pay my father's debts, and settled my brothers in eligible situations; but my attention was not wholly engrossed by my family, though I do not think it necessary to enumerate the common exertions of humanity. The manner in which my uncle's property was settled, prevented me from making the addition to the fortune of my surviving sister, that I could have wished; but I had prevailed on him to bequeath her two thousand pounds, and she determined to marry a lover, to whom she had been some time attached. Had it not been for this engagement, I should have invited her to accompany me in my tour; and I might have escaped the pit, so artfully dug in my path, when I was the least aware of danger.

"I had thought of remaining in England, till I weaned my child; but this state of freedom was too peaceful to last, and I had soon reason to wish to hasten my departure. A friend of Mr Venables [Maria's husband], the same attorney who had accompanied him in several excursions to hunt me from my hiding places, waited on me to propose a reconciliation. On my refusal, he indirectly advised me to make over to my husband – for husband he would term him – the greater part of the property I had at command, menacing me with continual persecution unless I complied; and that, as a last resort, he would claim the child. I did not, though intimidated by the last insinuation, scruple to declare, that I would not allow him to squander the money left to me for far different purposes, but offered him five hundred pounds, if he would sign a bond not to torment me any more. My maternal anxiety made me thus appear to waver from my first determination, and probably suggested to him, or his diabolical agent, the infernal plot, which has succeeded but too well.

"The bond was executed; still I was impatient to leave England. Mischief hung in the air when we breathed the same; I wanted seas to divide us, and waters to roll between, till he had forgotten that I had the means of helping him through a new scheme. Disturbed by the late occurrences, I instantly prepared for my departure. My only delay was waiting for a maid-servant, who spoke French fluently, and had been warmly recommended to me. A valet I was advised to hire, when I fixed on my place of residence for any time.

"My God, with what a light heart did I set out for Dover! – It was not my country, but my cares, that I was leaving behind. My heart seemed to bound with the wheels, or rather appeared the centre on which they twirled. I clasped you to my bosom, exclaiming "And you will be safe – quite safe – when – we are once on board the packet. – Would we were there!" I smiled at my idle fears, as the natural effect of continual alarm; and I scarcely owned to myself that I dreaded Mr Venables's cunning, or was conscious of the horrid delight he would feel, at forming stratagem after stratagem to circumvent me. I was already in the snare – I never reached the packet – I never saw thee more. – I grow breathless. I have scarcely patience to write down the details. The maid – the plausible woman I had hired – put, doubtless, some stupifying potion in what I ate or drank, the morning I left town. All I know is, that she must have quitted the chaise, shameless wretch! and taken (from my breast) my babe with her. How could a creature in a female form see me caress thee, and steal thee from my arms! I must stop, stop to repress a mother's anguish; lest, in bitterness of soul, I imprecate the wrath of heaven on this tiger, who tore my only comfort from me.

"How long I slept I know not; certainly many hours, for I woke at the close of day, in a strange confusion of thought. I was probably roused to recollection by some one thundering at a huge unwieldy gate. Attempting to ask where I was, my voice died away, and I tried to raise it in vain, as I have done in a dream. I looked for my babe with affright; feared that it had fallen out of my lap, while I had so strangely forgotten her; and, such was the vague intoxication, I can give it no other name, in which I was plunged, I could not recollect when or where I saw you; but I sighed, as if my heart wanted room to clear my head.

"The gates opened heavily, and the sullen sound of many

locks and bolts drawn back, grated on my very soul, before I was appalled by the creeking of the dismal hinges, as they closed after me. The gloomy pile was before me, half in ruins; some of the aged trees of the avenue were cut down, and left to rot where they fell; and as we approached some mouldering steps, a monstrous dog darted forwards to the length of his chain, and barked and growled infernally.

"The door was opened slowly, and a murderous visage peeped out, with a lantern. "Hush!" he uttered, in a threatening tone, and the affrighted animal stole back to his kennel. The door of the chaise flew back, the stranger put down the lantern, and clasped his dreadful arms around me. It was certainly the effect of the soporific draught, for, instead of exerting my strength, I sunk without motion, though not without sense, on his shoulder, my limbs refusing to obey my will. I was carried up the steps into a close-shut hall. A candle flaring in the socket, scarcely dispersed the darkness, though it displayed to me the ferocious countenance of the wretch who held me.

"He mounted a wide staircase. Large figures painted on the walls seemed to start on me, and glaring eyes to meet me at every turn. Entering a long gallery, a dismal shriek made me spring out of my conductor's arms, with I know not what mysterious emotion of terror; but I fell on the floor, unable to sustain myself.

"A strange-looking female started out of one of the recesses, and observed me with more curiosity than interest; till, sternly bid to retire, she flitted back like a shadow. Other faces, strongly marked, or distorted, peeped through the half-opened doors, and I heard some incoherent sounds. I had no distinct idea where I could be – I looked on all sides, and almost doubted whether I was alive or dead.

"Thrown on a bed, I immediately sunk into insensibility again; and next day, gradually recovering the use of reason, I began, starting affrighted from the conviction, to discover where I was confined – I insisted on seeing the master of the mansion – I saw him – and perceived that I was buried alive. –

[The following passage describing Maria's attempt to commit suicide is taken from Wollstonecraft's notes for the ending of the novel, and shows clear similarities to the original ending of *Caleb Williams*.]

"She swallowed the laudanum; her soul was calm – the tempest had subsided – and nothing remained but an eager longing to forget herself – to fly from the anguish she endured to escape from thought – from this hell of disappointment.

"Still her eyes closed not – one remembrance with frightful velocity followed another. – All the incidents of her life were in arms, embodied to assail her, and prevent her sinking into the sleep of death. – Her murdered child again appeared to her, mourning for the babe of which she was the tomb. – "And could it have a nobler? – Surely it is better to die with me, than to enter on life without a mother's care! I cannot live! – but could I have deserted my child the moment it was born? – thrown it on the troubled wave of life, without a hand to support it?" – She looked up: "What have I not suffered! – may I find a father where I am going!" – Her head turned; a stupor ensued; a faintness – "Have a little patience," said Maria, holding her swimming head (she thought of her mother), "this cannot last long; and what is a little bodily pain to the pangs I have endured?"

"A new vision swam before her. Jemima [Maria's former guard and current friend] seemed to enter – leading a little creature, that, with tottering footsteps, approached the bed. The voice of Jemima sounding as at a distance, called her – she tried to listen, to speak, to look!

"'Behold your child!' exclaimed Jemima. Maria started off the bed, and fainted. – Violent vomiting followed.

When she was restored to life, Jemima addressed her with great solemnity: " — led me to suspect, that your husband and brother had deceived you, and secreted the child. I would not torment you with doubtful hopes, and I left you (at a fatal moment) to search for the child! – I snatched her from misery – and (now she is alive again) would you leave her alone in the world, to endure what I have endured?"

"Maria gazed wildly at her, her whole frame was convulsed with emotion; when the child, whom Jemima had been tutoring all the journey, uttered the word 'Mamma!' She caught her to her bosom, and burst into a passion of tears – then, resting the child gently on the bed, as if afraid of killing it, – she put her hand to her eyes, to conceal as it were the agonizing struggle of her soul. She remained silent for five minutes, crossing her arms over her bosom, and reclining her head, – then exclaimed: 'The conflict is over! I will live for my child!'"

Appendix F: Contemporary Reviews

1. From the *Critical Review*, Second Series, 11 (July 1794): 290–96.

To anticipate the contents of this very interesting narrative, would be no kindness to the reader. We shall, therefore, not attempt an analysis, but simply observe, that the plot of this novel turns on the enmity of two neighbouring gentlemen, the one of whom is governed by all the vulgar passions predominant in uninformed minds, pride, interest, love of power, and envy; the other is externally amiable, but is internally directed, not by true principle, but by that very equivocal motive to virtue, the love of fame. Actuated by this principle, the latter is betrayed into the commission of a crime, which involves the remainder of his life in perplexity, gloom, distress, and cruelty.

The moral is excellent, but the necessity of *religious* principle, without which we are persuaded no real virtue can exist in the human heart, is not so strongly enforced, as the nature of the story would admit. The characters are extremely well drawn; and the pictures of modern manners are in most instances but too faithfully delineated. The political reflections, which however are not very numerous, might in general have been spared; and in a future edition, which we doubt not so very interesting and entertaining a book must soon come to, we would recommend to the author to expunge a considerable part of them at least.

It is but justice to add, that this work ranks greatly above the whole mass of publications which bear the name of novels, if perhaps we except the productions of Fielding, Smollet, and Burney. In the construction and conduct of the narrative, it is even, in our opinion, superior to them. It is no mean compliment, indeed, to Mr. Godwin's ingenuity to say, that though the passion of *love* (which has in general been considered as an essential adjunct in the composition of a novel) does not enter into the plot, so fascinating is the narrative, that few readers will have sufficient coolness to lay down the book before they have concluded it....

Mr. Godwin will by some be thought to have been guilty of a misnomer, since, instead of "Things as they are," the novel might, perhaps, as well have been intitled, "Things as they ever have been."

2. From the *British Critic* 4 (July 1794): 70-71.

This piece is a striking example of the evil use which may be made of considerable talents, connected with such a degree of intrepidity as can inspire the author with resolution to attack religion, virtue, government, laws, and above all, the desire (hitherto accounted laudable) of leaving a good name to posterity.

In this extraordinary performance, every gentleman is a hard-hearted assassin, or a prejudiced tyrant; every Judge is unjust, every Justice corrupt and blind. Sentiments of respect to Christianity are given only to the vilest wretch in the book: while the most respectable person in the drama abhors the idea of "shackling his expiring friend with the fetters of superstition."

In order to render the laws of his country odious, the author places an innocent prisoner, whose story he (avowedly) takes from the Newgate Calendar of the first George's reign, in a dungeon; the wretched, unhealthy state of which he steals (as avowedly) from one of the benevolent Howard's painful descriptions of a worse gaol than common. We will only add, that the character, on which the author seems to dwell with most pleasure, is that of a leader of robbers, one who dwells in a ruinous retreat; and dispatches felons and murderers, in parties, around the country.

When a work is so directly pointed at every band which connects society, and at every principle which renders it amiable, its very merits become noxious as they tend to cause its being known in a wider circle.

3. From the *British Critic* 5 (April 1795): 444-47.

A Friend, for whose opinions we have the highest respect, thinks it important that the unfair efforts of the author of *Caleb Williams*, to throw an odium upon the laws of his country, should be specifically and distinctly exploded. The whole of the fable, he alledges, and the reasoning which it is employed to introduce, is founded not upon mere mistake, or accidental misrepresentation, but upon a statement, with respect to the law of England, absolutely false; of which it is impossible that any man, who wishes to be informed, can be ignorant. As we did not hesitate to correct an accidental misstatement of our own respecting this book, so neither can we prevail upon ourselves to suppress the remarks of our friend and correspondent, which certainly are such as deserve particular attention. We shall allow him therefore, to speak for himself.

"The hinge upon which the fable turns is the persecution, and the consequent misfortunes and death of the Hawkinses. Without examining whether a landlord can be justified in turning out his tenants for not voting according to his direction, or whether there are many instances of persons who have been victims of this species of oppression, such a combination as Mr. Godwin supposes among the gentry of this country certainly does not exist; and if any gentleman should be inclined thus to sacrifice a victim to his resentment, he must hesitate upon two considerations; the injury to his own interests, by depriving himself of a tenant in the first instance, and by increasing the difficulty of finding tenants in future; and the probability, (which all who know the spirit with which elections are carried on will admit to be very great) that the man he turns adrift, will be taken under the protection of the opposite party, and that instead of bringing ruin upon him, he will be the means of making his fortune. I have taken notice of this because it might induce a doubt whether Mr. Godwin has even taken a common and superficial view of the state of society in this country, instead of having surveyed it with the precision, and sagacity of a Philosopher, and I proceed, to what is of much greater importance, those circumstances respecting the Laws of this Country, and the Mode of their Execution, which he has alledged in direct violation of truth....

We have next the story of Miss Melvile's arrest. It seems very improbable that what is there related would have been attempted or executed at the risk of incurring the penalty for murder; nor is it likely that a transaction, exciting such general indignation and resentment, should not have been prosecuted with all the rigour of the law. The murder of Tyrrell, the acquittal of Falkland, the trial, condemnation, and execution of the Hawkinses, succeed to our notice. There is no evidence to bring the fact home to Mr. Falkland, and the jury set his high reputation against the very slight presumption of his guilt, arising from his absence during a few minutes from his lodgings, about the time when Tyrrell was supposed to have fallen. To this no objection can be made, nor do I suspect that Mr. Godwin thinks the eloquent defence he has composed for Falkland could fail of its effect upon merely human judges. The circumstances stated against the Hawkinses are so strong as almost to amount to positive proof. There is no tribunal by which they would not probably have been condemned. But it is to be remembered that the narrative before us is fictitious, and though I neither mean to palliate, or deny, the fallacy of human judgment, I think it may fairly be questioned, whether it is possible that such circumstances should appear without actual guilt. Mr. Godwin's imagination has not been able to account for them, and the narrative in this instance may be considered as exceeding all the bounds of probability. From the story of the young man brought before Mr. Falkland upon a charge of murder, and released by him, it should appear, (a supposition confirmed by many other passages in the book) that Mr. Godwin is utterly ignorant of the nature of the office of a Justice of the Peace. Homicide is, primâ Facie, a capital Felony. The law has established distinctions arising from the circumstances of each particular case. The facts upon which these distinctions depend must be determined by the verdict of a jury, the only judges of fact which the law of this country knows. A Justice of Peace is bound to commit a man charged before him, by the oath of credible witnesses, if the case is not bailable, where the circumstances amount to any reasonable presumption of Felony. Where a man is slain, and the person confesses the fact, he must be committed. It is not material whether a justice of Peace ought to have the discretionary power attributed to him by Mr. Godwin. The Law of England certainly does not give it, and Mr. Godwin is in this instance either ignorant of the law, or wilfully misrepresents it. It is not easy to say what grounds are intended to be laid for the commitment of Caleb Williams himself. It is no where expressly said that Falkland added the guilt of Perjury to his other crimes, but he must have sworn to the robbery, or Williams could not have been detained. We must now follow Williams to prison, and here the circumstance to be remarked is the length of his imprisonment. This also is impossible to have happened under the law of this country. If no bill of indictment was found against him at the next assizes, he could not be detained.... But to return to matters of fact, the most extraordinary and gross misrepresentation, or I should say with greater propriety, the most palpable, and notorious false-hood concerning the law of England, and which pervades every part of this work, remains to be taken notice of. The author all along affects to believe that a man may be tried twice for the same offence. This is the less excuseable as it is of no use in carrying on the Fable. Falkland's jealousy and sensibility, on the point of reputation, was sufficient to account for his anxiety to prevent the truth, in regard to the murder of Tyrrell, from being brought to light. It was not necessary to call in the ter-rors of a public sentence, and execution, nor indeed is this con-sideration any where represented to have aggravated the solici-tude of Falkland, who must have known that his darling reputa-tion could not be more effectually blackened by a legal convic-tion, than by a bare manifestation of his guilt. But whatever motive may have influenced Mr. Godwin, it is certain, and uni-versally known, that a verdict of acquittal upon a criminal charge, is as complete a bar to any further trial for the same offence, as the King's Pardon, or an Act of Indemnity. Thus does it appear that a Philosopher who has already treated expressly of Political Justice, and has invented a Fable for the purpose of attacking the moral and political prejudices of his countrymen, and making them acquainted with the truth, in all the instances in which he has affected to state the law of the land, and to reason from it, has stated it falsely; and it is almost superfluous to say, that in so doing, he has outraged Philosophy, Reason, and Morality, the foundation, object, and end of which is Truth.

[Godwin's published response to this attack is printed above as Appendix A, 3.]

4. From the *Monthly Review*, 15 (September 1794): 145-49.

Between fiction and philosophy there seems to be no natural alliance: – yet philosophers, in order to obtain for their dogmata a more ready reception, have often judged it expedient to introduce them to the world in the captivating dress of fable. It was not to be supposed that the energetic mind of Mr. Godwin, long inured as it must have been to abstract speculation and sublime inquiry, would condescend to employ itself in framing a whining love tale; which, after having drawn a few tears from the eyes of a number of tender virgins, would have reposed in eternal peace on the loaded shelves of some circulating libraries. In writing the Adventures of Caleb Williams, this philosopher had doubtless some higher object in view; and it is not difficult to perceive that this object has been to give an easy passport, and general circulation, to some of his favourite opinions. Having laid it down as a first principle that virtue consists in justice, or the wise and equal pursuit of general good, he thinks it necessary, in order to carry his system into effect, to investigate many sentiments which, though hitherto considered as the legitimate offspring of nature, and even as possessing some degree of moral value, are in his judgment only the creatures of error and prejudice. In this class he appears to rank that sense of honour which seeks its ultimate reward in the good opinion of mankind. Accordingly, this fictitious narrative seems to have been written chiefly for the purpose of representing, in strong colours, the fatal consequence of suffering the love of fame to become predominant.

Mr. Falkland, who ought, perhaps, rather than Caleb Williams, to be considered as the principal actor in this drama, exhibits a character wholly formed on the visionary principles of honour. Early tinctured with extravagant notions on this subject, by the heroic poets of Italy, he cherishes a romantic pride; which, notwithstanding his natural propensity toward benevolence, displayed in the occasional acts of generosity, soon forms his ruling passion, and a length overwhelms him with accumulated wretchedness. He is the fool of honour; a man whom, in the pursuit of reputation, nothing could divert; who would purchase the character of a true, gallant, and undaunted hero, at the expence of worlds; and who thinks every calamity nominal except a stain on his honour.... [What follows is a synopsis of the events of Volume I.]

This visionary character is drawn with uncommon strength of conception and energy of language. The reader, while he respects and adores the virtues of Falkland, feels infinite regret that his mad passion for reputation should suppress every feeling of humanity, and become the source of unspeakable misery to himself, and of the most tragically calamity to others. The character, though original, will perhaps be admitted to be consistent; unless it should be thought difficult to reconcile the benevolence every where ascribed to Falkland, with the *deliberate* injustice and cruelty which were shewn in suffering the innocent Hawkins and his son to be executed, in preference to confessing his own guilt. – It will perhaps be said that the ruling passion of Falkland was not benevolence, but the love of fame; yet it may be questioned whether such benevolence, as is ascribed to Falkland, be not utterly incompatible with the tyrannical sway which is given in his character to the *selfish* passion of the love of fame.

A farther object in this story appears to have been to exhibit an example of the danger of indulging an idle curiosity, merely for its own gratification; and the fatal consequences of this folly were perhaps never so impressively exemplified as in the story of Caleb Williams, the confidential servant of Falkland. Williams, having been made acquainted with many particulars of his master's history by his steward, begins to suspect that the

murder of Tyrrel had been committed by Falkland: he is therefore determined, at all hazards, to detect the secret; he becomes
a perpetual spy on his master's actions, and practises a thousand
artifices to accomplish his purpose, till at length he extorts the
truth from Falkland, on a solemn oath of secrecy. Having
gained his wish, he finds the secret a most painful burden,
which, through his master's jealous apprehension for his reputation, brings him on a long series of persecution and perils; and
the relation of them forms a large and interesting part of the
narrative. Nothing can exceed the skilful management with
which that part of the story is conducted, in which the reader
remains unacquainted with the real occasion of Tyrrel's death,
till the suspicion against Falkland is gradually excited, and at
length confirmed by the persevering ingenuity of Williams.
The sufferings of Williams in prison, on a fictitious charge of
having robbed his master, – the contrivances by which he
repeatedly regains his liberty, – and the adventures through
which he passes, while he is wantonly persecuted as the perpetrator of a heinous felony, and flies in disguise from place to
place for safety; till, in the last extremity of danger, he discloses
the fatal secret, and becomes miserable under a load of self-
reproach: all are related with an interesting particularity that
evidently shews the hand of a master. The general result is a
forcible conviction of the hazard of suffering any foolish desire,
or curiosity, (that restless propensity,) to creep into the mind.
"Error, (as Caleb well remarks,) once committed, has a fascinating power, like the eyes of the rattlesnake, to draw us into a second error. It deprives us of that proud confidence in our own
strength, to which we are indebted for so much of our virtue."

This narrative seems, moreover, intended to give the author
an opportunity of making an indirect attack on what he deems
vulgar prejudices respecting religion, morals, and policy. On
these subjects, he expresses himself with that kind of latitude
which those, who are acquainted with his treatise on Political
Justice, will be prepared to expect. Striking pictures are drawn,
in various parts of the work, of the oppression which is often
practised under the form of the law, and of the hardships which
are inflicted in our prisons even on those whom the law has

not convicted of any crime. Artful apologies are put into mouths of professional robbers, without any adequate refutation. Law is said to be better adapted for a weapon of tyranny in the hands of the rich, than for a shield to protect the humble part of the community against their usurpation. Caleb Williams thinks with unspeakable loathing of those errors, in consequence of which every man is fated to be, more or less, the tyrant or the slave; and he is astonished at the folly of his species, that they do not rise up as one man, and shake off chains so ignominious, and misery so insupportable. Mind, to his untutored reflections, is vague, airy, and unfettered; the susceptible perceiver of reasons, but never intended by nature to be the slave of force. He thinks it strange that men should, from age to age, consent to hold their lives at the breath of another, merely in order that each in his turn may have a power of acting the tyrant according to law; and he *prays* that he may hold life at the mercy of the elements, of the hunger of beasts, or of the revenge of barbarians, but not at that of the cold-blooded prudence of monopolists and kings! – What all this means we cannot precisely say: but, before the old fences of law be broken down, we hold it prudent that some effectual provision should be made for taming the ferocious passions of those animals, who have never yet been turned loose into the wilds of nature without biting and devouring one another.

With due allowance for systematical eccentricity, (the reader will pardon the paradoxical expression,) this performance, interesting but not gratifying to the feelings and the passions, and written in a style of laboured dignity rather than of easy familiarity, is singularly entitled to be characterized as a work in which the powers of genius and philosophy are strongly united.

[William Enfield]

5. From the *Analytical Review* 21 (January 1795): 166–75.

We are somewhat at a loss how to introduce our readers to an acquaintance with this singular narrative. Of incident it presents little, of character and situation much. The power of genius is often seen in these pages to give efficacy to scenes and reflections, little calculated in their own nature to affect the human mind. Strong feeling, and a depth of reflection on the state and habits of society, claim our attention, and lead us forward at the will of the writer, while an almost total want or disregard of the rules of composition have betrayed him into faults of the first magnitude. We will first analyze the story, and then proceed to make a few remarks on the whole....

[A lengthy plot synopsis follows, including several passages from the novel.]

Such are the plan, execution, and effect of the novel, written by the author of the Inquiry concerning political Justice. The two great objects of fictitious narrative are entertainment and instruction. For mere entertainment it may be said, that intellectual relaxation or amusement is of more value, and attended with better effects, than any other employment commonly taken up as a relief from the more fatiguing duties of life: and in defence of the other object, instruction, nothing need be urged. The greatest sources of entertainment are those, on which the powers of intellect are most ardently employed. What are these? Universal benevolence on the ground of moral principle in the individual; and particular benevolence, on which the natural arrangements of society depend. Hence flow the duties of friendship, sexual attachment, parental love, filial affection, protection, gratitude, and every other object of amiable emotion. Will Mr. G.'s system of morality overthrow any or all of these? If it should, still they will remain as the beloved sources of exquisite enjoyment, capable of bringing forth all the powers of the understanding, and affording the most sublime entertainment. Whatever may be the portion of errour attached to the present state of society, still the errours in these great departments are as worthy the attention of the novelist, as the admiration of chivalry, the love of reputation, or the fatal effects of indiscreet curiosity. To us it appears, that the author is not sufficiently aware of the necessity of drawing a general outline of the plot of any work of imagination, before the narrative is entered upon; and that from this cause, as well as from a wish to avoid common place subjects, he has greatly restricted his power, and the effect of his composition. He has no tale of rational love, no marked instance of personal attachment, no fondly anxious parent, or child devoted to filial duty, in the development of his story; but by the exertion of genius, which is indeed astonishing, he rivets our attention to a minute dissection of the characters, feelings, and emotions, of three insulated men, in a great measure confined to their own individual ease and comfort. Hence he was reduced to fill his third volume with a series of incidents similar to those of the Newgate Calendar, though every where related with the imagination of a poet, and the discriminating spirit of a philosopher. If we were to give a character of this performance in few words, we should say, that it equals the Eloise of Rousseau in depth and accuracy of dissertation; approaches the sorrows of Werter in the gigantic energy of mental picture; but falls far beneath them both in felicity of subject.

We will not enter more minutely into the discussion of a plot so imperfect; or inquire into the degree of probability, that such characters should act as they are made to do. It does not appear to us, that any entire moral pervades this narrative. The author's occasional deductions, on the state of society, are but too well founded. The character of Tyrrel is not very uncommon, but his fate teaches us nothing. Falkland is extremely singular in his motives, his actions, and his wretched end; and this singularity pervades and governs the adventures of Williams. The adaptation of the causes to the effects, the merits or demerits of the personages, and the whole contexture of the story, apply too little to any thing within the ordinary course of observation, to afford any general moral.

6. From James Mackintosh, Review of Godwin's "Lives of Edward and John Philips," *Edinburgh Review* 25 (October 1815): 485–501.

Since the beautiful tales of Goldsmith and Mackenzie, the composition of novels has been almost left to women; ... Mr. Godwin has preserved the place of men in this branch of literature. *Caleb Williams* is probably the finest novel produced by a man – at least since the Vicar of Wakefield. The sentiments, if not the opinions, from which it arose, were transient. Local usages and institutions were the subjects of its satire, exaggerated beyond the usual privilege of that species of writing. Yet it has been translated into most languages, and it has appeared in various forms, on the theatres, not only of England, but of France and Germany. There is scarcely a continental circulating library in which it is not one of the books which most quickly require to be replaced. Though written with a temporary purpose, it will be read with intense interest, and with a painful impatience for the issue, long after the circumstance which produced its original composition shall cease to be known but to those who are well read in history. There is scarcely a fiction in any language which it is so difficult to lay by. A young person of understanding and sensibility, not familiar with the history of its origin, nor forewarned of its connexion with peculiar opinions, in whose hands it is now put for the first time, will peruse it with perhaps more ardent sympathy and trembling curiosity, than those who read it when their attention was divided, and their feelings disturbed by controversy and speculation. A building thrown up for a season, has become, by the skill of the builder, a durable edifice. It is a striking, but not a solitary example, of the purpose of the writer being swallowed up by the interest of the work; of a man of ability intending to take part in the disputes of the moment, but led by the instinct of his talent to address himself to the permanent feelings of human nature. It must not, however, be denied, that the marks of temporary origin and peculiar opinion, are still the vulnerable part of the book. A fiction contrived to support an opinion, is a vicious composition. Even a fiction contrived to enforce a maxim of conduct, is not of the highest class. And though the vigorous powers of Mr. Godwin raised him above his own intention, still the marks of that intention ought to be effaced as marks of mortality, and nothing ought to remain in the book which will not always interest the reader. The passages which betray the metaphysician more than the novelist, ought to be weeded out with more than ordinary care. The character of Falkland is a beautiful invention. That such a man could have become an assassin, is perhaps an improbability; and if such a crime be possible for a soul so elevated, it may be due to the dignity of human nature to throw a veil over so humiliating a possibility, except when we are compelled to expose it by its real occurrence. In a merely literary view, however, the improbability of this leading incident is more than compensated, by all those agitating and terrible scenes of which it is the parent. And if the colours had been delicately shaded, if all the steps in the long progress from chivalry to assassination had been more patiently traced, and more distinctly brought into view, more might have been lost by weakening the contrast, than would have been gained by softening or removing the improbability. The character of Tyrrel, is a grosser exaggeration; and his conduct is such as neither our manners would produce, nor our laws tolerate. One or two monstrous examples of tyranny, nursed and armed by immense wealth, are no authority for fiction, which is a picture of general nature. The descriptive power of several parts of this novel is of the highest order. The landscape in the morning of Caleb's escape from prison, and a similar escape from a Spanish prison in St Leon [Godwin's second novel], are among the scenes of fiction which must the most frequently and vividly reappear in the imagination of a reader of sensibility. His disguises and escapes in London, though detailed at too great length, have a frightful reality, perhaps nowhere paralleled in our language, unless it be seen in some paintings of Daniel De Foe, with whom it is distinction to bear comparison. There are several somewhat similar scenes in the Colonel Jack of that admirable writer, which, among his novels, is indeed only the second; but which could be second to none but Robinson Crusoe, one of those very few books which are equally popular in every country of Europe, and which delight every reader from the philosopher to the child. Caleb Williams resembles the novels of De Foe, in the austerity with which it rejects the agency of women and the power of love.

7. From William Hazlitt, *The Spirit of the Age* (1825).

The Spirit of the Age was never more fully shown than in its treatment of this writer – its love of paradox and change, its dastard submission to prejudice and to the fashion of the day. Five-and-twenty years ago he was in the very zenith of a sultry and unwholesome popularity; he blazed as a sun in the firmament of reputation; no one was more talked of, more looked up to, more sought after, and wherever liberty, truth, justice was the theme, his name was not far off: – now he has sunk below the horizon, and enjoyed the serene twilight of a doubtful immortality. Mr. Godwin, during his lifetime, has secured to himself the triumphs and the mortifications of an extreme notoriety and of a sort of posthumous fame....

Mr. Godwin is an inventor in the regions of romance, as well as a skilful and hardy explorer of those of moral truth. *Caleb Williams* and *St. Leon* are two of the most splendid and impressive works of the imagination that have appeared in our times. It is not merely that these novels are very well for a philosopher to have produced – they are admirable and complete in themselves, and would not lead you to suppose that the author, who is so entirely at home in human character and dramatic situation, had ever dabbled in logic or metaphysics. The first of these, particularly, is a master-piece, both as to invention and execution. The romantic and chivalrous principle of the love of personal fame is embodied in the finest possible manner in the character of Falkland; as in Caleb Williams (who is not the first, but the second character in the piece), we see the very demon of curiosity personified. Perhaps the art with which these two characters are contrived to relieve and set off each other, has never been surpassed in any work of fiction, with the exception of the immortal satire of Cervantes. The restless and inquisitive spirit of Caleb Williams, in search and in possession of his patron's fatal secret, haunts the latter like a second conscience, plants stings in his tortured mind, fans the flames of his jealous ambition, struggling with agonized remorse; and the hapless but noble-minded Falkland at length falls a martyr to the persecution of that morbid and overpowering interest, of which his mingled virtues and vices have rendered him the object. We conceive no one ever began Caleb Williams that did not read it through: no one that ever read it could possibly forget it, or speak of it after any length of time but with an impression as if the events and feelings had been personal to himself.

8. From a review of the 1831 edition of *Caleb Williams*, *New Monthly Magazine* 33 (May 1831): 209.

This is a volume which every novel-reader will be pleased to see. Caleb Williams is a production that will bear reading more frequently than most works of fiction, and, at least, as often as any modern book that we can call to mind. We know of no parallel to it in English literature. The profound knowledge of character, the subtle analysis of human nature, discoverable in it; the intense interest of its incidents and situations, and the polished grace and clearness of its style; the moral and intellectual power that dignifies every page of it, render it one of the most remarkable works that any age has produced; and it is, consequently, with no slight satisfaction, that we see an edition like this, that places it within the reach of the least wealthy of its admirers. It is one of the series of Standard Novels, publishing [sic] by Colburn and Bentley; three volumes in one, and at a price scarcely exceeding that paid for binding in its original form. The type is beautifully clear, and the "getting up" generally in excellent taste.

Works Cited/Recommended Reading

William Godwin's Works

Godwin, William. *Enquiry Concerning Political Justice and Its Influence on Morals and Happiness*. 3rd ed. 3 vols. Ed. F.E.L. Priestley. Toronto: U Toronto P, 1946.

——. *Enquiry Concerning Political Justice*. 3rd ed. Ed. Isaac Kramnick. London: Penguin, 1985.

——. *Political and Philosophical Writings of William Godwin*. 7 vols. Gen. Ed. Mark Philp. London: Pickering and Chatto, 1993.

——. *Things As They Are: or, The Adventures of Caleb Williams*. 3 vols. London: B. Crosby, 1794.

——. *Things As They Are: or, The Adventures of Caleb Williams*. 2nd ed. 3 vols. London: G. G. & J. Robinson, 1796; 3rd ed. 3 vols. 1797.

——. *Things As They Are: or, The Adventures of Caleb Williams*. 4th ed. 3 vols. London: W. Simpkin & R. Marshal, 1816.

——. *Caleb Williams*. 5th ed. London: H. Colburn & R. Bentley, 1831.

——. *Caleb Williams*. Ed. David McCracken. London: Oxford UP, 1970.

——. *Caleb Williams*. Ed. Maurice Hindle. Harmondsworth: Penguin, 1988.

——. *Caleb Williams*. Ed. Pamela Clemit. *Collected Novels and Memoirs of William Godwin*. Gen. Ed. Mark Philp. 8 vols. London: Pickering & Chatto, 1992.

Secondary Sources

Balfour, Ian. "Promises, Promises: Social and Other Contracts in the English Jacobins (Godwin/Inchbald)." *New Romanticisms: Theory and Critical Practice*. Ed. David Clark and Donald Goellnicht. Toronto: U Toronto P, 1994.

Barker, Gerard A. "The Narrative Mode of *Caleb Williams*: Problems and Resolutions." *Studies in the Novel* 25 (1993): 1-15.

Bender, John. "Impersonal Violence: The Penetrating Gaze and the Field of Narration in *Caleb Williams*." *Critical Reconstructions: The Relationship of Fiction and Life*. Ed. Robert M. Polhemus and Roger B. Henkle. Stanford: Stanford UP, 1994. 111-26.

Butler, Marilyn, ed. *Burke, Paine, Godwin, and the Revolution Controversy*. Cambridge: Cambridge UP, 1984.

———. "Godwin, Burke, and Caleb Williams." *Essays in Criticism* 32 (1982): 237-57.

———. *Romantics, Rebels and Reactionaries: English Literature and its Background, 1760-1830*. Oxford: Oxford UP, 1981.

Clemit, Pamela. *The Godwinian Novel: The Rational Fictions of Godwin, Brockden Brown, Mary Shelley*. Oxford: Oxford UP, 1993.

Clifford, Gay. "*Caleb Williams* and *Frankenstein*: First Person Narrative and 'Things as They Are.'" *Genre* 10 (1977): 601-17.

Corber, Robert J. "Representing the 'Unspeakable': William Godwin and the Politics of Homophobia." *Journal of the History of Sexuality* 1 (1990): 85-101.

Dickinson, H.T. *British Radicalism and the French Revolution, 1789-1815*. Oxford: Basil Blackwell, 1985.

Dumas, D. Gilbert. "Things As They Were: The Original Ending of *Caleb Williams*." *Studies in English Literature* 6 (1966): 575-97.

Everest, Kelvin, and Gavin Edwards. "William Godwin's *Caleb Williams*: Truth and 'Things as They Are.'" *1789: Reading Writing Revolution*. *Proceedings of the Essex Conference on the Sociology of Literature*. Ed. Francis Barker, et al. Colchester, 1982. 129-46.

Furbank, P.N. "Godwin's Novels." *Essays in Criticism* 5 (1955): 214-28.

Gold, Alex, Jr. "It's Only Love: The Politics of Passion in Godwin's *Caleb Williams*." *Texas Studies in Language and Literature* 19 (1977): 135-60.

Graham, Kenneth. *The Politics of Narrative: Ideology and Social Change in William Godwin's "Caleb Williams"*. New York: AMS Press, 1990.

Handwerk, Gary. "Of Caleb's Guilt and Godwin's Truth: Ideology and Ethics in *Caleb Williams*." *English Literary History* 60 (1993): 939-60.

Harvey, A.D. "*Frankenstein* and *Caleb Williams*." *Keats-Shelley Journal* 29 (1980): 21-27.

——. "The Nightmare of *Caleb Williams*." *Essays in Criticism* 26 (1976): 236-49.

Hazlitt, William. *The Spirit of the Age*. Ed. E.D. Mackerness. London: Collins, 1969.

Helfield, Randa. "Constructive Treason and Godwin's Treasonous Constructions." *Mosaic* 28 (1995): 43-62.

Hogle, Jerrold E. "The Texture of the Self in Godwin's *Caleb Williams*." *Boundary 2* 7 (1979): 261-81.

Kelly, Gary. *The English Jacobin Novel, 1780-1805*. Oxford: Oxford UP, 1976.

——. *English Fiction of the Romantic Period, 1789-1830*. London: Longman, 1988.

Kiely, Robert. *The Romantic Novel in England*. Cambridge, MA: Harvard UP, 1972.

Kilgour, Maggie. *The Rise of the Gothic Novel*. London: Routledge, 1995.

Klancher, Jon P. *The Making of English Reading Audiences, 1790-1832*. Madison: U Wisconsin P, 1987.

Leaver, Kristen. "Pursuing Conversations: *Caleb Williams* and the Romantic Construction of the Reader." *Studies in Romanticism* 33 (1994): 589-610.

Locke, Don. *A Fantasy of Reason: The Life and Thought of William Godwin*. London: Routledge and Kegan Paul, 1980.

Marken, Jack M., and Burton R. Pollin. *Uncollected Writings (1785-1822), Articles in Periodicals and Six Pamphlets, One with Coleridge's Marginalia, by William Godwin*. Gainesville: Scholars' Facsimiles and Reprints, 1968.

Marshall, Peter H. *William Godwin*. New Haven: Yale UP, 1984.

McCracken, David. "Godwin's *Caleb Williams*: A Fictional Rebuttal of Burke." *Studies in Burke and His Time* 11 (1969-70): 1442-52.

——. "Godwin's Literary Theory: The Alliance between Fiction and Political Philosophy." *Philological Quarterly* 49 (1970): 113-33.

——. "Godwin's Reading in Burke." *English Language Notes* 7 (1970): 264-70.

Miller, Jacqueline T. "The Imperfect Tale: Articulation, Rhetoric, and Self in *Caleb Williams*." *Criticism* 20 (1978): 366-82.

Miyoshi, Masao. *The Divided Self: A Perspective on the Literature of the Double.* New York: New York UP, 1969.

Myers, Mitzi. "Godwin's Changing Conception of *Caleb Williams*." *Studies in English Literature* 12 (1972): 591-628.

Ousby, Ian. "'My Servant Caleb': Godwin's *Caleb Williams* and the Political Trials of the 1790s." *University of Toronto Quarterly* 44 (1974): 47-55.

O'Quinn, Daniel. "Trembling: Wollstonecraft, Godwin and the Resistance to Literature." *English Literary History* 64 (1997): 761-88.

Paul, Charles Kegan. *William Godwin: His Friends and Contemporaries.* 2 vols. London: H. S. King, 1876.

Philp, Mark. *Godwin's Political Justice.* London: Duckworth, 1986.

Rajan, Tilottama. "Wollstonecraft and Godwin: Reading the Secrets of the Political Novel." *Studies in Romanticism* 27 (1988): 221-251.

Rothstein, Eric. *Systems of Order and Inquiry in Later Eighteenth-Century Fiction.* Berkeley: U California P, 1975.

Scheiber, Andrew J. "Falkland's Story: *Caleb Williams*' Other Voice." *Studies in the Novel* 17 (1985): 255-66.

Simms, Karl N. "Caleb Williams' Godwin: Things as they Are Written." *Studies in Romanticism* 26 (1987): 343-63.

St. Clair, William. *The Godwins and the Shelleys: A Biography of a Family.* New York: W.W. Norton, 1989.

Storch, Rudolf F. "Metaphors of Private Guilt and Social Rebellion in Godwin's *Caleb Williams*." *English Literary History* 34 (1967): 188-207.

Sullivan, Garrett A., Jr. "'A Story to Be Hastily Gobbled Up': *Caleb Williams* and Print Culture." *Studies in Romanticism* 32 (1993): 323-37.

Thompson, E.P. *The Making of the English Working Class*. Harmondsworth: Penguin, 1980.

Thompson, James. "Surveillance in William Godwin's *Caleb Williams*." *Gothic Fictions: Prohibition/Transgression*. Ed. Kenneth W. Graham. New York: AMS Press, 1989. 173-98.

Thorslev, Peter L., Jr. *The Byronic Hero: Types and Prototypes*. Minneapolis: U Minnesota P, 1962.

Tompkins, J.M.S. *The Popular Novel in England, 1770-1800*. London, 1932.

Tysdahl, B.J. *William Godwin as Novelist*. London: Athlone Press, 1981.

Uphaus, Robert W. "*Caleb Williams*: Godwin's Epoch of Mind." *Studies in the Novel* 9 (1977): 279-96.

Walton, James. "Mad Feary Father: *Caleb Williams* and the Novel Form." *Salzburg Studies in English Literature* 47 (1975): 1-61.

Wardle, Ralph M. *Godwin and Mary: Letters of William Godwin and Mary Wollstonecraft*. Lincoln: U Nebraska P, 1966.

Warren, Leland E. "Caleb Williams and the 'Fall' into Writing." *Mosaic* 20 (1987): 57-69.

Wehrs, Donald R. "Rhetoric, History, Rebellion: *Caleb Williams* and the Subversion of Eighteenth-Century Fiction." *Studies in English Literature* 24 (1988): 497-511.

Williams, Gwyn. *Artisans and Sans-Culottes: Popular Movements in France and Britain during the French Revolution*. New York: Norton, 1969.

MIX
Paper from
responsible sources
FSC® C103567
FSC
www.fsc.org

LIST
of products used:

995 lb(s) of Rolland Opaque50
50% post-consumer

RESULTS
Based on the Cascades products you selected compared to products in the industry made with 100% virgin fiber, your savings are:

 4 trees

 3,450 gal. US of water
37 days of water consumption

 874 lbs of waste
8 waste containers

 2,675 lbs CO$_2$
5,072 miles driven

 13 MMBTU
64,151 60W light bulbs for one hour

 8 lbs NOx
emissions of one truck during 11 days